LANCASTER
COUNTY
Secrets

LANCASTER COUNTY Secrets

3-IN-1 COLLECTION

Suzanne Woods Fisher

Revell

a division of Baker Publishing Group
Grand Rapids, Michigan

Published by Revell
a division of Baker Publishing Group
P.O. Box 6287, Grand Rapids, MI 49516-6287
www.revellbooks.com

Combined edition published 2014

ISBN 978-0-8007-6986-4

Previously published in three separate volumes:
The Choice © 2010
The Waiting © 2010
The Search © 2011

Printed in the United States of America

Published in association with Joyce Hart of the Hartline Literary Agency, LLC.

14 15 16 17 18 19 20   7 6 5 4 3 2 1

The CHOICE

To my family, whom I love.

1

*C*arrie Weaver tucked a loose curl into her cap as she glanced up at the bell tower in Lancaster's Central Market. The clock had struck 2:00 p.m. more than ten minutes ago, and an English couple was haggling with her stepsister Emma over the price of a crate of strawberries. After all, the man was saying, the market was closing for the weekend. "Certainly, you Plain folks wouldn't want this fruit to go to waste now, would you? Tomorrow being Sunday and all?" He rested his hands on his round belly and fixed his gaze on Emma, a satisfied look on his red face—as red and ripe as a late summer tomato—as he waited for her to buckle.

But this red-faced English man didn't know Emma.

Carrie saw Emma purse her lips and hook her hands on her hips in that determined way and knew where this standoff was headed. Emma wouldn't drop the price of her strawberries to anyone, much less an Englisher whom, she was convinced, had a lost and corrupted soul. Her sister would plant her big feet and squabble over the price of strawberries until the sun set.

Carrie picked up the crate and handed it to the man. "Abgschlagge!" *Sold!*

The man and his wife, surprised and delighted, hurried off with the strawberries as Emma spun to face Carrie. She lifted her hands, palms out. "Have you lost your mind? My strawberries are worth twice that price! What were you thinking?"

"I'm thinking that it's past two and the market has closed and the van is waiting." Carrie pushed the leftover crates of red ripe strawberries into the

9

back of the van of the hired driver and slammed the door shut, pinching her thumbnail. Wincing from the pain, she knew she didn't dare stop to get ice. There wasn't a moment to waste.

"Dummel dich net!" Emma muttered as Carrie opened the passenger seat door for her. *Don't be in such a hurry!* "You've been as jumpy as a jackrabbit all morning."

Carrie reached out an arm to clasp her younger brother on the shoulder, pulling him back as he started to climb in the van behind Emma. "I need to run an errand and take the bus home later today. Andy's coming with me."

Andy's eyes went round as shoe buttons, but he followed Carrie's lead and hopped back out of the van.

Emma twisted around on the seat. "What errand?" she asked, eyes narrowed with suspicion. "You know your dad wants you home to visit with Daniel Miller."

Carrie blew out a big sigh. Silent, solemn Daniel Miller. He and his father, Eli, were staying with the Jacob Weavers this summer. Eli Miller and Jacob Weaver made no secret of the fact that they had a hope for her and Daniel. Well, they could hope all they liked but Carrie's heart was already spoken for. Spoken for and claimed, and the thought warmed her.

"Daniel's mighty fine looking, Carrie," Emma said. "Your dad is hoping you'll think so too."

"If you think Daniel is such a looker, why don't you visit with him?" Carrie stepped back from the van to close the door. That had been mean, what she said to Emma, and she reached out to give her sister's arm a gentle squeeze in apology before she swung the door closed and the driver pulled away. Dear Emma, nearly twenty-seven and terrified that she would end up an old maid. Carrie felt a smile pull at her mouth and fought it back, as an unbidden image of a large celery patch popped into her mind—Emma and her mother, Esther, grew celery in the family garden in hopes that this would be Emma's year.

Carrie shook off her musing and grabbed Andy's hand and hurried to the bus stop. She wanted to reach the Lancaster Barnstormers' stadium before Solomon Riehl would start pitching. Last night, Sol told her he might be a closing pitcher in today's scrimmage, so she should be in the stands by the last few innings.

"What kind of errand?" Andy asked Carrie.

She shaded her eyes from the sun to watch for the bus. "It's a surprise for your birthday."

"I won't turn nine 'til October."

Carrie looked at him and tousled his hair. "Consider it an early birthday present." She knew she wouldn't be here on his birthday.

As Carrie and Andy climbed on the bus and sat among the English, she felt the happiness of her secret spill over her. She didn't even mind the pain radiating from her throbbing thumb. She was entirely preoccupied with the conversations she had been having with Sol lately. Last week, he called her at midnight, as planned, from the phone shanty across the road from his father's farm. During that call, he had talked to her about leaving the community and trying to make a living as a baseball player. And he told her he wanted her by his side, as his wife.

Sol had been crazy about baseball ever since he first held a ball in his hand. Although competition was discouraged on the schoolyard, Sol stood out. He could throw a ball faster, farther, and with more accuracy than anyone.

Just a few months ago, a baseball scout happened to be driving past their youth gathering and had pulled his car over to watch Sol pitch, mesmerized. The scout had quietly slipped a business card into Sol's hand and whispered something to him.

On the buggy ride home from the youth gathering, Sol had pulled out the card and showed it to Carrie. "They're having open tryouts next week. He wants to clock my pitch. He said he hasn't seen a fastball like mine in years."

Stunned, Carrie turned the card over. "You aren't serious. Sol, you can't try out for professional baseball. You shouldn't even go to a game! You know that. The elders will be at your folks' door by day's end."

"Not if they don't find out," Sol said, grinning mischievously. Then his face tightened and the smile disappeared. "I'm tired of all the 'shouldn'ts' and 'can'ts' in my life. *Can't* go to the movies. *Shouldn't* listen to the radio. *Can't* ride a bicycle. *Can't* own a car."

Carrie gave him a sideways glance. All Sol talked about lately was how smothered he felt, being born and raised Amish. At first she felt alarmed by such talk. But she'd grown used to it and didn't take his complaints too seriously. She was sure he couldn't really leave his family and church behind. Or her. He would never leave her behind. Of that she was confident. "Not being allowed to own a car sure hasn't stopped you. I still don't know how you've kept that heap-of-rust you call a car hidden from your folks for so long."

Sol's face relaxed into a grin. "Six months now." He turned the buggy off to the shoulder and faced Carrie, taking her hand in his. "It's *just* a tryout. There will be plenty of other guys pitching, guys who have been training their whole life for a tryout. Most likely, I won't even make callbacks." He lifted her chin so she would look at him. "But I've decided. I'm going to go to the tryouts next week. Now's the time in my life to have a taste of what the world has to offer. That's what the running-around years are for, aren't they?" He leaned over to kiss her, featherlight, on the lips, then gently rubbed his nose against hers before slapping the reins to urge the horse forward.

As the horse lunged ahead, Carrie mulled over Sol's reasoning. Was Rumspringa a time for trying worldly things? To be tried and found lacking? Or, just by trying, did it make a person long for another kind of life than the Plain one? Her father had a saying, "Was mer net hawwe soll, hett mer's liebscht." *What we are not meant to have, we covet most.*

Sol laughed when she quoted her father's saying to him and told her that even Jacob Weaver was young once. Sol made it sound so easy. He made everything sound so easy. Besides, she thought, dismissing concern about Sol's restless nature, he probably wouldn't be picked by that team. He's just feeling his oats.

One week later, Sol had tried out for the Lancaster Barnstormers and was offered a one-season contract with promises of more. The pitching coach had been impressed with this Amish kid who could throw bullets. And when Sol stood on that pitcher's mound in the Clipper Magazine Stadium, he was hooked, ready to sign. There was no turning back.

Carrie was the only one who knew about Sol's baseball contract. He had hidden the fact from his father, telling him he was working a construction job for an English company. It wasn't entirely a lie; he did work on a construction site in the morning, but come noon, he clocked out, with the foreman's permission, and rushed to the stadium for spring training. Sol and Carrie knew this ruse wouldn't last. Next week, the Barnstormers would start a three-game series on Long Island. It was time to come clean with his folks. Sol would be leaving and he told Carrie he wanted her with him.

"But what about your folks, Sol? And my dad and Andy?" Carrie had asked him, still unsure if she could live with herself after leaving home. Like Sol, she had mixed feelings about joining the community. They both struggled to believe the way their parents believed, and oh, the world with its infinite choices, it was calling to them.

"We haven't bent at the knee, Carrie," Sol reminded her. "It's all the difference. We won't be shunned. We can still visit and write letters and eat with them. Be glad we haven't been baptized yet. Trust me, they'll understand. They were young once."

After a few more late-night conversations with Sol, Carrie came to see things his way. But the next morning, she watched her father and Andy talking and laughing together, and she felt all churned up again. How could she do this to them? How could she leave them?

As soon as she had a chance to see Sol face-to-face, she told him that she had changed her mind.

He patiently listened to her and answered her concerns, even those she had about God turning his back on them. "If it doesn't work out, we can always go back to the church," he assured her.

And then he kissed her, first on each cheek, then her forehead, before grazing her lips with his finger. By the time his lips found hers, Carrie's objections had evaporated.

Still, Carrie wasn't so sure their parents would understand. She was even less sure that God would understand. But one thing Carrie didn't doubt was that she wanted to be wherever Sol would be. She loved Sol *that* much.

Warming up his arm in the bull pen, Sol Riehl felt a deep satisfaction he hadn't dreamed possible. He certainly never felt it when he was mucking out stalls or plowing a field. Here he was, an Amish kid plucked right off the farm, pitching for a professional baseball team. Who had ever heard of such a thing? It felt like a dream that he didn't dare to wake from.

The catcher gave Sol a signal to throw some pitches. "You sure do pack some heat, Sunday Sol," he told Sol, slapping him on the back as the pitching coach called for the two to come up to the field. Sol tossed the ball to the catcher and followed him out of the bull pen. He scanned the seats above the dugout for any sign of Carrie. He had told her exactly where to sit, right behind the catcher, so she would have the best view of the pitcher's mound. He frowned, disappointed that she wasn't there yet.

Then Sol heard his name announced over the loudspeaker as the closer. He hoped Carrie was somewhere in the stadium so she would hear that announcement. He tried, without success, to keep the grin off his face as he took his first jog out to the mound.

As Carrie and Andy plopped down in the stadium's hard plastic seats, she breathed a sigh of relief, hearing Sol's name announced over the loudspeaker. Sol had told her where to sit so he could see her from the pitcher's mound. It was one of the things she loved about him; he had everything planned out.

She saw him jog out to the mound and look up, right to where she was seated. He gave her a quick wave, did a double take when he noticed Andy, then turned his attention to the catcher to practice a few more warm-up pitches.

When Andy realized it was Solomon Riehl on that pitcher's mound, he blurted out, "Ein Balleschpieler?" *A baseball player?*

"Best not to tell Dad and Esther about this birthday surprise, Andy," Carrie said, flashing him a warning. "Nor Emma."

Andy nodded, sealing the pact, eyes glued on the field. "Dad wouldn't mind." A slow grin spread over his face. "Esther would, though."

Carrie laughed. "Yes, Esther would mind something fierce."

As she watched Sol pitch, her heart felt so full she didn't even notice that tears were running down her cheeks. She knew that feeling so proud was wicked, but she couldn't help herself. Down on the field was Sol Riehl, in a sparkling white-with-red-pinstripe uniform, pitching in front of thousands of people in a baseball stadium. Her Sol.

At dinner that evening in the Weaver house, all that was spoken of was Eli Miller's purchase of an apple orchard. Carrie was grateful that no one asked her where she and Andy had been all afternoon.

Carrie's father, Jacob Weaver, knew of an orchard owned by an English neighbor who wanted to retire to Florida. It wasn't even for sale yet, but Jacob and Eli spent the day talking with that neighbor. When they returned, hours later, Eli was the new owner of a twenty-acre apple orchard. Jacob was so pleased to help his friend that he couldn't keep the smile off of his kind face.

"I'm mighty fortunate to have a friend like you, Jacob," Eli told him, matching Jacob grin for grin.

"Fortunate for you, Eli, that you had money to buy land," said Esther, Jacob's wife, in a thin, tight voice.

Carrie braced herself, keeping her eyes fixed on her plate. She knew that Esther couldn't tolerate letting Jacob be the center of attention.

"This farm belonged to my first husband. Jacob was penniless when I met him. Penniless with two small children." Carefully, Esther buttered a roll and began to delicately eat it as an awkward silence covered the dinner table like a blanket.

"And a blessed day it was when I met you, Esther," Jacob answered back softly, dark brown eyes twinkling, causing everyone to laugh. Even Esther softened. He was long accustomed to Esther's sharp tongue and had a way of defusing her.

Carrie looked fondly at her father. Once she had asked him why he married Esther in the first place. "Carrie girl," her father said, "folks marry for all kinds of reasons." He hadn't really answered her question, but she thought she knew what he meant.

Eli rose to his feet and clapped his hands together. "Daniel, it's time we set off to the bus depot." Like his son, Eli was a man of few words and only gave a nod of thanks to Esther.

Daniel crammed one last roll into his mouth and hurried to join his father outside, helping him hitch the horse to the buggy. Before the sun set today, Eli planned to be back on the bus to Ohio. He wanted to finalize the sale of his farm, auction off his equipment, and fetch his widowed mother, Yonnie. Daniel was to remain at the Weavers' to finish up details of the sale of the orchards.

Why Eli was in such a hurry was a mystery to Carrie, but she didn't really concern herself with the Millers. Her mind was on Sol. Leaving with Sol.

"And," Emma told Carrie as they cleaned up the kitchen after dinner that evening, "I heard Eli tell Daniel to try and woo you while he was gone."

"Woo me?" Carrie asked, drying a bowl before tucking it in the cupboard. "Maybe he should woo you."

"I'm too old for him. Besides, I think Daniel likes you. He kept stealing looks at you during dinner tonight."

"Emma, please." Carrie rolled her eyes. "He's such a brooder. Haven't you noticed he never smiles or laughs?"

Emma handed Carrie another wet bowl and gave her a suspicious look. "You'd better not be holding out for that Solomon Riehl. You know how your dad feels about Sol. He thinks he's a fence jumper."

Carrie stiffened, irritated. "*One time*, Emma. *One time*, Dad saw Sol working in the fields with his shirt off. That doesn't make him a fence jumper."

"Well, my mother says it does." Emma put her hands on her hips. "I heard her tell your father that Sol Riehl was a fellow walking with one foot in the world and one foot in the church. She said that he was always spoiled, being the only boy after all those girls. She said that his parents never expected enough from—"

"Emma!" Carrie held up a hand in warning. "Wer lauert an der Wand sei eegni Schand." *If you listen through the wall, you'll hear others reciting your faults.*

The kitchen door burst open, interrupting them. "Carrie, it's set up!" Andy shouted.

Carrie threw the dish towel at Emma and hurried outside to join Andy in a game of horseshoes before the sun set.

Watering the vegetable garden, Mattie Zook heard Andy and Carrie's voices in their yard. She dropped the watering can and ran down the hill to see her friend. Now that Carrie was working at the Central Market, Mattie hardly saw her anymore. What little free time Carrie did have lately was taken up by Sol Riehl.

All of the boys were crazy about Carrie, but she acted as if she didn't notice or didn't care. Sol was the only one who had ever caught her interest. Mattie could see why Carrie was so sought after. Sometimes Mattie thought she looked like an angel. Big blue eyes fringed with thick black lashes, skin the color of cream in summer, a dimple in each cheek that framed a bow-shaped mouth. And her hair! Good thing the boys couldn't see her hair too, Mattie thought. Thick, honey blond curls that cascaded down her back. But Carrie was more than just pretty, she was smart and kind, and had a little bit of mystery to her, as if she always had something else on her mind. The boys had to work hard to get her attention. Whenever Mattie told her that, Carrie would laugh and say she was just imagining things. Mattie loved Carrie's laugh. It reminded Mattie of the church bells she heard ringing whenever she was in town.

As Mattie reached Esther's rosebushes that bordered the property, she slowed to avoid thorns. She and Carrie had beaten a path through those bushes the very first summer Carrie's dad had married Esther and moved to her farm. The path had made Esther furious, which secretly delighted the girls.

Carrie waved to Mattie to join them. "I bet I know why you're here, Mattie!" she called out, laughing. "But Daniel isn't here. He and Dad took Eli to the bus stop."

As Mattie broke into a run to join Carrie and Andy, she wondered why Carrie would assume she was interested in the Weavers' houseguest. Like most of the girls, she had noticed Daniel Miller at the Sunday Singing. And he was handsome, she couldn't deny.

But Mattie's heart belonged to one man: Solomon Riehl. She had loved Sol for as long as she remembered. Long before Carrie had even met him.

Mattie would never reveal those feelings, though. She loved Carrie too much. She wasn't sure what the future held, but she trusted that God had given her this love for Sol. And she knew God was trustworthy.

Near midnight, Carrie quietly tiptoed downstairs, jumping carefully over the squeaky third step because Esther had ears like a hawk. She slipped out the kitchen door and glided into a run as soon as she turned onto the road. When she reached the phone shanty, she jerked the door open and stared at the phone impatiently, willing it to ring.

While she waited, drumming her fingers, her thoughts drifted to the talk she'd had with Mattie tonight. She nearly confided to Mattie about the plans to leave with Sol, but she held her tongue. It wouldn't have been right to have Mattie keep such a secret. The truth, she realized, was that she didn't think Mattie would understand. There was something about Mattie that seemed . . . pure. Holy, almost. Like those orchids sold at Central Market. Once the Orchid Lady had told Carrie that she kept the orchids in the greenhouse because they were so delicate. That's what Mattie seemed like. Too delicate for Carrie to share her tangled thoughts.

The phone rang, startling her out of her muse. She lunged for the receiver and smiled as she heard Sol's deep voice.

"Did anyone ask where you were this afternoon?" Sol asked.

"No," Carrie said, still smiling. "Dad and Eli were so excited about purchasing the orchards that it was all anyone was talking about."

"Surprised me to see Andy with you. Think that was wise?"

"Aw, it was a birthday present for him. He won't tell." Carrie was quiet for a moment. "I won't be here for his actual birthday." Her heart caught for a moment.

Sol didn't seem to notice the quiver in her voice. "So we'll tell our folks Sunday afternoon, just like we talked about. On Monday, I'll be on the team bus to Long Island, but you can follow on a Greyhound as soon as you can. I thought we could get married in New York, the day you arrive. How does that sound?"

Carrie didn't answer right away. She glanced back at the big white farmhouse. The moonlight shone behind it, casting a bluish hue over it. The night was so quiet and peaceful; the house and the barn filled with sleeping people and animals. An owl hooted once, then twice.

Her eyes caught on a shadowy figure and she gasped. Daniel Miller was sitting on the fence across from the phone shanty, watching her.

"Carrie?" Sol asked, his voice tight.

She pulled her attention back to the phone. "Daniel's here."

"That fellow who's staying at your house? What does he want?"

"I have no idea."

Sol snorted. "I have a pretty good idea. He stuck to you like flypaper at last Sunday's singing."

Carrie rolled her eyes. "Sol, he didn't know anybody else."

"He knew Emma and he didn't get anywhere near her."

Carrie smiled. Sol had a jealous streak. She shouldn't be pleased, but she couldn't help it. "Maybe I should find out what he wants."

"Carrie, you haven't answered my question. Have you changed your mind?"

She turned away from Daniel's gaze. "I haven't changed my mind."

"Ich liebe dich," he said. *I love you.*

A blush warmed her face. She'd never said the words before, because it was not the Plain way. But Sol said the words often. He admired how the English expressed themselves openly. "Ich auch," she whispered. *Me too.*

"So tell Daniel Miller to find another girl."

Carrie waited until she heard the click of Sol hanging up before she put the receiver back in the cradle. She turned slowly and opened the door to the phone shanty.

"Evening." Daniel's low voice came as a shock in the whispering stillness of the night.

"I guess I didn't see you on the way here." She pulled the collar of her nightgown close around her neck. "Why are you up so late?"

He shrugged. "Too hot to sleep." He crossed his arms. "You?"

She glanced back at the phone shanty. "Business call. For Central Market. They get up early."

"My, my. That is early," Daniel said, sounding amused.

She stared at him and he stared back. Then her cheeks started to burn as if she'd been standing too close to a stove. She dropped her eyes and spun around to leave. "Well, goodnight."

"Wonder what Esther might say about you having a midnight phone call."

Carrie froze. She did not want Esther to know she was out in the night, on the phone. Once Esther locked on to something, she wouldn't let go until it thundered. For the first time, she thought that Daniel Miller might just have a thought or two in his quiet head. She pivoted around to face him. "Do you plan to tell her?"

He gave a short laugh. "She reminds me of a bear that treed me once. Not sure I want to be on the wrong side of that woman." Daniel took a few strides and passed by Carrie. "You got more business calls to make?"

In the moonlight, Daniel looked less stern and tense, a little gentler. She decided that Emma was right, he was a looker. He used more words tonight than he had all week.

"Wait up. I'm coming," she said, matching his stride.

When the van dropped Carrie and Emma off from work the next day, Daniel and Andy were waiting for them at the gate. Andy's face was red and puffy from crying.

"Nau, was is letz, Andy?" Carrie asked. *What's wrong?* Something terrible must have happened; Andy never cried.

"Dad," he sobbed, gulping for air. "It's Dad." He threw himself into Carrie's arms and buried his face against her.

"Was fehlt ihm?" Carrie's heart started to pound. *What's wrong with him?*

Daniel explained that Jacob had been shoeing a horse when it kicked him.

"Someone's taken him to the hospital, yes?" Carrie asked. Her pulse quickened as her breath came up short.

Daniel shook his head. "He's on the couch in the kitchen." He took a step closer to Carrie.

"We must get him to the hospital. He has hemophilia. He's a bleeder. He needs an infusion of Factor IX." She stroked Andy's hair. "Alles ist ganz gut, Andy." *All will be well.* She looked up at Daniel. "Did you call for an ambulance?"

Daniel glanced up at the house. "Carrie . . ."

Emma gasped as she seemed to understand what Daniel couldn't say. "Ach, nee! Ach, nee! Er is dot, zwahr? Ach, liebe Mamm!" *Oh, no! Oh, no! He's dead, isn't he? Oh, dear Mom!* She ran toward the house.

Carrie heard Emma's cries, but the words dipped and swirled like barn swallows in her mind. She watched Emma disappear into the house, heard her shout for Esther. Andy had tightened his grip around her waist, his small body wracked with huge, wrenching sobs. She took in the concerned look on Daniel's face and then the full sense of what Emma said struck her, a panic gripped her chest so tightly that she thought her heart had stopped beating. *No. There must be a mistake.*

"He was kicked in the head. It was too late—"

"Du bischt letz," she told Daniel in a voice that was too calm. *You are wrong.*

Daniel rubbed his forehead. After a moment, he lifted his head. "It was too late by the time Esther found him—"

"Esther found him?" Carrie's hands flew to cup her face. "She didn't call the ambulance, did she?" She started trembling. "Esther didn't think he ever needed infusions. She said they cost too much and didn't believe they were necessary." She started to gulp for air. "She has the money, you see. This farm, it belongs to her. She never lets him forget that."

Daniel took a step closer to her.

"And then the last time Dad was hurt," Carrie continued without stopping to breathe, "she talked him out of having an infusion. It took him months to recover. The blood pooled in his joints and caused him terrible pain. But if his head was ever injured, he would be in serious trouble because the blood would pool in the brain. The doctor said so. I heard him say so. Esther knew that." She was visibly shaking now. "She *knew* that."

Carrie looked to Daniel, hoping he would admit that it was a prank, a bad joke. That Jacob was waiting for her and for Andy in the kitchen. But Daniel wore such pain in his eyes that she knew it was real.

My father is dead. He's dead! A small startled cry escaped from her throat.

Daniel stepped closer and wrapped his arms around both of them—a grief-stricken woman and a sobbing little boy—and held them tight.

2

Jacob Weaver's body was embalmed by the English undertaker and returned, the next day, to the farmhouse for the viewing. All afternoon, Carrie, Esther, Emma, and Andy received friends and neighbors offering condolences, doing errands of kindness. It was a soaker of a day, gray skies that poured down rain, matching Carrie's dark, troubled mood.

Carrie was worried about her brother. Andy was silent, never far from her side. She wasn't sure how to help him. It was one thing to grieve the loss of a parent, but after Esther's outrageous accusation last night, she wasn't sure he would ever be himself again. There was no balm for this wound.

It started when Andy had arrived late to supper, having lost track of time. Andy's absentmindedness was a constant source of irritation to Esther, and last night she told him that Jacob's death was his fault.

"Your father had told you to come to the barn straight from gathering eggs in the henhouse," Esther said, pointing a long finger in his direction. "If you had just obeyed your father, instead of getting distracted like you always do, he could be alive today. You *knew* he was a bleeder. Every minute counted."

Carrie exploded at Esther's accusation. "Sie ist schunn ab im Kopp! Er ist ein Kind! Mei vadder hett's net erlaabt! Du settscht dich scheme!" *You are crazy! He is only a child! My father would not permit such talk! You should be ashamed!* Her fists shook as she screamed, her chin quivered with rage. "You don't care, Esther! You never did!"

Esther stared into Carrie's eyes, a standoff, before abruptly turning and leaving the kitchen.

Carrie rushed to put her arms around Andy, crumbled with grief, weeping silently. "Andy, Andy, don't listen to her. It was Dad's time. The Lord God decided that, not you. And not Esther, either." Carrie scooped Andy up on her lap and held him tight against her.

It surprised Carrie to hear those words about God burst out of her mouth, as naturally as if they came from her heart. Triggering a fresh wave of grief, it sounded like something her father would have said.

When Sol arrived with his family to pay respects, he slipped a note to Carrie to meet him in the barn. As soon as he viewed Jacob's body and shook Esther's hand, he hurried to the barn to wait for Carrie. He knew she had to wait until an opportune moment; no one was supposed to have any idea they were courting. Funny, he thought, leaning against the horse's stall, they both tiptoed so carefully around the brittle requirements of the church. In two short days, they would no longer need to worry.

The heavy barn door slid open with a rumble. Carrie waited until her eyes adjusted to the dim light, then ran to him.

"I'm so sorry," he mumbled, folding her into his arms. For a long time, neither of them spoke.

Keeping her head tucked under Sol's chin, Carrie broke the silence. "I should have been here. We came back late from the market. Maybe if I'd been here, I could have gotten him to the hospital. She didn't even call for an ambulance."

"It was just an accident, Carrie," Sol said, tipping her chin up to face him. "Esther is a lot of things, but she isn't cruel." He knew how Carrie adored her father. That was one reason he wanted them to leave before they were baptized. He didn't want Jacob to have to shun Carrie.

"Neglecting a head injury when someone has hemophilia is cruel."

"A kick in the head is pretty hard to recover from, bleeder or not."

"But she didn't even give him a chance."

"Aw, Carrie, be fair. From what I heard, it was too late by the time anyone found him."

She sighed deeply as if her argument had run out of steam. "Maybe you're right. Dad was unconscious by the time Esther got to him."

Sol pulled her close to his chest. "Things have a way of working out, Carrie."

She pulled back from him, a confused look on her face. "What?"

"I've been thinking this over. I know how hard it was going to be to say goodbye to your father—"

She tilted her head. "What are you saying?"

"Just that, maybe it's a sign. That it's right for us to leave."

"God gave us a sign to leave by letting my father die?"

Sol put his hands on her shoulders, but she flinched, shrugging them off. This wasn't going the way he had hoped. He decided to change subjects. "I struck four batters out yesterday and threw a runner out at second base. You know what they're starting to call me? 'The Riehl Deal.'"

Her eyes widened as if his words had hit her, a solid slap. "Sol, I can't leave Andy. I won't leave him with her."

"You can't be responsible for Andy for the rest of your life."

"Maybe not. But I'm responsible for him until he's grown. I'm his only sibling. We have no one else, Sol."

Sol felt his stomach tie itself into a square knot. "Carrie," he said, choosing his words with great sympathy, "we have to face facts. We need to be practical. I can't take care of a wife *and* a little boy. Especially one with hemophilia. Andy needs to stay on the farm, with his people. They can help him with his medical bills. I can't do that."

"I realize that," Carrie said. "But there's another choice."

He lifted his hands, exasperated. "Such as?"

She looked at him as if it was the most obvious thing in the world. "You could stay."

After Sol left with his family, Carrie went back to the house, so exhausted and emotionally spent that she felt numb. She was certain that Sol would think everything over and agree with her. It shocked her to hear him still talk about leaving. Why couldn't he see it? Remaining in the church was the best choice. The only choice.

When the entire Riehl family came to her father's funeral on Monday and Sol was absent, she tried not to panic. Then she thought of how he had kissed her in the barn before he slipped back out to join his family, and she knew. It was a goodbye kiss. She hadn't wanted to admit it to herself, but she knew. Er hat sei verlosse. *He had left, without her.*

Carrie didn't think it was possible that a heart could break twice, in just one week.

One month after her father's funeral, Carrie thought she might just commit murder. Esther had discovered that Andy had left the gate unlocked, and the sheep had wandered down the road into other neighbors' fields. It had taken Esther all afternoon to gather them. Afterward, she took a switch from the willow tree and beat Andy's backside.

When Carrie returned home from the farmer's market and saw Andy's bruises, it was like someone lit a match to kerosene, her temper flared so hot and fast. She marched to the barn to prepare the horse and buggy to take Andy to the hospital. She grabbed the bridle and hurried to the stall, clumsily thrusting the bit into the horse's mouth, her hands were shaking so badly. "Es dutt mir leed," she whispered, apologizing to the horse, trying to gain control over her emotions.

Later, at the hospital, Carrie sat by Andy's bedside in the emergency room as a long tube snaked from an IV bag into his vein, filling him with Factor IX to help his blood clot. Mesmerized by the television hanging on the wall, Andy watched it, slack-jawed. The sight made Carrie smile. It felt rusty, that smile, but it felt good.

With Andy occupied, Carrie grew restless and noticed a newspaper left on a chair. She picked it up and automatically turned to the sports section, just as she did every time she worked at the Central Market, scanning for news of Sol. Just last week, she had read that he was the closing pitcher for every game.

As she turned a page, her heart skidded to a stop. There was a picture of Sol, celebrating a win, with his arm wrapped around a girl. An English girl. A pang of longing pierced her heart. Carrie stared at the picture so long that she didn't even notice Daniel, standing at the door, until he cleared his throat. Startled, Carrie dropped the newspaper.

"Heard about Andy," he said, pulling up a chair to sit down next to the bed.

Carrie gathered the newspaper and tossed it in the wastebasket. It occurred to her that Daniel had a curious way of appearing out of nowhere. But she found she didn't mind. Daniel was good at just being there.

A few hours later, after Andy was released, Daniel and Carrie took Andy home. Carrie settled her brother into bed and read until he was asleep. Esther had gone to bed, a relief to Carrie. She still felt a mutinous anger toward Esther for harming her brother. She went out to the front porch to look at the stars and search out the tail of the Milky Way. It was something her father had liked to do. He said it gave him great comfort to see God's handiwork in the heavens. Sorely missing him, Carrie wished she could borrow some of her father's faith. Especially now.

The kitchen door creaked open. "Another midnight call?" Daniel asked, holding the door open as if waiting for an invitation.

"No," Carrie said. "I'm not expecting any calls." Not now, not ever again, she realized.

He closed the door and stood beside her, arms crossed, gazing at the sky, not saying a word.

"When is your father expected?" Carrie asked, breaking the silence.

"When? Or what?"

Carrie glanced at him, not understanding.

"He's due on Friday." Daniel cleared his throat. "But he's expecting that by now I've asked you to marry me." He kept his eyes fixed on the stars.

Carrie's eyes went wide with surprise. She opened her mouth but no words came to the surface. Suddenly, an image of Sol with his arm around that girl bounced, unbidden, into her head. She wanted to hurt Sol as much as he had hurt her. What could hurt Sol more than knowing she had married? Without thinking, she blurted out, "Andy comes with me."

Daniel gave a nod.

Carrie's mind started to spin. "I've started baptism instructions this summer."

Mattie had persuaded Carrie to take the classes together. Carrie finally agreed, hoping Sol would hear that she was going to be baptized. She knew his mother wrote to him each week. Sol had been right about that one thing; it wasn't like he was under the ban. His folks were deeply disappointed in him, but they held out hope that he'd get over sowing his wild oats and return home.

Well, Carrie wasn't waiting for him. As far as she was concerned, he chose baseball over her and nothing would ever change that. "I'll be baptized in a few weeks. Then I'd like a wedding soon after." She glanced up at the direction of Esther's bedroom window. "As soon as possible."

Daniel gave another nod.

Carrie took a deep breath. "I have to be honest about something. I don't love you."

Daniel smiled, a slow unraveling. "Makes things simpler," was all he said, leaning over the porch railing, gazing at the moonless sky.

Carrie looked at his profile for a long time, trying to understand him. She had a feeling that she never would. "I don't know how they do things in Ohio, but here, you need to speak to the deacon who will speak to me. About marrying, I mean. He acts like a go-between."

Daniel straightened up and turned to her, looking her straight in the eyes. He held out his hand. "Deal?"

Carrie's eyes dropped down to his large open hand and she shook it, sealing the bargain.

Not long after the deacon's visit, Carrie and Daniel set the day for their wedding. As Carrie pinned the top of her blue wedding dress, she felt as if she might faint dead away, caught in that horrible place between regret and resolution. She wondered how Daniel was feeling right then, if he felt as sick as she did.

She fit the organza prayer cap over her hair bun, tying the strings under her chin, feeling as if her world had just become very narrow and she couldn't get enough air. For one fleeting moment, as she heard the churned-up gravel made by the arriving buggies, she thought about running away. Finding Sol.

But then she thought about her father. And Andy.

A fierce grief welled up within her, nearly to the point of bursting. One thought spilled into another and soon Sol filled her mind again. Cold fury displaced grief, renewing her determination. She finished tying the cap and smoothed the creases on her apron. Carrie was just about to go downstairs when she heard a gentle knock on the door. She took a deep breath and opened the door to find Yonnie, Daniel's grandmother.

Soft wrinkles creased Yonnie's face as she studied Carrie. Then, a satisfied smile covered Yonnie's face, warm as a summer day. "So. Today is your wedding day," she said, in a voice tender and shaky with age.

In her arms was a bundle wrapped in tissue. It looked as though it weighed more than she did. Carrie took the bundle from her and helped her sit down on a chair.

"You can open it," Yonnie said.

Carefully, Carrie unwrapped the tissue and found a quilt inside.

"It's called a Crazy Quilt." Yonnie's words were slow and faltering, her voice as thin as a trail of smoke. "It seems more fitting to have brought you a Double Wedding Ring, but for some reason, I felt as if this one was the right one."

Carrie gave her a sideways glance. She fought a wave of guilt as she realized Yonnie assumed she loved Daniel.

Yonnie pointed to some blue triangles. "I used the scraps from Daniel's clothes. They're from his growing-up years."

Carrie's chin snapped up. "You made this quilt all by yourself?"

"I did." The strings on her organza kapp bobbed as she nodded. She wasn't being proud, just stating a fact.

"You're a fine quilter, Yonnie. It's wonderful." Carrie laid the quilt out on the bed, the place where she and Daniel would spend their first night as man and wife. Her last few nights in Esther's home, she realized, relieved. Last night she had learned that Esther's eldest daughter and her husband were moving in to take over the farm, dispelling any doubts that she had made the right decision. At least, for Andy's sake.

Yonnie's Crazy Quilt was stunning. Deep-colored jewels of purple and green set among bright turquoise. The pattern practically popped in the room against the stark white walls and simple furniture. It snatched Carrie's breath away, the same feeling she got after the first snowfall each year.

"Truth be told, some people don't like the Crazy Quilt so much," Yonnie said, gently smoothing her weathered hand across the tiny stitches. "It's usually made of scrap cloth. But for some reason it's one of my favorites. Daniel's too." She paused to take a breath.

"Thank you, Yonnie. I will always treasure it." Carrie's life felt like a Crazy Quilt right now, long before the pieces were brought together into a pattern. Would they ever?

Carrie looked in the mirror one last time, took a deep breath, and followed Yonnie down the stairs to go marry Daniel Miller.

All of the furniture in the front room had been moved out for the wedding to allow room for seating. The traditional celery-filled vases had been placed around the house, and a mountain of food had been prepared by the ladies in the church. As Carrie stood beside Daniel in front of the bishop, her name was forever changed from Carrie Weaver to Carrie Miller.

The wedding lasted the entire afternoon and evening. Two meals were served for over three hundred people. Emma was happiest at weddings, Carrie thought, watching her move from table to table like a bumblebee over a field of flowers.

Carrie and Daniel were seated for meals at the Eck, the corner table reserved for the bride and groom. She noticed that her school friends seemed childish and silly compared to Daniel. Many of them hadn't been baptized yet and were still in the throes of their Rumspringa, sampling temptations that the world had to offer before renouncing worldly pleasures for good. All but Mattie, Carrie realized, watching her as she talked to Andy. Mattie never seemed to need a Rumspringa to know who she was. She was born knowing. She was like the hymn sung at the wedding ceremony, always sung in the same, sure way.

Later that night, after the last buggy pulled out of the gravel driveway and the last dish had been washed and put away, Carrie went upstairs to get ready for bed. She felt all trembly and shaky too, as if she'd been sipping on Esther's sweet rhubarb wine. Her stomach felt like a knotted fist. This was the moment that she had been dreading, ever since she had agreed to marry Daniel. She reviewed in her mind all of the reasons she had married Daniel—that she needed a home for her and Andy, that her father had approved of Daniel and hoped for this union. In a far corner of her heart, she knew this was the right thing to do. But she had dreamed about her wedding for years now, and the man in her dreams who would be knocking on her door should have been Solomon Riehl.

She gazed out the window at the sliver of a new moon. Not a moment later, Daniel knocked at the door. Carrie cleared her throat. "C-come in," she said.

Daniel came inside and closed the door behind him, hand on the doorknob. He stood there for a moment, looking at her, his expression unfathomable. She wondered if he could tell that she was shaking, though he was across the room. It seemed to her as if he was in the middle of deciding something. Then the moment passed. He walked over to the bed and grabbed a pillow and Yonnie's quilt. As he spread out the quilt on the floor, he said, "Seems best to wait. I'll sleep here."

Carrie didn't know how to respond. "Daniel, I mean to be a good wife to you," she finally said, lifting her chin bravely.

He nodded. "We can wait. Till you're ready." He took his vest and shirt off and hung them on a peg on the wall. Then, as comfortable as if he had been doing this every night of his life and she wasn't even in the room, he took off his shoes and pants, stripped down to his longjohns, and stretched out on the floor, pulling the quilt over him. "Night," he said.

Arms crossed, Carrie remained at the window, hugely relieved. She listened as Daniel's breathing settled into the even rhythm of sleep. She realized how little she knew about Daniel Miller, this man she had married. She didn't even know how old he was, or what his birthday was, or his favorite meal, or how or when his mother had passed. She didn't even know he would be so kind.

3

A few days after Carrie and Daniel's wedding, a group of men arrived at the Millers' newly purchased property early in the morning to get to work on the house. There was a lot of work to do, undoing modern conveniences to make it suitable. They disconnected the electricity, unhooked telephone jacks from the wall, lugged out a washing machine and an electric dryer, pulled screens off the windows.

About midmorning Carrie went outside to get some fresh air. She spread old quilts over the pieces of plywood resting on sawhorses that would serve as makeshift tables. Then she set out jars of coleslaw, bean salad, and applesauce that she and Emma had canned last summer. She spotted a big boulder on the lawn, soaking up the sun, so she went over to it and sat down, resting a minute.

Carrie leaned back on her elbows, grateful for the sun's warmth on her face. She looked up at the big house, at the white clapboard siding and the green shutters with little cut-out pine trees, at the stone foundation the house rested on. It was fancier than the simple Amish farmhouses she was used to. A pretty house, to be sure, but would it ever be a home to her? Would she ever learn to be content in this life she chose? She felt so strange inside. Sad and lonely and missing the life she thought she would have.

A small red car without a top on it suddenly swerved onto the circular gravel driveway and parked by the front door. Out hopped a young woman, talking to herself. She had an odd black clothespin attached to her ear. She didn't notice Carrie as she hurried to the door. She pressed the doorbell, glanced at her wristwatch, then pressed the doorbell again.

Carrie watched the stranger for a while, amused by the woman's growing irritation. She had red hair, long and sleek, held back by a dark band around her head. Her white shirt hugged her body, with the shortest skirt and the longest legs Carrie had ever seen. The heels on her shoes were so tall that Carrie wondered how she could walk on them without tipping over.

Finally, the stranger turned around impatiently, scanning the yard, and noticed Carrie. "Miss? Oh miss?" She waved. "Your doorbell doesn't work."

"No. I guess it doesn't." Carrie got to her feet, dusted off her apron, and went over to finish setting the table for lunch.

"Are you the homeowner?" she asked, hurrying over to Carrie.

Carrie looked up at the big house. "Yes, I suppose I am."

Relief smoothed out her face. "Good! My name is Veronica McCall. Here's my business card."

The woman was very pretty, Carrie thought. She had creamy white skin, even features, but her green eyes . . . they had a sharpness to them, like the glint of a frozen pond reflecting a winter sky.

Carrie took the business card, read it, then slipped it into her apron pocket. "Hello, Veronica McCall." She gave her a nod and started to put cups at each place setting.

She trotted behind Carrie. "And you are . . . ?"

"I'm Carrie Miller." It sounded strange to her tongue to stick Miller after her name.

"Well, Carrie, if you don't mind giving me a few minutes of your time, I'd like to discuss purchasing your property."

Carrie laid out forks and plates at each spot. "Thank you, Veronica Mc-Call, but this property is not for sale."

Veronica McCall was not easily dissuaded. "I can guarantee a profit for you."

Carrie smiled and shook her head. She had forgotten napkins, so she turned to head back into the kitchen just as Davy Zook, Mattie's brother, burst outside, holding a big metal box.

Veronica McCall stared at him as he hoisted the box in the wagon. "Is that a microwave?"

"Would you like it?" Carrie asked her. "We have no use for it."

She looked mystified.

"You're welcome to anything in that wagon, Veronica McCall."

Her eyes were locked on the wagon's contents: an electric stove, two window air conditioners, a room heater, electric wall lamps. "Are you moving out? Or in?"

"Moving in. Fixing the house up. Soon, they'll be pulling down the walls inside to make it so we can fit a large gathering for Sunday meetings." The confused expression on her face amused Carrie. "Are you new to our county, Veronica McCall?"

She shook her head as if trying to remember why she was here. "Yes. I just moved here from San Francisco."

"Earthquake country."

"Well, yes, but I'd take an earthquake any day over these lightning and thunderstorms." She scanned the skies for any threatening clouds, frowning.

"It would take a leap of faith for me to live in earthquake country," Carrie answered. Suddenly, she smiled. She was trying to decide on a name for her new home but hadn't settled on any. Maybe she should call it Leap of Faith Farm. Or better still: Blind Leap of Faith Farm. That's exactly what it felt like. Like she was taking a gigantic leap of faith. With her eyes closed shut.

Veronica McCall laughed. "I hope we can become friends, Carrie."

Carrie thought she saw a glimmer of sincerity behind those cold, glittering green eyes. But maybe not.

"Anyway, as you can see on the business card—"

Carrie patted her apron pocket.

"—I'm in business development for my corporation. We're very interested in acquiring property we can convert into a golf course. Finding land around here is nearly impossible. Yours has ideal topography." She paused for a moment, looking out across to the even rows of trees in the orchards.

"The slopes help to minimize frost damage to the apples," Carrie said. She had heard her father tell Eli that very thing.

Veronica ignored her. "It's possible that the house could be converted to a clubhouse, and that area there"—she made a sweeping gesture with her hand—"could be torn down and used for parking. Really, it's perfect. We're hoping we won't even need double fairways." She turned to Carrie. "Safety can be a factor with double fairways, you know."

Carrie didn't understand her words, or the meaning behind them, so she answered with silence.

"Of course, we have to get rid of that old carriage house and that barn. So many rickety old barns in this area." She made a clucking sound.

"There's a saying in the Plain life: 'A farm is not a farm without its barn,'" Carrie said.

Veronica opened her mouth to say something, then snapped it shut and tilted her head at Carrie, puzzled.

"The Amish build their barns first. When the farm is successful, a good house follows. To the Amish, a barn is more important than a house."

Veronica shook that thought off, then resumed her sales pitch. "And this property holds excellent proximity to Honor Mansion, which is really why I'm here." She spun around to face Carrie. "The hotel was recently bought by my corporation, Bonnatt's Development Company. First, we have plans for a major renovation on the mansion. You know, day spa, tennis courts, and then, a golf course." She flashed a brilliant smile, revealing white, even teeth. "So, Carrie, how much would you like for it?"

Carrie admired this woman's tenacity, but she had work to do. "Thank you, but as I said, it's not for sale."

Veronica sighed. "Is there anyone else whom I could speak to?"

"You could talk to Eli Miller. He's just coming up from the barn now." Eli, Daniel, and a few other men were walking toward them from the barn. They had been examining where to put the blacksmithing shop that they planned as a sideline business. Apples alone weren't enough to pay the bills.

"Which one is he?" Veronica asked. "They all look alike! Blue shirts, black trousers with suspenders, straw hats—"

"He's the only one with whiskers. Only married men wear whiskers. The bachelors are clean shaven." Daniel's jawline just showed the shadow of a new beard.

She squinted her eyes. "The one who looks like he's got a shoehorn wrapped around his chin?"

"That's Eli."

"So a beard takes the place of a wedding ring?"

She nearly surprised a smile out of Carrie, the way this woman talked. Carrie nodded.

"Thank you, Carrie!" Veronica called out, as she hurried toward Eli.

Carrie couldn't resist a grin when she saw how quickly Eli shooed Veronica McCall off. They all stood and watched as she zoomed away in her little car. Her red hair flew behind her like a flag waving in the wind.

"Englisch," Eli muttered, shaking his head as he passed by Carrie to head into the house.

With help from neighbors, Carrie and Daniel moved into the farmhouse at the apple orchard by week's end. Since Carrie and Daniel married in September, with their apple crop ready to harvest and sell, they skipped the honeymoon visits to relatives.

Carrie knew that Andy was never fond of school, but she couldn't understand why, after the first few weeks, he seemed reluctant to leave the house each morning. "You're sure you're not sick?" she asked him, putting a cool hand to his forehead.

"Nah," he said, pulling away from her. "But maybe you should pack me another brownie. I get awful hungry."

"But I packed you two yesterday. How could you still be hungry?" Carrie asked, frowning. "And put your shoes on. You are not to go barefoot. Ever, ever, ever. You know that. Too much risk of cutting yourself."

Andy sighed wearily and bent down to put his socks and shoes on. Daniel was sipping his coffee, his eyes on Andy, narrowed slightly in the way of a man studying a mildly perturbing question.

Carrie packed up a third brownie and handed Andy his lunch pail, then opened the door for him. "Go, Andy! You'll be late!" Andy poked his head out the door, looked both ways before stepping out on the porch, then lit into a sprint and flew down the lane.

Carrie leaned against the doorjamb watching Andy for a minute, puzzled. As she closed the door, Daniel blotted his mouth with his napkin and got to his feet. He scooped his straw hat off of the peg and stepped around her.

"Where are you off to, Daniel?" she asked. "To the orchards? Should I tell Eli you'll meet him there?"

He was halfway out the door when he tossed a "no" over his shoulder. Then he hopped onto a blue scooter, resting against the house, to catch up with Andy.

Carrie turned to Yonnie and shrugged, exasperated. "Why use two words when one will do?"

Yonnie smiled and continued to drizzle white icing over cinnamon rolls, hot from the oven. "Daniel doesn't say much because he's busy listening. He hears what others miss because he listens more than he talks."

Carrie looked at her, puzzled.

"He feels the sounds deep inside him."

Solomon Riehl didn't receive his mother's letter until he returned to Lancaster after traveling with the Barnstormers to Maryland, New York, and New Jersey. All of the team mail for the players had been held at Clipper Magazine Stadium. Sol had started to receive so much fan mail that he didn't even notice his mother's familiar handwriting until he had read halfway through the pile of letters. He read the letter, then reread it. A clear stream of fear pooled from his throat to his stomach, the quick panic that comes when you realize something has gone terribly wrong, something that it is simply too late to fix.

"Who's that one from, Amish boy?" asked Pete, an outfielder on the team. "From the look on your face, you just got dumped." He guffawed loudly.

Sol looked over at Pete, not really seeing him. He took his mother's letter and hurried outside of the locker room, then ran to his car. The keys shook in his hand as he stumbled to unlock the door. Some paint flaked off in his hands as he yanked the door open to climb in. Carrie had called his car Rusty because it had so much rust under its chassis.

Carrie, he thought, *how could you do this? How could you have married someone else?*

He locked the door, sank down low in the seat, and cried like a baby.

For the next few days, Daniel rode Andy to school on the scooter and met him, each afternoon, as school let out. Emma passed by them one morning in her buggy as she came to help Carrie cut up apples to dry on racks for snitz.

"Morning, Carrie."

Somehow, Emma could make a simple greeting sound worried, Carrie thought, as she hung Emma's bonnet upside down on the peg, hanging next to hers and Yonnie's like three black coal scuttles. Emma lived most of her life in a near panic.

"You know why Daniel's doing that, don't you?" Emma asked.

Carrie bristled, irritated by Emma's nosiness. "Of course I know why." Though the truth of it was that she didn't really know why, but she was grateful that Daniel took an interest in Andy. Andy needed a man in his life. At least, that was Carrie's reasoning when she told Esther she was taking Andy with her to live. Carrie thought Esther would have been relieved, but instead, she reacted with a cold fury. She barely spoke to Carrie during the wedding and hadn't come to visit Carrie at all since. Esther always had something to be angry about, Carrie knew. She had learned long ago that the only way to handle her was to stand up to her, but Esther nursed her grudges with the same loving care she gave to her roses.

Emma pulled up a chair to sit down, eager to divulge her news. "Well, I heard that your new English neighbor boys take Andy's lunch on the way to school. They wait for him at the end of the lane."

Carrie looked out the kitchen window. "Who told you that?"

"I heard it at a comfort knotting at Ada Stoltzfus's farm. You should have gone to the frolic, Carrie. Yonnie too. You learn all kinds of things."

Carrie frowned. She wasn't ready for a frolic yet, for all the questions about married life. "So, what's he like then, this Daniel? What sort of man is he?" her well-meaning friends would ask. Carrie wondered those questions herself. She wasn't sure she knew Daniel any better today than she did a few weeks ago.

"Why would those boys be taking Andy's lunch?"

"Well," Emma started out breathlessly, cheeks turning pink with pleasure, "they found out he's a bleeder, and they told him they want to see him bleed. They're picking a fight with him so he'll bleed."

Carrie threw the dish towel down and ran down the lane. By the time she reached the end of the lane, Daniel was on the way back.

"Emma told me!" she said, out of breath, when she reached him. "About the boys teasing Andy."

Daniel glanced over at the neighbor boys, who were throwing rocks at a treetop, trying to knock down a bird's nest. The mother bird flew close by, making distress calls.

Carrie saw them too. She frowned at them, but said to Daniel, "You can't take him to and from school for the rest of his life. Maybe I could speak to their parents so they'd understand how serious hemophilia is." Andy was small, built like Jacob, and looked younger than his years. She worried about him. She always worried about him.

Daniel's eyebrows lifted in warning. "And shame him with a fuss?"

"I'm not making a fuss," she said indignantly.

Daniel's gaze turned toward the boys. "As soon as the weather gets cold, they'll lose interest in meeting him so early." Daniel put one foot on the scooter. "Coming?"

She sighed and hopped on behind him for a lift.

"Mother, you ought not to be eating dessert for breakfast," Eli said quietly when he came inside from the barn one morning.

Yonnie was seated at the kitchen table having a slice of pie. "The way I see it, just in case the day doesn't turn out well, at least I've had my dessert."

"I like that way of thinking!" Andy said, bouncing down the stairs.

Eli looked at Yonnie and shook his head. Carrie handed him a cup of coffee as he sat down. "You see, Mother? You're a bad influence on the boy. Carrie, I'm counting on you not to let her get away with this nonsense."

Carrie smiled at the teasing, but she knew Eli was counting on her for much more than minding Yonnie. She knew he had hopes that Carrie would be able to turn Daniel around from his burden. Daniel seemed to have an invisible cloud of sadness hovering over him. She hadn't figured out what Daniel's burden was, but she had a hunch it had something to do with Abel, his cousin, raised as a brother to Daniel, who had left the family during his Rumspringa. Every so often, a letter from Abel would arrive and she would see Daniel quietly tuck it into his pocket. The letter's contents were never discussed. But for the rest of the day, Daniel and Eli would go quiet, even by their standards.

Carrie was filled with wonderings about this Abel fellow, whether he was younger or older than Daniel and where he was now. But it was Daniel's place to tell her these things and he was not one to volunteer information. Abel's name was hardly spoken between Eli or Daniel, or even Yonnie. It was like he had stopped living, like he was shunned, even though that couldn't be right. Carrie knew Abel hadn't been baptized, so he wouldn't be shunned. Yonnie had let that slip once. Carrie tried asking Yonnie more, about where Abel was now, but she could see Yonnie's mind drift off to another place and another time. Yonnie never did answer. Yonnie was a Miller, to be sure.

Carrie had wanted a home of her own and a future for her brother. In exchange, she received the hidden secrets and heartaches of the Millers.

In the middle of the night, Carrie woke and went downstairs, out to the porch to look at the stars. A few minutes later, Daniel joined her, wrapping a quilt around her shoulders.

Daniel was a deep sleeper. He could fall asleep instantly, she could tell so by the sound of his breathing. But he always seemed to know when she left the room. Maybe it was part of his listening, she realized. Even in his sleep, he seemed to listen.

"I had a nightmare," she said, hoping he would stay for a moment. "Andy had fallen and needed my help, but I couldn't get to him. It was like I was in quicksand. He kept calling for me and I couldn't get any closer."

"Just a dream," he said.

Carrie pulled the quilt tightly around her. "If anything ever happened to Andy . . ." Her voice drizzled off.

"It won't." Daniel leaned on the porch railing and looked up at the night sky.

A barn owl flew over them so closely they could hear the whir of its wings.

"The winged tiger," Daniel said, watching the owl disappear into the treetops.

Carrie tilted her head toward Daniel. "That's what my father used to call owls! They fly silently as moths and seldom miss their prey." She gave a short laugh. "Esther would correct him and say they're just flying rat traps."

"You miss him." He said the words simply, his voice low and flat.

"I do miss him. So much that at times I . . ." She shrugged, pressing her lips together.

Daniel nodded, as if he understood.

"Mattie said that all of creation is meant to remind us that God is nearby. She said that God is closer than our own breath." She turned slightly to face Daniel. "Do you think she's right?"

She saw a flash of something in his eyes, the echoes of a longing, a sadness. "I'm not the one to ask." He went to the door and held it open. "Don't stay up too late. Morning comes early."

Sometimes, she thought, turning back to gaze at the night sky, trying to talk to Daniel felt like trying to pump a dry well.

One afternoon, Carrie went to town to run some errands. When she returned to the farm late in the day, Daniel came out of the barn to help her down from the buggy.

"I'm sorry I'm late. I'll get dinner started right off," she told him as he unhitched Old-Timer from the tracings.

Carrie hurried to the kitchen and saw Yonnie at the stovetop, stirring a sauce. Glancing at the table, she noticed it was already set for dinner. "Oh, bless you, Yonnie!" She hung her bonnet up on the peg and untied her cape when she remembered that she had left a few packages in the back of the buggy and rushed down to the barn to get them.

As she reached the partly open barn door, she saw Andy drag a sack of oats over to Daniel, talking as he pulled.

"He used to be Amish but now he plays baseball," she heard him say.

Daniel stopped in mid-turn. "The baseball player? The one everyone talks about?"

"Yeah. He's the one." Andy held up an English newspaper, pointing to the headline about the Lancaster Barnstormers, about Sol's pitching.

Carrie had found the newspaper abandoned on a bench near the hitching post in town where she tied Old-Timer's reins. She had picked it up. When she was nearing home, she had turned down a quiet lane and pulled the buggy over to the side to read the article about Sol. She read it and reread it, then realized how late it was. That foolish action had made her late getting home, late starting dinner. She clapped her hands to her cheeks. How could she have been so careless to have left the newspaper in the buggy?

Andy held the sack of oats open so Daniel could scoop them into Old-Timer's bucket. "Solomon Riehl was courting Carrie, but then he disappeared, right when my dad passed. So she married you."

Carrie slid open the barn door and walked in. "Andy!" she said sharply.

Startled, Andy nearly knocked over the sack of oats.

"Geh zu Yonnie im Haus." *Go to Yonnie in the house.*

Andy looked at Carrie in mute astonishment, surprised by the sharp tone in her voice, but he hustled past her to go to the kitchen without a questioning word or glance.

Daniel turned back to filling the bucket with oats as if nothing had happened. Carrie picked up the newspaper and folded it. She wasn't sure what to say. Maybe she didn't need to say anything at all. She turned to leave and stopped when she heard Daniel ask, "So Solomon Riehl was the midnight caller?"

Carrie spun toward Daniel, who still had his back to her. "Yes."

Daniel put the bucket down and turned to face Carrie. "It was like Andy said?"

Carrie looked down at her hands nervously, avoiding Daniel's steady gaze. "Yes," she answered quietly.

Daniel didn't say a word, he just stood there, waiting for her to continue.

"Sol wanted to play for the Barnstormers and wanted me with him. We had made plans to leave. We were going to be married that very week when my father died. But . . . then everything changed. I couldn't leave Andy." She looked down at the hay-strewn floor. "Sol left anyway. The night that Andy was in the emergency room, after Esther had taken the switch to him, I knew I had to get Andy out of Esther's home. When you asked me to marry you, it seemed like . . . an opportunity." She lifted her eyes to gauge his response, but his face was expressionless. "I told you that I wasn't in love with you. I've never tried to deceive you."

He glanced out the barn window. "But you didn't mention you loved someone else."

The silence between them felt as real as a brick wall. Finally, she asked softly, "Daniel, why did you marry me?"

He didn't move for a moment, didn't say anything. She couldn't read him well enough to know what he was thinking. Finally, he took a few steps

41

toward her and gently lifted her chin so that she would look at him. They were inches apart, close enough to feel each other's breath.

"Same as you, Carrie. Trying to forget."

Daniel strode past her, out of the barn and into the orchards, not returning home until long after dark.

4

The pitching coach slapped Sol on the back as he jogged in from the mound after practice on Monday. "We clocked you at over 95 miles per hour! Fastest ever!" He was nearly bursting with pride. "Not sure what you had for breakfast, but keep it up, Sol."

Sol nodded, before heading into the locker room for a shower. The other guys on the team congratulated him as he peeled off his uniform. "You must be as pumped up as a hot air balloon after that practice," said Rody, the catcher.

Sol shrugged. "Just a good day, I guess." But he knew why. Every time he wound up for a pitch, the image of Carrie in another man's arms popped into his head. He pictured the catcher's mitt as the man's face—he could barely remember what Daniel Miller looked like—and he threw that ball as hard as he possibly could.

"Some of the guys are going out for a cold beer." Seeing his hesitation, Rody threw a wet towel at him. "Come on. I'll treat."

Sol slammed his locker shut. "Okay. Give me ten minutes to shower."

Veronica McCall dropped by on a weekly basis to ask Carrie if she was ready to sell the property. Each time, Carrie said no. Today, Emma was visiting to help Carrie can applesauce. Veronica smelled the freshly brewed coffee and helped herself to a cup.

As she poured the coffee into the mug, she glanced out the kitchen window. "Do all Amish men look like him?"

"Who?" Carrie asked, cutting the apples and tossing them into a big pot.

"Him. He's a hottie." She pointed out the window. "He could be on the cover of *GQ*." She turned to Emma to explain. "*Gentleman's Quarterly*. It's a magazine that has a gorgeous hunk on its cover every month."

Carrie put her knife down, wiped her hands on her apron, and looked out the window to see who Veronica meant. "Why, that's Daniel!"

"Who's he?" Veronica asked.

"Carrie's *husband*," Emma said, raising an eyebrow.

"He's my grandson," Yonnie added, in a voice of quiet pride. Seated at the kitchen table, Yonnie had been peeling apples for a pie. She had a trick of peeling the entire apple skin in one long ribbon—a talent that impressed Andy.

Veronica shrugged. "Your husband is a babe, Carrie. He could be a male model." They watched Daniel lift a bale of hay from the wagon and toss it onto a wheelbarrow. "He's got muscles in his arms that look like ropes."

Carrie looked at her as if she was speaking a foreign language.

Emma pointed her paring knife in Veronica's direction. "Lusting after another woman's husband is a sin."

Veronica turned to Emma with catlike eyes. "There's nothing wrong with admiring nature's handiwork." She glanced at her wristwatch. "Gotta go." She picked an apple slice out of Emma's bowl of cut apples and sailed out the door.

"Carrie, we need to keep an eye on *that* woman," Emma said, scowling, turning her attention back to her apples. "The English aren't like the Amish."

"And the Amish aren't like the English, Emma," Yonnie said. "My Daniel does not have a roving eye."

Carrie stood by the kitchen window, watching Veronica as she walked over to Daniel. She wondered what Veronica said to make him laugh. Before turning from the window, she did happen to notice that Veronica was right. His arms did look like thick pieces of rope.

Mattie had asked Carrie to help her sew a new dress. After purchasing the fabric in town, they returned to Carrie's house to use one of her patterns.

While Carrie hunted for the patterns upstairs, Mattie started some coffee in the kitchen. She inhaled the aroma from the coffee grounds as she scooped the coffee out of the can and into the filter. As she filled the coffee brewer with water, her thoughts drifted to Carrie. She felt troubled about her friend, sensing a wound deep in Carrie's soul, a wound that wasn't healing.

Mattie knew that losing her father was a profound loss to Carrie. What she couldn't figure out was why Carrie married Daniel so soon after Jacob died. And why she never seemed bothered by Sol's leaving. Maybe, Mattie thought, it was because Daniel was the one Jacob had chosen for Carrie. As Mattie waited for the coffee to finish brewing, she looked outside the kitchen window and saw Eli and Daniel unhitching Old-Timer from the buggy the women had used to go into town.

Daniel treated Carrie tenderly, Mattie had often noticed. He lifted her out of the buggy as if she were made of fine china. He waited to sit at the kitchen table until Carrie sat first. He really was a fine-looking man, she thought, watching him lead the horse into the barn. Tall and broad shouldered, fair haired with sky-blue eyes rimmed by dark eyebrows. He had a cleft in his chin, still visible. His blond beard, circling his jawline, was just growing in. Mattie would have assumed he would be a younger version of his father Eli, slim and wiry and worried. Daniel was nearly as handsome as Sol.

As Mattie opened up the cupboard to find the coffee mugs, Daniel came into the kitchen. "Wu is sie?" he asked gruffly. *Where is she?*

"Carrie's upstairs." Just as Mattie was about to ask him if he wanted coffee, Carrie came downstairs with the box of patterns in her arms.

"Was is letz?" Carrie asked, seeing the look on Daniel's face. *What's wrong?*

He slapped an English newspaper on the kitchen table, open to the sports section with a large headline: "Amish Sol Pitches a No-Hitter." He kept his eyes fixed on Carrie, brows furrowed. Carrie kept her eyes on the newspaper.

The silence in the kitchen took on a prickly tension. "It's mine," Mattie blurted out at last. "I bought it in town."

Both Daniel and Carrie snapped their heads toward her, eyes wide in surprise.

"I saw the headline and wanted to read about Sol," Mattie said. As Daniel and Carrie continued to stare at her, she felt her mouth go dry. "I love Sol. I always will, no matter what he's done. He's coming back one day. I'm sure of it." Mattie's eyes started to fill with tears. She stole a glance at Carrie and saw hurt flood into her eyes.

Suddenly, Mattie understood.

Without another word, Mattie put the coffee mugs on the counter and quietly left to go home. She was almost to the street when she heard Daniel call her name as he ran up to her.

"Here," he said, handing her the newspaper.

Later that night, Carrie changed into her nightgown and took the pins out of her hair, braiding the loose strands into a long rope. She slipped into bed and peered over the edge at Daniel, stretched out on the floor. "Are you asleep?"

He turned to his side, facing the window. "Nearly."

"Daniel—"

"Mattie was lying." He rolled over on his back, eyes facing the ceiling. "Just not sure what part of it she was lying about."

All afternoon, Carrie had been thinking the same thing. Mattie had *lied*! Carrie was the one who had bought that newspaper. But was Mattie also lying about loving Sol? Carrie wasn't sure. She punched the pillow into shape and laid her head on it.

"Seems at times there are three people in this marriage," Daniel said in a low voice.

With that, Carrie's temper flared. "You're wrong." She looked over the edge of the bed at him. "There are *four*."

The words flew out of her mouth before she even thought about them. She was only making a guess. Until that moment, she didn't know for sure that the burden Daniel carried might have something to do with a woman. "I . . . I'm sorry," she said when she saw the stark pain in his eyes, as real as if she had struck him. "I shouldn't have—"

"It's all right," he said, in a voice that hurt her with its gentleness. "I'm going to take a walk."

Daniel grabbed his shirt, pants, and shoes, and went downstairs. She heard the kitchen door close behind him.

The next morning, Mattie finished her chores quickly to have time to get to Carrie's. She needed to set right yesterday's conversation. She was mortified with herself for blurting out that she loved Sol. That was a secret she had guarded so well, for years now, from the moment she had first laid eyes on him. Just as she was turning the buggy into the gravel lane, she saw Daniel come out of the barn. He stopped when he saw her and waited until she came to a halt.

"Morning, Daniel," she said shyly. "Is Carrie inside?"

He shook his head. "Hanging the wash." He tipped his head in the direction of the clothesline, where Carrie was hanging laundry. He took the reins and helped her down from the buggy, then tied her horse to the post.

When Carrie saw Mattie approach, she put the wet shirts back in the basket and sat on the big rock in the sun, patting a spot in silent invitation for Mattie to come join her. "The wash should dry in no time with this Indian summer." A light breeze stirred the rows of clothes on the line. Yonnie's faded lavender churchgoing dress, hanging right beside her, tossed out a faint whiff of laundry soap.

Mattie nodded, head tucked down as she sat beside Carrie.

Carrie leaned against her elbows. "I've always loved this time of year. The work of summer is nearly done. It's warm, but not hot. Sort of a lull, waiting for winter."

Mattie nodded again, not saying a word, feeling like she had a knot in her throat.

Softly, Carrie asked, "Mattie, what made you tell a lie?"

Mattie covered her face with her hands. "It just flew out of me. I'm so ashamed. I feel terrible! But I could see that Daniel was upset about the newspaper."

Carrie watched the breeze twist and luff the white sheets, filling them like sails on a ship. "It was kind of you, standing up for me like that."

"I shouldn't have lied. It was wrong of me. But Carrie, we're friends." She said it in a tone as if that explained everything—her loyalty, her compassion, her devotion.

"I don't deserve such a friend."

Mattie shook that comment off. "You deserve so much more, Carrie. You're the strongest person I know. I know it's been hard lately."

Carrie looked away, but Mattie caught the glint of tears in her eyes. She noticed Daniel, standing by the barn with his arms crossed against his black leather apron, listening to a neighbor who had just brought a horse by to be shod. "He's a good man, that Daniel."

Carrie's gaze followed Mattie's. "Why didn't you ever tell me about how you felt about Sol?"

Mattie bent down and uncoiled a shirt from the basket, shook it twice, then stood to pin it to the line. She had diverted herself on purpose to give herself time to answer carefully. "I could never help my feelings for Sol. I've loved him for as long as I can remember. But you know what a flirt he is. You know how he was with all the girls, taking a different girl home from every singing." Nearly every girl but her, Mattie thought, pausing to pick up another shirt. The truth was that Sol did not know Mattie existed for much of the time they had lived in the same town. She was far too quiet, too plain, to attract his attention.

She looked across the clothesline at Carrie. "But then, he started taking you home from Sunday singings regularly, and you didn't seem to mind." She fixed her eyes on the clothespin in her hand. "I just couldn't tell you, Carrie. I just couldn't. It's not our way."

Carrie nodded. Courting couples avoided teasing at all costs. "You're pretty good at keeping secrets, Mattie. I never would have guessed how you felt about Sol. Not ever."

Mattie smiled shyly at her.

"You must have felt some envy toward me."

"No, Carrie. Never that." Mattie meant that sincerely. She would never have let jealousy take root in her heart. "You must believe that."

Carrie grabbed the last piece of wet clothing in the basket, then hung it on the line. "Mattie, you're too good for Solomon Riehl. He has no *Demut*, no humility. He'll never return to the church."

"Don't say that," Mattie said sharply. Then she dropped her eyes to the ground. "No one is ever beyond help."

Carrie tilted her head, watching her friend. "I guess it all depends if he wants the help." She picked up the empty laundry basket and rested it on her hip. "Mattie, can I give you a piece of advice? Don't expect anything from Solomon Riehl. Then you won't be disappointed."

Sunday felt different from any other day. A day set apart. Carrie had always loved church gatherings. Even as a child, there was a quiet excitement in the air. The preaching and hymn singing started early in the morning and lasted three hours, topped off with a fellowship meal, brought by the womenfolk.

Glancing across to the men's side of the room, she could see Eli, sitting ramrod straight, a somber look on his serious face. Seated next to him was Daniel. She saw Daniel's eyes lift quickly to the ceiling, as if he didn't want to be caught looking at her. It made Carrie smile, to think he was watching her. Next to Daniel sat Andy, angry and sullen.

Andy had been trying to memorize the *Lob Lied*, the hymn of praise sung at every Amish church gathering, before his ninth birthday. He had been itching to sit with the big boys in the church service, but it was tradition to wait until an Amish boy turned nine. Andy's birthday was coming up and he was determined to go in now. Before breakfast this morning, he had recited the verses one more time. When he missed the last verse, he clapped his hands on his cheeks. "Aw, Carrie, let me go in. Everyone knows I'm almost nine. They'll call me a baby."

Carrie shook her head. "No shortcuts."

"Come on!" Andy pleaded. He was near tears. "Dad would let me!"

"Go upstairs and get ready," Carrie told him. "We need to leave in a few minutes so we won't be late."

Andy bolted up the stairs, almost knocking into Daniel as he was coming down the stairs. Daniel's eyes met Carrie's briefly, then he dropped his gaze. "Is knowing that hymn so important?"

Discouraged, Carrie turned to the sink to finish the breakfast dishes. "I'm trying to make things normal for him. Trying to do what my father would want me to do with him." She scrubbed a dish. "Besides, the bishop will be watching Andy."

"Don't blame it on the bishop," Daniel said as he plucked his hat and coat off the peg. "It's Esther you're worried about. She's the one who will be watching Andy." He put his hand on the kitchen doorjamb. "There's no such thing as normal for a grieving boy."

Through the kitchen window, Carrie watched Daniel head to the barn, thinking over what he said. It was the longest paragraph he'd uttered. Still, it amazed her that Daniel had only spent a summer in her father's home and seemed to have a better understanding of the family than she did. He was right. So was Andy. Her father wouldn't have cared about those verses. She was worried about Esther. Esther had brittle requirements for everyone, especially for Jacob's children.

Carrie threw the dish towel down, more confused than ever. She wasn't ready to be a parent, but she was thrust into that role when her father died. She decided this must be what it felt like to tuck an octopus into bed. An arm or two kept popping out.

The focus of the bishop's sermon that morning was on the sinful nature of man. He was very effective. Everyone finished the morning feeling especially convicted of their wickedness. Afterward, the benches were moved and the tables set up, and the women served a soup and sandwich lunch. Carrie joined several other young women as they brought the food to the men. After the men finished eating, the women and children took their turn. When the meal was over and everything had been cleaned up, adults usually gathered in small groups to visit as children played or napped.

Today, though, folks seemed quiet, subdued. Eli herded the family into the buggy for a silent ride home. Daniel sat down on Eli's right side and picked up the reins, clucking to the horse to get it trotting. Carrie and Yonnie sat in the backseat, Andy between them. The trip home seemed to last forever, and the cramped quarters in the buggy didn't help much, either. Finally, Yonnie broke the quiet. "I think that bishop is needing a little more fiber in his diet. Maybe I'll mix up some of my special prune tea for him. Helps when the plumbing gets backed up."

Turning to look back at her, Eli scolded, "Mother! You are speaking of a bishop! Of a man chosen by God!"

"And that man is older than Moses," Yonnie muttered under her breath.

Carrie let her own smile come out in a quick curve of her lips and a downward tuck of her chin. She avoided Andy's eyes. She knew she needed to be a good example, but sometimes she missed just being a sister, one who could share a private joke, the way they used to.

Later that day, Carrie finished feeding Hope and was leading the cow into a stall when she heard Daniel and Eli come into the barn. Through a crack between the boards she watched Daniel sit on a bale of hay, hands on his knees, chin to his chest, defeated.

Eli came over to him and put a hand on his shoulder. "You have a chance to make a new life here, a fresh start with Carrie. I knew she'd be good for you. She's a strong woman."

Carrie ducked down low by Hope's wooden wall, unnoticed. She felt as nosy as Emma, listening to people's private conversations, but from the serious way they were talking, she decided it would be worse to interrupt them.

Daniel lifted his head and said, "Didn't you hear the bishop today? Heaven's deaf to the cries of a sinner." He stood and walked to the barn door, then turned back to his father. "There's really no such thing as a fresh start. Our past doesn't let us go."

After he left, Eli sat down on the hay bale where Daniel had been. Carrie's heart nearly broke as she saw him start to shake, then hold his head in his hands as he wept. Quietly, she slipped out the back door to give him privacy.

The next morning, the weather turned cold. Carrie took some coffee to Daniel down by the barn. She watched him for a moment. Concentrating intently, he pumped the bellows to blow on the fire, then grasped a horseshoe with the tongs and thrust it into the burning coals. He looked up when he saw Carrie and gave a brief nod when his eyes rested on the hot drink. She watched him pick up the poker-hot horseshoe and plunge it into the trough of water, releasing a hiss and plume of steam.

"Every now and then, the bishop likes to remind us of our sinfulness, Daniel."

He put the tongs down and took the coffee mug from her.

"He's not usually so grim. He's really quite kind. And the ministers aren't grim. The deacon, Abraham, isn't a bit grim." She leaned against the workbench. "Yesterday, Mattie said that maybe the bishop has been reading too much of the Old Testament lately and not enough of the New Testament." She picked up a tool, studying it. "She says that the New Testament tells us our sins are wiped clean."

Daniel took a sip of coffee but kept his eyes fixed on her.

"Whiter than snow, Mattie says. I'm not exactly sure where in the Bible it says that, but Mattie is usually right about that kind of thing. If she were born a man, the Lord would choose to give her the lot so she'd be a minister one day. I'm certain of it. Mattie's grandfather was a bishop. Caleb Zook was his name. One of the finest bishops there ever was. Everybody loved Caleb Zook. Even Esther. He passed, just a few years ago." Her words fell into an empty silence. After an awkward moment, she put down the tool and turned to go when she heard him say her name.

"Carrie?" he asked.

She spun around to face him. Daniel's eyes met hers, wide and sea blue. She could see his heart in his eyes, a heart beating with hope and hurt. She saw all of his sadness wanting to pour out so he could be freed from it. But he kept hesitating, and then the moment passed, like a cloud swallowing up the sun.

All that he said was, "Denki." He tipped his head toward the coffee cup in his hand.

"Bitte."

It was a start, she hoped.

Mattie was riding her scooter down the road one afternoon when she spotted something peculiar moving in a tree. She pulled over on the scooter to examine what it was. As soon as she saw the sandy blond head, she knew. She slid off the scooter and walked to the tree. "Andy Weaver! What do you think you're doing up there?"

Startled, Andy looked down at her, eyes wide. "I'm trying to feed the baby birds. Those rotten English boys killed their mother and they're awful hungry." He put one hand in his pocket and pulled out a handful of wiggling worms. "I dug up some food for them. See?" One of the worms dropped from his hand and landed on Mattie's head.

She screamed and brushed it off. "Andy, you shouldn't be climbing so high up! You'll fall!"

"Nah. I'm nearly there." With that, he swung one leg onto the branch by his head. There was a huge *crack!* as the limb broke. Andy spilled on top of Mattie, knocking the breath out of her.

"Oh Andy, are you all right?" Mattie asked, as soon as she stopped feeling dazed. She tried to get up, but he was smashed on top of her like a pancake. "Say something!"

"I think I'm dead," he said, rolling off of her as he held up his arm. His wrist looked as crooked as a snapped tree twig.

"Oh no!" Mattie said as she sat up, eyeing his wrist. "Another visit to the emergency room."

Andy smiled weakly. "At least they got television."

Mattie managed to wheel Andy to Carrie's on the scooter, slowly and awkwardly. While she hitched up the buggy to take Andy to the hospital, Carrie wrote a note to leave on the kitchen table for Daniel.

After the X-rays had been developed, Andy waited on a bed in the far corner of the emergency room, close to the television. Carrie had just turned the channel to a cartoon when the doctor came in and sat on Andy's bed.

"Popeye! My favorite!" he said, after glancing up to see what Andy was watching. "I yam what I yam," he said in a funny voice. "My mom let me watch it so I would eat spinach. But I still can't stomach spinach."

Andy looked up at him, wide-eyed, surprised by his casualness.

The doctor picked up Andy's chart, reviewed the notes, and peered at the X-ray pinned against the light. "I'm Dr. Zimmerman. Doing my internship here at Stoney Ridge." He smiled at Carrie and Mattie. "So, Andy, you broke your wrist and you're a hemophiliac. Just to be sure, we're going to give you a dose of Factor IX." He looked at Carrie and Mattie. "So which one of you broke his fall?"

"That would be her," Carrie said, pointing at Mattie. "She has a knack for being in the right place at the right time."

Mattie's cheeks reddened at the praise. "I'm going to the cafeteria to get Andy something to eat."

Dr. Zimmerman gave instructions to the nurse to get the IV drip for Factor IX set up for Andy, then he opened the cupboard to get the supplies for the cast. "Let's see if I can remember what they taught me in medical school." He looked at the supplies as if he'd never seen them before.

"So you're new at doctoring?" Andy asked, a little worried.

"Well, I think a day-old degree is good enough, don't you?" Dr. Zimmerman answered, eyes snapping with good humor. Andy's eyes, as wide as saucers, made Dr. Zimmerman burst into laughter at his own joke. He started unwrapping the gauze. "What color cast do you want?" he asked Andy. "Neon green would make the school kids think you're a super action figure."

"White," Carrie interrupted.

Andy groaned.

The doctor looked at Carrie with a question.

"We don't like things showy or loud," she said. "We don't want anything that draws attention."

"What's so wrong with drawing attention to yourself?" the doctor asked.

Carrie wrinkled her brow. "What's so right about it?"

The doctor shrugged. "Good point." He turned to Andy. "White would be my choice too." He lowered his voice to a whisper. "That way, you can tell kids that it's really leprosy."

"What's leprosy?" Andy asked.

"It's a highly contagious disease that eats away at your skin," he said, mixing up the plaster to spread over the gauze. "Looks pretty disgusting. Very effective way to gross out your friends."

Watching him with fascination, Andy brightened considerably at that news.

After an hour's wait in the waiting room, Solomon Riehl had just been admitted into the Emergency Room. His shoulder was throbbing and he wasn't sure what was wrong with it. It had been bothering him for a few weeks now, but aspirin usually took the edge off of the pain. Not today, though. He didn't want to talk to the team's trainer; if he did, it would be noted on his records. That could tip off the pitching coach to a problem. The coach was conservative like that. Sol just had to get through another few weeks, then he could give his shoulder a good long rest. He was hoping he could get a cortisone shot or something, like the other guys on the team did.

On the far side of the room, past the nurse's station, the silhouette of an Amish woman caught his eye. He put his things down on the bed, then looked closer to see if he might know who she was. He knew most of the Amish in Stoney Ridge. The woman had her back to him, facing the doctor. The doctor had put the blood pressure cuff around his own head and started to pump, making the boy on the bed start to giggle, then to guffaw out loud.

Sol's heart started to pound. He knew that laugh. That was Andy's laugh. And if that was Andy, then the Amish woman was Carrie. He hadn't seen her since the day he had left. It still made his insides twist up, every single day, what he had done to her.

Sol watched as the doctor high-fived Andy's good hand before he left. The nurse started an IV on Andy. Sol figured it was that hemophilia stuff he needed. After the nurse left, Sol jumped off the bed and grabbed his jacket. In that instant, an Amish man arrived, hat in hand, and stood by the door, scanning the room until his eyes rested on Carrie. In a few quick strides, the man reached her side and stood close to her. She leaned in against him, to tell him something. Sol drew back, as if touching a hot stove.

After a while, Sol saw the man head out the door into the hallway and decided to follow him. He slipped into the hallway and saw the cafeteria doors swing shut. Sol peered through the small window of the door and noticed the man, standing in front of the coffee vending machine, feeding the machine with coins.

Sol pushed open the cafeteria door. "She likes her coffee black," he said, walking up to the man.

Daniel looked at Sol, puzzled.

"Carrie," Sol said. "She likes it black because that's how her father liked his coffee."

Recognition dawned in Daniel's eyes. "Solomon Riehl," he stated, a fact.

"I am," Sol said. "And you're Daniel Miller."

Sol and Daniel stood looking at each other for a long moment, sizing each other up.

Daniel turned back to the coffee machine and punched the buttons for cream and sugar. After the cup filled, he turned to go.

Sol blocked his path. "She loves me, you know. She'll always love me."

Daniel swirled the coffee in his hand, watching the warm shades of brown and cream blend together.

"I happened to be in Ohio awhile back, playing a scrimmage." Sol watched Daniel carefully to see if there was any reaction, but he could have been describing the weather. Daniel's face was hugely unreadable. "Met a few Amish guys who came to watch me play. Guess they had heard about me."

Daniel lifted his head to look Sol straight in the eyes.

"They told me an interesting story about you and your cousin. About why you left Ohio."

Daniel's eyebrows lifted.

"Made me wonder how much Carrie knows. About you, I mean."

Sol thought he caught a flash of something in Daniel's eyes, then there was nothing.

Daniel lifted the coffee cup. "She likes it with cream and sugar because that's the way her mother drank it." He opened the door to leave, tossing over his shoulder, "My Carrie is waiting for me."

Sol stood there for a moment, watching the doors swing shut. It was common for the Amish to call each other "my" or "our"; it was part of belonging. But that wasn't how he meant it, Sol thought. Daniel Miller said "my Carrie" like a claim.

A young woman's soft and soothing voice came from behind him. "Hello, Solomon."

Sol spun around to see who was talking to him. There, smiling ear to ear, stood little Mattie Zook.

On the way home, Daniel stopped the buggy at the tree where Andy had been climbing when he fell. Andy had begged him to save the birds and bring the nest home.

Daniel shimmied up the tree and peered in the nest. "They're Cooper's hawks!"

"So?" Andy yelled.

Daniel looked down at him. "They're predators. They steal other bird eggs. And go after small animals too."

"You said that every creature has a purpose, Daniel," Andy yelled back. "You told me that."

Daniel gave an exaggerated sigh. "So I did."

"Them birds need our help!"

Daniel untangled the nest from its crook. He tucked it under his arm and shimmied back down the tree. There were three baby birds in the nest, already near death's door, panting and gasping, hardly moving. Andy reached into his pocket with his good hand and pulled out what was left of the worms he had caught that morning. He cradled the nest in his lap and tried to jam bits of worm into the birds' beaks.

"They need water," Daniel said.

"Yonnie might have an eye dropper in her medicine chest," Carrie said. "You can try that." But the feeble condition of those baby birds worried her. Andy was just barely getting over their father's death, if such a thing were possible, she thought. She wasn't really sure she'd ever feel the same way she did before Jacob died. The pain wasn't as severe as it had been a few months ago, though it would catch her off guard sometimes. Just yesterday, she found a list with Jacob's handwriting on it and tears flooded her eyes. Most days, though, grief wasn't at the forefront anymore.

Still, neither was happiness.

By the next afternoon, with Andy's vigilant care, the baby birds made a complete turnaround. They were noisy and demanding houseguests. Smelly too. Carrie insisted that the nest be moved out of the warm kitchen and into the barn. Andy objected, certain they would freeze to death.

"They'll be fine, Andy," Carrie said reassuringly. "The barn is protected." She pointed to the barn. "Go."

Just as soon as Andy disappeared into the barn with the nest, Mattie came to the door bringing a box wrapped up in warm scarves. She unwrapped the box on the kitchen table. Inside were five creamy white eggs. "They're Canada geese eggs. Dad ordered a batch to restock the pond. You'll need to keep them incubated for about a month. I thought, in case the hawk babies don't make it, well, this way he'd have something else to take care of."

Mattie packed the eggs up again to keep them warm.

Daniel took the box out of her arms to take to the barn. Solemnly, he looked at her and said, "You have a good heart, Mattie Zook."

5

It was just about a year ago, Carrie realized, on a beautiful fall day just like today—crisp and cold, with leaves on the trees in shades from red to yellow—that she had made her last batch of sweet cider with her father. She had watched Jacob closely as he mixed juices from different varieties of apples to make his sweet cider. He was very particular about his cider.

"Folks count on my cider, Carrie girl, to help them get through the long winter, so we got to make it just right."

Together, they sampled blends before deciding on the perfect combination. "Thirty-six apples, not one more or one less, make a gallon of cider," he had said, counting them out.

Even then, she felt a shiver of precognition, to seal that memory—a perfect moment, a perfect day.

After Daniel sold the fancy-grade apples from this year's harvest to a packing house, Carrie decided to use the leftover apples to re-create her father's cider. In the carriage house, Daniel had found an old cider press and cleaned it up for her. All week, she had been trying to match the taste of her father's cider—sweet and tart. Carrie didn't think the taste of her cider rivaled Jacob's—her apple varieties differed from his—but it was close enough for the neighbors. At church on Sunday, Carrie told one person, the right person—Emma—that she was making Jacob's cider, and by Monday morning, neighbors were lined up at the farmhouse with empty plastic gallon milk jugs.

One of the first customers was Annie Zook, a school friend of Carrie's who married one of Mattie's cousins and was pregnant with twins.

"That girl is about ready to pop," Emma said, waving to Annie as she drove off in the buggy. Emma had come for the day, to help, she said, but she spent her time talking with visiting neighbors. She glanced curiously at Carrie's flat midriff. "Seems like we should be getting an announcement pretty soon, doesn't it?" Then she frowned. "Though Mother said that you might take after your own mother, who had trouble having babies. She said your mother was a frail and sickly thing. She said your mother was a carrier of hemophilia and that's why it was a double whammy with Jacob being a bleeder and Andy being a bleeder. She wondered if you might have trouble too."

Carrie stiffened but wasn't surprised. The Plain had a saying: a new baby every spring. "If Esther seems to know so much about me," she asked Emma, "why don't you just ask her?"

These days, Esther barely said more than a few words to Carrie other than to point out Andy's shortcomings. Yesterday at church, Esther had picked up Andy by the back of the collar, like a coat on a peg, and told Carrie that he needed a haircut.

Emma planted her hands on her hips. "There's no need to get huffy. I just figured you'd be—"

"Cinnamon rolls are burning, Emma," Daniel interrupted, passing the women on his way to the barn.

"Himmel! No! I told Yonnie to take them out thirty minutes ago . . ." Emma hurried to the kitchen, her legs pumping hard as if she were being chased by a swarm of yellow jackets.

Carrie turned to Daniel. "I saw Yonnie take those rolls out of the oven awhile ago."

His eyes crinkled at the corners. "Ach? Ich bin letz." *Oh? My mistake.* Into his mouth he popped the last bite of a cinnamon roll he had hidden behind his black leather apron. A smile flickered over Daniel's lips, so quick, so faint, that Carrie thought she might have imagined it.

The first snowfall of winter dusted Stoney Ridge on Christmas. Before dawn, Daniel woke Andy to show him the sight of moonlight casting shadows on the white earth. Afterward, the two went into the barn to feed the animals. Andy flew out of the barn and let out a thunderbuster bellow that shook the air. Carrie rushed down, thinking something terrible must have happened.

Instead, it was something wonderful.

Daniel had surprised Andy with a pony, Strawberry, and a cart of his own. When Carrie saw the look on Andy's face as he stroked the roan-colored pony in the stall, her eyes filled with tears.

"Aw, it's not so much, Carrie," Daniel said, but he looked pleased. "Just a way to get him to school and back."

The Zooks had invited Carrie's family over to share Christmas dinner, so later that day Eli readied the buggy. Carrie looked forward to being with Mattie, but she worried about the turn of weather. The day had grown dark and cold, and snow was starting to pile up. Carrie fussed over Yonnie in the buggy, covering her with blankets warmed by the kitchen stove. Daniel wanted to train Andy to manage Strawberry, so they followed behind in the cart. Carrie peered through the back window of Eli's buggy at the sight of them. Daniel stood with his arms wrapped around Andy, partly to block the wind and partly to help him control the reins. Andy's hat had blown off, his coat was open, his red cheeks looked windchapped. But the look of pure joy on his face warmed Carrie's heart like a summer day.

Winter storms hit twice in January, just enough to keep things interesting, Eli said, without making life too difficult. In the middle of the month, the skies were blue, but a cold snap kept the ground frozen solid, so Eli and Daniel decided the time was right to prune the orchards. If the weather turned too warm, the slushy snow would turn to mud, slowing them down.

Midmorning and midafternoon, Carrie brought a warm drink and snack out to Daniel and Eli in the orchards to keep them fortified. As they finished pruning the last few acres of apple trees, she noticed that Eli had to stop frequently. He had trouble catching his breath, like he was at the top of a mountain and couldn't get enough air. She thought he was just having a hard time climbing up and down the ramp, dragging heavy saws, but she could see that Daniel was concerned.

One day at lunch, Eli felt so worn out that he decided to lie down in his room for a few minutes. After watching Eli slowly make his way up the stairs, Daniel asked her if she knew of any heart doctors in town, but she only knew of blood doctors.

"Has your father had trouble with his heart?" Carrie asked.

Daniel didn't answer right away, so Yonnie filled in. "Terrible trouble. He has a bad heart. Doctor had to open him up. Doctor said it was like . . . like fixing a leaky sprinkler."

Daniel rolled his eyes. "Surgery to fix a valve."

"I'll ask around and see if someone knows of a heart doctor to recommend," Carrie said.

"Doctor can't fix it," Yonnie said sadly. "His heart is just broken to pieces."

Slowly, like a weathervane, Daniel turned and stared at her. All the world's sorrow, all the world's pain, filled those troubled blue eyes.

"Oh Daniel, I didn't mean . . ." Yonnie's hands flew up to her mouth, as if trying to stop the flow of words.

He dropped his head, then lifted it. When he turned to Carrie, his blue eyes went still again. She'd never seen a person's face change so fast.

"Tell Eli I'll wait for him in the workshop," he told her, plucking his broadbrim off the wall peg before heading outside.

Carrie wondered what had just been said between Yonnie and Daniel. Or not said, as seemed to be Daniel's way. She closed the kitchen door, watching him. She couldn't crack that man open with a sledgehammer.

Suddenly, Yonnie's fork clattered on the floor as she clapped her hands together and started whispering, "Gottes wille. Gottes wille."

Not a moment later, a loud tumbling sound came from overhead. It was followed by an eerie silence.

Carrie ran to the kitchen door and called out to Daniel. Nearly at the barn, he spun around and bolted to the house, almost as if he had been expecting Carrie's call. He burst into the kitchen and flew up the stairs, two at a time, and threw open the door to his father's room. By the time Carrie reached them, she found Daniel cradling his father in his arms, a stricken look on his face as he called out, "Dad! Dad!" Eli's mouth moved silently, like a fish out of water. His hands were gripping his shirt, in great pain. Then he went still.

Daniel looked up at Carrie with a horrified look. "Er is nimmi am scharfe." *He's gone.*

Carrie was grateful Andy wasn't home when Eli passed. She thought she would meet him at school to prepare him for the sight of Eli's body, laid out in the front room.

As she took her bonnet off of the peg, Daniel stopped her. "I'll go. Need the fresh air."

Carrie's heart felt heavy as she saw Daniel walk down the driveway, hands jammed in his pockets, head dropped low. He seemed so alone. The deeper the feelings, she was discovering about him, the more he withdrew into himself. She didn't know how to help him.

No sooner had Daniel disappeared down the street but Veronica McCall arrived, banging on the front door as if Carrie were deaf as a fencepost. When Carrie opened the door, Veronica squeezed past her to enter the house. When Veronica's eyes rested on Yonnie's quilts, stacked up in the corner of the front room, she gasped. She rushed over to the quilts, pulling them out to admire them.

"These are masterpieces! They're stunning! They should be hanging in a museum!" She yanked them open as if they were sheets for a bed. "Did you make these, Carrie?"

"No. Daniel's grandmother made them. She's upstairs, resting—"

"Well, you just hop upstairs and wake her up! I have a proposition to make her."

"This isn't a good time for a visit—"

"Carrie, I want these quilts for the inn when it reopens! Name your price!"

Carrie sighed. "They're not for sale. Yonnie makes the quilts for her family to use. There are other quilters in Stoney Ridge who want to sell quilts."

"I know. I've been looking. But there are none like these. I've never seen any like these." Veronica McCall planted her hands on her hips and tilted her head at Carrie. "For an Amish woman, you drive a hard bargain."

"But I'm not *trying* to bargain."

"*Everyone* has a price, Carrie. Everyone can be bought. Even you."

Carrie was losing patience. "It's not *our* way," she said firmly, hoping to end the discussion.

Suddenly, Veronica McCall's eyes grew as large as dinner plates. She had just noticed Eli's still body lying on the table behind Carrie.

"Um, uh," Veronica McCall sputtered, at a rare loss for words. "Perhaps this isn't the best time for a visit." She handed Carrie a business card. "Call me later."

Carrie lacked the energy to explain to her that there was no phone so there would be no call. But she did ask her for one favor: to drive to Esther's farm and tell her and Emma that Eli had passed. She tried to explain the way to find the farmhouse, describing landmarks, as was the Amish custom in giving directions. But Veronica grew impatient, tapping her toes and frowning. She wanted specifics—street names and house numbers.

Mattie appeared at the open front door, somehow knowing they needed her. For a moment she stood listening, observing Veronica's growing frustration. "The Lord will guide you there," she said at last, steering Veronica out to her car.

Daniel grew even quieter in the weeks after Eli passed. Carrie would catch him deep in thought at odd moments, his mind a million miles away, like the time he stood on a ramp in the barn leading up to the hayloft, hayfork in his hands, just staring off into the distance. Or when she found him standing beside his horse Schtarm, holding the harness, forehead bowed against the gelding's big neck. Either way, it seemed as though he was living in a world she couldn't reach.

One night in mid-March, Carrie woke suddenly. Something was wrong. Daniel's bed was empty. She heard Hope's bellow, calling from the barn, in great pain. This yearling heifer, given to Andy by Jacob when he turned eight, was not just an animal to them. She was an extension of the family. Hope was the first of the herd on their farm. *I'm counting on her, just like she is counting on me*, Carrie thought as she quickly threw on warm clothes, wrapped a shawl around her head, and hurried out to the barn.

When Carrie slid the barn door open, she saw Daniel in Hope's stall.

He looked up at her, surprised. "How'd you hear her with that wind howling?"

Carrie shrugged, her eyes fixed on Hope. She was in trouble. A tiny hoof stuck out between her hind legs. Swiftly, she reached for the thin chain hanging on the wall.

"No. Let me," Daniel said, taking it out of her hands.

He reached a gloved hand into Hope, catching the little hoof with the chain, before a contraction started that nearly squeezed his arm off. Carrie gasped when she saw his face contort, matching Hope's pain.

When the contraction subsided, he asked her to crank the chain as he gently tugged.

"Careful, Daniel, careful."

Carrie cranked, Daniel tugged, Hope pushed and bellowed. Slowly the calf began to ease out of the canal. Daniel motioned to have Carrie come next to him. He gently guided her hands into Hope's canal, under the calf's warm and slimy body.

"You make the delivery," he said.

So Carrie began to tug and tug, and ever so gently the calf began to come out. First the hoofs, then the shoulders. Then the neck. Before she knew it, a miniature white face emerged. Then the entire body slipped out, like shooting down a waterslide. Carrie collapsed to the hay-covered floor, the calf half in her lap and half on the floor.

"A girl!" Carrie said, relieved. Had it been a male, she would have to sell it soon to a farmer who raised steers.

Daniel and Carrie watched with wonder as the little white nose wrinkled, sneezed, and took in her first breath. Hope turned and began to rasp her rough tongue along the wet whorls of her baby's hide. With this stimulation, the calf began to struggle to get to her feet, wobbling toward her mother. They touched noses, a first meeting. Then the calf nuzzled to nurse as Hope continued cleaning up her newborn.

It was that quiet time of a new day, when the earth seemed to be holding its breath, gently turning from darkness to daylight. "The circle of life, once again completed," Carrie said softly.

Hope swung her heavy head at Carrie with big, soulful brown eyes, blinking her long white eyelashes as if in agreement with the assessment.

Carrie laughed and hooked her arm through Daniel's. "It's a sign, Daniel. Everything's going to be fine."

"Think so?"

"I do. I'm sure of it," she answered, sounding more confident than she felt.

He gave her a soft, slow smile. They looked at each other, sharing a mutual thought, a fragile hope. Gently, he leaned over to kiss her, grazing her lips with his. Then his arms slid around her waist and he pulled her to him, pressing his lips against hers as if a kiss could tell her what words would not.

That first kiss from Daniel made Carrie think about the last kiss Sol had given her. About how different they were. A beginning and an end.

As Carrie thought about Hope's new calf and the way Daniel had held on to her, as if he was a drowning man and she was throwing him a long branch to drag him to shore, she made a decision.

Ready or not, it was time that Daniel got off of that cold floor. He had never complained, but she knew he would jump at the chance if she invited him into her bed. More than once, she caught the hungry look on his face, watching her as she got ready for bed, combing out her hair. Not long ago, she had even put aside her modesty and talked it over with Mattie. Her response jolted Carrie. "Daniel is a man, not a saint. What are you waiting for?" Mattie told her, sounding like a seasoned woman of the world.

So what was Carrie waiting for?

It wasn't love. She was practical enough to know that she would never feel for Daniel what she had felt for Sol. She hadn't married Daniel with any schoolgirl notions. Still, she was growing fond of Daniel and his quiet, kind ways. She appreciated how patient he was with her brother, how tender he was with his grandmother, how thoughtful and caring he was to her.

So what was she waiting for?

After giving that question some serious thought, she realized she was waiting to feel as if she knew Daniel, really knew him. She remembered how she used to hear her mother and father talk with each other at the kitchen table after she had gone to bed. That's what she hoped for in a marriage, that kind of closeness. In that way, she wanted Bund. *Intimacy. A bond.*

But sometimes, she thought Daniel would never really let her know him any better than she did. He seemed so closed up, so private. He rarely spoke more than a few words at a time—even his sentences seemed economized.

Later that afternoon, Daniel and Andy went to the feed store in town to buy bird food for the Cooper's hawk babies. At the last minute, Yonnie decided to go too. Carrie put some hot water in empty milk jugs to keep Yonnie warm, and covered her with extra blankets in the buggy.

After they had left, Carrie went out to the barn to check on Hope and the new calf. She sat on the milking stool beside Hope, milking her for the first time. This first milking, filled with colostrum, would be put in a bottle for the calf's first meal.

She rubbed the indented spot between Hope's two ears. "Thank you, sweet girl."

Hope licked and huffed and looked at her with large, peaceful eyes. As Carrie bent over to pick up the bucket, she heard the barn door slide open and fill the room with afternoon sunlight. Carrie looked up to see who it was, but the sun, behind the barn's door in a blaze of glory, dazzled her eyes so that all she saw was a black silhouette.

"Hello, Carrie," a man said.

At the sound of that deep voice, Carrie's heart started pounding so loud she was sure Solomon Riehl could hear it.

"I didn't mean to frighten you," Sol said, taking a few strides into the barn. "I just want to talk to you, face-to-face."

As her eyes adjusted to the light, she took in the changes in Sol. His hair was shingled and short, like an English man. His face seemed a little older, tired. He had dark circles under his eyes as if he hadn't rested well.

"We have nothing to talk about." Her words came out harsh, coming from an old and festering anger that she still felt.

"Carrie," he said, coming closer, "I made a mistake."

He was close enough now that she could smell him. It was a familiar smell to her, a smell she had once loved. She took a step back, nearly knocking over the milk bucket.

"I had to give baseball a try. When your father died so unexpectedly, and you wouldn't come with me, I panicked. I never should have left without you. I never should have left without telling you I was going. That I'd be back for you."

He smiled at her, but she didn't smile back. She crossed her arms and looked away, just to avoid his gaze. She was afraid if she looked at him, she'd be drawn in, unable to resist him. She wasn't even sure she could get any words around the knot in her throat, a knot made of tangled threads of anger and hurt.

He took a step closer to her. His voice dropped to a whisper. "But how could you have married him? Why couldn't you have waited for me? You knew I loved you. You knew I'd be coming for you."

Her chin lifted a notch. Defiance surged through her. "You gave me no reason to think you'd be back."

He put his hands on her arms. "Carrie, we can still be together. It's not too late. And you can bring Andy. I'll take care of both of you."

She jerked his hands off of her. "I was baptized into the church. And I'm . . . I'm married now."

He gave a slight shrug, but he kept his eyes lowered to the ground. "People leave. They leave all the time."

He didn't really believe that, she thought. He couldn't be so far removed from their ways that he would think she would leave. "You made your choice, Sol. I made mine."

"But that's what I'm saying, Carrie. I made a mistake." He reached out for her hands and tangled his fingers with hers, the way he used to. "It doesn't have to fashion into a crisis."

"It's not a crisis. But it is decided."

"You just married him to spite me."

Carrie gave a short laugh. "You don't have any idea why I married Daniel."

Sol released her hands. "Carrie, you don't really know him."

"And you do?"

"I know things you don't know. He hasn't been honest with you. There's something in his past—"

She raised her hands to stop him.

"Carrie, listen to me."

"No. I stopped listening to you at my father's funeral." Anger spilling over, she took a step closer to him. "You want to know why I married Daniel?" she asked, her voice shaking. "Because he was there."

And you were not, echoed silently through the barn.

She picked up the milk bucket. "And you wouldn't be here today if you had a baseball game to play."

Sol blocked her path. "I'm here today because of you. I have never stopped loving you. Not ever. I have regretted leaving without you every single day. It was the stupidest thing I've ever done. I'm here to make it right. Carrie, I want you more than baseball. It's *nothing* without you by my side."

She stepped around him to leave, but he blocked her path again.

"At least read this. Then you'll know more. About him." He thrust a paper into her hands.

She left the barn and broke into a run, despite sloshing milk all around her, so that he wouldn't see the tears splashing onto her cheeks.

Carrie didn't say anything to Daniel during supper, but after they'd eaten and she'd cleaned up the dishes, she went out to the barn to find him. Daniel always went out to check on the animals one last time before evening prayers.

When she slid open the door of the barn, Daniel glanced at her from one of the horse's stalls. He had been filling the bucket with water, but put it down when he saw her. He closed the horse's stall, turned the latch, and approached her, a question in his eyes.

She handed him the paper that Sol had given her. "It's about your cousin Abel, Daniel. I know he caused a fire that killed some people. I know he's in jail."

Daniel unfolded the paper and quickly scanned it.

Softly, she asked, "Was she the girl you loved, Daniel? Is she the reason you carry such a burden?"

He didn't say anything.

"It hurts that you felt you had to keep this secret, instead of telling me. I would have understood."

He closed his eyes. He seemed to be searching for words. Then he lifted his head and quietly said, "The two women who were killed in that fire were Katie Yoder and my mother." He looked past her, out the open barn door. "Katie and I were to be married."

"That's what I—"

Daniel put up a hand to stop her. "There was another fire. Two other people were killed." He took a deep breath. "A man and . . . ," his voice broke on the word, ". . . and a child."

"Daniel—"

"Abel didn't cause the fires that killed them, Carrie." He held up the paper, a copy of a newspaper clipping. "It seems that way from this article, but the truth is that Abel was innocent. I caused the fires. I did it." He lowered his head. "Abel went to jail in my place. But I'm responsible for the fires. For the deaths. I'm the one."

She felt all fuzzy headed as if her head was wrapped in her wooly shawl and she couldn't hear him clearly. As understanding started to dawn, a panic rose within Carrie. She suddenly felt as if this man whom she thought was safe wasn't safe at all. She didn't really know Daniel. Or what he was capable of doing.

Carrie knew what she should do. She should stay. She should get Daniel to tell her the whole story.

Instead, she turned and ran.

Carrie didn't return home for hours. When she walked up the kitchen steps, Yonnie was waiting by the door.

"What are you doing up?" Carrie asked, as she hung her shawl up on the wooden peg.

"We were worried about you," Yonnie said.

"I'm sorry to cause you concern. I was over at Mattie's." Carrie had spilled everything out to Mattie, about Sol showing up and the newspaper article, about what Daniel had said. Mattie listened carefully, then told Carrie to stop making up her mind ahead of the facts. She told her to go home and *ask* Daniel about the fires, to give him the benefit of the doubt, to trust what she knew to be true about him.

Yonnie glanced at the grandfather clock. "Is Daniel still in the barn?"

"No. Isn't he asleep?"

Yonnie's chin jerked up. "No! He went looking for you about an hour ago. He took Schtarm because Old-Timer has a sore leg."

"Schtarm? He used Schtarm in the buggy?" At an auction last fall, Daniel bought Schtarm, a young racehorse that didn't cut it on the tracks. He wasn't buggy broke yet and had such a skittish nature that Carrie doubted he would ever be a good buggy horse, but Daniel had confidence in him. She glanced out the kitchen window. "I wasn't on the road. I cut through the orchard. We must have missed each other."

All of a sudden Yonnie clasped her hands together and started her chanting, "Gottes willes. Gottes willes."

Not a minute later, Schtarm galloped into the gravel driveway, skidding to a halt at the barn. Carrie ran outside and saw that he was lathered up, buggy traces hanging by his side. His eyes looked wild and she had trouble getting close to him. She spoke calmly to him and was able to grasp one rein, just as a police car turned into the driveway. Mattie was in the backseat. She opened the door and ran over to Carrie, throwing her arms around her. For a split second, Carrie thought that Mattie seemed as frantic and wild-eyed as Schtarm. She looked over Mattie's shoulder at the police car, expecting Daniel to come out the other door. Instead, it was a police officer. He approached Carrie and Mattie, standing a few feet back.

"I'm Chief Beamer. Are you the wife of Daniel Miller?"

Carrie looked curiously at the policeman. Why was he here? Mattie released her grip on Carrie. "Oh Carrie! There's been an accident. The buggy. A car."

"Slow down, Mattie. Take a deep breath and tell me what happened."

"Daniel's buggy was turning left into my driveway when a speeding car passed by him."

Carrie took a deep breath and squeezed her eyes shut. When buggies and cars collided, the buggies always lost. She glanced at Schtarm, grateful he wasn't hurt.

"You're going to need to come with me, Mrs. Miller," Chief Beamer said.

"Where's Daniel?" Carrie glanced at the police car. "Isn't he in the car?"

"No, Carrie," Mattie said, her voice breaking on the word. "He's not." She started to cry.

Carrie looked at Mattie and the officer. She tilted her head, trying to understand what Mattie meant. Her mind wasn't working right. She had been up so early with Hope's new calf, then Sol's visit, and then finding out about Daniel and his cousin Abel. The fatigue of the long day suddenly hit her.

Mattie braced Carrie's shoulders to make her look at her. "He's dead, Carrie. Daniel was thrown from the buggy and killed instantly."

Carrie tried to concentrate on Mattie's moving mouth, but she didn't think Mattie made any sense. *Poor Mattie. She looks so troubled.* Carrie felt like she might be getting a fever, all shaky and sweaty and cold inside. Her leg muscles felt wobbly and she kept forgetting to breathe. *I must breathe. I must.* Everything started to swirl around her before it all became fuzzy and blended together. She didn't even remember falling, but the next thing she heard was Chief Beamer's deep voice, hovering over her.

"She's fainted. Dropped like a stone. Does someone have a blanket?"

6

Over the next few days, Carrie took comfort in the long-established rituals and traditions of burying a family member, as they gave anchor to her churned-up feelings. The day before Daniel's funeral, the bench wagon was delivered by two men. They helped move out all the downstairs furniture to store in the barn. Then they set up the benches in the empty house. Neighbors stopped by all throughout the day, bearing dishes of food for the shared meal after the burial.

As long as Carrie stayed busy, she was able to push away troubling, stray thoughts. Just like when her father died and Sol left, she found that the sun rose and set and the days would come and go, and there was the washing and the cooking and the gardens to care for. One couldn't live on the crest of grief every single moment.

The day after the accident, the undertaker returned Daniel's embalmed body to the farmhouse for the viewing. Tears streaming down her face, Yonnie held the Crazy Quilt in her arms that she had given Carrie for a wedding gift.

"Do you mind, Carrie?" she asked her as they tended to Daniel's body, just as they had tended to Eli's only weeks before. "I know it's custom to use a white quilt to bury him, but I want to wrap him in the quilt he loved best."

"Of course not," Carrie said. "I think he would be comforted by being wrapped in the quilt you had made for him." She felt numb, exhausted to the bone, worried.

The police had taken her to the city morgue to identify Daniel's body. Mattie came too. It was nearly dawn by the time they returned to the farmhouse. When Andy woke, Carrie told him about the accident. What worried her most was that Andy didn't cry. He became quiet and still, like a candlelight right before it's snuffed out. Andy spent the day in the barn, playing with the Cooper's hawk babies, avoiding the steady stream of neighbors who heard the news and wanted to pay their respect.

At the end of the day, a car turned into the driveway. Mattie climbed out of the backseat, but the other people, clearly English, remained in the car. Carrie met Mattie at the kitchen door.

"Carrie, the girl who hit Daniel's buggy is in the car," Mattie said. "She's with her mother. She wants to ask you to forgive her."

Carrie braced her hand against the doorjamb as if she needed it to hold herself upright. "Oh Mattie, I can't. I just can't."

"Yes, you can," Mattie said, firm but kind. "Her name is Grace Patterson. She's only seventeen. She works part-time over at Honor Mansion. She needs your forgiveness. You need to give it to her for your own sake."

Closing her eyes for a moment against the pain and loss, Carrie asked quietly, "And what if I don't feel any forgiveness for her?"

Softly, Mattie whispered, "Feelings follow intention." Mattie took Carrie's hand and led her out to the car.

An elderly woman got out of the car first, her face solemn and sad. Then the girl got out. Carrie had to force herself to look at her. She was so young. Her eyes were swollen with crying. Her face was red and blotchy. Carrie recognized that kind of misery and despair; she felt it when her father died.

Without thinking, she opened wide her arms. The girl looked at Carrie as if she couldn't believe what she was offering to her. Then she rushed into Carrie's arms, breaking into big, heaving sobs.

When Carrie finally went upstairs that night, she saw that Yonnie had replaced the Crazy Quilt on her bed with another quilt. The cold March wind seeped through the windowsills, and she shivered as she undressed. She wore two pairs of woolen socks and a sweater over her nightgown and still couldn't get warm. She wasn't sure she had ever felt quite so alone as she did that night, slipping under the covers. Never had so many changes come upon her in so little time. It was as if she had left her old life and stepped into someone else's life. The last thought she had before falling asleep was: *And now I am a widow.*

The sun shone brightly on the day of Daniel's funeral, but the wind still had winter's bite to it. At the graveside, four young men shoveled dirt on top of Daniel's coffin. Carrie heard no other sound other than that—*whoosh-whump . . . whoosh-whump.* No airplanes flying overhead, no cars driving past, no squawking jaybirds, just the silence of grief. A cold breeze blew the strings of her prayer cap across her face. She must have flinched as the clods of dirt hit the pine box, because Mattie quietly linked an arm through hers, as if to say, "You're not alone."

Afterward, back at the house, as they cleaned up the kitchen, Emma asked Carrie, "Want me to stay? I could ask Mother to stay too."

Carrie shook her head. She was in no mood for more of Esther's advice. Her only word of solace to Carrie had been, "Folks should not overgrieve much, for that is a complaint against the Lord."

Throughout the long day, Esther made broad hints to Carrie about the bishop's grandson, John Graber. She had picked him for Carrie's husband years ago, often inviting him over for supper and family gatherings. Carrie had no interest in him; she thought John Graber was odd.

Carrie had enough to worry about right now. Ever since Eli had passed, the job of bill paying had fallen to her. The second installment of the property tax bill, still in Eli's name, sat on Daniel's desk, and she didn't have the money to pay it.

Just two weeks ago, she had shown the tax bill to Daniel after they had accepted help from the church to pay the last of Andy's emergency room bill. Carrie offered to go back to work at Central Market, but Daniel objected, saying Yonnie needed minding. The older woman had fallen recently after losing her balance. She wasn't hurt, but she couldn't get herself back up. Daniel had told Carrie not to worry, that he would pay the tax bill by doing extra smithy work.

But now that was over.

Deacon Abraham, a kind man with a smiling face, ruddy as a bright apple, and a great booming laugh that jiggled his big belly, brought over a spare buggy to use since Carrie's had been destroyed in the accident. He also asked to buy Daniel's blacksmithing tools. He insisted he needed them, and then offered her three times what they were worth, refusing to pay less. Still, it didn't come close to the amount due for taxes. And it wasn't just this tax bill that worried her, it was the one after that, and the one after that. How was she ever going to be able to make ends meet? These were all new worries for her, ones she had never known before.

After Emma and Esther left, Carrie got ready to go to bed, exhausted. Andy and Yonnie were already asleep. As she leaned over to turn off the gas lamp in the living room, Yonnie's stack of quilts caught her eye in the flickering light. She spread her hand over a quilt, admiring again the tiny, even rows of stitches, the even binding, the splashes of yellows, purples, and deep blues that Yonnie coordinated so skillfully.

Carrie's heart almost slammed into her chest. She would have to talk to Yonnie in the morning, but it was just possible that she had found the means to hold on to the orchards. At least for the foreseeable future.

"I don't mind a bit," Yonnie said the next morning, when Carrie explained to her the idea of selling a quilt to Veronica McCall. "I made those quilts for my family to use. This is just one more way the quilts can be of use." Yonnie went over to the quilts and pulled them out and spread them on the kitchen table. She was trying to decide which one to sell.

Carrie's heart ached as she watched her. She knew those quilts told the story of her life.

Yonnie pulled out a red and yellow quilt she called "Ray of Light." "Think that fancy redheaded gal would like this one? She seems flashy."

Carrie nodded. "I think it's perfect, Yonnie."

As soon as the skies cleared after a soaking rain, Carrie hitched Old-Timer to the buggy. The sun shone on Carrie's face, relaxing her a little, as she prepared herself during the ride for this visit to Honor Mansion. She hooked Old-Timer to a post at the hotel, stroked his face, and ran her hand down the length of his sore leg. He seemed fine today. The buggy looked glaringly out of place in the parking lot filled with construction workers' trucks and

Veronica McCall's red convertible. She gathered the quilt that Yonnie had carefully wrapped up in paper and knocked timidly on the door of the hotel.

When the door opened, Carrie inhaled sharply. Grace Patterson stood at the threshold, looking just as shocked to see Carrie.

"Hello, Grace," Carrie said. A surprising wave of tenderness filled Carrie as she looked at Grace. She took in Grace's appearance. Her hair was short and spiked, a funny color, and her eyes were traced with a thick black liner. But she wasn't as tough as she looked, Carrie thought. She really didn't know much about this girl other than she thought Grace seemed like a fragile teacup.

Grace's eyes went wide. "Did you come to see me?"

"No. I'm here to see Veronica McCall." Carrie tilted her head. "Is your hair . . . were you born with that color?"

Grace ran a hand through her hair. "Oh no! I dyed it. It's called Manic Panic red."

"Well, it is really . . . bright." She tried to sound positive. "Thank you· for coming to Daniel's viewing. I know that was hard. Please thank your ·mother too."

"Mrs. Gingerich? She's not my mother. She's my foster mother. More like a foster grandma, actually. She's pretty ancient." Grace came outside on the porch and closed the door behind her. "But she's cool. I mean, like, her viewing habits totally bite, but other than that, she's okay."

Carrie didn't understand what Grace meant. She answered with silence.

"And she eats weird stuff. She only buys organic and won't eat glutens and . . . what is a gluten anyway? I don't have a clue but it's all anybody talks about anymore."

Carrie was mesmerized for a moment, watching Grace carry on a conversation by herself. There was something very earnest about her, something sweet and likable.

"It sounds so lame," Grace rolled her eyes, "but I thought the Amish people might bring shotguns and try to off me." She shook her head. "But everyone was so kind."

"My people?" Carrie asked. "You thought my people would shoot you?"

"Yes. I've lived in Lancaster County most of my life, but I really don't know squat about the Amish."

Carrie smiled. "You could probably say the same thing about how little we understand the English."

"So, um, I have to go before the judge in a few months. To see if . . . I might be charged . . ." Her voice trailed off as she looked out at the street.

Carrie's heart felt a tug of pity. Grace was so young to carry such a yoke. "Perhaps I can help in some way. I could write letters to the judge asking for mercy."

Grace's head snapped back at Carrie in astonishment. "Would you? Would you really do that for me?" She crossed her arms tightly against her chest and her eyes filled with tears. "But why? It's my fault that your husband is . . . dead. I don't deserve that. I don't deserve mercy."

For some reason, Carrie thought of Mattie. She knew just what Mattie would say and found herself echoing it. "None of us do, Grace."

Grace pointed down the hall to Veronica McCall's office and went back upstairs. Before Carrie knocked on the door, she noticed a reflection of herself in a hall mirror. She hadn't looked in a mirror since she had left Esther's home. She walked up to it, slowly, unsure of what to make of what she saw. There stood a woman, not very tall and a little too thin, in a black mourning dress and apron and cape. Her cheeks were flushed pink, for it was a cool spring day. What surprised her most was that she didn't look like a girl anymore. She thought of herself as barely old enough to be a wife, let alone a widow.

But her eyes, they showed her youth. They looked a little frightened, like a cottontail caught in a flashlight's glare.

Veronica was typing furiously at a computer and looked up when Carrie knocked, stunned, as if she wasn't sure who she was. "Carrie? Sit down, sit down." She moved some papers from a chair and pointed to it. "Listen, if you're here about Grace, I can assure you that Honor Mansion can't be held liable for the accident. First of all, she's only part-time, and secondly, she was off-duty and had left the property—"

"No." Carrie waved a hand to stop her. "No. I'm not here to discuss that . . . with you."

A wide smile spread across Veronica's face. "So, you're ready to sell."

"Not the property." Carrie put the quilt on her desk top and carefully unwrapped the paper. "But a quilt."

Veronica McCall leaned back in her chair. "It's beautiful." She spread it out and looked it up and down. "It almost looks as if it were done by hand."

"It was. Even the pieces are sewed together by hand, not on a machine. It took Yonnie thousands of hours to make it."

Veronica McCall's eyebrows shot up. "How much?" she asked, narrowing her eyes at her.

Carrie took a deep breath. Bargaining was new to her, but she had given the price a great deal of thought. "One thousand dollars."

"Five hundred," Veronica volleyed back. She smiled, but her eyes stayed cold.

She enjoys this, Carrie thought. "One thousand dollars."

"There are plenty of other quilts out there."

"Yes. There are many fine quilters in Lancaster County. None quite like Yonnie, though." *But Veronica knows that.*

One thinly plucked eyebrow raised up. "You drive a hard bargain."

"But I don't bargain, Veronica McCall. I've told you that before. It's not our way. One thousand dollars is a fair value for the quilt."

"Seven fifty."

Carrie started to pack up the quilt. She wasn't sure where she would go next, but she wasn't going to accept less for Yonnie's handiwork.

"Fine! Fine," Veronica McCall said, laughing. She pulled out a checkbook from her desk drawer.

"Would you mind giving me cash?" Carrie asked her. "I don't have a bank account." It was one of the things on Carrie's to-do list, under the heading, "Things to figure out now that I am a widow."

Veronica's eyes narrowed, as if she thought Carrie didn't trust her. She left the room for a moment and came back with the cash, counting it out in her hand.

As Carrie stood up to leave, Veronica said with a smug smile, "Nice doing business with you. I would have gone as high as fifteen hundred."

"But the fair value is one thousand dollars."

"Well, all's fair in love and war."

Carrie cocked her head at her and wondered why the English spoke in riddles. Her gaze shifted to the computer on Veronica's desk. "Do you use that often?"

"Oh, yes." Veronica gave a confident nod. "I'm a computer whiz."

"Someone told me that it's like a library." It was something Sol had told her once. He loved computers. He used to go to a coffee shop where he could "surf the internet." He tried to teach Carrie, but she had felt guilty for a week and could hardly look her father in the eye. She knew her father felt that the internet was a gateway to evil, just like television. It was one of those areas she had felt conflicted about, because through Sol's eyes she could see the good in those worldly things too.

"Sure is! I can google anything."

Carrie was nonplussed. It almost sounded like Veronica was trying to speak their dialect. "You can ferhoodle anything?"

"No! Google. It's a search engine." Veronica read the confused look on Carrie's face and waved away an explanation. "Never mind. Is there something you want me to look up?"

Carrie wasn't entirely sure she was doing the right thing, but Daniel's untimely death left her with missing pieces of a story. She felt as if she needed to know the truth about those fires in Ohio, and Yonnie couldn't or wouldn't discuss them. Just yesterday, Carrie tried asking her, straight out, but Yonnie went pale and started to tremble, then went upstairs to lie down. "I'm looking for some information about two fires in Holmes County, Ohio, that caused the death of two women, a man and his son, a few years back."

She gave Veronica McCall the few details that she remembered from the copy of the newspaper clipping Sol had given her. Veronica pecked at the buttons on the computer, stared at the screen for a long while, asked a few more questions, then typed more buttons.

Suddenly, Veronica let out a yelp. "Voilà! Found it." She gave a satisfied smile to Carrie. "I can find anything." She pressed a button and another machine spit out a paper. "Here's what you're looking for, Carrie." She reached over, grabbed the paper from the printer, and handed it to her.

Carrie folded it up, quickly, so Veronica wouldn't read it. Then she thanked her and left with the quilt money and the information about Abel Miller. Just as she closed the door, she heard the printer click into action a second time. Carrie's heart rose in her throat. *Veronica McCall wouldn't have made a copy for herself, would she? No, of course not. Why would she bother?*

About halfway home, Carrie pulled Old-Timer off to the side and read the paper. It was a report from a newspaper article, with a grainy picture of Abel Miller on it. She started to read the article: "Amish Man Fined and Sentenced to Prison."

Abel Miller, 21, was sentenced today to three years in prison and fined $250,000. He pled guilty to two acts of negligence that resulted in involuntary homicides. Miller had a business supplying kerosene fuel to local Amish farmers. Last November, gasoline had contaminated the containers, causing explosions in two Amish homes that resulted in the death of two women, forty-eight-year-old Lena Miller, a relative of the defendant, nineteen-year-old Katie Yoder, thirty-two-year-old Elam Lapp and his seven-year-old son, Benjamin Lapp. Against advice of counsel, Miller refused to appeal the conviction.

Carrie sighed. The story only raised more questions than it answered. She reread it, looked again at Abel Miller's photograph and stared at it for a long while. Her heart felt a pity for this Abel. How humiliating for an Amish man to have his photograph taken and printed in such a way. For the first time, Abel seemed real to her. Not just a shadowy figure in the Miller family, but a real man.

She wondered why Abel took Daniel's place in jail. More importantly, why had Daniel let him?

She folded the paper up carefully and placed it in her apron pocket. She didn't want Yonnie to come across this, adding to her suffering. Yonnie carried on bravely, but Carrie knew she was grieving deeply over Eli and Daniel.

One evening, Carrie went through Eli's accounting books to see what kind of expenses she would be facing. She knew there would be feed bills, a propane gas bill, and in a few months, yet another tax bill to pay. She knew they needed to sell another quilt or two to pay for expenses until the harvest, but it pained her to ask Yonnie.

Carrie was doing her best to keep the farm up, but it was already looking like the weary efforts of two women and a boy, not the pristine condition that Eli and Daniel had kept it in. Every few days, a kind neighbor or two stopped by to lend a hand with a chore or two, but they had families and farms of their own to care for. Thankfully, Daniel had finished pruning the trees in January and had returned the beehives to the orchards in early March, but her vegetable garden—food that she counted on for summer canning and for roadside stand sales—looked limp.

As Carrie closed Eli's accounting book, she suddenly felt a weariness that settled and went bone deep. She felt anxious about the future, and then anxious about being anxious. She put her head in her hands and squeezed her eyes shut.

Yonnie came up behind her, rested her hands on her shoulders and said, "Try not to worry. The Lord God hears our prayers."

Carrie patted Yonnie's hands and told her she was right, of course. But a part of her mind told her that maybe Daniel was right. Heaven had gone deaf.

As Carrie said goodnight to Andy, he asked her if they were going to lose the farm.

"What makes you think that?" she asked.

"I heard you and Yonnie talking. I saw you scribbling down numbers on a pad of paper." He climbed under the quilt covers. "Maybe I should quit school and stay home. I could do stuff. I could make money choring for people."

Carrie smiled at him and tousled his hair. "Your job is to stay in school and learn all you can. Someday, these apple orchards will be yours. You'll need to know all about numbers." She stroked his hair.

"I know plenty already. More than that ol' teacher. Bags of fat on her arms bounce when she writes on the board!" He lifted a skinny arm and pinched it, trying to mimic his teacher.

Carrie tried to frown at him but broke into a grin. "Enough of that talk. Like I said, you do your part by doing well in school. It's my part to think about making ends meet." She reached over and turned off the gas lamp. "Night, little brother."

"Night, Carrie."

Before she closed the door, she asked, "Are those English boys still bothering you?"

"Nope."

"Daniel was right, then. He said they would lose interest."

Andy didn't respond. He just rolled over on his side.

"Andy, do you miss Daniel?"

"Nope."

Carrie leaned on the doorjamb and watched him for a moment. She worried about him, her Andy. She knew he must be hurting. She wondered how he really felt about Daniel's death. He didn't show any emotion during the viewing and funeral. He didn't really show much emotion about anything, she realized, except for caring for the baby Cooper's hawks and Mattie's hatched goslings.

Those downy goslings looked like yellow balls of cotton that followed Andy around like he was their mother. It was incredible how quickly they grew; in just a few weeks, they were the size of leghorn chickens. Carrie and Andy made a makeshift cage for them in the barn. She was grateful that these creatures hadn't died. It made her sad to think Andy had grown calloused to death, at the tender age of nine.

She had to admit, she wasn't really sure how she felt about Daniel's death, either. She pushed thoughts of him off to the side before they could settle in for a stay, just like she did with Sol.

Spring training was under way. Sol thought he might be able to add a little more speed on his fastball after the weight training he'd done in the Clipper Magazine Stadium workout room all winter. The manager had even used him as an example to the other players.

"If the rest of you players would work as hard as this guy," he patted Sol on the back during the team meeting, "you'd have a chance for making the All-Star game this fall."

The way the manager said it, it seemed as if he was hinting that Sol had a chance for a pitcher's spot on the All-Star team. Just thinking about it made Sol all the more determined to speed up his pitch. It was all so close to him, within his grasp, this dream of making something of himself, he could practically see himself in the All-Star uniform, jogging out to the mound in Newark or Camden or Long Island, wherever the games were going to be held.

The only thing missing was no one would be there to watch him.

But then he got to thinking, with Daniel Miller gone—and it shamed him to admit it but when he heard the news from his mother he was elated—he and Carrie were given a second chance to get it right. Maybe by fall, she'd be at that All-Star game, watching him.

Late one afternoon, Veronica McCall walked right into Carrie's farmhouse. "Hello? Hello? Is anybody here?" she called out, before spotting Carrie by the far window in the living room, letting down the hem on Andy's trousers. "There you are! I knew someone would be home." She blinked her eyes. "Why is it always so dark in here?"

"We use the sun's light. And it's a cloudy day." Carrie put down the trousers and stood to meet her guest. "Is something wrong?" She could tell Veronica McCall seemed more on edge than usual today.

"There's a flaw in this quilt of Yonnie's." Veronica threw the quilt on the kitchen table, searching it over. "There! There it is! See?" She pointed to a corner piece in which a mismatched fabric was sewn in, disrupting the pattern.

"I do see," Carrie answered calmly.

"So she needs to fix it."

"No. It's meant to be there."

Veronica McCall looked at Carrie as if she were a dense child. "I can't have a flawed quilt. She'll have to fix it."

Carrie smoothed a hand over the red and yellow quilt. "Yonnie's quilts have a mark of humility."

"A what?"

"It's a sign of imperfection. Man will never achieve perfection, and we don't want to be prideful in even trying to achieve it. So many Amish quilts are made with an intentional flaw."

"Every one?"

"Not all, I suppose." Carrie folded the quilt gently. It pained her still, to have sold Yonnie's quilt.

"Well, that's . . . interesting, I guess." Veronica tapped her chin. "Hmmm . . . I wonder if I could spin it? Maybe I could even point customers to the flaw, to prove it isn't machine made . . . oh, this could be good!" She clapped her hands together, delighted. "Bet I could charge more too." She scooped the quilt out of Carrie's arms and left, nearly knocking Andy over as he came in from school. "Toodles!" she called out, banging the kitchen door behind her.

Just an hour later, Andy sat at the kitchen table eating a snack while Carrie was making dinner. Suddenly, he spotted something out the window and flew out the door, tossing over his shoulder, "Gotta check on my birds!" Instead of going straight to the barn like he always did, he slipped around the side of the house and behind the vegetable garden, out of sight. Carrie saw a young Amish woman walk up the path to the kitchen door. When she reached the house, Carrie could see it was Andy's teacher, Rebecca King.

She started the teapot to boil as Rebecca took off her cape and bonnet. "What a nice surprise, Rebecca! On such a cold spring day too." Carrie took two teacups down from the cupboard and filled them with hot water from the kettle. "Seems as if we should be getting warm weather by now."

Rebecca's round cheeks were bright red with cold. She wrapped her hands around the cup to warm them. "I wish I could say that the reason for my visit was just because we're overdue, Carrie, but . . ." She glanced at Yonnie, quilting in the other room.

"Something about Andy?" Carrie straightened. "He's not giving you trouble, is he?" She had a sinking feeling in the pit of her stomach, like something terrible was coming.

"No, I wouldn't say that," Rebecca said. She took a sip of tea. "You see, he's not at school. Ever since . . . your Daniel passed . . . he hasn't been to school."

"But that's been weeks now!" Carrie said, shocked. "Where has he been all day?"

"I don't know. All I know is that he told the kids he was very sick. He said it was extremely contagious. I can't remember exactly what the disease was."

Carrie looked out at the barn. "Was it leprosy, by any chance?"

"Yes! That's it!" Then her face grew worried. "Does he really have it?"

Slowly, Carrie shook her head.

"I didn't think so." Rebecca finished her tea and picked up her cape and bonnet. "I'd better get home. You'll speak to Andy about returning to school?"

"Yes. He'll be at school tomorrow," Carrie said, walking Rebecca to the door. "You can count on it."

For the next few weeks, until the school term ended, Carrie rode the scooter alongside Andy to school every morning. She even waited to leave until Rebecca rang the bell and she knew he was inside the one-room schoolhouse. Carrie never could get Andy to confess where he had been spending his days; out by Blue Lake Pond, birding, most likely. Once Daniel introduced him to birding, he preferred watching nature to watching Rebecca's jiggly arms dance on the blackboard. But it bothered Carrie to discover that Andy was so at ease with telling lies. He insisted that they weren't lies, he just didn't volunteer the truth.

"And the part about the leprosy?" Carrie asked, one eyebrow raised. "Your cast has been off for months now."

"Well, the doctor said it *looked* like leprosy," he told her solemnly. "And my skin did look gross when the doctor took off the cast. All wrinkled and white."

She tried to make him understand that not telling the truth *was* an untruth, that lies start with a seed of untruth that quickly grows into vines—jungles—of deceit. She could tell she wasn't making much of an impact. What he really needed was his father. She couldn't do anything about that, but she could make sure he finished out the school year, like it or not.

7

Spring inched to summer and the apple blossoms in Carrie's orchards faded and died, leaving in their place the promise of a crop to harvest, come autumn.

One August afternoon, the sun burned the back of Carrie's neck as she drove the wagon over to the Stoltzfuses' roadside stand to deliver tomatoes to sell. She stayed too long for a visit with Ada Stoltzfus, a woman known to be blessed with the gift of conversation. Carrie ran a few errands in town but was later than she wanted to be as she returned to the farm. Angry, dark clouds had choked out the sun, the air was gummy and heavy, foreboding a downpour, and the wind whipped fiercely against the trees. A summer storm was coming and she wanted to get home as fast as she could.

As the wagon clattered into the covered bridge, Old-Timer balked. Carrie snapped the reins but he wouldn't budge. Government workers had been reconditioning the covered bridge and had placed sawhorses with blinking lights so people would stay clear of their equipment. She got out of the wagon and tried to lead Old-Timer, but the horse would not move forward. He was frightened by the white cuts of lightning that lit the sky, making strange shadows in the bridge.

"You old fool," she said to Old-Timer. "Now what am I going to do?"

Out of nowhere, Carrie heard a young man's voice. "If you trust me, ma'am, I think I can help you." He had a gentle voice, soft-spoken, polite.

She whipped her head around to see where the man was standing. She couldn't make him out in the darkness, only his profile, but she could tell he was English. The stranger told Carrie to hop back on the wagon. He took off his coat and covered Old-Timer's head with it, talking to him softly. Old-Timer took a tentative step forward, then another, and finally made it through to the other side. The stranger removed his jacket and gently stroked Old-Timer's head.

"See?" he said with a grin. "It's as simple as that."

"Thank you for your help," she said. "Can I be offering a ride to you? This weather is turning bad." She looked up at the bruised, dark sky.

"I'm looking for the Miller home," he said.

Carrie felt a smile tug at the corners of her mouth. "Millers abound among the Amish. Any idea which Miller?"

"I'm looking for the home of Daniel Miller. Moved here from Ohio last summer. Father's name was Eli."

She snapped her head up to look at the man for a second time. Her heart started pounding so loudly that she heard it in her ears. She recognized the man from the article printed out by Veronica McCall's computer.

This man is Abel Miller.

Carrie shouldn't have been surprised by now that Yonnie seemed to be expecting Abel—the woman had an uncanny sense of knowing these things. She was standing outside on the kitchen steps as the wagon wheels rolled into the driveway. Abel jumped off the wagon and ran to her, hugging her little elderly body tightly to his, tears flowing down both of their faces. Carrie thought it was pure sweetness to watch. It felt good to see Yonnie happy. At times she was amazed at how Yonnie carried on, despite so much sadness in the last few years. It almost seemed as if she poured her feelings into her quilts, and that's why the colors were so dramatic and bold. Carrie left the two of them alone and went in to get dinner started.

On the ride to the house, Abel had told Carrie he had received a letter about Daniel's passing. He didn't say from whom and Carrie didn't ask. He said it was hard for him to get his mind around the fact of losing his cousin.

His uncle too. "I needed to see Yonnie, as soon as I could," he said. "She's all I have left."

Yonnie was practically glowing as she joined Carrie in the kitchen. "Abel is unhooking Old-Timer from the wagon and said he'd brush him down." She smiled. "A good Amish man takes care of the buggy horse first."

Carrie glanced sideways over at Yonnie as she peeled the carrots for dinner. *Was* Abel an Amish man? He was dressed in English clothing, his hair was shingled. Maybe he was wearing clothes he had been given when he left prison, Carrie reasoned. But another curiosity: Yonnie spoke English to him, not Deitsch.

By the time Abel came in from the barn, Carrie had supper in the oven.

"I filled your horses' water buckets and gave them all two flakes of hay. But your cow looks like she's about to burst. If you'll give me a milk bucket, I'll take care of her," he said.

Abel Miller was no stranger around horses, she decided, gathering clues about him. Maybe he was a smithy too.

"Thank you," Carrie said, "but my brother should be home by now and that's his chore."

As if on cue, Andy burst in the door, doffed his hat, reached a hand into the cookie jar, but froze in motion as his eyes landed on Abel.

"Andy," Carrie said, pulling his hand out of the cookie jar, "where did you disappear to? You were supposed to weed the garden. We're just about to eat. Hope needs milking, first." She led him by the shoulders to meet Abel. "This is Daniel's cousin, Abel. He's come for a visit."

Andy looked Abel up and down. "Ich gleich sei Guck net." *I don't like his looks.*

Carrie squeezed his shoulders in warning. "Andy! Was in der Welt is letz?" *What in the world is wrong with you?* She turned to Abel. "Kannscht du Pennsilfaanisch Deitsch schwetze?" *Can you speak Pennsylvania Dutch?*

Abel shrugged. "I'm pretty rusty."

Carrie turned to Andy. "Speak English."

Andy frowned at her. "I only said, 'You don't look like Daniel.'" A frown looked funny on such a young face.

Abel's mouth deepened at the corners, trying not to smile, yet he seemed amused. Carrie couldn't tell if he could understand what they were saying or just found them entertaining.

"Maybe not. But he's my grandson too, Andy," Yonnie said with surprising firmness. She still hadn't stopped smiling since Abel's arrival.

Andy shrugged, grabbed the clean milk bucket off of the bench, and ran outside to milk Hope, who was lowing unhappily from the barn.

As Abel washed up, Carrie set the bowl of stewed beef, carrots, and green beans on the table and passed the bread to Yonnie to slice. As soon as Andy returned, they sat down to dinner, closed their eyes, and bowed their heads for silent prayer. Abel held his hands open as if he was receiving a gift, eyes wide open, and launched into an out-loud prayer.

"Father, thank you for all the prayers you've answered for me today. For bringing me safely here to Yonnie, Carrie, and Andy. Help us to trust you more with each day that passes. In Jesus' name we pray, Amen."

Yonnie's, Andy's, and Carrie's heads bobbed up in surprise. Carrie was appalled by the familiarity with which Abel prayed, as if the Lord God himself was sitting next to him. Abel was raised Amish, Carrie thought; he must know their ways. Why had he prayed aloud?

Abel reached a hand out to the bread basket, passed it around, then picked up the butter knife and slathered a slice. "Mmm, good!" he said, after taking a bite. "They sure didn't have food like this in the slammer."

Carrie was so startled by his blunt remark that her fork slipped out of her hand and onto the floor.

Abel didn't notice. He started asking a lot of questions about the farm—the acreage, the kinds of apple trees, the outbuildings, and the livestock, of which there was little, for now.

"Hope just had her first calf, Lulu," Carrie said, passing the bread and butter to Andy. "So we finally have fresh milk. Up to a few months ago, I've had to buy milk from the Stoltzfuses, next farm over."

"You named a cow Hope?" he asked, his eyes laughing.

"Carrie named her Hope because she has high hopes for her," Yonnie said. "Carrie likes to give things meaning with their names. Her calf's name is Hallelujah because we're so happy she was born."

Abel grinned. "Sounds fittin'."

"We always name the calf after the initial of the mother." Andy spoke in a tone of someone who was firmly in charge of this farm. "That's the way my dad did it, so that's the way we do it."

Carrie looked at Andy curiously, wondering what was running through that boy's head. That was the first flicker of interest he showed in Abel, and it sounded nearly like an accusation.

Unfazed, Abel nodded at him. "Sounds like a solid system."

"So how long were you in jail?" Andy asked, eyes narrowed, his voice cold as winter earth.

"About a year and a half."

Andy's eyes roamed up and down Abel's arms. "Any tattoos?"

"Andy!" Carrie said, frowning, but Abel only laughed and shook his head before asking Carrie more questions about the property.

As Carrie answered Abel, she surprised herself by how much she knew about the orchards. She must have picked up more from listening to Eli and Daniel than she realized. "We only have twenty acres, but the trees were planted pretty dense. About one hundred trees to an acre, give or take a few. We have two acres of Northern Spy, three of Rusty Coat, two of Newtown Pippin, three of Smokehouse, two of Golden Russet, five of Honey Cider, and three of Pumpkin Sweet."

"I've never heard of those varieties," Abel said.

"They're Mid-Atlantic heirlooms," Carrie said. "Then we made cider from the apples that didn't make fancy grade."

Abel looked confused. "Fancy grade?"

"Eating quality," Carrie said. "Crisp to the bite and good looking. Those get sold to the packing house for top dollar."

"Carrie's known for her cider," Yonnie said. "Some say it's the best cider in the county."

"It was my dad's cider recipe," Andy said, without looking at Abel. "We use five kinds of apples."

"That's right," Carrie said, eyes shining. "We called it Jacob's Cider and can't make enough of it. On cider press day, folks line up at the crack of dawn, holding their own empty milk jugs."

"Saved 'em a quarter if they brought their own jugs," Andy said, with the voice of authority.

Abel cocked his head, watching them intently as they talked. "Well, you all sound like apple experts."

"There's much still to learn about taking care of an orchard," Carrie said, more to herself than to Abel.

"That's why I'm quitting school," Andy said. "To stay home and take care of our apples."

Carrie pointed a finger at him. "You'll do no such thing."

Yonnie turned to Andy and said, "The Lord God answered our prayers, Andy. Our Abel is home to help us." She reached over to squeeze Abel's hand.

Abel seemed perplexed for a moment, as if he had something on his mind, then he smoothed out his puzzled look. "That was a fine dinner."

For a split second Carrie had a vague impression he was hiding something. But maybe not. What did she really know about this English man? She'd only known him a few hours.

After dinner, Abel surprised Carrie by taking dishes to the sink, stacking them to wash. She had never seen her father, Eli, or Daniel touch a dish unless they were eating off of it.

"Did a lot of dish washing in the joint," he said, adding soap to the hot water. He smiled at the look on her face when he mentioned prison. "Kind of silly to pretend it didn't happen, isn't it? That's where my last seventeen months, thirteen days, and two hours—or so—have been spent." He had a dimple in one cheek that gave him a slightly crooked smile, as if he was grinning about a private joke. "Not that I was keeping track."

"You don't mind talking about it?" Carrie asked as she dried a wet dish.

"Not a bit." He handed her another dish to dry. "Truth is, I met the Lord Jesus in prison. And all things considered, I consider that to be a gift."

Carrie nearly dropped the dish when she heard him say that. She stole a look at Yonnie who had stopped her chair mid-rock, leaning forward as if she wasn't sure she heard him right. Even Andy, who had crammed so many cookies into his mouth that his cheeks puffed out, looked wide-eyed at Abel's declaration.

Abel laughed at them. "Now, ladies, pick your jaws up off the ground. I'm telling you the gospel truth. I found the Lord in a jail cell. I'm mighty grateful he saved my sorry hide." He grinned at both of them. "Sort of sounds like a country song, doesn't it?"

Abel Miller was a strange one, Carrie decided.

Abel insisted on sleeping out in the barn instead of in the house. The storm had passed mostly by, leaving the air fresh and sweet smelling. Abel carried a lantern, lighting the path ahead of Carrie. When she nearly slipped, he insisted on holding her elbow to steady her. In her arms were a stack of Yonnie's quilts, topped with a pillow for him.

"I'd forgotten how dark it can be in the country," he said, looking up at the heavens. The sky was a thick, cloudy soup. The only visible light came from a tiny slice of moon.

Carrie showed him where the workshop was, at the back of the barn, and the cot he could sleep on, and how to get the woodstove started. One of the horses whinnied from his stall.

"That's Schtarm, saying hello," she said, handing a pillow to Abel.

"You named him Storm?" Abel asked.

Carrie nodded. "Daniel named him. His name suits him. He's a retired racehorse that Daniel bought at an auction. A little high-spirited. He's too much for me to handle, but Daniel was trying to gentle him for the buggy when he . . ." She found she didn't know quite what to call it. Had an accident? Before he died? She pointed to the other horse's stall. "I use Old-Timer for the buggy. He's old, very, very old. Sometimes I think if he went any slower we'd be going backward, but at least he doesn't shirk in his traces like Schtarm."

Abel smiled. "Daniel had a keen eye for horseflesh." He took the quilts out of her arms. "Folks in Ohio used to ask him to go to horse auctions, just to offer his opinion."

Carrie wondered what magic those Ohio folks had used to pull an opinion out of Daniel. "In the far stall is Strawberry. Daniel bought her, along with a pony cart, for Andy last Christmas." She spread some sheets on the cot and tucked in the edges. "Andy hasn't ridden her since . . . Daniel passed."

Abel turned his head slowly and gave Carrie a long, steady stare.

"Tomorrow I'll take you out to where they—Eli and Daniel—are buried."

She shuddered when a clap of thunder, lingering from the storm, sounded close to the house. "I hope the lightning doesn't hit the house or barn."

"I noticed you have lightning rods on the house," Abel said. "But not on the barn?"

"Leftover from the English owner. He didn't keep any livestock in this old barn so he didn't have lightning rods on it. We haven't taken them down yet from the house. Been too busy with . . ." With funerals, Carrie realized. She changed the subject. "Sure this will suit you?" she asked, looking around the room. "It's not much more than a workshop."

"A big improvement to my former surroundings," he said with that crooked grin of his. Something about his smile made it impossible not to smile back.

She watched him for a moment as he cracked some kindling over his knee to spread on top of the fire he had started. She would never have known he and Daniel were related. If a man could be called beautiful, that would have been the way to describe Daniel. Abel wasn't as fine boned and handsome as Daniel, but he moved with a confidence and assurance that Daniel had lacked. Abel had a toughness about him, like a boxer in a ring that she had seen once on a trip to town. And yet, Abel's eyes—as soft and warm as melted chocolate—belied his tough exterior. They gave him away.

Abel glanced at Carrie, aware she was appraising him. "Thank you, Carrie. It's good to finally meet Daniel's wife."

The way he said it made her feel funny, like he knew more about her than he let on. And, in return, she knew nothing about him. She was halfway through the door when he asked, "So, Carrie, have you made a plan?"

She swiveled around. "What do you mean?"

"I just wondered, have you thought of moving back home with your folks?"

She stepped out of the shadow and into the light. "*This* is my home. Mine and Andy's. *That's* my only plan." She lifted her eyebrows. She suddenly realized why he had that odd look on his face at dinner, when Yonnie said he was an answer to their prayers. He wasn't planning on staying. "What about you, Abel Miller? Do you have a plan?"

They looked at each other for a moment, a standoff. Then lightning lit the sky and thunder rumbled loudly on its heels.

"Let me walk you back to the house," he said. "Don't want you slipping and hurting yourself."

He had neatly avoided her question, she noticed.

Later, after turning off the switch on the gas lamp next to her bed, Carrie peered outside from her bedroom window at the soft moonlight of the apple orchards. She saw the buttery glow of lantern light coming from the small windows of the barn. It felt strangely comforting.

In the pale dawn of the morning, Carrie woke, half expecting Abel to be gone, but she saw he was up, coming in and out of the barn like he'd been up for hours. When she went out to the barn, she found that he had shoveled manure out of the cows' and horses' stalls, fed them, filled the egg basket with fresh eggs, and milked Hope.

"Denki, Abel," she said when she found him sweeping out the workshop. She handed him a cup of hot coffee.

He gratefully accepted the cup and took a sip. "For what?" He looked genuinely surprised.

"For your help."

That odd look passed over Abel's face like it did last night, the same look Andy got whenever she caught him with his hand in the cookie jar. "I should be thanking you," he said. "Best sleep I've had in years. I've nearly forgotten what it was like to fall asleep to the sound of night birds instead of prison gates clanging shut. Or closing my eyes in a room that was dark. Cells are never completely dark. The lights in the hallways stay on so the guards can make their rounds."

Carrie's eyes went wide. And what could she say to that?

After breakfast, she told Abel she would take him to the cemetery as soon as she had finished hanging the laundry. He gave her a brief nod and went back out to the barn. Awhile later, she found him out in the barn, Schtarm's right front hoof up on his thigh; he was scraping caked dirt and dung out of it with a hoof pick. He straightened up as soon as he saw her.

"This horse is a beauty."

She came around to the horse's left side and patted Schtarm's velvet nose. "True, but I can't handle him," she said. "Been thinking about selling him. He has a skittish nature."

"There's usually a reason why a horse acts so nervous. He just doesn't know how to say what's troubling him," Abel said, gently rubbing his hand along Schtarm's glossy cinnamon hide. "So, he misbehaves. But the truth is he's just trying to be heard."

His gaze fell away from hers and he picked up a curry comb to brush Schtarm, running it over his neck and withers. The way Abel touched the horse gave Carrie a shiver. It was so gentle and tender. "Are you skilled at blacksmithing?"

Abel gave a hard, short laugh. "No, ma'am. I'm no horse pedicurist. Left that particular skill set to Daniel and Eli. I prefer to keep my distance from the back end of a horse." He unhooked the halter from the post and led Schtarm back into the stall.

Abel had no trouble hitching up Old-Timer, Carrie noticed. He did it in the same careful pattern as all Plain folk did, like he'd been doing it all his life. He helped her up on the buggy and took the reins without asking, holding them loosely in his hands. The sky was bright blue, washed clean from last night's rain. Large puffy clouds chased each other in the sky. Abel pointed out the different farms along the way and asked about each of her neighbors.

At the cemetery, Abel's lighthearted mood dimmed, like a cloud passing over the sun. After showing him the graves, Carrie left him alone and walked over to her father's small tombstone, identical to all of the others; a sign of humility. Carrie stood by her father's grave for a long while, remembering. Then she went back to wait in the buggy and distract herself from dwelling on loss. Esther's voice echoed in her mind, "Overgrieving is a complaint against the Lord." But it was so hard, so hard to accept the mysterious will of God.

From the buggy, Carrie watched Abel. He sat down on the damp ground in between Eli's and Daniel's graves. He held out his hand, gently running one hand over the rounded edge of the stones, the same gentle way that he had touched the curve of Schtarm's neck. She could see his lips moving, as if he was talking to them. After a long while, he wiped his face with both hands and brushed off his pants. The damp ground had soaked the knees of his pants in large dark patches. He looked a little embarrassed, but relieved too, as he climbed in the buggy.

"So glad that six feet under isn't the end of things," he said. "Their souls are with the Lord Jesus."

"That's our hope," Carrie said, automatically.

He shifted in the buggy seat to look at her. "The Bible says that when we're absent from the bodies, we're present with the Lord. Second Corinthians 5:8."

Carrie didn't want to argue with him. He knew his Bible better than she knew hers, she could see that. He spouted off a few verses last night like he had the whole thing memorized. Besides, she had another question burning inside of her. As forward as it seemed, Carrie felt she had to ask, especially once she figured he didn't seem likely to be sticking around.

She slapped the reins to get the horse moving. With her eyes fixed on Old-Timer's rhythmic back quarters, she said, "There's something I need to ask you. About Daniel."

"Ask me anything," Abel said, regarding her with inquiring eyes, his head slightly tilted.

"Daniel said he caused the fires."

Abel made a small sighing sound, as if he'd heard this story before. "Is that what he told you? That he caused them?"

She nodded. "He said he was responsible for them." Her gaze returned to the reins. "I don't understand why . . . how . . . he could ever harm someone."

"Do you know much of what happened in Ohio?"

She shook her head, her heart pounding so loudly she was sure he could hear it.

Abel was quiet for a moment, as if gathering his thoughts. He reached over and took the reins from her, then pulled Old-Timer over to a stop at the side of the road. He shifted in his seat to look at her. "A few years back, Daniel started a business of delivering kerosene to the Amish. I helped him out when Eli didn't need me in the fields. Most of the folks lived down macadam roadways, and it was easier for us to make deliveries using horse and wagon than for the delivery truck. We built a shed to keep the containers clean and dry, separate from the barn. Separate from anything that could contaminate the containers. Only thing we had in the shed was a telephone, to take orders. In Eli's district, folks were allowed a phone for business, as long as it wasn't in the house."

Carrie nodded. It was the same allowance for her district.

"You know about Katie?" he asked.

Carrie nodded again, though all she really knew was her name.

"A week before Daniel and Katie's wedding," Abel continued, "the containers became contaminated with gasoline. Kerosene and gasoline don't mix." He glanced over at a farmer's field of tall corn, yellow-brown stalks rustling in the breeze. "We still don't know how it happened. They had arrived clean as a whistle, without a trace of gasoline. Daniel signed off on them and put them in the shed. Later that day, he made the deliveries. By that evening, two households had explosions. Lena, Daniel's mother, happened to be at Katie's, preparing for the wedding, when the kerosene was lit. It exploded and killed her instantly. Katie was burned badly and died the next day. Another man and his son were killed too." He stopped for a moment, as if the words had caught in his throat. "We just don't know *how* it happened."

The air had grown thick and heavy, as before a storm, though the sky was empty of clouds. Carrie's eyes prickled with tears; she kept her eyes on her hands, folded in her lap. As he spoke the words, she knew them to be true. She had known, deep in her heart, that Daniel could never have caused harm to anyone. As the truth slipped in and pushed away any lingering doubt about Daniel, on its heels swept in an overwhelming sorrow. A single tear fell onto her lap, followed by another and another. She wiped them away with the back of her hand as quickly as they came, hoping Abel didn't notice.

From the corner of her eyes, she saw his chest move as he drew in a breath. "The police traced it back to the shed. They found small traces of gasoline on a shelf. Since it was a business, Daniel was held liable, even if it was an accident, even if Amish families would never sue him. He was still negligent. The judge gave him a stiff fine and an even stiffer prison sentence—he wanted to make an example because there have been other problems with fuel delivery companies. He knew the sentencing would make headlines and he knew the Amish would never appeal. But he didn't care who went to jail, so I told the judge it was my fault, and next thing I knew, I was a long-term houseguest of the Ohio State Penal System. Soon as I was paroled, my parole officer gave me permission to leave the state, as long as I check in with him."

He turned to her. "I guess to answer your first question, Daniel *felt* responsible, but he didn't *cause* those accidents. We'll never know how it happened, but Daniel was innocent. I know that." He gave her a gentle smile. "It's good that you asked, Carrie. You deserve the truth. The Bible says that the truth will set us free."

Well, she had the truth now, but it didn't make her feel free. It made her feel weighted down with regret. She smoothed out her apron, as if trying to push away the sadness. "Seems to me you lost over a year of your life."

"Oh no." Abel looked right at Carrie. "No, I didn't. I gained my life."

Before Carrie could even wrap her brain around that statement, a little red convertible roared past. It startled Old-Timer, who jerked the buggy off the street.

"Oh dear," she said without thinking. "We'd better get back to the house. Gschwind." *Fast.* She took back the reins from Abel and urged the horse forward.

When they arrived home, Veronica McCall's red convertible was parked by the front door.

Abel looked amused. "Who does that car belong to?"

"A woman who works at the Honor Mansion, up the road. She keeps badgering me to buy this property."

Abel gave Carrie a sharp look. Then he hopped down and helped her out of the buggy. "You go on in. I'll put away the team."

Carrie went inside and found Yonnie spreading out quilts all over the kitchen table, with Veronica McCall picking and choosing which ones she was interested in.

"Hello," Carrie said as she took off her cape and untied her bonnet strings.

Veronica McCall spun around on her high heels. "Carrie! Where have you been? Our interior designer went berserk when he saw that quilt you brought to me. Over-the-moon berserk! Now he wants Yonnie's quilts in all of the rooms at Honor Mansion!" She turned back to the quilts and started snatching them up, to make a pile. "He's using them as his focal point in every room."

Carrie searched Yonnie's face, wondering what she thought about that plan. "Perhaps we could get back to you, Veronica McCall."

Just then, Abel came through the kitchen door.

"Veronica, this is Abel Miller," Carrie said quickly, hoping to distract Veronica from piling up Yonnie's quilts. Veronica glanced quickly at him, then did a double take. It reminded Carrie of how Veronica looked when she first saw Yonnie's quilts. And how she always looked when she talked about Carrie's property. Like a hunter who found her prey.

Carrie looked over at Abel. Jaw wide open, he was gaping at Veronica McCall as if he had never seen a woman before.

8

The next afternoon, Veronica McCall found Carrie picking cucumbers in the vegetable garden. "Yoo-hoo, Carrie! I need to talk to Abel. Where is he?"

Carrie pointed to the barn. "In the back. There's a room where he's staying."

"Thank you!" Veronica called out, spinning on her high heels as she turned to hurry to the barn.

Carrie wondered what Veronica McCall would need with Abel. Before long, she heard the car engine start up. She straightened up from bending over a cucumber bush just in time to see Veronica McCall drive off. Abel was in the seat beside her.

It was dusk when they returned. Carrie was at the kitchen sink, cutting vegetables for the stew. She saw Abel get out of the car, and Veronica McCall reach over to hand him a large manila envelope, as if he had forgotten it. He gave a sideways glance at the house before accepting it from her. For a split second, Carrie thought she saw that uncomfortable look on his face again. Then he tucked the envelope under his arm before heading to the barn.

At dinner, Abel talked and asked questions but didn't volunteer an explanation about his outing. It still surprised Carrie to have conversation at the dinner table. Silence wove itself through most of her day; even meals were quiet. At least, it had always been so at Esther's table, and Eli's too. But Carrie found herself enjoying Abel's stories. Tonight, he told about the friends he made in prison, fellows with odd names like Five and Steelhead.

Andy, Carrie noticed, was trying his best to look bored. But he didn't bolt from the table as soon as they prayed a quiet prayer after the meal was over, like he had been doing since Abel had arrived. Carrie thought Abel would make a good preacher; he seemed to have a habit of slipping Bible phrases into the conversation whenever he could, which was often.

Clearing the plates from the table, Carrie asked, "Why did his parents name him Steelhead? Was it after the trout?"

After Abel stopped laughing at Carrie, he said, "No. He actually had a steel plate put in his head after he got shot at during a botched robbery."

Her eyes went wide. Even Andy couldn't hold back a look of surprise. "Oh, he didn't have a gun," Abel said. "Steelhead would never hurt a fly. It was the store owner's gun. It went off, by accident, when Steelhead sneezed during the holdup."

Andy tilted his head. "What about Five?"

"Five went to jail for the five-finger discount." He wiggled his fingers in the air.

Andy and Carrie exchanged a confused glance.

"Shoplifting," Abel said. Realizing they still didn't understand, he added, "He stole things from stores." He leaned back in his chair, folding his hands behind his head. "Now those are two characters I will miss."

After dinner, Abel joined them in the living room. Yonnie had decided that Abel needed a quilt, so she started laying out fabric pieces on the cardboard table. She asked Abel what colors he liked and which patterns and shapes. Abel patiently answered her questions, helping her come up with a final vision for the quilt.

"When you marry," Yonnie said, "I'll make you another one. For your bride."

Abel laughed. "Don't get started yet on that one, Yonnie. I'm in no hurry to find love."

Yonnie peered at him in that knowing way she had. "But love might be in a hurry to find you."

An image of Veronica McCall bounced into Carrie's head.

When the clock struck nine, just like always, Carrie took out her father's Bible and knelt down to read a chapter.

"Carrie, do you mind if I read?" Abel asked.

"No, I don't mind at all." In fact, she was pleased. She held the Bible in her hands, thinking back to all of the moments of her childhood, kneeling in the living room, listening to her father's dear voice read from the Good Book. The sweet memory was as firmly imprinted on her heart as were the words of God in the worn old leather Bible.

She handed the Bible to Abel, but he shook his head and pulled a small book out of his coat pocket.

He opened his book, leaned back in his chair, and started reading, "'Yahweh, investigate my life; get all the facts firsthand. I'm an open book to you, even from a distance, you know what I'm thinking. You know when I leave and when I get back; I'm never out of your sight. You know everything I'm going to say before I start the first sentence. I look behind me and you're there, then up ahead and you're there, too—'"

"Abel," Carrie said. "It's time to be reading the Bible now."

"It is. This is from Psalm 139. David wrote it."

She frowned at him. "That's plain old English."

"It's a modern translation. It's called *The Message*. It's a Bible I read from in jail every day—"

Carrie's back stiffened. "Just seems you ought not to be talking to the Lord God like that." She looked to Yonnie for support, but she had nodded off to sleep, like she always did during the evening Bible reading. She glanced at Andy, but he had quietly returned to his puzzle when she and Abel started to talk.

Abel lifted his head and looked at Carrie with genuine puzzlement. "Like what?"

"Like . . . well, like . . . he's one of your odd-named friends from jail."

Abel closed the book and smiled. "But the Bible says we can talk to God like that."

Abel's talk about God made Carrie fidget in her chair, uneasy. She knew her father faithfully read Scripture, but he didn't pause and ponder any of it or ask questions of anyone about what he read. And he never would have talked to God like he was . . . a . . . fishing buddy. That was thought to be grossfiehlich. *Haughty or high-minded.*

Carrie told Andy to go to bed and followed him upstairs to make absolutely sure that's where he was headed. Just last night, she found he had crawled out his window to sit on the porch roof, searching the sky for night birds with Daniel's binoculars. While she said goodnight to Andy, she heard the buzz of low voices downstairs, Abel and Yonnie's. She waited until she heard Yonnie climb the stairs to bed in her cautious, creaky way. Carrie figured Abel had gone to the barn so it was safe to go downstairs, but there he was, seated at the kitchen table. She wanted to turn tail and head back upstairs, but he heard her footsteps on the stairs and stood, waiting for her.

"I wanted to finish our conversation," he said.

Awkwardness covered her like a blanket. "I ought to be getting to bed. Dawn comes early." She went into the living room to turn off a gas lamp.

"Carrie, I do know the Amish ways."

She turned off one more light, then spun around in the dimly lit room to face him. "Then why don't you follow them?"

"Because I pray out loud? Or read an English Bible? Or both?"

She nodded, but the truth was, it was Abel's praying that rankled her the most. He talked to God like he was sitting up there in heaven, taking down notes so he wouldn't forget what Abel wanted. She knew God was going to do whatever he wanted to do, regardless of anyone's pleading.

"I've learned more about God in the last year or so than I ever did in Eli's home. There's so much more to God than what we've been taught."

"Like what?"

"Like, there's a difference between religion and relationship. It's all right here," he said, tapping his Bible.

"Christ came not for relationship, but for our will," Carrie said. "I've heard the bishops and ministers preach that all of my life."

"Maybe he came for both," Abel answered quietly.

Carrie wasn't sure what to say to that. She hadn't thought these things through. It occurred to her that she had always just accepted what her father had told her, what her church had told her, then what Sol had told her. As she was finding herself doing frequently around Abel, she became uncomfortable. She crossed her arms defiantly against her chest. "So, you're not planning on joining the church? You would leave your faith?"

An ill-at-ease look swept over Abel's face. He went to the kitchen table and sat down, pulling a chair out for her. Reluctantly, she sat down. He put his hands together.

"Carrie, my faith is mine. I'll never leave it. It doesn't matter what church I go to." He looked at his folded hands. "I'm just not sure I can act Amish."

"You don't 'act' Amish. You live it. You *are* it." Even as she said the words, she felt the sting of her own hypocrisy. Here she was, lecturing Abel as if she had never had doubts about bending at the knee. Not much more than a year ago, she was willing to throw it all away for Sol. "You'll turn out the kitchen light?" she asked him, waiting for his nod before she went up the stairs.

She whispered an apology to the Lord God for sounding so proud. She also hoped that God would understand that Abel Miller was a fence jumper and not blame her for bringing him into her home. Like Esther would, if she knew.

Carrie shuddered, hoping she could hold that off as long as possible.

Later that week, Mattie dropped by Carrie's house with fabric for Yonnie. Mattie's mother was hosting a comfort knotting the next Wednesday, and Yonnie had offered to help by cutting fabric into squares to be sewn into a comforter. The quilts would be sent to homeless shelters in Philadelphia.

Mattie set the box down on the table and pulled out *The Budget*, the Amish newspaper, for Yonnie. "Here you are. Just like I promised. Mom said she's done reading and you're welcome to it."

Yonnie was thrilled. She loved *The Budget*. She spent hours sitting and reading the letters sent in by the scribes all over the country. She settled into her favorite chair, basked by sunlight, and spread out the newspaper on the quilting frame in front of her. First, she always turned to the obituaries.

"Why do you like the obituaries?" Mattie asked, watching Yonnie scan the page.

"Making sure I'm not dead yet."

Smiling, Mattie came in to join Carrie in the kitchen, boiling jars and lids to fill with blackberry jam. "A hot day for hot work! How can I help?"

Carrie pointed to the box on the table. "Those are jars that need washing before I can sterilize them."

Mattie washed her hands and rolled up her sleeves. "I always look for weddings in *The Budget* first. Then I read about the visiting." She started taking the jars out of the boxes and put them in the sink to wash. "What about you, Carrie? Don't you always look for wedding news?"

Carrie lifted the hot jars out of the boiling water and set them carefully on the countertop. "I used to. Not so much anymore." She ladled the thick, lumpy, hot purple liquid into the jars, then topped them with a metal lid.

"Oh, it won't be long before you're married again. Remember when we were girls? If we held a ripe dandelion seed head and blew three times, then the number of seeds left would tell us how many children we'd have." Mattie smiled, rinsing out the sudsy jars before handing them to Carrie to sterilize.

Carrie didn't answer at first. "I don't want to marry again." She put the jars Mattie had washed into the large pot of boiling water. Drips of sweat were streaming down her neck.

Mattie looked up at her. "You don't mean that. I thought—"

"You thought I'd be thinking about Sol?" Carrie asked. "I'm not." Her voice sounded crosser than she intended. But it had occurred to her that Mattie might feel worried Sol would start coming around now that Daniel was gone. Carrie hadn't heard from Sol in months. That suited her just fine. She might not know how she felt about Daniel, but she knew how she felt about Sol: zannich! *Angry!*

"Did I say such a thing?" Mattie handed Carrie two jars. "I just thought you'd want to marry again. That's all."

The gentle reproach in Mattie's eyes stung. Carrie turned her eyes to the filled jars. "All I want is to be able to give these apple orchards to Andy one day. If I can hang on to them."

Mattie tilted her head. "Are you having money troubles?"

Carrie hesitated a moment, listening for the pop of the jam jars to indicate the lid suctioned into a seal. "Not troubles, exactly. Not yet." She had refused Veronica McCall's offer to buy Yonnie's quilts. She just couldn't let Yonnie part with any more of them. She was sure there had to be another way to pay the bills.

"Can't you ask Esther for help?"

Carrie winced. Esther had never truly forgiven Carrie for insisting that Andy come live with her. "Her solution would be to move back in with her."

"You could talk to the deacon. He would be able to help."

"I know. If I need to, I will." She wiped the counter with a clean rag. "For now, we're all right. It's looking like this will be a good apple year." She took the jars out of the water and set them down. Mattie ladled the jam into the clean jars and put a lid on each one. "So if keeping the orchards is what you want for Andy, what do you want for yourself?"

Carrie shrugged a shoulder carelessly. "We don't get everything we want, Mattie."

Mattie bent an ear down to hear the *pop! pop!* of the lids. When she heard them, she smiled, satisfied. "No, maybe not, but the Lord promises us everything we need."

A few days later, Carrie made hotcakes with apple butter for breakfast. She was pouring Yonnie a cup of coffee as Abel came in from the barn.

"Mmmm! They smell delicious." Abel grabbed a plate and forked a few steaming hotcakes onto it, spooning apple butter on top.

"Daniel loved Carrie's hotcakes too," Yonnie said.

"Only time I ever saw him give an all-the-way-to-the-toes smile," Carrie said.

The words flew out of her mouth before she caught them. She clamped her lips shut as Abel's chin snapped up. He looked straight at Carrie, but she kept her eyes lowered to her plate.

The morning was already so hot that Carrie went down to the barn to make sure the animals' water buckets were filled. Abel came in from the workshop when he heard her.

"Got a minute?" he asked.

She finished pouring water into Lulu's bucket, then straightened. "No. I've got an apple snitz in the oven."

"I was pulling off some rotted boards on the barn to replace them and got a nasty splinter in my hand." He held up his hand to show her.

"Come over to the window."

He held out the hand with the wood splinter. As she tried to pull it without breaking it off, he said, "Those Cooper's hawks need to be set free. They're nearly grown." The hawks were squawking a raucous call at them from the cage Andy had made for them by converting a horse stall.

She nodded.

"They're wild creatures. Keeping them in a barn is no place for them."

"I've said as much to Andy, but he won't part with them. I think it's the last link he had to Daniel."

In a voice low and kind, Abel asked, "Carrie, was Daniel good to you?"

She dropped his hand as if it was a hot coal. Abel's gaze was steady—he looked at her with brown eyes that were warm and concerned. He made her uneasy, though, asking her questions that no one ever asked. Sometimes she couldn't believe he and Daniel were related. He must have been a perfect complement to Daniel. Abel liked to talk. He probably filled in the emptiness of Daniel's silences, she decided, turning her attention back to the splinter, ignoring his question.

"Done," she said. "Best to put a bandage on that." She turned away quickly.

Abel put his hand on her forearm. "Was he good to you, Carrie?"

Her gaze shifted to the birds in the stall, staring at her with their beady black eyes.

Abel waited. And waited. The silence in the barn took on a prickly tension. Carrie knew he expected her to pour out all the grief and sorrow she had stored up for so long. She felt close to tears and she didn't know why. How could she admit to him that the sadness she felt whenever she thought of Daniel was caused by guilt, not grief?

Keeping her eyes averted, she answered, "Daniel was always good to me. Very, very good to me."

Walking back to the farmhouse, she realized she had spoken the truth. Daniel had been good to her. Still, her feelings about Daniel were a tangled mess. She felt terrible about how things had been left between them. She felt a deep guilt that shadowed her, the way Daniel's burden had shadowed him. But most of all, she felt a sorrow that things were left unfinished between them.

The following day, Veronica McCall came to Carrie's house and walked right into the kitchen without knocking. She didn't close the door tight, so Carrie hurried past her to shut it before hot sticky air could rush in.

"Where's Abel?" she asked.

"I heard him nailing some boards on the back side of the barn," Carrie said. "That barn is so old it's nearly falling apart."

"I came to ask him if he could do some carpentry work for us at Honor Mansion. A carpenter is having surgery for a hernia or a kidney or something like that."

Carrie tilted her head. "A hernia or a kidney?"

"Well, something's wrong with him." Veronica waved the thought away. "So he's out for a while and we need to get the interior woodwork finished. I thought of Abel. Don't all Amish men know carpentry?"

Carrie turned to Yonnie, who was watching Veronica McCall with a curious look on her face. "Yonnie, does Abel do carpentry?"

"Oh sure," Yonnie said. "And he knows all about electric. And motors too."

"He's an electrician?" Veronica asked. "Even better! Our electrician hasn't shown up in three days. They all keep quitting. Perfect! I'll go talk to him." She blew out the door, not bothering to shut it. Hot, heavy air swooped in.

If Veronica McCall hired Abel on, Carrie thought, maybe he would stick around and help them get through the harvest. Just one harvest, she prayed, whispering cautiously to God above, if she could just make it through this first harvest without Daniel. She closed the door and turned to Yonnie. "What else can Abel do?"

"He's good at fixing things. Abel can fix anything." She looked up to the ceiling, pensive, as if trying to pull down a memory like a book from a shelf. "I'm pretty sure he could build a nuclear submarine if he put his mind to it."

Carrie stared at Yonnie, trying to make sense of her. "Yonnie, what do you know about nuclear submarines?"

Yonnie smiled, and the wrinkles on her face fell into their natural grooves. "I know about all sorts of things."

Carrie went over to sit next to her. "Well then, what do you think Abel plans to do with himself, now that he's out of jail?"

She picked her quilting up off her lap. "Stay here, of course, and help us. We're his family. He belongs here."

"I'm not so sure that others are going to understand an English-looking fellow just set free from jail is family."

Yonnie kept her eyes on her quilt pieces. "Abel is still in his Rumspringa."

Carrie doubted that. Abel seemed a little old for running-around years. "So you think he just hasn't decided yet about joining the church?"

"Oh sure," she said, but not with conviction. She started to concentrate on a row of tiny stitches.

"Yonnie, was Abel so . . . ," she hunted for the right word, ". . . devout before he went to jail?"

She gave a short laugh. "Oh my, no."

"He's changed, then?"

Concern pulled down her wrinkled features. "Haven't we all." She started humming, which was her signal that she was done talking.

Abel didn't return for supper that night. He wasn't even home in time for evening prayers. Carrie was nearly asleep when she heard a car zoom up the driveway, skidding to a halt in front of the barn. She got out of bed and looked out a corner of the window to see who it was. In the full moonlight, she saw Veronica McCall reach out to plant a kiss right on Abel's lips. She quickly stepped away from the window and jumped back in bed, ashamed of herself for spying on them like, well, like Emma. But one thing she did notice: Abel didn't seem to be objecting to the kissing.

A few days later, about dinnertime, the bishop's grandson, John Graber, showed up at the farmhouse, carrying a big smoked ham. "My mother thought you might be needing this," he said in his awkward way.

"Oh my, yes. This will feed us for . . . weeks," Carrie said, taking it from him. Months, even.

Abel came in from the barn, bursting through the kitchen door. "Well, hello there!" he said. "Just noticed your buggy out front." He reached a hand out to John Graber. "I'm Abel, Yonnie's grandson."

John Graber looked at Abel's hand as if he didn't know what to do with it. Then his head turned from Abel to Carrie, completely confused. But then, the wheels in John's mind had always turned slowly.

"This is the bishop's grandson, John," Carrie said, filling in the silence.

John just stood there, looking ill at ease and bewildered. It was one of the many reasons Carrie thought he was strange. He ran clean out of words after the first greeting.

Abel, not a bit put off by John's lack of loquacity, went on merrily ahead and invited him to stay for supper. Carrie tried not to let a relieved smile spread over her face when John declined and abruptly turned to leave. She could only imagine what John would report to his grandfather after hearing Abel pray like he was on a first-name basis with the Lord God Almighty.

"Another time, then, John!" Abel called out cheerfully from the kitchen door.

Carrie scowled at Abel after he closed the door.

"What? What did I do?" he asked her.

"John Graber is sweet on her," Yonnie whispered. "She doesn't want to encourage his attention. She thinks he is strange."

"He does seem a little strange." Abel grinned at Carrie. "Maybe a little weak on the social skills."

As Carrie watched John's buggy turn onto the road, she wondered how long it would be until Esther showed up. She hurried upstairs and pulled open a trunk where she had stashed Daniel's clothes. She had meant to pass them on to someone in need but hadn't found time yet. She picked up the shirts and trousers and held them close to her, burying her face in them and inhaling deeply. There was still a lingering hint of Daniel in them—the sour smell of wood smoke mixed with the sweet smell of hay. She took them downstairs and handed them to Abel.

He lifted his dark brows at Carrie, puzzled.

"Perhaps you could look Plain while you're here," she told him.

Abel frowned, scratched his chin, then dropped one hand to rest on his dead cousin's shirt.

The next morning, after breakfast, Esther arrived in her buggy with Emma and a large suitcase. "I've decided you need help," she told Carrie, eyeing Abel suspiciously. "Emma will stay for a while."

At least Abel was wearing Plain clothes, Carrie thought. Daniel was much taller so the pants legs puddled around the ankles, but Abel could pass for an Amishman.

Emma clomped upstairs to claim a spare bedroom while Carrie made coffee for Esther and brought out a day-old cake. For as long as Carrie could remember, Esther had an effect on folks like a thundercloud that had just poured rain on their picnic. Abel stayed for coffee and did his best to try to engage Esther in conversation, but she nearly ignored him. It wasn't long before the conversation at the kitchen table drizzled to a cold stop.

Esther waved away Carrie's offer for a second cup of coffee, hurried to her buggy, and left. Carrie stood at the kitchen door for a moment.

Abel came up behind her, folding his arms across his chest as he watched Esther slap the reins to get the horse moving. "So, that's your mother."

"No, no," Carrie quickly said. "That's Emma's mother."

"So what happened to your mother?"

"My mother died right after Andy was born. My father moved us to Stoney Ridge to be closer to a hospital for Andy. When Dad married Esther, he took over managing her land."

"Oh," Abel said. "So Esther brought into the marriage her farm."

The farm and her godly self, Carrie thought but didn't say. Instead, she just nodded.

Abel gazed at her as if reading her thoughts. "She has a way of making clear her expectations."

Carrie's gaze shifted to Esther's buggy, turning right onto the street. "Even heavenly angels would find it hard to live up to Esther Weaver's expectations."

That evening, Carrie tried to avoid Emma's glare as Abel read from his Bible, but inside, she was cringing. After he finished, she hurried upstairs to check on Andy. He always kicked off his covers as he slept, so she smoothed the sheet over him. She had just changed into her nightgown when Emma knocked on the door. Carrie braced herself.

Emma came in, wringing her hands as she sat on the bed. "Carrie, Abel ought not to be reading that Bible. It ought to be in our language. You know that as well as I do. And he shouldn't be praying like that at dinner, either. When Mother hears of this—"

"Emma, this is not Esther's home. This is my home," Carrie said sharply. "And it wouldn't do you any harm to listen to Abel." The words spilled out so fast she surprised herself with their boldness. Emma was only saying things Carrie had thought herself, just a week or so ago when Abel first arrived.

Emma's brow wrinkled, creased with worry. She drew her lips in a tight line as she folded her arms against her chest.

"I'd rather Esther not be told about Abel's way of Bible reading."

Emma went to the door. "It's not our way."

"I'm a Miller now."

"Amish is Amish. There's no difference." Emma closed the door behind her.

Carrie used to believe that, but now she wasn't so sure.

Sol had been named Pitcher of the Month for August. His image flashed up on the large screen in the stadium the day it was announced, and he was interviewed by three newspapers—one of which was the *Philadelphia Inquirer*. His baseball career was taking off, just like he had planned.

In his apartment, he kept a stack of copies of all of the newspapers that wrote about him, even though there was no one to show them to. Not yet, anyway. Soon, he hoped, when the season wrapped up, enough time would have passed that he would be able to call on Carrie. He was sure she'd have forgiven him by now and things could go back to being the way they were before. The way he had planned.

It had been over a month since Abel had come. The long hot summer had flown by fast and the end of the growing season was almost in sight. The tree branches in Carrie's orchards were heavy with fat, ripening apples.

One afternoon in late September, threatening dark clouds raced across the sky. The wind blew so strong that Carrie took the clothes off of the line, still damp, before the rain started. As she took the last sheet down, she raised her face to the molten gray sky and felt a foreboding. This had the makings of a winter storm. The rain began as the day drew to a close. By supper, the rain had turned to stinging ice pellets.

"Good thing our neighbors got their third cutting of hay done last week," Emma said.

"But not good for apples," Carrie said quietly.

"What's so bad about the rain?" Abel asked, reaching for the butter.

"There's nothing wrong with rain, but it's cold enough to hail," Carrie said, more to herself than to him. "Between the wind and the hail, a lot of apples could get knocked to the ground."

In the middle of the night, Carrie woke to hear hail bouncing off the roof. She looked out the window and couldn't believe her eyes. The hail looked the size of Ping-Pong balls, ricocheting off the ground. "Oh God," she whispered. "Please help."

In the morning, the sun shone bright and cruel. Carrie dressed quickly and rushed out to the orchards. Andy heard her and followed close behind. Abel was already out there, turning in a circle, stunned. Bright red apples covered the ground like autumn leaves. Carrie picked one up. When she saw the bruise and cuts on it, she nearly cried. Most of the crop had been damaged.

Why, God? she asked silently. *Why do you have to keep knocking me down?*

Without a word to Abel or Andy, she turned to walk back to the house. She was almost to the barn when she heard Abel yell out, "Cider!"

Carrie stopped and turned toward him.

Abel ran up to her, holding a bruised apple, and held it out to her. "Andy said you made the best cider in the county." He spun around. "Didn't you say that, Andy?"

Andy nodded, not understanding what Abel meant.

Carrie looked at all of the apples on the ground. "You think we could salvage the crop by making cider?" A glimmer of hope showed in her eyes, but then faded as practicality swept in on its heels. "I only have one old cider press."

"I can put a gasoline motor on it to speed things up."

Carrie shook her head. "Can't. You can't have gasoline around food. I know that from working at Central Market."

Abel's brow furrowed as he scanned the farm. Then his eyes rested on the old waterwheel, attached to the barn. His face lit up. "There's nothing wrong with using water power, is there?"

Carrie nodded slowly. "But that old waterwheel hasn't been used in years."

"Just the other day I took a look at it. Nothing's broke, it just needs a little elbow grease. And thanks to last night's storm, there's plenty of water running in the creek. Won't take much to get it turning. You clean out the cider press and get it ready. I'll work on the waterwheel—a couple of belts and pulleys and we're in business. Andy can ride Strawberry over to the Zooks' and see if Mattie's brothers can spare some time to get these apples picked up today." He turned to Andy. "If you don't mind, you might need to stay home from school today. I'm going to need a partner."

A wide grin spread across Andy's face.

Carrie looked around again at all of the apples. Maybe Abel was right. Maybe it could work. Why not try? She had nothing to lose. "I'll need empty jugs."

"Make a list. Write down everything you need and we'll get it today."

She looked at him, amazed and excited by the idea. "Denki, Abel."

By noon of that day, the waterwheel slowly creaked to life, then spun as a gust of wind sent it whirling. Abel had rigged a system of belts and pulleys to turn the screws on the cider press. As pressure pounded down on the apple mash, sweet clear cider spilled out. The Zook boys, all eight of them, even their father, had arrived to help pick up the apples and load them into crates.

Carrie and Emma had washed the apples and started adding them into the press, trying to get just the right blend of flavors, as Grace Patterson rode her bicycle up the driveway. Carrie wiped off her hands with the rag and waved to her. Though they were only a few years apart, Carrie's heart felt a motherly tug when she saw Grace. Today, Grace was dressed with a long flowing skirt and a man's shirt rolled up at the sleeves. On her feet were combat boots. Her hair was now blond, nearly white. Watching her, Carrie thought it seemed as if Grace wasn't quite sure who she really was, so she kept trying on a different façade until, one day, she might stumble on the one that suited her.

Grace bit her lip. "I came to ask you something."

Carrie filled up a paper cup with the cider and handed it to Grace to sample. "So, ask."

Grace took a sip of the cider, then her face lit up. "That is *money*! Tastes like I bit into a ripe apple."

Carrie smiled. "It's my father's recipe. The storm knocked the apples down so we had to make the cider, just to save the crop. I'm surprised at how good it tastes, though. I was afraid the apples would be underripe but they seem to be plenty sweet." She pointed to the cider press. "That old thing was made in the 1980s and still works."

"Dang, that is old." Grace filled up another cup of the cider. "So . . . ," she took a sip, throwing a glance in Emma's direction, "so my arraignment has been scheduled and I hoped . . . you . . . might be able to come to it. To talk to the judge." She swirled the cider in the cup and watched the bubbles form on top.

"I'll be there, Grace," Carrie said without hesitation. "I've already written a letter."

Grace's eyes flew up to hers. "Thank you so much," she said, almost a whisper. She drank down the cider and looked around at the filled jugs as Abel and Andy pulled up in a wagon. "Won't the cider go bad without refrigeration?" she asked Carrie. "Unless you're making hard cider. A kid in my biology class did that. Took about two weeks to ferment." Her forehead furrowed. "Then he came to school drunk and got suspended."

"The devil's brew?" Emma gasped. "Mother would never approve."

Carrie stopped suddenly and looked at Abel, who looked just as surprised. "Oh no!"

Abel blew the air out of his chest in a great gust. "No, we're not trying to make hard cider." He rubbed his chin. "Maybe we could keep the jugs cold in the creek."

"You could probably stick them in the freezers at Honor Mansion. The kitchen is empty." Grace swallowed the last drop. "I'll ask Veronica."

"That's a great idea," Abel said. "Better even to freeze it than to keep it refrigerated."

Grace crinkled up the cup and handed it to Carrie. In a low whisper she added, "Better still, get Abel to ask Veronica. She won't say no to anything he asks. She's got the hots for him."

Overhearing, Abel looked alarmed. Grace waved and hopped on her bicycle to head back to work.

"Come on, Abel," Andy said, hopping back up on the wagon after drinking a cup of cider. "I'll go with you to ask that fancy red-haired lady with the short skirts." He glanced at his sister. "I meant, the fancy lady with the red car."

Carrie frowned at Andy. He was worrying her a little.

By the time they returned, given permission by Veronica to use the freezers, Carrie's cider mill was in production. Mattie had offered to sell the cider at Central Market, where her family had a market stand.

"Maybe Esther would let Emma sell it too," she told Carrie. "I've seen her there, working with Emma at the farm stand now and then."

Emma had been working for Esther at Central Market every other day as the crops finished up their summer bounty.

"Maybe so," Carrie said, but she doubted Esther would agree.

Carrie, Emma, Abel, and Andy pressed cider over the next few days. The Zooks loaned their cider press too, so they were able to double the output, and the weather stayed cold so the apples weren't going soft. Word spread among the neighbors that Carrie's cider was even better this year than last, and they stopped by the farm throughout the week to buy a jug or two.

After spending so much time side by side with Abel, Emma concluded that he was no longer to be viewed with suspicion. Andy, too, relinquished his lingering hostility toward him, helped along by Abel's request to skip school that week. Carrie noticed that he shadowed Abel the way he used to shadow her father, and later, Daniel. All week long, she almost never had to nag him to do chores as long as Abel worked alongside him. The sight should have gladdened Carrie's heart, but instead it made her feel sad. She was pretty sure Abel wouldn't be sticking around. And that meant one more loss for Andy.

By Friday, Mattie had sold every jug of cider at Central Market. Carrie fought back tears as Mattie handed the large wad of cash to her. Mattie had been bold enough to double the price Carrie wanted for the cider, and still, she sold every jug with people asking for more. The cider had brought in more money than selling the fancy grade apples to the packing house ever had.

Before the sun set for the day, Abel found Carrie wiping down the cider presses in the barn. "Mattie told me that she had more customers than cider."

Carrie smiled. "Thanks to your quick thinking, Abel."

He brushed the compliment aside. "That's not what I meant. I meant that it could be we've found a niche here."

"Maybe next year we don't even bother with the packing house. Maybe we just make cider."

"I'm not talking about next year. Other varieties are coming on the market now. We could buy them and make the cider, then sell it at the Zooks' stand at Central Market. They're staying open until Christmas."

Considering the option, she asked, "I don't see how we could make much money after buying the apples."

"Hear me out. Mattie thinks she could have priced it even higher than she did." He took the rag from her and started rubbing the sides of a press. "I think we might have something here. Jacob's Cider is a hit."

It made her stomach feel funny, to hear him say *we* like he did. "I don't know. We'd need our own freezer. We can't be using Veronica McCall's much longer. She's told me more than once that she should be charging me rent." She gathered the rags in her arms to take up to the house to wash.

Abel nodded. "I might be able to find a used freezer someplace and convert it with a generator." He opened the barn door for her and waited until she crossed the threshold to slide it shut. There, in front of her, was a wagon filled with crates of apples.

"Did I mention that I happened to stop by a farmer's market today?" he asked with a big grin. "They're not your heirlooms, but I did get five varieties of apples for your five-apple cider. The farmer said they had a high sugar content for cider. That's good, right?"

"But . . ." Carrie suddenly felt panicky about the cost of those apples. The wad of cash in her apron was about to disappear, and with it, hopes to pay the next installment of the property tax.

As if reading her mind, he added, "And they didn't cost a thing. They're misshaped apples." He held an odd-looking apple up to her. "The farmer said they taste just as good, but he can't sell them as eating apples."

"He didn't charge you?" she asked.

"Well, we bartered back and forth. He told me he needed some shelves built in his garage, and I told him I needed those apples. An even exchange."

Wrapping her shawl tightly around her, Carrie felt so grateful for Abel's help that she could hardly breathe. Maybe Yonnie was right. Maybe he could fix anything.

"I think I've settled on the right name for my home," she said, eyes shining. "Cider Mill Farm."

9

Carrie was just latching the chicken coop after throwing feed to the bossy leghorns when she heard Andy's screams coming from the barn. She dropped the bucket she was carrying and ran down to see what had happened.

When she peered inside the open door, she saw Andy doubled over, as if he was sick. Scattered around the barn were feathers and beaks and bloody pieces of meat and bones. The Cooper's hawks had attacked and killed Mattie's goslings. Carrie stood, frozen, taking in the morbid sight, unsure of what to do next. Andy picked up a broom and tried to hit the hawks, but they were too quick. They just flew above him and rested on a rafter, peering down at him with an insolent stare, mildly interested in his tirade. When Andy finally gave up, out of breath, he threw the broom down.

Abel came up behind Carrie, hearing the commotion. "No, let me," he whispered to her, as she made a move to go to her brother. "You go on back to the house." He walked over to Andy.

She turned to leave, then stopped, leaning against the doorjamb. Andy was turned in the opposite direction and didn't notice she was still there.

"The Cooper's hawks were just doing what they're meant to do, Andy," Abel said softly. "It's in their nature to hunt for food."

Andy kicked at a hay bale. "I gave them plenty of food! Why did they have to eat my geese? Why couldn't they be satisfied with what I gave them?"

"Someday, they'll be satisfied. There's a verse in the Bible that says the lion will lie down with the lamb. That's what heaven will be like."

Andy sank to the floor and leaned against a hay bale, hugging his knees. "Why does everything have to die?" Abel leaned against the hay bale, close to Andy—but not too close. "It was my fault."

"How so?" Abel asked.

"I left the goslings' door unlatched." Andy looked miserable, before resting his head on his knees. "Last night. I got watching an orb spider spin her web and catch a horsefly and wrap it up for dinner that I just plain forgot." Then he mumbled something that Carrie couldn't hear.

"What do you mean?" Abel asked, crouching down next to him, eyes fixed on him.

Andy lifted his head. "I had a dream about Dad and went to wake up Carrie. She wasn't there so Daniel said he would go get her." His voice started to break. "If I hadn't done that, he wouldn't be dead."

Abel took that in for a moment. "It was just an accident, Andy. Listen to me. It wasn't your fault. *It wasn't.* Daniel wouldn't want you feeling responsible. It just happened. We don't know why bad things happen."

Carrie leaned her forehead on the doorjamb. It broke her heart to think that Andy had carried such a heavy burden, all this time. A burden that belonged to her alone.

"It's just like my dad. It was my fault my dad died. Esther said it was. Esther said that if I don't find trouble, trouble finds me. Everything I do always goes wrong."

Abel didn't say anything for a moment. It seemed to Carrie as if he knew how important his response would be and was shooting off one of his one-sentence prayers to the Lord God before he uttered a word.

"There's a verse in the Bible that says God has the length of our days planned out. He knows when it's time for a person to pass. The psalmist wrote that God has the days of our lives all prepared before we'd even lived one day. It's all part of God's plan. Some die sooner than others, and that's hard, real hard to understand, but that's God's business. Our work is to trust him about those things." Abel stroked Andy's hair. "You are *not* responsible for Daniel's death or your dad's. I promise you that, Andy."

Andy started to weep, great sobs that shook his body. Abel pulled him close to his chest and let him cry. Carrie turned and ran to the farmhouse. She couldn't stay and watch Andy's tears; she was barely holding back the avalanche inside of herself.

Later, Carrie saw Abel and Andy carry the carnage out of the barn in a big black bag to bury in the manure pile. Then they caught the Cooper's hawks and took the cage to Blue Lake Pond to set them free. Andy came back looking taller, Carrie thought, like he'd grown a year in a day. When he went upstairs, Carrie threw on a shawl and went out to the barn. Abel was feeding hay to the horses. He threw the last of the hay in the stall, then came up to Carrie.

She searched for words, spirit-lifting words like those he had given as a gift to her brother. All she could think to say was, "Denki. For Andy."

He gave her a nod and then picked up the broom to sweep the fallen hay.

"Andy's not good at confiding his troubles. He seems to feel safe, talking to you. He's at that age where he needs . . . well, I'm not very good at . . . making Andy feel like a man."

"You're good at it." He said it so softly, while he kept sweeping, that she thought she might have imagined it. "When I first got here and saw those hawks . . . well, I've been holding my breath, just waiting for a problem." He stopped sweeping and straightened up. "At least we know they can hunt for food." He swept the rest of the hay into a stall and leaned the broom against the wall. "Kind of surprised me that Daniel would have let Andy keep those hawks. Daniel didn't like predators." He looked at Carrie as if expecting her to explain.

How could she try to explain a man she never knew? Even after all of those months together, she still had no idea who Daniel really was. "To tell you the truth, Abel, I didn't know Daniel all that well."

Abel raised his eyebrows. "I can't deny he had a jaw as tight as a beaver trap. It was hard for him to share his thoughts and feelings."

And his secrets, Carrie thought.

"At least by talking." Abel studied her for a long moment, a quizzical look in his eyes, before he cocked his head and pointed a finger at her. "Stay here. I'll be right back." He went into the workshop. She heard him pull open a drawer, rummage through it, shuffle some papers, then close it again. He came back into the barn and handed her a bundle of envelopes, secured by a rubber band. "These are the letters Daniel wrote to me while I was in jail. Maybe it would help you get to know him better."

She hesitated.

"Go ahead, Carrie," Abel said. "There's nothing to hide."

Carrie took a deep breath, still reluctant.

He pressed the envelopes into her hand. "In some of the letters, he writes about you."

Later that night, Carrie took the lantern up to bed with her and slipped the rubber band off the envelopes Abel had given to her. She looked at the postmarks of Daniel's letters and sorted them from beginning to end. She unfolded the first letter and read the pen-written note. Daniel's handwriting was angular, careful—the script of one who had been taught penmanship at school all those years ago, a skill he had never forgotten.

April 5th

Dear Abel,

After such a long and hard winter, as this past one was, I felt a small stirring of pleasure at seeing the first redwing blackbird return, and heard the clamor of northward winging geese, and the warbling song of the bluebirds as they claimed their nesting boxes. All signs that spring is coming.

I received your letter telling me about your newfound faith. I can hear the change in your voice, even through your letters. I'm glad you've found such peace. I wish I could find that, Abel. You've always been a 100% guy. Whatever you've done, it's with your whole heart. I've always admired that about you. Me? I'm a fence-sitter. And now even my faith has gone dormant.

Looks like we might have an offer on the farm. Ervin Lapp, next farm over, wants to buy land for his youngest son. He offered Dad a decent price, considering land prices are low. Dad wants to use the money and move to Pennsylvania. His old friend, Jacob Weaver, has been encouraging him to come, to make a fresh start. But is there really such a thing?

Yours, Daniel

Carrie's hands almost shook as she held the letter. It seemed as if she was reading Daniel's mind and his heart. She opened another letter postmarked a few weeks later.

May 10th

Dear Abel,

We've had a lot of soakers lately, back-to-back. Glad we got the fields plowed under before it all turned to mud. Had to stop plowing the north field for a few days until four speckled bobolinks had hatched.

Well, it's done, Abel. Dad sold this farm, with all of its memories, good and bad. We're heading down to Pennsylvania next week to stay with the Jacob Weavers and look for property to buy. It will be a small farm, no doubt, after paying off the court fine. Yonnie will stay with cousin Miriam while we're gone.

In your last letter, you mentioned that there is a grace that is greater than all of our sins. How can you be so sure, Abel? How can you truly know that we can ever satisfy God's demands for holy living?

Will write to you when we get to the Weavers and send you the address.

Yours, Daniel

Carrie slipped the rubber band around the rest of the letters. She knew Abel meant well by giving them to her, but they made her guilt over Daniel's death bubble to the surface. It was a long time before she fell asleep.

A few days later, the light clop of hooves on gravel announced the arrival of the bishop and the deacon. As the buggy stopped in the driveway, Carrie threw Emma a look of disdain.

"It wasn't me! I didn't say a peep to them."

Hands hooked on her hips, Carrie asked, "And not a peep to your mother?"

Emma's lips puckered in an "Oh."

Carrie knew they were here to check up on the mysterious Abel Miller. There were organized ways of doing things—certain days and times set apart for such matters. If a concern had been brought to the church leaders, the deacon might pay a visit first. That would never be a cause for worry. Deacon Abraham was a caring man. Whenever she saw him in town or about the farm, two or three of his grandsons rode beside him in the wagon or shadowed him as he worked. He had been widowed recently and decided to move into the Grossdaadi Haus, to let his youngest son take over the farm. "Alles hat seine Zeit," he was fond of saying. *There's a time for everything.*

But to see the bishop climb out of the buggy—now that was a cause for concern. The bishop was known to be influenced by Esther. If there was any principle that Esther lived by, it was abiding by rules, the way things had always been done. It was the pattern of her life. If Esther had convinced the bishop that Abel might have a worldly influence over Andy, he would insist that Abel leave.

Carrie saw the deacon head out to the barn to talk to Abel while the bishop came inside and sat at the kitchen table. Carrie brought him coffee and a piece of shoofly pie, while Emma shared her observations about those who weren't properly dressed at church last Sunday.

"And did you notice that Amos Fisher had on his cream-colored shirt under his coat?" Emma asked the bishop. "He thought no one noticed that it wasn't white, but I saw it, straight off." She peered at him with a look that said she expected him to feel just as alarmed as she did over the gravity of the incident. He didn't.

Carrie kept trying to kick Emma under the table to quiet her from tattling on their friends and neighbors, but Emma prattled on, oblivious. Finally, the deacon came into the kitchen. He accepted Carrie's offer of coffee and pie, and happily settled in at the table.

As Emma cut the slice of pie at the counter, Carrie whispered, "Aw, Emma, why do you have to say such things? Amos Fisher probably just got busy that morning and forgot. He wasn't trying to be proud."

Emma looked injured. "I'm only trying to help the bishop. He's as blind as a bat." She poured the coffee. "Mother always said that she was the eyes and ears of the congregation."

"Mostly the mouth," Yonnie whispered, reaching behind the women to get another piece of pie.

"Carrie," Abraham said, "if there is anything you need, being a widow and all, if you have any financial worries, the church is here to help. That's what we take the alms for."

Carrie handed him the pie and reached a hand out to cover Yonnie's wrinkled hand. "Thanks to Yonnie, we had what we needed to pay the property tax bill."

"And our Abel helped us save the apple crop by turning it into cider," Yonnie added.

"Speaking of," the bishop said. "I understand Daniel's brother is here."

"Daniel's cousin," Emma said. "Abel is Yonnie's grandson."

The bishop nodded. "I have taken notice that Abel Miller isn't a church member."

"Abel is in his Rumspringa," Yonnie said.

The bishop raised his sparse eyebrows, surprised. "It has come to my attention that he reads from an English Bible. A modern one. Now, you know it isn't our way to be reading from a modern English Bible."

Carrie knew he was just speaking what he believed.

"What other English influences might Abel Miller have on this home?" the bishop asked. "What about his influence on our Andy?"

With that comment, Carrie knew for certain she could thank Esther for filling the bishop's head with those worries. Just as she was about to object, Abel came through the kitchen door.

"Thought I should come in to say hello to the bishop." Abel offered a stiff, one-pump Amish handshake to the bishop as Carrie got a cup of coffee for him. She wished there was some way she could have warned him to stay in the barn.

The bishop fixed his eyes on Abel, measuring him. "You read from a modern English Bible." It wasn't a question. "The Bible has never changed."

Abel glanced at Carrie, who tipped her head toward Emma. "Well, you see, I never learned German. I came to Eli's home when I was thirteen."

Abraham slapped his knees in delight. "You see, Atlee? He can't read German! Of course!"

"If he can't read the *Luther Bible*, then he should be reading from King James," said the bishop.

Abel didn't respond to the bishop, but he looked as if reading those translations hadn't occurred to him and he was only sorry he hadn't thought of it himself.

"Abel has been away from Plain folk for a while," Abraham said. "He needs time to be reminded of our ways. We will pray he will choose to become baptized in due time." The deacon smiled. "And he'll be a fine helper for Yonnie and Carrie since our Daniel's passing. Sent by the Lord God." He stood. "Better get back to my dairy." He leaned close to the bishop and quietly added, "Ich have er gut ausgfrogt."

The bishop nodded, rising from his chair. "So then, Abel Miller, we will expect to see you in church on Sunday."

Abel had been going to an Amish-Mennonite church in town on Sundays. Carrie thought Yonnie would have minded that he wasn't going to their church service, but she never said anything to him, so Carrie didn't, either.

Afterward, as the deacon's buggy rolled onto the street, Abel turned to Carrie, "What did the deacon say to the bishop? In Deitsch?"

"That he had thoroughly interrogated you."

"That's what I thought he said." Abel gave a short laugh. "We talked about horses."

Carrie could hardly look at Emma for the rest of that day. Abel was unfazed. He acted just the same toward Emma, friendly and warm and teasing, like he understood she was a rule follower. But that night, he kept right on reading aloud from his modern Bible too.

The next morning, Carrie slid open the heavy door of the barn and walked inside. The heady scent of hay and sweet grain was so familiar. Hope shuffled when she heard her and rolled her heavy head in Carrie's direction. Abel gave her a nod as he came in from his workshop. He unlatched the hook of the nearly empty rubber water bucket from the eye on the wall and carried it outside to the hose.

Carrie sidled into Schtarm's stall to add a scoop of sweet grain to his feed. She watched his graceful head bend to the fragrant, honeyed oats when Abel came to get Schtarm's water bucket. As she stroked Schtarm's large neck, she said, "I'm sorry Emma raised a concern about you."

"Are Esther's other daughters like Emma?" he asked, his mouth turned up at the corners.

"No. Emma is just . . . Emma. My favorite stepsister, Sarah, she lives in another district now, she always said that Emma's prayer cap was on too tight."

Carrie still wasn't sure what Abel's plans were, but she couldn't deny that she hoped he might stay on, even though the harvest was done. He spent his days at Honor Mansion doing carpentry work, but he still found time to do plenty of chores around Cider Mill Farm. He had found an old freezer for the cider that he was able to get for free if he would haul it away. It wasn't in working condition, but Abel said that was a minor detail. He fixed it and got it running with a generator.

Abel slid Schtarm's stall door shut and latched it. "So Yonnie said you're not too keen on being courted by this bishop's grandson, right?"

Carrie nodded, unsure of what he was getting at.

"Last night, Yonnie mentioned that she thought Emma and John might be a good pair."

Carrie's eyes went wide. "She wants to try her hand at matchmaking? With Emma?"

"Yonnie has a way of knowing about these kinds of things." He grinned. "So what do you think?"

She could feel a slow smile stretch across her face. "Emma would love to be married. And John would love to be loved." It suddenly seemed like such a funny coupling that she started to giggle. She could just picture worried Emma seated on a buggy seat next to John Graber, thin and long and angular and solemn. She laughed so hard, she buckled at the waist, and it felt so good. She hadn't laughed like that since—why, she couldn't even remember how long it had been. When she finally stopped laughing, she wiped away the tears streaming down her face.

"Here," Abel said, grinning, as he pulled out his handkerchief. He held the back of her head with one hand and began dabbing her face with the handkerchief. They stood just inches apart, closer than they had ever stood before. All of a sudden Abel stopped wiping, everything stood still. His gaze traveled Carrie's face, from her starched prayer cap to her lips. Carrie's heart started thumping foolishly.

Suddenly, Emma's voice rang out from the farmhouse. "Carrie? Yoo-hoo! Carrie? Where are you? Andy won't eat his oatmeal."

Abel slightly turned his head in the direction of the farmhouse but kept his eyes on Carrie. "Emma's oatmeal? Who could blame him? She's a fine cook, but her oatmeal tastes like library paste."

Carrie jumped back and hurried past him into the house.

All day long, she couldn't stop thinking of that gaze.

Ever since Veronica McCall hired Abel to work at Honor Mansion, she stopped by Carrie's farm on her way to work to give him a ride. Early one Saturday, Veronica McCall burst into the kitchen, brushing past Carrie at the door, looking for Abel.

"He's down in the barn. I'm sure he heard you honking your car horn and will come up to the house in a minute," Emma said with a frown, as she put a match to her Coleman gas iron. "Two counties over heard you," she muttered. Emma didn't care much for Veronica's ways.

Oblivious to Emma's disdain, Veronica poured herself a cup of coffee and sat down at the kitchen table, close to the ironing board. "So what's that you're ironing?" she asked.

"My churchgoing dress. I'm getting it ready for the singing." Emma held up an organza prayer cap. "And these too." She ironed with a vengeance, making sure every little pleat in her cap was crisp and starched. Her white prayer caps sat in a row on the kitchen table, like roosting chickens.

"What's a singing?" Veronica McCall asked, picking an apple out of a bowl. She examined it, put it down, and picked up another.

"A singing is a wonderful thing," Yonnie said. "All of the young folk go, saying they want to sing hymns, but they're really stealing looks at each other when they think nobody's looking."

"So it's dating, Amish style?" Veronica McCall asked, amused. "Figures. Seems like churchgoing is the Amish's National Sport."

Emma opened her mouth to correct her for blaspheming when Veronica shocked her silent by saying, "Maybe I'll tag along. What time should I be here?"

Carrie's eyes went wide. "Why?"

"I want to learn more about the Amish."

"But . . . why?" Carrie asked again.

Veronica looked at Carrie as if she were very slow-witted. "I live and work near the Amish and I should know more about them."

Just then, Abel came through the kitchen door. An awkward silence fell over the room.

"What are you ladies talking about?" he asked as he went to the sink to wash up.

"Veronica McCall wants to come to the singing with us," Emma said to him, sounding concerned.

He spun around, hands dripping soapsuds on the black part of the floor where the linoleum had rubbed away. "Why?"

"I just thought I'd come! Why is that such a big deal?" Veronica McCall asked, frustration rising.

"It's not . . . common . . . for Englishers to go," Carrie tried to explain. "We sing hymns."

"I like music," Veronica said, putting down the apple.

"Some of the hymns are from the Ausbund," Emma said.

"What's an out band?" Veronica asked.

"Ausbund," Abel said. "It's the Amish hymnal; it's hundreds of years old. There's no music score. The verses are in high German, and songs can last fifteen to twenty minutes."

Veronica McCall's arched eyebrows shot up.

"But some of our hymn singing gets a little lively," Emma added, eyes narrowing at her. "And downright raucous."

Veronica McCall lifted a shoulder in a careless shrug. "I'll try anything once."

Abel looked cornered, like a trapped animal. He turned back to the sink to finish washing his hands.

"What time should I arrive?" Veronica asked.

Abel winced. "Come tomorrow night at six."

Veronica stared at him, but he kept his eyes on his soapy hands. "Fine, then. Six."

"Better wear something that covers those limbs," Emma said, peering at

Veronica McCall's long legs. "And button those up to keep from displaying a good bit of the Lord's bounty." She wagged a finger at Veronica McCall's blouse.

Abel froze at the sink. Carrie had been setting the table and stopped, forks suspended in midair. Emma's and Veronica McCall's eyes locked on each other, a standoff, two stubborn women with their hands firmly planted on their hips.

"Fine," snapped Veronica McCall, before scooping up her purse and blowing out the kitchen door.

"Fine," said Emma triumphantly.

Abel, Carrie noticed, didn't look so fine.

That night, as Carrie was getting ready for bed, she pulled out Daniel's letters. Every few days, she steeled herself to read another letter. Tonight, she wanted to finish them.

July 8th

Dear Abel,

You'd better sit down for this.

I asked Carrie Weaver, Jacob's daughter, to marry me and she said yes. I'm still a little stunned, myself. It all happened rather fast. Ever since we arrived at the Weavers', Dad had been encouraging me—downright badgering—to take an interest in Carrie. More than an interest. She's a lovely girl—don't get me wrong—but I still have Katie in my heart. Then, suddenly, Jacob Weaver died and Carrie was grieving so, and next thing I knew, I asked her to marry me. We're to be married in September. Carrie wanted to marry quickly and move out of Esther Weaver's house. (When you meet Esther, you'll understand.) So, there you have it. There are moments when I wonder what I've done . . . but I will tell you that it's a great relief to see Dad looking pleased. As for Carrie, I think she deserves better.

Yours, Daniel

October 7th

Dear Abel,

I'm writing this in the middle of a violent storm. Lightning is splintering the dark sky, and the thunder booms so loud it's as if the heavens have cracked open to spill forth the rain.

Carrie and I have been married for four weeks today. Strange, how one day in a person's life can change its course forever. Married life is an adjustment, though I think Carrie does a better job of it than I do. She is suddenly caring for a household of Millers—Yonnie, Dad, and me. Her younger brother, Andy, too. And she has been unfailingly kind. Dad calls her "my great blessing." I think he's right.

But for the life of me, I can't figure out why I should be blessed.

You asked me if Carrie knew of the Ohio incident. I wanted to tell her, straight off, but Dad counseled me not to. "Some things are best left behind," he told me, and I couldn't really argue with that. I hesitated to tell her and the moment passed.

You also asked me if I have forgiven myself yet. How do I do that, Abel? I see the loneliness etched on Dad's face when he doesn't realize I'm watching. Mom should be by his side. I think of my Katie and the happy life that was robbed of her. I think of how old that little Benjamin Lapp would be by now, and if Elam Lapp would have taken him fishing and birding, like Dad did with you and me. I think of you serving time in jail when I should be there, and Dad having sold his farm to pay the fines. Both of you have paid a steep price for something I was responsible for.

How can I ever forgive myself? How, Abel? And if I can't forgive myself, how could I ever expect God to forgive me?

Yours, Daniel

February 4th

Dear Abel,

It's been over a week now since Dad died. I'm sorry you weren't here for the service. The local church showed up, even though they hardly knew him.

Quite a few folks came from Ohio on a bus, mostly greybeards. It would have pleased him.

During the service, Carrie did something that touched me deeply. When the first clods of dirt fell on Dad's coffin with a gentle thud, she reached over to take my hand. Such a simple act, but it was like she was sharing her strength. I have felt frozen, Abel, and Carrie is helping me to thaw. I wished I could have told her how much it meant to me. I tried to, but the words just get jumbled in my head, like when we used to go fishing at Black Bottom Pond and couldn't untangle the lines. When the last shovelful of dirt covered Dad's lifeworn body, I couldn't help but hope you might be right. That six feet under isn't the end.

Yours, Daniel

Carrie read and reread the letter. The part about when she reached out and held Daniel's hand nearly broke her heart. The sound of the dirt clods hitting Eli's coffin reminded her of her own father's funeral. Her mother's too. She had reached out for Daniel's hand for *his* strength, not to *give* him strength. She felt a fresh wave of crushing guilt over failing Daniel so miserably. Memories of him pressed like a pile of stones on her chest.

Her feelings about Daniel were so tangled up, his death so unexpected, that she had managed to push thoughts of him away. In fact, she had gotten pretty good at ignoring sorrows. It was in the still of the night, when she had nothing to listen to but her own thoughts, that she couldn't hide from them. Her heart echoed with hollowness and her sorrows found her, as if they were patiently waiting for her to acknowledge their presence. It was then that she had trouble shooing them away.

Daniel's letters changed all of that. They brought her sorrows out in the daylight. They revealed a side of him that she sensed was there but could never seem to find a way to break through to it. It was the very side of him that had given her the assurance to say yes when he asked her to marry him. She felt safe with Daniel. But when he finally shared his burden with her, she panicked like a skittish horse. Why couldn't she have just stayed and listened to him?

She felt a grieving for what might have been with Daniel. It wasn't just that he had lost his life; they had lost a life together. She was all mixed up inside, like pieces to one of Yonnie's crazy quilts before any sense was made of them. She kept hoping the pieces would come together into a beautiful pattern, and everything would turn out all right.

But it was too late for that. Daniel was gone.

The next day was a churchgoing Sunday. Carrie got up early to start breakfast so they'd be ready to leave by 7:30. When Abel came inside, she poured a cup of coffee and handed it to him.

As he took the steaming cup from her, he cocked his head. "You okay?"

"Of course," Carrie said.

He peered at her with worried eyes. "You look awful pale."

She put her hands up to her cheeks. "Been indoors too much, lately, I s'pect."

"He's right," Emma said as she came downstairs. "You look as wilted as last night's lettuce."

Carrie went upstairs to wake up Andy, but stopped at her bedroom. She looked at the bed and felt its pull, climbing beneath the heavy quilt, her gaze on the window that framed a gray, brooding sky. She listened to the creak of the wind battering the walls and felt bruised with weariness. Her head hurt, nearly as much as her heart.

When Emma came past her door, she peered at Carrie. "What's wrong? Are you sick?"

Slowly, Carrie sat up. "I don't know. Maybe. I think I should skip church today and try to rest."

Yonnie poked her head around Emma. "I'll make up some of my sassafras tea. Whenever you're feeling poorly, sassafras tea will soon have you fit as a fiddle."

One bright spot, Carrie realized as she pulled the covers up to her chin, trying to stay warm, she had a firm excuse to get out of tonight's singing. She didn't want to encourage John Graber's interest in her. She didn't want to encourage any man's interest in her.

Later that evening, Veronica was down in the kitchen with Emma, loudly insisting that she refused to go in the buggy to the singing, saying she would freeze to death. Just as loudly, Emma told Veronica that she would only be cold because she wasn't wearing enough clothing, that she was showing more curves than a country lane. Insulted, Veronica insisted on driving her car. Emma and John Graber left in the buggy, and Abel joined Veronica in her car.

After they left, Andy came up to Carrie's room to play checkers. Two hours later, Carrie heard Veronica's car swerve into the driveway, a car door slam, then the car zoom off. Andy heard Abel come into the kitchen, so he flew downstairs to hear a recap of the evening. He couldn't wait until he was old enough to go to the singings.

Andy had left her bedroom door open, at the top of the stairs. Carrie could heard them talking as if they were just a few feet away. Abel was explaining that Veronica McCall wanted to leave early. "She was already mad that she showed up an hour early. I forgot to tell her the Amish don't follow daylight saving time. And then she complained that it smelled like a cow barn," he said.

"Wasn't it in a barn?" Andy asked.

"Yeah, but she was talking about the people."

Andy let out a hoot of laughter, then Yonnie shooed him upstairs to get ready for bed.

"How's Carrie doing?" she heard Abel ask. "Any idea why she's not feeling well?"

"It's her spirit," Yonnie said, sounding like a doctor. "She's ailing."

"Might be the flu."

"No. No fever, no stomach sickness. It's in her heart. She's struggling over something."

Carrie felt a chill run through her. Yonnie's keen perception always made her feel peculiar.

Just after Andy left for school on Monday morning, Veronica McCall walked into the kitchen at Cider Mill Farm. Usually, when she picked up Abel, she didn't bother to come into the house. Only when she wanted something.

Veronica McCall helped herself to coffee and pulled out a chair at the kitchen table, prattling on about how cold it was and that the mud was damaging her new leather boots. Carrie kept looking out the kitchen window, hoping Abel would come in from the barn and take Veronica off of her hands.

Veronica McCall was talking so fast and furious it took her a minute to see that Carrie wasn't listening. "You haven't heard a word I've said! And . . ." She stopped in mid-sentence. "Why, you look terrible! Raccoon eyes. We need to get some makeup on you to cover up those dark circles." She reached for her purse and started to hunt through it. "Why don't you people have any mirrors in your houses?" Out of her purse, she pulled a small bag with a zipper.

"Because mirrors reflect vanity," Emma said, coming into the kitchen with her arms loaded with sheets to wash.

Yonnie eased out of her rocking chair and came over to Veronica. "Carrie is grieving over our Daniel," she said softly.

Veronica McCall looked up at Carrie. She pointed to a chair. "Sit, Carrie. I'm going to fix you right up." She unzipped the bag and pulled out a metal tube and a small plastic compact.

A switch tripped inside of Carrie. With one hand she swept Veronica's makeup onto the floor.

Just then, Abel came inside on the wings of a frigid swirl of air. He hung up his coat and turned around, aware of a sudden silence as thick as blackstrap molasses. His eyes darted between Veronica, Carrie, and the spilled makeup on the floor, quickly sizing up the situation.

In a few quick strides, he was at Carrie's side. "Veronica, wait for me outside." As Veronica hesitated, he added firmly, "Now."

"I was *trying* to help," Veronica snarled. She scowled at him, packed up her makeup, snatched her purse off the table, and went outside.

He turned to Carrie and put his hands on her shoulders. "Carrie, you need to go upstairs and rest for a while. Yonnie and Emma will take care of Andy. I'll take care of the chores." He glanced through the kitchen window at Veronica, leaning against her car, fingers punching at her black telephone, angry. "Really, you need to rest."

Carrie jerked her shoulders out of his grip. "Stop telling me what I need! Nobody knows what I need."

Emma stared at Carrie with her mouth gaping wide open, like a hooked fish.

"What do you need, Carrie?" Abel looked at Carrie with such sweet sorrow it took the fight clean out of her. Gently, he added, "How can we help you if you don't tell us?"

Suddenly exhausted, Carrie's fists unclenched and she turned to go upstairs.

Abel's words echoed in her head as she tried to sleep. She felt terrible for treating Veronica so rudely. It was so unlike her—unlike any Amish woman, except for Esther and Emma—to snap at someone like that, especially an Englisher. And then she was rude to Abel too, who was only trying to help. *What do I need? I don't have an answer. I don't know. I just feel weary and lonely and scared.* She shuddered as if a cold wind had blown through the room.

What do I need? Something for my soul that I can't seem to find.

The next day, Veronica McCall drove up as Carrie was hanging laundry to dry. For the first time, she didn't start talking a blue streak the minute she laid eyes on Carrie. She just quietly picked up some clothespins and started hanging things.

"I'm sorry I spoke sharply to you yesterday," Carrie said. "You were just being kind."

"I was, and you did," Veronica answered crisply.

"You see, we don't wear makeup."

"Maybe you people should be a little more open-minded."

Carrie decided to not pursue that particular territory with her. "Just make sure you hang similar things together on the line."

"Why?"

"It's much more orderly to hang all the dishcloths together in a row, and Yonnie's aprons, and Abel's trousers."

"Dry is dry, if you ask me."

"It's just our way."

"It's faster if you just hang them."

Carrie stopped, exasperation growing. "I'm not in a hurry. A task takes as long as it takes."

"It's supposed to rain this afternoon. If you don't speed it up, you'll end up with laundry as wet as when you started."

Clothespins in her mouth, Carrie suddenly remembered a day with her mother, hanging the laundry out on a windy winter day, just a few weeks before her mother had died bringing Andy into the world. The clothes came in so stiff, frozen solid, that they could stand up by themselves when they brought them inside. Her mother took a pair of frozen pants, topped it with a frozen shirt, then topped that with her father's straw hat, and suddenly they had a scarecrow in the kitchen. Within minutes, that frosty scarecrow melted in a heap, like a snowman on a sunny day. Carrie and her mother had laughed and laughed.

Veronica McCall shook Carrie out of her muse when she reached for a clothespin. "You people make such a big deal about the silliest things." Veronica secured a towel to the third clothesline without any more arguing. When she finished, she picked up a dropped clothespin and handed it to Carrie. "I want you to teach me all about being Amish."

Carrie's eyes went wide. "Why?"

"I *told* you. I live near the Amish. I need to know more about them."

Veronica looked very sincere as she said it, but somehow Carrie thought this sudden interest had nothing to do with being Amish and everything to do with Abel. She had an image in her mind of a picture she'd seen in a book once: a lion tracking a gazelle.

Poor Abel. He doesn't stand a chance.

10

John Graber turned his attention to courting Emma, who was thrilled to have a suitor. Carrie was even more pleased not to be the object of John Graber's affection. He had taken Emma for a buggy ride one afternoon and home from a hymn singing on another.

In the night sky was a Hunter's moon, round and creamy that, Emma said, beckoned her to take a walk. Carrie thought that perhaps John Graber was outside doing the beckoning. Esther would be pleased to think the bishop's grandson might become part of the family, after all.

Yonnie, Abel, and Carrie were in the living room; Andy had gone to bed. Abel was oiling his carpentry tools, Carrie was mending Andy's britches, and Yonnie had fallen asleep in her rocking chair, like she always did, mismatched quilt pieces spread on her lap.

When the clock struck nine, Abel and Carrie put their things away. Abel pulled out that Bible he carried with him. Carrie had stopped worrying about Abel's Bible reading and out-loud prayers. In fact, she looked forward to them. Abel's deep voice had a soothing effect. He read just like he prayed, like God was right in the room with everyone.

"This passage is from the book of Lamentations," Abel said. "Jeremiah was a prophet, a very emotional guy, who was called to speak for God during the siege and fall of Jerusalem. When he focused on the terrors around him, Jeremiah felt personally assaulted, even abandoned by God: 'He shot me in the stomach with arrows from his quiver.'"

Those words echoed in Carrie's mind. *He shot me in the stomach with arrows from his quiver.*

Suddenly, her heart started hammering. "That's it!" Her hands flew to her cheeks. "That's what I need! I need to have God stop piercing my stomach with his arrows."

Yonnie startled awake, but then drifted back to sleep.

Embarrassed by her outburst, Carrie jumped out of her chair. Why did her mouth always run ahead of her brain?

Abel jackknifed to his feet. "Carrie, wait." He whispered loudly, throwing a glance at Yonnie. "Please wait." He made her sit back down in the chair and crouched in front of her. She was trembling and didn't really know why. "Listen to me, Carrie. When Jeremiah focused on those circumstances surrounding him, he felt assaulted, even abandoned by God. But when he focused on God's past mercies, he found strength and encouragement." He opened up his Bible and hunted for the passage. "'I remember it all—oh, how well I remember—the feeling of hitting the bottom. But there's one other thing I remember, and remembering, I keep a grip on hope: God's loyal love couldn't have run out, his merciful love couldn't have dried up. They're created new every morning. How great your faithfulness! I'm sticking with God (I say it over and over). He's all I've got left.'"

Abel took Carrie's hands in his, and as he did, she felt the peace of the moment settle into her soul, like a leaf slowly making its way to the bottom of a pond. "Carrie, Jeremiah had it all wrong. God wasn't slinging arrows at Jeremiah. It was God who was helping him through his troubles."

Carrie lifted her head and searched Abel's dark eyes. She wanted desperately to believe him.

During the off-season, the Barnstormer players were required to participate in community events—speaking at schools and Scout meetings, cutting the ribbons at new store openings. "It's all part of building community spirit," the manager said. "And Sol, we want you at every event. We think you're the reason for a surge in attendance last summer. Everybody loves this Amish spin."

Sol was happy to do anything he could to solidify his worth to the coaches. He didn't end up snagging that All-Star spot, after all. In fact, it worried him a little that he didn't close the last two games of the season. He didn't even play a single inning. He knew that things changed fast on the roster. He'd already seen a number of players come and go.

The comment the manager made about fans' interest in Sol's Amish upbringing was spot-on. During the question-and-answer period at every event, Sol was hammered with questions about what it was like growing up Amish. It always amazed him that the English had been living among the Amish all of their life—sharing the roads with the buggies—but knew so little about them. And what they did know was usually wrong. One kid at a Cub Scout meeting even asked him if the Amish were a cult.

"No," Sol told him, surprised by the question. "The whole thing about being Amish—going all the way back to the 1600s—is to be an adult when you get baptized. Church leaders want each person to make their own decision before God. Being Amish has nothing to do with cults. Being Amish means you're trying to live a simple life that pleases God. Being Amish is about being part of a family, a big church family. It's having people care about you and look out for you, all of your life."

"So then," the kid asked, chewing a big wad of gum, "why'd you leave?"

Sol stumbled, not knowing how to answer, not wanting to say a word against his people. It surprised him to see how tightly his upbringing held him, even now. The Scout leader used the pause to wrap up the meeting because the janitor wanted to sweep up the gym and go home.

One afternoon, Carrie climbed up the ramp to the hayloft in the barn to throw down a bale. With one eye looking out for mice, she dragged a heavy bale from the far corner as she heard Andy run into the barn. She heard him say to himself, "Box, twine, gloves. Gotta remember gloves." Then there was some scuffling and the sound of something being dragged outside.

Looking out through the small barn window, she saw Andy load the ramp to the loft onto the back of his pony cart and head down the driveway to the street. She shouted to him, but he didn't hear her. She finished pushing the bale over the loft's edge, then sat on the edge, debating her options, wondering how long a wait she would have until Andy returned home, when Abel came into the barn.

"Um, Abel?"

Abel turned in a circle, trying to locate her voice, before looking up. "What are you doing up there?" He looked around. "What did you do with the ramp? How'd you get up there?"

"Andy took the ramp."

Abel nodded. "I did hear something about a rescue."

Carrie narrowed her eyes. "What kind of a rescue? Is he bringing home another stray?"

Abel scratched his head. "How are you planning to get down?"

"I don't have a plan. I need help."

"I see, I see." He walked around the barn, arms folded against his chest, deep in thought. He kicked the hay bale she had thrown down over on its side. "Tell you what. I'll stand on the hay and try to catch you."

"It's too far. I'll break something! *You'll* break something!"

Abel ignored her protests and jumped up on the hay bale. "I'll catch you."

"Abel, that's crazy! I'll hurt you!"

"No you won't. Just jump."

"Abel, be serious."

He shrugged. "Guess you don't mind waiting for Andy to return."

Carrie bit her lip. She knew that could mean waiting for hours, if he even remembered to bring the ramp back. "Okay, fine. But you have to promise to break my fall."

"Trust me, Carrie."

She looked down at Abel, about eight feet below her, held her breath and jumped. She tumbled onto him and he fell off the hay, breaking her fall as promised, but banging his head on a barn post.

"Abel, are you hurt?" She scrambled off of him and onto her knees. His eyes were closed and he didn't respond. He started moaning, as if in great pain. She leaned closer to see if his head was bleeding. "Say something."

He groaned again and whispered in a weak voice, "I'm so . . . so . . . glad it was you falling on me like a ton of bricks and not Emma." Then he broke into a grin.

She sat back on her knees and threw some hay at him for teasing her. He sat up, laughing, then stopped abruptly as a strange look came over his face. She could almost feel his gaze moving over her hair, like the touch of a gentle breeze. Her hair! In the fall, her bandanna had slipped off, pulling hairpins out along with it. Her hair had fallen thick and loose over her shoulders and down her back. She looked around for her bandanna and scrambled to get it. Abel pulled himself up to stand. As she tried to gather her hair to tie in a knot, she dropped her bandanna. Abel reached down and picked it up, then crouched down to gently tie it around her head. He tied a knot and let his knuckles slide down her jawline, brushing his fingertips lightly over her mouth, his eyes locked on hers the whole time. Then Abel went utterly still, but the air around them seemed to vibrate.

Carrie stood and backed away from him, first one careful step and then another. The barn door rumbled open as Andy led Strawberry by the halter into the barn. In the back of the pony cart was a large box filled with three hungry, angry owlets. Next to the nest was the mother owl, angry, feet tied together with twine. Her right wing was broken, bent at an odd angle. The hayloft ramp was nowhere in sight.

"In less than twenty-four hours, those baby owls have climbed out of their box twice to peck at my toes while I was feeding Hope and Lulu," Emma scolded Andy at breakfast. "Then their mother comes running at me, full speed, dragging that broken wing behind her, trying to protect her babies. As if I wanted them pecking at me! And the way they screech!" She shuddered. "The whole lot of them have to go!"

"They're part of our family! They need us!" Andy looked to Abel for support. Abel had set the mother owl's wing with a makeshift splint and tried to keep her tied to a post in the barn so it could heal, but she kept pecking apart the twine that held her feet.

"Soon as she's healed, Andy, they need to be set free," Abel said. "Humans can't really raise owls as well as their own parents. Fall is the time of year for great horned owls to raise a brood and teach them how to learn to hunt and fly. It wouldn't be right to keep them locked up in a barn."

"They can catch mice in the hayloft," Andy said. "There's plenty of 'em!"

"We can build an owl house and hope they'll stick around, but they're not pets." Abel took a sip of coffee and cast a sideways glance at Andy. "Any idea where my gloves went?"

Andy widened his eyes in a useless effort to look innocent.

"Speaking of missing things, Andy," Carrie asked, "when is the ramp coming back?"

Andy's face scrunched up. "See, that's a problem. I had to climb the ramp to get the nest out of the tree, but on the way down, it slipped."

"What caused that mother owl to have a broken wing, anyway?" asked Carrie.

"Beats me," Andy said, reaching over her for the raspberry jam. "Probably those English devil boys."

Carrie gave her brother a look.

"Andy Weaver!" Emma scolded. "You should be pitying those boys for their lost ways. Not blaspheming."

"Let's take Strawberry and the cart and go bring back the ramp," Abel said.

"See, that's another problem," Andy said, stuffing his mouth with bread.

"How so?" Carrie asked.

"Ramp fell into the water and sunk."

Carrie covered her hands with her face.

Abel shook his head. "Let's go down to Blue Lake Pond and you can show me where it sank." He waited until Emma left the table, then whispered to Andy, "Might have to catch a fish or two while we're there. Our last chance before the weather turns too cold. Feels like the wind is already practicing for winter." Loudly, he added, "Then we'll clean out the goslings' pen for those owlets so they'll stop thinking Emma is their mama."

It was that gloaming time of day, nearly dusk, when Andy and Abel returned home, wearing cat-in-the-cream smiles. Her brother's face, with its windchapped cheeks, shone with happiness. Andy preened like a starling, Carrie saw, feeling her heart swell.

"Took all day but we got the ramp," Andy told Carrie, sounding like a man of the world. "Happened upon Abel's gloves too." He handed Emma a string of trout and tracked mud onto her freshly cleaned linoleum floor.

Carrie went out in the barn to help Abel with Strawberry. "Andy said getting the ramp took all day." She picked up a bucket of oats to toss in Strawberry's manger.

"The ramp took five minutes," Abel said, slipping the bridle out of the pony's mouth. "The fishing took all day." He led the pony into the stall and grabbed her water bucket to fill it.

Carrie wanted to tell him how grateful she was that he spent time with Andy and helped him with his bird rescues. She knew Andy could be vexing. More than a few times, he had driven Esther to the brink of exasperation with his careless ways. She wanted to express all of her appreciation for what Abel did for them, but all that came out was, "Denki, Abel."

He grinned. "A day like this is so *good*, it makes you want to praise God for his goodness, and thank him for giving you the life to enjoy it," he said, watching Strawberry's throat ripple as she drank. He turned around and leaned against the bars, crossing his arms against his chest. "Nicht wahr? *Don't you agree?*"

She looked at him, unclear about what he meant. "About what?"

"About God's goodness." He pulled the stall shut, latched it, and swiveled to face her. "Carrie, do you believe God is good?"

"Of course," she replied without hesitating, hoping to stave off a preaching. She pulled her shawl around her shoulders. "I'll see to warming your dinner."

Abel put a hand out to stop her.

Oh no, Carrie thought. *Too late. Here comes the sermon.*

"For all of my growing up years, I only knew that hard side of God. His wrath and punishing ways, but I never really knew about the other side of God. The good side."

"If he is so good, then why does he make us suffer so?" As soon as the words spilled out of Carrie's mouth, she wanted them back, but of course it was too late. That was the risky thing about words—once said they couldn't be unsaid. She closed her eyes, ashamed. How dare she question the mysterious ways of the Lord?

"Carrie, God doesn't cause the suffering. He helps us bear it." Abel spoke with such gentleness that it almost hurt to hear it. "There was a chaplain in the jail who taught me about the parts of God I had missed. He showed me how to study the Scriptures and learn about God for myself."

Abel dropped his hand and crossed his arms again. He turned and looked straight at her, leaning one hip against the railing. They stood together in silence for a long moment. "That's why I'm here. I want Yonnie and you and Andy to know about this side of God. I don't want you to miss out."

"Miss out?"

He put his hands on her shoulders and softly said, "On the part about life being hard but God being good, and not confusing the two."

Her stomach did a flip-flop, with Abel standing so close and giving her such an intense look. Nervous, she said the first thing that popped into her head: "And Veronica McCall?" she asked in an accusing tone. "Do you want her to know about this too?"

He dropped his hands and tilted his head, genuine puzzlement on his face.

Instantly, Carrie regretted her words. What was the matter with her today, with her mouth flying ahead of her brain? What Abel did with Veronica McCall was none of her business. "She was here today, looking for you," Carrie said in a kinder tone. "She was awful mad you weren't at work today."

He didn't answer right away. Finally, he said, "God cares about Veronica, if that's what you mean."

But Carrie saw that look flash across his eyes again, the look that said he was hiding something.

Spring training had started well for Sol, but once the season began, things had spiraled south. Other teams had wised up to his fastball pitch, and he was losing his effectiveness as a closer. He hadn't struck anyone out in three straight games. The pitching coach had told him he was relying too heavily on one pitch. The problem was, he didn't have another pitch. He hadn't grown up spending years on Little League and school teams, like the other players did. He studied the pitchers to try to pick up their junk ball or curveball tricks, but when he would ask about their grip or delivery, they avoided answering him. He couldn't really blame them. They were competing for the same playing time.

Rody, the catcher, had been his only true friend, often staying late to help him practice. Tonight, Rody finally threw down his mitt and took off his catcher's mask. "I'm done for the day. I'm gonna go hit the showers. Let's go meet up with the guys and grab a beer."

Sol shook his head. "Thanks, but no." When he first joined the team, he had gone out with the guys after practice, but the clumsy way he had played at practice the next day brought a quick end to late nights and beer. Plus, the players were like magnets for girls—fancy girls. Forward girls, who sat too close in their tight little dresses. One girl, Alicia, latched on to him and called or text messaged him on his cell phone a couple of times a day. When he got the bill that month, he couldn't *believe* it! He had to pay a dime for every time she text messaged him, whether he wanted to read it or not. Amish girls would never act in such a brazen way.

He had quickly discovered that the party life of the English wasn't all that different from Amish Rumspringa parties, and he soon tired of it. Anything that interfered with baseball just wasn't worth it to him. He knew he had this one opportunity. The other guys had jobs to fall back on if they didn't make the cut. Sol had an eighth grade education and one fastball pitch. If he lost this chance, it was back to the farm, mucking out stables.

Sol spent the evening in his sparsely furnished apartment, eating cold pizza, icing his shoulder, and reading a book about training tips for pitchers. He fell asleep in a chair, with the book splayed across his chest.

In the dark of an early dawn, Carrie went downstairs and set the coffeepot to brew. Abel liked to come in for a quick cup before breakfast to warm his hands. She found she looked forward to those moments she had with him, before Andy and Emma and Yonnie came downstairs and the day had started. Abel would discuss with her what needed to be done on the farm and ask her opinion before making a decision. She'd never had a relationship like that with a man before, not with her father, or Sol, or Daniel. She would catch herself, though, whenever she found herself relying on Abel, and pull herself back from the edge.

She put some eggs in a bowl and peeked out the kitchen window. The snow was falling thick and heavy. She saw Abel climb up the kitchen steps, stamping snow from his feet, his cheeks and ears raw from the cold. She met him at the door with a mug of steaming black coffee.

"Thank you," he said, pulling off his gloves. He wrapped his hands around the mug and took a sip. "Best taste in the world."

Carrie held three eggs in her hand. "How do you want your eggs cooked?"

Just then Andy galloped past Emma heading down the stairs and went straight to last night's dessert, cutting off a hunk of cake. Seamlessly, Emma grabbed the knife out of his hand and used it to slice pieces of bread to toast in the oven. As Emma went to the table to get butter for the toast, she reached over to pinch some curls back into Carrie's cap. "Those curls that keep escaping aren't becoming, Carrie."

"Actually, they're quite becoming." Abel promptly turned a shade of plum as he realized what had blurted out of him.

Carrie felt a little flutter of pleasure from what he'd said, though she knew such thoughts were vain. A deep flush spread up her neck and over her cheeks so she spun around to face the stove, clumsily knocking the hand that held the eggs. One by one the eggs landed, cracking on the linoleum, yolks and whites and broken pieces all running together. There was a moment of stunned silence, until Andy let out a hoot of laughter.

Abel stared down at the cracked eggs, then looked at Carrie. "Scrambled would be fine."

A few days later, Carrie woke to the strong, sour stench of smoke in the air. As she prepared breakfast, she saw no sign of Abel in the barn like she usually did—no glow of a lantern light, no wisp of smoke from his woodstove chimney, no opening or shutting of the barn door, no wave when he saw her through the kitchen window.

For one brief moment, she thought he had left them without saying goodbye. The notion sent her into such a panic that she could barely stop her hands from trembling as she filled the coffeepot with water. But then she spotted Abel riding into the yard on Schtarm and let out a sigh of relief that surprised her with its depth.

Abel tied the horse's reins to the post and came directly into the kitchen. "Stoltzfuses' barn burned down early this morning," he said, looking concerned. "I smelled the smoke so I rode over to see if I could help, but the barn was nearly gone."

"Oh no! They're in Indiana, aren't they?" Emma asked. "Ada was over here the other day, talking about it, so excited to see her new grandbaby. They go every year about now, as soon as they close up their roadside stand for the year."

"The deacon is trying to reach them," Abel said. "I'm going to go back over there and help clear out the debris."

"I'm coming too!" Andy said, jumping up from the table to head to the door.

Carrie reached out and grabbed his arm. "Slow down. You're going to school." She smiled. "Perhaps Abel wouldn't mind seeing that you get there."

Crestfallen, Andy sat back down at the table to finish his oatmeal, sighing deeply.

"Any idea how the fire started?" Carrie asked.

He shrugged. "The police were there, looking for signs of arson."

"What?" Emma asked, alarmed. "Why would they think such a thing?"

Before Abel could answer, a car pulled into the driveway. Emma peered outside. "There's two English women, an old one and a young one."

"They're here for me," Carrie told Emma. "I'm going into town today to help the girl who . . . caused the accident." She took her black bonnet off of the wall peg. "She's having an . . ." She couldn't remember the word.

"An arraignment?" Abel said.

Carrie nodded, wrapping her cape around her. Going into a crowded courtroom scared her to death; she was already anticipating the bold stares of curious English. She felt like a fish out of water, but she had made a promise to Grace to come. "I hope to be back long before Andy returns from school," she told Emma.

"Grace told me what you did for her, Carrie," Abel said, as he reached to open the kitchen door for her. "About forgiving her. She said you changed her life."

Carrie tied the strings of her bonnet and kept her head down.

"You did a fine thing." He spoke quietly, so Emma wouldn't overhear.

Carrie kept her eyes downcast. "It was the right thing."

"Forgiveness is always the right thing," Abel said softly.

By ten in the morning, Carrie and Mrs. Gingerich, Grace's foster mother, were seated closely behind the defense table at the Stoney Ridge District Court. Arraignments were a rubber-stamp process, the lawyer explained to the women. The prosecutor riffled through a big box of files as defendant after defendant was brought in. Carrie's eyes went wide as one woman was arraigned for stealing a blender from Wal-Mart. A boy was brought in for possession of drugs. Carrie shivered. He wasn't much older than Andy. Seeing the wickedness of the world made her long to return to the safety and security of her apple orchards. It made her grateful for her people and their gentle ways.

Carrie had been relieved when she saw Grace's appearance earlier in the car. Someone—probably Mrs. Gingerich—had made her look more like a normal teenager. Her hair color had changed from platinum blond to a color that actually existed in nature. She wore a white blouse and a dark skirt. Gone were the combat boots too. In their place were dark, plain shoes and nylon stockings. Grace felt self-conscious in her clothing, Carrie noticed. She kept scratching her legs as if they itched. She could only see the profile of Grace's face, but she felt a tenderness toward her. She could see so much pain in Grace's eyes. In a way, she reminded her of Daniel. Carrying a burden.

Just as the bailiff was calling out Grace's docket number, Abel slipped into the seat next to Carrie, startling her.

"Strength in numbers," he whispered.

The courtroom doors opened again, disrupting the proceeding. Carrie turned and saw Veronica McCall, followed by Emma. Behind Emma trailed Mattie, one arm around Yonnie for support.

When the judge glanced up, his jaw dropped at the sight: a row of Amish women settling into a bench, black bonnets lined up like a row of crows on a telephone wire. Bookended on the bench were an Amish man and an English woman with carrot red hair.

After the judge shook off his surprise, he acknowledged the show of support for Grace. "But the defendant admits she was speeding on a foggy night. A careless thing to do which resulted in the needless death of a young man. Because of your request for leniency, Mrs. Miller, I'll disregard the prison time." He gave a nod toward Carrie. "It was a gracious thing for you to do, considering this accident caused your husband's death. However, the defendant must serve 300 hours of community service. And, her driver's license is revoked for three years." He banged the gavel. "Next."

Grace jumped up from the table and leaned over the railing to hug Carrie. "Thank you, Carrie. It could've been a lot worse if it weren't for you."

"So you're not disappointed?" Carrie asked, over Grace's shoulder.

Grace pulled back and crossed her arms. "No. I mean, my license getting revoked bites, but the service hours were lighter than I expected." Shyly, she added, "Thanks to you." She looked at the row of Amish people. "And to all of you."

"Don't mention it," Veronica McCall said, claiming credit. She tapped her watch. "But now, you need to get to work. You're on the clock. You too, Abel." She took both of them by the elbow and steered them to the door.

Carrie saw Abel try to turn back to her, but Veronica slipped her hand into Abel's and pulled him along, much like someone would lead a cow to a stall.

11

The church leaders planned to build the new barn for the Stoltzfuses while the land was resting and farmers had more time, a commodity usually in short supply. When the day came, sunny and mild for a winter day, Andy was the last one in the buggy after breakfast and chores, stepping carefully around Abel's tools, paper bags full of nails, and baskets of food. They waved to Yonnie, who preferred to stay home and quilt in the warm kitchen.

The four walls of the barn lay flat on the ground, getting assembled, by the time Old-Timer trotted into the Stoltzfuses' driveway. Andy hopped out of the buggy before it came to a stop and ran to join his friends, practicing their hammering on blocks of wood. Abel reached for his tools, gave Carrie a nod, jumped down, and hurried to the site where the barn gables were being assembled. Emma and Carrie watched as he looked for an empty spot among the men. Then Emma grabbed a basket and hurried to join the ladies in the kitchen. Carrie picked up the reins to lead Old-Timer where rows and rows of buggies and wagons were parked in the pastures.

"Carrie!"

She turned in the direction of Abraham's voice. Abraham gave her a warm grin and reached up to shake her hand. He whistled for a boy to come and take the buggy. "Put the horse in the paddock with the others," he told the boy. He helped Carrie down and picked up the two remaining baskets of food. "Our Andy gets bigger each time I see him."

"And you probably see him squirming in church."

The deacon laughed. "And why not? The good Lord never expected a growing boy to be able to sit still for hours."

The good Lord might not, but Esther certainly did. At last Sunday's gathering, she sent Carrie dark looks from across the bench whenever Andy got restless, which was often.

"Just look at those colts over there." Abraham tipped his head toward the field. A mother horse was grazing, heavy head hung low, while a foal danced around her, jumping and kicking his heels in sheer joy. "God understands the young." He put the baskets on the table. "Even the young at heart."

Abraham headed back to the building site, pulling out his hammer and nails from his canvas waist pouch. For a moment, before going inside to join the women, Carrie gazed at the bare bones of a barn, flat on the ground, waiting for life to be breathed into it.

A barn raising was the most beautiful sight in the world to her. The sounds, a symphony of pounding by dozens of hammers, took her breath away. It always had, even when she was a child.

"Hello, Carrie," said a voice behind her.

Carrie stiffened, instantly recognizing Solomon Riehl's voice. She kept her gaze fixed on the barn. "Why are you here?"

Sol took a step to stand next to her. "I heard about the Stoltzfuses' barn burning down and wanted to do my part." He kicked a stone on the ground. "They've always been good to me."

"Everyone has been good to you," Carrie said, her glance sliding at him. Maybe too good, she thought. She turned to go to the kitchen, but he blocked her path.

"I'm sorry, Carrie. About Daniel."

"What's done is done," she said, but it came out scratchy and uncertain. She felt her eyes prickle with tears. She didn't want to cry.

Softly, he said, "Please. Let's talk."

"Not here, not now," she whispered, more to herself than to Sol. She straightened and took a step back, putting even more distance between them.

His eyes searched hers. "Then when? When can we talk?"

Carrie's heart softened, just a little, as she saw the earnest ache in his eyes.

Suddenly, a loud, persistent ringing noise came out of his pocket. A dozen white caps turned instantly toward Sol's direction. Panicking, he pulled out his cell phone. Carrie used the interruption to step away from him. She picked up the baskets on the table and hurried to the kitchen, feeling the onset of tears burn the back of her throat. *Just stay busy,* she told herself, *so you won't dwell on the way things turned out.*

She started emptying out the baskets, putting the desserts she had made last night on the counter with the others, as if nothing had happened. In her heart, though, she felt sore and lonely.

Mattie's heart started pounding when she caught a glimpse of Solomon Riehl out of the corner of her eye. She was setting the table for lunch, determined not to look at him. She would not, would not, would not look at him.

She looked at him.

She scolded herself, feeling like she was back in sixth grade, Sol in eighth, when she would steal glances at him all day long.

She noticed that others were avoiding Sol. He was in that strange place in their community of straddling two worlds, Amish and English. He wasn't being shunned since he hadn't been baptized, but he wasn't one of them anymore, either. She wondered how Sol felt to be among his people but standing on the fringe. How terrible, she thought, to be living on the wary edge. To never feel like you belonged anywhere, to anybody.

When Carrie's buggy arrived, Mattie noticed how Sol put down his hammer, poising himself for a moment to find her alone. She tried to keep her eyes off of them when Sol approached Carrie, but she could tell Carrie seemed uncomfortable. Then his cell phone went off and Carrie turned abruptly to leave. Mattie's eyes stayed on Sol. A look of stark pain crossed his face. He turned his head and caught her watching him. Their eyes met and held. Her heart started hammering so loudly she was sure he heard it, twenty feet away, but he dropped his head and went to the building site.

As Sol swung himself up on a beam, at ease in a precarious spot, Mattie couldn't help but admire his grace. Barn raising was an activity he'd been a part of since he was a toddler. She whispered a prayer for him, asking the

Lord to show him all that he was missing and to bring him back where he belonged.

As Carrie set clean dishes on the long picnic tables, she saw one man cup his hands around his mouth and yell, "Fix un faerdich!" *All ready!* Almost in unison, the hammering ceased. The women hurried out of the kitchen, wiping their hands on their aprons. Someone hollered out a count, as a few men picked up one frame of the barn wall and hoisted it upright. A few others swarmed to the base of the wall, hammering it securely into the cement foundation of the barn. The opposite wall went up, then the two ends, puzzle pieces locking into place. The youngest men, Sol and Abel included, climbed the wooden rigging as easily as if it were a ladder, hoisting the roof gables up with ropes. Within minutes, the skeleton of the barn, raw and yellow, stood silhouetted against the blue winter sky.

Lunch was served before noon. The men laid down their hammers and nails, untied their waist pouches, and dropped their bundles of tools, right where they'd be working. Emma and Carrie had filled up an old washtub, set outside the kitchen, with warm water, soap, and towels. Even with a brisk wind, the men were red-faced and sweating as they hurried to wash up and find an empty spot at the table. With the jerk of his head, Bishop Graber gave the signal for silent prayer. Automatically, the men dropped chins to chest, quietly communing with the Lord God. Then the bishop coughed, the signal to end the prayer, and the men grabbed their forks and shoveled the food in their mouths.

Abel arrived late to the table, lagging behind after examining something at the work site. Scratching his head, he went straight up to Abraham, seated at the end of the table, eating quickly so the next group, standing on the side, could sit and eat.

"In Ohio, we're bolting the walls to the foundation."

Abraham looked up at him curiously.

"It makes the barn sturdier to bolt instead of nail. Against storms and such," Abel said.

Seated a few seats from the deacon, Sol said loudly, "And how many barns have you built in the last few years?"

Abel jerked his head in Sol's direction, a confused look on his face.

Abraham intervened. "I have heard about this new bolting from my cousin in Ohio. It helps to protect against tornadoes, especially."

"But not fires," Sol said, looking straight at Abel. "What's to stop a fire?" Abel locked eyes with Sol.

Abraham slid down on the bench to make room for Abel. "Abel, please sit and eat. I want to hear about your bolts."

Watching the exchange, Carrie hurried to set a place for Abel. As Carrie swiveled around to return to the kitchen to fill up a platter of pork chops, she saw Emma leaning over John Graber to pour lemonade into his glass. John was eagerly working his way through a pork chop and didn't seem to notice her. She wondered if Abel had seen Emma fussing over John, but he was deep in conversation with Abraham about bolts. She could feel Sol's eyes watching her, aware he noticed how she had tried to catch Abel's eye, but she kept her gaze from meeting his.

As soon as the men and boys were finished, they returned to pick up their hammers. The volley of pounding began again as the women sat down to eat. Esther sat across from Emma and Carrie.

"So, where is Yonnie today?" Esther asked.

"She's home, working on a quilt," Emma replied.

Esther looked at Emma. "She should be coming to the quilting frolics."

"She says she likes to quilt alone. Says it's like praying to her," Emma said, taking a bite of a pork chop. She wiped her mouth with her napkin and leaned forward on the bench, eyes shining. "She's been teaching me all that she knows, all about combinations of colors. Her stitches are as tiny as baby teeth. And she doesn't even use patterns, she just makes them up out of her head—"

"Lancaster Amish do not quilt like Ohio Amish," Esther said. "And you would do well to remember the difference, Emma."

Esther's rebuke had the effect of dousing a candle. Emma's smile faded; her neck drooped low as a cygnet's. The brightness left her and her mouth tightened. Carrie had to look away.

What Esther was saying was right, Carrie had to admit. Lancaster was the first Amish settlement, and most of the church leaders clung tightly to traditions. As settlements spread throughout the Midwest, a willingness to change and adapt spread with them. Esther's quilts were just like the Lancaster Amish, Carrie realized. Each one looked like the one before. Yonnie's quilts, well, no two were alike. She brought combinations of colors and patterns together in ways no one could imagine.

Still, Carrie's heart was touched with pity for Emma. Each night when she and Andy and Abel gathered after dinner—to read *The Budget*, or play Scrabble or Checkers—Yonnie and Emma would bend over the frame of a quilt. It was as if Yonnie was passing on all of her knowledge to Emma. Emma was a quick study too. The quilt they were making for Abel reminded Carrie of a kaleidoscope Andy had found once and brought home.

Andy ran up to Carrie and pulled on her elbow, whispering loudly enough to warrant a raised eyebrow from Esther. "Here comes that fancy red-haired lady." He pointed to the driveway. A few of the teenaged boys who hadn't been baptized dropped their hammers and hurried over to examine the car.

Carrie left her lunch and walked to meet Veronica. "Come to see the barn raising?"

"Abel invited me."

Carrie raised her eyebrows. That didn't sound quite right to her.

"Oh fine." Veronica rolled her eyes. "I'm sure he would have if I had asked. Where is he?"

Carrie pointed to Abel's figure, straddling a gable on the barn roof.

"Are you sure that's him? They all look alike."

"That's him."

They walked a little closer to the barn, smelling the sweet smell of fragrant pine.

"Isn't it a sight to behold?" Carrie asked her. "To build a whole barn in a single day." She pointed to the sides of the roof. "The framing is completed before the noon meal. And in the afternoon, the roofing is installed. That's what Abel is working on now."

Veronica squinted in the bright sunlight. "Nothing you people do is fast. Why in the world would you be building a barn in a day?"

"The point isn't its haste, Veronica McCall. Wonderful things can happen when people work together. A barn raising is an amazing project of brotherly love."

"Maybe I should hire them all to finish up Honor Mansion." Veronica walked closer to the barn. "Abel! Abel! Yoo-hoo!" She waved up at Abel.

The staccato of hammers drowned out her shout, so she went back to her car.

As if in a dream where her feet were caught in quicksand, Carrie slowly realized what was about to unfold. She tried to stop Veronica, but it happened too quickly. Veronica leaned over the door of her car and honked the horn, then yelled out Abel's name again and honked again. Startled, Abel turned, lost his balance, and slipped off the roof.

Abel's fall was first broken by a beam, then by boards laid for the loft. Before others knew what had happened, Carrie ran into the barn and scrambled up a ladder, stepping carefully on the unnailed flooring. Abel lay crumbled on his side, moaning, one arm bent at a grotesque angle.

"We need to get him to the hospital," Abraham said, peering at Abel from the top rung of the ladder. He turned to the crowd below and spotted Veronica. "Can you call for an ambulance?"

"I'll drive him!" Veronica McCall yelled, standing among the Amish men and women. "It'll be faster than an ambulance!"

Abel put his good hand on Carrie's forearm. "Komm mit, bitte?" *Please, come?* Carrie nodded.

The men made a gurney to hoist Abel down to the ground and carried him to Veronica's car. Carrie found Emma to tell her she was leaving, to make sure Andy got home. As she hurried to Veronica's car, Sol stopped her. "I'll come too, Carrie. I could help."

The words spilled out before she could stop them. "Like you helped Daniel?" She shook his hand off of her arm and climbed into the passenger seat, avoiding the hurt in Sol's eyes.

Abel's body went stiff as he stifled a moan of pain, intensified by Veronica's wild driving. It was as if she took aim to hit each pothole and bump in the road.

Sol watched Carrie leave with that Abel Miller, moaning like he was dying, the big baby. He wondered who the good-looking English woman with the sports car was. It bothered him to see that Carrie had a life filled with people he didn't know. Discouraged, he went back to work on the roof with the other men and hammered shingles until the sun started sinking in the sky. When the men were satisfied the barn was watertight, they packed up their tools. Sol handed his tools and carpenter belt to his father. He wanted to leave quickly, before his mother cornered him, asking him to come home again. It wrenched his gut, the way she asked. Almost begging.

He walked down the street to catch a bus at the crossroads. He wished he had just driven his car. He worried it would stir up trouble, but no one would have even noticed, he decided. Crossing his arms against the wind, his mind drifted to Carrie. He had been looking forward to seeing her all week, as soon as his mother had written to him about the barn raising. But it didn't go at all like he had hoped. He thought Carrie might be eager to see him, but she wasn't. Her lips held in a thin tight line as she spoke to him, all three or four words. And then the cell phone went off! He frowned, rolling his eyes. He could still feel the measuring glances of the women as he spoke on the phone. And it was that Alicia girl!

Sol sighed, discouraged. He thought he and Carrie might be able to get back to where they were before. When he saw her today, he felt a sharp pain as he realized again how beautiful she was, how big those blue eyes were. He felt such a longing for her. But his relationship with Carrie had veered off course like a runaway horse and he didn't know how to get it back on track.

Sol thought back to a conversation he had, a year or so ago, with Carrie's father. He was shining a flashlight on Carrie's bedroom window one night when Jacob Weaver surprised him.

Jacob was standing on the porch, watching him. "What's on your mind, Solomon?"

Hardly anyone called him that, only Jacob Weaver. Sol always thought it was Jacob's way of reminding him what his name represented. Sol decided to be frank with him. He turned off the flashlight and approached Jacob. "You know about Carrie and me."

Jacob's chin dropped, his bushy whiskers rested against his chest, as if he was thinking. He wasn't a big man, but he had a way of making Sol feel small. He lifted his head, as if he had decided something. "I'm sorry, son. You ought not to be expecting my blessing."

Sol looked at Jacob, shocked. "And why not? You've known me since I was a boy. What makes you think I'm not good enough for your Carrie?"

Jacob leaned on his hands against the porch railings, slowly gathering his thoughts. Finally, he said, "I've known you plenty long. That's why I'm saying no."

"What?!"

"As long as I've known you, at church and barn raisings and other gatherings, I've noticed that you always eat first, with the older men."

Sol shrugged. "I worked hard. I was hungry."

"Yes, yes, I'm sure you were. So were the other boys. But they waited, to show respect to the elders. Seems like a small thing, I know, but it's more than that. It's the reason behind it. You always think first about yourself." Jacob shook his head. "I won't let my daughter marry a man who takes care of himself first."

Squarely meeting Jacob's gaze, Sol said, "I would take good care of her."

Jacob let his gaze slide away. "I'm sorry, Solomon." After a moment he lifted his head. "But I don't believe you would." He turned to leave.

"Then who?" Sol asked him. "Who, Jacob? Who could be good enough for your Carrie?"

Jacob stopped, stood still for a moment, then walked into the house. This time, Sol let him go. By the way he squared his shoulders, Sol could tell that Jacob had someone else in mind for Carrie. He could also see that Jacob's mind was made up.

That was the first time Sol started to think about leaving, with Carrie.

All of a sudden, he realized that at the barn raising today, he had eaten with the first shift of older men. He hadn't even thought about it, he just grabbed an empty spot. He clapped his hand against his forehead, as if he had just proven Jacob's point. But on its heels came a renewed vigor to win Carrie back.

To prove Jacob wrong.

A buggy clattered past him, then pulled over to the side of the road to stop. A capped head popped out of the buggy window. "Need some help, Sol?" Mattie shouted.

Oh, you don't know the half of it! he thought, as he broke into a jog to catch a ride with her.

At the hospital, Carrie helped Abel walk into the emergency room while Veronica parked her little red convertible. A nurse took one look at how he clutched his arm, face contorted in pain, and pointed toward a bed behind a curtain. Abel stretched out carefully on the bed, took hold of Carrie's hand, and wouldn't let go. He held it so tightly that her hand turned a mottled white.

"Abel, they need to examine you," Carrie told him. "You need to let go of me. I'll be in the waiting room the entire time." But he wouldn't let go.

"Just stay," the nurse said, yanking the curtain around the bed. "Men like their women right by their side."

Carrie shook her head. "I'm not—"

The nurse interrupted Carrie with questions about the accident. Then she cut off Abel's shirt. Carrie felt her cheeks grow warm at the sight of his naked chest, but what made her even more anxious to leave was Abel's arm, bent askew. Still, he wouldn't release her hand.

Veronica's voice, raised in argument with a nurse, floated in from the hallway. "What do you mean, only family can be with him? I'm his girlfriend!"

Carrie leaned over to whisper to Abel, "I think Veronica McCall would like to be with you." She hoped this would convince him to let go of her hand.

"Nee," he whispered back, wincing as pain shot through him. *No.*

"Since when have you been speaking the dialect?" Carrie asked, smoothing his hair back out of his eyes with her free hand to comfort him, the way she did with Andy when he was sick or upset.

He tried to smile but gave up.

"Okay, pal," the nurse said, wrapping a blood pressure cuff around Abel's good arm. "Let go of her hand. I need to get your blood pressure."

Relieved, Carrie pried her fingers out of his, freeing her hand from his grasp.

After recording Abel's blood pressure, the nurse took his pulse. Frowning, she asked, "Why is your pulse going so fast?" She peered at him, then at Carrie, who was stroking his hair. "Hey, buddy, stop looking at her and look at me for a second."

Abel turned his head toward the nurse, puzzled, as she kept two fingers on his pulse.

"That's what I thought. Now it's going down." She rolled her eyes. "We're going to wheel you to X-ray, then the doctor will tell you what a mess you've made of your arm." She snorted. "As if we all didn't know that." She yanked back the curtain and jerked his gurney, pushing him down the hall to X-ray.

Abel looked back at Carrie with pleading eyes. "Bleib do!" *Stay here!*

"Druwwelt nix, Abel," she said reassuringly. *Don't worry.* "Someone will be here."

Carrie heard the nurse mutter to Abel, "Sheesh, pal. You got it bad."

Carrie walked into the waiting room rubbing her hands, trying to get feeling back into the one Abel had squeezed for the last hour.

"Sis Schaade! Sei Dod waar ganz unverhofft!" someone called out, thinking Carrie was wringing her hands in grief. *What a pity! His death was so unexpected!*

Startled, Carrie glanced up to see a half-dozen Amish men and women from the barn raising, patiently waiting for news about Abel, Abraham and the bishop among them.

"Oh no! He's not dead," she reassured them, still wiggling her fingers. "He's got a broken arm, but he's not dead."

"Atlee, perhaps you should take Carrie home. You should all go home," Abraham said, looking around the room. "I will stay."

"Would you? He wants someone to stay, but I . . ." *I want to go home*, Carrie thought. It had been a long day.

"I'll stay with him," Veronica McCall said, rounding a corner, a cup of coffee from the vending machine in her hand. She gave Carrie a measured look.

"Thank you," Carrie said gratefully, meaning it.

Abraham called a Mennonite taxi driver who owned a van to take them all home. It was dark now, and Carrie briefly wondered about the new barn at the Stolztfuses', but then her thoughts bounced to Sol. When the van pulled up to Cider Mill Farm, she thanked everyone for their help.

Even the bishop, not known for his sensitivity, could tell Carrie was troubled. "That boy will be fine, Carrie. He's a young fellow. They heal right quick."

Carrie nodded.

"That English gal. She's the one who ought to be feeling upset. She brought this on," Abraham said.

Carrie shrugged. At this moment, she didn't care about Veronica McCall. She didn't even much care about Abel's broken arm.

A light snow was falling when Veronica McCall returned to Cider Mill Farm. Abel was next to her in the passenger seat, his arm wrapped in a stiff, freshly plastered cast, hanging in a blue sling. Emma and Carrie went outside to help him, but he looked like he wasn't feeling any pain at all. His eyes were dilated and unfocused.

Carrie put one arm around Abel's waist and Emma took the other side. "Emma, he shouldn't be out in the cold workshop. I think he should sleep in your room for now. You can stay in my room."

Abel started singing at the top of his lungs, something silly about leaving his heart at a Greyhound bus station.

"He's totally doped up," Veronica McCall said. "Here are the meds that the doctor prescribed." She handed Carrie a white paper bag. "He was only supposed to have one of those pink pills, but I gave him two so he could sleep." She looked at her wristwatch. "Gotta run. I have a video conference call in the morning. Tell Abel toodles!"

"Toodles?" Emma asked, astounded. "You want us to tell him 'toodles'? How about 'I'm sorry for honking the horn and causing you to fall off the roof of the barn'?"

Veronica's eyes narrowed like a cat. "It was an accident. Accidents happen."

Emma helped Carrie get Abel into bed for the night. He kept singing, one song after another, until Emma scolded him. "I'm just about ready to stick a sock in your mouth, Abel Miller, if you don't hush up! You'll wake up Yonnie and Andy!"

At that fierce reprimand, tears started trickling down Abel's cheeks. Emma threw up her hands and left the room.

Carrie slipped off his shoes and pulled the blanket over him, being careful not to put weight on his cast. "Good thing you don't touch the devil's brew, Abel Miller. You're a mess."

"Why did you leave me, Carrie?" he asked in a gruff whisper.

"Aw, Abel, you nearly broke off my hand. I stayed as long as I could. You had a whole crowd of people there. Filled up the waiting room." She straightened. "Besides, you had her. You didn't need me."

"But I wanted *you*," he said, before closing his eyes.

Carrie touched him then, on the cheek with the tips of her fingers. "Hush this crazy talk now and go to sleep." She watched as his breathing settled into an even rhythm of sleep. She took the pill container out of her apron pocket and set it on his nightstand. Two pain pills, Veronica McCall said she had given him, when there was a warning right on the label not to exceed one pill every six hours. What had she been thinking?! The logic of that woman defied her.

She leaned over to turn off the gas lamp by his bedside, pitching the room into total darkness.

When Carrie went into her bedroom, Emma was combing out her long hair and braiding it. "Is he asleep?" Emma asked.

"I think so," Carrie answered. She hung her apron on the peg and reached for her nightgown.

Emma put down her brush and leaned her chin on her elbows. "Mother said that John Graber is now Alva's John."

"Alva Brenner?"

Emma nodded sadly.

Carrie went over to sit on the bed near her, her nightgown in her lap. "Oh, Emma. What does your mother know about such things?"

Head bowed low, Emma added, "He doesn't come around anymore."

Now that Carrie thought about it, Emma was right. John Graber hadn't been at Cider Mill Farm for the last few weeks. How could she have missed noticing that? Just the other day, Abel asked her if something was bothering Emma. When she asked why he thought so, he said, "She seems more worried than usual."

Was she getting so absorbed in her own problems that she was blind to Emma's? she wondered, pulling pins out from her hair bun, dropping them in her lap. "Are you awful disappointed?"

Emma gave a quick nod. "Yonnie promised me . . ." She clamped her lips shut.

"Promised you what?"

"Yonnie made up a special tea and gave it to John so that he would love me forever." She looked at Carrie out of the corner of her eyes. "Don't look at me like that, Carrie." Emma's eyes swam. "I only want . . ."

Carrie handed Emma a handkerchief to wipe her tears. "Want what?"

Emma blew her nose loudly. "I want someone to look at me the way, well, the way Abel looks at you."

"What?" Carrie asked, stunned. "Stop talking nonsense."

Emma finished braiding her hair. "It's not nonsense, Carrie. He's sweet on you."

"Emma, Abel has an interest in Veronica McCall."

She shook her head. "I asked him, flat out. I said to him, 'What do you think you're doing, courting that fancy English gal?' I told him it was wrong, wrong, wrong—being unequally yoked and all—and that gal has trouble written all over her. He said to me, 'Emma, I'm not courting her!' He said he was only working for her because she needed help and he needed work and that he was trying to teach her the Bible." She pointed her finger at Carrie in warning. "But she wants him like a mudhen on a tin roof wants rain."

"Well, she may be doing the wanting, but he's not doing any running, as far as I can tell." Emma didn't know about all the times Carrie caught Veronica and Abel in the convertible car, windows steamed up. Late one night when Carrie couldn't sleep, she even saw Veronica leave from Abel's workshop. Carrie stood and started to unpin her dress, then stopped. "You don't need Yonnie's silly remedies to make a man love you, Emma."

"Then what do I do?" Emma asked, a forlorn look on her face. "I don't want to be a Maedel. I'm getting old. My wrinkles are multiplying like cow flies. I want a husband and a family of my own."

Carrie went over to her and finished braiding the long rope of her hair. "Then tell the Lord God about it, not Yonnie."

Emma gave her a weak smile. "Now you're starting to sound like our Abel when he's in a preaching mood."

Actually, Carrie thought that comment sounded more like Mattie. Abel quoted Scripture and spouted theology, Mattie talked about trusting God for everything. Both of them, though, loved God with their whole hearts. She yawned, trying to get comfortable, scrunching far against the edge because Emma had taken up the entire bed.

It took a long while to fall asleep. She wished she could have started the day all over again. It had not been a good day, this day, and she felt miserable. When was she ever going to be able to be around Sol and not leave feeling all churned up inside?

As Emma's breathing settled into loud snores, Carrie covered her ears with a pillow.

Whatever pills Veronica McCall gave to Abel knocked him out. Finally, by lunchtime, Carrie worried that he might have passed in the night. She tiptoed to his bedside and laid her hand on his forehead. He stirred at her touch, then opened his eyes and blinked a few times.

"Hi," she said. "How are you feeling?"

"Don't know." He closed his eyes again. "Just woke up."

"Think you could eat something?"

He inhaled deeply. "That coffee smells awfully good."

"I'll get you some."

"Carrie, wait . . ."

She put a hand on the doorjamb and turned back to him. "I'd better get you that coffee. No doubt your throat is sore from singing last night like a lovesick coyote." When she saw the look of alarm cross his face, she added, "Silly English songs. Out of key too. They were terrible."

Downstairs, Yonnie and Emma were washing dishes.

"How's our Abel doing?" Yonnie asked.

"He's going to survive, I think," Carrie said. "He'd like some coffee if there's any left."

"That's a good sign," Emma said. "Think he's hungry? There's leftover hotcake batter."

For reasons Carrie couldn't explain, she suddenly felt shy around Abel. She handed the mug of steaming coffee to Emma. "Why don't you take this to him and ask him yourself?"

As soon as her chores were done, Carrie threw on her shawl and headed out to the orchards, walking up and down the rows of trees through the slushy snow and mud. Still unsettled from seeing Sol, she knew she needed to fix her mind on something else. She examined the spindly arms of the apple trees and decided the time for pruning had come. Winter was halfway over. Ready or not, spring was right around the corner.

She went into the barn and started collecting the saw blades she would need to start pruning the trees. She tried to remember which saws Daniel and Eli had used. She was grateful they had pruned the trees so well a year ago so she would only need to follow the footprint they'd left behind.

She had never sharpened a blade before, but she had watched her father do plenty of them. She lit a gas lamp and sat at the grindstone, starting to tread the pedals to make the wheel spin.

Suddenly, the barn door slid open. "Just what do you think you're doing?" Abel asked Carrie as he approached the grindstone.

She stopped pedaling. "You should be in bed."

"I'm not sick. I just hurt my arm."

"I'll say." She turned her attention back to the blade.

"Carrie, what do you think you're doing?"

"I'm sharpening the blades so that I can prune the apple trees."

His jaw dropped. "By yourself?"

"If I don't, it won't get done."

"I'll do it for you. Just give me a little time to get back on my feet."

"Not with that broken arm, Abel. Can't wait that long."

Abel's frown deepened to genuine displeasure. "Carrie, a few more days won't make any difference."

She stopped again and looked straight at him. "Abel, these orchards are my responsibility. I need to do this. I need to take care of my farm."

He got that funny look on his face again, like there was something he was hiding. "I can cut the lower branches."

She thought he was crazy to even offer, with an arm in a big cast. "Suit yourself. But I'm starting tomorrow morning."

"Well, you're sharpening those blades on the wrong side, so you're going to have an awful hard time with it if you don't let me help you, now."

She jumped off the seat and swept her hand in a be-my-guest gesture.

At breakfast the next morning, Carrie explained to Emma that she and Abel were going to be starting the pruning. Emma's lips pursed tightly together, then she listed off all of the reasons why this was a foolish idea. Abel sat in his chair, eating his scrambled eggs, a smug look on his face.

Emma pointed a finger at Abel. "And what makes you think he'll be any good to you? He's a one-winged bird."

Abel's dark eyebrows lifted, but he didn't say a word.

Carrie sighed. "Emma, I need your help with chores while I prune those trees." She stood up and took her dishes to the sink.

"If Mother knew—"

Carrie whirled around. "She doesn't know and she doesn't need to know. This is my home, Emma, not Esther's."

Emma clamped her lips shut.

Carrie threw on a cape. After hitching the wagon to Old-Timer, she hurried into the barn and lugged the hayloft ramp out to the wagon. Abel lifted the back end of the ramp, helping her scoot it onto the wagon bed. He remembered the tool box and shoved it next to the ramp. She climbed up as he hoisted himself into the seat. She stopped the horse at the farthest grove of trees and didn't even bother to tie his reins to a tree. Old-Timer was too old to think about running off.

From the wagon bench, Abel was studying the endless rows of trees. "These trees are shaped well. Room for lots of light to get in. We just have to trim back the new growth."

She climbed off of the wagon and yanked the ramp down, then started dragging it to the nearest tree.

Abel climbed down carefully, moving as slow and cautious as an old man. "Listen, Carrie . . ."

She knew by his tone of voice that he was about to tell her how she didn't know what she was getting herself into. She crossed her arms and flung her head back to stare at him. "What, Abel?"

He looked at Carrie for a long moment, then gave a little nudge to the brim of his hat. "I found some clippers too. You use the clippers and I'll use the saws."

Carrie had always loved working outdoors, much more than she did the cleaning and cooking and keeping up of the house. Emma preferred doing woman's work. The menial work, Carrie thought, and then, out of habit, whispered an apology to the Lord for her prideful heart. All work was sacred in God's eyes.

But after an hour Carrie had barely pruned the upper branches of one tree. A blister had formed on the palm of her hand and her toes were numb with cold. It was harder work than she could have ever imagined. Already, the muscles in her shoulders and arms ached as she leaned on the ramp to clip the branch. She paused and looked down the long, even row of trees. Last night she had done the math: about one hundred trees per acre, and there were twenty acres. She sighed. This job was unending.

It was slow going for Abel too. He had been trying to saw the lower branches, but with his arm in a sling he was weak and off balance. Though the morning was cold, she saw beads of sweat on his brow. He even looked pale. She was sure his broken arm was aching, but he was too stubborn to admit it.

"Let's take a rest," she said, after he had stopped to wipe his face with a handkerchief.

She climbed down from the ramp and sat on a blanket against the tree trunk, drawing her knees up to stay warm. She rested her forehead on her knees. "I can't do it," she said aloud. "I can't do it alone."

Abel leaned against the wagon. "Well, thank you very much."

She lifted her head at him. "I didn't mean it like that." She sighed and bent her head down again.

"It's hard work to manage orchards, Carrie," he said.

She snapped her head up. "So you want me to just give up?"

"No, that's not what I . . ."

When she finally risked a glance at Abel, he was staring at her with that guilty look on his face. She saw his eyes lift quickly to the trees down the row, as if he didn't want to be caught looking at her.

She stood up and stretched. "Could I ask you something?"

"Ask away," he said, grabbing a rag from the back of the wagon.

"What happened to your folks? How is it you ended up with Eli?"

He looked at her, startled, as if that was the last thing he expected her to ask. Then he took the rag and started to wipe down the tree saw. "Eli was my mother's older brother. My mother left the church to run off with my father, who was English. He never did marry her, so that's why I have my mother's last name." He put the saw down and picked up Carrie's clippers. "She died in a car accident when I was five."

"What about your father?"

He shrugged. "Well, the police didn't see the potential in selling drugs that my father did. So they hauled him off to prison and I was deposited in foster care."

It was hard for Carrie to believe there were parents like that, people who could drop their responsibilities to their children like they were changing clothes. To the Amish, family is the very center of life. To have a child is a great blessing, given by God.

Abel picked up the water jug and offered it to Carrie. She shook her head so he took a drink.

"Then what happened to you?" she asked.

He wiped his mouth with the back of his sleeve. "I got into a few scrapes while I was in the system, ended up in juvey a couple of times."

"What's that?" she asked.

"Juvey? Juvenile Hall. It's like, well, sort of like jail for kids."

His eyes were laughing at her, at the shocked look on her face. Her cheeks flamed, aware of how naïve she seemed.

"So, when I got out of juvenile hall the last time, I was told that a relative was willing to take me in. An Amish uncle." He smiled. "At that point, all I knew about the Amish were buggies and beards."

"How old were you?"

"Thirteen." He rubbed the part of his neck that his sling rubbed against. "Daniel was two years older. He and I hit it off, right from the beginning." He grinned. "Not such a good thing. I talked Daniel into a lot of mischief making. A lot."

She gazed down the long row of apple trees before looking up at him. "So even back then, you weren't thinking you'd be baptized into the church?"

He gave her a sharp look. "Back then, I did everything I could to try and prove I didn't need anything or anybody." He picked up a dried, withered apple left on the ground from last year and threw it as far as he could. "Like I said, I was a bad apple."

It must be terrible to never belong to anyone, Carrie thought. Being Amish meant a certainty of always belonging, always being a part of a whole. She wondered if Abel could sustain being alone forever. She wasn't like that. She needed others, she needed that place at the table. It occurred to her that if she had left with Sol, she might never have felt again like she belonged somewhere. She was quiet for a long moment, mulling that over. Slowly she lifted her eyes to meet Abel's. "If you were such a bad apple, why did you go to jail for Daniel?"

"Carrie, you knew Daniel. You knew how sensitive he was. Do you really think he could have survived prison?"

Startled, Carrie realized Abel was right. Daniel wasn't . . . sturdy.

Abel lifted his eyebrows. "Now don't go thinking I was a saint. Daniel was the closest thing to a brother I would ever have." He kicked the ground with his foot. "I would have done anything for him."

Carrie looked at his profile, silhouetted against the canopy of a deep and endless blue sky overhead. "Abel Miller, sometimes I think you're more Amish than the rest of us."

Early the next morning, Carrie dressed to head out to the orchards, wondering how many days and weeks it would take to get those trees pruned. Her entire body ached, muscles she never knew she had felt stiff. Since it was Saturday, at least Andy would be joining them.

Just as she was pouring coffee into a thermos to take out to the orchards, she heard buggy wheels roll into the driveway. It was still too dark to see anything but a lantern, but then she saw another lantern, then another. Then another. She threw on her cape and went outside. Abel heard them too, and came out of the barn holding a bucket, brimming with Hope's steamy milk, fragrant and fresh, in his one good hand.

Abraham greeted them as he hopped off the first buggy. "Wie geht's!" *Good day!*

Abel and Carrie walked up to meet him, puzzled.

"With Abel's arm broke, did you think we'd forget you needed help with those apple trees?" Abraham laughed. "How is that broke arm, Abel?"

As Abel answered the deacon, Emma came up behind them. Carrie gave her a suspicious look. "Did you go telling Esther I was trying to cut those trees myself?"

"No! I promise." She looked as surprised as Carrie did.

Somehow, Carrie realized, they just knew she needed help. "Well, Emma, we'd better get more coffee brewing, then," she said, barely able to contain her relief.

In one day, working together, the neighbors finished pruning every apple tree and stacked the limbs and kindling to dry in the shed, ready to use next winter. As Carrie waved goodbye to the last buggy, her heart brimmed with gratitude. It was the Plain way for neighbor to help neighbor, she *knew* that. But for the first time, she *felt* it. This is what it means to be Plain, she thought. This security, this sense of belonging. She never should have worried. She had neighbors.

She walked down to the first row of trees in the orchard. She tilted her head back to look at the deep blue of the evening sky. As darkness descended, the stars began to pop out, clear as a map of the skies. The long, even rows of trees would soon finish their winter's nap, waiting for the call of spring. She couldn't wait for those first pink blossoms. Spring had always been her favorite time of year, when the earth warmed and erupted into dazzling colors. She was as excited as she could remember being about anything. Cider Mill Farm was the first home she'd ever really had to call her own. She had grown to love it, every rock and tree. She felt as if she was just starting her life again.

Later that week, Carrie took a letter for Abel that arrived in the day's mail and a stack of his freshly ironed clothes down to the workshop. She pulled open one drawer to put away his shirts and closed it again, but something jammed. The drawer wouldn't shut. She pulled it open and reached her hand in the back to see what was jammed. It was a large yellow envelope addressed to Abel Miller, with a return address of Veronica McCall's company. She smoothed out the envelope and placed it flat in the drawer, then closed it tight.

What was in that envelope? The thought kept nagging her, like a sliver in a finger. Before Abel returned from Honor Mansion, she went to the barn and opened up his drawer. She picked up the envelope, knowing full well it was wrong, that it was wicked. But still, she opened it up and read the papers. She read and reread until her knees went weak and her heart started pounding in her ears. It was a contract from Bonnatt Construction Company with an offer for Cider Mill Farm.

My home. My orchards.

She stopped reading as a chill shivered through her. With shaking hands, she slid the papers back in the envelope. "I don't believe it," she murmured.

"I just can't believe Abel would betray me like that." But even as she said the words, doubt flickered in the back of her mind like fireflies darting in the night.

That evening, she had trouble falling asleep, until a wheel clicked over in her mind. The thought made her finally relax. Even to smile. The joke was on Abel, really. She was surprised she hadn't thought of it sooner. There was no way he could sell Cider Mill Farm.

You can't sell what you don't own.

12

On an off Sunday in late February, when church wasn't being held, a loud roar rumbled into the driveway, so loud it sounded as if a train had arrived. Abel and Andy were in the living room and hopped up to see what the racket was. Emma stood next to Carrie by the kitchen door, wiping her hands on a dish towel.

Abel came up behind Carrie and looked over her shoulder. "No way!" He shoved open the kitchen door and flew down the steps. A giant of a man with a big silver helmet on his head, wearing a black leather jacket, climbed off of a motorcycle.

"Abe!" the man shouted, spotting Abel as he approached, enveloping him in a bear hug. "Dude—you got a broken arm!"

Coughing from the man's tight embrace, Abel looked back to the house and waved. "It's Steelhead!"

Emma, Carrie, and Andy, wide-eyed, walked out on the kitchen steps.

The man pulled off his helmet, revealing a large, shiny bald head. He walked around in a circle, taking in the house and the orchards. "I feel like I just walked into a Christmas card." Then he whirled around to face Carrie and Emma, slowly appraising the two women. He whistled. "Wow. What a babe."

"A babe?" Abel asked, glancing back to the house. "Oh, that's Carrie. I wrote you about her."

"The big gal?"

"Emma?!" Abel's eyes went wide. "A babe?"

"I like a woman with a little meat on her bones," Steelhead said. "Man, she is one hot mama."

Overhearing, Emma spun around in disgust and slammed the kitchen door.

At dinner that noontime, Andy's eyes stayed fixed on the eagle tattoo on Steelhead's right arm. When Steelhead noticed Andy's fixation, he flexed the muscles in his arm, making it look as if the eagle was about to fly. He tore off a crusty chunk of bread, dunked it in his soup, and stuffed it in his mouth. He grinned and winked at Andy.

Carrie wondered if the tattoo would look like an expired balloon, faded and sagging, when Steelhead grew old. Emma wasn't at all impressed by Steelhead's tattoo, or anything else about him. Steelhead didn't seem to notice. He would tell Abel a story or make a joke, then glance at Emma to see if she was paying attention. Emma ignored him and concentrated on her meal.

Andy was fascinated by him. "How did you get so bald?" he blurted out.

Carrie gasped, but Steelhead only grinned. "I like to think I've been liberated from the burden of hair," he said, elbowing Andy.

Andy pondered that answer for a moment, then started laughing so hard he bent in the middle. Carrie started laughing too, just watching him. It felt so good to see Andy laugh again.

"So, Mr. Steelhead, what brings you to Stoney Ridge?" Yonnie asked. She seemed a little dazed by Steelhead, but so did Carrie.

"Well, I'll tell you ma'am, Abe and I had always talked about starting our own business someday, and he didn't seem to be coming back up to Ohio." Steelhead slapped Abel on the back so hard he winced. "When my parole officer gave me the okay to leave the grand state of Ohio, I got to thinkin', why not go find my little buddy and see what's taking him so long?"

Abel bit the corner of his lip and kept his eyes on his plate.

"Is everyone finished?" Emma asked, ice in her voice.

Abel gave the signal for a silent prayer to finish the meal, then Emma hopped up and started to clear the table, banging dishes as she set them down on the counter. She was making such a racket, slamming pots and kettles, that Steelhead looked worried, as if she might start throwing things at him.

"Are you vexed with me, ma'am?" he asked her.

Emma didn't even glance his way.

"She's always like that," Andy whispered to him. He twirled his finger beside his head like the spring of a clock. "A little crazy."

"Am I talking too much for you, Miss Emma?" Steelhead asked her.

Starting to fill the sink with hot water, Emma said stiffly, "Plain folks believe that needless words are a displeasure to God."

"Oh, honestly, Emma," Carrie said. "Steelhead is our guest."

"No, she's absolutely right," Steelhead said. "I'm known for making a short story long." He laughed and stood to stretch. "And now, I'll be on my way. I'm staying in town." He went over to Emma and took her hand gently in his. "Thank you for the meal, Miss Emma."

Emma's cheeks colored, but she gave a short jerk of her head before pulling her hand out of his.

After Abel went outside with Steelhead, Carrie turned to Emma. "Why were you so rude to him?"

Emma scowled and pointed her finger at Carrie. "You should be too! He's going to take our Abel away."

"Don't be ridiculous, Emma." But she looked out the window and saw the two men standing by the motorcycle, talking and laughing. Even though Abel was looking more Plain as his hair grew long, he still seemed English.

"You mark my words," Emma said from behind her, "that kind of man can talk anybody into anything."

Carrie rolled her eyes at Emma's worldly wise airs.

Suddenly, Andy screamed from the other room. "Carrie! Come quick! It's Yonnie! She's dead!"

Carrie found Yonnie on the floor by her quilting frame, unconscious. She was breathing, but her pulse was racing. Emma shouted out the kitchen door to Abel to come quick.

"Call 911," Steelhead said.

"Can't," Abel said, hovering over Yonnie. "No phone."

"What?!" Steelhead looked around the kitchen in disbelief. "I'll go for help. I'll take the little dude with me."

Before Steelhead could finish that sentence, Andy was out the door and on the back of the motorcycle. They returned a few minutes later with Veronica McCall following close behind. She walked into the kitchen like a football coach talking to his players before the big game.

"Everyone? Remain calm. I called for an ambulance," she said, pointing to the black clothespin on her ear.

Emma and Andy stayed at the house while Abel rode in the ambulance with Yonnie. Veronica and Carrie followed behind in the car. Carrie was so distracted she didn't even say goodbye to Steelhead. She hoped Emma wouldn't run him off too quickly. He was an odd fellow, but there was a sweetness to him.

At the hospital, Abel, Carrie, and Veronica sat in the waiting room outside of emergency for a long while as the doctor ran tests on Yonnie, trying to determine why she was unconscious. With a captive audience, Veronica McCall thought it would be a fine time to discuss selling the property.

"Not now, Veronica," Abel said in a warning voice, trying to cut her off.

"Why not now? We have time—"

"Not now," he said, giving her an angry look.

A dark cloud passed over Veronica's face. It was obvious that she didn't like having someone tell her what to do.

Just then, the nurse came in and told them they could see Yonnie. "The doctor will be in shortly. He's reviewing her initial test results."

Yonnie slipped in and out of consciousness. She lay in the bed, so tiny and frail. Carrie leaned over to smooth some wispy gray strands into her prayer cap. Abel stood on the other side of her bed, holding her wrinkled hand, his face full of worry. She was the last leaf on his family tree.

Dr. Zimmerman came in through the door, reading Yonnie's chart. When he looked up, he said, "Well, well! My favorite Amish family! My, you people seem to be in the emergency room a lot." He pointed to Abel's cast and asked him how it was mending.

"Too slow for my liking," Abel said.

"That was a nasty break, Abel. Bones need time to heal." Dr. Zimmerman turned his attention to Yonnie. He asked Abel a few questions to get Yonnie's medical history. "She's stable, but I'd like to admit her and run more tests."

Veronica, Abel, and Carrie got into the elevator, trailing behind the orderlies as they pushed Yonnie's bed to the floor where she would stay for the night. Dr. Zimmerman tagged along to answer their questions.

Just as the elevator doors were about to close, a hand reached in. The doors jerked open as Solomon Riehl stepped inside. His eyes scanned those in the elevator, then stopped when they landed on Carrie, as if he knew she was in the elevator. Shocked by the sight of him, Carrie felt her palms start to sweat and her heart pound, but no one else in the elevator had any idea of her discomfort.

Awkwardly, Sol sidled next to Carrie. "Carrie, how are you?" he asked her in a kind voice.

"Very well," she answered, lifting her chin a notch.

"Good. That's good."

Suddenly, Veronica McCall let out a gasp. "Solomon Riehl! The pitcher for the Barnstormers!"

Veronica's face was lit up like a firefly on a summer night. Carrie didn't really blame her. It wasn't so long ago that Sol had the same effect on her. Veronica rooted through her purse for a paper and pen, thrusting them at him for an autograph. Dr. Zimmerman got caught up in Veronica's excitement and reached in his pocket for a prescription pad for Sol's autograph.

"How do you know Carrie?" Veronica asked Sol, as he scribbled his name on her paper.

Sol turned to look straight at Carrie. "We go way back. Way, way back."

Veronica looked from Sol, back to Carrie, then back to Sol. "Well, small world."

Carrie inched farther away, against the wall. She kept her eyes lowered on Yonnie, but she knew that Abel was looking straight at her. That was one thing—the only thing—about Abel that reminded her of Daniel, she realized. He didn't miss a thing.

As soon as the elevator opened, Carrie squeezed past Sol and followed the orderlies. She and Veronica waited in the hallway while Abel went into Yonnie's room with the doctor. A nurse spotted Veronica using her cell phone and ordered her outside on the deck. "It's freezing outside!" Veronica wailed, but the nurse insisted. She finally complied, leaving Carrie alone.

Carrie knew Sol was waiting by the elevator for such an opportune moment. As he approached her, she stiffened and crossed her arms. "You have a habit of popping up in unexpected places."

"I'm here with the team for an autographing event in the pediatric ward," Sol said. "A couple of the players are on the ward signing baseballs and photos and things. To cheer up the sick kids."

"How nice," Carrie said in a flat voice.

Sol took a step closer to her. "Carrie, we need to talk."

She turned her head away.

"I didn't realize Daniel had died on the same day I came to your barn with that . . . information. I'm sorry, Carrie. Until Mattie mentioned the date . . . I didn't know . . ."

Carrie kept her eyes lowered. "You didn't cause his death, if that's what you mean." *I did that*, she thought. Still, the chain of events that started by a single act astounded her.

Sol leaned in toward her. "Does that fellow mean something to you? The one dressed Plain but acts English?"

Her eyes flew up to meet his. "I suppose Mattie told you about Abel too?"

Sol nodded.

For a split second, Carrie wondered when Mattie had talked to Sol. Then she caught herself and dismissed the thought; she had no claim on Sol. "It's not any of your concern."

"But you *know* what he's done, back in Ohio. Why would you be letting yourself get taken in by these kinds of guys? I'm worried about you."

"You don't know anything about the Millers, except for that old newspaper clipping."

"I know enough. I know that Jacob Weaver would never have let you near them had he known what they'd done."

"My father knew," she said coldly.

Sol was shocked silent. He put his hands on her upper arms and his voice dropped to a whisper. "Carrie, don't you see? We've been given a second chance. To get it right."

Carrie's brows lifted. "That's not the way it works."

He sighed. "One choice? One wrong choice? That's all it comes down to?"

Carrie turned her head to the side.

He dropped his arms. "When did you get so hot hartzfich?" *So hardhearted?* His voice broke as he asked, "Did my leaving do that to you?"

Suddenly Abel stood at the open threshold of Yonnie's door, just as Veronica joined them from the patio. They gathered around Carrie and Sol, watching them curiously. As Carrie realized she had an audience, her cheeks flamed. Sol didn't seem to notice; he kept his gaze fixed on her.

"Is Yonnie dying?" Veronica asked Abel.

"Who's Yonnie?" Sol whispered to Carrie.

Abel looked at Sol, annoyed. "Who *are* you? And why are you here?"

"Yonnie is Abel's grandmother," Veronica answered Sol. "She must be ninety if she's a day." She turned back to Abel. "A body can't live forever, you know."

Abel scowled at her. "She's only eighty-one. And who is this guy?"

"This is Solomon Riehl, the famous baseball player." Satisfied that she had made the proper introductions, Veronica turned to Dr. Zimmerman as he approached them. "So, is she dying?"

Abel threw his arms up in the air in a gesture of *oh, you can't be serious!*

Even Dr. Zimmerman looked surprised by Veronica's bluntness. "I hope not. Not on my watch, anyway." He turned to Abel. "We'll call you if there's any change in her condition."

"Better call me," Veronica McCall said with a smug smile. "These people"— she nodded her head in Carrie's direction—"don't have telephones." She followed Dr. Zimmerman down to the nurse's station to give him her phone number, talking the entire way.

As the elevator door opened, a large man in a Barnstormers' jacket stepped out and spotted Sol. In a rusty and deep voice, he shouted, "Riehl! Where'd you go? Coach is looking for you!"

Sol gave Carrie an awkward glance. "I'd better go." Lowering his voice, he added, "I'll see you soon. Think about what I've said. Just think about it, okay?" He squeezed her arm and hurried to reach the elevator before the doors closed.

Abel stared at her a moment, in that intent way of his. "What was *that* about?"

Carrie kept her eyes on the ground. "What was what about?"

"What's the story with that Sol guy?"

"It's like Veronica said. He's a baseball player."

Abel crossed his arms against his chest. "So she said. What else?"

"Nothing else," she said, lifting her head to meet his gaze. But she couldn't hold his stare.

"Well, let's see. For one thing, he's clearly Amish."

"What makes you say that?" Sol didn't look at all Amish, she thought, not anymore. It was more than the shingled hair and blue jeans. He had never moved like an Amish man, slow and cautious. He had always moved quickly, with the confidence of an athlete.

"What makes me think he's Amish? One: his accent. Two: his name. Three: the way he was looking at you."

She spotted Veronica walking toward them in the hallway. "Maybe Veronica could drive us home. Emma is probably driving Andy crazy with her worry about Yonnie."

"You go. I'm going to stay here overnight."

She glanced at Yonnie's door. "Will you tell her I'll come to see her tomorrow?"

Abel nodded, distracted, and turned to go back into his grandmother's room.

Veronica McCall drove Carrie home, talking on the black clothespin the entire time. Just before they reached Cider Mill Farm, she said, "I'll call you back. I have another call. Uh-huh, uh-huh. Wait a minute." She handed Carrie the clothespin. "Here, Carrie. Abel wants to talk to you."

With one hand, she pointed to the part that Carrie should listen to.

Awkwardly, Carrie lifted it up to her ear. "Carrie?" she heard Abel ask. "Yonnie is awake now."

Carrie hesitated before answering, unsure of where on the clothespin she should speak into. Irritated, Veronica pointed to the speaker. "How does she seem?"

"Better. She's even talking a little. Dr. Zimmerman thinks she had a small stroke. They're going to put her on anticoagulants to thin her blood. He thinks she'll be fine. He said he'll probably release her tomorrow, so I'll stay the night and hire a driver to bring her home."

"Tell him I'll come and get him," Veronica interrupted, eavesdropping.

"Oh. Okay," Abel said flatly, overhearing Veronica. There was a pause. "Carrie, are you okay?"

"Everything's fine," she said briskly, not wanting to discuss Sol. She handed Veronica McCall her black clothespin telephone.

When they pulled up to the house, Carrie thanked Veronica for coming to the rescue. With one hand on the door handle, Carrie shifted her body to turn to her. "I'm grateful for your help today. But I'm still not going to sell you my property."

"*Your* property?" she asked, arching one thin eyebrow. "Abel is the rightful owner."

Carrie shook her head. "Eli left the home to Daniel. To me and Andy."

Veronica stretched in her seat like a cat. "It's a matter of public record, Carrie. Go look it up at the county. The name on the deed of the property is Abel's."

"That couldn't be right." But even as Carrie said it, a knot of doubt started to grow.

"Ask Abel who owns the property, if you don't believe me."

Carrie felt the beginning of a slow burn. "So Abel knows?"

"Of course he knows," she crooned, with a triumphant little smirk. "He's known all along. He paid the taxes on it just last week." At Carrie's bewildered expression, Veronica smiled the smile of one who knew something that another did not. "Why do you think he's staying here? Why do you think he's here at all?"

Samuel Zook, Mattie's brother, was passing Cider Mill Farm in his buggy as the ambulance pulled away. He stopped for a moment as Emma filled him in on Yonnie's emergency. When he arrived home and told Mattie the news, he offered to take her to the hospital. "But you'll have to catch the bus to get home or Dad will skin me alive for missing the afternoon milking," he told her.

Mattie grabbed her bonnet and cape and hopped in his buggy before he could finish the offer.

As soon as Mattie walked through the hospital door, she looked for someone to help her find Yonnie. A hospital volunteer led her to Yonnie's floor and pointed down the hallway to the room. Mattie gently knocked on the door, not knowing what to expect, but was surprised to see Yonnie sitting up in bed, talking with Abel. His face lit up and he sprang to his feet when he saw her.

"Mattie! How did you hear? What are you doing here? Is Carrie with you?" A crestfallen look passed over his face as he realized she was alone.

For a split second, Mattie found she couldn't answer. *Why, he's falling for Carrie! Dear Lord, anyone can see that a mile away.* When Abel asked her again why she was at the hospital, she said, "To check on our Yonnie."

"The doctor thinks that Yonnie can be discharged tomorrow," Abel said, looking affectionately at his grandmother.

Mattie took hold of Yonnie's wrinkled hands. "That's wonderful news, Yonnie!" She turned to Abel. "My dad has a hired driver scheduled for tomorrow afternoon. He has a doctor's appointment across the street. I'm sure he wouldn't mind bringing you both home, if that would help."

Abel sighed with relief. "That would mean Veronica won't have to pick us up." He winced. "She's been calling the nurse's station every fifteen minutes. They're about ready to pull the phone cord out."

Sol stood outside the hospital, stunned from the news his pitching coach had given him after the event in the pediatric ward. His contract for the upcoming season wasn't going to be renewed.

"I'm sorry, Sol," the coach told him. "We found another pitcher who can match the speed on your fastball, but he's got a few more parlor tricks up his sleeve." The coach patted him on the back, as if that made it all right. "I like you a lot. You've got a great work ethic. This is nothing personal. Baseball is a business, a tough business. It was a good run while it lasted." He then said that he would look around and see if there might be a AA team that needed a pitcher, but he knew there was no interest in the Atlantic League. "And the thing is, Sol, you're going to keep running into the same problem. I even thought about having you help coach the Junior Barnstormers team, cuz I think you'd be good with kids, but what could you offer? You haven't been taught the mechanics of pitching, or hitting, or catching. You're just now catching on to keeping stats. You've had a lucky streak with one fast pitch."

Sol sat on a bench, head in his hands. A lucky streak. A good run while it lasted. Now what? He had such plans. He was going to skim the surface of the world, and here he was, stuck in Stoney Ridge.

He had no idea what he was going to do next. His baseball dream had just died. Carrie was still mad at him; she was staying mad. His folks had told him not to come around anymore. He knew it wasn't his mother's idea; she looked as if it was killing her to hear his father say those words, but they decided it was high time Sol came back to the fold. He figured a church elder, or maybe Esther Weaver, might have paid them a visit.

The thing was, he wasn't really Amish anymore. But he wasn't really English, either. He felt small and very, very alone.

Absentmindedly, he watched a young woman, dressed Plain, walking to the bus stop. Sol jackknifed to his feet and jogged over to her. "Mattie?"

Startled, Mattie spun around to see who was calling her name. Then she smiled.

Sol was grateful to see a friendly face, any friendly face would do. "What are you doing here? Would you have time for a visit? A cup of coffee, maybe?"

"I heard the news about Yonnie so I came to see if I could help. And to answer your other questions, yes and yes."

In the cafeteria, Mattie sat across from Sol as he poured out the story of getting cut from the team. He didn't mean to tell her so much, but Mattie had a way of listening and talking at just the right places. When he told her the coach wanted him to come back for "Salute to Whoopie Pie Day" because it would boost attendance among the Pennsylvania Dutch fans, she laughed so hard it made him start to laugh too. Put that way, it did sound ridiculous.

After he finished, he asked, "Any idea what I should do now?" He peered at her as if she could provide him with answers to all that plagued him.

Mattie stood, walked to the window that overlooked the parking lot, and then turned back to him. She spoke the truth that was in her heart, because that was the only way she knew how to be. "When you get to your wit's end, Sol, you'll find God lives there."

"Why didn't you tell me Eli left you these orchards, Abel?" Carrie asked, then waited, hands on her hips, letting her silence demand an explanation from him.

They had just settled Yonnie up in her bed after returning from the hospital. Emma hovered over Yonnie like a bee over blooming lavender and Andy was at school, so Carrie followed Abel out to his workshop in the barn. Since Veronica McCall's revelation about the property deed, she had been waiting for this moment to come.

Abel spun around, confused. He looked exhausted from spending the night upright in a hospital chair. "Who told you that?"

She told him everything Veronica had told her.

His eyes went wide, but Carrie knew she had the truth. "That's not how things went . . . I didn't . . . I would never . . ."

She glared at him, standing her ground.

"Can you stop looking at me like that? You're sort of scaring me."

She kept glaring at him.

He raked a hand through his hair, searching for the way to say what he had to say. "The house and orchards were left to me after Daniel died, Carrie. I received a letter from Eli's attorney before I was released from jail. He's the one who told me about Daniel's death." He rubbed his face with his hands. "Eli didn't put you in his will."

She felt anger boil up like a kettle on a hot stove. "Or Andy?"

"Or Andy."

"And you knew about this, the *entire* time."

He nodded slowly, looking miserable.

She was so upset she was shaking. "I have been working to pay the next tax bill on this property all winter. We are paying our feed and gas bills one at a time. Why, even Yonnie has been parting with her quilts! It's been that way ever since Daniel passed." She took a few steps to the open door of the workshop and swept an arm out toward the apple trees. "Do you have any idea what this land means to me? These orchards are meant for Andy to have one day. You arrive out of the blue and think you're going to walk away with it? To sell it and walk off?"

Abel was stunned. "But I never knew . . . why didn't you tell me you needed money? I could have been helping. I want to help. That shouldn't be your responsibility."

"It *should* be my responsibility! All along, I've thought they belonged to me! To me and my brother!" She spun around to leave.

With his good hand, he grabbed her arm to make her face him. "I admit, I came here thinking I would sell the place. I figured you would want to live with your folks, and Yonnie would come back to Ohio with me. Steelhead and I had plans to start a business. But then, I met you, and I saw how you love this place. I see how your face lights up and how hard you work at it. I never *signed* those papers, Carrie. I could never do that to you."

"Why should I believe you?"

"Why shouldn't you?"

"For a man who keeps spouting off that the truth will set us free, I don't see you doing much truth telling. You had plenty of chances, Abel Miller."

Stung, he dropped his hand to his side. In a quiet voice, he said, "I know. I kept looking for the right time to tell you, but it never seemed to come. And then it got harder to tell you. When the property tax bill came in the mail last week, with my name on it, and you put it in my workshop, I just went ahead and paid it. I thought I was helping, but the truth is, well, I just didn't know how to tell you the truth. Not after all this time." He rubbed his jaw. "Eli left this property to me because he was trying to set things right. For me. He wasn't trying to hurt you. Neither was I."

Just then, Andy came running to the workshop to show Abel a hummingbird's nest he had found on the way home from school. Abel bent down to examine it.

"Wow, Andy, what a find!" he said with such fondness in his voice that it made Carrie's heart hurt.

Carrie watched the two heads bent over the nest for a long moment, then as her eyelashes spiked with tears, she turned quickly to go to the house.

13

Sol drove to Central Market right about the time he thought Mattie would be done working for the day. Just this week, her family had opened up their stand to sell the first fruits of the year: asparagus and spring onions. He smiled at the pleased look on her face when she spotted him. He flashed her his most dashing grin, the one he used only when girls were around. "Hello there, Mathilda Zook."

Mattie gave him a measured look in that way she had. "Sol, please wipe that dipped-in-honey grin off your face. I know you well enough to know when you're trying to charm someone. Why don't you stop playing games and just tell me what you need."

Sol's grin faded. "I could sure use a friend, Mattie."

Mattie closed up the stand and locked it, put the money in her pocket, and turned to Sol. "Let's go for a ride."

Sol drove down to Blue Lake Pond. In the late afternoon sun, it was so cold they decided to stay in the car. With their eyes facing the silver shimmer of the pond, Sol found himself spilling out everything about the turmoil he felt over the last year. Mattie was easy for him to talk to, easier than Carrie, he realized. There was a little part of him that wasn't entirely surprised Carrie wouldn't forgive him. As if he always felt he might disappoint her, after she really got to know him. Maybe that was why he went ahead and disappointed her. He couldn't deny a part of him felt relieved about trying to play baseball without worrying about a wife. But in the back of his mind he figured he and Carrie would eventually work things out, that they were meant to be together. He underestimated her stubborn streak.

He looked over at Mattie in the car. Her face was turned to the sky, like a flower, and she smiled softly as the sun washed over her. Things felt so comfortable with Mattie. In a way he didn't understand, she knew him better than he knew himself.

"The thing is, I could always have any girl I ever wanted." He snapped his fingers. "Just like that. Amish or English. Carrie knows that."

Mattie nodded, shifting in the seat to look straight at him. "Until now."

Sol frowned. He knew what she was probably thinking, just like his mother and sisters, that he was being punished for leaving the flock. "I don't know how you can handle all of the rules, Mattie. I got so tired of bumping into rules every time I turned around."

"I guess I don't see the rules as taking something from me. I see them as giving to me."

He glanced at her, surprised. How could he describe freedom to someone who was raised in a cage? "Do you mean to tell me that you honestly think God would label you a hopeless sinner if . . . ," he tugged on a string of her prayer cap, "if you had one less pleat in your cap? Or one more? Will the wrong number of pleats in your cap send you to the devil?" He felt a twinge of guilt to say such things aloud, to cause doubt in Mattie the way it used to when he said such things to Carrie.

But Mattie didn't look to be filled with doubts. In fact, she looked as if she was trying to suppress a smile. "Sol, you're missing the point. My clothes and prayer cap, the way I look, they aren't making me *suitable to* God. They're reminding me, every day, that I *belong* to God."

Sol looked at her, amazed, as if seeing her for the first time. Before him was a girl with steady gray eyes, wide cheekbones that narrowed to a dainty chin, giving her face a sweetheart shape. Her skin was like freshly skimmed cream, her hair the pale yellow of a winter sun. Mattie had a shy innocence common to Amish girls, yet he found that nothing he said shocked her. All those years he'd known her, yet he had hardly ever noticed her. He had to admit, the reason he was spending time with Mattie now was because she was Carrie's best friend, and this was the closest he could come to Carrie.

He shook his head. "It's amazing you and Carrie are such good friends.

She's always been tempted by worldly things. She wants more choices." He stopped himself. *Or was that me?* He thought Carrie wanted more, but suddenly he realized he might have blurred her wants with his. He gave a quick shake of his head. "Wanted. She wanted more choices. I guess I don't really know what she wants anymore." He cast Mattie a sliding glance, hoping she might expand on Carrie.

Mattie's eyes were fixed on the pond. "I do have one rule, Sol. I'm not going to talk to you about Carrie."

There was no mincing words with *that* girl, he pondered after he dropped Mattie off at the end of her lane, far enough away from her house that her folks wouldn't see his car. Mattie surprised him with her forthrightness. His sisters had catered to him the same way his mother catered to his father. Wasn't that the way things worked in the Amish world? He wasn't sure he liked the change.

A few weeks later, as Carrie was setting the table for supper, Esther's buggy rolled into the driveway of Cider Mill Farm. She had been visiting Ada Stoltzfus, she said, who kept her longer than she should have. On her way home, she felt a wheel on the buggy come loose. Abel took out his tools to fix the wheel, while Emma invited her mother inside and encouraged her to stay for supper. Esther seemed to be in a rare pleasant mood and agreed to stay. She even asked to see Yonnie's quilts. Still, a feeling of dread rose in Carrie, the same feeling she got before a storm was due in. Well, this was going to be interesting, she thought, setting an extra place at the table for Esther. Because like it or not, chances were that Esther was going to meet Steelhead.

On the afternoon that Yonnie had her stroke, Carrie had returned to the house thinking Emma would have run Steelhead out hours earlier. Instead, she found the two of them playing Scrabble at the kitchen table and laughing over made-up words. Andy said they'd been playing for hours. Since then, Steelhead dropped by every day to see Abel, he said, but he spent his time at the kitchen table, talking to Emma while she cooked or ironed. Today, Andy had talked Steelhead into a motorcycle trip to Blue Lake Pond to see a heron.

When the two came roaring in from their adventure, it was suppertime.

Carrie bit her lip. There was no opportunity to flag off Steelhead. He and Andy came bursting into the kitchen, Andy talking a mile a minute until he saw Esther sitting at the table, and his mouth clamped shut. But Steelhead, oblivious as usual, plowed through the sudden silence and walked right over to give Esther a warm welcome. As Esther shook his big hand, her pleasant mood evaporated, the way a wisp of steam vanishes above a cup of hot tea.

It was so quiet during the meal that Carrie could hear Esther's chewing and swallowing echo through the kitchen. Finally, Steelhead broke the silence.

"Would you pass me more of that shepherd's pie, Miss Emma? It's mighty fine."

Carrie noticed that it was getting so that Emma couldn't pass him a serving dish without blushing the color of a plum.

Steelhead turned to Esther. "Emma is a good cook. Really good. I've never known as fine a cook as Emma."

Esther didn't respond. She just fixed her eyes on Steelhead, and he was looking like a bird caught in her lair. Carrie almost laughed out loud at the look of mild panic in his eyes.

"She might be the best cook in the state of Pennsylvania," he started to blather, "certainly better than that whack job who called himself a cook that we had in prison. Ain't that right, little buddy?"

He nudged Abel to help, but Abel knew enough to not step into that particular landmine. He tried to look off into the distant corners of the room as Steelhead, unstoppable, carried on.

"Hooboy!" Steelhead continued, his head turning shiny. "I never want to eat another morsel of prison grub. Been there, done that, got the T-shirt. Know what I'm saying?"

Esther's eyes went wide with shock and her lips puckered as if she'd just eaten a pickle. Emma covered her face with her hands. Carrie tried to kick Steelhead under the table but missed. Abel cleared his throat, trying to get Steelhead to stop talking, but Steelhead was cornered. His mind was whirring along, and his mouth dragged along behind it, spilling out any thought that passed through his head. Finally, after he had described prison life in its entirety, he ran clean out of words.

Esther slowly stood. "I must go."

As Carrie closed the kitchen door behind her, it was all she could do to lean against it, her forehead against the doorjamb. Esther didn't even wait for the silent prayer at the end of the meal, she was *that* perturbed.

"Too bad Esther Weaver didn't stay for my snickerdoodles," Yonnie said, still seated at the table. "She could use a little sugar."

Steelhead snorted a laugh, then another. Andy's eyes went round at the sound. A slow smile spread over Abel's face. Emma's eyes darted between the two men, as laughter started to rise up and carry them away. Then, to Carrie's astonishment, Emma started to giggle.

Carrie leaned her back against the kitchen door, studying them. Emma looked positively . . . happy.

One afternoon, Sol had just dropped Mattie off near her home and decided to take the long way back, a route that went past Carrie's farm. To his delight, he spotted Carrie getting the mail at her mailbox. He pulled up to her and rolled down his window. "Please, Carrie?" he asked. "I've got something to tell you."

She hesitated, but got in the car. "I'm surprised this old rust heap still drives."

"My baseball contract was cancelled. It's over."

"I'm sorry," she said faintly. "I know that means the world to you."

He was trying to hold her eyes, but she looked away. "No," he said firmly. "You mean the world to me." He reached over to take her hand and slowly brought it up to his jaw. She curved her palm against his cheek; he turned into the caress. He felt encouraged as he saw the anger in her eyes dissolve. "Carrie, what is it going to take for us to find our way back to each other? Do you want me to join the church? I will, if that's what you want. I'll do anything you want."

Carrie shook her head. "I don't want you to join the church for me. If you join the church, you do it for you." But even as she said it, sounding so sure, he saw her face soften, then her stiff shoulders, then, finally, her resolve.

Softly he said, "We could pick up from where we left off last summer."

"I'm not the same person I was last summer."

"Come on, Carrie," he said, his voice gentle and kind. "I know. I know all about you and Daniel."

"What do you mean?" She slid her hand out of his.

"I know it wasn't a real marriage. I know that he slept on the floor."

She recoiled as if she'd been slapped in the face.

"I saw that fancy red-haired lady in town the other day. She told me. She said Andy told her. When I heard that, I knew. I knew for sure you still loved me." His tone was as much a statement as it was a question, but his eyes were pleading with her.

A look of utter disbelief covered Carrie's face. "You've turned my marriage to Daniel into being all about you." Her hands tightened into fists. "Daniel and I, we were finding our way to each other. The way we were, it had nothing to do with you. Nothing!"

"It had everything to do with me! I got to thinking, why would any normal, red-blooded man agree to sleep on the floor? With a girl like you just a few feet away? Then it dawned on me . . . he knew you loved me too."

"Again, it's back to you! As if the whole world spins on your axis."

Now Sol was getting indignant. "So you think making a man sleep on the floor isn't selfish?"

An angry flush streaked Carrie's cheeks.

"Admit it, Carrie. Aren't you even a little relieved he's gone?"

She didn't say anything for a long moment. Then she turned to him, with a look in her eyes as if something just became clear to her. "No. I'm not relieved at all." She got out of the car door and ran up her long driveway.

He banged his head over and over on the steering wheel, frustrated, wondering why everything he said lately didn't seem to come out right. They were such good thoughts, they sounded so reasonable when he worked them out in his head, but when he put them into words, they sounded haughty and proud. Downright vain.

Carrie found Andy in the barn milking Hope. "Did you tell Veronica McCall that Daniel slept on the floor?"

"What's the big deal?" Andy asked, surprised at how upset she looked. "I saw him there, sometimes, when I had a bad dream and came in to get you. I thought it was neat that he slept on the floor. Like he was an Indian or something."

The next day, Abel took the buggy into town for an errand. When he returned, he unhooked the buggy from Old-Timer, but left the tired horse at the hitching post to tend to later. He found Carrie in the vegetable garden, filling up her apron with spring peas. He had a large manila envelope tucked under his arm. "Carrie—"

She looked at the envelope, gathered the corners of her apron, and brushed past him.

He followed behind her. "I know you're upset. You've hardly said a word to me all week. Look, about this deed—"

Something inside of Carrie snapped as anger flooded through her. "Nemme dich die Baamgaarde! Nemme dich das Haus!" she shouted, choking over her own breaths. "Nemme dich alles!" *Take the orchards! Take the house! Take it all!* She ran from him, peas from her apron scattering on the ground. When she saw Old-Timer at the hitching post, she untied his reins and jumped on his back. She rode away as fast as she could, which, considering Old-Timer's advanced age, wasn't much more than a steady trot.

When she reached the pond, she slid off Old-Timer and led him down to the water's edge to drink. His throat rippled as he drank. Finally satisfied, Old-Timer lifted his head and whiffed the air with flaring nostrils. She sat down, her arms hanging loosely over her bent knees, and stared at the calm water. With one hand, she fingered the horse's reins. She was always amazed at the ability of those narrow leather straps to control the instincts of such a mighty beast. Did God hold such reins to this strange, sad world, she wondered?

Wrapping her arms around her legs, she rested her chin on her knees and watched a golden eagle soar over the still pond. An oriole trilled sweetly as a woodpecker drilled into a nearby tree. This was where she had come during those hard days right after her father had died and Sol had left. This was where, many years before, she had played with Mattie, skipping stones over the pond's surface. This was where she could sit and hear the music of the wild birds. This was where she could always find peace.

She didn't know how much time had passed when Abel sat down next to her on the ground, breathless. "Took me awhile to find you."

She frowned at him. "I didn't want to be found."

He ignored her comment. "Where'd you learn to ride a horse like that?"

She shrugged, her gaze straight ahead. "I used to ride bareback a lot. Made Esther mad."

He smiled and leaned back on his elbows, crossing his legs at the ankles. "Why did you ever get baptized? Sounds like you grew up breaking every rule."

She tilted her head toward him. "I know myself well enough to know that I need the rules."

They sat in more silence after that, taking in the view of the eagle, hanging above them like a kite snagged in the sky. "Whatever problem you're facing, I can help," Abel said softly.

She turned her head slightly toward him, asking in icy anger, "Before or after you sell my home out from under me?"

He sighed. "I'm not taking your home. I'm not taking your orchards. I'm not taking anything. If you'd just let a man finish what he's trying to say, you'd know these things." He handed her the large manila envelope. "This is the new deed, changed to your name. Yours and Andy's. It's official. I had a notary witness it."

Carrie took the envelope from him, speechless. She opened it up, slowly, and pulled the papers out. Right in the middle of the deed, in a boldly typed font, was her name and Andy's. Gratitude welled up inside of her, choking off the words. She needed to tell him that he could never know how much this meant to her. They had always felt like visitors in Esther's house, never family. Never truly wanted. She needed to tell him how much she appreciated this gesture, and that she knew what it cost him, but all that came out was, "Denki, Abel."

The edges of his eyes softened, as if he understood all she was trying to say. "I told Veronica the deed has been changed. She wasn't too happy." He gave a short laugh. "One time in jail we were shown a TV documentary on erupting volcanoes. Kinda reminded me of that." He grinned. "She fired me too. Said she didn't need a one-armed carpenter."

"I'm sorry," Carrie said.

He lifted one shoulder in a careless shrug. "I'll find work someplace. Surely somebody needs a one-armed carpenter." He reached into his coat pocket and pulled out a thin envelope. "There's something else. There's one more letter from Daniel. I just wasn't sure if this letter would help or . . . well, anyway . . . seems as if you should know what it said." He hesitated, then handed it to her.

Carrie's heart started to pound when she saw the postmark. It was mailed on the day Daniel died. Carefully, as if it were made of tissue, she unfolded the letter.

March 18th

Dear Abel,

Spring is late this year. We had howling wind and blowing snow yesterday. Only the downy woodpecker didn't seem to mind. He clung to the beef suet Andy and I put out on the bird feeder. He just kept pecking on the high-energy food, finding sustenance for another cold winter night.

Speaking of finding sustenance, the strangest thing happened today. After a long struggle, Andy's cow gave birth before dawn to a new calf. Carrie helped through the whole thing without complaining or fretting. Afterward, I felt so glad she was by my side. I didn't think I would ever feel anything again for a woman, not after my Katie. I married Carrie because Dad wanted me to, and I wanted him to stop suffering. To be honest, I just didn't really care. But somewhere along the way, I started feeling something for her, a fondness. I guess the plain truth is that I needed her. And then came love. I love her, Abel.

I know in the next letter you're going to be preaching me a sermon. I can hear it now, the text will be Romans 8:28, your favorite verse in the Bible, about God working things out for our good, even things that didn't start out so good.

Maybe you're right, Abel. Maybe there's hope for a sinner like me.

I see the mailman coming so I'll say goodbye and get this in the mail.

Yours, Daniel

Something broke inside of Carrie in a terrible gush of guilt and pain. Tears started to flood her eyes. "I let Daniel bleed. Just like Esther let my father bleed. Daniel told me about the kerosene fires that very day, just hours after he must have mailed this letter. And I turned and ran out on him. I was so upset, that he hadn't told me, that Sol—of all people on this big earth—had been the one to tell me about those fires. I felt so angry and I just . . . I just had to get away from him . . . but I never dreamed he would die that night." She took a big gulpy breath. "I failed him miserably. I'm just like Esther."

She went through her handkerchief, then soaked Abel's, and finally, he gave up patting her on the back. He wrapped his arms around her and told her to go ahead, have a good cry. He just held her until she had no more crying left inside of her. She cried for her father's death, and for Daniel's life cut short, and for her own sorry mess. In between sobs she told him about Sol leaving and about grabbing Daniel's offer to marry.

"I didn't love Daniel," she sobbed. "Not the way he deserved to be loved."

Abel rested his chin on the stiff pleats of her prayer cap and held her closer. When she was finally able to look up at him, she noticed tearstains on his cheeks as well.

"Carrie, maybe you needed Daniel as much as he needed you. I'm not sure why he died when he did. It's just one of those mysteries God sends our way. But God has a way of fixing our messes, bringing good out of them." He tipped her chin so she would look at him. "I do know that Daniel would never want you feeling like you failed him. You didn't. One moment doesn't erase all the good."

She wiped her face with her hands. "But what if that was the last moment?"

"Even then." Abel rose to his feet and walked to the water's edge. He picked up a stone and skimmed it across the pond.

Carrie was quiet for a while, watching the stone skip on the glassy surface a few times before it sank deep. "I just wish I knew, for sure and for certain, that he forgave me."

Abel turned to face her. "You knew Daniel well enough to know the answer to that."

A loud, raucous call came from the sky, and Carrie lifted her eyes to find its source.

"Hear Mrs. Mallard honking?" Abel asked quietly, eyes fixed on the V formation of the ducks. "Three quacks mean she's telling the ducks that all is well and it's safe to come down." He reached out a hand to help Carrie to her feet. "Es is alles in Addning." *All is well.*

Sol sat on a gray plastic chair in the LaundroMat, flipping through old magazines, waiting for the clothes dryer to buzz. It always surprised him to see men doing their own laundry. Amish men took a pass on laundry. And cooking and cleaning too. Sometimes, he felt like he had arrived from another planet, he had so much to learn. He watched a man separate clothes into bundles of light and dark colors and wondered why he would bother. Then it dawned on him. *That's why my white T-shirts are always gray!*

There were many aspects to the English that bothered Sol—their obsession with television, for example. But there was one thing about the English that Sol really admired. They gave themselves plenty of opportunities for second chances. Guys on the team had started college, then dropped out to play professional baseball. When they were ready, they could go back again. People moved from house to house. Even marriages could be easily dissolved. Two guys on the teams had been divorced and were already remarried, and it wasn't a big deal. But for him, once he bent at the knee, if he changed his mind it would have harsh consequences. He hadn't even been baptized yet and he was already getting a taste of feeling shunned.

He thought the English were a lot kinder about giving people second chances, a margin of error. If the Amish were known for forgiving, why did they have to be so rigid when someone changed his mind? He was going to have to ask Mattie about that. He found his thoughts often bounced to wondering what Mattie would say about these things. Lately, it seemed that thoughts of Mattie filled his mind more than Carrie. He shook his head, as if to clear it.

The next day, Mattie was watching for Sol's car after she was done with work. She was careful to keep her expectations in check. She never assumed he would come to pick her up—she just *hoped* he would. When she saw his car, she could hardly hold back a grin. He opened the car door for her and had barely turned the ignition when he told her his theory of second chances and the English.

Mattie listened quietly, wondering what he was really asking. It seemed as if Sol was measuring things out lately, trying to convince himself that what he was doing was the right thing. He had been asking her a lot of questions about being Amish. After praying, she decided it wasn't up to her to convince him whether to join the church or not. That would be up to God.

"So, what do you say to that?" he asked, almost accusingly, after he finished. "About how the English give people a margin of error? About how unforgiving the Amish can be sometimes?"

"The Amish aren't perfect. And there are certainly flaws in our culture, just like there are flaws in the English culture." She looked at him. "You know the flaws of the Plain way, you've thought them out. So now, Sol, what are its good points?"

Sol spent his days working at the construction site where he had been hired a year ago, before he left for the Barnstormers. After he was cut from the team, he spoke to the foreman who said he'd be glad to take him on. Today he finished putting away his tools in the foreman's truck as he heard someone yell out "quittin' time." He tossed the rest of the tools in the truck and hurried to his car; Mattie would be expecting him.

For the last few weeks, Sol picked Mattie up after work whenever she was working at Central Market. It saved her bus fare and allowed them extra time together before her folks expected her home. He wasn't sure how her folks would feel about her spending time with him, but he trusted Mattie's judgment. If she wasn't worried, he wouldn't worry either. He just knew that he looked forward to their time together. They talked about all kinds of things, important things, and he was always a little sorry when she said she had to go.

Ever since Mattie had asked him the good points about being Amish, Sol found himself flooded with memories. At the time, though, he had looked at her, unable to answer.

"But you've always known what is truly good, Sol," she had finally said. "Our families and the church."

And how could he answer—that those things weren't good? He knew they were.

But her simple words revealed a piercing wisdom. He couldn't stop thinking about his family, meals, barn raisings, hay making with the neighbors, even Sunday gatherings. It stirred something in him, deep inside; he felt something vital was missing. He was less than himself, missing an arm or a leg or a hand. But he always felt better when he was around Mattie.

The last time he dropped her off, he asked her, half teasing, half serious, "Mattie, why do you even bother with me?"

She looked at him in her solemn, frank way. "I've always thought you had so much potential."

He gave a short laugh. "Right about now, I think you're the only one who does. I doubt my dad would even think I could run the manure spreader in a straight line."

Then she said something that took his breath away. "Not that kind of potential, Sol. Not for farmwork. Not even for baseball. But this kind of potential." She rapped on her chest. "This kind. In the soul."

Finishing her morning chores earlier than usual, Carrie hurried over to Mattie's to help the Zooks prepare to host Sunday church. Once a year, each family in the district took a turn hosting church and the fellowship afterward. Every female relative and neighbor would come over a few days ahead to clean and sweep and dust and scrub and cook and bake.

She found Mattie alone in the kitchen, getting things ready for when the women arrived to prepare for the noon meal on Sunday. She was trying to warm up honey in a large honey jar, placed in warm water. The honey had crystallized and she needed it to make pies.

Carrie came over to look in the pot on the stovetop. A spoon stood straight up. "Hopelessly stuck," she said.

Mattie laughed. "I was just thinking about how it seems as if people get stuck just like this spoon in the honey."

"What?" Carrie asked, starting to fill the sink with warm water so she could wash the dishes Mattie had piled in the sink. She was only half listening.

"Think about it." Mattie tried to loosen the spoon in the honey jar. "Folks think they're traveling on the right road and something happens to stop them—something big, like a mistake they made, or a sin. Then, even though they feel so bad, they just stay stuck."

Carrie added the soap to the hot water and swished it around as bubbles started rising up.

Softly, Mattie said, "Daniel was like that, Carrie. Daniel was stuck."

Carrie stopped what she was doing, and slowly turned to Mattie, not even aware that her hands were dripping bubbles on the floor.

"Eli was trying to help him move forward, so was Abel. Without realizing it, so were you. But he just stayed stuck." Mattie was quiet for a moment, then added, "Sol's another one. He's just stopped in his tracks." The spoon loosened a little. She released it and turned away from the stovetop to face Carrie. "If you don't mind my saying so, sometimes I think you're stuck too, Carrie. Unable to move forward, just filled with regrets about the past. About things you can't change."

As tears started prickling Carrie's eyes, she turned back to the sink.

"I don't think that's what God is wanting from us. I think he wants us to get on with things." Mattie looked out the window at Abel and Andy, who had just arrived to help move furniture out of the downstairs so the benches in the church wagon could be set up. "Take Abel. Now there's a fellow who isn't stuck. He's faced some hard things, but he just keeps moving forward, doesn't he?"

Then she reached over to the honey jar and pulled out the spoon. "Well, look at that!" she said triumphantly, holding it in the air.

"No one will want me there," Sol told Mattie after she had encouraged him to come to church held at her home on Sunday.

"That's not true."

"No, Mattie. They'll only want me there if it means I'm coming home."

"The church is your family, Sol. They only want the best for you."

He frowned at her. "You make it sound so simple. But you know it's not."

For some reason he agreed to go. Afterward, he decided it was the worst idea he had ever let a woman talk him into. The only place to sit was on the edge in the back row, a bystander. From that vantage point, he was able to notice how often Abel Miller's gaze roamed to Carrie during the service. Carrie never even glanced Sol's way, and he knew that for a fact because he kept himself slightly turned so he could watch her. Plenty of other folks were snatching a look at Sol, eyebrows raised in disbelief. Why weren't they measuring that Abel Miller? he wondered. *He's* the new bird in the flock. *He's* the one they should be raising an eyebrow over.

Sol's mind drifted to the first time he laid eyes on Carrie, when Jacob had moved his family to Stoney Ridge to marry the starchy widow Esther Blank. Carrie was only twelve, but the sight of her snatched his breath away. She held her back as straight as a plumb line, her chin lifted slightly in the air. It was one of the reasons Esther accused Carrie of being proud, but she wasn't proud. She was just being Carrie.

When Carrie finally turned sixteen, it took Sol two full years of asking before she agreed to go home with him in his courting buggy. She told him he was a flirt and not to bother her until he was done making eyes at other girls. He couldn't help flirting with the other girls; it was just too much fun. But he never really thought about anyone but Carrie, not seriously.

Today, Carrie sat next to Mattie on the women's side, chin to her chest, as if concentrating carefully on what the minister was preaching about. Once, she reached up and tucked a ringlet of honey blond hair that had slid loose back into her prayer cap. The gesture, one he had seen her do hundreds of times, brought Sol a bittersweet ache. The only time he saw her look across at the men's side was when Andy dropped his hymnal after nodding off, causing a startling bang when the heavy book hit the floor. Carrie raised her eyebrows at her brother in exasperation, then quickly looked at Esther, who was scowling at Andy. Mattie, he noticed, had to bite her lip to keep from laughing.

On the other side of Mattie was Carrie's spinster stepsister, Emma, sitting with her chest lifted high, as if she'd just sucked in a deep breath and didn't dare let go. Sol's gaze drifted to Mattie. He had never noticed Mattie in church before, though of course she'd been there. She'd always been there. He saw that her eyes were closed and her face was lifted, her lips were moving silently, as if praying to God. He marveled at the depth of her faith, almost envying her. Watching her, he wondered how he had ever considered her plain. She looked so filled with joy and the glory of the Lord, she could have nearly burst with it.

As soon as the service was over, everyone poured outside to help set up for lunch. Sol saw Abel Miller make a beeline toward Carrie. She was lifting a tablecloth high in the air to spread over the table and didn't notice him until he was a few paces away. When she saw Abel, Sol's belly clenched with a sick dread.

She looks at him the way she used to look at me.

Nearly everyone ignored Sol, or kept conversations with him quick and to the point, even his friends. His mother asked when he was coming home, but when he hemmed and hawed, she turned away sadly.

He felt irritated with Mattie for encouraging him to come. She didn't understand what it felt like to have those you've known and loved all your life treat you with distance. They knew he was there, he felt their curious glances. But most acted as if he were a stranger they'd met once but couldn't remember who he was or why he was here.

And he wasn't even under the ban.

Afterward, it occurred to him that might have been the very reason Mattie had wanted him to attend.

14

Carrie returned to the farmhouse late one afternoon after taking the last of their frozen cider to the Zooks to sell at their Central Market stand. She tied Strawberry and his cart to the post and hurried inside to see if Emma had started dinner. She found a note from Emma on the kitchen table, saying she had gone on an errand and not to worry if she missed dinner.

"I wonder why she went to town so late in the day," Carrie said to Yonnie, after crumpling up the note. "Usually Emma will only go into town in the morning. She's always said that any Englisher who is drunk and hungover from the night before will still be asleep in the morning and off the streets."

Yonnie gave a slight smile. "Sounds like our Emma."

Carrie started making a batch of brownies for Andy's after-school snack. "Any idea where Abel went to?"

Yonnie looked baffled. "I don't recall him saying where he was going. Or when." She pressed her fist to her mouth, as if willing herself to remember. "I think Veronica McCall swooped in. Maybe she left with him. I think I nodded off."

Carrie glanced at her, a little worried. Yonnie had been sleeping an awful lot lately. Carrie noticed how thick and swollen her ankles were. Sometimes it seemed as if she was like a clock winding down. Carrie looked around the kitchen to see what Emma had started for supper, but she couldn't find any fixings. "Yonnie, what did Emma do today?"

Yonnie looked to the ceiling, as if the answer was written up there. "She was ironing her cap."

"Oh, Emma and those pleats," Carrie said, grinning. Making dinner would be up to her today. She went over to the refrigerator and opened it, loading up her arms with lettuce and cheese and hamburger meat. As she whirled around to set things on the counter, she happened to notice a curl of black smoke coming from the back of the barn, where Abel's workshop was. Her heart started to pound. Trying to sound calm, she said, "Yonnie, I'll be back in a minute."

Carrie flew out of the house and down to the back of the barn. First she tried to get into Abel's workshop but the door handle was too hot. She ran to the barn door and slid it open, as smoke poured out. She heard terrible noises inside, noises she knew would be etched forever in her mind: Schtarm's frightened neighing, Hope and her calf's bawls of panic. She unhooked Hope from her stanchion, pushed on her to back up and then led her out the door. Her calf had enough sense to trot behind her.

"Geh!" she screamed as she opened Schtarm's stall door, stepping back as the horse lunged forward and galloped out of the barn. The other stalls were empty. She could see flames lick the stacked hay bales and knew she had to get out. She tripped over a rope and tried to get to her feet, but bent over coughing and wheezing from the thick smoke. Her raw eyes ached. She felt her way out of the barn and gasped for fresh air.

Soon neighbors started to arrive, one after another, signaled by the smell of smoke in the air. Men and boys formed two bucket lines from the water pump, where Carrie pumped until her hands were raw with blisters. The fire department turned up the driveway and took over with their long hoses. Within an hour, the fire was extinguished, but all that was left were smoking timbers, blackened beams, stone and metal. She was amazed to see the waterwheel remained untouched.

Carrie stood there, stunned by a fire's power.

The deacon came up beside her. "Go on in the house, Carrie. Let Yonnie know all is well. A few of us will stay to make sure the fire is out." He shooed her away. "Go, get some salve on those hands."

As she turned to go inside, Andy rushed up the driveway on his scooter, his eyes wide and frightened. "Where are the horses? And Hope and Lulu?" he asked, staring at the fire truck.

"Strawberry's there," Carrie said, pointing to the frightened pony, still hitched to the post with his cart attached. "The others ran off, Andy, but they're not harmed. You might be able to find Hope and Lulu in the orchards. Maybe Emma could help you look for them when she returns." *Where was Emma, anyway? And where was Abel?*

"I'll help him," Abraham said.

Carrie went inside to assure Yonnie that the fire was out. Her nose and throat kept stinging and she couldn't stop coughing. She finally went upstairs to take a long shower, to get the ash out of her hair and smoke smell off of her body. It was dark when she heard Old-Timer trot the buggy up the driveway, Steelhead's motorcycle on its heels. From the bathroom window, she saw Emma step down slowly from the buggy, stunned, staring at the blackened hole where the barn used to be. "Die Scheier is ganz verbrennt," Emma kept saying, over and over, as if she couldn't believe her eyes. *The barn is completely burned.*

Steelhead looked like Carrie felt: dazed. He just stared at the smoldering barn site.

She saw Abraham walk up to them, so she closed the window and went to her room to lay on the bed, exhausted, just wanting to close her aching eyes for a moment. She put a cold cloth over her eyes to stop them from burning. At first she thought she was dreaming when she heard the clop of Schtarm's hoofbeats pound up the driveway. Awhile later, she woke again when she heard Abel's voice, calling out frantically to the men who remained around the blackened structure, asking where Carrie and Andy and Yonnie were and if all of the animals had been accounted for. Satisfied that they were all safe, she heard him holler, "What on earth has happened to the barn?" Drifting back to sleep, it struck her as strange that he didn't ask about Emma.

The next morning, Carrie was woken by a ray of sun that filtered through her window. She eased out of bed and pulled a fresh dress off of the peg, then stopped suddenly as her tender, blistered hands reminded her of yesterday's fire. Pinning her dress as quickly as she could, she peeked out the window and saw Abel and Abraham emptying out the carriage house. Abel didn't have his sling on, she noticed. She was relieved to see Hope and Lulu tied to stakes, munching hay. Her eyes wandered to the charred remains of the barn. She shuddered at the sight.

By the time Carrie went downstairs, nearly thirty Amish men had arrived. They walked carefully around the blackened structure, tapping on the timbers to see if any could be saved, raking through the ashes. Mattie was in the kitchen, having come over early to help with her father and brothers. She and Emma had prepared hot coffee and made cinnamon rolls, knowing neighbors would be coming soon. Even Esther had arrived; she was folding mayonnaise and chopped celery into a large bowl of shredded chicken to make sandwiches for lunch.

When Emma saw Carrie, she turned her hands over, looking at them, clucking like a mother hen. "Wie entsetzlich!" *How painful!* "Let me bandage them for you." Emma looked as if she hadn't slept well, her eyes were troubled and worried.

"Let me," Yonnie said. "I have some special ointment."

"They don't really hurt that much. I was so tired last night I hardly noticed," Carrie said, holding her palms up as Yonnie covered the blisters with ointment.

"Schtarm came back last night, all on his own," Emma said. "And Andy found Hope and Lulu in the orchards."

"The deacon decided to wait until spring planting is over to have a barn raising," Mattie said, stirring a batch of cookie dough, "so he thought the men could convert the carriage house for the animals. That's why we're all here today."

It warmed Carrie's heart to hear those words. Already, her neighbors were helping her move forward. Life was meant to be lived as it came. It wasn't their way to dwell on hardships; instead, they carried on.

As Yonnie finished wrapping the gauze around her hands, Carrie asked, "Emma? Where were you yesterday afternoon? And where was Abel?"

Emma's head snapped up. She shot a glance at Esther, then looked out the window at Abel. "He said to say he was awful sorry he wasn't here."

Carrie looked out the kitchen window. She saw Abel lugging a piece of lumber off of a wagon. Andy was alongside of him, chattering the whole time. "Yes, but Emma, where were—"

Just then, Yonnie started chanting, "Gottes willes, Gottes willes." When Carrie spun around to look at her, she saw Yonnie hugging her arms around her middle. Carrie's insides seized, knowing trouble was coming but not sure from which direction.

Not a minute later, a police car pulled up to the house. Carrie hurried out the kitchen door and down the steps to meet them, Emma and Mattie trailing behind her. Two police officers got out of the car, staring at what was left of the barn.

"Anybody hurt from the fire?" a beefy officer asked Carrie, a cluster of keys jingling from his belt.

She recognized him. It was Chief Beamer, the police officer who had told her that Daniel had been in an accident. She doubted he would remember her. To the English, the Amish looked as alike as peas in a pod. "No. My neighbors came and helped to put it out."

"Any idea how it started?" he asked her.

She shrugged. "Lightning, maybe."

Chief Beamer looked doubtful. "I don't remember any lightning yesterday. Do you, Jim?"

The officer named Jim shook his head. "Mind if we look around?"

Carrie cocked her head. "Why?"

The two policemen exchanged a look. "This is the second fire in this area in the last few months," the chief said. "We think they might have been set intentionally."

"Why would you think that?"

"Arson fires have a pattern. Splash patterns of flammable liquid, and they have multiple points of origin." He put his hands on his hips. "You just have to know what you're looking for."

The two officers went down to the burnt barn and walked around, examining the area where the fire started. They used some large pitchforks, turning ashes and smoking piles over.

"Found it," Chief Beamer yelled to the other policeman. He held up a burnt-out gasoline can. When he passed by Carrie to get to his car, he said, "We found the same can at the other fire."

Carrie's bandaged hands flew to her cheeks, shocked. "Who would do this? Why would anyone do this?"

Chief Beamer glanced around at the men. "Any chance there's a fellow here named Abel Miller?"

"What do you want with Abel?" she asked, her heart pounding.

"Is he down there?" he asked her, pointing to the group of men surrounding the barn.

Carrie remained silent.

The chief looked at her as if he knew she wasn't going to help, then walked out in the yard and shouted out, "Abel Miller? Is there an Abel Miller here?"

Thirty Amish men stopped what they were doing and looked at the policeman. They looked at each other, a silent communication passing between them, until the deacon, standing in front of the carriage house, gave a nod.

A man, carrying a piece of lumber to give to Abraham, dropped the wood and said, "I am William Abel Miller."

Another fellow put his hammer down. "I'm One-Eyed Abe. Last name's not Miller but my wife's a Miller. Folks get my name mixed up all the time."

Two more men came forward, all claiming some variety of the moniker "Abel Miller." They weren't lying. It was their given name. But Carrie knew what they were doing. They were caring for their own.

The chief and the other policeman looked bewildered. "Now, look—"

Abel had been watching the entire thing. He slid a board back onto the wagon and walked up to the policeman. "I think I'm the Abel Miller you're looking for."

Chief Beamer breathed a sigh of relief. "Can you tell us where you were yesterday afternoon?"

Abel shot a glance at Steelhead, standing nearby. "Out birding."

The chief looked confused. "You mean, hunting?"

He shook his head. "No. I was coming home and stopped to watch a flock of black ducks heading south over Blue Lake Pond. This time of year it's a highway in the sky, with all the migrating birds heading north. Kind of a flyway."

"Black ducks?" Abraham asked, stepping forward out of the group of Amish men, clearly interested. "Why, they're getting about as scarce out here as sunflowers in January."

The chief frowned at Abraham. "Anyone see you?"

"Don't you mean, can I prove it?" Abel asked.

"Yep," said the chief.

Abel turned his head to look at Esther, standing with her arms tightly crossed against her chest. Next to her stood Emma, hands clutched together as if she was praying. Then his gaze shifted to Carrie. When Abel's eyes met Carrie's, a current passed between them. He hesitated just a moment too long. "No. I guess I can't."

It was at that moment that Carrie knew Abel was lying. She knew it.

Chief Beamer took a step closer to Abel. "Then you'll have to come down to the station."

"On what charges?" Abel asked, chin lifted high.

"No charges yet. We've got some questions we want to ask you."

"Just because I wasn't here?"

"We got a tip that you've had a history with fires," Chief Beamer said. "And a little history with the law."

From behind her, Carrie heard Emma let out a gasp. The officer called Jim put a hand on Abel's shoulder to guide him into the back of the police car.

"No!" Andy shouted. "You can't do that to our Abel!"

Abraham gently put his hands on Andy's arms, then steered him up to Carrie. Andy threw his arms around Carrie's middle, as they watched the car with Abel, head held high, pass by them.

Emma met Carrie at the kitchen steps. "He didn't do it, Carrie. He would never do anything to hurt us."

Carrie brushed past her and went into the kitchen.

Emma followed behind. "Carrie, are you listening to me?"

Carrie picked up a rag and started rubbing clean the floury countertop where Emma had made the cinnamon rolls. "I heard you."

Emma grabbed Carrie's shoulders. "You know he's innocent, don't you?"

Carrie looked right at her. "Yes. I know."

Emma dropped her arms and looked at Carrie, puzzled.

"But I also know he is lying, and if I know Abel, that probably means he is protecting someone." Carrie put the rag on the counter and crossed her arms. "So who is he protecting, Emma? And why?"

"What I want to know," Mattie asked, leaning on the kitchen doorjamb with her arms crossed, "is who gave the police that tip?"

Sol had read about Carrie's barn burning in a newspaper at work that morning, but he didn't let on to Mattie that he knew when he met her for a walk at the pond in the late afternoon. He listened carefully as she filled him in on the details of the fire.

Then she added one little piece of information that he had missed—the actual day of the fire. For some reason, he thought it must have happened a few days ago, but Mattie said it happened yesterday. He should have read that newspaper article more carefully, he realized. His stomach made a slow, sickening twist.

"Something bothering you, Sol?" Mattie asked as they walked along the pond shore. "You're awful quiet."

He looked into Mattie's soft, kind eyes, then turned back to the pond, as still as glass. Like a stone thrown into the pond, he knew his words would disturb the calm, set into motion a rippling effect he couldn't stop. Mattie had always believed the best in him, and now he was about to change that.

He released a puff of air. "I told the police that Abel Miller set those barn fires."

He winced, bracing himself for her fury, but nothing stirred behind those pale gray eyes.

Then he felt a jolt that went straight through him, as real as lightning.

Mattie knew! She knew what he had done.

"It wasn't a lie, Mattie," he said quickly. "I had some information about him. Something you don't know about. In Ohio, he had gone to jail for killing some folks in a fire. I thought he might try and hurt Carrie."

Yesterday afternoon, Sol was sent to City Hall by the construction site manager to pick up some building permits. As Sol left City Hall, permits in hand, he noticed Abel Miller run up the stairs as if he was late for something. When Sol read about the fire early this morning, the more he convinced himself that Abel was responsible. It infuriated Sol to think this man could cause harm to his people, especially his Carrie. He asked his boss if he could take an early break and went straight to the police station with a copy of that newspaper clipping that he kept in his wallet.

But Mattie had just told him that the fire had been started at about the same time he had seen Abel Miller at City Hall. She added that the police had already come to take Abel away. That was when his stomach started feeling it was twisting like a pretzel. As much as Sol distrusted Abel, even he knew there was no way the man could have been in two places at once.

Mattie's gray eyes showed her disappointment in him. They almost changed color, darkening to a smoky gray. Her eyes were like that, he'd learned. A weathervane for her feelings.

"Abel didn't kill anyone. Neither did Daniel. Not intentionally. Those Ohio fires were just a terrible accident. Carrie told me all about them." She explained to Sol about the kerosene containers contaminated with gasoline.

He felt a stinging heat in his chest and eyes. What had he done? What terrible blunder had he made? "I thought I was doing the right thing, Mattie. Everything pointed to Abel Miller. I was trying to help. You're always saying that if we love someone, we want the best for that person. I only want the best for Carrie."

A trace of color rose under Mattie's fair skin. "I also said only God knows the best for a person." She looked at a duck, skimming the surface of the pond. "Sometimes, I think you aren't as interested in Carrie as you are about winning." She marched up to the road, skirts swishing, and tossed over her shoulder, "Winning her back is like a game to you."

Sol took a few quick strides to catch up with her. "That's not true, Mattie!"

She stopped. "And since when have our people ever, *ever* judged another?" She stamped her foot. "You think you can banish anyone who doesn't fit in your scheme . . . like Daniel." She shook her head, disgusted. "And now Abel."

Sol felt as if she had knocked a punch to his solar plexus. So Carrie *had* told her about his visit on the day Daniel died. He had never brought it up to Mattie, hoping she hadn't known. She had a look on her face that suddenly panicked him, a bright, painful look that glittered in her eyes. Oh God, could he lose her too? When he reached out to her, she backed up and crossed her arms over her chest.

"Sol, you sit on the fringe, not Amish, not English, and you still think you can have everything you want." She wagged a finger at him like an angry mother. "Well, you can't!"

Sol's eyes went wide. "Mattie—"

"Don't Mattie me!"

"Please, Mattie. Calm down. Don't be mad. I'm not like you, Mattie. You . . . you're like a furrow, plowed straight and deep. You always knew right where you wanted to go, how you wanted to be. I'm trying, but it's just not that way for me. I'm not . . . strong like you." The words shocked him coming out as they did, without thought or premeditation, but he knew them to be true. He suddenly knew what was making his chest hurt. It was fear. It was nothing like he'd felt before. He felt a fear of never being able to make things right with the people he loved. He felt a fear of losing Mattie. He felt a fear of God turning his back on him.

He slid a cautious glance at Mattie and watched her eyes fill with a soft pity, stinging his pride, but he could see the fight slip away from her.

"Oh Sol," she finally said. She came close to him and wiped the tears off his cheeks with her palm. She smiled again, a warm, slow smile and the warmth of it spread down deep into Sol's chest. "Don't you understand? It's never too late to be the man you were intended to be."

You have to know what you're looking for.

Those words of Chief Beamer kept echoing in Carrie's mind. She spent the afternoon poking through the ashes of the barn.

Emma came down to help. "What are we looking for?"

"Anything. Anything that might tell us how this fire started."

"Carrie," Emma started, looking worried, "maybe we should let the police handle this."

Carrie looked up. "I thought you didn't believe Abel could have set this fire? The police seemed pretty sure he did."

Emma bit her lip, then gave a quick nod of her capped head, picked up a stick, and started looking.

Covered with gray ash, hands black with soot, Carrie was just about to give up the hunt when she found something. Something that split her heart down the middle.

Steelhead arrived, but before he could dismount from his motorcycle, Emma hurried to tell him Abel needed his help. She explained quickly what had happened and where Abel had been taken.

Steelhead winked at her. "Don't you worry, little muffin. I'll see what I can do."

The neighbors returned home to do their own chores after completing the work on the carriage house, but Esther and Abraham lingered and agreed to stay for dinner. When supper was ready, Carrie found Esther at the carriage house, giving Abraham, a man known for his skilled carpentry, suggestions about how to hammer the final hinges onto the gates.

"You've got the patience of a saint," Carrie whispered to Abraham as he packed up his toolbox, out of earshot of Esther.

His eyes smiled as he said, "Always good to have a supervisor."

The way he said it reminded her so much of something her father would have said that Carrie felt a sharp pang. Her father had such an easy way about him and never took offense. Not unlike Abel, she suddenly realized.

With everyone seated at the kitchen table, Abraham gave the signal to offer silent grace for the meal, just as Steelhead returned. Hanging tightly on behind him was Abel. Andy leaped up like a puppy to greet him, opening the door and bouncing down the kitchen steps. Abel wrapped an arm around Andy's shoulders and climbed the stairs to give everyone an awkward nod.

"I just wanted you all to know that I've been released. No charges." He and Steelhead stood by the door, tentatively, as if they weren't sure they would be welcomed.

"That is a great blessing," Abraham said, smiling warmly. "I could not understand why they thought you would have started a fire in your own barn, anyway."

"Carrie's barn," Abel said, glancing at Carrie. "And Andy's."

"Our barn," Yonnie interrupted. "These orchards belong to all of us."

"Sit," Abraham said, pointing to the empty chairs. "Eat with us."

Emma and Carrie rose to set places for Abel and Steelhead. Emma filled up two heaping plates of food while Carrie set the utensils at their places. Abel went to the sink to wash up. He looked at Carrie, a question in his eyes, but she turned away.

Abel and Steelhead sat down at the table and automatically bowed their heads. "Thank you, dear Jesus," Steelhead started. Emma and Carrie froze. "Thank you for setting free my brother Abel. Thank you for this fine meal made by these two fine women."

Carrie dropped her head into the palms of her hands.

"Thank you, sweet Jesus. We love you, Lord. Amen. Amen. Hallelujah." He popped his head up, grinning widely. He patted Abel on the back. "Chow time, little buddy."

Esther sat there stoney-faced, watching Steelhead. Tonight Carrie noticed that there were deep lines around her mouth and eyes, and the hair that showed from beneath her prayer cap was turning as gray as a winter day. She was still beautiful, Carrie thought, aware that her father had always thought so too. Emma, seated next to her mother, was in sharp contrast, as plain and plump as one of Yonnie's buttermilk biscuits.

Abraham smiled broadly. "So, Abel, tell us how it came to be that you were released."

Abel looked up, exchanging a glance with Steelhead. "Turns out Steelhead had seen me, during the time of the fire. So, I had an alibi, after all."

"It's the gospel truth, I did see him," Steelhead said, before shoveling a forkful of food into his mouth.

"You couldn't have thought to tell the police officers that piece of information when they asked?" Esther asked Abel.

The same thought occurred to Carrie.

"Isn't it wonderful that Abel is done with that nonsense?" Emma asked.

"Then just as Steelhead arrived, another fellow came in and said he had seen me in town yesterday afternoon. I think you all know him." Abel cast a sideways look at Carrie. "A fellow named Solomon Riehl."

Silence fell over the table. Finally, the deacon cleared his throat. "Emma, I'd like more of your wonderful chicken pot pie." He reached over to her with his empty plate. "And in a month's time, we will build a new barn. A farm is not a farm without its barn."

"So, Abel, with the workshop gone, where do you plan to live?" Esther asked, frowning.

"Right here, with us," Yonnie said, frowning right back at Esther.

Carrie put up a hand in warning. "Actually, he might prefer to stay with Steelhead for a while."

Abel kept his eyes on his plate.

"Good," Esther said, satisfied. "We should be going. Abraham, it's time for prayer." She bowed her head.

"Not yet, Esther," the deacon said.

Meekly, Esther lifted her head.

Abraham handed Esther the casserole. "Have another piece of your daughter's chicken pot pie. It's a fine dish."

"It sure is," Steelhead said as Emma's face flamed.

Esther and Abraham left soon after supper. Carrie made Andy take a bath to wash off soot and ash after being near the barn all day. The stench of sour smoke was everywhere. As she was gathering his dirty clothes to launder, she heard Yonnie's knees creak up the stairs and her door quietly close. Carrie listened for the roar of Steelhead's motorcycle to start up before she went downstairs, sure that Abel had left with him. But there he was, at the kitchen window, staring out at the place where the barn had been. He spun around when he heard her.

Carrie stiffened. "I thought I heard Steelhead leave."

Abel's smile dimmed. "He did. He, uh, took Emma out on a motorcycle ride."

Carrie's eyes went wide. Emma was starting to worry her a little.

Abel walked over to her. "Carrie, I'm sorry I wasn't here yesterday. If I had been here, the fire wouldn't have started." He looked at her bandaged hands. "Are your hands awfully sore?"

She put her hands behind her back. "Not so much. Yonnie put some ointment on them that helped."

"You believe me, don't you?" He took a step closer to her, searching her eyes. "You know I wouldn't have started the fire."

She brushed past him to start putting away the dishes that Emma had washed.

"Carrie, look at me!"

She stopped. "I know you didn't set that fire, Abel." She put the dishes down and fished something out of her apron pocket. She opened her palm—there was Veronica McCall's little black clothespin cell phone.

Abel looked puzzled. He reached out and picked up the cell phone. "Where did you find this?"

"I spent the afternoon raking through the ashes in the barn."

He turned it over in his hand. "Do you know what this means?"

"I do." Her chin lifted a notch. "I know *exactly* what it means. You're trying to protect Veronica McCall. Same way you tried to protect Daniel."

He couldn't have looked more stunned if Carrie had clubbed him on the back of the skull with a two-by-four. "Protect her?" He took a few paces around the kitchen, rubbing his jaw, thinking something out. Stopping with his hands on his hips, he said again, "You think I'm trying to *protect* Veronica?" He threw his hands up. "What, you think I'm sweet on her?"

"I've seen you in her car, kissing!"

"One time, Carrie." He held a finger in the air. "She tried kissing me that one time and I put an end to it!" He shook his head as if he couldn't believe what he was hearing. "I've been trying and trying to teach her about what it means to have a faith!"

Carrie rolled her eyes and crossed her arms tightly across her chest. "I've seen her coming out of your workshop once or twice, late at night."

"That's where I keep my Bible and books." He scratched his head. "At least, I did until the fire." He took a step closer to her and put his hands on her upper arms. "How is it everyone seems to know but you that I—"

A knock on the front door interrupted him. He sighed, dropped his arms, and went to answer it.

For a split second, Carrie worried Veronica McCall had arrived, but the visitor at the door was Grace. She followed Abel into the kitchen.

Carrie gasped when she saw her. "Your hair!" This time, it was purple.

Grace's hand flew to her hair. "What? Is it too much?"

"No, no," Abel said soothingly, pulling a chair out for Grace. "It's very nice." He flashed a warning look at Carrie to stop staring at Grace's purple hair. "Carrie, why don't you sit down? Grace said she has something she wants to tell us."

Grace tossed her bulging backpack on the kitchen table. "Dang, that's heavy. I can't stay long. But I need to show you something."

"Did you bicycle here carrying that?" Carrie asked.

"Yup," Grace said, all business. She pulled out a big steel tube from her backpack, and a stack of papers.

"What's all this?" Carrie asked.

"When I heard about the fire," Grace said, "something just kept bugging me—like stuff wasn't adding up. Yesterday afternoon, Veronica came rushing into her office. She was acting kind of odd—I mean, she acts all wound tight and freaked out a lot, but this was even more so, like she'd overdosed on sugar—talking loud and saying hello to everyone. Like she wanted everyone to know she was there. She asked me what time it was. Twice, she asked, like she wanted me to remember. Then she closed her door to make a phone call, but she was in such a tizzy she forgot to close the back door. Her office has two doors. I heard her talking to someone to report a fire burning. I could have sworn I heard her give Carrie's address. Then she made another call—I heard her say something about a convicted arsonist named Abel Miller, violating his parole." She pulled out a stack of papers. "So this afternoon, I went online and printed out the telephone bill that had yesterday's call log. Busted!" She waved the bill in the air. "She made a call to the fire department to report the fire and to the police department to tell them about Abel." She handed Carrie the bills.

Carrie and Abel exchanged a glance.

"There's more." Grace reached down and pulled out a metal tube. "These are the properties adjacent to Honor Mansion, the very ones Veronica is chomping at the bit to buy." Popping the cap, she tipped it over and out rolled a set of architectural blueprints. "You need to see these." She unrolled the blueprints on the table—plans drawn for Bonnatt Company's golf course.

"Carrie," Abel said, pointing to one section. "Look at how they've incorporated the Stoltzfuses' land."

"Where their barn was before it was burned down," Carrie said.

"Yup," Grace said. "The Stoltzfuses sold those couple of acres to Veronica."

Carrie and Abel exchanged a look. When the Stoltzfuses' barn was rebuilt, it was built closer to the house, but it was a smart thing to do. A good opportunity to move it, in fact. That original barn was so far from the house that a street ran between the house and barn. Abner and Ada had always complained about their barn's location.

"The Stoltzfuses never knew about the golf course," Grace explained. "Veronica gave them twice as much as it was worth and they wanted to help their son in Indiana buy a farm." Her cheeks went pink. "I, uh, happened to be eavesdropping when they were in Veronica's office." She pointed to another area on the blueprints. "Look here."

Grace pointed to surrounding properties, neighbors to Cider Mill Farm. "They're going to need a few other chunks of Amish farmland too." She put her finger on Cider Mill Farm's property. "Now look at your farm."

The golf course incorporated *all* of Cider Mill Farm. It was as plain as day.

"Grace, did you take these from Veronica's office?" Abel asked.

"Yup, and I need to get them back before she returns to the office later.

She's at a business dinner with Bonnatt tonight." She rolled the papers up again. "I don't know what you want to do with this information, but I knew I had to get it to you."

"Thank you, Grace," Carrie said.

Grace bit her lip. "There's one more thing." The anxious tone in her voice made Carrie and Abel look up sharply. "I'm sunk if I lose my job. I still have court fees to pay from the accident and I'm still on probation and if I get fired, then—"

"Not to worry," Abel said. "We won't involve you."

After Grace left, Abel came back into the kitchen, shaking his head.

Carrie sat at the kitchen table, leaning on her elbows. "Could this be true? Would Veronica McCall do such a thing?"

"Could and would." He sat down in the chair across from her. "The deacon said something tonight that made it all so clear. He said, 'A farm is not a farm without its barn.' Get rid of the barns and you have an easier time getting rid of the farmers." He leaned back in his chair. "She knew enough about the Amish to know that."

Abel was deep in thought, drumming his fingers on the tabletop. His fingers froze. "And someone had tipped the police off that I had done jail time for fires. It's like Veronica knew just enough to try to pin the fires on me. The police were talking about holding me for forty-eight hours—and calling my parole officer in Ohio because I would be violating parole even if they didn't press charges. In the nick of time, Steelhead came in, but they weren't too impressed with an alibi provided by another ex-con. But then Solomon Riehl and Mattie came in and the police decided two witnesses cleared me."

Mattie was with Sol? Carrie felt her mouth go dry. Emma had told Carrie she had seen Sol at Central Market, hanging around Mattie's stall, nearly every time she worked there lately.

Abel started drumming his fingers again. "But how could Veronica possibly have known why I had been in jail? I never told her any of that. I never even told her I'd *been* in jail."

Distracted, Carrie was only half listening, then the full sense of what Abel just said struck her. "Oh Abel, I told her!" She swallowed hard, and told him about the day in Veronica's office when she asked her to look up

Abel Miller on the computer. "I'm sorry. I had a dreadful feeling about that as I left her office."

He raised an eyebrow as he listened, then gave a slight shake of his head. "It's not a secret. It would've been easy for her to find information."

Abel and Carrie disagreed about what to do next. They went back and forth, but Carrie wouldn't budge. "I won't do it, Abel. It's not our way to seek vengeance."

"I'm talking about justice, not vengeance."

"How many times have we said the prayer, 'Not my will but thine be done'?"

Abel threw up his hands. His voice had an edge of impatience to it. "Carrie, if we don't stop her, she'll just do it again. You saw those blueprints. She's after more land. How many more people have to lose their barns?"

Carrie knew he was right; Veronica McCall wouldn't quit. She stood up and went to gaze out the kitchen window, crossing her arms. "It's not our way, Abel. We don't pick and choose how and when we trust in God. We either trust him or we don't." She surprised herself, saying those words, but she knew she believed them to be true.

Abel leaned forward, kneading his strong hands together. He was quiet for a full minute, and then he rubbed his hand over his face. He stood and took a few strides toward her, his hands hooked on his hips. "Du machst mich ferhoodled." *You make me crazy.*

Her eyes met his and held just a beat too long, and before she realized what was happening, he leaned toward her and his lips, so soft and warm, found hers. She thought she might be dreaming, even as she felt the grip of his strong arms slip around her waist. He kissed her with such sweetness it was almost unbearable, a kiss that lasted forever and was over too soon.

Abel pulled away first and looked into her eyes, whispering, "I was trying to tell you something before Grace arrived: why is it everyone seems to know how I feel about you . . . except for you?"

Just as he was about to kiss her again, she heard Steelhead's motorcycle. By the time Emma had climbed off the motorcycle and came up the stairs to the kitchen door, Abel was already opening it for her. Her eyes darted from Abel's to Carrie's, sensing the tension in the air, as if they were angry.

"What's happened? What did Abel say?"

Abel's lips tightened. He adjusted the brim of his black felt hat. "Nothing.

217

Nothing at all." He paused at the door, before giving a nod to Carrie. "It's been a long day. Sleep well, Carrie."

Carrie closed the door behind him. She could still feel Abel's lips on hers, his arms holding her tightly. Slowly, she turned around, then did a double take.

"Emma? Wu is dei Kapp?" *Where is your cap?*

15

a few days after the fire, Carrie took Andy and Yonnie in the buggy over to the Stolztfuses'. It was a warm spring day and Andy was eager to see their new colt, born just a day before. After lunch, Ada Stoltzfus shooed Carrie off.

"You go on home. I'm sure you have lots to do. I'll have Abner bring Yonnie and Andy back later today, after we have a good visit." She handed Carrie a few jars of homemade raspberry jam. Carrie smiled, accepting her kindness.

Carrie was eager to go; she had plenty of chores waiting for her back at Cider Mill Farm. She saw Abel working in the carriage house, so she left Old-Timer tied to the hitching post and hurried to the house to start dinner. Ever since that kiss in the kitchen, she had been taking pains to avoid being alone with Abel. As she hung up her bonnet on the peg, she heard a strange noise coming from Emma's room. Cautiously, she tiptoed upstairs and opened Emma's door. In the bed were Emma and Steelhead. Carrie backed up and knocked into the wall. Steelhead and Emma looked up, horrified.

Carrie ran downstairs and outside and burst through the open door of the carriage house, shouting Abel's name.

He dropped Old-Timer's water bucket and spun around fast. "What's happened?"

Carrie was breathing hard, in such a state that she couldn't speak, which only alarmed Abel more.

"What's wrong?"

219

She put the palm of her hand against her pounding heart, as if to quiet it. She couldn't move, couldn't breathe. "It's . . . it's . . . Steelhead is in . . . bed!"

Abel looked at her as if she were speaking another language.

She took a gulpy breath. "With Emma!"

The kitchen door banged open and out flew Steelhead, running toward the carriage house. He had dressed hastily and forgotten his shirt and shoes altogether. He was still putting one arm into a coat.

"Carrie!" Steelhead shouted, hopping on the gravel driveway as if it were made of hot coals. "It's not what you think!"

She whirled around to avoid looking at Steelhead's hairy chest, embroidered with another large tattoo. "Steelhead, what have you done?" she asked, her voice breaking. "How could you do such a thing?"

"I couldn't help it," Steelhead sputtered. "Emma is, well, she's like no other woman I've ever met."

Carrie spun around, then covered her eyes. "Zip your coat!" Muffled from behind her hands, she asked, "How could you take . . . advantage . . . of my sister?"

Steelhead put up his hands in warning. "I didn't! I would never hurt Emma." He took a deep breath. "I did right by her. We got married. We got our license, the other day, at the county courthouse." He gave Abel a guilty look. "We waited three days, like the law says to do, then this morning we went to the Amish-Mennonite preacher in town, to get married. Proper-like. In the eyes of God."

Carrie reached a hand against the beam, feeling as if she was nearly going to pass out. Abel's arm encircled her waist, supporting her, as he led her to sit on a hay bale.

Steelhead came closer. "I love her, Carrie. From the minute I saw her, I knew. This was the only girl in the world for me."

Carrie looked at Abel. "Did Yonnie give him her tea?"

Abel shook his head. "I don't think so. He's telling the truth. He's been crazy about her since the day he met her."

Carrie's shoulders sagged. "Steelhead, Emma is . . . she's Amish!"

Steelhead nodded. "I know. I know. We have a few things to figure out."

"A few things to figure out?" Carrie put her hands against her head; she couldn't believe what she was hearing. "She's broken her vows to the church. She'll lose everything."

Steelhead looked uncomfortable, but unconvinced. "We'll work it out." He crossed his large arms over his chest. "I've never felt like I belonged to anyone before meeting Emma. The times I've spent sitting in your kitchen, talking to her, getting to know her, I knew—we both knew—we belonged together."

Carrie stood to face Steelhead, astounded. "If you truly loved her, *why* would you . . . *how* could you . . . take everything meaningful from her?"

Steelhead looked dazed, stumped. He scratched his head, as if he hadn't thought that deeply in a long time. Slowly, he turned to head back to the house, then stopped. "We were going to tell you, Carrie. In fact, Emma was coming to tell you what we'd done, but that barn fire kind of threw us for a loop. Then Emma didn't want to tell you, on account of that little police problem with Abel, then Esther was here . . ." Steelhead snorted. "And she's a little scary. Even for me." He zipped up his coat, as if he suddenly realized he was barechested. "We came back to tell you today, but when we got here, no one was around, and then . . . well, our passion just overtook us."

Carrie clapped her hands over her ears as Abel made a cutting motion at his throat, trying to warn Steelhead to stop talking.

Steelhead dropped his head. "Won't you at least come and talk to Emma? She's awful upset you found us like that. You mean the world to her, Carrie."

As Steelhead turned and left, Carrie plopped back on the hay bale. "Abel Miller, did you know about this?"

An awkward look covered Abel's face. She knew that guilty look on his face meant he was hiding something. Carrie fixed her gaze on him and sure enough, he just started spilling.

"I went to City Hall to try and stop them, Carrie. I knew what they had planned and I felt responsible, bringing Steelhead here. They were determined to go through with it. Emma was just as determined as Steelhead. But it wasn't my place to tell you." He paused. "That's why I couldn't tell you where I'd been."

She crossed her arms, still glaring at him. "Just how many more secrets are you keeping?"

He stiffened. "Don't go throwing stones, Carrie. You know as well as anybody how secrets get started."

She looked at him, puzzled.

"Planning to leave with Solomon Riehl was no small secret."

Her cheeks flushed, stung by his words. Yet he wasn't wrong. How many times did she lecture Andy about the seed of deceit beginning with an untruth? How often did she remind him that an untruth grows, so quickly, so quickly, into a lie?

For a long time, neither of them spoke. Then Abel sat down next to her on the hay bale, so close she could smell the faint scent of detergent on his clothes. "Aw, Carrie, she loves him. He loves her."

"Her way of life is as different from his as cheese from the moon. It isn't as simple as falling in love, Abel."

"Maybe it is," he said. "Maybe it should be."

Then a thought, a ray of hope, cut through the fog. "Maybe . . . maybe Steelhead could go Amish."

Abel looked at her as if she had lost her mind. "And give up his motorcycle?"

"A motorcycle is easier to give up than a family." Her voice dropped to a whisper. "Would it be so awful bad to go Amish?"

He shrugged. "Expecting an English guy, especially one like Steelhead, to go Amish would be, well, it would be like asking Schtarm to be a buggy horse."

She covered her face with her hands.

He pulled her hands away from her face. "Would it be such a terrible thing to go English?"

Carrie looked him straight in the eyes. "You know the answer to that. She'll lose everything she holds dear. She'll be shunned, like she doesn't even exist anymore." She shuddered.

"So it's better that she end up alone, or with an Amish fellow she doesn't even love, than marry a man she does love? They share the same faith, Carrie, the same beliefs. They just express them in a different way."

Carrie knew he wasn't talking about Emma and Steelhead anymore, but she hadn't meant to get into that particular territory. She still hadn't sorted it all out. Each time her mind drifted to that kiss, which was often . . . oh, that sweet, sweet kiss . . . it made her feel lightheaded and her stomach all dizzy, just like she felt as a girl when she swung too high on a tree swing.

She pulled her hands out of his and stood to leave. "Maybe that's what the will of God might be for her."

He stood, facing her. "Is that really how it seems to you?"

"For the Amish, that's the way it is."

They stared at each other, a standoff. The silence between them was as thick as blackstrap molasses.

"She hasn't lost everything." Abel picked up Old-Timer's water bucket. "She has him."

The sound of wheels churning up gravel made them both turn their heads toward the road. Esther and Abraham rolled up the driveway in a wagon. Seated between them was Yonnie. Andy sat in the back on top of a bale of hay.

"Abraham brought some hay for your animals. On the way, we stopped for pecan pie at the Stolztfuses' stand and saw Yonnie and Andy, so we gave them a lift," Esther said, helping Yonnie ease out of the buggy. "Ada insisted we bring a pie for you too."

Carrie glanced at the house and saw Emma peering out the kitchen window, a stricken look on her round face. Then Steelhead came up behind her. A cold chill shuddered through Carrie.

The next day, Abel found Carrie hanging sheets on the clothesline. He picked up some clothespins and handed them to her. "Carrie, we still have a problem we need to take care of."

She glanced at him and took a clothespin out of her mouth to speak. "Which problem would *that* be, Abel? My sister, marrying your English friend? Or my barn burning down?"

Ignoring her, he handed her a wet sheet. "I think we need to go to the police and tell them you found Veronica McCall's telephone at the fire site."

She pinned the sheet to the clothesline. "No."

"Why not? What's wrong with just telling them?"

"Vengeance belongs only to God."

"Who's talking about vengeance? I'm talking about justice."

"I won't judge another person. It's not our way."

"Carrie, I'm just talking about telling the truth." He rubbed his face, exasperated. Then he dropped his hands and hooked them on his hips. He was studying her as if he didn't quite know what to make of her. "Is it so wrong to want to stop her from doing this to anyone else?" He took a step closer to her and lifted her chin so that she would look at him. "Is it, Carrie?"

Abel's words rankled her. As Carrie went about her chores that day, she prayed to God about what to do with Veronica McCall. By early afternoon, an idea came together in her mind. She felt in her heart it was the right thing to do, that God had given her this plan, but she knew she had to do it alone. She wanted to keep Abel out of this. This was between Veronica McCall and her. So she waited until she knew Abel had gone birding with Andy. She threw on her cape, put the black clothespin cell phone in her apron pocket, and hitched up the buggy to go to Honor Mansion.

When she arrived, she stood at the open door of Veronica McCall's office. "A farm is not a farm without its barn," Carrie said, in a voice so steady it could not be her own.

Veronica's eyes lit up. "So you're ready to sell?"

Carrie sat down in the chair across from her. "That's not what I meant. Do you remember I told you that Amish proverb, the very first time we met?" She placed the black clothespin cell phone on the desk in front of Veronica.

Veronica's eyes went wide in shock. Then she got up and closed the door to her office. "Where did you find this?"

"In the remains of the barn at Cider Mill Farm. I spent the day raking through the ashes. Just when I was about to give up, I found that."

She reached across the desk to grab it, but Carrie closed her fist around it. "I must have left it there when I was visiting Abel."

Carrie fixed her eyes on her.

"What?" Veronica asked. She snorted. "You couldn't possibly be insinuating that I set that fire."

Carrie held her gaze, then Veronica dropped her eyes. "You can't prove anything. A lost telephone earpiece does not implicate me."

"No, not alone, but a number of things put together do." Out of her apron pocket, Carrie fished the page about Abel's arrest that she had printed for her, months ago. She unfolded it and set it before Veronica. "It even has the date that you printed it." She pointed to the top of the page.

"That's not much to go on."

"Your phone records show that you made calls to the fire department about fifteen minutes after the Stoltzfuses' fire had been set and then fifteen minutes after the Cider Mill Farm fire."

A stain of color spread across Veronica's sharp cheekbones. "That's outrageous! How dare you accuse me of such lies!"

"Not lies." She pulled out both sets of phone bills that Grace had given her, one from Veronica's cell phone company, the other from Honor Mansion's telephone service.

"Where did you get these?" Veronica asked, eyes narrowed in suspicion.

Carrie chose to deflect that. "There's one more thing. Yonnie saw your car at the house around three o'clock. She was in the kitchen and saw you go into the barn. Then she fell asleep and didn't see you leave." She looked at Veronica. "But she did place you at the site, at just the right time. And the police said a woman gave an anonymous tip about the fire and about Abel Miller setting it. So even though one piece of evidence alone isn't much, put it all together and it's a convincing picture. Like a puzzle, all filled in."

Veronica stared at Carrie, furious, bested. "What is it you want?"

Carrie took the paper and folded it up again. "Nothing."

Veronica raised an eyebrow in suspicion.

"It's not my place to judge you, Veronica McCall. I've made plenty of mistakes myself." She took a deep breath and looked Veronica straight in the eyes. "I forgive you. For burning my barn."

The only evidence of nervousness that Veronica showed was of a pencil, twiddling back and forth in her hand. Other than that, she remained still.

"But if anything else were to happen, I will go to the police. It wouldn't be right of me to let you continue to hurt people. Innocent people." Carrie slipped that paper back into her apron for safekeeping, then lifted her eyes to meet Veronica's. "I forgive you, but I don't trust you."

Veronica stood and walked to the window, crossing her arms tightly against her chest.

Carrie rose to leave and was almost to the door when she turned back. "I just don't understand why you would harm Abel. He's been so good to you."

"Sure you do." Veronica spun around. "You're nobody's fool, Carrie."

As Carrie's hand turned the door handle, Veronica's voice dropped to a whisper, almost a hiss. "He treats you like spun sugar."

Keeping her hand on the handle, Carrie lifted her chin a notch. "I know."

Veronica's eyes hardened. "I don't think I've given you enough credit."

And I might have given you too much, Carrie thought as she closed the door behind her.

When Carrie returned to the farmhouse from Honor Mansion, she found Emma and Steelhead in the kitchen, seated at the table, looking solemn. Emma's suitcase was at her side.

Carrie took a deep breath. "Where's Andy and Abel?" she asked, hoping to stall what she knew was coming.

Steelhead answered. "Abel is down in the carriage house with the little dude."

Carrie looked at Emma's nervous hands, wringing her handkerchief. "Have you told Yonnie?"

Emma wiped her eyes with her handkerchief. "She's upstairs, resting. She said she'll miss me, but she won't be pointing a long bony finger in judgment at me. She said that she's a sinner too, of the worst kind, and she's too old to worry about shunning. She said I'd be getting plenty of that from . . . the others."

From Esther, Yonnie meant. Carrie hung her cape and bonnet on the peg. "Does Abel know you're leaving today?"

Steelhead nodded. "Just so you know, Abel tried to talk us out of it."

"So he said." Carrie pulled out a chair and sat down.

"This morning we fixed up a back room in the carriage house for Abel to stay."

"Where are you and Emma going to live?"

Emma blew her nose loudly. "Over in town. I'm going to start a quilt shop with my savings from work at Central Market." She looked at Carrie with pleading eyes. "You could stop by. Yonnie said she would come."

Carrie's eyes dropped to her lap. She wasn't sure how to answer her. She needed time to sort it out.

Tears leaked down Emma's cheeks. "And Seymour"—she nodded her head toward Steelhead—"found a job as a sanitation engineer."

"Seymour?" Carrie asked, trying to hold back a grin in spite of the seriousness of the moment. She looked at Steelhead. "Your name is Seymour?"

Steelhead looked sheepish. "Yeah." He squeezed Emma's hand. "Carrie, I want you to know that I love Emma and just want her to be happy."

Carrie pressed her hands against her temples. "If you love her so much, then why won't you go Amish?"

Emma and Steelhead exchanged a glance.

"I offered," Steelhead said. "She said no."

Carrie looked at her, stunned. "Emma?"

"You know it's nearly impossible for the English to go Amish, Carrie. Steelhead would be miserable being Plain. Look at how our Abel is struggling. He's been living with Plain folks for years, off and on, and he can hardly string two words together of the dialect to make any sense. I can't do that to Seymour." Emma blew her nose. "Oh Carrie, this is my chance at love. A real, true, heartfire love. You know what I'm talking about."

Carrie did. She knew.

Emma squeezed her hands together. "I hope you'll forgive me. I know I've disappointed you, but I feel peace in my heart that I'm not disappointing God." Emma took a letter out of her apron pocket and handed it to Carrie. "Would you give this to Mother?"

Carrie closed her eyes. "No, Emma."

"Please, Carrie, please." Emma was nearly begging, her voice teary.

Carrie shook her head. "I can't. Esther should hear this from you. She deserves that."

"She's right, cupcake," Steelhead said. "It's just what I've been telling you. We'll go right over and tell her together."

Emma looked as if she was about to face the firing squad. As Carrie handed the envelope back to her, Emma grabbed her for a hug. Then Steelhead wrapped his large arms around the both of them, squeezing the breath out of them before releasing them.

"We'd better hit the road, lambchop," he said to Emma.

As they climbed onto the motorcycle, Abel and Andy came out of the barn to say goodbye. Just as Steelhead started the engine, Abel pulled Andy by the shoulders to get him out of the way. Emma took off her prayer cap and her apron and handed them to Carrie.

Her eyes blurry with tears, Carrie said, "I'm going to keep these for you, Emma, just in case you change your mind. You can *always* change your mind and repent and be forgiven by the church. Remember that." Then she gave Emma one last hug.

Carrie, Abel, and Andy followed the motorcycle down the driveway and watched it roar down the road until it disappeared from sight.

"You okay?" Abel asked Carrie.

Carrie looked at the cap and apron in her hands. "She's my favorite sister."

Abel smiled. "I know," he said, slipping her a handkerchief.

Then a thought jolted Carrie and stopped her tears. Even if she felt confused and heartsick about shunning her own sister, she knew Esther wouldn't think twice. "I'm guessing Esther will be rounding the corner into this driveway with a new helper by sundown."

Color drained out of Abel's face. Carrie felt the same way.

Andy, who had seemed stoic about Emma's leaving, glared at Abel accusingly. "I suppose you'll be leaving next."

Abel looked taken back. "What makes you say that?"

"Emma told me you fixed it so the house belongs to Carrie and me."

Abel and Carrie exchanged a glance.

"Yeah. That's what I figured," Andy said, running off before Abel could answer.

Within a few hours after Emma left Cider Mill Farm, Esther's buggy clattered into the driveway. Seated next to her was Clara, a cousin thrice removed, tall, thin, and unhappy. "Clara will help you now," Esther said in a voice that had a vinegar tang to it.

Scarcely nodding at Carrie, Clara took her bag up to Emma's empty room and started to unpack.

"She's the one who's allergic to everything, isn't she?" Carrie asked miserably. "Maybe I could find someone else."

"For now, she stays," Esther said, casting a mutinous look at Abel.

Carrie took a deep breath. "I just found out about Emma, Esther, same as you."

Esther stiffened her spine at the mention of Emma's name. Adhering to the Ordnung, she would never again utter her name. "But he knew." She gave a brief nod in Abel's direction.

"Yes, ma'am, I knew," Abel said.

Arms akimbo, Esther glared at Abel. "This is your doing. Your English Bible, your talk about God being bigger than being Amish. Emma—" she shuddered, "—she told me about the things you've said. You turned her thinking inside out."

That wasn't true, Carrie knew that. Abel looked pained, but he didn't defend himself nor did he back away. He just let Esther say her piece.

"And how long until you convince my Carrie to leave?" Esther glanced over at Andy, standing next to Abel. "And take my Andy with her?" And then, to Carrie's shock, Esther's eyes started to well up with tears. Embarrassed, she turned to leave.

Carrie's heart swelled with an unexpected softness toward Esther. In her own brittle way, she realized, Esther loved them. She had lived her life hanging on to tight rules and didn't know what to do when those rules didn't work.

Carrie ran to her buggy to stop her before she left. "Andy and I aren't leaving, Esther. We're staying right here. I won't take him from you. You can count on that."

With one leg hoisted on the buggy step, Esther stopped and gave a quick nod. She reached a hand out to grasp Carrie's and gave it a light squeeze. Then, she lifted herself up onto the buggy seat, her face all stern and stiff again, and slapped the horse's reins.

Carrie watched her go, realizing she had just come to a final decision. She turned around to face Abel. Their eyes locked, filled with unspoken thoughts, then his gaze fell away from hers and he returned to the barn.

A week to the day after Emma left, Yonnie didn't come downstairs for breakfast when she usually did. Carrie made a cup of her favorite hot tea and sent Andy upstairs to give it to her. Not a minute later, she heard him scream.

Carrie hurried upstairs to Yonnie's bedside and could see that she was in trouble. Her breath sounds were labored, rattling, spasmodic. Her skin was cool and ashen blue. Carrie reached for her hand, the skin thin as tissue.

Yonnie grasped Carrie's hand. "I need . . . Abel." Her face was pale and tired and tense.

It was the tension on her face that worried Carrie the most. She knew

Yonnie was dying; she recognized the signs. But she'd never seen an Amish person pass with their face tense and troubled, only with peace.

"Get Abel," Carrie told Andy. "He's in the carriage house." She turned to Yonnie. "Hush, now. Don't talk. Save your strength. He'll be here soon."

Yonnie's labored breathing marked time in the somber room until a door slammed and Abel rushed up the stairs, two at a time. He stopped so abruptly at the doorjamb that Andy, following close behind, nearly ran into him.

"Should I get an ambulance?" Abel asked Carrie.

"Nee, nee," Yonnie whispered. "No hospital. I need to make something right before I pass."

Noticing how frightened Andy looked, Carrie said quietly, "Go milk the cow."

The boy's wide-eyed gaze jerked to the window that faced the carriage house, then back to her. "But I already did."

"Go," Carrie said firmly, pointing to the door. "Take Clara with you." She shut the door behind him, whisper-soft, as Abel knelt beside Yonnie's bed, holding her hands in his.

Yonnie's voice came out in little puffs. "My sin . . . is like a cancer that spread and choked our family."

Abel gently kissed her hands. "Yonnie, please—"

"Let me say it." She closed her eyes as if gathering strength. "The kerosene, contaminated with gasoline. Daniel didn't do it. He thought he did, but he didn't." She took a deep breath. "I did it."

He raised his head, startled. "You? But how?"

Tears leaked out of the corners of Yonnie's eyes. "I needed gasoline for the washing machine."

Abel stared at her, his eyes wide open, unblinking. "Yonnie, what are you getting at?"

"I found a red can in the barn with some gasoline still in it. I was coming back to the house and heard the phone ringing in the shed." She took another deep breath, gathering strength. "Cousin Miriam was on the phone, calling about Daniel and Katie's wedding. We gabbed a long time."

Abel's expression on his face grew absolutely still.

"I must have put the can on top of the containers when I picked up the phone. When I hung up with Miriam, I noticed the can was on its side. But nothing had spilled. Oh Abel, I was sure nothing spilled out."

He was silent for a moment, then quietly said, "The spilled gas would have evaporated."

Yonnie was panting, sucking in great gasps of air like she was drowning. She pressed her hands to her cheeks. "Lieber Gott, I didn't know what I'd done. Not till later that day, after Daniel had come back and delivered the kerosene to the neighbors. And then, the fires." She shuddered. "By the time I realized what had happened, the police were all over the farm. I was so frightened. That night, I tried to tell Eli. I tried, but I couldn't. And then it was too late."

"Yonnie . . ."

She put up a hand, heavy and swollen at the knuckles, to stop him. "Things started happening so fast. There wasn't time to think. Oh, to lose Eli's Lena, and Daniel's Katie, all at once. Four funerals, four funerals in one week. And next thing I knew, you and Daniel and Eli were standing before the judge. The longer I waited, the harder it got to tell the truth." She drew in a draught of air. "And then off you took yourself to jail. And still I didn't tell. I let my sweet Daniel think he was responsible." She gave out a gasp, as if in pain. "Oh Abel, I am the worst of sinners. The Lord God will punish me."

Abel dropped his head. His fists were clenched tight, but he remained silent. Carrie could see the pulse beating in his neck, fast and hard.

"Tell her, Abel," Carrie said softly but firmly, kneeling down beside him, resting her hand on his back. "Tell her you forgive her. You've got to let her know."

Time was running out. Yonnie's confession had sapped her energy and she was fading. Carrie saw the signs of approaching death—skin as thin as crepe paper, shallow gasps, a slowing pulse.

"Abel, we know, both of us, how secrets get started. You said it yourself . . . that we have no business throwing stones. Don't let her down the way . . . ," Carrie's voice broke on the words, ". . . don't disappoint her the way I let my Daniel down. Tell her you forgive her."

Her words fell into an empty silence. Slowly Abel lifted his head and Carrie thought he was going to speak, but then he dropped his chin to his chest.

Somebody had to do *something*. The only prayer Carrie ever said aloud was the Lord's Prayer, but she felt the need to speak what was on her heart, like Abel always did, as if the Lord God himself was standing beside her.

Carrie placed one hand over Yonnie's, and one hand over Abel's. "Um, dear God in heaven, none of us deserve your forgiveness, but still, we're asking for it. We're hoping for it. Please have mercy on our Yonnie. She made a mistake, a dreadful mistake, and she's sorry. She's so very sorry. Please, God, have mercy. Amen."

As soon as Carrie finished, Yonnie inhaled deeply, as if filling up her lungs, then exhaled, a sigh of great relief.

One moment Yonnie was there, and the next she was not.

Abel fell on his grandmother's still chest and wept for all that had died with her, heartbreaking cries that Carrie knew would heal him in the end.

If only Daniel could have heard this truth, she thought, stroking Abel's back. If only he could have wept like Abel was weeping. If only Daniel could have known that grief was meant to heal.

16

Abel and Andy, quiet and solemn, went birding for the afternoon. As soon as the undertaker arrived for Yonnie's body, Carrie told Clara she'd be gone for a long while, and she went straight to Mattie's house. If Yonnie's passing had taught her anything, it was not to wait on important things.

One of the Zook boys opened the kitchen door when he saw Carrie marching up to it.

"If you're looking for Mattie, she's upstairs," he said, eating a sandwich.

Carrie took the stairs two at a time, just as she had when they were girls. She found Mattie in her bedroom, whipping a sheet in the air, letting it float over the bed. Standing across the bed from her, Carrie pulled the sheet taut, tucking it into the corners.

"Yonnie died this morning."

Mattie froze. Her eyes went wide with shock. Slowly, she sat down on top of the bed.

Carrie sat next to her and told her about Yonnie's confession, choking up as she spoke about Daniel. Mattie listened carefully, wiping away tears with a handkerchief.

"I need to go, Mattie, there's so much to do to get ready for Yonnie's viewing. But first, there's something I have to ask you."

"Anything," Mattie said. "How can I help?"

"I need to find Sol. How do I get in touch with him?"

Mattie closed her eyes and moved her lips silently, as if whispering a prayer, then opened them as she slipped off the bed. "I'll get his address."

Carrie took the bus into Lancaster to Sol's apartment. She had never been to that particular part of town before; she felt apprehensive, but she knew she needed to see him. She held the piece of paper that Mattie had written on and looked for the apartment number on it. She knocked on 13B and took a step back. Sol opened the door, looking as if he had just walked in the door from work, still in blue jeans and a dirty T-shirt and work boots.

For a long moment, he blinked a few times, as if he thought he was dreaming. Then he swallowed, and opened wide the door. "Carrie, come in."

Carrie looked around the dingy apartment. She thought she saw cockroaches scurry out of an empty pizza box.

"Do you want to sit down?" Sol asked tentatively, tucking his shirt into his blue jeans, looking around to see if there was an empty place to sit.

She shook her head. "No. I need to get back soon. I just came to tell you something."

His eyes flew to meet hers.

"You asked me to forgive you," she said, her voice shaking. "You asked me several times. I'm sorry I didn't offer it to you." She folded her hands against her stomach. "It was wrong of me to hold on to that anger. It hurt you and it hurt me and it wasn't fair to Daniel. And it just . . . it's no way to live." She looked up at him. "I forgive you. I'm not mad at you anymore. That's all. That's all I came to say."

Sol's eyes started to swim. "I don't know what to do, Carrie. Tell me. Tell me which way to turn." He looked as if his very soul ached, as if he had finally come to the end of burnt-out solitude.

In all the years she had known Sol, she had never seen him look helpless. Her every memory of him was marked by his sure smile and his confident way of handling whatever life threw at him. He looked so hurt, so frightened and broken, and she couldn't bear it. She felt something turn over in her chest.

"All that I can tell you is that I'm not afraid of God anymore. There's peace in my heart. I don't feel God's finger wagging at me. I had that part of knowing God all mixed up. But the past is the past. What's done is done. I don't want you feeling bad about it. I'm grateful for the life God has given me." She looked deeply into his eyes, hoping he understood.

Sol reached out for her hand. Carrie smiled, a sweet conciliation, and put her hand in his.

Within a few days, a funeral service was held for Yonnie. Emma and Steelhead came to the cemetery, standing at a distance, on the edge. Carrie noticed that Emma still wore Plain clothes but her prayer cap was absent. Carrie exchanged a smile with her, but she didn't leave the graveside to go speak to her as Abel did. Emma was happy, Abel said. She wanted Carrie to know she was happy. Seeing her made Carrie's heart ache; she missed her sorely.

Afterward, back at the house, Carrie carried an empty plate to the kitchen to refill with cookies. She thought of Yonnie eating cookies for breakfast and felt a wave of grief, missing her quirky ways. It saddened her that Yonnie had waited so long to set things straight. Maybe, at the very end, people need the truth to be known. Abel was right, the truth did set people free. If only Yonnie had told the truth to set Daniel free. Yonnie's secret had kept Daniel in a prison, of sorts.

Abraham lingered after others left to return to their farms for chores. "Would you have a moment, Carrie?" the deacon asked her as she handed him his coat. He gave her a warm smile.

Carrie threw a shawl over her shoulders and the two went outside.

"Shall we walk to the orchards? They're in bloom, aren't they?" he asked, knowing full well they were. "Springtime is a testament to the goodness of the Lord. He maketh all things new." He clasped his hands behind his back as he walked, looking so very content. "It's been over a year now since Daniel passed."

Carrie nodded. "It was a year on March 18."

"Hard to understand why the Lord God took such a young man as he did, but it's not for us to question God's ways, is it?"

"No."

A soft, strong breeze swept up through the trees, scattering a confetti of apple blossom petals down on them. He stopped and cupped his ear. "Do you hear that mourning dove call out, Carrie?"

She listened for the familiar cooing sound.

"Did you know that some birds use the nests of other species? Oftentimes a mourning dove will use an old robin's nest to raise her family—a nest that is a lot sturdier and more secure than her own."

The deacon kept walking along in that slow, thoughtful gait of his. "Great horned owls have even taken over crows' nests. There's a powerful instinct God put in nature to keep life going." He stopped and looked at the curtain of flower blossoms that covered the trees, quiet for a long time.

Suddenly, Carrie realized that he had been praying the whole time he was talking, his head tilted to the heavens, as if including the Lord God in this conversation.

"He put it in humans too. The ability to love again. Not to remain so tied to the past that we can't keep living."

He started walking back toward the farmhouse. "I had a visitor yesterday. A young man. Said he was ready to start instructions so he could be baptized in the fall." The deacon fished out his handkerchief from his pants pocket and blew his nose loudly, then put it back in his pocket. "I can feel the Lord God's pleasure when a young fella is ready to make that decision." He took his hat off and rubbed the indentation on his hair that his hat had made. "Of course, I always ask the young fellas—each one, I ask—'now, son, you wouldn't be making this decision because you're sweet on an Amish girl, would you?'" He put his hat back on. "Why do you think I ask that question of the fellas, Carrie?"

She knew how important it was to have pure motives for baptism. She had struggled with it herself. "Otherwise, one day he might regret the decision. Maybe even resent that girl."

He nodded. "That's right. So I asked him, straight off. Know what this fella said?"

She tilted her head, curious.

"He said he's been struggling a long time, a real long time, about whether he should be baptized in the Amish church." The deacon chuckled. "He said that he loved the Lord God with all his heart, soul, and mind. Being Amish came after that. But he wanted me to know that he did love an Amish girl. He prayed about it, and God finally gave him peace. He thought God understood."

Suddenly, as understanding flooded Carrie's mind, her heart felt too big for her chest.

The deacon nodded. "So I told this young fella, as long as he knew that God came first, above all else, then I would approve him for baptism. Because that's the most important thing of all, to know that God comes first." He took a few steps forward, then stopped to wait for Carrie, a smile lighting his eyes. "Just exactly what I told him."

Walking back toward the house, they finished the rest of their talk. An important talk.

The following week, at first light, teams of men arrived at Carrie's farm, hauling in beams and boards and wooden pegs. By midmorning, wagons with women and children arrived, loaded with hampers of food. When Carrie saw Esther's buggy, she hurried to greet her and help her down. Esther gave her a thin smile, rusty from disuse.

As Carrie watched everyone working on her behalf, she felt flooded with gratitude. Watching the barn rise before her gave a catch in her heart. These were her people, her family. She almost sensed her father's pleasure, as real as the sun shining. Her mind drifted to Daniel too, wondering what he would think about this beautiful new barn. She found thinking of him didn't cause the sorrow that it used to. She gave thanks to God for bringing Daniel to her, and her to Daniel.

By late afternoon, nails had been gathered up in brown paper bags and hammers tucked beneath the bench seats of buggies. Carrie left Esther and Clara in the kitchen, cleaning out the Tupperware to return to the women who'd brought the food.

She gazed at the new barn, proud and tall against the cerulean sky, the freshly sawn boards still raw and yellow. Inside, she found Abel and Andy examining the posts and rafters. Carrie stood in the center and peered up at the thick beams that crossed over her head, inhaling the fragrance of new wood.

Andy climbed up to the loft and tossed a handful of sawdust on Abel's head. Carrie laughed—it covered his dark hair like a snowfall. He brushed it off, grinning.

"What are you thinking?" he asked her as she turned in a circle, soaking up the sight of the new barn.

"I was thinking that everyone I know has something at stake in this barn. The women brought the food, the men brought the wood and supplies, all of my neighbors gave the gift of their hard work. There's a little part of everyone here." She wrapped her arms around herself, deeply satisfied. "It's a fine barn, Abel."

Andy started climbing down the ramp, then decided to jump off, midway, but as soon as he hit the floor he doubled over, clutching his foot in pain. He had landed on a hammer that had been left behind, and the sharp edge sliced into his heel.

Carrie crouched down and pulled out a handkerchief to mop up the blood seeping out of the wound. "Why are you running around barefoot, Andy? You know better!"

Abel bent down to examine the cut. "That's pretty deep. It's going to need stitches."

Carrie took Andy's hand and placed it against the wound. Straightening up, she said, "Abel, would you mind getting the buggy ready? I'll need to take him into the emergency room." She rubbed her face with her hands. "Just the other day, I realized Andy hadn't needed an infusion of Factor IX in months and months."

"I'll go with you," Abel said.

"So will I," Esther said, standing at the open barn door.

Abraham peered around her shoulder. "I'll come too."

Carrie looked at Esther, stunned. Esther had never gone with her father or Andy to the hospital when they needed attention. Not once.

Abel smiled. "That would be nice, Esther."

Andy's eyes went wide. "But if she comes that means I can't watch television," he whispered to Carrie, who gave him a look that read, "Too bad."

Abel went down to the carriage house to get the horse. Carrie dragged the tongue of the buggy to help him hitch the horse. As Abel backed the horse into the buggy traces, Carrie looked up in surprise.

"Abel Miller, bist du narrisch?" *Are you crazy?* "You've got the wrong horse."

Abel shook his head, eyes fixed on fastening the buckles to Schtarm's bridle. "I've been working with Schtarm. He thinks he's finally ready to be a buggy horse."

Carrie raised her eyebrows. "He thinks so? Or knows so? Because I'm not climbing in a buggy with a runaway horse."

Abel finished clasping the last buckle, then turned to her. "He knows. He's ready."

As Abel went to the barn to pick up Andy, Abraham approached Carrie, waiting by the buggy. "Abel has been bringing Schtarm to my farm for the last few weeks. We've picked up where Daniel started, getting that horse buggy broke." He helped Carrie up. "I think Schtarm has finally worked out all the things that were troubling him." He covered Carrie's hands with his big, worn ones and gave them a squeeze. "You know, about being a buggy horse."

Carrie nodded, knowing exactly what he meant.

In the emergency room of the hospital, Andy's heel was stitched up while he was given another infusion of Factor IX. Abraham kept Andy amused with stories about his boyhood. Esther seemed amused too, Carrie noticed, wondering if something sweet was brewing between Abraham and her. Abel offered to get coffee for everyone, so Carrie walked with him to the cafeteria.

Abel bought the coffees and pointed to an empty table in the crowded room. "Let's sit for a minute, since Andy has company."

"I still can't get over having Esther here," Carrie said, pulling a chair out.

Abel nodded in agreement. "God is always working to bring folks together."

He really should be a preacher, she thought. He had a way of gently redirecting people to God. "Schtarm did well, Abel. We were here in half the time that it usually takes." She stirred cream and sugar into the coffee in her cup. "Yonnie was right about you."

He lifted his eyebrows in a question as he took a sip of his coffee.

"She said you could fix anything. Engines, motors, horses." Carrie blew on the top of the Styrofoam cup to cool the coffee. "People too." *Like me*, she thought. *He helped to fix me.*

Abel shrugged off her compliment, but seemed pleased. "Grace bicycled over this afternoon while you were cleaning up after lunch. She was on a break and had to get back to work, but she wanted you to know that someone new is managing Honor Mansion. Veronica has been promoted and is moving to New York City. In fact, Grace said she had already left." He took another sip of coffee. "Grace also mentioned that you paid a visit recently to Honor Mansion."

Carrie made her eyes go all round and innocent, like Andy's did when he tried to act as if he didn't know what she was talking about.

"So, were you planning on telling me anytime soon about that particular visit?"

Carrie inhaled, as if she was about to say something, then shook her head.

Abel leaned forward on the table. "Let's make a pact. No more secrets." He held out his hand to her. "Deal?"

She smiled and took his hand, giving it the one-pump Amish handshake. "Well, then, since we're not keeping secrets, I suppose there's something I should tell you. Mattie gave me some news today when she came over to help with the raising. Sol is moving back home. Come summer, he's starting baptism instructions."

"This summer? He's taking the baptism classes this summer?" A strange, almost sickened look came over Abel's face.

She nodded. "That's what Mattie said." Carrie looked down at her coffee. "She said they're to be married in November."

"What?" Abel inhaled sharply, leaning back in his chair. He whistled. "I never saw that coming."

"My dad used to say that folks marry for all kinds of reasons."

Abel gazed at Carrie, his eyes dark and fathomless. "So what do you say about it?"

"I'm happy for Mattie and Sol. I really am." She and Mattie had time for a long heart-to-heart talk while cleaning up today's lunch dishes. She admitted to Mattie that she had loved Sol like crazy for a while, and in some ways she always would. "But it wasn't you who came between us, Mattie," she told her sincerely. "That was God's doing." She and Sol weren't meant for each other. And one thing Carrie knew: no woman but Mattie could ever help Sol to be his best self.

When Abel didn't respond, she glanced at him and saw him quickly look away. He was holding his hat in his hands, running it around and around by the brim. When he finally looked at her, his face was solemn. "Things haven't exactly turned out the way you thought they would, have they? It isn't exactly what you asked for."

In Carrie's mind, she reviewed the day, this wonderful day, of barn building and family building, a day filled with hope. "No. It's not. It's more. My life is more than what I ever could have asked for."

Their eyes caught and held, and held and held, and this time they both knew that neither one was letting go. He reached out a hand, palm forward, and she placed her palm against his, weaving their fingers together. Her stomach did a flip-flop; she'd been waiting for this conversation since the walk with the deacon last week. She could tell Abel was measuring his words carefully. She saw him swallow hard.

"Carrie, I can't imagine living the rest of my life without you. I love you. Be my wife." He grinned that crooked grin. "Be my Amish wife."

Carrie studied him for a moment, his brown hair curling at the ends around his collar, his beautiful melted-chocolate eyes, the cleft in his chin. Sometimes, she realized, the very thing we think is a problem turns out in the end to be God's protection. When Sol left her for baseball, she thought her heart was permanently broken. God had a different idea for her, a better one. God led her to Daniel, who led her to Abel.

She tilted her head. "Is it as simple as that? You love me, I love you."

"As simple as that."

They shared a smile, as deep and as intimate as a kiss.

Acknowledgments

First, last, and always, to the Lord God, for giving me the opportunity to write for his sake.

A special thank-you goes to the Lancaster Barnstormer baseball team for letting Solomon Riehl pitch his fastball for their team. And also for sharing time and knowledge, answering my questions, and reading through the manuscript to help correct errors.

Thanks also to my favorite first readers who graciously agreed to read and critique that first draft. The Ugly Draft. Lindsey Ciraulo and Wendy How. Your keen insights and guiding comments ("Now, did you happen to notice that Carrie has three arms in that scene?" and "Why are there two Mondays in that week?") are invaluable!

Thanks to my dream team: agent Joyce Hart of The Hartline Literary Agency and those at Revell: Andrea Doering, Barb Barnes, Janelle Mahlmann, Twila Brothers Bennett, Claudia Marsh, Deonne Beron, Carmen Pease, Sheila Ingram, Donna Hausler, and everyone else who has worked so hard on my behalf.

Many thanks to the Amish families I met, who graciously opened their homes and their hearts and let me share their world for a little while.

And, of course, thanks to my family for being so supportive of this writing gig: Steve, Lindsey and Josh, Gary, Meredith and Tad.

The WAITING

Love and thanks to all my family,
near and far.

1

$\mathcal{M}$orning dew shimmered in the warm summer sun as Jorie King led the last horse to a paddock by the road. She unhitched the halter and gave the horse a swat on his hindquarters to hustle him into the pasture. She couldn't help but smile. A stubborn one, he was. Must be part mule.

As she swung the gate closed, she noticed a car at the end of the driveway. A stranger leaned against the hood of the car, his arms crossed against his chest. When the man spotted Jorie, he waved to her and called out, "Hey there! Ma'am! Any idea how far to a gasoline station?"

Jorie latched the paddock gate and walked over to him. "About two miles," she said, pointing up the road.

The man regarded Jorie with mild curiosity, tilting his head as he appraised her prayer cap and Plain clothes. "My car ran out of gas."

Jorie spotted her neighbor across the street, leading some cows to their pasture to graze. "Ephraim!" she called out, waving to the boy. "Ephraim, would you bring a can of gasoline down here?"

Ephraim did a double take when he noticed the stranger. Jorie swallowed a smile at the boy's reaction—not many men in Stoney Ridge had skin the color of chocolate. A few cows split off and wandered into the cornfield before Ephraim suddenly remembered them and rounded them up. He guided them through the pasture gate, locked it, and waved to Jorie as he ran up the long drive to the barn.

Jorie waited for the tall dark man to speak again. The stranger seemed at ease with silence. His gaze followed Ephraim until he disappeared into the barn, and then the man's eyes swept across the countryside in front of them. "I think that might just be the most beautiful place I've ever seen."

Jorie looked over to take in the sight of the farm: the two-story white frame house nestled against a hill. A gray-topped buggy leaning on its traces by the large barn. About halfway up the drive, a ribbon of a creek wove parallel to the house. On the banks of the creek sat an enormous willow tree that provided shelter to a handful of sheep. And surrounding the house were acres and acres of fields, straight and even rows of corn and wheat. The only sound punctuating the stillness was a distant neighbor calling for his cows. "That's Beacon Hollow. It belongs to my neighbors, the Zooks."

"Clear to see they're good farmers," he said as his eyes scanned the farm.

They stood silently, waiting for Ephraim, listening to the husky whisper of the dry August corn in the fields. "The Zooks have always been farmers," she finally said, breaking the quiet. "They were some of the first settlers around here. Now the land is farmed by four brothers." She looked up the drive to see Ephraim on his way down the hill, lugging a red can of gasoline with two hands. "Ephraim is one of the brothers."

"Don't tell me they're all as young as him, managing a big farm like that!"

Jorie smiled. "No. He's the youngest. The oldest brother is Caleb. He and his wife Mary Ann are really running the farm. Matthew—he's eighteen—he does quite a bit of work."

"Where's the third brother?"

Jorie hesitated. "That would be Ben. He's in Vietnam."

The man looked at her curiously. "Pardon me for asking, ma'am, but I thought the Amish didn't fight in wars."

Jorie's chin lifted a notch. "He's *not* fighting. He's a conscientious objector."

Ephraim crossed the road with the full gas can and gave a shy nod to the stranger. The man poured the gasoline into his tank and tightened the cap, then handed the can back to Ephraim. He reached into his back pocket and pulled out a wallet, opened it, and took out a few dollars to hand to Ephraim. "Let me pay you for the gasoline."

Ephraim shook his head. "No n-need."

The man offered the money to Jorie, but she waved it away.

"I'm beholden to you. And I like to pay my debts." He peered into his wallet. "Say, do you like wild animals?" When Ephraim's eyebrows shot up with interest, the man smiled and held out two tickets. "These are tickets to the Mezzo Brothers' Circus & Menagerie that just came to Lancaster. Most of the animals are on the shady side of retirement, but there's a young cougar. The trainer said he just bought it off of a trapper in West Virginia last week."

Ephraim shot a sideways glance to Jorie before accepting the tickets. She smiled and gave a brief nod. If Cal and Mary Ann objected, she would explain the circumstances, maybe even offer to take Ephraim to the circus. Everybody knew how he loved animals.

He put down the gasoline can to study the tickets, a look of wonder on his face. "They r-really have a c-cougar?"

"They used to roam free in Pennsylvania," the man said. "The last one was killed in the 1930s." He put a hand on his car door, but his gaze had settled on the horses behind Jorie, as if watching them eat was the most fascinating thing in the world. "Are those Belgian drafts?"

"Percherons," Jorie said.

Ephraim pointed to Jorie's driveway. "That l-leads to S-Stoney Creek, the K-Kings' farm. They b-breed Percherons." He looked back at the man. "Most every P-Percheron around here is f-from the K-Kings. N-No one knows horses l-like Atlee K-King." He gave Jorie a shy smile.

She was surprised and pleased that Ephraim spoke to the man. He didn't talk much, especially around strangers, self-conscious of his stutter.

"They sure are beautiful creatures," the man said. A colt peered over the pasture fence at them for a moment, then tossed his dark mane and trotted off down a dirt trail to join his mother.

The clang of a dinner bell floated down on the wind. Ephraim's head jerked toward the farmhouse at Beacon Hollow. "Friehschtick!" *Breakfast!* He gave a quick nod to Jorie and the man, grabbed the empty gasoline can, and set off at a sprint up the long drive to the farmhouse.

Jorie shrugged, lifting her palms. "When you're thirteen years old and growing like a weed, mealtimes are serious business."

The man got into his car, turned on the ignition, leaned his head out the window, and grinned. "Meals are serious business at any age." As he drove off, he called out, "Thank you, ma'am, for your help."

Ma'am? Wasn't that a term the English used to address older women? Jorie put her hands up to her cheeks. She knew it seemed vain, but being called ma'am made her feel older than her twenty-four years. A horse leaned his heavy head over the fence, sniffing for grass, and pushed his nose at her, making her stumble a step. She caught herself and whirled around, laughing. "Leave it to you, Big John, to remind me not to take myself too seriously." She stroked his forelock. "Especially on a beautiful Sunday morning like today." She gave him a pat and went up to the farmhouse to get ready for church.

As soon as Caleb Zook tucked his beard to his chest, a signal for silent prayer before breakfast, Ephraim bowed his head slightly and watched for Cal to close his eyes. Then he quietly stretched out his hand so that it rested on the handle of the syrup pitcher, ready to make his move as soon as the prayer ended. He closed his eyes, and halfway through the prayer, he felt Cal gently place his hand over Ephraim's and squeeze hard, really hard, until Ephraim released his grip and slipped his hand into his lap.

"What do you think we should do tomorrow?" Cal asked as soon as prayer ended, reaching out for the syrup pitcher.

Ephraim settled for the bowl that held steaming scrambled eggs. "C-cut hay," he said, dishing out a spoonful of eggs onto his plate before taking a mammoth bite.

The sound of footsteps thundering up the wooden porch stairs, two at a time, interrupted the discussion as the door swung open and warm air swooped in. "Sorry to be late," Matthew said, scraping his boots on the mat. He gave Ephraim a sideways glance. "Thought you were coming back to the barn to help me sterilize those milk cans."

Ephraim shrugged. He had gotten distracted when Jorie called him down to help the man who needed gas, then completely forgot about Matthew waiting on him for help.

As Matthew pulled out a chair and sat down, he picked up the bowl of scrambled eggs and started to dish them onto his plate.

"First, wash up," Cal said. "Then, prayers. Then, eat."

Matthew pushed himself away from the table and went to the sink to wash his hands. "Where's Mary Ann and Maggie?"

"Upstairs," Cal said. "Maggie's having trouble with her hair. We can't be running late today for meeting."

Ephraim's eyes followed the syrup pitcher as Cal set it down, and Matthew grabbed it as he sat down at the table. Ephraim sighed as he watched his brother pour a small river of syrup on his scrapple, dripping down the edges, pooling on his plate.

"I think cutting hay sounds like a good plan, Ephraim," Cal said. "The front that came through last night left us a beautiful day. Maybe it'll stay clear for a while." He smiled as he handed the pitcher to Ephraim. "Though I always have to laugh at myself when I try to plan for the week. Weather is God's way of keeping a farmer humble."

Ephraim tried pouring the few remaining drips of syrup onto his scrapple, gave up, and reached past Matthew to grab a piece of toast before that, too, was gone.

"Did Jorie King say yes to teaching?" Matthew asked.

"She did," Cal said, looking pleased. "Took a month of convincing but she finally agreed. How'd you guess that?"

Between bites, Matthew said, "Ephraim said he saw her in the schoolhouse yesterday."

"She was s-sweeping it out," Ephraim answered in a mournful tone.

"Getting it ready for next week's start," Cal said. "Did you offer to help her?"

Ephraim stopped chewing his toast. The thought hadn't occurred to him. Cal rolled his eyes.

"Ha! Our Ephraim keeps as far a distance as possible from a schoolhouse when he doesn't have to be there," Matthew said.

Ephraim tried to kick him under the table, but Matthew, expecting it, quickly moved his legs out of reach.

Seven-year-old Maggie galloped down the stairs with her hair firmly pinned into a tight bun, covered by a freshly starched prayer cap. Her mother, Mary Ann, followed behind her. They sat down at the kitchen table, bowed their heads for a moment, then Mary Ann jumped up. The toast was burning and she hurried to yank the toast tray from the oven.

Mary Ann seemed flustered today. Ephraim thought it might have something to do with lots getting drawn today for the ministers for the new district. He had heard plenty of neighbors say they were hoping and praying Caleb Zook would draw the lot.

"So Jorie King is going to be the teacher?" Maggie asked, poking her glasses higher on the bridge of her small nose.

"Maggie, sometimes I think you've got ears like an Indian scout," Cal said. "Yes, Jorie will be your teacher this year."

Maggie dusted her oatmeal with brown sugar. "Why is she called Jorie?"

"Her grandmother is Marge and her mother is Marjorie, so Jorie's name is shortened to avoid confusion," Cal explained.

"Why ain't Jorie married?" Maggie asked, using a fork to saw her scrapple into tiny bite-size pieces. "She ain't *that* old. And she's awful pretty."

"Isn't. She *isn't* that old," Cal said. "And whom a teacher courts is none of our concern." He pointed to her plate to keep eating.

"Matthew said she's been asked a dozen times." Maggie took the smallest possible bite of her scrapple. "Matthew said she always says no."

"Matthew needs to remember that careless words are a displeasure to the Lord," Cal said, as he gave Matthew "the look"—one eyebrow raised over a stern face.

Ephraim grinned. He could tell Cal's heart wasn't in it. He saw Cal cast a glance at Mary Ann, at the sink scraping burnt edges off the toast, before leaning over to whisper to Maggie. "Jorie and your Uncle Ben have an understanding. As soon as he gets back from Vietnam, they'll get married. She's just waiting on him."

"Ephraim's hoping Jorie will hang on a few years and wait till he can grow some whiskers," Matthew interrupted, elbowing Ephraim. "If I were you, little brother, and had a schoolteacher who looked like Jorie King, I'd be offering to sweep that schoolhouse morning and night." He turned his head toward Mary Ann, whose back was to him while she stood at the counter, buttering toast. Satisfied she was preoccupied, he whistled two notes, one up, one down, while outlining an hourglass shape with his two hands.

Ephraim blushed furiously, made a grab for the milk pitcher, and knocked it over.

Cal jumped up and tried to mop up the milk before it spilled onto his lap. "Matthew, you fulfilled your teasing quota for the day and it's only seven in the morning."

"Will you teach me how to whistle, Matthew?" Maggie asked.

"Can't, Magpie," Matthew answered. "Not until your front teeth grow in." He peered into her mouth. "I declare, all of your teeth are falling out and nothing's coming in. I'm starting to think you're going to be toothless, like ol' Amos Esh." He sucked in his lips and chomped down on them, trying to look toothless. "Don't worry, though. I'll get you a pair of store-bought choppers for your birthday."

Maggie looked to her father with saucer eyes.

"Matthew is trying to upset you, Maggie," Cal assured her. "Your teeth will come in when they're good and ready. Finish up so we won't be late. It's a big day."

Leaning against the sink, wiping her hands with a towel, Mary Ann said, "I'm worried you're going to end up in the lot."

Cal got up to refill his coffee cup. "Now, Mary Ann, the Lord didn't intend for his people to worry."

As Ephraim inspected the remaining quarter of his toast, butter on the edges, red raspberry jam heaped on top, Cal's thought forever struck him as odd. Cal worried almost as much as Mary Ann.

Cal put down the coffee cup and placed a hand on Mary Ann's shoulder. "I have more faith in our people than you do. They have better judgment than to vote for me as a minister."

She covered Cal's hand with hers, but Ephraim could tell she had a different idea of how folks would vote.

Twenty minutes later, after Ephraim's and Maggie's faces were scrubbed so they shone, Cal herded everyone into the buggy and slapped the reins on the horse's hind end to set off down the long drive to the road. At the end of the drive, he stopped the horse and let Matthew jump out to get yesterday's forgotten mail from the mailbox. Matthew walked back to the buggy, sifting through the mail, then stopped abruptly. He tore open a thin gray envelope.

"Shall I get a rocking chair for you, Matthew, so you can read in comfort?" Cal asked.

Matthew held up the envelope and its contents. "It's from the U.S. Selective Service. 'You have been reclassified from 1A to 1W and must report to the Armed Forces recruitment office in Philadelphia, Pennsylvania, for a physical exam on September 1st, 1965.'"

His news had an impact on the family of a thunderclap out of a clear blue sky. Mary Ann shot Cal a look of alarm. Ephraim felt the breakfast in his stomach do a flip-flop. Even Maggie stopped humming, and she was always humming to herself. She opened her mouth to ask a question, but Ephraim nudged her.

"Not n-now," he whispered in her ear.

Quietly, Cal said, "I'll go with you for that meeting."

"No, you won't," Matthew said firmly. "I can handle this myself." He tucked the letter in his coat pocket and climbed onto the back of the buggy.

"How long has Ben been gone now?" Maggie asked.

Mary Ann turned her head to look at her daughter in the backseat. "Nearly two years."

Matthew leaned toward Ephraim. "How many times do you think we're going to get asked today if we've heard from Ben? Last time, I counted thirteen." It was a question that confronted them every time they went to church or to town or to any gathering.

"Will Matthew be sent to Vietnam too?" Maggie asked.

"No," Cal said in a tone that meant the discussion was over. He slapped the reins on the back of the horse to get it moving.

Ephraim elbowed her as an awkward silence covered the buggy.

"What?" Maggie whispered to him, palms raised.

"He's worried M-Matthew will get s-signed up t-to g-go," Ephraim whispered to Maggie.

"I don't get it," Maggie whispered loudly.

"Me n-neither."

"There's two types of conscientious objectors," Matthew explained in a longsuffering voice. "There's the conscientious objector who won't serve. And then there's the C.O. who will serve. That's what Ben got signed up for. He got tricked. So that's why he was sent to Vietnam."

"Why didn't Ben just tell the government he was tricked?" Maggie asked. "That he didn't want to kill anyone?"

"He's *not* killing anyone," Cal said sharply.

Mary Ann turned and placed a hand over Maggie's small hands. "What's done is done. But we pray every day that Ben is safe and well and coming home to us."

"But why couldn't he just explain—"

Ephraim covered Maggie's mouth with his hand. Maggie was too young to realize that those unanswerable questions about Ben grieved everyone. But Ephraim knew.

"That's enough talk about war and killing," Cal said. "It's a beautiful Sunday morning and our thoughts should turn to the Lord."

They *should*, Ephraim thought, but thoughts were hard to control. Sometimes his thoughts bounced around like a game of ping-pong. Mostly, his ping-pongy thoughts had to do with getting his chores done as fast as he could so he could sneak off to the Deep Woods. But anytime Ben's name was brought up, which was often, his thoughts hung there, suspended. He couldn't stop thinking and worrying about him. Where was he? Was he in danger? Could he be captured and tortured as a prisoner of war, like stories he overheard when he went to town with Cal?

After meeting ended that morning, the children and non-members went outside while the members remained in the house to choose two new ministers for the newly split district. The bishop, Isaac Stoltzfus, would oversee both districts.

"It always gives me the chills, this lot choosing," Jorie said to Mary Ann, as they stood in line to whisper their choice of a minister to the bishop. "All that separates one man from the other is a slip of paper and the will of God."

Mary Ann turned to her. "I'd forgotten that your father was a minister too. Then you understand how hard it can be—adding those duties on top of a busy farmer's life."

Jorie nodded. "The day Dad drew the lot, Mom cried all afternoon."

"How are your folks?" Mary Ann asked.

"It's taken awhile, but they feel as if Canada is home now," Jorie answered. Three years ago, her parents and siblings had moved, with four other families, to start a new settlement. She had chosen to stay behind to help her grandparents with their horse breeding farm. She never regretted her decision. She loved those Percheron horses as much as her grandfather did. And, of course, there was Ben. He had asked her to stay.

Jorie glanced across the room at her grandfather. With his thick head of snow white hair and bushy eyebrows, he reminded her of a white polar bear, big and strong. He winked when she caught his eye. His familiar deep-lined face was dear to her heart, and she knew there were more lines etched into his face this year than last. Atlee King was doing all he could to keep the farm solvent. Their best broodmare, Penny, died while trying to deliver twin foals. Penny was an older horse, but she'd always been a sweet, gentle mother, producing strong and healthy babies. There were always problems with the horses, but that particular setback—losing Penny and her foals—was an enormous loss.

When Caleb Zook asked if Jorie would teach, at first she said no, but he kept asking and she kept thinking about it. The extra income could help her grandfather and she wouldn't have to go far from home. Still, the thought of what she had agreed to made Jorie's stomach churn. It wasn't the teaching part—it was that blasted state exam the eighth graders needed to pass in late May. Mr. Whitehall, the superintendent of public schools, was not shy in sharing his opinion that one-room schoolhouses were an antiquated system. He was only making concessions to the governor of Pennsylvania, he pointed out, to allow for them. But if those eighth graders didn't pass that state exam in late May, she knew it could have repercussions for all of the Amish schools.

When she admitted to Cal her concerns, he insisted that if anyone could help those scholars pass that test, he knew it would be Jorie. "Our district needs you," he told her. "It's an unusually big eighth grade class this year, and either they are woefully behind in their studies from the school they've been attending, or they might—not all, mind you—be a little . . . slow to learn. Either way, you're the only one I can think of who can bring them up to standard."

Oh, she hoped he was right. She was starting to wake up regularly in a panic, dreaming it was already May and the scholars all failed the test. She shook her head to clear it of that thought, and suddenly realized that she was next in line and the bishop was waiting for her.

She quickly whispered her choice to him and found a seat next to Mary Ann. "Folks are praying the lot will fall to Cal."

Mary Ann smoothed out her apron as if sweeping away her concern. "There are plenty of other good candidates."

Sylvia, Mary Ann's sister, seated on her other side, slipped an arm around her sister and gently squeezed her shoulder. "Caleb is far too young," Sylvia said, giving Jorie a thin smile. "We need ministers who are old and wise."

Cal may be young, but Jorie knew there weren't many men who had the effect on others like he did. When Cal spoke, others always listened. If he walked into a room, everyone in it seemed to breathe a little sigh of relief. As if all would be well.

But Sylvia obviously disagreed. The way Sylvia was staring at Jorie right now, with those piercing dark eyes, reminded her of a Cooper's hawk, arms out wide like wings stretched protectively around Mary Ann. She knew it wasn't right to let her mind meander down such lanes, comparing people she knew to birds and animals. The images just popped, unbidden, into her mind. Silently, she asked the Lord to forgive her for such foolishness and managed a smile in return for Sylvia.

The bishop announced that five men had been recommended by the members. Caleb Zook's name was indeed on the list. Jorie felt torn between relief for the church and empathy for Mary Ann. Isaac reminded everyone that each nominated man would choose a hymnal, the *Ausbund*, and in two would be a slip of paper. From those lots would come God's choices to lead his flock.

A library hush fell over the room as the hymnbooks were placed on the tabletop. A prayer was offered, then the nominees stood, one by one, to claim a hymnal. "Please not Cal, Lord, please not Cal," Mary Ann whispered, unaware that others could hear her.

Samuel Riehl was the first to open the hymnal. He held up a slip of paper and his wife, Rachel, gasped. Then two more men opened empty hymnals. It had come down to Cal and Henry Glick. As Cal opened his hymnal, his shoulders slumped. He turned around, looked at his wife, raised his eyebrows, and held up the hymnal for all of the church members to see the white slip of paper.

Henry Glick grabbed Cal's hand and pumped it enthusiastically. "May God be with you, Caleb."

Jorie had to bite her lip to keep from laughing at the look of relief on Henry's face. She felt Mary Ann lean into her shoulder, and she shifted to look at her—as Mary Ann slumped over into Jorie's lap in a dead faint.

2

When Mary Ann came to, people were standing above her like nurses puzzling over a patient. As her vision came into focus, she recognized her husband's light blue eyes, filled with worry. Then she realized that Jorie was the one cradling her head in her lap.

"She didn't expect Cal would be chosen," she heard her sister Sylvia say. "None of us did. She's just plain overcome."

Marge King, Jorie's grandmother, put a cool hand on Mary Ann's forehead. "Any fever?" Marge demanded. She fancied herself a healer, but everyone steered clear of her remedies.

Slowly, Mary Ann shook her head.

Marge looked unconvinced. "Still feeling dizzy and light-headed?"

Mary Ann tried to wave Marge off. How could she possibly put into words all that she felt right now? She had dreaded this morning, knowing in her heart what was to come. As soon as she saw that slip in Cal's hymnal, a deep foreboding settled over her, a portent that life would never be the same. She pulled herself up to her elbows and insisted she was fine.

"I'll stay close by," Marge said, clearly disappointed.

As Cal helped her to her feet, Mary Ann was glad Maggie was outside with Ephraim and Matthew and hadn't seen her faint. Deeply embarrassed, she wondered if her sister was right. Maybe she had been overcome by the news of Cal drawing the lot. Being a servant of God was a burden and a responsibility, she knew that to be true. It was an unpaid position without any training, and a man was appointed for his lifetime. On top of an already heavy workload, Cal would be called upon to drop everything for the needs of the church members. The duties would follow Cal like a shadow. He would be a fine minister for the new district, she had no doubt. But at what cost?

"That's twice you've fainted in one week," Cal said quietly as he helped her stand. "Two days ago, in the kitchen, when you were canning tomatoes, and now today. Maybe you should see the doctor."

She shook her head. "Drawing the lot just . . . shook me up, is all."

"I can't blame you," Cal said. "I wanted to faint dead away, too, when I saw that slip. Sure you're feeling all right? You still look a little pale."

"I might be fighting a virus," she answered, slipping her hand through the crook of his elbow. "I've been a little tired lately."

After a time of lunch and fellowship, Cal pulled Maggie and Ephraim out of a softball game to return to Beacon Hollow for the afternoon milking.

"Dad?" Maggie asked, as she climbed up into the buggy. "Will you be marrying and burying folks now?"

Mary Ann turned in the buggy to look at Maggie, seated next to Matthew. Once Maggie got started with her questions, there was no end in sight. And the comments she could make! Mary Ann never knew what would come out of her daughter's mouth.

"So maybe you can marry off Matthew to Fat Lizzie before he leaves!" Maggie puckered her mouth and made kissing sounds. "I caught her making googly eyes at Matthew during meetin'."

"Maggie Zook!" Mary Ann waved a finger at her daughter. "Lizzie Glick is a fine girl. She's . . . she's just big boned." She turned to face forward. "Besides, only a bishop does the marrying."

"M-Matthew's s-sweet on Wall-Eyed Wanda," Ephraim said quietly to Maggie.

Whipping her head around to glare at Ephraim, Mary Ann said firmly, "Wanda Graber can't help having a lazy eye."

"I'm not ready to be tied to any woman's capstrings quite yet, little brother." Matthew doffed Ephraim's straw hat and sent it spinning into the back of the buggy.

As Ephraim scrambled over the back of the bench to retrieve his hat, Mary Ann noticed how much he had grown this summer. He was slight and gangling, with a freckled complexion and straight, blond hair—nothing like Cal, who was tall and broad shouldered, with thick dark hair and skin that was tanned by the sun. Ephraim wasn't a boy any longer, nor was he a man. He was at that difficult in-between stage.

Cal, uncharacteristically solemn, hardly noticed the teasing. Mary Ann knew he was thoroughly preoccupied with the changes being a minister would bring for the family. And he was losing Matthew's help on the farm just as he would be so busy with new duties. They would all grieve over losing Matthew—and it wasn't just the help he gave. Matthew was the heart of their family. She had raised him like her own since he was ten years old—he had been a beautiful, golden-haired boy, and now he was a handsome young man, sturdy and bold, with laughing eyes. What would their home be like without his rascal's smile and teasing ways? She didn't even want to imagine it.

Cal went to bed early that night, worn out by the day's events. Mary Ann tiptoed into the bedroom to get ready for bed. The moon was coming up full over the sloped roof of the barn, casting its light through the window. She listened to her husband's steady breathing and stood by the bed for a moment, watching him. Even though it was vain to think it, she loved his looks. He had such a remarkable face, a truly breath-catching face: strong-boned but refined, with a hint of a Roman nose. It still caught her by surprise, to be Cal's wife, even after eight years of marriage.

She had wanted to marry Cal from the first time he had taken her home from youth group. There were plenty of other girls who had a hope pinned on Caleb Zook. He was handsome, intelligent, kind, all of those things, but what set Cal apart—what had always set him apart—was that he had been given more than his share of wisdom. Even when he first took over Beacon Hollow, after his folks' accident, neighbors would watch for the day when Caleb Zook bought his seed and then they would start planting. They knew Cal could call the weather like no one else. It ran in the family with those Zooks, her father used to say. They were just known for having more than their share of common sense. Except for that Ben, her father would add. It might have skipped a generation with Benjamin Zook.

Once or twice, Cal stopped by her farm on a summer evening for a long walk. She had assumed she wasn't really his kind of girl. She was attractive enough, but there were prettier girls. She was flat where she should have been flounced out, thick where she should be thin. And she was two years older than him.

Then the Armed Forces started conscripting men for the Korean War and Cal was called to serve two years in a hospital in Philadelphia. She never heard from him, not a single letter, the entire time he was away. He came home every so often for a weekend, but he never stopped by her farm. She started to think he wasn't planning to return after his duty was served. But then his folks were in a terrible accident. A truck sailed through a stop sign and crashed into his parents' buggy, killing them instantly. The government released Cal from duty and he was suddenly back again, stepping into the gaping hole of his parents' absence. He cared for his younger brothers and managed every aspect of Beacon Hollow.

Cal was far more serious than when he left, far more grown up. He asked to take Mary Ann home from a Singing one evening, and five months later, asked if she would marry him. She was so surprised that eager words tumbled out of her mouth before she could stop them: "Oh yes! Oh yes, yes, yes!" And then, to her great embarrassment came the words, "But . . . why?"

Then it was his turn to look surprised. It was her heart, he told her. That was what made a woman beautiful.

Cal was a kind and good husband to her. He never expressed disappointment that their family was so small, though she was sure he must have felt it. Most of her friends had four or five children by now. She had given him Maggie. And a beautiful little boy, Sammy, who never took a breath.

She said her evening prayers in silence while she changed. As she unpinned her dress to change into her nightgown, something caught her eye in the moonlight. She went over to the window and held out her arm. A large bruise ran from her shoulder to her elbow. She couldn't remember banging herself to cause such a mark, but life on a farm was filled with heavy work. It probably happened when she was helping the boys pour a milk can into the bulk tank.

She promptly put the bruise out of her mind and slipped into bed next to her husband.

In late August, on the first day of school, Jorie arrived before 7:00 a.m., though school took up at nine. Cal was already there, opening up windows to air out the heavy smell of linseed oil he had used to seal the wooden floors and keep down dust. The schoolhouse sat on a corner of Beacon Hollow's farmland, donated to the new district. Cal had organized a work frolic in late July to build the schoolhouse in one day. The aromas of raw wood and fresh paint mingled with the linseed oil, permeating the room.

Cal smiled when he saw her. "I missed all of this. We didn't have parochial schools when I was young." He turned in a slow circle, admiring the building. "I was bused to a public high school about an hour away. We spent so much time on that bus my father used to call it a dormitory on wheels."

"I'd forgotten that you finished high school," Jorie said. "You have a diploma, don't you?" She raised her eyebrows. "Maybe *you* should be teaching."

He was grandly dismissive of that notion. "Oh no. A public school education only gave me a headful of useless information about the kings and queens of England, and how the human being evolved from a one-celled organism." He lifted open another window. "This little room, all that goes on within these four walls—this is where our scholars will be prepared for our way of life." He spun around and pointed to her. "And you're just the one who can do that."

He laughed when he saw the look of panic on her face. "You'll do fine, Jorie King. The Lord will not fail you."

"It's not the Lord I'm worried about. It's those eighth grade boys." At the front of the classroom, she crossed her arms across her chest and walked a tight little turn, back and forth. "It's such a large amount of eighth graders. And all boys! Out of a classroom of twenty-five scholars, I only have six girls. I noticed those eighth grade boys in church yesterday." She stopped to look at him. "Some of them *must* be fifteen!"

"Two are sixteen. They still haven't passed the test. This will be the year, though, that we will clear that logjam of boys. They've spent the better part of ten years on a long journey through eight grades."

She clapped her hands against her cheeks. "Cal, you are expecting me to be a miracle worker. Seven scholars have to pass that test come May or the superintendent is threatening to close our school. I don't know what I've let you talk me into."

Cal winced. "Eight. Ray Smucker is coming today too."

She shuddered. Those Smuckers were legendary for contrariness.

"I have confidence in you, Jorie," he said kindly. "But . . . there is a big stick up on the wall, just in case you need it." He pointed to a large ruler, hanging by the blackboard. He put on his straw hat and tipped it. "Looks to be another hot day today. Good for the hay."

She scowled at him. "Bad for the scholars."

He grinned. "Don't forget. School lets out at four."

Forget? How could she forget when school let out? She was already counting the hours.

Jorie spent the first hour taking enrollment and reassigning seats. The front row was the first graders, the populous eighth grade took up the last three rows. When she got to the sixth grade, she saw a hand waving, frantically reaching to the sky to catch her attention. "Esther Swartzentruber?"

Esther sprang up. "I just thought you should know that Ray Smucker is eating an apple." She spoke with great authority and jerked her pointed chin in Ray's direction. "In class."

"Oh?" Jorie said. "Thank you, Esther. Please sit down."

Esther sat down, pleased with herself. She had her mother Sylvia's fragile elegance, with sharp brown eyes and finely cut features. Jorie knew Esther also had Sylvia's capability to slice peoples' hearts to ribbons.

Jorie looked at Ray. The chair was too small beneath his bottom and his knees did not fit under the desk, so he stretched out his long legs into the aisle and crossed his ankles. On his face was a look of defiance. "Ray, please put your apple in the trash."

Ray didn't budge.

"Ray, didn't you hear me?" Her voice was steady but forced.

Ray met her gaze. "Soon as I'm finished with it," he said, letting a broad smile escape. "Don't want to be wasting it." He took another bite of the apple.

Jorie hesitated on the edge of a decision. She knew this was her make-or-break moment to earn the scholars' respect. She walked down the aisle toward Ray, who sat there, defiantly eating his apple. "You must not have had enough for breakfast today." She spun around. "Does anyone else have any apples in their lunch?"

Twenty hands shot up. "Please get them." The scholars rummaged in their lunches and handed Jorie the apples. She walked up and down the aisles, collecting the apples in her apron. "Here you go, Ray. Eat up." She put the apples on his desk and went back to the front of the class to resume roll call.

Ray looked victorious. At least, until the eleventh apple. By then, he was looking a little sick of apples. By the fifteenth, he was barely chewing, and by the twentieth, he grew still and his face was pale.

"Whoa, pal," Eli Graber said, seated next to Ray. "You're looking a little green there. You're not going to puke, are you?"

"No," Ray answered, clearly annoyed.

Suddenly, his eyes went wide. A wrenching heave rolled up from his stomach and he vomited in the direction of Esther, seated in front of him. Esther froze, her shoulders hunched up by her ears, then she screamed as if an arrow had pierced her back. Ray wiped his mouth with his sleeve, glared at Jorie, staggered outside, and took off down the road.

Jorie came to herself with a start. "Ephraim, go get a bucket of water and a rag." She turned to Esther. "Stand still, Esther, so I can clean you up. Really, he hardly got anything on you. In fact, take off your apron and you'll be as good as new." The rest of the children started to gag from the smell and clumped by the windows, trying to breath in great gasps of fresh air.

"Er is sich alles verblut!" Esther shouted, pointing at a first grader. *He is all bloody!* "Er is am Schtarewe!" *He is dying!*

Jorie looked to see Tommy Fisher, standing against the wall, start to cry. A red rivulet ran down his chin from one nostril, dripping blood onto his light blue shirt.

Maggie came up to Jorie and quietly whispered, "Aw, he was just picking his nose."

Jorie grabbed a tissue from the box on her desk and slid down onto one knee in front of Tommy, working fast. She rolled the tissue tight and stuffed it up into his bleeding nostril, trying to staunch the flow. "You're not going to die, Tommy. Now hold this," she said, putting his hand up on his nose and leaning his head back.

Breathing a little hard, with sweat dripping down her back from either the excitement or the heat of the morning or both, Jorie closed up the enrollment book. "Grab your tablets and pencils and let's go outside."

The class poured out behind her.

Jorie supposed, with such a day as she was having, it was inevitable that she would get a visit from Sylvia Swartzentruber. She always found herself surprised by the fact that Sylvia and Mary Ann were sisters. They were as opposite as two women could be.

Ben used to say that Sylvia looked as if she had a popcorn kernel stuck in a back tooth. "I would bet money on the fact," he had said more than once, "that Sylvia has never once had a laughing jag. Not once in her life."

Jorie would scold him for saying such a thing, but she wouldn't deny it.

Sylvia wrinkled her nose at the lingering smell when she stepped into the main room of the schoolhouse. Then her eyes went wide at the sight of the window that had been shattered by a fly ball during a lunchtime softball game. "Caleb Zook donated the land and built this school," she said, her voice as sharp as a pinch, "and within one day, you have already let this building fall into disrepair." She huffed. "According to Esther, today was a complete and total disaster."

"Not entirely, Sylvia," Jorie said. "I admit there were a few . . . unexpected twists and turns . . . but by four o'clock, things were pretty well organized." All in all, she felt rather satisfied. The books were taken out of the cupboards and distributed, letters and numbers were written on the blackboard, and no other injuries had occurred.

Sylvia cocked her head like a wary sparrow. "Esther told me you are planning to have a Christmas program. That's the most ridiculous thing I've ever heard. Those things end up just filling their heads with nonsense and taking away time that ought to be put on lessons." She crossed her arms against her chest. "Plus, it makes them vain and forward."

Jorie heartily disagreed, but she kept that opinion to herself. How could learning—any learning—be thought of as nonsense?

"And the next time someone loses their breakfast on my Esther, I expect you to have the good sense to send her home to change her clothes. She came straight home, took a long bath, and is lying down with a frightful headache."

"I'll keep that in mind," Jorie said.

She breathed a sigh of relief as Sylvia, finally exhausted of scoldings, turned and left for home. She knew God loved each and every soul, but she wondered if even the Almighty Lord found it took a little more effort with Sylvia Swartzentruber.

Matthew was almost done sawing up a large tree branch that had fallen during a heavy rainstorm so it could be split, seasoned, and used for firewood. He stopped to wipe his brow and noticed Jorie King drive a buggy up the long lane that led to the farmhouse and barn. He dropped the saw and took a few strides to the water pump. He quickly pumped some water and washed off his face, then smoothed his blond hair back under his black felt hat. He ran his hand over his chin, checking to see that he had shaved his whiskers properly. He wiped his hands on his pants and hurried to meet her, hoping she had time for a talk. Jorie King might be his brother's girl, but his heart beat faster when he saw her. He knew it wasn't the Plain way to believe in luck, but sometimes he thought Ben was such a lucky dog. He was always lucky. Lucky in life, lucky in love.

Matthew had never seen such a color of hair as Jorie's. When the sun hit it just right, like it did in church yesterday, it looked like it was nearly on fire. For a moment, his mind wandered to a daydream of liberating her hair from that starched bonnet and those nasty-looking pins, then his vision was interrupted when Jorie said, "Mary Ann told me your news, Matthew." In a flash, she hopped down from the buggy. "What do you think about leaving us behind and living in the big scary city of Lebanon?"

Matthew grinned and squared his shoulders, trying to look like a man. "Truth be told, Jorie, I think the federal government isn't a bit interested in what I think about it." He wouldn't admit it to her, but he was disappointed he ended up getting sent to the Veterans Hospital in Lebanon, just an hour away by bus, to work in the psychiatric rehabilitation ward. He was worried Cal would ask him to live at home, but his brother never said a word about it. That was Cal, though. He believed a man had to make his own decisions in life.

Matthew had his heart set on New York City. Once, while he was in town, he heard a song on the radio at the hardware store about New York City being a place where people never slept. Imagine that!

"I'm hoping you'll be able to return for our Christmas program in December," Jorie was saying, jolting him back to the present. "Ephraim will be the angel Gabriel, announcing the coming birth of the Christ child. We've already started to work on it."

Matthew's heart soared. Jorie King wanted to see him again! "Well, I'll be sure to—"

"If you're looking for Mary Ann, she's in her garden," Cal said, coming toward them from the barn.

Matthew tried not to scowl at Cal for interrupting.

"It's you I'm looking for, Cal, if you have a moment to spare," Jorie answered.

"What is it?" Cal asked, leaning against the fence. He shot his brother a look to give them a little privacy, so Matthew went back to the woodcutting. He used the hatchet to hack twigs off of the branch so he could keep one ear on the conversation.

"It's about one of the boys at school."

"Someone giving you a hard time? I hope it's not Ephraim."

"No, nothing like that. In fact, it's just the opposite."

"How so?"

"Did you mean what you said in your sermon yesterday? About how husbands should be listening to their wives? That a wife's opinion should be considered a gift of wisdom to the husband?"

"Of course I meant it. What are you getting at?"

"Ray Smucker came for an hour on the first day of school, just long enough to get on the attendance roll, and left."

"So I heard," Cal said, eyes laughing. "He had a hankering for an apple. Or two. Ephraim said you handled it as calm as a summer day."

"Ray hasn't been back since. I stopped by the farm and spoke to Lyddie." She tilted her head. "Gideon told her that Ray doesn't need any more schooling."

"Gid has never set much store in book learning. He only went through the fourth grade himself. He raised his older boys the same way, letting them miss months at a time when he needed them on the farm. Guess he feels they turned out all right."

"That was a different time," Jorie said. "The school districts had a more lenient eye toward farming families. And Gid had a different wife for those boys. I know this is a late-in-life child for him, but Lyddie is young. She wants Ray to get some schooling. He's older than Ephraim and hardly knows any English. How's . . . ," she glanced at Matthew, who ducked his head down, "will he get along in life without knowing English?"

Matthew covered a grin. Those Smuckers weren't known for being the brightest lanterns in the barn. They were a difficult bunch to deal with. They hardly knew any English, so they had to depend on others for dealings outside the Amish community. And they were always borrowing money from others and forgetting to pay back the loan. Cal loaned Gideon Smucker hundreds of dollars to buy tools and start up a blacksmithing business. Gideon started the business, then soon lost interest. Once or twice, he overheard Mary Ann gently chide Cal to remind Gid to pay back the loan, but Cal refused. He said their money belonged to the Lord, and it was the Lord's business to remind Gid to pay back his debts. Mary Ann wasn't inclined to challenge her husband, but after Cal left the kitchen, Matthew heard her muttering to herself that the Lord probably had better things to do with his time than be a debt collector.

Matthew was surprised that Jorie even bothered worrying about Ray; other teachers sure didn't waste any time worrying about a Smucker. Maybe it was because she was new to teaching this year and there'd been so much controversy about the Amish having their own schools. Cal felt Stoney Ridge had an example to make for other Amish communities who were having terrible times with the Department of Education.

Just last week, Matthew saw some letters in the *Sugarcreek Budget* about fathers in Indiana and Ohio who were getting tossed into jail for not wanting their children to be bused to large public schools. Over a decade ago, the same thing had happened in Pennsylvania. Matthew's father was one of those men who had been tossed in jail and fined, repeatedly, for not letting Cal go to high school. Finally, a superior court ordered Cal to go. He remembered how mad his mother was, banging pots and pans in the kitchen and telling his father they should up and move to Canada or Mexico. His father worked in a different way, much like Cal, moving calmly toward a goal. He started a letter-writing campaign to the governor. He wrote a letter every day and encouraged others to write too. The governor finally agreed to a compromise—Amish children over the age of fourteen went to a vocational school until they were sixteen. Cal said he was hoping the Pennsylvania Compromise would be so successful that it would clear the way for Amish brethren in other states.

Cal had just set the date for the work frolic to build the schoolhouse and was heading home from town when he nearly ran his buggy into Jorie, walking down the middle of the street on her way home from town. She was reading a book and didn't even hear his buggy. Cal said he pulled over to see what the Sam Hill was the matter with her, noticed the book she was reading was *Silent Spring* by Rachel Carson, and offered her the teaching job, right on the spot. She didn't accept at first, but Cal had made up his mind and, once decided, nothing could budge it loose. He kept on asking her until she said yes. Matthew wasn't really sure why Cal was so all-fired determined to hire Jorie, especially since she didn't really want to teach. There were at least three other girls he knew of who wanted the job, but Cal didn't think they would inspire the scholars.

"Matthew," Cal said, jolting him out of his reverie. He pointed to the fallen tree limb. "The branch isn't going to trim itself." Then he turned back to Jorie. "Seems like this is a job for the deacon."

"I agree." She crossed her arms over her chest. "So before coming here, I went and spoke to Jonas. He said he agreed with Gideon."

Cal kicked at the ground. "Aw, Jorie, I can't go over there and start telling a man how to raise his son."

At Cal's hesitation, Matthew noticed Jorie's back stiffen a notch. She was exasperated, Matthew realized, and it looked like steam trying hard not to rise from a kettle. He thought being mad made her look especially beautiful. A stain spread up her cheeks and her eyes got all wide and fiery. Passion, he thought. She was a woman with passion. Not like most girls he knew. Girls like Fat Lizzie, whose large eyes followed him around during meetings. He was looking forward to meeting more girls like Jorie King while he was living in Lebanon. There was a big world to explore and the United States Government was going to help him do it.

"But you're a minister now," Jorie told Cal.

Cal took off his hat and raked a hand through his hair. "My job is to take care of our members' spiritual needs."

She put her hands on her hips. "Why shouldn't you be teaching a man how to be a good father? Maybe then you won't *have* to worry so much about spiritual needs."

Matthew stopped hacking off twigs and glanced at Jorie and Cal. He got a kick out of watching her speak her mind to Cal. With her hands hooked on her hips, Matthew couldn't help noticing how small her waist was. His gaze drifted to her face. He wondered what it would be like to kiss those lips—they were so full. He had tried to kiss Cindy Yoder once, but she started giggling and couldn't stop. He had been looking forward to kissing since he was Ephraim's age, but kissing Cindy was a dire disappointment. She was too young, only sixteen. He was pretty sure kissing a mature woman like Jorie would be different. He shook his head. His thoughts were going down twisted, dangerous paths.

Matthew's gaze shifted to Cal, who held his hat in his hands and was turning it around, fingering the brim. That meant his brother was thinking about what to do. He was thinking hard. The more times he turned his hat around, the stickier the problem. Jorie's head was tilted up to look at Cal, much taller than she was, waiting patiently for him to respond. For a split second, he thought he saw something else in Jorie's eyes. Some kind of feeling for Cal that made Matthew uneasy. Then the look in her eyes passed, and she turned her gaze to the setting sun.

Maybe it was just a look of admiration. People often looked at Cal like that, as if they expected him to spout forth wisdom with a Solomonic flair. Yet Cal would be the first to say he was just a man, like any other man.

Softly, Jorie added, "In the English system, a truant officer could arrest Gideon Smucker."

Cal bristled.

She gripped her elbows and looked past him to the willow tree hanging its limbs over the little creek. "How many times have you said that the new superintendent is watching our school? You said we need to comply with what he's asking of us or we may end up having to bus our scholars to that big public school."

Cal raised an eyebrow. "That's pretty ironic coming from a teacher who seems to be spending most of her time outside of the classroom with those scholars."

"That classroom is stifling hot. Besides, we *are* studying. We're studying nature. Making observations."

"And when the time comes for that year-end state exam, you'll end up spending the month of May cramming those eighth grade heads with book learning."

"They'll pass," she said, drawing her five-foot-three self up tall. "They'll all pass."

"I'm sure they will." Cal smiled down at her, obviously enjoying her indignation.

She waved her hand away. "Those state tests don't tell everything. They don't test a child's curiosity, or intuition, or sensitivity . . ." She looked down at the ground. "I just don't believe in letting the classroom interfere with an education."

He gave a short laugh, amused. "A sentiment best kept to yourself."

"Maybe you could talk to Gideon and remind him that he's got a boy who needs to be educated. And he should've stayed awake during your sermon yesterday. He could've learned something."

Cal put his hat back on and adjusted the brim, a matter decided. "Well, now you've pointed out something that is a serious grievance. If a man is sleeping through one of my sermons, well, that's something that's got to be dealt with."

"Oh, you!" She threw up her hands in mock despair and started walking to her buggy, but Matthew could see she was smiling.

Cal followed behind and helped her climb up. "I'll talk to Gid."

"When?" she asked him.

"Jorie King, you are more free with your opinions than—"

"Than a new minister?" she asked with a sly grin. "Soon, Cal. Please pay a call on Gideon Smucker soon." She slapped the reins on her mare and drove down the lane.

Matthew threw down the hatchet and joined his brother, watching Jorie's buggy drive down the long lane.

Cal glanced at him. "Heard everything, I suppose."

"Yup," Matthew answered. He folded his arms across his chest. "I like her. She's got spunk."

"I'll say," Cal said, shaking his head. "Go tell Mary Ann I had to run an errand."

"Shall I tell her the minister is off on his first mission of mercy?" Matthew grinned.

Cal bent down, picked up the big axe, and thrust its handle against Matthew's chest with his two hands. "Might be gone awhile, so you'll need to finish up that branch by yourself."

Matthew's smile faded.

When Cal went to speak to Gideon about sending Ray to school, he heard an earful about Jorie's teaching style. "That Jorie King don't teach nuthin' worth learnin'! Those kids spend half their time up in trees. I seen 'em with my own two eyes." Gideon poked two fingers at his eyes to emphasize the point. "Ain't it true, Lyddie?"

Lydia, a quiet, defeated-looking woman, refilled the cups of coffee. "Ray might like going to school, Gid. Jorie makes learning real interesting."

Gideon snorted. "She's encouragin' them kids to have a early death! It makes my blood run cold to see the boys climbin' to the very tops of those big trees at Blue Lake Pond last Friday."

"Oh *that*," Cal said. "Ephraim told us they needed a crow's nest for nature study. Fridays are their field afternoons. Then they have to write compositions on what they've observed in nature."

Gid snorted again.

Cal saw the hunting guns lined up in a wall shelf and tried a different tack. "Did you hear that pesky bobcat got into Amos Esh's sheep pasture?"

"Yeah, I heard."

"Jorie had the scholars memorize a quote by Ernest Thompson Seton: 'Animal tracks are the oldest known writing on earth.'"

Gideon looked bored. "Book learnin' don't make a hill of beans of difference."

Cal took a sip of coffee. "Now hold on, Gid. That quote got Ephraim thinking. It was Ephraim who tracked down that bobcat. He laid a trap for it."

Gideon raised an eyebrow. "That Ephraim always was a boy for the woods."

"Maybe so, but Jorie gave him the idea of how to trap him. She had told Ephraim, just the day before, that bobcats have insatiable curiosities. Almost everything attracts their attention. So he put out a trap with a little bit of catnip oil. He learned that from school."

"Humph." Gideon stroked his gray beard, listening to Cal. "That's an old trapper's trick."

From behind Gid's back, Lyddie lifted her eyebrows at Cal, a small gesture of appreciation. Gideon leaned back in his chair.

Cal looked out at the fields. "Looks like you've finished your second hay cutting."

Gideon followed his gaze, then let out a deep sigh. "I suppose I could spare Ray for a little while. Since the harvest is near done."

"I think that's a wise decision, Gid." Cal stood up. "Well, Mary Ann will be wondering what's happened to me. Thank you, Lyddie, for the good-tasting coffee."

Gideon walked him to the door. "Just so's you know, I didn't vote for you for minister."

Cal turned to him and gripped Gid's shoulder with one hand. "Now that just tells me how wise you really are, Gid. I didn't vote for myself, either."

"But I did!" Lyddie called out. "I voted for you, Caleb!"

Cal turned around to wave and heard Gideon scold his wife, "A woman ought not to contradict her man in public."

Before heading into the hardware store late one afternoon, Cal handed Ephraim two dimes. "One for you and one for Maggie too. But no Tootsie Rolls for her. Too chewy. Not till those front teeth make their grand appearance."

Ephraim grinned and went inside to the racks that held the candy bars. His mouth watered at the sight. He loved candy.

Cal walked down the center aisle until he came to the nail bins. As he searched for the type of nails he wanted, Ron Harding, the owner of the hardware store, walked out of the back room. "Hello there, Cal. Sure has been a dry spell we've been having." He looked out the window at the dark clouds. "Those clouds look threatening, though. Always threatening, never delivering. Weather can sure be aggravating."

"It has been dry lately," Cal said agreeably. Ephraim knew he was just being kind. He was always amazed at how much the English carried on about the weather. What was the point? Weather belonged to God.

Ron arched an eyebrow at Ephraim, who was closely following this back-and-forthing. "Say, would you have time for a word?" he asked Cal. "Outside?"

"Give me a minute," Cal said.

"What's your favorite?" Ephraim heard someone ask.

When Ephraim jerked around, he saw the friendly face of Fat Lizzie, the girl whom everyone knew was sweet on Matthew.

Ephraim pointed to the Tootsie Rolls.

"Mine too," she said.

Cal came up to them and handed a bag of nails to Fat Lizzie to weigh so he knew what he owed.

"How's the new school doing?" Lizzie asked him. "I think you were awful smart to hire Jorie King as the teacher." She leaned over the counter and whispered to Cal, "She knows more than most folks about all kinds of things, especially those horses. It makes Ron mad when folks ask Jorie's advice before they buy his harnesses."

Cal grinned. "She's got her work cut out for her, making sure those eighth graders pass that state test next May." He motioned to Ephraim. "Every single scholar needs to pass that test, including our Ephraim."

Ephraim put a Tootsie Roll and a package of Life Savers on the counter and hunted for his dimes as Cal went outside to talk to Ron Harding. Ephraim searched the ground, still couldn't find the dimes, and looked at Fat Lizzie in a panic.

She just waved it off. "My treat today," she told him, with a finger to her lips like they were sharing a secret.

Ephraim didn't know why Matthew was always making fun of Fat Lizzie. He liked her. She was always doing stuff like that for him and Maggie, buying them candy and gum. Matthew said it was only because she was trying to make a good impression. She *was* making a good impression, Ephraim told him. A fine impression. He thanked Fat Lizzie with a grateful nod and walked outside to join Cal.

"I hear you're the head honcho now," Ron Harding was telling his brother.

"Just a minister," Cal corrected.

"Well, I'm just a hardware store owner. But I know that citizens look to us leaders to guide them." He leaned against the porch pole and crossed his arms. "Cal, I was hoping you might use your influence on the Amish folks."

"I would never do that," Cal said. "I only take care of my people's spiritual needs."

"Sure you do! Remember how your people weren't going to take that polio vaccine? Then you gave them a talk, and next thing we knew, your people were taking part in the national vaccine, lined up getting their sugar cubes just like real Americans."

Cal crossed his arms. "What's on your mind, Ron?"

"Seems to me that when you live in this country, you need to be a good citizen."

"We pay our taxes and volunteer as firefighters."

From behind Cal came a drawling voice. "And your people chew up our roads with those danged horses. You won't fight in our wars, but you benefit from being safe in this country."

Cal spun around to face Jerry Gingerich, who worked at the gas station across the street from the hardware store. Cal didn't say anything, he just held Jerry's gaze. Jerry dropped his eyes first and looked over at Ephraim.

Jerry had a neck thicker than any Ephraim had ever seen. His arms and hands were also massive, but what scared Ephraim were his eyes. He thought they were blank and stupid most of the time, but when Jerry looked him up and down, they narrowed into tiny slits. Ben, like Cal, had gone to public schools and had been friendly with Jerry. Ephraim didn't have many memories about his folks—he was only four when they passed—but he did remember the look on his mother's face when Ben hung around with Jerry. Even now, Jerry had a reputation for being a troublemaker. Everybody knew he played gambling card games in the back room of the gas station.

The only thing good about Jerry Gingerich, Ephraim had always thought, was his hunting dog, Rex, a black mutt. Ephraim held out his hand and Rex trotted over to investigate, sniffing tentatively. Satisfied, Rex backed up a few feet and sat down by Jerry's side, like a sentry guard. If Rex could pump gas, Ephraim was pretty sure he could outwork Jerry.

"Now Jerry," Ron said in a calming voice. "Cal's brother Ben is serving as a conscientious objector. He's over in Vietnam." He looked at Cal. "And I heard that your brother Matthew just got called up too. That right?"

Jerry spat on the ground. "Those C.O.'s are safe and sound and cozy, while my brother is serving active duty in the Marines."

"Jerry!" Ron said, clearly exasperated. "Your brother is stationed down in North Carolina." He frowned at Jerry before turning to Cal. "Alls I'm saying, Cal, is that it would be a good thing for this county if you would help us in a sensitive matter."

Cal glanced at Ephraim. "Speak your mind."

"If you want to keep living the way you're living, then you need to do what we tell you to do," Jerry added with a sneer.

"That's enough, Jerry!" Ron looked across the street at the gas station. "You've got a customer." He waited until Jerry ambled back across the street. "All that I wanted to say is that you folks have enjoyed your way of living out here, set apart, and able to mind your own business. We want to keep things that way. But there's a fellow trying to buy a house in this town. He's not our kind of man. If he buys in Stoney Ridge, we'll all lose. Others will be coming in right behind him. That's the way it works with those people. I've seen it with my own eyes. Our land value drops and before you know it, we're looking like Philly or Camden. No townsfolk will sell to him, I made sure of that. So I'm thinking he might try next to find something out in the country. So I'd like you to talk to your people and make sure no one sells to him."

Cal looked at Ron Harding as if he was speaking in Chinese.

"A fellow named James Robinson."

"The veterinarian that's buying Doc Williams's practice?" Cal asked. "We need a good vet. Doc Williams said he's never seen a young vet as capable as James Robinson."

Ron snorted. "Well, we don't need this one."

Cal looked at him, puzzled.

"This one is a colored man."

3

On the morning of September 7, after Maggie and Ephraim went to school, Cal and Mary Ann waited at the bus stop with Matthew to say goodbye. "Well, Matthew," Cal said. "Just as well to get it over with and not have it hanging over your head. The time will fly like a flock of birds. Soon, you'll be back home with us. Ben too. Then we'll see to splitting up Beacon Hollow or buying you both a farm, just like we always said we would."

Mary Ann listened to the two, talking in low voices. *Oh Cal, don't you see? Leaving isn't hanging over Matthew's head. He can't wait to go.* There was a glint in Matthew's eyes that was hard to miss. She always worried he was like Ben in that way. Matthew had a bent toward English things. Worldly temptations.

Yes, two years will fly by. But then would he really come back?

As soon as they saw Matthew off on the bus, Cal and Mary Ann drove the buggy to town for an appointment with their family doctor. More inexplicable bruises had been popping up on her arms and legs, heavy and purple. She finally went to the doctor earlier in the week and he arranged some tests for her right after the visit. She wasn't too concerned about the results; Marge thought she was just anemic. But now she noticed that Dr. Lachman—whom she had known all her life—avoided her eyes, and her heart started to pound as if it was clubbing her chest.

Seated across from them at his desk in his office, Dr. Lachman said the bruising was caused by acute myeloid leukemia. She couldn't understand all that the doctor was trying to explain, that a rapid increase of immature blood cells was crowding out her bone marrow, making it unable to produce healthy blood cells. But she did understand that leukemia meant blood cancer.

"How long, Mary Ann?" Cal asked her, all color drained from his face. "When did you first notice the bruising?"

She looked down at her hands and noticed they were trembling. It was suddenly so hot in the office. She could feel a trickle of sweat roll down her back, but strangely, her hands were ice cold, so she wrapped them in her apron. "A few weeks ago," she answered quietly.

"Why didn't you say something?" Cal said.

"I thought it was the flu," she said, fumbling for the words. "There was just so much going on . . . Matthew's news, you became minister, school started up . . ." She started to cry but bit her lip to stop. She didn't want to cry. Once she started, she wasn't sure she could stop.

Cal crouched down beside his wife. "Oh Mary Ann, please don't cry. I can't bear it if you cry." He covered her hands with his.

Mary Ann looked down at her husband's large, calloused hands. How she loved those strong hands. She tried to draw in a breath, but it caught in her throat. "How long?" she asked the doctor in a quiet voice. "How long do I have?"

"No, no. We're not going to be thinking like that," Cal said, rising to his feet. "You can do something, can't you, Dr. Lachman?"

"This is a rare cancer, Mr. Zook, and a very aggressive one."

Mary Ann flinched as if the doctor had reached across his desk to strike her. Cancer. *Slap.* Aggressive. *Slap.*

"There's got to be *something* you can do," Cal insisted.

The doctor kept his eyes on his desktop.

"What are you saying?" Cal asked, his face ashen. "You can't be telling me she only has a short time to live. She's only thirty-two years old!"

"How long?" Mary Ann repeated. She had a hard time talking around the knot in her throat, a knot made of tangled threads of fear, worry, and unbearable sadness. "A year? Six months? Just tell me the truth."

Dr. Lachman took a deep breath. "Not months. A matter of weeks and days."

"Lieber Gott." Cal leaned forward, palms on the doctor's desk. *Dear God.* After a long moment, he spoke in a hard, desperate whisper. "Please, Dr. Lachman, there's *got* to be something."

Dr. Lachman rubbed his forehead. "I suppose we could try some treatments, but—"

"See, Mary Ann?" Cal jumped on that, his eyes filled with hope. "See? I knew there could be something to try." He looked at the doctor. "I've read there are all kinds of new medical discoveries going on, all the time."

"That's true enough," Dr. Lachman said. "Breakthroughs in research are going on all the time. Why, just last year, the Surgeon General announced that smoking can cause cancer."

"I don't smoke," Mary Ann said sharply. She didn't mean to sound so harsh; it just seemed like such a ridiculous comment to make.

Dr. Lachman looked away. "What I meant was that scientists are on the brink of discovery."

"Do I have time to wait?" she asked, but the doctor had no answer for her.

The first thing Matthew did after getting off the bus in Lebanon was to find a place to live. Lottie, the supervisor at the Veterans Hospital where he had been hired to work, gave him the address of a lady named Mrs. Flanagan, who lived close to the hospital and had a room to rent. Lottie must have tipped Mrs. Flanagan off that Matthew would be a good tenant because the older lady seemed to be expecting him. The front door opened as he approached it and a heavyset woman with dyed orange hair, penciled eyebrows, and a thick, doughy face lumbered out to meet him. She showed him the room to rent and within minutes, he had a new home. If you could call the tiny room a home; he thought of it more like a shoe box. Still, he was grateful.

After unpacking, he retraced his steps back to the bus stop, certain he had passed a barbershop on the way. He had never been in a barbershop before. His mother, and then Mary Ann, had always cut his hair out on the back porch. The barber, a short man with a round belly, pointed to a pedestal chair bolted to the cracked linoleum floor, then flung a plastic apron over Matthew's chest and spun him around, peering at his longish hair. "We don't get too many hippies coming in here."

"But I'm not a hippie," Matthew said. "I'm starting a new job tomorrow at the Veterans Hospital."

"Well, then, how 'bout a buzz?" he asked Matthew with a glint in his eye.

Matthew nodded, not quite sure what to say, nor what a buzz meant. Just a few minutes later, he was educated.

He paid for the haircut, mumbled a thank-you, and looked for a shop where he could buy a baseball cap to cover his conspicuously bare head.

Dr. Lachman scheduled Mary Ann to start chemotherapy immediately—the side effects were so intense that she was nauseous, fought fever and chills, and was exhausted. Her sister, Sylvia, organized a steady stream of helpers from the church so that Mary Ann was never alone. She tried telling Sylvia that all she really wanted was to be alone, but Sylvia was not convinced. Her sister came every day, right after school, and brought eleven-year-old Esther to play with Maggie, which meant Ephraim disappeared into the woods and Maggie was in a bad mood for the rest of the evening. Mary Ann empathized. Esther bossed Maggie and Ephraim around just like Sylvia used to boss Mary Ann. As much as she loved her sister, Sylvia had an effect on others like a dark cloud on a beautiful day.

Shortly after breakfast on Saturday, Marge King came to pay a visit at Beacon Hollow. Mary Ann was resting in her room when Marge burst in, Jorie trailing behind with an apologetic look on her face. Marge went right up to Mary Ann, took her pulse, and rested her palm against her forehead. Mary Ann knew that Marge was happiest when she was playing doctor, and she had a feeling she was about to get the full treatment.

Marge peered into her eyes and said, "I've got just the thing for you. I'll go downstairs and whip it up."

"She's been itching to come," Jorie whispered to Mary Ann after Marge went downstairs. "She's been working on a curative since she heard your news. I recommend tossing it out the window when her back is turned."

Mary Ann smiled at her friend. Being around Jorie was like a breath of fresh air. She found she even felt a little more energetic. "Would you help me get dressed so I can go downstairs? I'm tired of being in this room."

Sylvia swept in as Jorie was brushing Mary Ann's hair to pin it into a bun. She walked up to Jorie and snatched the brush from her hand. "You are *not* her sister."

Mary Ann blanched as Jorie backed away with a hurt look on her face. Sylvia meant well, but she only knew one way of helping others, and that meant total control. It had been that way since they were children. Their mother had passed when the sisters were young, and even though Sylvia wasn't much older than Mary Ann, she assumed the role of mother and big sister, rolled into one. Mary Ann even thought Sylvia intimidated their father. He had tried courting a few women, but Sylvia found serious character flaws in each prospective bride. He didn't take a second wife until Sylvia married Noah Swartzentruber. And as soon as Mary Ann married Cal, he sold his farm to Noah and Sylvia and moved with his new wife to Sarasota, Florida. When Noah died, unexpectedly, Mary Ann thought Sylvia and Esther might go live with their father, but Sylvia didn't have any reason to leave Stoney Ridge. Though it wasn't spoken of, everyone knew Noah Swartzentruber had been a wealthy man.

"Not so hard, Sylvia," Mary Ann said, wincing, as Sylvia pulled a brush through her long hair.

But it was too late. Sylvia suddenly dropped the brush on the floor. The three women stood there, staring at it. Clumps of long hair were on the brush, fallen from Mary Ann's head.

It was too hot to sleep. Ephraim tried to dwell on thoughts of winter: sledding down Eagle Hill, ice-skating on Blue Lake Pond. But in the middle of September, cold weather was a distant dream.

Lying in bed, listening to the crickets, Ephraim found himself swirling in worries. In just a week's time, Mary Ann had gone from feeling a little poorly to barely able to get out of bed. Her sister, Sylvia, had taken over their home and dished out chores like she owned the place. Cal assured him that it was only for a short while, that Mary Ann would be as good as new soon. But what if Mary Ann didn't get well?

He let his thoughts drift to Vietnam, a place that seemed about as foreign as a place could be. What if Ben didn't come home? It was a question he tortured himself with on nights like tonight, when he couldn't sleep. The worrisome thoughts came too fast. He wanted Ben at Beacon Hollow, to throw softballs against the barn and to teach Maggie to swim at Blue Lake Pond. He'd tried to help her swim a couple of times this summer, but she sunk like a stone.

Ben had taught Ephraim a few cuss words that he tried to practice when he was alone. He tried them out today, when he was hiding from Esther, but found he didn't have the heart for cussing, and he didn't know what the words meant, anyway. Ben said he would teach him the meanings of the insults when he came back home. So Ephraim quit trying, prayed for forgiveness, and went home for dinner.

Early Sunday morning, Cal took a cup of tea upstairs to Mary Ann and was surprised to find her getting dressed. "Just what do you think you're doing?"

She pinned the top part of her dress together. "Going to meeting."

He set the teacup down on the nightstand. "You must be out of your mind. You're not strong enough."

"Going to meeting gives me strength. There's no place I'd rather be today than at church with my family, hearing you preach."

Cal sat on the bed. "You shouldn't even be around so many people coughing and sneezing. You could get sick and . . ."

"And what, Cal? Catch cold and die?"

As soon as the words tumbled from her mouth, she wished them back. Cal's shoulders drew back as if he'd been hit. She hadn't meant to sound mean. Harsh words were not said in their home. But something needed to be said. They both needed to face the truth of how sick she really was.

She saw Cal's glance shift toward the door. Maggie was peeking around the open door, overhearing their conversation. Mary Ann reached out her arms for her daughter, who rushed into them.

"I'm feeling fine, Maggie. Truly, I am." Mary Ann smoothed her daughter's soft cheek. Her heart ached in a sweet way as she watched the relief ease Maggie's small face.

Rehearsing for the Christmas program had gone so badly during Monday's practice that Ephraim told Maggie to go home without him, and he darted past her before she could start up with any of her endless questions. He hurried through the pasture field, crossed the creek and several fences and fields, and reached his favorite place on earth: the Deep Woods. The Deep Woods belonged to Bud Schultz, their English neighbor to the north. Bud didn't mind people traipsing through the woods, as long as they left it unspoiled. Ephraim knew there were folks—both English and Plain—who borrowed Bud's woods without a care. Sometimes, Ephraim would bring a sack to carry out empty bottles of beer and spirits he came across. He couldn't let garbage remain in that beautiful place. The Deep Woods was a remnant of virgin woods, bordered by a stream and a marsh. It was impossible to log by horses, and somehow, over the last three centuries, those majestic trees had slipped by unnoticed and been spared the axe.

His father had taught all of his sons from an early age to love the Deep Woods. He remembered his father saying, in a voice of reverence, that these woods were what the country looked like when the first settlers arrived from across the Appalachians.

Ephraim knew these woods like he knew Beacon Hollow. Even in the deep shadows of the setting sun, the place was familiar to him, filled with landmarks of childhood memories: an enormous old oak where he had once taken refuge from a skunk passing by; a makeshift blind where he could watch white-tailed deer; a stream where he had been able to catch fat fish in no time. He found his favorite spot—a felled beech tree, covered with a cushion of moss. On the tree was carved his father's initials: "SZ, 4/8/26, caught 3 cottontails." He sat down and became utterly still. Soon, the woods came alive with creatures. Around Ephraim's neck hung his binoculars. He slept with them nightly and polished them weekly, and nothing was as dear to his soul.

High above Ephraim's head came a *peck-peck-peck* sound. He slowly lifted the binoculars to his eyes and followed a branch until he saw a redheaded woodpecker drilling for insects in a nearby tree. Two squirrels raced through the treetops. Then the woods became silent, like a curtain had been drawn. He heard the steps of someone approaching and jumped up.

"Ephraim!" Jorie reached him, panting. "I was just about to give up looking!"

"W-what's w-wrong?" His first thought was of Mary Ann.

She held up a hand to catch her breath, then plopped down on a fallen log. "I just wanted to give something to you, but you lit out of school so fast!" She handed him a sketch pad, along with a charcoal pencil. "It's for you. To make observations of nature. When I graduated eighth grade, my teacher gave me a set of paints and a sketch pad, so that I would keep painting. I guess I had thought it would end, after school ended, but she was right. Learning never ends."

After he took it from her, she looked all around her. "Isn't this a wonderful place? It's like a primeval forest! These trees must be hundreds of years old." She looked almost dazzled. "Imagine how much these old trees have seen and heard over the years." She ran her hand along the giant beech, gave a satisfied sigh, and turned back to Ephraim. "So. Rehearsal didn't go too well."

Ephraim shook his head. "I c-can't." He had a gut-wrenching fear of speaking in front of class. In the Deep Woods he had no such fears—the trees and flowers and birds and squirrels that thronged the forest never laughed at him like the other kids would. Like Esther Swartzentruber did on a daily basis.

"Sure you can, Ephraim," Jorie said. She nudged him with her elbow. "You're a Zook."

"I'm n-not. I'll n-never b-be like them."

Jorie's sky blue eyes looked intently at him. As if he was worth something. "Why wouldn't you want to be like your brothers? I don't know another family who is as well respected as the Zooks. It's been that way as long as I can remember."

Ephraim glanced away. She didn't understand. His brothers—each one so different from the other—were smart as a whip. He couldn't even talk fast. When he tried, the words piled up in his throat like sticks in a beaver's dam.

"And the Zook stubbornness is legendary. I can see right now that you've got that trait."

Ephraim tried not to smile.

Softly, she added, "Ephraim, don't you know you're more like Cal than Ben or Matthew?"

He felt tears prickle his eyes and looked away. "I c-can't m-memorize the whole thing. I t-tried."

"Memory is such a mystery. You don't have to have the whole thing in your head, like reading from a book. Your mind will lead you from one thing to the next, the same way a flashlight can light a step ahead of you. In time, you'll learn to trust your memory."

They sat there quietly, listening to the songbirds, while he took in what she said. Then she rose to her feet. "If you want some help memorizing your lines, I'd be happy to help you after school."

A stain of flush brushed his cheeks. "Since M-Matthew's away and M-Mary Ann is ailing, C-Cal n-needs me at h-home right after school t-to help chore."

"Saturdays, then. You can usually find me at the schoolhouse on Saturday mornings." She pointed to the sketch pad she had brought him. "I've noticed you have a knack for sketching. I thought it might be helpful if you had a real pad to draw your observations. About birds and trees and all kinds of wild creatures." She looked up at the sun beaming through the treetops. "Nature like this, it's a sanctuary, isn't it? A solace. To me, the God who created all this beauty must be a wonderful and loving Being. A realm of limitless love." She sighed happily. "I'd better get back. Don't stay too late. You know how Mary Ann gets to fretting." She turned to leave, then spun around to add, "Everything's going to be fine, Ephraim." She headed out the way she came.

Ephraim watched her for a while, then opened the sketch pad and scribbled his name on the inside corner.

As often as she could, Jorie stopped by to visit Mary Ann at Beacon Hollow, but this time the sight of her dear friend had her close to tears.

"I brought some books for Ephraim," she said, putting the books on the side table where Mary Ann sat in a porch rocker. She tried to keep her voice sounding lighthearted and carefree, but the truth was, she was shocked by how quickly Mary Ann's appearance was deteriorating. When she arrived, Mary Ann had been folding laundry, but she had to stop and rest after each garment, as if it was too heavy to lift. Her skin was milk pale, nearly translucent, and there was a bruise on the hollow of her throat.

Mary Ann's eyes swept over the titles on the books' spines. "Did Cal ever tell you why he was so determined to have you be the schoolteacher?"

"No. He just kept telling me I needed to do this, for the good of the community."

"That sounds just like Cal, doesn't it?" she said with a fragile smile. "It has been good for the community, but the real reason was because he knew you would be good for our Ephraim." She looked out to the pasture where Ephraim and Maggie were tossing hay to the horses, carted from pasture to pasture in a little red wagon. The horses nickered and rumbled and stretched out their necks, snatching mouthfuls of hay before it even hit the ground. "Ever since Ben left, he's grown quieter. And his stuttering seems to be getting worse. We've all tried to encourage him to talk. But still, he's just getting quieter. The sight of him fighting to form words never fails to pierce my heart."

"He's a fine boy, Mary Ann. He's just at that age where he's very bashful."

"Think he'll ever outgrow his stuttering?"

"Absolutely. As his confidence grows."

"He reads all of the books you loan to him. Sometimes in the same day." Mary Ann sighed. "I always wished I was more of a scholar. Like Cal. So that I had more things to talk about with him. I just never liked to read much."

Jorie patted her on the knee. "I don't think your marriage to Cal is lacking in any way."

"Jorie, why didn't you marry Ben before he left?"

Jorie grew still. As close as they were, she hadn't expected such a personal question from Mary Ann.

"I don't mean to pry," she hurried to add. "I just have always wondered, that's all, and this sickness has given me boldness. Why would you wait for him but not marry him? You might have had a child by now. Maybe two."

Jorie took a towel from the laundry basket and folded it. "Ben never asked me."

Mary Ann's eyes went wide. "What?! Then . . . what have you been waiting for?"

Jorie shrugged and picked up another towel to fold. "I guess I've been waiting for Ben to grow up." She put the towel on top of the stack and picked up a sheet.

"There are other men to consider. They've certainly given *you* a lot of consideration."

Jorie anchored the corner of a sheet under her chin to fold and rolled her eyes to the heavens.

"Jacob Schwartz? Daniel Riehl?" Mary Ann spread out her fingers and started counting. "Levi Lapp. Zach Glick. His cousin Sam Glick. Then there's—"

Jorie put up a hand to stop her. "It's always been Ben for me. You know that." She put the folded sheet in the basket, on top of the towels.

Mary Ann leaned back in her chair and closed her eyes, as if spent. "Oh Jorie. What if you're waiting and waiting for Ben to be something he's not?"

Jorie had nothing she could say to that. It was not a new thought to her. She stood. "Well, there just aren't enough Caleb Zooks to go around. The rest of us have to make do." She reached down to lift the basket. "I'll take this laundry in. Shall I bring you a lemonade?"

Mary Ann's eyes flew open, as if something just occurred to her.

"Are you all right?"

"Yes. Yes. Lemonade would be fine."

Jorie hoisted the basket on her hip and took a few steps, then turned back for a moment. "Sure you're all right?"

Mary Ann nodded, a serious look on her face. "I'm just fine."

By the time Jorie was leaving to go home, the sky was lit with color as the sun started its descent into the horizon. Cal was outside harnessing a buggy horse as she passed by him on her way down the driveway.

"Cal, stop for a moment and look up! It's a spectacular sunset," Jorie said. "I've always thought of a sunset as God's last painting of the day. It's the last gift he gives to us before he gives us the gift of a sunrise."

Cal looked in the direction she was pointing. "'His name shall endure for ever: his name shall be continued as long as the sun: and men shall be blessed in him: all nations shall call him blessed.'" He glanced over at her and read the question on her face. "Psalm 72:17." He turned back to the setting sun. "Thank you, Jorie. I needed a spectacular sunset today."

The horse nudged Cal with his long nose, as if to remind him that he was waiting. Absentmindedly, Cal reached out a hand and stroked his forelocks.

"I appreciate you stopping by when you can. The two of you had your heads bent together, whispering like schoolgirls."

"I was telling her stories about our scholars. How are you holding up, Cal?"

"God will not lead us where his grace cannot take us." He spoke the words and he knew them to be true, and the thought behind them was true, but still, they didn't quench the fear in his heart of what was coming.

"That doesn't mean this isn't a hard thing to endure." Her gaze met his over the horse's head. "So how are you holding up, really? You look . . . positively wrung out."

He fit the bit into the horse's mouth, slipped the bridle over its head, and buckled its chinstrap. "Truth be told, I'm a little stunned. Like I'm going to wake up any day now and realize it's all just been a bad dream." He hooked his hands on his hips. "It's all happening so fast. It's like time has turned into a fast-running river. And all I want is for the river to run backward."

Jorie's eyes filled with tears. "She's like a sister to me."

He gave her a gentle smile. "She feels the same way about you." His attention turned toward the clip-clopping of horses' hooves on the driveway. "Speaking of sisters. Here comes Sylvia."

"I'd better be getting home," Jorie said quickly. She slipped away, taking the trail behind the barn, so that she would be out of sight before the buggy reached the rise.

"What's your hurry?" Cal called out, grinning, watching her go.

It didn't seem right to smile, under such circumstances, but he couldn't help himself as he watched her scoot off. Sylvia had always been hard on Jorie. Mary Ann thought it was because, long ago, Atlee King insulted Sylvia's father by not selling a Percheron to him. Atlee was particular about his horses and wouldn't sell to just anybody. Sylvia's father had a reputation for being too harsh with animals. It would be Sylvia's nature to bear a grudge even if it wasn't her grudge to bear. But Cal thought Sylvia's rancor had more to do with the close friendship between Jorie and Mary Ann.

Sylvia's horse came to a halt and he knew he should go greet her. He usually tried to make himself scarce when Sylvia paid a visit. Mary Ann often teased him that it was strangely coincidental how many chores in the barn demanded his immediate attention when her sister came calling.

Today, with Mary Ann feeling so poorly, it wouldn't be right to leave his wife alone, unfortified.

The rain came down in waves, making up for weeks of bone-dry weather. Cal was trying to spend every spare minute he could with Mary Ann, so he was doubly grateful for the rain. It gave him an excuse to go inside the house and not have Mary Ann accuse him of hovering. She was curled up on the living room sofa, looking out the window at the rain as it fell sideways in the fierce wind. Cal was at his desk, paying bills. They hadn't spoken in a long time, but it didn't bother him. He just wanted to be near her.

Interrupting the tranquility, Ephraim burst into the kitchen. "Cal!" he shouted when he spotted his brother in the living room. "There's an important l-looking l-letter for you." He thrust the letter at Cal. "From the g-government." He pulled off his raincoat and hat and hung them to dry on the wall peg.

"Is it about Ben?" Mary Ann asked.

Cal nodded. Shock coursed through him and it took all of his willpower to appear calm as he finished reading the letter. "They want his dental records."

"Now why would they ask for those?" she asked. "I don't know if he has any."

"He doesn't." Cal folded up the paper and tucked it back in the envelope. He walked over to the sofa and sat down with the letter in his hand. "Ephraim, please go feed the sow."

"Aw, Cal! I just c-came in! It's p-pouring b-buckets."

"Go!" Cal said firmly, pointing to the door.

Choking over words of protest, Ephraim snatched off his hat and slammed it on his head, jerking open the door.

Mary Ann put a soft hand on Cal's forearm.

"They want dental records to identify his body," Cal said quietly, covering her hand with his. "It's probably a mistake. The Army is famous for making all kinds of mistakes. Until we hear more, we'll keep this news to ourselves. No point in worrying anybody about something that is most likely wrong."

As soon as the rain let up, Cal walked over to Bud's and made a call to the government phone number listed on the letter.

❧❧

The wait was over three days later. Two Army officers arrived at the house in a dark green car with news about Ben. "We're confident that we have a positive identification on Benjamin S. Zook," they told Cal after he greeted them on the front porch where Mary Ann was taking some sun. "He was killed by an enemy sniper while he was evacuating a wounded soldier. He died a hero's death and is eligible to be buried in a military graveyard." One officer held out Ben's dog tags in his hand.

Cal picked up the dog tags as if they were made of spun sugar. After a long moment, he lifted his head and said in a voice roughened with pain, "No. He belongs here, with us." He ran his finger over the indentation that read BENJAMIN S. ZOOK. "We didn't have dental records, but if I saw his body, I could confirm his identity. Maybe there's been a mistake."

The officers exchanged a glance. One cleared his throat and said, "The body is . . . well, there was a misunderstanding when the body, I mean, your brother's body . . . well, you see . . ." He looked to the other officer for help.

"Sir, Benjamin S. Zook was cremated," the other officer said. He started out boldly, then he too, watching Cal's and Mary Ann's horrified faces, lost his composure. "Apparently, the jungle heat . . . bodies decompose so quickly . . . and the commanding officer made a decision . . . well, we're terribly sorry. I realize—now—that cremation isn't your religion's customary way of . . ." His words drizzled to a stop.

"Lieber Gott . . ." Mary Ann put her head in her hands. *Dear God.* Cal put his hand on her shoulder.

"I have his remains in the trunk. I'll go get them . . . uh, it." When he returned, he held out a small metal box for Cal and a flag. "Here's the flag for you, for the funeral."

Cal shook his head. "Thank you, no. We don't fly flags."

The officers exchanged another look of confusion, then quickly said good-bye and drove off.

Together, Cal and Mary Ann sat for a while, staring at the small metal box that held all that was left of Benjamin Zook.

"I'd better tell Jorie," she said, breaking the quiet.

"I'll go," Cal said as he stood up, raking a hand through his hair. "You need to rest. We have a funeral to plan. I'll stop by a few other neighbors and let them know too. And I'll stop at Bud's to call Matthew at work."

Mary Ann rose to put her arms around his waist. "I'm so sorry."

Cal wrapped his arms around her. Over her shoulder, he looked down at the dog tags, clenched in his fist. "I just thought I would've known, deep in my bones, if something had happened to one of my own."

Cal was told by Atlee that he could find Jorie at the schoolhouse. He came over the hill and saw the yellow light of a lantern glowing. He knocked on the door, waited, then knocked again before she came to the door.

"Oh, Cal!"

"You working?" he asked.

"Yes." She opened the door and stepped back so he could enter.

Cal took a deep breath. "I have some news. About Ben."

Her face lifted to his, filled with hope. It broke his heart, having to tell her this terrible news. He dropped his eyes to the ground, unable to look at her any longer.

"He's been killed, Jorie." He glanced up as the shock registered through her. She sank down on the bench behind her. "Two Army men came to the house this afternoon to give us the news."

She didn't say a word. She just sat there, looking stunned. It wasn't proper for him to touch her in any way and so he didn't, but he wanted to do or say something that would help to ease her hurt. He shared the pain she was feeling.

"Jorie," he whispered as he sat down on the bench beside her. "Say something."

She looked at him, startled, as if she had forgotten he was there. "Things were left so badly between us."

"What do you mean?"

"Ben. He did it on purpose."

"Did what?"

"At the Recruiting Office. He knew to sign up for being willing to serve. He knew the difference."

"That's not true. He didn't know. He was fooled."

She shook her head. "He knew. This was his chance to see the world, he said."

Cal leaned back. "Why would he tell me he had been tricked?" He found he wasn't entirely surprised, as if he himself had a doubt in his mind but kept it stifled.

She sighed. "Cal, you always believe the best in others. Ben didn't want you thinking he was less than he was." She put her hands against her face. "When he told me what he had done, we argued. I told him I wouldn't wait for him." Then her eyes started to fill with tears. "But I *was* waiting. I've been waiting and waiting for him to come home."

Cal felt hot tears burn the back of his eyes. "He cared for you, Jorie."

"I know. I know he did. But not enough to keep him home." A tear leaked down her cheek. "And I didn't love him enough to leave."

And what could he say to that? It was the truth. He had known Ben had tried talking her into leaving the church with him, before he was even drafted, but she refused. He had always admired Jorie for standing her ground with Ben. "I'll walk you home."

"No. Thank you. I'd rather be alone for a while."

He stood and walked to the door. "As soon as I speak to Isaac, I'll let you know when the funeral will be held."

She nodded and followed him to the door. "Tell Mary Ann that I'll come help dress him for the viewing."

"There will be no viewing, Jorie." He looked away. "They cremated him."

She had to grab the doorjamb to steady herself. "Oh Cal, have we seen our Ben for the last time?"

He did touch her then. Ever so gently, he squeezed her shoulders with his hands. "No, Jorie. Not for the last time. We have hope for a life together in the presence of Almighty God."

Ben's funeral was planned for Saturday. The night before, in the predawn hours, Mary Ann woke up, realized Cal was not there, and tiptoed downstairs. She saw a lantern light in the barn and grabbed her shawl to pull around her. Before she even reached the barn, she heard the sounds. Sounds of Cal weeping. She had only known him to cry once, four years ago, when they buried their stillborn son. She stopped, knowing he would feel shamed if she found him grieving so deeply. It wasn't their way to express deep emotion. Doing so would seem like a complaint against the Lord.

She knew it would be best to let Cal grieve for his brother in private. Besides, Ben was a sore spot between them. Mary Ann couldn't pinpoint why, but she never quite trusted Ben. Cal would hear none of that; to him, Ben was a Zook. She dropped her head and returned to the house, finding her pathway in the dark with a flashlight.

When she passed by Cal's desk, she stopped and took out four sheets of stationery. She wrote and wrote, words from her heart, then sealed each letter in its envelope and addressed one to Matthew, one to Ephraim, one to Maggie. And one to Cal.

When Matthew asked Lottie for time off to attend his brother's funeral, she threw her plump arms around him and hugged him so tightly that he nearly felt the wind was getting squeezed out of him.

"Oh baby, you take all the time you need," she told Matthew, rocking him back and forth, her eyes brimming with tears. Lottie's son was a soldier in Vietnam and she talked about him every single day.

Ben's death seemed more real to Lottie than it did to Matthew. He just couldn't believe he would never see his brother walk up the steep incline of Beacon Hollow with that long stride of his, or pitch a softball to Ephraim on their front lawn, or toss Maggie in the air, or watch Ben drive off in his courting buggy with Jorie by his side. Or . . . skipping out the side door of the barn to head to town—letting Matthew finish up choring for him. Ben was famous for that. Matthew could never stay mad at him for long, and he never let Cal know how often it happened, either.

After work on Friday, Matthew caught the bus to Stoney Ridge and was surprised to see Cal waiting for him at the station. Matthew knew something was on his mind when Cal didn't even comment on his hair, hidden under his black felt hat. He left the baseball cap back at Mrs. Flanagan's, along with his new English clothes. He had expected to get a raised eyebrow and a gentle lecture about staying on the Plain and narrow way. Instead, on the drive to Beacon Hollow, Cal explained that Mary Ann had a type of blood cancer.

"You might be surprised when you see her," Cal said. "She's as frail as a bird."

"But I just saw her a few weeks ago. How could she get so sick so fast?"

"That's the acute part, I suppose, of acute myeloid leukemia."

"But she'll be okay, won't she? I mean, those doctors can work miracles. At least, that's what they tell us at the Veterans Hospital."

Cal swallowed hard. "I don't think so, Matthew. It's like she's fading away, right before our eyes."

Matthew was quiet for a long while. First Ben, then Mary Ann. Here he had been enjoying his new life, even if it was in tired old Lebanon, while Cal was coping with tragedy after tragedy. Without thinking, he took off his hat and turned it around and around by the brim. "Life can sure change fast, can't it?"

Cal nodded. "That it can."

Matthew glanced at Cal, at the strong set of his jaw. His brother reminded him of a plowed field, with furrows straight and deep. "Cal, we all count on you. Who do you count on?"

Cal's eyes turned to the ridgeline that defined Stoney Ridge. "'I will lift up mine eyes unto the hills, from whence cometh my help. My help cometh from the Lord, which made heaven and earth.' If the Lord God is wise enough to manage this world, he knows enough to help me through these troubles." A brief smile passed over his face as he gave a sideways glance at Matthew. "So, little brother, I see you got your money's worth at the barbershop."

Later that afternoon, after Ben's funeral service, the last of the women washed and dried dishes in Beacon Hollow's kitchen while husbands gathered outside by the buggies. Jorie stayed as long as she could, but the moment came when she had to get off by herself. She slipped out the back door and walked down to the willow tree by the creek. It was a glorious September afternoon, almost cruel in its beauty. She saw Ephraim walking around in the creek, barefoot with his pants rolled up, watching the water swirl around his ankles.

"Hello there, Ephraim."

He whirled around, looking as if he expected to be called back to the house. Instead, Jorie sat down on the creek bank.

"Nice to have a few moments to yourself, isn't it?"

He nodded.

"The creek is so clean that you can see to the bottom. Did you know that water is actually made up of different colors? All clear, but colors all the same."

He dug a toe into the creek bottom, kicking up a swirl of dirt.

"I'm sorry about Ben. I know you and he were especially close."

Ephraim gave a big nod. "I'm s-sorry too. F-for you."

She nodded, then swallowed hard to fight back the tears that started to prickle her eyes. They came so suddenly, those tears. "It's hard to understand God's will sometimes. It's hard to understand why he took our Ben."

"A-about Mary Ann t-too."

Jorie studied Ephraim's profile as he watched the ripples on the top of the water. He was so dear to her, her Ephraim. He reminded her of one of her colts: gangly, long limbed, awkward, skinny as a broom handle, but filled with so much promise. She shouldn't have been surprised that he had figured out Mary Ann wasn't going to get better. Ephraim was perceptive like that. They sat there quietly for a long time, watching bugs land on the top of the water. "The bishop's words at the very end of Ben's funeral today helped me feel better. Do you remember what he said? He repeated it twice."

"God a-always h-has a p-plan."

"Promise me you'll say that to yourself whenever you start thinking about Ben and feeling sad. And whenever you feel worried about Mary Ann. I promise to do the same."

She rose to her feet. "I'd better get back up there. My grandmother had her eye on Sylvia's sour cream coffee cake. I don't think Sylvia would understand if that entire cake went missing."

She smiled a little, and that made Ephraim smile. It felt good to smile, she thought, even on a day like today.

On the bus ride back to Lebanon late Sunday afternoon, Matthew's heart felt heavy. He didn't know what troubled him more: the reality of Ben's death or the sight of Mary Ann. Both, most likely.

When he had walked into the kitchen, the sight of her tore a choking gasp from his throat. She was thin and pale, with dark circles under her eyes.

He could hardly say hello, trying to get it past the knot in his throat. He noticed bruises on her arms and suspected they were on her legs too, though she covered them in stockings. For the first time since he had left home, he found himself wishing he was still at Beacon Hollow, to help his family. He had planned to spend his days off exploring the area, maybe even take the bus to Philadelphia. He wanted to visit museums and well-stocked libraries, to attend different churches, and even to sit downtown on park benches and watch people. Mostly girls. So far, he had hardly seen any girl under fifty in Lebanon, and the one he did meet—a candy striper at the hospital—had a very impressive overbite.

Instead, he decided he would head back to Stoney Ridge as often as he could. Cal needed him.

The last few nights when Mary Ann woke in the night, she found Cal in the chair next to the bed, watching her, like a mother looking after a sleeping child. She wished his last memories of her wouldn't be these but of other times, when she had been young and full of life. She smiled and patted the bed so he would lie down beside her. He slid into bed, stretched out, and put his arm around her, so that her head was on his chest. She could hear his heart beating. What a beautiful sound, she thought. The sound of your husband's heartbeat.

"Cal, I told Dr. Lachman today that I am going to stop the treatments." She listened for him to respond, but he didn't say a word. "The treatments aren't working. The cancer is going too fast. I need to die well."

She glanced up at him. He was staring at the ceiling.

"Dr. Lachman agreed with me."

A tear slipped from the corner of Cal's eye and rolled down his cheek.

She propped herself up on her elbow to face him. "I need to show Ephraim and Maggie, even Matthew, that our faith matters, even facing death. Maybe especially then. I can't do it while I'm sick from the chemotherapy, lying in bed, looking and feeling like a plucked chicken. This is my time. I'm at peace with it." She reached over him to pull the nightstand drawer open and take out the letters. "There's one for Matthew and Ephraim and Maggie. To be given to them on their wedding day." It could have been hours later or only moments when she lifted the fourth letter and placed it gently on top of his chest. "This one is for you, Cal. For your wedding day."

"Don't," he said, his voice breaking.

She brushed the tears off of his cheeks. "I've never asked anything of you, Cal, but I am asking you to consider this. After I am gone, it's normal to grieve. I hope you'll miss me sorely." She paused and took a deep breath. "But after a time I want you to ask our Jorie to be your wife."

Mary Ann could read the shock of her words on Cal's face by the moon that was casting its long pale light through the window.

He turned away. "You can't pick out another woman and tell me to love her," he said after a long moment. "You can't be thinking I'll marry her after you're gone. You can't will someone into taking your place."

She touched his cheek, turning his face back to hers. "I've given this thought and prayer, Cal. Jorie would be just the kind of mother our Maggie and Ephraim need. And the right wife for you too."

"Jorie King is my brother's girl."

"Not anymore." She felt him take in a hard breath. "It might take awhile to think of her in a different way, but I hope you won't let that stop you, Cal. Not Ben's memory, not meddling relatives." She sighed. "Things have changed, for all of us. I'm blessed, in a way, having this time. Knowing I'm dying. Your folks never had that chance." She laid her head back down against his chest, her cheek nestling into the hollow above his heart.

In a voice roughed by pain, Cal said, "I just don't know how I'm going to live through your dying."

A cold spell hit the next week, complete with gusting wind and frost on the roofs of the farmhouse and outbuildings. It took them all by surprise after such a long hot summer.

"M-Mary Ann, are you . . . g-going to g-get b-better?" Ephraim asked her one morning when he brought a pail of steaming milk into the kitchen from the barn.

Mary Ann turned slowly, careful to keep her face calm, for even with the gusting wind she'd caught the note of fear in Ephraim's voice and it touched her heart. He was standing in front of the wall pegs that held Cal's hat and large coat and looked so small by comparison. His bony wrists, chapped red from the cold, stuck out from the ends of his coat sleeves. She came up to him, her gaze moving gently over his face, a face that was so dear to her.

"I don't think I am, Ephraim," she said.

The words flew from Ephraim's mouth, fierce and whole. "Please don't die."

Mary Ann dug her fingers into his shoulders as she pulled him against her. It was hard, so hard sometimes to accept God's will.

The weather warmed up by week's end. One evening, Mary Ann had just enough strength to ask Cal to carry her outside to watch the day end. He bundled her up in quilts and sat her in the porch swing so she could watch Maggie and Ephraim play softball. Cal sat next to her, holding her hand. Her heart was suddenly too full for words as she let her gaze roam lovingly over Beacon Hollow: the corn shocks built like tepees, her vegetable garden that had been started and tended by Cal's mother, the neat shed that held their winter wood supply, the lofty white barn. Flat, carefully plowed fields with rich, loamy soil. And a creek that ran almost the year round to give water to their cows and sheep and horses that liked to graze under the willow tree's shade. Cal kept the farm in immaculate condition, just like his father had. Beacon Hollow, it was part of them; this place was their history. This farm—it was a good home to raise a family.

They watched the sun slip under the horizon, slowly and silently. She wondered if this was what dying would feel like. Slipping away slowly and silently. She didn't fear death, for she would be in the loving arms of her Father in heaven. But it was the thought of the loving arms of those she was leaving behind that broke her heart, the thought of all those joyful moments they shared that would be lost.

She knew she didn't have much longer. She had grown so weak, so tired. Her body was covered with deep, eggplant purple bruises. Dr. Lachman had told her such bruising would be a sign that her time was near. He said that most likely, hemorrhaging would occur in her brain. He wanted her to come to the hospital, but she and Cal refused to consider it.

"It's not our way," Cal explained. "Our people pass at home, surrounded by loved ones."

Cal and Maggie made hot chocolate and brought it out on the porch to watch the full and creamy moon rise in the evening sky.

"What will it be like in heaven?" Maggie asked Mary Ann as she handed her a warm mug.

Mary Ann wrapped her arms around her daughter. Maggie had hardly left her side in the last few days, only leaving to go to school, and then she rushed home as if she feared the worst. Mary Ann knew she had to answer this question well to help her daughter find peace. She didn't want to leave Maggie with bitter feelings about God, as if he had played a mean trick on them by taking her too soon. The way Mary Ann felt growing up without a mother. It was through knowing Cal that she came to understand God didn't play tricks; his ways were good and wise.

"Maggie, how do your hands feel right now, holding on to that warm mug after playing in the cold?"

"Good."

"Really good?"

She nodded.

"But after a while, that good feeling fades away."

She nodded again.

"In heaven, that good feeling won't go away. That warm, good feeling is like the presence of God, and it will last for all eternity."

Cal's gaze settled gently, lovingly, on his wife.

That night, Mary Ann died in her sleep.

On the kitchen counter at Beacon Hollow were pies and casseroles, sliced cheese and ham, bowls of black and green olives and sweet pickles, slices of bread slathered in peanut butter. Sylvia examined the bounty with a critical eye and moved the mayonnaise and mustard closer to the sliced ham. Marge King tried to shoo her out of the kitchen to take her place with the family near Mary Ann's coffin, but Sylvia wouldn't budge. She was determined to oversee the food. The last time Marge King helped in the kitchen for a funeral, she absentmindedly added marshmallows to the chicken salad. Sylvia was going to make sure things were set out right. It was the least she could do for her only sister.

Besides, Sylvia knew she had to keep moving. She had to stay busy. If there was one thing she knew, keeping busy helped ease a heartache.

Jorie could not eat much of anything today, but Sylvia kept thrusting plates at people and encouraging them to "Eat, eat!" Finally, Jorie accepted one just to appease her. Watching Sylvia, knowing how her heart must be suffering with her sister's body laid out in the other room, Jorie was filled with compassion for her. Sylvia was a devout woman, trying to do the right thing, whose greatest need was to be needed.

Jorie had driven her grandparents over for Mary Ann's viewing and stayed close by Marge's side. Sometimes, her grandmother could be a little . . . unpredictable. Downright inappropriate, Atlee would say, though with amused respect for his wife. Jorie felt almost relieved to focus on Marge; it helped her set aside the heartache of loss that shadowed her lately.

When their turn came to view Mary Ann's body, Marge reached out and stroked Mary Ann's cold cheek, as tenderly as if she were a sleeping child. "If only she could have just hung on a little longer. I was working on a remedy that could've healed her for sure."

Jorie bent over and kissed Mary Ann on the forehead. "Goodbye, dear friend," she said, before turning quickly away to stop from tearing up.

Her eyes caught Cal's across the room, and he gave her a brief nod. She didn't know how he was able to cope lately. Two funerals in scarcely two weeks' time. Such grief, such grief. She knew she felt speechless under its weight.

As the line continued, she followed her grandparents to shake the family's hands. Cal spoke soft words of gratitude, but his eyes were two flat, smooth stones. Even Matthew, who usually couldn't wipe the laughter from his eyes, answered everyone who spoke to him in a polite, subdued voice. Maggie was silent, not even humming. Ephraim was nowhere to be seen.

When the twentieth buggy turned onto Beacon Hollow's lane, Ephraim felt as if he couldn't breathe. He had to get out of the house, away from the neighbors who kept patting his head and telling him Mary Ann was in a better place. He knew that couldn't be true because, for Mary Ann, there was no better place than Beacon Hollow.

He decided to go across the road to Stoney Creek and see how big the yearling Percherons had grown. He was crossing the road when he noticed a car stopped at Marge King's roadside fruit stand. He recognized the driver: that dark-skinned man who had run out of gasoline back in August.

"Hello there! Remember me?" the man called out to Ephraim.

Ephraim walked up to his car and leaned down to peer inside. A woman was next to the man, about the same age. She was just as dark as the man but her hair wasn't kinky—it was long and straight—and her stomach was as round as a volleyball.

The man smiled at Ephraim. "I don't think I caught your name, last time we met."

"Ephraim Z-Zook."

"I'm Dr. Robinson, Ephraim. I'm the new veterinarian in town. This is my wife, Mrs. Robinson." He turned to his wife. "He's the boy who helped me when I ran out of gas a month or so ago."

So *this* was the man, Ephraim realized, who Ron Harding was talking about at the hardware store. For the life of him, he couldn't understand why people would listen to Ron Harding and Jerry Gingerich. He'd rather have a man like Dr. Robinson live in Stoney Ridge than the likes of those two. He had asked Cal why folks wouldn't let a colored man live here, especially a vet when they needed one so desperately. "Folks can be mighty ignorant," was Cal's explanation.

Ephraim had told Cal *that* sounded like another thing to add to his list of questions without answers. Lately, Ephraim's mind, his whole being, was questions.

Seeing the frustrated look on Ephraim's face, Cal spoke up again. "Give people a chance to get to know him. Then he'll change their minds. You just watch and see."

Dr. Robinson broke in on Ephraim's musings. "We just came from a house down the road that was up for sale, but when we got there, the lady said she had changed her mind. Wasn't for sale, after all."

Ephraim felt a twisting in his stomach.

"I noticed that roadside stand and thought we'd stop to get some tomatoes. I don't see anyone working, though."

"That's M-Marge's s-stand. She's over at B-Beacon Hollow. At the f-funeral."

"Who died?" Dr. Robinson asked.

Ephraim looked down at the ground. "My s-sister-in-law."

"Oh. I'm sorry, Ephraim."

He didn't want to have to answer any questions about Mary Ann. He pointed to the stand. "M-Marge usually l-leaves an h-honor j-jar."

"No kidding?" Mrs. Robinson asked, leaning forward in her seat to look at Ephraim. "An honor jar? What happens if people forget their honor and walk off with the money?"

Ephraim shrugged. "I g-guess they n-need it m-more than we d-do."

Dr. Robinson looked at Ephraim for a long while. "Have you been able to get to that circus yet?"

Ephraim shook his head.

"I think it's only in town another month before moving on to Harrisburg."

Ephraim nodded. "I'll try to g-go soon."

Dr. Robinson stuck out his hand to shake Ephraim's. "Glad to have seen you again, Ephraim."

"H-hope you find a place s-soon."

"I hope so too," Mrs. Robinson said. "We're staying in a dumpy little motel in Stoney Ridge and eating our meals at the diner. We'd better find a place before this baby comes or I will go stir-crazy." She twisted her fingers around her head like she was winding a clock.

Ephraim didn't expect that; he felt a smile tug at his lips.

"Lisa, that's the farm I was telling you about." Dr. Robinson pointed to Beacon Hollow. "That's your home, Ephraim. Isn't that right?"

Ephraim turned and looked up at the farmhouse. A buttery glow from kerosene lanterns lit the windows. Buggies were lined up, shoulder to shoulder. The sun was setting low in the west, casting a long reddened light onto the carefully tended fields.

He turned back to Dr. Robinson. "Me and my f-family, that's where we l-live."

The weather turned unseasonably warm again after Mary Ann's passing. Sylvia dropped by Beacon Hollow every day to help. She organized meals to be delivered for the next month and hired two teenaged girls to clean the farmhouse, do laundry, and cook.

"Caleb, I realize now is not the time, but—" Sylvia started before leaving to return home one afternoon.

"Then perhaps it's a conversation that could wait until some other day," Cal interrupted wearily.

"There has been quite a bit of talk about what's going on in that schoolhouse," Sylvia continued, as if Cal had asked her to elaborate. "Actually, about what's *not* going on in that schoolhouse. Do you realize that they spend more time outdoors than in?"

"It's been beastly hot this fall, Sylvia. Soon enough, they'll be stuck indoors. Until then, Jorie feels spending time out in nature actually helps promote learning."

"Promote fiddlesticks!"

Cal put a hand up to stop her. "Let Jorie do the teaching, Sylvia. You have enough to do, taking care of your own farm." What he wanted to say was that Sylvia didn't need to stop by every day.

"Speaking of my farm, Caleb," she said, "I've been thinking that Maggie should come and stay with us for a while."

Cal was just about to take a sip of coffee when he froze. "*Take* my Maggie?"

Sylvia sat down next to him. "It would give you time to get used to things, get a new routine established. You know how close she and Esther are. It would be good for her to be around females."

Cal kept his eyes lowered. "She's my daughter, Sylvia. My only child. It would be like taking the light from the sun. I just couldn't bear it."

"Think about what *she* needs, Caleb. And what Mary Ann would want for her."

After Sylvia finally went on her way, a sadness welled up inside of Cal. He wanted Mary Ann alive, to take care of their daughter and to deal with Sylvia's meddling. He wanted his brother Ben alive to help run Beacon Hollow. He pressed his lips together against his weakness. His wife and his brother knew a better life now. The eternal life, warm and safe with God and the glory of heaven. It was selfish of him to miss them. If only for the sake of Ephraim and Maggie, he had to find the courage to surrender to God's will. Mary Ann and Ben were no longer with them—they'd gone to God.

The Lord giveth and the Lord taketh, but it was wrong of him to dwell so much on the taking. God had given him so much too. Happy years with Mary Ann and a beloved daughter in Maggie. Two other brothers to share the work of Beacon Hollow.

Death was certainly a hurtful thing, he couldn't deny that, but only to those left behind.

As Jorie watched Maggie working at her desk, she wondered what was going through her head lately. How did a little girl make sense of death? Maggie often had a knowing look on her face, the hint of a smile that made Jorie think she knew more than she was letting on. Jorie had always gotten the impression that Maggie was smart beyond her years. Her gaze turned to

Ephraim, sitting in the far back row. She worried about him, sweet Ephraim. His stutter had grown worse since Mary Ann's passing, and that was when he did talk, which was seldom. It seemed as if he was trying to be invisible, but Jorie refused to let him. She hoped that by having him do well in the role of the angel Gabriel in the Christmas play, it might give him some confidence he lacked.

She glanced up on the wall to see the growing list devoted to an inventory of first sightings. It was an idea she came up with to try and encourage the scholars to become more observant of nature. As her eyes scanned the list, she realized that most of the first sightings were Ephraim's. Red fox. Cooper's hawk. Northern bobwhite. Great egret. Ray added a cottontail, which made the scholars laugh at its ordinariness, but then he looked so offended that Jorie added it to the list.

On the opposite side of the blackboard was another growing list, titled "Very Important Questions." Whenever the scholars had a question they couldn't answer, they wrote it up on the board for the class to discuss. "How does the moon stay up in the sky?" "When bees head to the hive, how long until it rains?" "What do you get if you cross an elephant with a rhinoceros?" She was pleased with the questions and the discussions they prompted; she wanted to ignite the children's curiosity about this big, beautiful world God gave them. If there was one thing she wanted to leave them with, it was . . . wonder.

Ephraim thought briefly of telling Cal about the circus tickets, but quickly dismissed the notion because he was pretty sure Cal wouldn't let him go. He just wanted to see the wild animals, up close, but Cal would be worried he'd be tempted to see the entertainment. His brother Ben had gone once and came home with jaw-dropping tales of circus ladies who wore practically nothing. No, he thought it would be best not to bother Cal with this right now. Cal had enough on his mind. He thought of what Ben often advised when faced with such a knotty problem: "Better just go now and apologize later."

Ephraim would need to skip school to go to the circus. He had given this plan a lot of thought and settled on Friday. Jorie took the class out on all-day expeditions on Friday, and Ephraim figured that, if absolutely necessary, he could use the excuse that he was late to school. Once, Levi Yoder was so late that the class left without him. There wasn't church this Sunday, either, which reduced the chance of Cal crossing paths with Jorie, and hopefully, she might even forget that he was absent. Jorie could be forgetful like that, especially if she got excited about something the scholars found on a Friday expedition. He might just get away with it.

On Friday, he and Maggie left for school like always, but he stopped at the road. "You g-go ahead, I'm g-gonna head through the D-Deep Woods."

"I'll come too."

"No!"

Hurt, Maggie spun around and marched up the street toward the school-house. Ephraim bent down to tie his shoe. As soon as she disappeared around the bend, he ran down the street in the opposite direction to catch the bus.

At the part of the road where the bus usually stopped, Ephraim waited anxiously, hidden behind a tree. He was worried a buggy would pass by and spot him playing hookey. Suddenly, behind him came a familiar tuneless humming.

He whirled around to face Maggie. "Aw, Maggie. C-can't I d-do anything alone?"

She pushed her glasses up on her nose. "If you don't let me come with you, I . . . will . . . tell."

He scowled at her but explained the plan for the day and told her that if she went along with it, she might have to lie. She cocked her head and thought about it for a split second. "Dad says that repentance is a daily thing. So I'll just plan on doing some extra repentance-ing today."

As soon as she finished the sentence, they heard the bus chugging up the hill and waved their arms so the driver would stop. Less than an hour later, they stood at the Lancaster bus station, wondering which way to go. It wasn't hard to determine that West Lampeter Fairgrounds was the answer to that question—circus posters covered every surface. Before even reaching the fairgrounds they caught sight of the unmistakable peaked top of a canvas circus tent, thickly striped in white and red.

"There it is," Maggie said, eyes wide.

They found the ticket booth at the circus entrance. Ephraim handed the ticket taker his two prized tickets. "W-which w-way t-to the menagerie?" he asked, trying not to stare at how small the man was. This man was smaller than anyone in Stoney Ridge.

The dwarf pointed a finger down the path along the large tent. "Animal dens are that way. It's feeding time now, if you hurry."

Ephraim and Maggie wandered around the tents, led by the smell of animals—a smell that wasn't much different from a barnyard.

"Oh, Ephraim, look!" Maggie called out. "See the horses? They're Percherons, aren't they? Just like the Kings'!" A makeshift corral held a half-dozen draft horses, their heads buried in mounds of hay.

"K-Kings' horses are b-better," Ephraim said loyally.

Spotting the animal dens, he grabbed Maggie's hand and pulled. In a long row, shaded by the tent, were cages on wheels, brilliantly painted scarlet with gold trim. Their sides were propped open to reveal an assortment of unusual animals. Three chimps, with large patches of missing hair, were huddled in a corner of a dirty den. Next den over, an old black bear with paws as big as dinner plates squatted in front of his food dish. Then there was an angry-looking eagle, tied to a post. A tired and toothless lion lay on his back in another den. At the very end was the cougar den. *This* was the reason Ephraim had come. He walked up to the cougar cage, as close as he dared, and quietly watched. The cougar licked its paws, tail swinging, before noticing Ephraim. Its lithe, tawny-colored body jumped off of a ledge and went up to the bars, as if sizing Ephraim up. The cougar sniffed the air, then settled back on its haunches. Ephraim had never seen anything so beautiful. The cougar and Ephraim exchanged a long look. He took a step closer.

"Not so close, Ephraim," Maggie whispered.

"It's ok-kay. She knows," Ephraim said, eyes still glued to the cougar's.

"Knows what?" Maggie asked, hiding behind him.

"She knows I th-think she should b-be free."

A sudden clanking of metal surprised the cougar and she turned toward the sound, curling back her lips to bare her teeth. It was a circus worker, not much older than Matthew, throwing lunch to the cougar. He had an electric prod that he kept in front of him and used it to poke the big cat in the flank as she ate. The cougar lunged toward him, but he shocked her with the stick, then laughed when she fell back in pain.

"S-stop!" Ephraim shouted with such force that his spit sprayed through the air.

"Beat it, kid," the worker yelled. "Or I'll try it out on you." He pretended to jab the prod toward Ephraim.

"Come on," Maggie said, pulling Ephraim away. "Let's go find the human cannonball." They had seen large banners for the human cannonball, plastered on sides of the big tents. "And I want to see the world's fattest lady. And I want cotton candy too."

Ephraim scowled at the worker but went off with Maggie. They walked into the main tent and saw trapeze artists and a tightrope walker, but the human cannonball, they were told, was at the dentist with a toothache. When they found the fattest lady in the world, they decided that Fannie Byler, a woman in their church, was even fatter. Ephraim bought Maggie cotton candy on a paper cone. Too soon, he knew they needed to catch the bus to get home by the time school let out.

Before they left the circus, Ephraim wanted to walk past the cougar den one more time. The cougar was waiting as if she had been expecting him. She stuck her nose through the bars, drawing in a scent of him. Her golden eyes were bright and she stared right at him, and he had the strangest notion that she was begging him to set her free. Ephraim put a hand up as if he was going to touch her, but the trainer shooed him off.

On the bus ride back, Maggie fell asleep. A bump in the road woke her up and she looked at Ephraim. "This was the best day of my life." Then her eyes drifted shut again and she leaned her head against his shoulder.

Today had been worth it.

It was purely accidental that Jorie was walking on the road when the city bus pulled up and Maggie and Ephraim hopped off. She was heading home and thought she might stop by Beacon Hollow to see if they were sick, but the timing of the bus was just a coincidence. They didn't notice her following behind them. She knew they were up to something, and she was pretty sure Cal wouldn't be happy about it. But they were safe and they were home. She thought she even heard Maggie humming. The sound of it tugged at her heartstrings like a well-loved hymn. Whatever they had been doing, she knew they needed time for things like that, where they could just be two happy children.

She crossed the road and turned left at Stoney Creek's drive.

On a rainy morning in late October, Matthew surprised Cal by showing up for breakfast. The windows were open and an acrid smell of burnt oatmeal filled the room.

"Did you burn the coffee too?" he asked, when Cal opened the door for him.

"No, but I can't guarantee that it's drinkable," Cal said. "How'd you get here?"

"Bus. I have a couple of days off and thought you might need some help getting that third cutting of hay in."

Cal looked a little confused. "I hadn't given much thought to that third cutting yet."

"Hadn't thought about it? This time last year, you had that third cutting stacked and in the hayloft."

Matthew was worried about his brother. Cal was always the strong one. He kept the family together after their folks died, stepping into their father's footsteps as if he was born for it. But Cal seemed as if he were walking around in a fog, preoccupied and distant. As Matthew looked around, he could see only the bare minimum was getting accomplished at Beacon Hollow. The cows were getting milked, of that he had no doubt. And the milk was getting picked up regularly by the milk truck every other day, just like always. But not much else of the normal farm routine seemed to be happening. Even the fields—usually plowed under with manure as soon as the harvest was in so that they would spend the winter gaining nourishment—looked about as well-plowed as if a cat had scratched around on them. He looked outside at the steady rain. Well, the hay wasn't going to get cut today.

Cal went to the stairs. "Ephraim! Maggie! Time to wake up!"

"They're not here. I met them on the road. They were on their way to Jorie's."

"What?" Cal said, dropping a spoonful of paste colored oatmeal into a bowl. "Why would they be going there at such an early hour?"

"Something about hunting for a beaver's den. Ephraim said he had just read that beavers have extra-large lungs and that's why they can go underwater for seventeen minutes. Said he wants to time them." Matthew stirred the oatmeal, took a bite and frowned, then pushed it away. "They went early to get breakfast at Jorie's." Quietly he added, "I shoulda gone too."

"There's fresh eggs," Cal said, pointing to the basket, still on the counter. "You can help yourself."

Matthew looked for a clean bowl in the cupboard, couldn't find one, so he rinsed one that sat piled up in the sink. He cracked three eggs, tossed the shells in the sink, and started whipping up the yolks. He cooked the scrambled eggs in the only fry pan he could find that wasn't dirty, then looked for a clean plate, and finally just gave up. He sat down at the table and ate the eggs directly out of the fry pan. "I saw Sylvia in town. She said to tell you she'll be stopping by around noon. Said she's bringing Esther to play with Maggie."

"Oh no," Cal said. "Oh no, no, no." He glanced at the clock on the wall. "Matthew, you need to run over to Jorie's and fetch Maggie. Ask Jorie to come too. Tell her . . . it's an emergency." He grabbed Matthew's fry pan and started filling the sink with hot water.

Matthew pushed himself back from the table. "What's the emergency?"

"Sylvia wants Maggie to live with her."

Matthew's eyes went wide. "You gonna let her?"

"No, I am not. But we have to show her that we're doing just fine and that Maggie isn't running all over the county like a wild Indian." He grabbed the liquid soap bottle and squirted its entire contents into the sink, then started scrubbing dishes like a madman.

Fifteen minutes later, Jorie and Maggie and Ephraim arrived, trailing behind Matthew. When Cal caught sight of Maggie, he could practically hear the squawking Sylvia would do if she caught sight of her. Barefoot, Maggie was wearing Ephraim's shirt and a pair of old pants, held up by twine. Her hair was tucked loose in a bandanna, flowing down her back in tangles and snarls.

Cal ran outside. "Jorie! Maggie needs to be—"

"To be turned back into a girl," Jorie said, laughing. "Don't worry, Cal. Matthew explained the situation."

"No, I do not!" Maggie said, scowling, an indignant look on her face.

"Yes, you do," Cal answered, in a tone of voice which meant she had to obey.

"This is all because of Sylvia . . . and Ephraim says she's not really even his aunt!" Maggie shouted.

"Maggie, calm down." Cal gave Ephraim "the look." "That's true, she's not Ephraim's aunt."

"Mine either," Matthew chimed in.

Cal rolled his eyes.

"You can't deny," Matthew said, "that somehow Sylvia Swartzentruber manages to exude disapproval at fifty yards."

At first, Cal wanted to put a stopper in Matthew, but as the meaning of his words sunk in, he let out a laugh. It surprised him, that laugh. A small laugh. In that messy kitchen, with dishes piled up in the sink and a floor so dirty that shoes could stick to it, with Matthew and Ephraim and Maggie looking at him as if he was coming unhinged.

A small, tiny laugh, but it was there. His first laugh since Mary Ann had passed.

Jorie seemed to understand; her eyes were smiling as Cal tried again to persuade Maggie to change into girl clothes.

"But I *am* a girl!" Maggie said, stamping her feet.

"Of course you're a girl," Jorie said. "We just need to have you looking like one." She put a hand on Maggie's head and gently guided her upstairs to get a bath.

Downstairs, Cal, Matthew, and Ephraim swept and cleaned and hid the dirty laundry down in the basement. Jorie came back down and tried unsuccessfully to swallow a grin at the sight of Cal with an apron around his waist. "Maggie says she doesn't have any dresses."

"That's not entirely true," Cal said, feeling his cheeks grow warm. "She just doesn't have any *clean* dresses. That's why she's helped herself to Ephraim's hand-me-downs."

"What happened to the girls who were cleaning for you?" she asked.

"They're working as waitresses for that new restaurant in town." He swept an overlooked pile of dirt into a dustpan. "I haven't had time to find someone else." Truth be told, he was overjoyed when the girls told him about their job offer. They made him nervous in his own house, and he knew Sylvia grilled them for details—which only added to Sylvia's ability to leak a constant stream of complaints about him, like a rowboat with a hole in it.

Jorie glanced at the kitchen wall clock. Ten thirty. "Where do you think I could find some of Maggie's dresses?"

Cal pointed to the basement stairs. "Down there, in the basement. In a pile. The machine broke down and I haven't had a chance to fix it."

At eleven, Jorie brought Maggie to see Cal. She was wearing a lavender dress with a starched white apron over it, black stockings, and polished shoes. Her shiny clean hair was tightly pinned down under a stiff prayer cap.

"Maggie," Cal said, a smile lighting his face, "you look like—"

"A dumb girl." She wiggled. "These dadburn pins keep poking at me. I wish I was a boy like Ephraim."

Cal crouched down. "I'm sure glad you're my little girl."

"If I were a boy, then I wouldn't have to play with Esther," Maggie said. "She likes to play house and make me the baby just so she can boss me around."

"S-she tries to b-boss me t-too, Maggie," Ephraim said. "She'd b-boss you whether you're a b-boy or a g-girl. She's just p-plain b-bossy."

Jorie looked around the kitchen. "You men worked a wonder!"

Matthew leaned over to whisper loudly in her ear, "Just don't look in the oven. You'll see a week's worth of dirty pans."

"Maggie, stop wiggling," Cal said.

"I can't help it!" she said with a scowl. "These clothes are still wet."

"They'll dry soon." Jorie squeezed Maggie's shoulders. "We'll go find that beaver's dam another day." Something at the window caught her eye. "Sylvia's here. I think I'll just slip out the back." She went out the side door as Ephraim darted upstairs.

Mary Ann's garden! Cal hurried out behind Jorie. He saw the shock register on her face when she saw the garden, overgrown with weeds as scraggly as the pumpkin vines. Mary Ann had loved this little plot of soil. She had treated it like a sanctuary. When the house got crowded, he could always find her in the garden, fussing over her plants.

"It's been a little hard to find time to weed," he said. That wasn't entirely true. Everything just seemed to take him longer these days, as if his head was stuffed with cotton and he wasn't thinking clearly.

Jorie spun around on her heels. "Lizzie Glick! She'd be just the right girl to keep house for you. I've never seen anyone work as hard as Lizzie."

"What makes you think she'd quit a good job at the hardware store to keep house for me?"

She looked at him as if it was the most obvious thing in the world. She pointed toward the window. "Because of Matthew."

Cal turned toward the house. Through the window, they could see Matthew attempting to juggle three eggs. Maggie was clapping her hands in delight until Matthew dropped an egg on the floor. Cal turned back to face Jorie, puzzled. "What about Matthew?"

She gave him a patronizing smile. "Why are men so smart in some things and—"

He held up a hand, grinning. "No need to finish that thought."

"Talk to Lizzie."

"Jorie, thank you." His eyes held hers just a beat too long, and then he looked away, feeling guilty, as if he had done something wrong.

Jorie didn't seem to notice his discomfit. She pointed to his waist. "Don't forget to take off that apron."

The kitchen door banged shut and he knew he needed to go back inside to face Sylvia. He yanked off the apron and tossed it behind a bush, then returned to the kitchen with a sigh.

Sylvia wasn't fooled by Maggie's freshly scrubbed look. "I saw Maggie running along the road this morning in Ephraim's old trousers. And her hair was tied back, looking like a tail on a runaway horse."

Cal scratched his head. "Well, you see, she likes to help outside and those dresses and pins just . . ." He stopped himself. There was no point defending it. The truth was that he let her dress the way she wanted.

Within five minutes, Sylvia found the dishes in the oven and the mountains of laundry in the basement. "What happened to those girls I hired?"

"They were offered jobs in town at the new restaurant. They offered to stay, but I told them to go on, take the jobs. They'd make more money than I could pay them and they'd get to be around young folks."

"You're too soft on people, Caleb. Always have been." Sylvia sighed, then waved her hand. "I'll find you new helpers."

"Well . . ."

Esther smiled a Cheshire cat smile as her mother added, "And Maggie will be coming home with me today."

Maggie's eyes went wide.

"Maggie is a strong-willed child, Caleb. It's not your fault you can't manage her. She needs a firm hand."

"Sylvia, I know you mean well—" Caleb started. He knew from the set of Sylvia's chin, lifted high and aimed dead straight at him, that he was in for a fight. He had enough experience with Sylvia to know it was wise to tread carefully when she was in this frame of mind.

"I'm only doing what's best for my niece. It's what my sister would have wanted. No little girl is going to grow up properly in an all-male household. She's already wearing pants. Next thing you know she's going to cut her hair short and carry a slingshot to shoot down a duck for dinner." Sylvia looked Ephraim over, head to toe. "Perhaps Ephraim should come with me too." Her crisp words knifed through the air.

Now Cal set his jaw. As calmly as a frustrated man could, he asked, "You're saying that these children are better off without me?"

"No, of course not. But you're a minister now. That was God's doing." She rolled her eyes as if God should have consulted her first. "He knew Mary Ann would be taken from us. You don't have time to be doing laundry and ironing clothes and cooking meals and milking cows and taking care of two children. I can't imagine how you're doing your minister duties too."

What she meant, Cal knew, was that he probably wasn't doing his minister duties. It wasn't far from the truth, either. He felt like he was treading water and barely able to keep his head up.

Sylvia started up the stairs. "I'm going to pack a few things for Maggie."

Matthew scooted his chair next to Cal's. "Are you going to let that happen?" he whispered forcefully. "I know you're grieving, but get hold of yourself."

Cal planted his elbows as if anchoring himself into the tabletop. "Sylvia!" She stopped, midway up the stairs, and came back down to the kitchen with a curious look on her face. "I am the head of this family. And I will not let you take my family from me." He stood, his palms facedown on the table, drawing strength from all that a family table symbolized. "That's the last I want to hear on this subject."

Sylvia's face grew hard and her mouth set in a stern line. She grabbed Esther's hand and marched out the door.

Matthew stood by the window, watching them climb into their buggy. "Why do I feel you just poked a sleeping bear?"

On the buggy ride home, Sylvia silently fumed while Esther, bored, dozed off. Sylvia reviewed the many red flags of trouble she observed at Beacon Hollow. First and foremost, *what* was Jorie King doing there? She saw her talking to Cal by Mary Ann's garden, saw them look into each other's eyes. Sylvia knew she wasn't supposed to hate, that it was a sin. But it was a sin to think you were something special too, and that was Jorie King, in a nutshell. She remembered Jorie as a little girl, with an impish face and unruly hair. She had been headstrong and daring. No doubt spoiled, as the daughter of a far-too-lenient minister. And as a young woman, Jorie was famous for the number of suitors she had turned down. It dawned on Sylvia that Jorie might be trying to set her cap on a prize like Cal, now that Ben and Mary Ann were gone.

Poor Cal. He was distraught without Mary Ann, that was plain to see. He looked as haggard and worn out as his clothes, all wrinkled and rumpled. And that house! Why, she had never seen such an unkempt house. Her sister would be shamed.

Somehow, she needed to help Cal. *If only he weren't so stubborn! Why couldn't he accept help?* As Sylvia turned onto her drive, she came to a decision: she would not let poor Mary Ann down. Maggie needed her, Ephraim needed her, and, clearly, Cal needed her.

After Sylvia left, Cal sent Maggie and Ephraim to the garden to weed. Matthew offered to help fix the wringer washer, so Cal went to the workshop in the barn to look for the tools he would need. Bud Schultz walked over from his farm and joined him.

"I saw Hurricane Sylvia leave." Bud whistled. "Roar in, roar out." A beefy man in his late sixties, Bud's eyes grazed over the tools hanging on Cal's neatly organized pegboard.

Cal found his toolbox and looked through it for his wrench. "She wasn't too happy."

Bud unhooked a hammer from the wall and held it up, lifting his bushy upswept eyebrows in a question to borrow it. Cal gave a nod and Bud tucked the hammer claw on the hook of his overalls. "Any reason in particular this time?"

"She doesn't think I'm much of a mother, I suppose. Or a father. Or a minister, for that matter."

Bud leaned against Cal's workbench. "You know, Cal, people have been known to marry again."

Cal jerked his head up. "She hasn't been gone very long."

Bud breathed loudly through his nose. "Have you even thought about it?"

"No."

"Maybe you should. That's all I'm saying."

"Marrying a woman I do not love is apt to be a cure worse than its affliction." Cal found the wrench he was looking for and closed up his toolbox.

"Who said anything about marrying a woman you don't love?" Bud said, lifting his shoulders in a shrug.

"Aw, Bud, I just never expected to grow old with anyone else." Cal looked at his neighbor, a man who was dear to him.

Over the years, Bud had become a part of the Zooks' family. He joined them for supper nearly every Sunday. They felt comfortable borrowing Bud's telephone and asking for rides. Bud had a son who left farming behind to become a stockbroker in Philadelphia and visited once a year, only to badger his father into selling the farm and moving to the city. Every year, Bud refused and his son left in a huff.

"You're going to have an awfully long and boring life if you don't give yourself the freedom to love again," Bud said, thumbs hooked under his overall straps. "Why, you're a young fellow—scarcely thirty years old! Unless of course, you don't feel the need . . ." His voice trailed off as a mischievous glint came into his eyes.

Cal stiffened. "I am a man yet."

Bud grinned. "Hoo-boy, that's a relief." He leaned against the wall and crossed his arms. "You know, you Amish folk do a better job than most of us by facing the future as it is."

"You've been alone an awful long time, Bud. You seem to be doing just fine."

Bud walked over to the open door of the barn and scanned his fields. "Maybe I'm a little sorry I didn't take my own advice."

When Jorie returned home from Beacon Hollow, she spotted Doc Williams's car in the driveway. She went first to the barn, assuming she would find him there. The Kings' barn was a huge structure, made of stone at the bottom and whitewashed wood at the top. Beyond the barn were forested hills that followed the entire perimeter of the property. Jorie stopped for a brief moment to take in the sight. In autumn, the hills were spectacular— aflame with trees of red, orange, and yellow foliage.

As Jorie slid open the door, a slice of fading sunlight fell across the freshly swept barn floor. She breathed in the familiar smell of animals and hay. The main part of the building consisted of two aisles of box stalls, separated by a dark, narrow corridor. Most of the stalls were empty at this time of the day. Atlee managed the barn with a precise regimentation: the horses were turned out to graze by rotating pastures. A barn swallow swooped over her and landed on a mud-plastered nest; she could see the hay sticking out of the layers of mud in the nest. She walked through the center of the barn and out the other side, and there she found her grandfather talking to Doc Williams. Standing beside them was that tall, dark-skinned man whom Jorie had met awhile back, when his car ran out of gas in front of Stoney Creek. So *he* was the new veterinarian.

"Jorie, I was hoping to see you." Doc Williams waved her over. "This is Jim Robinson, a vet from Virginia who's going to be taking over for me. I've been showing him around, introducing him to my patients."

Jorie knew Doc Williams better than she'd ever known an English person. She always thought he had the makings of a Plain man—when he didn't know the answer to something, he said so.

"We've met once before." Jorie shook hands with Dr. Robinson. "Do you know much about horses?" She hoped the answer was yes. Doc Williams knew cats and dogs, but when it came to sheep, cows, and horses, he had to consult his books. He had retired from a city practice and moved to the country, then ended up practicing because there was no nearby vet in the area to handle the Amish farms. Last year a series of misfortunes—a mastitis outbreak at Jonas Lapp's dairy, bloated sheep from sweet clover at Samuel Riehl's, and the loss of Stoney Creek's prize broodmare—and Doc Williams knew it was time he found someone else.

"My specialty is large animals," Dr. Robinson told her. "I grew up around horses." He walked over to the fence where a stallion, Big John, looked at him curiously with glossy black eyes. Big John stuck his nose over the fence to see if Dr. Robinson might be hiding a carrot or two in his pocket. The doctor chuckled as Big John sniffed his face and hands. "He is absolutely huge! Must be at least seventeen hands."

"Eighteen," Atlee corrected. He wasn't being proud, he was just stating a fact.

"These Percherons are such gentle giants." He stroked Big John's long forelock.

"Are you familiar with the breed?" Jorie asked.

"A little," Dr. Robinson answered, rubbing his hands along Big John's large-boned face. "Let's see, Percherons are from the northwest part of France. Their Arabian ancestry is evident in their large, dark eyes, and gives them an elegance despite their massive size—"

Jorie's eyebrows lifted in surprise. It almost seemed as if he was reading from a textbook.

"—a versatile breed known for their intelligence and gentle temperaments. Easy to train, gentle and patient around children."

Jorie and her grandfather exchanged a look, impressed.

Dr. Robinson turned to Jorie. "I knew of a man who lost his voice to throat cancer. He was able to guide his horses with the slightest touch of his hand." He looked around the pastures. "Your horses are magnificent. Beautiful conformation. They're compact and muscular, the neck is crested, with a little feathering on their legs. Are they all dapple gray in your line?"

"Most," Atlee said. "We've got a new broodmare, though, who looks like she's been dipped in ink. Name is Fancy."

"Because she thinks she's something special," Jorie added.

Dr. Robinson noticed the chalkboard on the barn wall with statistics written about expected foaling dates. "Any chance you keep breeding records?"

Jorie smiled. "My grandfather keeps very precise records. He's been breeding these horses for thirty years. Why do you ask?"

"Not sure if you're in need of customers, but I have a friend from vet school who's asked me to keep a lookout for a good Percheron stud."

Jorie exchanged another glance with her grandfather. Atlee took a few steps toward Dr. Robinson. "Welcome to Stoney Ridge. We're delighted to have you here."

Two months had passed since Mary Ann's funeral. The initial shock had worn off and some of the Zook family routines were established again. Ephraim and Cal spent a morning in the fields, pitching ears of dried corn into the stake-side wagon. It was a finger-cold day, when a farmer was forced to accept that winter was right around the corner. Cal had been trying to pasture the livestock each day to save on winter feed, but it was time to keep the animals in the barn, protected from the rain and cold.

"M-most of the b-birds are gone," Ephraim said, as they walked between rows.

"Sometime during this month, we can expect a few northern visitors," Cal said. He pointed out some northern juncos, feeding on weed seeds along fencerows. "We're going to have to keep those feeders stocked. Those birds depend on us for handouts."

"We'll be ice-skating on Blue Lake Pond soon," Maggie said.

"Not too soon, I hope," Cal said. "I have a lot to do before nature ends the year."

Ephraim gave a little whistle and the two horses stirred. They leaned patiently into their load and pulled ahead fifteen or twenty feet, then stopped. They were so well trained that they could be started and stopped and held in place with nothing more than a whistle or cluck. Matthew was the horse trainer at Beacon Hollow. He had picked out these two horses—then foals—from the Kings' three years ago and spent time every day working with them.

Maggie ran back and forth to the house, returning with a fresh water jug. By midmorning, they were ready to let the horses rest and take a break.

Cal sat, leaning against a fence post, when Ephraim saw a look of crushing weariness come over him.

Cal took his hat off and raked his fingers through his hair. "We've barely made a dent," he said, more to himself than to Ephraim. "So far behind and there are still acres and acres to go."

"We'll g-get it d-done, Cal," Ephraim said, trying to be encouraging. He looked up at the gray flannelled sky and wondered himself how they were going to get all of the corn into that silo. The day had begun with clear skies, but now a layer of threatening clouds had come in and the temperature was dropping, which meant snow was on its way. Rain and snow could ruin the silage, causing it to mold. "I could s-stay home from s-school."

"Me too," Maggie volunteered.

"No," Cal said. "You need your schooling. Somehow, it will get done." He smiled. "Might take a small miracle, but it will get done."

Sometime later, they heard the clip-clopping of horses' hooves turn into Beacon Hollow's drive. When the buggy driven by a chestnut gelding reached the yard, five bearded men hopped out. They looked around and waved when they saw Cal and Ephraim and Maggie in the field. Cal stood, brushed off his pants, and left the cornfield to cross the pasture and reach the men. Ephraim and Maggie followed behind him.

"Thought you could use a hand getting the corn in before the snow starts," said Samuel Riehl, the other minister. Without waiting for an answer, he led the other four neighbors out to the place where Cal and Ephraim had stopped working to rest.

Ephraim looked up at Cal and saw him blink back tears. Seeing the relief flood his brother's face made his chest ache.

The men fanned out, working row by row, clucking the horses to move forward as if they were their own. Cal put his hat back on and adjusted its brim while looking at the men as they worked.

"You're right, C-Cal," Ephraim said, grinning. "Somehow, it'll g-get done."

Cal rested a hand on Ephraim's back. "The Lord answered our prayers, Ephraim. He gave us neighbors." He grabbed Maggie's hand and the three walked over the hay stubble to join the men.

That evening, as they sat down to evening prayers in the living room, Ephraim noticed that the weariness on Cal's face was gone, replaced by a look of satisfaction. The fire was crackling in the hearth as Cal read aloud from his Bible. Maggie snuggled close to him on the couch.

When Cal finished reading, he closed it, and his hands lovingly grazed the top of the old leather Bible. "It was a good day."

It was, Ephraim agreed. *A very good day.*

5

Thanksgiving came and passed. It brought the first real snowfall that harkened winter's arrival. Ephraim woke in the night to the sound of a woman's scream. He threw off his blankets and ran to the window, lifting it open. He heard Cal's footsteps heading down the stairs and hurried down to catch up with him before he left the house.

"D-did you hear it?"

Cal pulled the rifle off of the wall. "I did. Now go back to bed." He opened the kitchen drawer for cartridges.

"W-what w-was it?"

"I don't know. Some kind of wild creature. It's not a sound I've heard, at least not since I was a boy."

"I'll c-come. I c-can t-track for you."

"I need you to stay here with Maggie."

"But Cal—"

"Stay." Cal spun around to give him a look that said he meant it. Then he grabbed his hat and coat from the wall pegs and left.

Ephraim watched him head out past the barn, down to where the sheep were in the meadow. He wanted to go with Cal so badly he could taste it. He thought for a moment of sneaking off anyway, but knowing Maggie, she would get up and wander outside looking for him. He sighed, deeply annoyed, and went back to bed.

He tried to stay awake to listen for a shot—to know Cal had found the animal—but next thing he knew, someone was shaking him on the shoulder to wake him up.

"Milking time." It was Cal's voice. Sometimes his brother was like a human alarm clock.

Ephraim opened one eye and saw that the sun was starting to rise. He bolted up. "D-did you get it?"

"No. But it got our Delilah."

Delilah was their best ewe. Matthew had named her Delilah because she welcomed the attention of the rams—any ram—never failing to get pregnant each year. She usually gave them twins too. As Ephraim leaned over to put on his pants, a tear dropped on the floor. He wiped his eyes with his hands, mad at himself for going so soft on a dumb sheep. But he hated animals getting killed. When he trapped the bobcat that kept getting into Amos Esh's sheep pasture last September, he didn't mean for it to be killed. He wanted to catch it and take it far away, but Amos Esh got to the trap first and shot it dead.

Each December, when the air grew cold enough for hog-killing, Ephraim had always found a way to absent himself. He would be in the house or in the barn, far enough away so that he wouldn't hear the squeals of the hog as it was tied up before being shot in the head, mercifully quick. The hog was dipped in boiling water and hung from a tree next to the toolshed, then gutted and butchered into a thousand pieces. From it they got bacon, ham, loin, sausage, and ribs. Everything was used—"Everything but the squeal" was a line he'd heard all his life. Cal tried to explain that if you wanted ham and bacon, you had to kill a hog. It wasn't for sport, he said, but for eating. Still, the first time Ephraim witnessed a hog-killing, he ran behind the barn and threw up.

Ephraim had never even killed a chicken. If Mary Ann asked him to go get a hen for dinner, even an old hen that had stopped laying eggs, he would find Maggie to do the killing for him. She had watched Mary Ann do it so often she was already good at it. A quick twist of the neck and the hen never knew what had happened. Maggie offered to show him how, thinking Ephraim just couldn't get the hang of it. He would decline, saying it was girl's work, but that wasn't true. He just couldn't stomach it.

On this morning, out in the barn, Cal let out a big yawn as he wiped down the cows' teats with antiseptic before attaching the milking pump. The diesel generator that ran the pump hummed in the background. "Ephraim, I'm sorry about last night. I know you could've probably found it."

Ephraim shrugged.

"If you get time after choring, go out looking for tracks to see which way it was heading. I need to know if I should sleep in the barn tonight in case it comes back."

"Did it t-take Delilah?"

Cal looked away. "Most of her. So we know it wasn't a coyote."

Ephraim knew that coyotes go for the neck of their prey and usually come back later for the kill. A coyote wouldn't drag it away, like this one did. "C-Cal, have you ever heard a s-sound like that?"

"Once," Cal said. "When I was a boy. It was the scream of a mountain lion. There are still a few of them around."

From the barn, Cal could hear a horse and buggy turn into the lane of Beacon Hollow. He hurried outside and was surprised to see Jorie King in the driver's seat, out of breath.

"What's making you look as pleased with yourself as a pig in pokeweed?" He couldn't help but smile when he saw the shining intensity in her eyes.

She was so pleased she beamed a smile back at him. "I have an idea! I was driving to town and saw it and I just knew! I knew it could be fixed up and it could be just the place. I turned the horse right around to tell you!"

"Slow down and catch your breath. I have no idea what you're talking about."

"For the new vet! A place to live! It's that old cottage that my grandparents lived in when they first bought Stoney Creek, before they built the farmhouse. It's not in good shape, but we could fix it up. And maybe he could even use that room off the back for his patients. It's got a separate entrance."

Cal turned around to look at Stoney Creek's large barn, the rooftop visible from Beacon Hollow. "That's on your land," he said in a flat tone.

"Practically on the main road, though. That's why my grandparents wanted to live on this side of the farm. But for a vet, he'll be close to the major roads during winter. And it's wired for electricity. We just need to get someone from the electric company to come out and turn everything back on."

He gave her a wary look. "I don't think you should be getting involved in this."

She cocked her head. "I already am involved. Stoney Creek needs that vet as much as anybody else."

"What does Atlee say?"

"I haven't told him yet, but I'm sure he'll agree with me."

"Jorie," Cal said in a warning tone.

"He's a *good* vet, Cal. You know that. We need to help him." She picked up the horse's reins, preparing to leave. "If you have time soon, would you mind going through the cottage and making a list of repairs? I'll talk to some of the neighbors and see about getting some curtains made and furniture donated. Maybe we could have a work frolic. Then Dr. Robinson and his wife could move out of that motel well before the baby arrives."

He nodded, trying to follow everything she said, as a small needle of worry began to plague him.

All morning, Cal and Ephraim worked in the barn, side by side. After Ephraim finished his chores, he went out to see if he could find any animal tracks. As he passed by the sheep grazing under the willow tree, he was glad to see that Cal had already taken care of what was left of Delilah. All that remained were some tufts of wool. Ephraim knew Cal had probably put her in the manure pile to return to the earth. It was hard, loving animals like he did. They were always getting themselves into some kind of trouble.

Along the fence was a low spot where puddles had formed from melting snow. He looked carefully and spotted tracks in the mud where an animal had jumped over the fence. The paws were large, nearly four inches. He wished Matthew were here this weekend. He would have liked to show Matthew those paw prints before they were washed out with rain or snow. With paws that big, it could be a bear. But then he dismissed that notion. The sound of that scream, that was no bear. He hopped over the fence and picked up the trail again as it led into the Deep Woods. He knew that wild animals were most active at dawn and at dusk, so he wasn't too worried about meeting it face-to-face in the broad daylight. He hoped he would, though, but as he went farther along the creek, the paw prints vanished.

The persistent rumble in his belly reminded him it was past lunchtime, so Ephraim gave up the hunt and returned home.

Cal was in town later that week and saw Marge, Jorie's grandmother, in the hardware store. He had been planning on stopping by the Kings' on the way home, so this was a pleasant coincidence. He wanted to talk to Marge about Maggie.

Marge King might fancy herself as a healer, but Cal had always thought of her as being more of a fixer. She liked to fix people, mostly. She had a keen insight that he respected and rarely gave him poor advice, with the exception of her medicinal know-how.

Some people thought Marge was far too outspoken and a little quirky. Maybe so, but he had always liked quirky. In fact, now that he thought about it, Jorie was quirky. He'd assumed she was more like Atlee with her devotion to those horses, but there was a side of Jorie that lived up in the clouds. Maybe she got some of that cloud living from Marge.

"Just the person I've been wanting to see," he told her and she looked so pleased. "Marge, you've raised five daughters of your own."

"Indeed I did. Twenty-seven grandchildren at last count! But they're scattered all over the countryside now—Ohio, Indiana, Illinois, even Canada." She clucked, deeply distressed. "My own parents could never have imagined the changes we're facing."

"Every generation faces a set of unique challenges," Cal said. "But we can handle those challenges with the Lord's help." The clerk rang up his batteries on the cash register. Cal paid for his purchase and walked outside with Marge. "I've been wanting to talk to you about Maggie."

Marge looked at him, interested. "Something ailing her? The flu is going around."

"No, no, nothing like that." He wanted to veer away from talk about home remedies. "She doesn't like anything to do with being inside, kitchen work, or any woman's work, for that matter. Just the other day, Sylvia offered to take her to a quilting bee and we couldn't find Maggie anywhere. She hid herself in the hayloft to avoid going." He winced. "Sylvia wasn't too understanding."

Marge covered her mouth with her hand, her eyes widening with near laughter. Jorie had the same habit, he realized, when she was amused by something but knew she shouldn't show it. Maybe Marge and Jorie were more alike than he had realized. Mercifully, Jorie had no interest in doctoring.

"Maggie just wants to be outside, choring with Ephraim and me," he continued. "I'm worried she won't learn the . . . feminine skills . . . she'll be needing."

Marge nodded.

"What would you advise, Marge?"

"Well, since you've asked my advice," Marge said amiably—she dearly loved to be asked for advice—"I would just let her be."

Cal just looked at her, nonplussed. "Really?"

"Maggie's grieving for her mother, Caleb. Doing women's work probably just reminds her of Mary Ann. It's easier to be outside. She just wants to be near you."

Cal took that thought in for a long moment.

Marge patted his arm, as she would a small child. "If you're worried that Maggie won't learn the things she needs to know about being an Amish woman, you can quit your worrying. When she's ready, she'll learn. Just give her time." She tilted her head. "But you sure look a little careworn. How about if I bring you a new tonic I whipped up? I call it 'Phoenix Wings.' It'll boost your energy. You'll rise like the phoenix!" She lifted her arms as if to take flight.

Cal's dark eyebrows shot up. The last time he tried Marge's remedy—a cough syrup—just to be polite, he couldn't hold anything down in his stomach for the rest of the day. And his stomach hadn't been the problem. "Thank you, Marge. I think I'm fine, though."

Marge shrugged, disappointed. "Suit yourself." She peered out into the street, searching left and right, and for a split second Cal could see how lovely she must have been as a young woman. "Now where did I put that horse and buggy?"

As a habit, Jorie went to the schoolhouse early to start the stove and get the room warmed up. On Monday morning, the door swung open as if it hadn't been latched. She couldn't believe she hadn't shut it tight. She walked in slowly and carefully, sensing something wasn't quite right.

She saw nothing out of the ordinary. Nothing looked out of place, but she couldn't shake the feeling that someone had been inside.

Cal couldn't postpone cleaning out the barn any longer. Under normal circumstances, he kept it in pristine condition, but these times weren't normal. However, Bud—a man unconcerned about pristine conditions of *any* barn—looked around Beacon Hollow's barn with disgust just yesterday and wondered aloud when the milk inspector would be coming through. That was the moment when Cal knew it was time to get the barn back into shape.

At breakfast on Saturday morning, he told Ephraim and Maggie the plans for the day. They responded by folding their arms on the table, clunking their heads, and groaning.

But Matthew saved the day. He walked into the barn, unannounced, as Cal was doling out pitchforks. Matthew told Cal that it was a good thing he had come, because he could smell that barn as he stepped off the bus. By late afternoon, they had milked the cows, mucked out all of the stalls, replaced the straw bedding, swept the aisles, and knocked down cobwebs . . . and the barn was back to the Zooks' previously high standards of tidiness. A small thing it was, really, just an ordinary thing, but for the first time in months, Cal felt as if he wasn't draining the sea with a pail. That tidy barn made some broken part of him begin to feel whole again.

Cal had just come into the kitchen and started to open cupboards, wondering if Ephraim and Matthew would object to scrambled eggs and cold cereal for dinner. He knew Maggie wouldn't care one way or the other; she was fussy about food and turned up her nose at most things. He found it just one of many mysteries attached to raising a girl.

"Uh-oh, the aunties is coming," Maggie said, looking out the window.

"Are coming. The aunties are coming," Cal corrected, trying to hide his disappointment. Ada and Florence were Cal's two elderly maiden great-aunts, his grandfather Zook's sisters. They lived in a small house on the far south end of Beacon Hollow's property. "What do you think they want?" Cal wondered as he peered out the window over Maggie's shoulder. What he really wondered was, how long would they stay? Once they settled in, those aunties could talk the air full. "Matthew! Come downstairs and visit with the aunties."

Cal heard an exaggerated moan float down the stairs. He went to the kitchen door and opened it wide. "Ada! Florence!" he said, in as delighted a voice as he could muster. "Come in and sit down."

The aunties walked in and glanced around the cluttered kitchen, hands on their bellies, frowning. Cal moved books and papers off of the kitchen table. He cringed when he saw drops of raspberry jam from today's lunch on a chair seat. He hoped the aunties might not notice, but of course, they did and exchanged a disapproving glance. Before sitting down, Ada wiped the sticky seat with her handkerchief.

"Caleb," Ada began, after easing into a chair, "you need a wife."

His dark eyebrows lifted in surprise. He hadn't expected this: an ambush from the aunties. "It's only been a few months."

"Yes, we know," Ada said. "But these are special circumstances."

"How so?" Cal asked, distracted by Matthew who had come to the bottom of the stairs and was trying to quietly slip out of the room, unnoticed. Cal shook his head and pointed to an empty kitchen chair. Matthew remained where he was, poised, ready to escape.

"You're a minister," Ada said. "You need to be an example to others, even in your grieving. It's time you think about remarrying. We know this is what Mary Ann would've wanted."

"Absolutely would have wanted you to marry again," Florence echoed. Some folks thought Florence never had an original thought in her head; she only finished whatever Ada was thinking.

Wide-eyed, Cal looked at them as if they had just told him they were flying to the moon. He turned to Matthew for help. To his chagrin, Matthew looked back at him with laughing eyes, enjoying every moment of Cal's discomfort.

"So, Caleb, we have an idea," Ada continued, milky eyes flashing. "We're quite excited."

Cal's heart sank. Once Ada had an idea in her head, nothing on earth could shake it from her. A Zook trait, his mother had dubbed it.

Ada slipped on her reading glasses. "We have made a list of suitable wives for you."

As Ada searched through her apron pockets for the list, Cal's gaze wandered to the window. He hoped to spot a cow straying out of its stall, or a loose horse, or something that could give him an excuse to bolt.

"This won't be at all difficult," Ada said. "You are a rarity. An eligible bachelor among a sea of women whose lonely hearts ache for a husband."

"Oh, that's lovely, Ada," Florence oozed.

Positively dripping with self-satisfaction, Ada unfolded the list with a flourish. "Every other Saturday night, we have invited one of the women on this list to come and make supper for the family." She held up a cautionary hand. "Hold your horses. We know that Saturday-before-meeting is your busiest day, so we've only invited the ladies to come on off-meeting Saturdays."

Now intrigued, Matthew pulled up a chair and sat down, leaning his chin on his elbow. Cal shot him a look to intervene, but Matthew only shrugged his shoulders in a gesture of surrender.

"First Saturday," Ada said with a birdlike smile, "will be tonight. Laura Mae Yoder. She's a lovely girl."

"A charming girl," Florence echoed. "She's a good cook too."

"W-who's a g-good cook?" Ephraim asked, bursting through the kitchen door with a swoop of cold wind following behind him.

Cal got up and closed the door tight.

"Laura Mae Yoder," Matthew said. Cal noted that his tone was entirely too jovial. "So who else is on your list, Ada?"

"In two weeks, Emma Bontrager will come."

"Who else?" Matthew asked. "How long is the list?"

Florence pulled the list out of her sister's hands. "So far we have eight on the list."

"What's she t-talking about?" Ephraim whispered to Cal.

Cal crossed his arms and leaned his back against the doorjamb. "Ada and Florence think I need to be married off, Ephraim. So they've made a list of single women and have invited each of those ladies to come over and cook for us." At any other time he would have laughed, for it was such a preposterous thing. To tell him, a grown man with a child of his own, whom he must marry and when. But he shouldn't laugh. Doing so would hurt the aunties' feelings and he knew their hearts were in the right place. They were just trying to help.

"A g-good dinner once in a w-while?" Ephraim asked, as if that were the most wondrous thought in the world.

Cal doffed the tip of Ephraim's black hat, sending it spinning. "You got a complaint against my cooking?"

Matthew snorted and went back to reading the list. "Where Ephraim is concerned, a good meal is nothing to joke about."

Cal pressed his lips together, trying not to smile. Even Mary Ann, who had far more patience with the aunties than he did, was known to hide once or twice when she saw them coming up the road. The aunties kept up a constant stream of dialogue, finishing each others' sentences, and a person ended up feeling exhausted after listening to their chatter.

"We came up with this idea because the way to a man's heart—" started Ada.

"—is through his stomach," finished Florence.

Interesting logic from two maiden ladies, Cal thought.

Maggie sidled up to Florence's side. "Jorie King isn't on there," she said, running a finger down the list.

Ada and Florence exchanged a look. "No."

"Why n-not?" Ephraim asked.

Ada's lips drew in a tight line as Florence blurted out, "She didn't add her name to it."

"What are you talking about?" Cal asked. "I thought you came up with this list yourself."

Florence looked as if she might start to cry. Ada scowled at her and explained, "We were at a quilting frolic the other day and passed around the sign-up list to the unmarried gals."

Cal groaned.

"Jorie King didn't sign up?" Matthew asked.

"Not only that, she said it was a terrible idea and that you were a grown man who could think for yourself." Ada looked indignant. "But all of the other women thought it was a fine idea."

Cal sat down at the table. "Ada and Florence, I know you mean well, but I'm perfectly capable of deciding if, when—and whom—I will marry."

Ada covered his hand with hers. "We think so too, Caleb, but you don't seem to be doing it."

Cal cringed. Whenever the aunties got a certain look on their faces, they weren't going to budge. He was going to have to be tough, really tough. "No, Ada. Absolutely, positively no."

Out of the corner of his eye, he saw Laura Mae Yoder walking up the drive that led to the farmhouse, carrying a large basket.

A few hours later, after the kitchen had been cleaned up and Laura Mae Yoder went home with her emptied basket, Matthew held his stomach and moaned. "I ate so much I'm nearly wobbling on the chair." He opened one eye at Cal, seated across from him at the kitchen table. "So, what did you think?"

Cal patted his stomach. "Laura Mae is a wonderful cook."

"Sure. She's a fine cook. But what did you think about her as a wife?"

Cal glanced at him. "She's a sweet girl," he answered without much conviction. "A real sweet girl. But she isn't the one for me."

Matthew grinned. "I'll say!"

Cal tried not to laugh but couldn't help it.

Matthew grabbed another cookie Laura Mae had left for them on a big plate. "I'll go make sure the barn is locked up tight." He put on his coat and hat, reached for the door, then stopped and turned around, eyes twinkling. "Don't you worry, big brother. You know our aunties. They are going to keep at it until they find you Mrs. Right."

Cal threw a cookie at his head, but Matthew caught it, stuffed it in his coat pocket, and grinned.

"Why, Cal, how thoughtful! For later."

"Line up, everyone," Jorie told the scholars. "Time for a spelling bee."

The class jumped out of their chairs and raced to their well-rehearsed spots—alternating grades on each side of the room. Jorie liked to pair classes together to build teamwork. She thought it kept the shine off of any scholar who had a tendency to puff himself up by spelling the pants off of everyone else.

The big-eyed first graders were paired with the third graders and went first, pitted against the second and fourth graders. "Bough," Jorie said, enunciating it clearly.

Maggie gasped. "I know!" she told the third graders.

"Wait," Davy Mast said. "It's a twick." Davy had trouble pronouncing his *r*'s. *L*'s, too. He looked to Jorie. "We-peat and give in a sentence, pwease."

Jorie smiled at Davy, impressed. "The tree bough broke in the storm."

The first and third grade spelling bee contestants sobered. They whispered in a frenzied conference, made a unanimous decision, and gave Davy the honor of spelling aloud: "b-o-w."

Esther hollered, "Wrong!" The older grades hooted with laughter until Jorie shushed them. She gave Esther a warning look.

"Second and fourth grade team: bough."

They had an advantage after knowing how it was *not* spelled. "B-o-u-g-h," fourth grader Arlene Blank proudly spelled.

"Correct," Jorie said. She turned to the crestfallen first and third graders. Davy Mast hung his head and went to his seat. There was a risk to being spokesman: whoever spoke, if a word was spelled incorrectly, had to sit down. "Davy, you were absolutely right. Words can be very tricky. It's important to know the context, just like you asked for a sentence. Well done." Davy sat a little straighter in his chair, but he still looked as if he had been duped.

After that, the rounds went faster and faster. Finally, the entire eighth grade, all big boys, was pitted against Esther, who was spelling them down, one by one. With every correct word, the scholars went wild with claps and hoots. When a word was misspelled, groans and boos echoed throughout the room.

"Xenophobia," Jorie announced to the last standing contestants: Ray Smucker, Ephraim, and Esther.

Ray looked as if he had been tossed a hot potato. "Z," he started and got no farther before Jorie raised a hand to stop him. Ray lumbered to his chair like a big bear, woken from his hibernation and not happy about it.

"Xenophobia," Jorie repeated.

Esther gave Ephraim a catlike smile. "You go first."

Ephraim looked panicky.

"Remember the roots, Ephraim," Jorie said. "Always look to the root word."

Ephraim looked up at the ceiling as if trying to pull the root words down from the sky. "Xeno . . . stranger," he muttered to himself, "ph-phobia . . . fear." He looked at Jorie and enunciated the letters slow and spoon-fed, as if he was terrified he would make a mistake.

"Correct." Jorie turned to Esther and delicately pronounced, "Cormorant."

Esther scrunched up her face.

"Look to the roots, Esther," Jorie coached.

"Put it in a sentence," Esther demanded.

"Cormorants devour fish voraciously."

Esther looked completely blank. "C-o-r-e . . ."

Jorie put up a hand. "No. Ephraim, your turn."

Ephraim looked up at the ceiling again. "Cor . . . raven . . . mor . . . sea . . . raven of the sea. A g-greedy person." He dropped his gaze and looked right at Jorie. "C-o-r-m-o-r-a-n-t."

The entire class looked to Jorie for confirmation. She smiled. "Correct." They burst into hoops and hollers for Ephraim, who blushed furiously. Jorie was pleased for him; it was the first time he had won a spelling bee. It was the first time he had won anything at all.

Esther squinted in annoyance at this display of high spirits. As she walked past Ephraim to get to her desk, she whispered loudly so everyone could hear, "G-g-g-good j-j-j-job."

A horse's whinny floated up the hill to the barn on the wind. Cal knew the visitor was Isaac Stoltzfus coming up the lane before he even saw him in the buggy. He recognized Isaac's sorrel mare, a horse that arched her neck and trotted proudly, glad to be working. He wiped his hands on a rag and went out to meet the bishop.

"From the looks of those clouds we are in for more bad weather," Isaac said when he climbed down from the buggy.

"Would you like to come in for coffee?" Cal asked. He had to offer, but he hoped Isaac would decline the coffee. The breakfast dishes were still piled high in the sink, and Maggie and Ephraim had tracked muddy footprints through the kitchen.

"Thank you, no. Nell is expecting me home soon."

Cal waited a moment, certain Isaac had something other than the weather on his mind. He had to wait, though, for Isaac to shape his thoughts. Isaac was a deliberating man. Such deliberateness could be exasperating in a minister's meeting, especially when it was time to get home for the milking, but Isaac made few mistakes and Cal held great respect for him.

"So," Isaac started, looking down the driveway toward the road. "Jorie King has offered the old cottage on Stoney Creek to the new veterinarian."

"Yes, she has. The English won't sell or rent a house to him."

"And why is that?"

"I was told because he is a dark-skinned man." Cal took his hat off and started spinning the brim in his hands. "I was warned by some Englishers in town to not allow our people to sell or rent to him."

Isaac stroked his long beard. "Caleb, do you think it's wise to get involved in English problems?"

"The way I see it, Isaac, we already are involved. We need that vet. Dr. Robinson knows farm animals much better than Doc Williams. And Doc Williams has a lot of confidence in him."

"And did you tell Jorie this?"

"I did," Cal said.

"I'm concerned that she may be creating problems for herself, for Atlee, and Marge."

"She believes she is doing the right thing, Isaac." No. It was more than that. "And truth be told, I think she is too. I'm helping her get the cottage prepared."

Maggie and Ephraim burst out of the house and ran down to the barn, laughing loudly, stopping only long enough to throw snowballs at each other.

"I'm going to get you, you yellow-bellied coward!" Maggie yelled as Ephraim ducked into the barn.

Cal cringed as he saw Isaac do a double take when he recognized Maggie: she was wearing Ephraim's hand-me-downs.

"I can explain," Cal quickly said, knowing Isaac was horrified to see a little girl in boys' clothing. "I'd forgotten how often the washing needs to get done. We ran out of clean clothes yesterday so the laundry is drying on the line." He pointed to the clothesline; the clothes hung frozen solid like popsicles. "They'll be dry in no time."

Isaac looked at the clothesline for a long moment, as if he had never seen such a sight. "Shall we walk?" he asked when he finally spoke. They strode out past a field of freshly cut hay, now stubble, and walked along the fence line. Cows in a pasture stopped grazing and stared at them. "Have you given some thought about marrying again, Caleb?"

"No. Others have, though."

"Some folks are worried about you."

Cal grimaced. "Any chance you spoke to Sylvia?"

"As a matter of fact, I did. She stopped by the farm yesterday. Said you don't have any household help."

"Well, not at the moment. I'm looking around, though."

"Sylvia said she's offered to take Maggie for a spell. What do you think of that?"

"Aw, Isaac, you know Sylvia. Maggie would be miserable staying in that house. I'd be miserable without her. She's all I have left."

"Our Sylvia can be quite . . . determined," Isaac said.

Mule-headed, Cal corrected but kept the sentiment to himself.

"Her heart is in the right place. Beacon Hollow is a household filled with males. Maggie needs to be around women, to know how to do women's things." He stopped for a moment and looked out at some cows grazing in the pasture. "There's something else to consider. You're a minister now. You have added responsibilities."

Cal looked directly at Isaac so that he might know the truth of what he said. "Mary Ann is still in my heart."

"There's no greater way to honor her memory than by marrying again."

Cal crossed his arms and looked out over his fields, a mixture of snow with yellow stubble. Empty fields. Frozen earth. Like his heart. "Isaac, I would need to feel something for a woman. And right now, I'm not feeling much of anything. Except for wishing the good Lord might have spared Mary Ann." As soon as he said the words aloud, he regretted them and braced himself for a chiding look from Isaac, to remind him that God does not make mistakes.

Instead, Isaac nodded, seeming to understand. "You might be too young to remember my Annie."

Cal looked at him sharply. "I'd forgotten, Isaac. Nell's been your wife for so long, I just plain forgot you had been married before."

"Nell and I have been married for twenty-five years. But Annie Riehl was my first wife. We'd only been married a year and she died giving birth to our first child. A little girl who died a day later."

Caleb felt a jolt. Isaac didn't have any daughters, only sons. *At least I still have my Maggie, a part of Mary Ann.*

"I felt just like you did, numb inside. But I prayed that God would renew my heart and give me a fresh wind. No sooner had I prayed that prayer when Nell came into town to visit her cousins. One look at her and she swept me away." He stroked his long white beard. "I'm not saying it's the same. A part of my heart will always long for what might have been with my Annie. But Nell has been God's good gift to me."

"Nell's a fine woman, Isaac."

Isaac nodded. "It isn't good for man to be alone. Marriage had always been God's intention." He started to walk back toward the buggy, hands linked behind his back, and Cal matched his stride. "God's ways are mysterious, and I'm not denying they can be hard to understand and accept, but they are always best. We don't trust God because we *should*. We trust God because he is *good*." Isaac paused and crossed his arms across his big chest. "Give some prayer to the notion of marrying again, Caleb. Or maybe reconsider Sylvia's offer to care for Maggie."

"I just need a little time to sort things out."

The barn door blew open and out ran Maggie, then Ephraim, who scooped and picked up snow to toss at her. Maggie gave a yelp when the snowball hit, then scooped up one of her own. She aimed it for Ephraim, but he was too quick for her and ducked. The snowball hit the bishop on the back of the head and knocked his hat off.

With big eyes, Maggie said, "Oh no! I'm sorry, Bishop Isaac!"

"Maggie," Cal said in a voice of dismay. He bent down and picked up Isaac's hat.

Isaac shook the snow off his hat, placed it on his bald head, and said, "Maybe not too much time, Caleb."

That afternoon, Cal took Maggie and Ephraim to the hardware store to ask Lizzie Glick if she'd be willing to come work for him. She said yes before he even finished asking and said she would give Ron Harding two weeks' notice starting today.

Afterward, when he returned home, he packed up all of Mary Ann's belongings—her letters, her Bible, her clothes, even her recipe box in the kitchen with her handwriting on those recipes—and put them in a box in the attic.

Remembering Mary Ann was just too hard. So he decided to try to forget her, to fill his life with new memories. It was time he stopped living in the past and face the future, whatever it would hold.

The morning frost crackled beneath Cal's boots as he crossed the yard, passing under the deep shadow cast by the barn. It had been over a week since Jorie had asked him to look over the Kings' cottage and make a list of needed repairs, but this was the first morning he could spare the time.

He was pleased to see there weren't too many repairs to be made. A few new shingles were needed to patch a hole in the roof, and there was evidence of mice. He pulled the cottage door tight, checking to see that the lock still worked. The cottage wasn't large, but the water worked, the electricity and heater could be turned on, and it would suffice.

Cal walked through a field to reach the Kings' farmhouse. He came from the back side of the farm, past the barn, and noticed that Atlee's buggy was missing. He was bending to slip the list under the mat at the kitchen door when a flash of fire caught his eye through the window. Sitting in front of the fireplace was Jorie, brushing out her wet hair to dry by the fire's heat. It was long and thick, curling down to her hips, the color of burnished copper. He was transfixed; for a moment, he allowed himself to drink in the sight of her. He'd never seen anything so lovely in all his life. No wonder the Bible said an uncovered woman ought to be shorn. He quickly turned away, trying to keep his thoughts focused on the Lord. He slipped the list of repairs under the doormat and left, before Jorie knew he was there.

A soft smile touched his lips as he walked back home. He felt the stirrings of a faint breeze, the hint of a fresh wind in his spirit.

In the middle of the night, Ephraim woke with a start. He heard the bawling of his favorite heifer, Gloria, and knew her time had come to deliver her first calf. She had been off her feed at dinner and her eyes had a glazed look. He threw on his clothes, grabbed a flashlight and blanket, and ran downstairs and out to the barn. There, he waited for another hour or so, but he had watched plenty of birthings before this one, and something wasn't right. She was pushing but nothing was happening. He rubbed his head with his hands, and then he jumped up and ran for the house.

Ephraim took the stairs two at a time and burst into Cal's bedroom. "C-Cal, Cal, w-wake up," he said as he shook his brother's shoulder. "I think s-something is wrong w-with G-Gloria."

"Hmmm?" Cal mumbled, then sat up. "I'll be right out."

When Cal got out to the barn, he checked Gloria. "I don't see the calf's legs." He reached into her. "And I don't feel the feet. Could be it's twisted up inside there." He checked the clock on the wall. "It's three in the morning, Ephraim. Run over to Bud to call the vet."

Ephraim practically flew over fences and through a dark pasture to get to Bud's. He pounded on the door until a sleepy-eyed Bud answered it.

"C-could you c-call the v-vet?" Ephraim's voice caught in his throat, and he had to swallow hard.

"Slow down," Bud said. "What's wrong?"

"It's G-Gloria," Ephraim said. "She's c-calving, but we c-can't s-see the c-calf."

"Okay, Ephraim, you head on home. I'll call Doc Williams. I'm sure he'll be right along."

Ephraim ran back to the barn and stood by Gloria's stall. "It won't be long now," he soothed her. He waited for twenty anxious minutes until he heard the sound of the car coming up the drive. He ran to the barn door, but it wasn't Doc Williams's car, it was the new vet's.

"I'm Dr. Robinson," he said to Cal as he strode into the barn. He gave a nod to Ephraim. "I understand you've got a heifer in trouble."

"She's been pushing for hours now," Cal explained. "Nothing's happening." He led the doctor down the aisle to reach Gloria, laboring in a straw-filled stall.

After examining the heifer, Dr. Robinson said, "Looks like that calf is just too big for her."

Ephraim drew in a sharp breath.

Cal noticed the look on his face. "Not to worry, Ephraim, I'm sure the doctor has seen this plenty of times."

"It's pretty common," Dr. Robinson said, smiling, "but I'll need some help."

Ephraim watched as the doctor took some chains and a large metal frame out of the back of his station wagon. Dr. Robinson and Cal put Gloria in a frame with a clamp that caught her across the hips. Dr. Robinson reached inside of Gloria and attached chains to the calf's small hooves so he could pull it out. He ratcheted the handle to keep the chains tight. Despite the cold winter air, sweat was running down his face and arms as he tried to manipulate the calf. Finally, relief covered his face as placenta water started to flow from Gloria, in drips and drabs, a sign that things were starting to happen.

"Steady and gentle," he told Cal and Ephraim, who were pulling the chains.

As Gloria bawled, distressed, the other cows began to stamp their hooves and stir in their stanchions, aware that something was happening.

Ephraim blew out a long breath when the calf finally emerged, a dark brown slippery mass on the straw bed.

"Here," Cal said, and he handed Ephraim a straw. "Tickle its nose."

Ephraim put a piece of straw up the calf's nostril and it half snorted a breath as its lungs filled up with air for the first time. Ephraim's eyes met Cal's; they both smiled at the sound. It meant all was well. They took the frame off Gloria, and it wasn't long before she pulled herself up and looked at her calf, surprised.

"You did g-good, Gloria," Ephraim said. "I knew y-you would." He stroked the cow's neck and scratched under her chin where she liked it best. "You're n-not a heifer anymore! Y-you're a real c-cow. I promise having a c-calf will n-never be that hard again."

The three of them stood for a while, mesmerized, watching the calf try to stand on its wobbly legs. When it began to nurse, Dr. Robinson packed up his bags.

"How is business going?" Cal asked.

"Little by little, it's building up," Dr. Robinson said. "I expected it to take time."

Cal nodded. "It's good you're here. Gloria's glad too."

"I'm just glad Gloria didn't wait any longer to go into labor," Dr. Robinson said. "My wife is due in just a few weeks." He turned to Ephraim. "Ever get a chance to go to that circus?"

Ephraim shot a horrified look at Cal, who spun around, curious. Ephraim gave Dr. Robinson an infinitesimal shake of his head, which he read perfectly.

"I meant, uh, I wondered if you heard what happened at the circus in town? When they were getting ready to move out, a cougar broke free from her cage. She's loose."

On Sunday, Cal closed the service with a prayer, then announced where church would be held, two weeks' hence. Standing in between the men and the women, he had been preaching mostly to the men, but as he finished up announcements, he turned to face the women. "And we'll meet again in two weeks at—" His eyes caught Jorie's and his mind was suddenly filled with the sight of her brushing out her long coppery red hair in front of the fireplace. Her hair almost *looked* like it was on fire. "At, uh . . ." Where *was* church to be held? For the life of him he couldn't remember. "Uh . . . um . . ."

"The Eli Stutzmans'," called out Eli Stutzman.

Cal spun around to face Eli, who was peering at him as if he might be a little touched in the head. Cal's cheeks stained red. "Thank you, Eli." He then dismissed everyone with a final benediction.

A squirrel scampered in front of Ephraim, its tail and whiskers twitching, and then disappeared into the trees. Ephraim spotted a downed log cushioned with moss, and he sat on it. He loved these moments, when chores were done and he could have some time to be off in the Deep Woods by himself. He didn't mind school so much, not since Jorie was his teacher, so long as he didn't have to open his mouth and talk about anything. Answering questions aloud made Ephraim's school day a misery.

But as hard as speaking aloud was, nothing made his day worse than Esther Swartzentruber. He knew it was a sin to hate, but Esther Swartzentruber made it hard. Esther mocked him for his stammering nearly every day. When he had to stand in front of the class and he saw Esther's face just waiting for him to get caught on a word, the words jammed in his throat and wouldn't come out. Then Esther would start snickering and the rest of the kids would join in. She was clever enough to wait until Jorie's back was turned, occupied with another child. Maggie told him not to pay any mind to Esther, even if she was kin.

"Don't let her know she bothers you, Ephraim. That's what Dad tells me to do when Matthew teases me."

But Matthew's teasing wasn't mean-hearted, not like Esther's.

Ephraim walked down a trail he hadn't been on since Ben had left for Vietnam. It seemed like some days, like today, everything reminded him of Ben and Mary Ann. Then he was stabbed, suddenly and unexpectedly, by grief for the parents he hardly remembered. He tried to swallow down the wad of tears building in his throat. It just hurt so much to think of the people he loved who had passed.

The brush rustled behind him.

Ephraim whirled, nervous. He let out a shaky breath. It was only the wind.

He started walking again, quiet as a cat in felt boots. Then he heard the crackling, rustling noise again. Ears straining, he scanned the woods before he saw it. Standing high up on a rocky ledge was the cougar. She looked at Ephraim with a wild cat's insolent stare. His heart missed a beat. She was the same one from the circus, he knew for a fact. Short ears and a ringed bobbed tail. He knew he shouldn't move a muscle, but he didn't think he could have, anyway. She and Ephraim exchanged a long look, underscored by his shallow breathing. Then she turned and walked away in the opposite direction. He released a shaky sigh of relief.

As soon as Ephraim was satisfied that the cougar had gone a distance, he took a peanut butter and honey sandwich from his pocket, unwrapped the wax paper, and placed it carefully on the rock . . . just in case the cougar returned that way. Then he backed away slowly, and after he broke out of the woods, he took off for home at an all-out run, holding on to his black hat.

On a gloomy, gray morning with drizzling rain, Cal, Bud, Ephraim, and Maggie filled the wagon with tools and went to the cottage on the King property. Jorie and her grandparents were inside, sweeping and cleaning and dusting.

"The electrician came yesterday," Jorie told Cal when he found her. She flipped on the switch and an overhead light went on.

A blush pinkened her cheeks, he noticed, either from the chill in the air or excitement. Maybe both. She looked happy.

"I'm a little surprised that there aren't more neighbors here to help," Jorie said.

"It's still early," Cal said, sparing her feelings. He knew that there would only be a few helpers showing up today. During the week, many neighbors came by to privately tell him they wouldn't be coming. They didn't think they should be getting involved in English problems. It was one of the first times he felt truly like a minister. His job was to shepherd a flock of helpless sheep; except that these were not witless animals, they were his neighbors, and he loved them.

"It's our problem too," he told each one. "If you have trouble with a horse with colic or a breech calf one night, Dr. Robinson won't be asking if it's Amish or English."

By the end of the day, the cottage was in move-in condition. Dr. Robinson insisted on paying rent to the Kings, but Atlee preferred a barter arrangement: free veterinary care for his beloved Percherons in lieu of rent. Dr. Robinson told him, under those generous conditions, he would throw in consulting too, when they were considering a stud or an addition to their brood stock. Atlee was delighted with the arrangement. This way, he whispered to Cal and Bud, he could avoid having to pay taxes on rental property, and it suited him just fine to have a vet on the premises for his beautiful horses.

As Cal packed up his tools, he smiled at the sight of Jorie and Lisa Robinson talking together in the kitchen. An unlikely pair: a petite, bonneted Plain woman in a green dress with a white apron and black ankle boots, facing a tall, dark-skinned woman wearing bell-bottom pants and a brightly flowered maternity smock, with large hoops hanging from her earlobes. Despite their obvious differences, he could tell the two would become friends. They shared an interest in flower gardening, and he saw Jorie's eyes lit up in that animated way she had, as she described which flowers would attract butterflies.

It was a good thing—the *right* thing—to offer a home to the vet and his wife, especially with their baby soon to come. Cal just couldn't rid himself of a nagging feeling that, by doing so, they had poked a hornet's nest.

6

The first day that Fat Lizzie started working at Beacon Hollow, Ephraim came in from the dairy with Cal and thought he'd died and gone to heaven. The scent alone was overwhelming. Breakfast was fresh eggs, a mountain of potatoes, sausages, salt-cured ham, and hot biscuits. By dinner, he found a clean white shirt laid across his bed. Another ironed shirt was hanging up on a peg in his room. He brought the shirt to his nose; for the first time in his memory, he was conscience of the sweet scent of laundry detergent. Maggie's hair had been properly combed and pinned, and even Cal's weary eyes lit up with delight when he caught a whiff of Lizzie's chicken pot pie.

Matthew had a day off in the middle of the week and came home to see Ephraim and Maggie perform in the Christmas school play. He arrived early, in time for breakfast, and seemed surprised—annoyed, actually—to find Lizzie in the kitchen. Cal explained that he had hired Lizzie and she was doing a fine job. Matthew scowled, as if Cal should have spoken to him first, and Ephraim caught the look of abject disappointment on Lizzie's face. Matthew helped himself to breakfast and pointed to a pillowcase full of dirty laundry he had brought with him from Lebanon that he wanted Lizzie to wash.

All of the parents crowded into the schoolhouse to watch the scholars perform the Christmas story from the book of Luke in the Bible. Ephraim had memorized his lines with Jorie's help and didn't even stutter when he delivered them. Matthew felt like cheering, though it wouldn't be appropriate to single out one child's performance over another. He looked over at Cal and had to swallow hard when he saw tears burning down Cal's cheeks like a mini-fountain.

Maggie and the other first graders were given the job of moving props on and off the makeshift stage by Jorie's desk. Afterward, cookies and punch and coffee were served, and parents had a chance to look around the room and appreciate the scholars' artwork on the walls.

Matthew saw Cal sidle up to Jorie and whisper, "Did you hear him? Did you hear how smooth he spoke?"

"As smooth as syrup over pancakes," Jorie whispered back, smiling, interrupted by Maggie, who dragged everyone over to look at her pictures on the wall.

"And there's Ephraim's cougar," Maggie said, pointing to a pencil drawing of a mountain lion.

"How could he have captured such detail?" Cal asked aloud.

"It's amazing, isn't it?" Jorie said, stopping to admire it. "Like he's seen one close up."

"He did!" Maggie said, her face lifted high to peer at the drawing. "At the circus!" As soon as she realized what she said, she slapped her hands over her mouth as her eyes went wide as silver dollars.

"So *that's* where you both were when . . . ," Jorie began to say, then she, too, snapped her mouth shut.

"*That's* where Maggie and Ephraim were on the day they skipped school," Esther finished Jorie's sentence. "I knew it! I knew it!" She gave everyone a sweet-as-pie smile before she turned, yanked her mother's sleeve, and pulled Sylvia into the conversation. "I told my mother that Ephraim and Maggie weren't sick! I knew they were playing hookey!" Esther pointed to Ephraim's picture. "Look! He went to the circus and saw a cougar!"

Completely confused, Cal looked from Esther to the drawing to Ephraim, who was turning the color of beets. Sylvia grabbed Esther's hand and went to find Jonas.

Even though Ephraim's instinct was to bolt and run, he knew better. As they walked home, he tried to explain to Cal about the circus tickets that Dr.

Robinson had given to him. "I j-just wanted to s-see the animals," Ephraim told Cal. "N-nothing else." That was the truth. Maggie was the one who wanted to see the two-headed man, but he was too loyal to say. He should admit it, though, because she was the squealer. She kept looking at him out of the corner of her eyes, biting her lip. He ignored her.

"Aw, Cal. Don't be too hard on 'em," Matthew said. "You and Ben would have done the same thing in your day. Probably did a heck of a lot worse than that, knowing our Ben." He grinned. "Remember the time when you and Ben 'borrowed' Amos Esh's rowboat to fish at Blue Lake Pond and it sunk?" He elbowed Ephraim. "It's still down there."

Ephraim flashed Matthew a grateful look.

Cal frowned at Matthew. "It's the lying I don't like," he said. "Lying is a terrible habit to start. One lie leads to another." He stopped and looked right at Maggie and Ephraim. "You have to promise me you won't lie to me, ever again."

Maggie promised and ran ahead home, to help Lizzie get dinner ready she said, but Ephraim thought she was smart enough to vanish before Cal changed his mind and decided to dole out punishments. Unsure of the ground he was on with Cal, he stayed by his side. He almost wished Cal would have just inflicted him with an added after-school chore for a month or forbidden him to go to town. Disappointing him felt worse.

Before they even reached the kitchen, a delicious smell drifted out to greet them: Lizzie's pot roast. It was made with beef and onions, and it smelled heavenly. As they walked inside, all thoughts of the circus vanished, replaced with a hearty appetite of sweet and savory expectations. Maggie was setting the table and Lizzie was at the stove, frying potatoes.

Over her shoulder, Lizzie said, "Hope you're all hungry. I've been waiting dinner for you and just kept adding things to the pot. I'm going to call it 'Late for Dinner Because of the Christmas Program Pot Roast.'"

Matthew tossed his hat on the wall peg like he was playing a game of horseshoes. "Ha! You should change the name to 'Found Out Maggie and Ephraim Ditched School and Went to the Circus Pot Roast.'"

A smile spread across his face at the scowls he was getting from Maggie and Ephraim. Then his smile faded. Behind them, he noticed the bag of dirty clothes in the same spot that he had left it in the morning.

When Matthew asked Lizzie about it, she froze, spatula in the air. Then, cucumber calm, she stepped away from the frying pan and let the potatoes sizzle. She put her hands on her hips and squinted at him. "Caleb Zook hired me to care for him, Ephraim, and Maggie. He never mentioned cleaning up after the high and mighty Matthew Zook."

Matthew looked to Cal, who only shrugged his shoulders. From that point on, Lizzie pretended Matthew didn't exist, which Ephraim thought was pretty smart, especially for a girl. It made Matthew crazy.

It was the Kings' turn to host church. The bench wagon had been brought over a few days before, and the men who delivered it helped move the down-stairs floor furniture into the barn. The large interior doors in the kitchen were opened wide so the benches could be set up, facing each other, taking up the footprint of the entire first floor.

Early Sunday morning, as more and more buggies started to arrive, Jorie hurried down to the barn to lead Big John out to the farthest paddock before meeting started. Last time the Kings hosted church, when the hymn singing started up, Big John started to stomp and snort and carry on as if he wanted to join them. His noise stirred up all of the horses to whinny and neigh until they practically drowned out the singing.

As if triggered by an invisible signal, the men and women, huddled in tight little knots to keep warm, began to file toward the house just before eight. The children came running up from the barn; the girls joined the women, the boys joined the men. As soon as the older women, wives, and widows filed inside, the young bachelors flanked the doors to watch the young girls walk through. The girls' eyes stayed straight ahead, but their lips curled into pleased smiles and blushes pinkened their cheeks. Jorie's eyes suddenly blurred with tears. Sometimes if she just held her breath and concentrated really hard, she could almost see Ben standing beside the other young men, one booted foot hooked over the other in that way he had, watching her.

Jorie followed behind the unmarried girls, but she felt, with Ben's passing, as if she didn't know where she belonged anymore.

As soon as school ended each day and before he was due home for milking, Ephraim ducked out and went into the Deep Woods, cougar snooping. He found coyote tracks, bobcat tracks, and lots of deer tracks, but no cougar tracks.

One day, after a light snowfall, he found a trail of large paw prints. He followed the trail as long as he could. His concentration kept slipping because he had the feeling that he was being watched. It was a foolish notion, he thought, because of course he was being observed: by the deer he passed by, by birds in the trees, and probably a host of critters he couldn't even see. Suddenly, the birds stopped singing. The feeble winter sun that had been shining fitfully through the dense treetops disappeared. The forest grew silent and a chill went down his spine.

He paused for a moment to get some water out of his thermos. As he lifted his head to drink, his eyes caught sight of the cougar. She had already spotted him. She crept slowly out of the shadows, her round belly low and brushing the rough edge of a rocky ledge, high above him. When their eyes met, she went still.

Ephraim stayed motionless as a held breath. The cougar moved first. She whirled and dashed along the top of the ledge, her body floating against the shafts of sunlight that lit the rocks like streaks of fire. He watched her poise for a leap and then disappear into a crevice in the ridge.

Now he knew where she lived.

It had snowed so much during the night in Lebanon that cars weren't able to get out of their driveways. Matthew wasn't expected at work until nine, so he grabbed the shovel he had seen at the side of Mrs. Flanagan's garage and started to clean the snow off of her sidewalk, then her driveway. The feel of the shovel in his hands, the way his shoulders and back muscles ached after a while—it felt good. A good ache. This was the work he was used to. It surprised him to realize how much he missed hard labor. Even though he worked long shifts at the hospital, most of what he did was push patients around in wheelchairs or run errands for the staff.

He was enjoying himself so much that he got a little carried away and kept going. He shoveled Mrs. Flanagan's neighbor's sidewalk and driveway, and then the neighbor after that. When he got back to the house, cheeks chapped red from the cold, Mrs. Flanagan stood on her glassed in porch with black thunder on her face.

"What do you think you're doing?" she asked him, holding the door open for him as he stomped snow off of his boots.

"Just shoveling."

"Why did you shovel those neighbors' sidewalks? Especially two houses over?" She sounded mad.

"I was just enjoying the work." He pulled off his coat and scarf and gloves and hung up his coat. "Is there a problem?"

She stood there with her hands on her hips, angry. "Yes, there's a problem! I don't like that neighbor!" She marched into the kitchen.

Matthew was stunned. Part of being Amish was helping your neighbor. They didn't decide first if they liked someone or if that person deserved help. Helping each other throughout the year—loading the silos, shocking cornstalks in the fields, building barns—well, it went without saying. It was as much a part of being Amish as driving a buggy.

He couldn't even imagine a single person in his church who wouldn't agree to help if someone asked. Not one. Often, a person didn't even need to ask. Like after Mary Ann passed, the neighbors stepped in and helped Cal with his third cutting of hay, stacking it neatly in the hayloft to help them get through the winter. Cal didn't ask for help; he was too careworn to even know what was needed on the farm. But one day, they just arrived and went to work.

It took leaving that community for Matthew to realize all it meant to him. He remembered a time when a photographer came to the farmhouse to try to sell his father an aerial shot taken of the entire neighborhood. His father called all of his sons to come see as the photographer spread out the photograph on the hood of his car. His dad pointed to Beacon Hollow's fields and the dark section of the Deep Woods that bordered it. Matthew remembered looking at the map and marveling at the landscape from the air: the view the turkey vulture had when it soared high over the fields. The creek, meandering through the pasture fields, where he and his brothers fished and swam on hot summer afternoons. He saw things in that photograph he had never noticed before, just by seeing it from a different vantage point.

Living here in Lebanon, he felt like that man in a quote by Emerson: "A man standing in his own field is unable to see it." His nose was too close to the picture. He didn't realize what he had until it was gone.

Late one evening, Jorie King was working in the schoolhouse. She heard a knock at the door, went to answer, and peeked her head out, then opened it wide. "Cal, what are you doing here?"

He came inside and stamped the snow from his feet. "I could see the light on from the barn and thought maybe you'd forgotten to turn it off," he said. "What are you doing here so late?"

She closed the door behind him. "Getting some work done," she answered.

Cal walked up and down the center aisle of the classroom, looking at the walls. "Is Maggie behaving for you?"

"Of course. She's a bright girl."

"She prefers out of doors to being inside, in the kitchen."

"I was like that. Still am. My biscuits could break a man's tooth."

She saw a smile crease over Cal's face, then it faded. He seemed to have something on his mind. He looked up at the artwork hanging on the walls, his hands clasped behind his back.

"Is Lizzie working out?" she asked, hoping he would relax. He seemed nervous, jumpy, almost. She had never seen him like that.

"Yes. She's a big help, just like you said she'd be. But Maggie needs a mother."

"I know how she misses Mary Ann. She'll never forget her, Cal, if that's what you're worrying about." She noticed that he winced slightly when she said her name.

Cal put his hands to his temples and rubbed. "I'm asking if you would consider becoming her mother."

Jorie stopped in her tracks. She had not expected *that*. Her mouth dropped open, then she closed it tight, nearly laughing. "This is about the aunties' list."

His cheeks colored up just like the boys in her classroom did when she caught them. It touched her heart—she was discovering that Cal couldn't mask his feelings. He looked down on the ground, avoiding her eyes, as the awkwardness between them widened into a large gulf.

"It's only been a few months," Jorie said softly. She put the books on the desk. "I'm sorry, Cal. I can't be a substitute for Mary Ann. No one can." She walked up to him. "There's not a girl in the county who wouldn't jump at the chance to marry Caleb Zook. But I think you should wait. Mary Ann is still in your heart. You just need some time. Sometimes the heart takes longer than the body to mend."

She wanted to smooth the dark hair off of his pale forehead like she did with one of her scholars when he had fallen down and hurt his knee or elbow. To let him know he would be all right. But, of course, she didn't dare touch him and Cal turned to leave.

He was almost at the door when he turned around to say, "I can't remember the color of her eyes. I lived with her for eight years and I can't remember what she looked like."

He started to open the door but stopped when Jorie called out, "Brown. They were dark brown." She walked up to him. "I loved her too, Cal."

He lifted his head to look at her. "How much time? How long until life feels normal again? Until the house doesn't seem cold and empty? Losing Mary Ann was like losing . . . light and warmth and joy. Have you ever loved someone enough to feel as if a limb has been torn from you?" As the impact of what he just said dawned on him, he covered his face with his hands. "I'm sorry, Jorie. Forgive me. I don't know what's wrong with me tonight. I shouldn't have come. Please . . . forget what I said, what I asked."

She leaned against the doorjamb, watching him walk down the lane. "Yes, Cal. I loved someone like that."

She said it so softly that he couldn't have heard. Yet he stopped and turned, locked eyes with her briefly, before turning around and picking up his stride.

7

Cal didn't see Jorie again until Sunday meeting, which happened to be Christmas morning. After services, he gave her a crisp hello, trying not to remember how soundly she had turned down his foolish, bumbling, impulsive marriage proposal. He still couldn't *believe* he had proposed marriage to her. What had he been thinking?! He supposed it had to do with walking home on a cold night and seeing that warm buttery glow in the schoolhouse windows. He had suddenly felt a desperate longing, as if the blaze of the lanterns was a beacon, a sign of hope, to him. The next thing he knew he was knocking on the schoolhouse door and proposing marriage! Every time he was reminded of it, like now, he felt his cheeks grow hot with embarrassment.

But Jorie seemed, or at least acted, as if she didn't even remember it had happened. She caught up to him as he walked to his buggy. "Did you hear that Dr. Robinson's wife had her baby last night? A little boy. A Christmas baby!"

He started to say something, then changed his mind. He couldn't help but smile as she told him the news. "No, I hadn't heard. Maggie and Ephraim will want to know." She was wearing a bright blue dress that made her eyes look bluish-green. How would he describe that shade? Turquoise? Jewel blue? He wondered if that's what the color of a sea surrounding a tropical island might look like—mesmerizing and endlessly deep. They were incredible eyes.

Were her eyes as blue as the sky? He looked past her to study the sky.

"And I've been meaning to tell you that Ray Smucker is starting to speak

355

English in the classroom. He's still far behind where he should be, but he's making quick progress. Thank you again, Cal, for talking to Gideon that day. I couldn't persuade him, but you seemed to know just the right thing to say to make him change his mind. It's a miracle."

"It was God who worked the miracle," he said, reminding himself as well as Jorie, so that he would not be tempted to the sin of pride.

She smiled slightly, before turning to go speak to someone else.

Those eyes, Cal realized. They were definitely bluer than the sky.

During the first week of January, the weather was so cold that an icy crust formed on top of the snow. Jorie told the scholars they could bring sleds to school. Some had real sleds, Lightning Guiders with shiny runners and handles to steer by. Others had homemade wooden sleds with cast iron runners. Those sleds couldn't be guided and the children always landed in a ditch. A few brought whatever they could find that would do the job: an old dishpan or a scoop shovel. Ray Smucker had a twenty-inch square board that he sat on to slide down the hill. It worked a few times and Ray was feeling pretty pleased with himself. He started down the hill a fourth time and—about halfway down—the edge of the board dug into the crust. The board stopped, but Ray went on for quite some distance. When he stood up, the seat of his pants had been worn to a thread, showing off a sizeable portion of his long underwear. He backed down the hill away from the laughing children, jumped over the fence, and ran home. He didn't return for the rest of that day.

On a bitterly cold Saturday afternoon, Matthew sat at the kitchen table while Lizzie ironed Maggie's prayer caps. The iron hissed as it glided over the damp cap and the smell of hot starch filled the kitchen. Matthew told her stories about the kinds of people he met working in the hospital.

After he finished, Lizzie gave him a look of mild interest as she carefully placed the cap over a roll of toilet paper to keep it stiff as it cooled. "After working in that hardware store for the last two years, I came to realize that—English or Amish—people are people. There are plenty of good English out there and plenty of bad ones. We Amish, we're not so different. Good ones and bad ones."

Matthew took a long sip of coffee, mulling over Lizzie's remark. She wasn't much for book learning, but he thought she had plenty of common sense and a knack for sizing up people.

Carefully, she set another freshly ironed prayer cap on the counter next to the two she had finished. "So, how do you like city living?"

"I like everything about it but the sounds," Matthew said. "Sounds in the country are soft and gentle. City sounds are harsh: tires squealing, shouts in the night, constant wailing of sirens. Fires, police, ambulances. Even when I'm working, the patients in the ward make weird sounds. Almost like they're moaning."

He wasn't really sure if she was interested in his thoughts or just being polite—as she ironed she hardly threw a glance his way—but he kept talking. "And the people—they're different. City folks constantly complain about the weather. It's either too hot or too cold or too wet. Even if it's dry and the crops and garden desperately needed moisture, the weatherman would say that the weekend would be miserable because of the threat of rain. For me, coming from a farm that's tied to the weather, that way of thinking is crazy talk. Whoever heard of an Amish man complaining about the weather?"

"That's because we know that God controls everything," Lizzie said quietly. "The sun, the clouds, the wind, and the rain. We know that complaining is finding fault with God."

Matthew tried to hold back a grin. Lizzie Glick was finally talking to him.

The next morning, Matthew poured hot coffee from a chipped white enamel pot into two mugs. He handed one mug to Cal. A pot of oatmeal sputtered on the stove. It was a cold, snowy morning and the wind was blowing hard enough to take the bark off the trees. So cold that Cal let Ephraim and Maggie sleep in while he and Matthew milked the cows and fed the animals.

"I'm starving. Shouldn't Lizzie be here by now?"

Cal gave him a questioning look over the ridge of the mug. "It's Sunday."

Matthew frowned. That meant breakfast was going to be pretty slim pickings. He took a bowl from the cupboard and spooned oatmeal into it. "Want some?"

Cal shook his head.

"Suit yourself." He sprinkled brown sugar on top of his oatmeal and sat down at the kitchen table to eat.

Cal sat with his hands wrapped around the mug of coffee, watching the steam rise. "Matthew, I think you are the only person in this town who isn't trying to tell me who to marry and when."

In between spoonfuls of oatmeal, Matthew asked, "Want me to?" He grinned, knowing what was on Cal's mind this morning.

Last night's Supper List prospect, Katie Miller, had been particularly disappointing. Not only was Katie a poor cook, which dismissed her immediately in Ephraim's mind, but she started to cry when everyone refused second helpings of her overcooked moon pie. She didn't stop crying until they finally ate more, just to appease her. Matthew wasn't sure he could ever stomach another piece of moon pie again, as long as he lived.

One of Cal's dark eyebrows arched at him. "No, I don't."

"Want to hear how the odds are running?"

Cal gave him a look of disbelief.

"Half the town thinks you're going to marry Laura Mae Yoder because you ate two pieces of her chocolate cream pie."

Cal rolled his eyes.

"And the other half thinks you're going to marry Susan Stoltzfus because she signed up for two Saturday nights in a row."

Cal sighed. "Where are you getting this information?"

"Lizzie told me."

Cal eyed him. "Thought you didn't care much for Fat Lizzie."

"Oh, she's not so bad," he said with a careless shrug. "Not so fat anymore, either. Then there are a few stragglers who are rooting for Jorie King." Matthew glanced at Cal to see his reaction but there was nothing. "Folks are saying that since you're a minister and all, you've probably been told to hurry up and get hitched."

Cal clenched his jaw. "I will not marry just because I've been told to."

"*That's* what I told Lizzie," Matthew said, eyes twinkling. "And besides, even if you were to consider Jorie, you'd have to get in line behind me." He picked up a banana and started to peel it. "I've given some thought to marrying her myself."

"You've given some thought to marrying most every girl in town," Cal said. He glanced at Matthew. "What, you're serious? You? You're nearly six years younger than her."

"Quit looking at me as if you think I'm addle-brained." Matthew broke off a piece of banana and popped it in his mouth. "Dad was ten years older than Mom. And Mary Ann was older than you, big brother." He grinned. "It could work."

"And what makes you think a woman like Jorie King would be interested in an eighteen-year-old boy?"

"Well, brother Caleb, I never thought I'd see the day." Matthew laughed. "And here I thought you were immune to women."

"What are you saying?"

"You're a little sweet on Jorie King."

Cal stood up abruptly, walked to the sink, and poured his coffee down the drain. "I never said such a thing."

"No? Well, then, you're blushing like a ripe summer tomato for no good reason."

Later that afternoon, Cal had just finished milking the cows when he saw Jorie walk up the long incline to Beacon Hollow. A smile crept over his face, then he remembered Matthew's teasing and quickly sobered up. His mind wandered to Katie Miller weeping over the moon pie; that pie still sat like concrete in his stomach. He just didn't think he could stand one more evening of the aunties' Saturday Night Supper List.

Jorie waved to Ephraim, who was cleaning out the metal milk cans. "Where's Maggie?" she asked as she slid the barn door shut.

"In the house with Fa—" Cal caught himself. "With Lizzie. I have *got* to stop calling her Fat Lizzie."

Ephraim snorted and Cal tossed a rag at him.

"Lizzie dropped by this afternoon to play a game with Maggie," Cal added.

"With M-Matthew, you m-mean," Ephraim added, grinning.

Jorie smiled. "I stopped by to ask if you heard that cougar scream last night. Sounded close by."

Ephraim's grin faded. He tucked his chin to his chest.

"I did," Cal said. "No stock was hurt last night. Same for you?"

"No, none hurt. But I worry about it scaring my pregnant mares into early labor. Not to mention what a cougar could do to a foal."

"If you're worried, I'll get a few neighbors together to hunt for it."

With that, Ephraim dropped the metal can and ran out of the barn. Jorie and Cal watched him go, a puzzled look on their faces.

"What's troubling him?" she asked.

"It's that cougar. Any time someone brings it up, he jumps like a jackrabbit." Cal closed the door behind him. "Not really sure why he's so frightened by it."

"He bolted when you said you would hunt it."

"You're right. He did." Cal cocked his head. "But you've always understood him better than the rest of us."

"Ephraim has a tender heart. And a soft spot for animals. He's like you that way." An awkward silence spun out between them. "I'll go say hello to Maggie before I leave for home." She turned and reached for the handle of the barn door.

Cal put his hand over hers to stop her from sliding open the door. "Jorie, I was hoping someday, maybe before too long, you'd be thinking of Beacon Hollow as home." *Lieber Gott, did I really just say that?* He felt his face grow warm, but he kept his hand on hers.

Jorie seemed to be studying his hand. She was quiet for a long moment, as if gathering her thoughts. Finally, she lifted her head. Their eyes locked, hers as dark as the sea. "Men seem to ask women to marry them for all the wrong reasons. Daniel Riehl asked me to marry him to combine our land, which basically meant he wanted Stoney Creek because his land is a sodden marsh. Jacob Schwartz wanted me for my fine features. Said it would be nice to look at me each day. Never mind that he's thirty years older than me and I might not be as interested in looking at him. And never mind that he talks so much and in such a loud voice that he can burst a person's eardrums." She released a sigh. "Ben wanted someone waiting for him back at home, whenever he was *ready* to come home." She pulled her hand out from under his. "And you want me to raise Ephraim and Maggie."

Cal turned her shoulders so she would face him. "So what is it *you* want, Jorie?"

She looked at him. "I don't want to be just a convenience to someone. There's got to be more to a marriage than that. I want a marriage . . . ," she gently rapped her fist against her chest, ". . . from the heart." She stepped back from him and slid the door open, avoiding his eyes as she closed it behind her.

"She said no. Flat out, no doubts about it. No." Cal walked over to Bud's house on the pretext of borrowing a tool, but it was really to talk. He still couldn't believe he had asked Jorie to marry him, *again*. And again, she said no.

"How did you ask?" Bud asked, sitting in his favorite easy chair by the fire. The Sunday newspaper was spread around him on the floor, as if he hadn't moved all day. He had been working on a crossword puzzle when Cal interrupted him.

Cal moved some newspapers off the sofa and sat down across from Bud. "I said I was hoping she'd start to think of Beacon Hollow as her home."

"Hoo-boy! And that didn't sweep her off her feet? Imagine that. It's right up there with your first winner, when you told her Maggie needed a mother." Bud shrugged his shoulders. "Well, maybe this aunties' list will get your mind on some other gal."

Cal jerked his head up. "No."

"So she's the one you want?"

"Yes." Yes, she was. Yes! He suddenly realized that Jorie was the only one for him.

"Tell me again what she said."

Cal repeated the conversation.

"Sounds to me like she wasn't saying no at all. Sounds to me like she was giving you another chance by telling you what she *didn't* want."

Cal felt a pang of regret. He leaned back on the sofa. "It wasn't so hard with Mary Ann."

"Aw, you were just kids. You grew up together. This time, Cal, you're going to have to woo her."

"*What?*" Cal asked, mild panic rising in him.

"Woo her! She's a woman, Caleb. What does she like?"

"We're Amish," Cal said, as if that explained everything.

Bud rolled his eyes to the ceiling.

"I guess I don't know that much about her," Cal said.

"Try to think of something," Bud said in a longsuffering voice.

Cal exhaled, resigned. "She likes reading books. She likes taking walks in the Deep Woods. She loves her horses. She likes teaching. And children, even the difficult ones. She's able to find the good in people." He leaned forward on the sofa. "She's got a flair for drawing, especially things she spots in nature. She loves church—I can tell by the look on her face. In fact, it's usually pretty easy to tell what she's thinking or feeling. If you can't see it written on her face, she'll tell you. She speaks her mind, that Jorie. She's not much of a cook—"

"Well, well, well," Bud said, interrupting, folding his hands behind his head as he leaned back in the chair.

"What?" Cal asked.

"Thought you didn't know her."

8

*A*fter church one Sunday, Isaac asked Cal to stop by his farm on Tuesday for an informal meeting of the ministers. Cal braced himself for some kind of sticky problem with a church member. Hardly a few weeks went by without some kind of need arising. Being a minister was harder than he could have imagined. It wasn't the time he gave to sermon preparation—that he found nourishing to his soul. It was knowing so much about the inner life of his people. In the last few months, he had learned things he would rather not have known: Petty quarrels. Flirtations with worldly temptations. Young couples who got ahead of their wedding night. It was hard for him to shake off.

After Isaac's wife served the men coffee and pie, Jonas jumped right in to explain the reason behind today's gathering. "There's concern brewing about Jorie King," he said. "About her teaching methods."

Isaac crossed his arms against his chest. In his slow, meditative way, he asked, "Caleb, Samuel, what do you think?"

A short, stocky man with a kind heart, Samuel Riehl shifted in his chair as if he felt uncomfortable, then shrugged his rounded shoulders. "Maybe I've heard a few things."

Then all three men looked to Cal for his opinion. He felt his stomach tighten into a knot. "She might be a bit unconventional—"

"A bit?" Jonas sneered. "Her class spent the better part of December counting birds over by Blue Lake Pond."

"There's a reason, Jonas," Cal said. "That bird count helps the government keep track of bird populations. Birds are an indicator species. They reveal a lot about the health of an ecosystem. If their numbers are down, there is a problem somewhere."

Jonas leaned back in his chair. "Her job is to teach those scholars how to read and write. That's all."

Cal stole a sideways glance at Jonas, a man he had always considered a friend. He wondered how much of Jonas's complaint toward Jorie had to do with the fact that he had chosen her to teach over Emma, Jonas's eldest daughter, who didn't have an interesting thought in her head. Cal knew what kind of teacher Emma would make. He had plenty of those kinds of teachers when he was in school. He had decided that he would have to risk disappointing Jonas; he just couldn't foist Emma Lapp on those scholars.

"First things first, I always say," Jonas continued. "We need to make sure those scholars are getting their basics in, before they go traipsing off to the woods to count birds."

"Counting those birds is a lesson in arithmetic," Cal said, trying to keep his voice calm. "And science too. Maggie said they had to memorize the birds' names in Latin so they could identify the species. That's a language lesson, right there."

Jonas leaned forward. "That state exam in May has two hundred questions on it and I don't think there will be any questions in Latin."

Cal lowered his head. He didn't know why he felt such a strong need to defend Jorie, but he knew he would do anything for her.

"Maybe you could talk to her, Cal," Samuel said.

Isaac stroked his long white beard, a sign he was thinking. "Samuel has a good point. Perhaps, Caleb, you could speak to Jorie. Just to remind her to get the basics in, *before* the bird counting."

Cal folded his hands together. He couldn't say no to Isaac. "I'll talk to her."

Later in the week, Cal stopped by the schoolhouse as Jorie was locking up the door for the evening. "Hello, Jorie."

She spun around. "Hello, Cal. What are you doing out tonight?"

"Earlier today, old Eli Stutzman stopped by to say his wife was done."

"Done what?"

"That's just what I asked him. 'Done living,' he said."

"Clara's passed?" Jorie's eyes went wide.

Those eyes of hers, they kept changing colors, he realized. Tonight, in the dusk of winter, they looked as blue-gray as an ocean storm. "She did. Very peacefully. Her heart gave out on her. I'm just coming back from their place now."

Jorie locked the schoolhouse door. "Now she'll be seeing those sunsets from high above."

They stopped for a moment and looked at the setting sun. Its rays were casting long shadows that appeared blue on the pure whiteness of the powdery snow.

"E. B. White once wrote, 'I am always humbled by the infinite ingenuity of the Lord, who can make a red barn cast a blue shadow,'" Cal said softly.

Jorie caught his eye, smiled faintly, and looked away, as if she was a little embarrassed he caught her looking at him. He noticed a couple of tendrils of hair, loosened by the breeze, curl about her ears.

The wind kicked up hard as they started walking up the road that led to their homes. Cal's hand flew to his head, barely snatching his hat before it went sailing.

She pulled her cape around her, shivering. "How does Matthew like living in the city?"

"He hasn't said. Probably means that he likes it very much."

"I can't imagine why anyone would choose to live in a city. Out here, most everything around us has been made by God: the grass and trees and birds. But in the city, so much is made by humans: those hideous electric wires, telephone poles, asphalt, cars, pollution."

Cal half listened to her, looking for a segue to broach the real reason he had stopped by. To talk to her about the scholars, like Isaac wanted him to. "Jorie, I know you like taking the class out on nature hikes . . ." He swallowed hard.

She stopped and turned to him, her blue eyes wide with happiness. "Oh, I do. I do! And you understand why, don't you, Cal? Do you see how knowing about God's earth only brings us closer to him? How it helps us to feel the awe and majesty? That's what I want the scholars to discover. So that all of their lives, they know to look around them, at nature and up at the heavens, and they remember God."

Her face was so lit up with joy that the sight of it took his breath away. Imagine what it would be like, having a teacher like her to open scholars' minds and point them to God's majesty.

"Well, I'll be on my way," she said, when they reached the turnoff to Stoney Creek. She turned and started down the long drive.

"I'll walk you to the farmhouse," he offered, falling into step beside her. "Don't want you crossing paths with that cougar."

She glanced at him, alarmed. "Do you think it's still a danger? I haven't heard of anyone losing stock."

"Samuel found the remains of a deer carcass near his field. Thought it looked like a mountain lion had taken it down."

A worried look passed over her face.

"Don't you worry about that cougar," he said in a voice of gentleness. "It's probably moved on by now. Cougars don't want to tangle with people."

Her mouth curved into a smile. "Well, come springtime, it had better not try to tangle with my new foals."

"How many are you expecting?"

"Four, Lord willing."

As she described each mare and what traits she had been looking for in the studs and what she hoped to get from the pairing, Cal watched her. He thought her face was even lovelier when it was animated by excitement. The intensity of her look, the sparkle of eagerness in her eyes, made him lose track of what she was saying. In the fading sunlight, he noticed a light sprinkling of freckles over her nose. He had never noticed those before.

Too soon, they arrived at her farmhouse. He saw that the moon was rising, yellow as a wolf's eye. Somehow, they had stopped walking and were facing each other. Without thinking first, he reached out, and pushed a loose strand of her hair back under her cap. Then he stepped back, worried that he offended her. But she only smiled and said, "Good night, Cal."

On the way home, Cal slapped his forehead when he realized he never did get around to the subject of sticking to reading and arithmetic in the classroom.

Oh well, he thought. Another time.

Caleb Zook kept surprising Jorie. Tonight, he seemed genuinely interested in what she was trying to inspire in the scholars. Maybe she shouldn't have been surprised. Cal was known to plow a field with a book in his coat, so that when the horses rested, he could read. After hearing his sermons, she could almost imagine him more as a professor at a fancy English university than as a dairy farmer. Yet he loved his dairy and his farm. And more than anything, he loved being Plain.

Last week, he surprised her another time with that marriage proposal, said in his roundabout way, with a stain of flush brushing his cheeks. She knew he was getting pushed by the aunties to remarry. Probably others too. As fond as she was of Cal—and she couldn't deny she felt a little flutter of pleasure in her chest when he asked—something held her back.

Sometimes, Jorie wondered if something was wrong with her. Most of her friends were keen to get married. If they were still single, as she was at the age of twenty-four, they were more than keen. They were desperate. Half the girls in Stoney Ridge would like to marry Cal. Maybe it was vain and foolish, but Jorie wanted more out of marriage than to be a poor substitute to the memory of a first wife, especially to dear Mary Ann.

Her grandmother complained that her grandfather had spoiled Jorie for marriage by expecting too much. By that she meant the conversations Jorie and her grandfather would have about the Bible and other books they'd read, plus their late-night discussions about breeding and training Percherons. Marge was never especially interested in the horses, and Atlee preferred she not go near them, anyway, after she nearly killed one with an herbal remedy for worms. But he would always ask Jorie's opinion before choosing a pairing. Jorie would spend hours poring through files, with measurements, notes, charts, cross-references—going back five generations into the horses' lineage. Atlee grumbled that all she did was point out a horse's fault. "But the first question about any potential pairing," she would insist, "is not how great the offspring will be but what problems it might produce."

Ben never understood her love of horse breeding. She tried to teach him about the mysteries and complexities of genetics. "Just put two horses you like together and they'll make a horse you love," was his response.

"It isn't just one or two traits we're looking for," she tried to explain to him, "but how the horse combines all these things. The whole of every horse is always greater than the sum of its parts." Ben would listen for a while but soon lose interest. Anything that smacked of farming bored him.

But he did like book reading. He was a Zook in that way. Their shared love of books was one quality that had drawn her to Ben. Her grandmother often said that Ben was charming, gregarious . . . and handsome as the devil. "That man could charm the spots off a leopard and sell them to a zebra," Marge would say, though she was fond of Ben. Everyone was fond of Ben. And the weaknesses in him—his wild streak, his fiery temper, his tendency to be a fence jumper—Jorie had hoped those would change in time as he grew into manhood.

But Ben was gone now. And she had never imagined herself married to anyone else.

Before going inside the farmhouse, Jorie stopped to make sure the barn doors were locked tight. The wind blew her apron up against her face. As she smoothed it down, she thought again about changing her apron from white to black, from unmarried to married. It would be a significant step, a message to others that she was choosing to remain single. At least she had been thinking about it . . . until yesterday. She had dropped by the Robinsons' cottage with a meal and a baby quilt. Lisa let Jorie hold the baby—a warm little Easter egg of a body. With his tiny belly full of milk, he fell sound asleep in her arms. A pang of longing pierced her heart as she realized she might not ever have a child of her own. Yet for all that was hard about it, remaining single might be what the Lord wanted for her. And the Lord knew best.

Maybe she would wait to change her apron, though. Just in case.

9

On a cold and sunny afternoon, Ephraim went cougar snooping, hoping he might spot her. Every few days, he left a big chunk of raw meat for her on that rocky ledge where he first saw her. When he returned, it was always gone. He hoped Cal hadn't noticed that the meat packages in the freezer might be diminishing faster than usual, but he wasn't too worried. Cal still seemed pretty distracted and wasn't paying attention to details the way he used to. The way Ephraim reasoned it out, if he could make sure the cougar could get food, she wouldn't be as tempted to kill their stock or their neighbors'.

When he reached the ledge, he took out the frozen meat, a roast, from his sack, unwrapped the paper and laid it out in the sun to thaw. Then he hid in a small crevice in the rocks. Out of his sack, he took the charcoal pencils and sketch pad Jorie had given him. He settled down to wait, hoping to see the cougar. He wanted to try to draw her, not from memory, but from real life. While he was waiting, he went ahead and polished off his lunch.

He didn't mean to doze off, but the winter sun was shining down on him, the rocks were warm, he was sheltered from the wind, and Lizzie had made him an enormous lunch. He startled awake when he heard a man's voice, then another. He crouched down low and hid until the men passed by him. He heard one say, "We warned him. We told him what to do—what to *not* do. I think we need to teach them a lesson so they'll all take notice."

Ephraim didn't see their faces but he did see Rex, Jerry Gingerich's dog,

369

trotting along behind them. Rex spotted him and let out an earbusting woof, but Jerry whistled and Rex ran off to join his master. That dog was too good for the likes of Jerry Gingerich, Ephraim thought. He wondered what warning they were talking about. And why. He thought he might ask Cal. His brother had a way of fitting things together, like the last piece of a tricky jigsaw puzzle. He made things Ephraim couldn't understand seem so clear. But then he thought better of it. Cal would ask why he was out in the Deep Woods when he should have been home, choring. And that might lead to questions he didn't want to answer about cougar snooping.

Remembering why he had come in the first place, Ephraim eased out of the crevice and walked over to the ledge.

The meat Ephraim had left for the cougar was gone.

After Maggie and Ephraim were sound asleep, Cal took out all of his books and spread them on the kitchen table. Matthew, home for the weekend, had gone out with friends and wouldn't be home for hours. Cal had been looking forward to this evening of quiet study. He needed to infuse himself in the Word of God, like steeping a tea bag in hot water. He shook down the ashes in the woodstove and added new wood. The new wood settled into the fire with a hiss and pop. As he sat down at the table, he released a contented sigh, opened his Bible, and prayed for God's Spirit to give him understanding.

He was engrossed in a passage of Scripture and didn't know how much time had passed when a noise of hooves outside interrupted him. The kitchen door blew open, bringing in a swirl of frigid air. Matthew stood, feet planted, at the open door threshold.

"Was fehlt dir denn?" Cal jumped up to pull Matthew in and closed the door tightly behind him. *What's the matter with you?* He was alarmed by the angry look on his brother's face.

"It's Lizzie Glick. You've got to fire her."

Cal gazed steadily at Matthew. He had to work to keep a grin off of his face. "Do I?" He went to the stove and picked up the teakettle. "Any particular reason?"

Matthew pulled the kitchen chair out and sat down, leaning on his elbows, hands clasped together. "I'm sorry to say I have discovered a serious moral lapse in Lizzie Glick." He had a very earnest look on his face. "It's Maggie I'm worried about. Lizzie could be a bad influence on our Maggie."

Cal pulled out two mugs, dropped a tea bag in each one, then filled them with steaming water. "And what seems to be the cause of this moral lapse?" He handed a mug to Matthew and sat down beside him.

"She went home tonight with Mose Riehl." When Cal didn't seem to look shocked, Matthew leaned closer. "He is *seven* years older than she is."

Cal had to swallow a retort about how age didn't seem to matter when *Matthew* was doing the considering. He took a sip of tea and tried to look as if he was giving the matter serious reflection. "Did you happen to ask her home?"

"I did," Matthew said, leaning back in his chair. "Out of kindness."

Cal felt a smile tug at his mouth and fought it back. "Kindness?" He knew his brother wasn't used to putting himself out to make a girl notice him. When it came to girls, Matthew rarely, if ever, met with failure.

"Yes. Kindness. I thought she might be needing a ride home after working all day here. And that was when she told me she was going home with Mose Riehl. I pointed out the age difference between them, and she said she *prefers* mature men." He pointed his finger at Cal. "Now that is just what I mean by being a terrible influence on our Maggie." He shook his head. "There's no telling where that thinking will lead." He blew on the top of the tea, cooling it. "So, you should fire her."

"Lizzie has done a fine job for us, Matthew. She runs this house like a tight ship." In fact, he had noticed that having Lizzie in the house gave the place a feel of ticking along to a natural clock. Life had some semblance of order again.

"It's only Maggie I'm thinking of, Cal."

"I haven't seen this serious moral lapse affect our Maggie yet, Matthew." Just the opposite, Cal thought.

Maggie enjoyed Lizzie so much that she spent more and more time with her in the house. That meant less time shadowing Ephraim, which was probably for the best. Maggie could be pesky, he was aware, and Ephraim required more and more time to himself lately, to wander in the woods and think out the troubling thoughts that plagued a thirteen-year-old boy. Lizzie

Glick was the best thing that had happened to them in the last few months. Why, just the other afternoon, he had walked inside and found Lizzie and Maggie in the living room, heads bent together over a quilting frame, with the midday sun streaming over them. The sight would have pleased Mary Ann, he was sure.

Still, Cal knew enough not to say those thoughts aloud to Matthew. "Well, I'm thinking there might be another option than firing Lizzie."

Matthew looked at him, confused.

"You could try being a little more mature yourself."

Insulted, Matthew pushed away his teacup, stood, spun on a booted heel, and headed out the door to put away the horse and buggy, leaving the door unlatched so the wind blew in again. Cal got up, closed the door tight, and sat down at the table again. He couldn't stop grinning.

Jorie arrived at the schoolhouse on Monday morning to a door flung wide open. She heard voices and stepped inside with caution. Her eyes went wide when she saw what had happened: the schoolhouse had been vandalized. Desks were knocked over, profane words were scrawled on the blackboard, her desk was turned upside down. In the center of the room stood Cal, Ephraim, and Maggie, looking just as stunned as she felt. "Was is do uff?" she asked. *What happened here?*

Cal spun around when he heard her voice. "I don't know. We just got here ourselves. Ephraim remembered that it was our turn this week to refill the coal bucket, so we came early and found it like this."

Jorie fought back tears as she read the abusive words written on the blackboard. At first, she felt defeated. Then, a new feeling swelled up within her. She wasn't going to let whoever did this triumph. "Ephraim and Maggie, would you mind running to Stoney Creek? Ask Atlee for black paint and a brush."

"It'll be quicker to get the supplies at Beacon Hollow," Cal said. "Ephraim, you know where they are."

Working silently, Cal started righting desks on one side of the room, Jorie on the other.

"Once or twice," she said quietly, "when I arrived in the morning, I had the feeling that someone had been inside."

He stopped working and turned toward her. "Why didn't you say something?"

"I couldn't be sure. It was more of a feeling."

He hooked his hands on his hips. "I don't want you working here at night anymore. Not as long as it's dark so early."

"Cal, do you have any idea who would do this?"

He took the broom off the wall hook to sweep up broken glass. "Es macht nix aus." *It doesn't matter.*

"Es macht aus." *It does matter.*

"What would be the point of knowing? It's not our way to seek confrontation with outsiders who seek to do us harm."

"All I'm wondering is *why* this happened." They stood looking at each other for a long moment, a standoff. Then Jorie tucked her chin to her chest. "It's because I rented the cottage to Dr. Robinson."

Cal leaned the broomstick against a desk and walked over to her. "You did what you felt God led you to do. Our people have always faced persecution because we have tried to do what God asked of us. This is no different."

Tears prickled her eyes. "I'm not so sure the parents of twenty-five scholars will see it the way you see it."

She wasn't sure how it happened—did Cal reach for her? or did she lean toward him?—but suddenly she was in his arms and he was gently telling her not to worry herself about those parents. Her face was buried in his shirt, the top of her head under his chin. And oh, he felt good. He smelled good and felt so good.

When they heard the thundering footsteps of Ephraim and Maggie approaching, Cal pulled back, but before he released her, his fingers barely brushed her cheek, sliding softly down her neck. She felt his touch all the way to her toes. She turned away, suddenly shy.

The door burst open as Maggie and Ephraim came in with a can of paint and a brush. The four of them went to work cleaning up the schoolroom. She overheard Cal tell them that he thought it might be best not to tell the other scholars about the vandalism. She was grateful for his decision to keep it quiet. Ephraim wouldn't tell, she knew, because he didn't like to talk, but Maggie had a tendency to talk first and think later. By the time the scholars started to arrive, all that was left was a broken window to repair.

Jorie decided that even though it was Monday, it would be a good day for a field outing to see if there were any signs of an early spring in the Deep Woods. That way, she reasoned, the blackboards could dry, undisturbed, and Cal could quietly replace the broken window. She just couldn't stay inside the schoolhouse today. Not after *that*.

A few nights later, Cal sat at the kitchen table, studying the Scriptures for Sunday's sermon. He was reading about the ark of the covenant and the symbols placed inside—a jar of manna, Aaron's staff, the stone tablets of the Ten Commandments. He knew the Lord wanted the Israelites to remember these signs as evidence of his faithfulness, but he kept feeling as if there was something else he wasn't quite grasping from the text. He heard a soft humming and looked over to see Maggie, standing at the foot of the stairs. He held out his arms and she ran into them. He scooped her onto his lap.

"Have a bad dream, Maggie?"

"No," she said softly. "A good dream."

He tucked his chin on the top of her small head. "Want to tell me about it?"

She screwed up her nose and concentrated on remembering her dream. "I dreamed that I saw Mom in heaven. She was holding baby Sammy in her arms. He was looking up at her and trying to pull her cap strings. And she was laughing. She looked so happy."

Cal took a sharp breath. He didn't realize Maggie remembered little Sammy. She had only been a toddler when he was born.

"We don't talk about Mom very much," Maggie said, stroking his beard gently with her small fingers. "Have you forgotten her?"

"No," he said quickly. "Of course not. I could never forget her." But the truth was, he *was* trying to forget Mary Ann. That was one of the reasons he didn't bring her name up very often.

"Jorie says that sometimes remembering Mom can hurt, but it's still good to do. She says that remembering is part of who we are. That remembering Mom helps make me Maggie." She yawned loudly. "She told me I'm the keeper of Mom's song." Maggie slipped off of his lap. "Mom is happy now, Dad."

Cal listened to her light step climb up the stairs, accompanied by a sweet, tuneless humming, and the sound lifted his spirits. He gave up a silent prayer of thanks for his Maggie.

The keeper of Mary Ann's song? He sat there for a while, pondering that, then glanced at the grandfather clock against the wall. He closed his Bible, grabbed his hat, coat, and gloves, and went to Stoney Creek to see Jorie.

As he strode up the gentle rise that led to the Kings' farmhouse, his feet crunching through the half-frozen mud, Cal noticed a bobbing lantern crossing from the house to the barn. He knew the lantern would be held by Jorie, checking on the horses one last time. He called out to her and picked up his stride to reach her.

"What are you doing out so late, Cal?" She held a shawl tightly around her and her hair was covered with a bandanna. Her voice was quiet, practically blending in with the inky night.

"I . . . was hoping to talk to you," he said. "But don't let me stop you from checking the horses."

Cal followed her into the barn and watched as she walked past each horse, checking the locks, looking in each stall to make sure each one was safe and sound for the night.

Satisfied, she turned to face him. "Now you've got my full attention. What's on your mind?"

He took one step closer to her. "What did you tell Maggie about being the keeper of the song?"

"The keeper of the song?" She looked confused, then understanding flooded her eyes. "You mean, Mary Ann's song?"

Cal winced when he heard Mary Ann's name spoken aloud, even though he was aware he was doing it. She noticed too.

He looked around and pointed to hay bales, lying side by side. He sat down on one, leaning his back against the wall. She followed him over and did the same. It was easier this way, he thought, not having to look right at her.

"Maggie has been staying after school to help me clean off the blackboards and sweep up. She's been asking me questions about her mother. She wants to remember her, Cal."

And he wasn't helping her do that, he knew Jorie was thinking. He kept his eyes on the hay-strewn floor. This was hard, so hard.

"I think it's a good sign, that Maggie is working through her grief. I told her that by remembering her mother, she was the keeper of her mother's song." Softly, she added, "I'm the keeper of my grandfather's song, here at Stoney Creek. You're the keeper of your folks' song, by caring for your brothers and Beacon Hollow."

Cal looked away. "Memory can be a curse too."

"It's true, memories can be painful. But it's what makes us unique in all of God's creation. Animals run by instinct, but they can't call things to mind the way God tells us to." She turned her head to look at him. "Why, you mentioned it yourself in a sermon just two weeks ago. About how the Israelites were told to gather stones as a means of remembering."

Cal's gaze lifted to the barn rafters. "'That this may be a sign among you, that when your children ask their fathers in time to come, saying, What mean ye by these stones? Then ye shall answer them, That the waters of Jordan were cut off before the ark of the covenant of the Lord; when it passed over Jordan, the waters of Jordan were cut off: and these stones shall be for a memorial unto the children of Israel for ever.'" He dropped his gaze. "Joshua 4:6 and 7."

She smiled. "Sometimes I think you and Samuel and Isaac have the entire Bible memorized." She tucked a strand of loose hair back under her bandanna. "The stones were meant to remind them of how faithful God has been to them, but also to remind them of their dependence on him. It's like keeping that jar of manna in the ark of the covenant. God wanted them to remember their hunger too. That hunger drove them to God for his mercy."

Cal felt his heart miss a beat. That was the *very* section of Scripture he had been puzzling over when Maggie came downstairs, not thirty minutes ago.

"Our memories, good and bad, they shape us. God uses them all for his purposes. He wants us to embrace our past, not forget it. That's what I've been trying to tell Maggie." She searched his face. "I hope that's all right with you."

He nodded. He rose to his feet and walked to the barn door to slide it open, then waited for Jorie. "She's humming again, our Maggie."

She picked up the lantern she had set on the floor and followed him to the door. "I know. Esther complains about it on a daily basis. Says no one can concentrate with all that racket going on." She slid the door shut and latched it. "But no one else seems to notice the humming."

A big grin spread over Cal's face.

On Sunday, Cal woke to a sky filled with low iron-gray clouds, so close they almost seemed to touch the earth. When it was time to leave for church, Cal, Maggie, and Ephraim ran to the buggy with their heads covered to keep the driving rain off their faces. But as the horse turned into Walter Schlabach's farm, where church would be held that morning, the rain tapered off and sunbeams broke through the clouds.

How fitting, Cal thought, as he handed the reins of his horse to Walter's eldest son, Eli, to stall in the barn during the service. The sun streaming through the heavy clouds was a symbol of the morning, rich with the promise of what was to come.

It was not as if Cal felt God more on these church mornings, for he knew God was everywhere and with him always. But when he heard the rustling of members filling up the benches, he never failed to be filled with a sense of the glory of the Lord. It was all done in silence, in quiet expectation, a time of waiting.

Then Amos Esh, the vorsinger, slowly rose to his feet. He lifted his head and opened his mouth in a big *O*, releasing a perfectly pitched note to begin the first hymn. The men's deep baritone voices joined in, filling the room with slow waves. The women's voices, an octave or two higher, blended sweetly with the low tones of the men to create one voice, an embodiment of their unity, making the church one with God. For three hundred years, the Amish have sung their beloved hymns in just that way. Slow, unrushed, almost chanting.

When the time came for the first sermon, Cal and Samuel and Isaac each tried to defer to the other. "I'd prefer if you spoke, Samuel," Cal said.

"And I'd prefer to have you speak first, Caleb," Samuel told him.

Cal and Samuel turned to Isaac, but he preferred to have the others begin. It wasn't a show, it was a sign of sincere humility.

After a few more preferrings, Cal rose to deliver the sermon. He looked around the room for a moment, catching as many eyes as he could, making sure he had their concentrated attention. He started preaching from Joshua 4, about gathering stones of remembrance. A baby cried out and Cal turned toward the women's side, still preaching, when his eyes met Jorie's and his heart missed a beat and his mind went completely blank. He turned back to face the men, quickly recovering his train of thought.

What was happening to him? He was starting to act like Matthew around Lizzie.

A few hours later, after returning home from church, Cal went up to the attic and brought down the box of Mary Ann's things. Her Bible and her recipe cards and her letters from her father. He found Maggie in her bedroom, reading a book on the bed. He set the box down on the floor and opened it.

"Maggie, these are your mother's belongings. I think she'd want you to have them." He picked up the recipe box and sat next to her on the bed. "They'll help you remember her." He opened the recipe box. Leafing through the index cards, he pulled out one and smiled. "Now, here's one. When we were first married, your mom wanted to make this cake just like my mother used to make it. But she forgot to add the sugar!" He pointed to it. "See how she's underlined 'two cups of sugar'? So she wouldn't forget, next time."

Maggie took off her glasses and held the card up to her nose to read it up close.

Cal reached down in the box and picked up the Bible. "Your mom made little notes in the margins when she read a verse that meant something special to her." He opened it to Psalm 139 and ran his finger along the text until he found verse 14. "'I will praise thee; for I am fearfully and wonderfully made: marvelous are thy works; and that my soul knoweth right well. My substance was not hid from thee, when I was made in secret, and curiously wrought in the lowest parts of the earth.'" He pointed to Mary Ann's small margin note: "'Went to midwife today and heard baby's heartbeat with a stethoscope.'" He put a hand on his daughter's head. "That was you, Maggie. That was your heartbeat."

Maggie reached over and threw her small arms around Cal's neck, hugging him tightly.

10

*J*orie brushed out her long, thick hair and rolled it into a bun, then carefully pinned her prayer cap into place. Any minute now, she was expecting to see Ephraim and Maggie run up Stoney Creek's drive, eager for their planned hike to a golden eagle's nest by Blue Lake Pond. When she looked out the window and saw Ephraim and Maggie, she was surprised to see that Cal had tagged along, uninvited but welcome. She smiled.

The day was cold, even for February, though it was bright and clear. Lizzie had made a snack for them that could have fed half the town of Stoney Ridge. After spotting the eagle's enormous nest, six feet wide, made of sticks and branches, Jorie led them to a sheltered spot overlooking the pond. They leaned against rocks that were warmed by the winter sun and shared Lizzie's picnic. Through his binoculars, Ephraim saw the mother eagle return to the nest with food in her mouth, so he and Maggie took off to see if they could get high enough to catch a glimpse of how many eaglets were in the nest.

Cal smiled as they scrambled up the hill. "I thought we'd have leftovers, but Ephraim eats more than all of us put together."

Jorie looked out over the pond. "This is my favorite place on earth. I used to spend hours here with my brothers in the summers."

"What do you hear from your folks?" Cal asked, stretching out his long legs.

"The settlement is doing well. Good farmland and opportunities for growth." She took an apple out of the basket and tossed it to Cal. He shined it on his shirt and took a large bite out of it. "They want us to come and join them."

Cal stopped chewing and looked at her. "You're not thinking of going, are you?" His cheeks reddened slightly. "I mean, the Percherons. We farmers need those horses. You can't breed them fast enough for us." He swallowed.

"How well I know. We have a two-year waiting list." She looked up at the mother eagle, soaring in the sky. "I don't want to go, but my grandfather has been talking about it some. He's getting older, and Mammi is not . . ." Her voice tapered off.

"Not quite herself?" Cal took another bite of apple and chewed. "I've noticed. I brought her home from town awhile back—she had forgotten to tie her horse and buggy to the hitching post—and she was determined to have me turn right on the main road when she knew the way to Stoney Creek was left."

"Oh," she said flatly. "I hadn't heard about that." She wondered if her grandfather was aware of it and just didn't tell her.

His dark brows lifted. "If you need extra help with her, all you need to do is ask."

She smiled. "For now, we're doing all right. She takes a little extra watching."

"Seems like something the aunties would take to. They love a cause. And I would love to direct their attention away from getting me married off." He slapped his hand against his forehead. "Judas Iscariot! Tonight is another Saturday Night Supper. I completely forgot."

She laughed at the stricken look on his face. "How are those suppers going?"

"Depends who you ask." He took another bite out of the apple. "If you ask Ephraim, they are heaven on earth. Mark my words—his future bride will win his heart through his stomach."

"So the aunties haven't located your perfect match yet?"

"Not yet. But they won't give up. They're moving into the next district over now. Six weeks ago, they brought a widow lady who was rather . . . long in the tooth. And that's putting it kindly. Four weeks ago, they found a gal who sneezed her way through dinner. At the end of the evening, she confessed that she was allergic to cows."

"Oh, that would *never* do for a dairy farmer." Jorie drew a line through an imaginary list in the air.

He grinned and rose to his feet, stretching. "Two weeks ago, it was a stern woman who felt children should be seen and not heard. Matthew happened to be home, and you know what a relentless teaser he is. He got Maggie giggling so hard that milk came out of her nose. That did not sit well with Miss Manners. She left early, in a huff." He reached a hand down to help her up.

Jorie laughed as she took his hand and let him pull her up. "Well, maybe tonight will be the night."

Cal didn't release her hand; instead he reached for her other hand and entwined their fingers together. Jorie thought she could hear her heart beating and wondered if he could hear it too. His eyes locked with hers, watching, waiting, when suddenly a loud whoop from Ephraim burst through the tree branches. Cal dropped Jorie's hands and took a step back as Ephraim and Maggie scrambled through the brush to join them.

"We s-seen 'em with our own eyes!" Ephraim said. "Three eaglets!"

Jorie was surprised to feel a twinge of disappointment. She couldn't help but wonder what might have happened next, had Ephraim not swooped in when he did.

On the way back to Beacon Hollow, the shadows were growing long and Cal was getting anxious to get home in time for milking. Ephraim led the way through the endless woods. He was at that age when boys have more energy than they know what to do with, so he was usually one hundred yards or so ahead of them. But Maggie was wearing out. Her small legs were made for playful scamper, not for a long hike, and she dropped behind constantly, so that Cal and Jorie had to stop and wait for her to catch up. Finally, Cal swung Maggie on his back and picked up the pace.

Ephraim was far enough ahead that they couldn't see him. As they came around a bend, they stopped abruptly. They hadn't seen the three men until they had nearly run right into them. One of the men had a hold on Ephraim's jacket collar like he was hanging him on a wall peg. The men's faces were haggard with rough growths of beard, their eyes red-rimmed. Jorie recognized one face: Jerry Gingerich. He was the one holding on to Ephraim.

"Well, what have we here?" Jerry asked, his words thick and slurred. "Hey, Pete, Jim. I think we got us some Plain folks!" In one hand, he held a bottle filled with amber-colored liquid. He started to bring the bottle back up to his mouth, then let it fall as recognition filled his bloodshot eyes. He knew Cal. A satisfied look covered his face, as if he couldn't believe his good luck.

"Let us pass," Cal said in a calm, relaxed voice, but Jorie could tell by the stillness of his features that he was dead serious.

Another man circled around Jorie. "This here is that uppity red-haired gal. I've seen her in town." A few bits of spittle from his mouth careened through the air.

Jorie met his animosity in the way her people always did: by turning silently away from it, but her heart was thumping wildly in her chest.

"Oh, you think you're too good for me!" He reached up a hand to pull her prayer cap off, but Cal quickly sidestepped between Jorie and the man, causing the man to lose his balance and stagger back a step.

"Let us pass," Cal repeated, lowering Maggie to the ground.

"Or else . . . what, Plain man?" Jerry said, waving his bottle in the air. He took another gulp straight out of the bottle. "What are you going to do about it, huh?"

He dropped his hold on Ephraim and pushed Cal. Cal swayed back a little but his feet didn't budge.

"We warned you. We told you not to let that colored man move in, but you went ahead and ignored us."

"Jorie, take Ephraim and Maggie," Cal said, "and run on back to the house." His voice was flat, quiet, and he stood with his hands loose at his sides, his head a little bent. But the air around him pulsed and thrummed.

"Hold it," the third man said, talking around a thick wad of chewing tobacco that puckered his mouth. "You don't give the orders around here." He spewed a thick glob of tobacco juice onto Cal's boots.

"Let my family go," Cal said. "It's me you've got the quarrel with." He turned his head toward Jorie. "You heard me. Go, now."

Jorie grabbed Ephraim's arm, but he pulled away from her. She grabbed him again, more firmly. Leading Ephraim and Maggie by the hands, she backed away, then turned and started running the way they had come. She heard one of the men object, but Jerry said, "Let 'em go. He's the one we want."

As soon as they had gone a distance, she stopped. "Ephraim, lift Maggie onto my back. I know a shortcut to Bud's."

Ephraim linked his fingers together to give Maggie a leg up.

"I'm scared," Maggie whispered into her ear.

"Then say a prayer, Maggie," Jorie said in as calm a voice as she could manage. She followed a chain of animal trails through the dense woodland until she found a narrow passageway through a bramble thicket that bordered Bud's field. She put Maggie down and grabbed her hand to run, not stopping until she reached Bud's farmhouse. He was passing from the barn to the house and saw them waving and calling to him.

"What's the matter?" Bud asked, looking alarmed. "Is there a fire?"

Jorie spilled out the story to Bud in big gulpy breaths as Maggie pulled on her dress sleeve. Bud told her to sit tight while he went in the house to get a gun.

"No, Bud! No gun," Jorie said. "It's not our way."

"But I'm not Amish," he said, then he turned and walked to the house.

Maggie kept pulling on Jorie's sleeve. Still panting, Jorie looked at Maggie. "What is it?" she asked.

"It's Ephraim! He's still in the woods. He didn't come with us!"

As Bud came out of the house with his shotgun and his hunting dog, Jorie told Maggie to go to Beacon Hollow and stay with Lizzie until they got back.

"You go on with her, Jorie," Bud said. "This is no place for a woman. Besides, Maggie needs you."

Jorie looked down at Maggie and knew that Bud was right. Maggie looked so small and scared. Jorie nodded. "Please hurry, Bud."

An hour later, Bud and Ephraim brought Cal, bruised and bloody but upright and walking, to Beacon Hollow. Relief washed over Jorie, and she was surprised at the strength of her own emotions. She had feared the worst. She couldn't bear to lose him—and with that sudden awareness came a rush of tears. Maggie ran toward her father, hugging his middle. Cal winced as her arms tightened around him.

"I'm fine, Maggie. I really am. Just a bump or two." He exchanged a look with Jorie and she knew he wasn't fine.

"Put him up in his bed," she told Bud and Ephraim.

"Wait," Cal said in a voice as dry as toast. "The cows need milking."

"Lizzie, Maggie, and I took care of it, Cal," Jorie said. It had helped keep them busy and their minds off of worrying about what those men were doing to Cal.

"And the aunties?" he asked.

"They came and left," Jorie said. "Lizzie said you weren't feeling well, which was the truth."

After Cal was settled upstairs, Jorie set about doctoring his injuries with calm efficiency. A solution of powdered golden seal and myrrh for his cuts, first boiled and steeped for twenty minutes. A lavender and almond oil infusion for his swollen eye. She took ice from the kitchen, wrapped it in a dish towel, and gently placed it on his sore ribs. "Hold it there," she said, placing his left arm over the bag.

When the ice touched him, his entire body went rigid, but he relaxed as the numbness set in. Within seconds, he closed his eyes and breathed deeply.

Jorie stayed for a moment, watching as he fell asleep. His face was so bruised and battered, it nearly broke her heart. She felt a strange tenderness toward Cal. She always had. Impulsively, she leaned over and kissed his forehead and quietly left his room.

When she went downstairs, Bud was sitting at the kitchen table with Ephraim. Lizzie had made dinner but no one was hungry.

"I think he needs a doctor," Jorie said. "He might have some broken ribs."

"I'll go home and call for a doctor," Bud said. "I'll let Matthew know too, but first I'm calling the police to report this."

"No!" Jorie said, more loudly than she meant to sound. "No, Bud. I'm sorry, but that's not our way."

Bud slammed a fist down on the table, upset and angry. "That's the very reason you folks get harmed. It never stops. Fellows like Jerry Gingerich know you won't fight back. You won't press charges. You Amish don't do a dadblasted thing about it!"

"Vengeance belongs only to the Lord," Jorie said in a shaky voice. She spoke those words and believed them to be true, but in her heart, deep down, she was struggling to accept them. She *wanted* those men to pay for what they did to Cal. It was a terrible thing that people felt they could do anything to the Amish and get away with it.

Bud seemed to realize her inner turmoil. His craggy face softened around the edges. He eased out of the chair and tousled Ephraim's hair. "Here's the hero, today. He stayed right by Cal until I arrived. By the time I got there, those yellow-bellied cowards were gone."

Ephraim didn't look like he felt like a hero. Jorie thought he still looked frightened. She wondered what he had witnessed of the beating Cal took.

"Don't worry, Ephraim," Maggie said, patting him on his arm. "Dad just has a bump."

When Cal woke, Jorie was sitting in a rocker by the window. "You shouldn't be here," were his first words. "It'll get people talking. It isn't proper."

"Well, good thing I've got an understanding minister." She stood and came to his bed. "I went home for the night and just came back a short while ago." She smiled. "Marge is working on a curative for you."

He laughed, a soft laugh that turned into a cough. He tried to sit up and moaned, then leaned back down.

"You've got broken ribs. And a concussion. The doctor said you're going to need to take things slow for a while." She pulled up the chair beside him. "Can I get you anything?"

"No." He closed his eyes for a moment. "Ephraim's all right, isn't he?"

"Yes. He's downstairs. He's quiet. But then, he's always quiet."

Cal opened his eyes. "It was the strangest thing. I remember seeing him come back, alone. I knew he was watching the men beat on me. Then, suddenly, there was a scream—one prolonged scream, and then another. I thought maybe it was you, but then I got hit and blacked out."

"It wasn't me," Jorie said. "While I was running to get Bud, Ephraim slipped away and doubled back."

"Maybe it was Ephraim, trying to distract them." He closed his eyes again. "Next thing I knew, Ephraim and Bud were standing over me."

He was quiet for so long that she thought he had fallen asleep. She went to his bedside to pull the blanket, slipping off the side of the bed, back over him. She gazed fondly at him. He was young, only thirty, and despite his battered face, he was a handsome man with his thick mane of dark wavy hair and his sparkling blue eyes. Though she was brought up believing that no man was better than another, Cal was an anchor in their community. How could anyone dare to lay a hand on him? The thought of what happened in the Deep Woods sickened her.

"Aw, Jorie. Quit looking at me like I'm such a pitiful sight."

She laughed. "Right now, you are a pitiful sight, Caleb Zook." Then she sobered. "I'm the one who brought this trouble on you."

"What's done is done. We're all in this together." He fixed his eyes on her. "But while you're feeling beholden, there is something you can do for me."

"What's that?"

He took a deep breath. "I've been lying here, thinking and praying. I feel, more than ever, that it's the right decision." He bit the corner of his lip. "I want you to marry me."

She stopped smoothing the blankets and stilled for a long moment. Then she straightened up. "Yes." This time the answer came from her heart.

"I'm going to keep asking you till you say yes."

"All the more reason I should say yes."

"Jorie, we're a good team, you and I. Maggie adores you, so does Ephraim. You belong here at Beacon Hollow."

"Cal, are you listening? I said yes."

He was just about to start talking again when he realized what she said and snapped his mouth shut. His left eye, the one that wasn't swollen nearly shut, widened in surprise. "You mean it? You're not just saying that because you're feeling sorry for me?" His cheeks stained red.

"I mean it." She had no doubts. It just felt right, like lemonade and picnics by the lake on a warm summer day. There was another long silence where their eyes locked and they both knew they had an agreement. Silent, but there. She smiled and reached out to stroke the hair off of his forehead. "We can talk it all over when you're feeling better."

A tenderness came over Cal's face. He reached for her hand and brought it to his mouth, pressing his lips to the inside of her wrist, where the blue veins pulsed beneath her pale skin. "If I could sit up, and if I didn't look like I've been sent through a washer wringer, I would kiss you properly."

She felt breathless, the way she got when she was climbing the ramp to the hayloft. "Matthew is here," she said, suddenly shy. "He wants to see you."

"Not like this. I'll come downstairs."

She nodded and walked to the door. As she turned the knob, she heard him ask, almost in a whisper, "Jorie, do you really mean it?"

She kept her hand on the doorknob, though she did turn to look at him. "Preacher Caleb," she said in a lightly teasing tone. "My no is no, and my yes is yes."

As Ephraim saw Cal wince with every step as he made his way to the kitchen table, he felt his throat tighten. How could those men have hurt his brother like that? Cal was such a good and kind man. He didn't deserve that treatment. It disturbed Ephraim deeply to have seen those stupid, drunk men pummel Cal, over and over. Just thinking about it made his eyes start to prickle with tears, so he went out on the stoop and called for Maggie to come in to see her dad. He held the door open as Maggie raced inside, then practically bumped into her when she skidded to a stop, shocked by the sight of her father. She had seen him last night, but he looked even worse this morning, swollen and bruised. Cal spread out his arm so that Maggie would stand close and lean against him.

Jorie brought Cal a cup of hot coffee.

"How do you feel?" Matthew asked, handing Cal the milk and sugar pitchers for his coffee.

Cal stirred his coffee, then took a sip, carefully avoiding the cut on his lip. "Like someone dropped an anvil on my chest."

"Looks like someone dropped it on your face," Matthew said, peering at Cal's cuts and bruises.

Cal glanced over at Ephraim. "You should have stayed with Jorie, Ephraim. I'm sorry you had to see that. But I'm grateful for your concern."

Jorie sat down next to Ephraim. "What's troubling you?"

Ephraim looked at Cal. "You n-never th-threw a p-punch. You just s-stood there. You just s-stood there and l-let them hit you." He had never seen men so riled up, not even his brother Ben, who had a temper on him.

"If I had, Ephraim, I wouldn't have been any different from those men," Cal said. "I would become just like them. The rage and hate that lives in them would become a part of me. Vengeance belongs only to God."

Maybe, but Ephraim still wanted to hurt them back. Especially that Jerry Gingerich. He didn't recognize the other two men, but he hated them too.

"I sort of remember the sound of a scream," Cal started. "But then I blacked out. What was that all about?"

All of the eyes at the table turned to Ephraim. His eyes went wide and his mouth fell open, but no sound came out. A knock on the door diverted everyone's attention. Ephraim jumped up and opened it to Flora Miller, bearing a hot casserole. Flora gasped when she saw Cal's battered appearance.

After Flora left, Jorie said she should be getting home. "The news is out. Every woman in our church district will be bringing you a casserole, so I think I will be getting home to help Atlee with the horses."

Cal tried to get up, but Jorie shook her head. "Stay put. I'll stop back later to see how you're doing. Maybe my grandmother will have a remedy cooked up for you."

Matthew snorted. "Last time she gave me a remedy, I spent two days on the john. No, big brother, if you're smart, you will run for the high hills if Marge King tries to get anywhere near you with one of her curatives." He tipped his head toward Jorie. "No disrespect to your grandmother."

Jorie tried to look stern but broke into a laugh as she tied her bonnet under her chin. "None taken. He's right. Run for the hills."

Matthew was spreading blackberry jam on his toast. Maggie was stirring spoonfuls of sugar into Cal's coffee. Ephraim was sure he was the only one who caught the look that passed between Cal and Jorie as she turned at the door to wave goodbye.

Something had changed between them, something had been sealed.

When Jorie returned home, she found her grandmother in the kitchen making sweet rolls. As she hung her bonnet and cape on the kitchen wall peg, she braced herself, expecting her grandmother to drop everything and insist on going to Beacon Hollow. A few hours earlier, as Jorie left to see Cal, her grandmother had been poring over books to find just the right painkiller. She half-expected Mammi to have shown up at Beacon Hollow this morning, holding in her hands some vile-tasting liquid to force down Cal's throat. But Mammi stood at the kitchen counter, in the middle of a cloud of flour, kneading dough as if her life depended on it. Books were still open on the kitchen table, surrounded by all kinds of dried herbs in jars, but Mammi never even mentioned Cal, which struck Jorie as strange.

She went out to the barn to help her grandfather feed the horses. She smiled when she heard the shuffling of the horses' feet in anticipation of their noon meal.

Atlee stopped pitching hay into a wheelbarrow when he saw her. "How is our Caleb?"

"He looks worse, with all of the swelling and bruises. But he was up."

Atlee grabbed a forkful of hay and tossed it in the wheelbarrow. "You're looking pretty chipper this morning," he said, in between heaving the hay.

"Oh?" she said. "I saw the first robin on my way home. A foretaste of spring."

Atlee gave her a look as if he didn't really think a robin alone deserved the credit for giving her that kind of happiness.

Briefly, Jorie thought about telling him that she and Cal were going to be married. If she were going to tell anyone, it would be her grandfather. But she thought better of it. It was hard not to spill her secret; she felt as if she was nearly bursting with the news. Her heart had almost stopped when Cal asked her. When it started up again, it felt like it was beating in unsteady lurches. It still surprised her, saying yes like that, but she found she had no doubts. For now, it would remain a secret, shared just between her and Cal.

Instead, she said, "Surprised me a little to see that Mammi had forgotten all about making a remedy for Cal. When I came home, she was making rolls."

Atlee lifted his eyebrows. "Guess she forgot about it."

"Doesn't it seem as if she's getting more than a little forgetful about things like that lately?"

Atlee continued to heave hay into the wheelbarrow. "What else?"

"She left the oven on all night the other day. And last week I went out to get a casserole from the freezer, and there was her knitting project, frozen solid."

"Well, she's getting older. We old folks get a little forgetful now and then."

"Maybe. But usually that's about insignificant things. Her doctoring has always been so important to her."

Atlee didn't answer, which meant that he didn't want to discuss it. Jorie grabbed another pitchfork and joined her grandfather as he wheeled the barrow down the corridor of the barn.

As soon as he finished helping Cal milk the cows, Ephraim tucked another frozen package of meat under his coat and took off for the Deep Woods at a fast run. It wasn't easy to get away this week. He felt bad about Cal, but a little sorry for himself too. Cal needed extra help, which meant a lot more choring for him and less time for cougar snooping.

The scream Cal had heard before he got whacked on the head was the cougar's scream. She was in a tree above them, her lithe body poised on a branch, peering down at the men beating on Cal. Then she spotted Ephraim, hiding behind a rock, and exchanged a long look with him. That was when she let out a scream that made the hair on the back of his head stand up straight. One of the men had been holding Cal up under his arms and the other two were taking turns pummeling him. When the cougar screamed, they stopped, looked up, and saw her. She screamed again. This time, they dropped Cal and ran.

After the men left, he ran to Cal's side, praying he wasn't dead. He also wanted to protect Cal in case the cougar decided to come down from the tree. Her expression was unmistakably belligerent. He threw his body over Cal's and covered his head with his arms, bracing himself for an attack. After a long wait, satisfied that Cal was still breathing, Ephraim stole a glance up at the tree. The cougar had gone.

Not a minute later, Bud arrived. Ephraim knew the cougar was a wild creature and that it couldn't really have known he needed her help. Even still, today he wanted to leave an offering, a thank-you for saving his brother's life. And one thing else Ephraim noticed. The cougar's belly was round with life.

"It's warming up some, don't you think?" Jorie asked Cal when he stopped by the schoolhouse on Friday afternoon.

He laughed, a sound rich and thick. "Only you, Jorie King, could find the good in a bitterly windy March day."

"At least it's not snowing," she said as a smile wreathed her face. She was so happy to see him up and around and looking like himself that she wanted to laugh and throw her arms around him in a big welcoming hug. Instead she stood before him, assessing his face, with her hands linked behind her back. His eye looked nearly normal; the swelling was almost gone. The bruising had gone from angry red to blue and yellow and purple. But she saw he still held himself stiff and upright, as if he couldn't bend over without fear of snapping in two.

Cal looked down at her and held her gaze. "If it's not making you feel rushed, I'd like to talk to Isaac on Sunday afternoon about how soon he could marry us."

"That sounds fine," was all that she said, but she knew her eyes were smiling. Ever since she had agreed to marry Cal, she was nearly floating with sweet anticipation. She felt lighter than air.

"Good. It's settled then. Sunday it is. And that will be the *end* of the aunties' Supper List."

She couldn't help but laugh at that. Cal's smile deepened, his eyes warmed. He took a step closer to her and reached for her hands. His calloused hands felt large and strong. He studied her face for a long moment, before he leaned into her, tilting his head, and his mouth came down onto hers. His lips were warm, his beard gently tickling. He kissed her with such sweetness it was almost unbearable. And when he pulled back, she had to look away because she had tears in her eyes. Something had become very clear to her: she loved him.

12

Matthew's night shift was nearly over. He had finished up cleaning the bathrooms and stopped at the nurses' station to study the updated patient board. "Morning, Lottie," he said. "Did you just get here?"

"Hello to you, farm boy," Lottie said with a big toothy grin. "How'd you get stuck on night duty?"

"Only way they let me off on weekends is if I pull a Saturday night once in a while." He leaned his elbows on the counter and turned his head to look down the hall at a cluster of Plain People, hovering by a patient's door like bees over flowers. "What's going on?"

Lottie tilted her head. "Say, you speak German, don't you?"

"They're not speaking German. They're speaking Deitsch, a dialect. But yes, I do speak it."

"Well, if you can understand what they're saying, get yourself down that hall and make yourself useful. Those folks came in this morning to see a new patient. They seem upset, but no one on the floor can understand them."

"Sure. I'll go."

Matthew walked up to the group in the hallway. An older woman was crying. He spoke to the eldest man and asked, in Deitsch, if he could help him. The man looked at Matthew, startled to hear his own language coming out of a hospital worker. "Er is net mein Sohn!" He pointed to the door. "Er is net mein Sohn!" *He is not my son.* He gripped Matthew's shirt with his two hands and clung to him. "Warum is mein Sohn?" *So where is my son?*

Matthew spotted Dr. Doyle, the floor physician, coming out of the elevator. "Let me go tell the doctor what you've told me." He unclasped the man's strong fingers from his shirt and hurried to the elevator.

"You're sure?" Dr. Doyle asked the Amish farmer, after Matthew explained the situation. "You're absolutely sure?"

Matthew translated back and forth between the doctor and the Amish farmer. The farmer kept insisting, "Er is net mein Sohn!" *He is not my son.* "Warum is mein Sohn?" *So where is my son?*

The doctor looked through the charts. "This man had identifying dog tags. They sent him here to Pennsylvania *because* of those tags."

"Er is net mein Sohn! Warum is mein Sohn?" the farmer kept repeating.

"Why don't you folks go down to the waiting room with me and we'll see if we can get things straightened out." Dr. Doyle turned to Matthew. "You'll help with the translating?"

"Sure, sure," Matthew said.

"Then who *is* this patient?" Lottie whispered to the doctor. "How are we going to ID him?"

"Write him up as a 'John Doe,'" the doctor told her. Exasperated, the doctor blew air out of his cheeks. He led the family down the hall, but before Matthew went to join them, Lottie asked him to take the new patient his breakfast. Matthew balanced the breakfast tray in one hand and slipped open the door with the other. The patient, a young man with a nearly shaved head, sat in a chair, facing the window. He was entirely still except for his fingers, which drummed restlessly along the arm of the chair. How sad, Matthew thought, to be a John Doe. A no-name. To not belong to anyone. He felt a sweeping gratefulness for the family he had, the place at his table. Even Ben's spot had never been sat in.

He walked a few steps closer to the patient. "Can I get you anything?" Matthew asked him softly.

The patient didn't respond.

"Some water? Or juice? I know where Lottie keeps a box of candy hidden, if you like chocolates." Matthew's words fell into an empty silence. "Okay, then. I'll come back and check on you later. Maybe by then you'll want some of Lottie's chocolates. Everything's going to be all right. You'll see."

The patient had stopped his finger drumming. He had grown so still, so motionless, that it almost seemed to Matthew as if he had died. An eerie feeling crept up Matthew's spine. How could he explain a dead patient to Dr. Doyle? He took a tentative step closer to the patient, hoping to see his chest expand with a breath. He crouched down carefully in front of him and placed a hand on his knee.

The patient suddenly lifted his head and looked straight at Matthew with blank, empty eyes.

Matthew lurched back, nearly falling. "Judas Iscariot!" He felt his heart miss a beat. "Er is noch lewendich!" *He's still alive!*

All during meeting, Cal tried to keep his mind on the Lord and off of Jorie. Still, whenever he walked or turned around as he preached, he found himself searching for her face among the sea of prayer caps. He'd known her all his life, but lately, out of nowhere, the sight of her could snatch away his breath and make his chest hurt. As he closed the service, Cal made a few announcements: a barn raising would be held next week at the Reuben Yoders'. A comfort knotting would take place at Sylvia Swartzentruber's on Friday. "And next meeting will be held at the Roman Stoltzfuses'." He looked over at Jorie and they shared one of those special smiles that came only into their eyes. Maybe as soon as next meeting, he would be making the announcement that he and Jorie were planning to marry. This very afternoon, he would speak to Isaac about it.

Just as Cal opened his mouth to give the benediction, the door blew open and Matthew burst in, scanning the room until his eyes found Cal's.

"I found him! Cal! He's alive! Our Ben's alive!"

When Bud heard the news about Ben, he offered to drive the Zooks over to Lebanon in his station wagon. Maggie squeezed between Cal and Bud in the front seat. Matthew and Ephraim sat in the backseat. "Shall I stop by the Kings' and pick up Jorie?" Bud asked Cal.

"No," Cal said, firmly. He was still reeling from Matthew's discovery—that Ben was alive, in a hospital, just an hour from Stoney Ridge. It was all he could do to finish the church service and rush back to the farm to find Bud.

"She's not expecting to come?" Bud asked.

Cal's jaw clenched tight. "She doesn't know we're going to Lebanon."

"Think that's being fair to her?" Bud said.

Cal didn't answer.

Bud looked at him. "Or are you just being fair to you?"

Cal looked out the window. He couldn't think about Jorie right now. He just couldn't. He avoided her after church. He didn't even look at her, though he knew she was watching him as he grabbed Maggie's hand and hurried to the buggy. Right now, all he could think about was Ben.

Bud shrugged. "Suit yourself."

Cal asked Matthew to tell the story about discovering Ben over and over again. "Are you sure he didn't recognize you, Matthew?"

"Not at first. Then, when I realized he was our Ben and talked to him in Deitsch, he got real upset and the doctor told me to leave. I was so shaken I didn't even know what to do next. I thought I'd better just get word to you, Cal, so I hitchhiked from the Vet Hospital all the way to Stoney Ridge." He took off his hat. "But I really couldn't tell for sure if he recognized me."

"Matthew's changed an awful lot since Ben's been gone," Bud said quietly. "He's gone from being a boy to a man. And with that fancy haircut, he doesn't look Amish anymore."

Cal turned his head slightly. "Yes. So much has changed since he left us."

Maggie looked up at Cal. "Dad, I don't hardly remember Ben."

Cal rested a hand on her small head. "Two years is a long time when you're seven years old. But now you'll have plenty of time to get reacquainted."

At the Veterans Hospital, Matthew led them to the psychiatric floor and started to head into Ben's room, everyone following behind, until the doctor stopped them.

"Matthew, you can't just waltz in there—" Dr. Doyle started.

"Nobody's waltzing," Cal said. "We just want to see our brother."

"And you certainly can't bring children onto this ward," Dr. Doyle said, frowning at Maggie and Ephraim. He turned to Lottie, who was watching, with wide eyes, from the nurses' station. "Maybe you could take them to the cafeteria and get them something to eat."

Lottie wiggled her finger toward Ephraim and Maggie, who looked to Cal for permission. He nodded, so they followed her down the hall.

"Let's find someplace to talk," the doctor said. "Follow me to the waiting room. You'll overwhelm your brother if you all charge in there, claiming him. If he really is your family member, let's do this in a way that is best for him."

Cal, Bud, and Matthew followed the doctor into the waiting room and sat on stiff plastic chairs. The doctor looked through a chart and told them what he knew about this patient's history. "He was a conscientious objector doing nonmilitary assignments but got involved in an offensive. Within a few weeks of the incident, he started to show signs of instability. He was sent to Bangkok for psychiatric evaluation, his breakdown continued to escalate, and was sent here for long-term care."

"When will my brother be able to come home?" Cal asked.

The doctor held up a hand in warning. "Whoa. Slow down. Let's get an identification on him first."

Cal stood to go.

"Look, Mr. Zook," the doctor said. "If he is your brother, he's not well. He's . . . he's going to need care."

"We can care for him at home," Cal said.

Dr. Doyle looked like he'd had a long day. "His wounds aren't physical. He's a little scrambled up."

Cal looked at him. "Speak plain."

Dr. Doyle stood to face Cal. "He's going to need psychiatric rehabilitation. He's very withdrawn. He has what we call a clinical depression. He suffered some kind of traumatic incident that has made him shut down."

"He needs to be home," Cal insisted. He was losing patience with this doctor who spoke of Ben like he was reading from a medical book. What did he really know about his brother? Or about being Amish? About God's strength that helped them heal?

"Well, let's take this one step at a time. Matthew can accompany you, Mr. Zook." The doctor turned, then spun around. "Stay calm. No big show of emotion."

Bud gave a short laugh. "Doc, you're preaching to the choir. These folks are Amish."

"Let's go," Cal said. "I want to welcome my brother home."

In the hospital room, Matthew walked quietly up to Ben, who was seated in the same chair, staring out the window, fingers drumming. Dr. Doyle stood protectively by the door. "Ben, I've brought someone to see you. It's Cal. Our big brother Cal."

Cal crouched down in front of Ben as his eyes studied his face. Ben was barely recognizable to him. The laughter in his eyes—so much a part of Ben—was gone. In its place was an emptiness. His face was thin and pale. His head was shaved. Different, broken, yet the same. This man was indeed his brother. "Zwaar?" Cal asked, his voice cracking with emotion. *Can this be true?* "The good Lord has seen fit to return our brother Ben to us."

Ben showed no sign of recognizing Cal; his eyes remained fixed on his right hand, drumming restlessly on the arm of the chair. Cal wasn't disappointed—Matthew had prepared him for such a lack of response. His heart, though, was overflowing with joy . . . just to be near his brother Ben.

In a soft, gentle voice, Cal started talking to Ben as if he'd seen him only last week and wanted to let him know what crops were going to be planted soon and which cows were due to calve. Too soon, he felt, the doctor interrupted, saying he thought Ben had enough excitement for one day.

Slowly, Cal stood. "Ben, the Lord God answered our prayers and protected you. He brought you home to us. I'm so glad you're back with us." He cleared his throat; it felt as if he had ground glass in there. "So very glad." He clasped Ben on the shoulder as if he was afraid he might disappear again.

Out by the nurses' station, Cal crossed his arms against his chest and locked eyes with Dr. Doyle. That little doctor couldn't be much older than Matthew, Cal thought, and acted as jumpy as a cricket. "He needs to be home with us. He won't get better here."

Dr. Doyle shook his head emphatically. "I'm sorry, Mr. Zook. He's still under evaluation. There are procedures we need to follow."

Cal threw up his arms. "I am tired of the government telling me about my brother. First, you tell me he's dead. Then, that his body has been *cremated*.

Now, we find out—through no help from the government, mind you—that he's alive! I want to bring my brother home. He belongs at home."

Bud sidled up to the doctor. "Remember, Doc, these folks are Amish. They aren't gonna sue you. They just like to take care of their own."

The doctor looked curiously at Bud, standing there with his hands jammed into his overall pockets, his straw hat tilted back on his wispy gray hair, his heavy boots giving off a faint whiff of manure. "This patient is suffering from a severe clinical depression. It's given him dissociative symptoms." At the blank look on everyone's faces, he tried again. "Something like amnesia."

"Amnesia?" Matthew asked. "So he *has* forgotten us?"

"No," the doctor sighed, deeply and grievously. "He hasn't forgotten you. He's tried to suppress painful experiences that are too difficult to endure. It's like his mind has shut down as a way to cope. It's not unusual behavior in a veteran, but it's not understood very well. If he went home too soon, with expectations from all of you heaped on him, it might cause the opposite response. He might withdraw even further, because he can't fulfill your expectations of him."

Cal spun the brim of his black hat around and around in his hands. "We don't want to cause him any more pain."

"That's why I want you folks to go home, let the professionals evaluate your brother, and let us decide what the best course of action to take will be," the doctor said.

"Could we come back to see him soon?" Cal asked. When the doctor hesitated, Cal quickly added, "We thought he was dead. For months now, we thought my brother was dead."

The doctor's face relaxed slightly. "Of course. Of course you can visit him. Look, we all want the same thing. We want your brother to get well. Matthew will be here every day and can call you with updates."

Bud made a snorting sound. "These folks don't have phones, Doc."

"How soon?" Cal asked. "How soon can we come and visit?"

"Next weekend," the doctor said. With visible relief, he noticed Lottie approaching from the elevator with Maggie and Ephraim. "Lottie has some paperwork for you to fill out about your brother. You have information we need."

He hustled away as if there was a fire on the ward.

Lottie had a large file folder in her hands and plunked it on the counter of the nurses' station. "The government loves its paperwork," she said to Cal, as if that explained everything.

Matthew offered to keep Maggie and Ephraim busy, so Cal began the process of filling out forms. When he was drafted in the Korean War, there was one simple form to sign. Why would it be so much more complicated to declare someone alive? he wondered, after filling out the sixth form. Thirty minutes later, Cal found Matthew, Ephraim, and Bud in the waiting room.

"Where's Maggie?" he asked.

"I thought she was with you," Matthew said, suddenly alarmed. "I was showing them around the hospital and Maggie said she needed to go to the bathroom. When she didn't come back to us, I figured she had found you."

"Matthew," Cal said, frowning, "you know Maggie's tendency to wander off."

They spent time retracing their steps, going floor to floor. They finally split up and each took a floor, until Lottie waved to Cal down at the elevator. "Come look what I found." She took him back to Ben's hospital room. There was Maggie, sitting on Ben's bed. Maggie was reading out loud from a comic book she had found in the waiting room. Cal watched them for a while.

"Well, well, look at that," Lottie whispered.

"What?" Cal asked. To him, Ben hadn't changed a wit. He was still in the chair, staring out the window.

"See his hands? They're still. First time I've seen his fingers not drumming a beat."

Cal's eyes shifted to Ben's hand, resting calmly on the armchair. Maggie looked up and noticed her father at the door. Gently, she laid the comic book in Ben's lap. "Next time we come, we'll finish up the story and see whether Archie ends up with Veronica or Betty." She patted her uncle on the shoulder. "See you soon, Ben."

Bud drove Matthew to the house where he was renting a room. "I wish we could stay and take you to dinner, Matthew," Cal said. "But the dairy . . ."

Matthew waved him off. "I understand. I'm kind of beat anyway." After he got out of the car, he shut the door and leaned through the window. "Maggie, what made you think to read to Ben?"

She pushed her glasses up on the bridge of her small nose. "Jorie told us to read whenever we got the chance. When I saw the comic book in the waiting room, I just thought Ben might like it."

Matthew reached in to give her a big wet noisy kiss on her cheek. "You did good, little Magpie."

Cal loved his dairy, but there were days, like today, when the relentless demands of thirty cows waiting to be milked felt like a ball and chain around his leg. They had left the hospital so late that he knew they wouldn't be back to Beacon Hollow in time for the milking. A whole set of problems could be waiting for him back home, the least of which would be the noise of thirty bawling cows with bursting udders. He kept glancing at the speedometer, wishing Bud would pick up his pace.

Bud scowled at him. "Stop staring at me. I'm driving the speed limit and that's all there is to it!"

"Aw, Bud," Cal said. "Little old ladies are passing us by!"

"So much for the slow life of the Amish, is all I got to say," Bud said, but he did speed up a little.

When Bud finally turned the station wagon up Beacon Hollow's long driveway, nearly two hours late for the milking, Cal was about to leap out of the car. He tossed a thank-you back to Bud and rushed into the barn, expecting to hear a chorus of thirty unhappy cows. Instead, the cows were quietly eating, udders emptied, manure shoveled off behind them in their stanchions, and the barn had been swept clean. Maggie and Ephraim skidded to a halt behind him.

"Wer hen schunn die K-Kieh g-gemolke?!" Ephraim said, looking around the tidy barn in amazement. *Who milked the cows?!*

Cal turned around in a circle, amazed. "Our good friends and neighbors. That's who milked our cows. They knew we needed help and they just stepped in." He sighed, deeply satisfied with this day of many miracles. "And *that*, Maggie and Ephraim, is what being Amish is all about."

In the kitchen, they found the table set for supper, the smell of a casserole baking in the oven. On the table was a bowl of pickled cucumbers, sliced tomatoes, and a basket of sliced bread, covered with a napkin.

As Ephraim made a lunge for the bread basket, Cal grabbed his wrist. "First, we wash up. Then, we thank the Lord for a day such as this. Then, we eat."

"Who do you think made us dinner?" Maggie asked, scrubbing her hands at the kitchen sink. "Same folks that milked our cows?"

Cal laughed. "I hope not. I think it was a female who made us this fine dinner. Maybe two. She didn't leave us a note. I'm guessing she didn't feel the need to be thanked. But we can sure thank the good Lord for this meal and the hands that provided it." He tucked his chin to his chest and offered a prayer, filled with gratitude, to God for this day's events, including a request for healing for Ben. *And dear Lord,* he added silently to his prayer, *please help me know what to do about Jorie.*

On Monday afternoon, as soon as school let out, Cal was waiting on the steps of the schoolhouse. The scholars poured out, scarcely noticing him, but Maggie and Ephraim stopped in their tracks.

"You both head on home before the rain starts up," he told them. "I'll be there soon."

Cal waited until the last scholar left, then went into the schoolhouse and stood by the door, awkwardly. He was hoping Jorie would say something. She sat at her desk, engrossed in writing on a paper. She didn't acknowledge him in any way.

He cleared his throat. "We went to see Ben yesterday." He took a tentative step inside and took off his hat.

"I heard," she said, without looking up.

So she did know he was here. Cal took a step closer. "He isn't . . . well. The doctor said he's suffering from a type of stress brought on by trauma. A depression. He's sort of in his own world." He took another step. "But there was a bright spot. Maggie read to him and it seemed to calm him. We thought that was a real good sign."

Jorie gave a slight nod. He noticed her hand was clasping the pen so tightly that her knuckles were white.

Cal rambled on for a while, trying to remember the details that the doctor had told him. "Matthew is going to call over to Bud's each night, a little after five when the long-distance rates go down, and tell us how Ben is doing. If there's some improvement, we're hoping we can bring him home soon. That doctor, though, he might take some persuading."

Jorie stood and went to the window that overlooked the playground. Rain had begun and it hit with a fury.

"Jorie," Cal said in a soft voice, coming close behind her.

She spun around. "You know what really makes me mad? You took Maggie! You took a little girl to a *psychiatric ward* of the Veterans Hospital. Yet you didn't take me! You left church yesterday with no intention of asking me to come. I saw you leave!"

"But—"

Her eyes were fiery. "I care about him too."

He tossed his hat on a nearby desk and raised his hands. "Jorie, please try and understand. I couldn't handle . . . having both . . ." He sighed. "We may as well have this out now as later. We've got a problem that's going to need some working out."

"I realize we've got a problem! But for you to exclude me yesterday, well, that's hard for me to understand. You're the one who's always saying that men need to listen to women, that a woman's point of view is like a gift." She lifted her chin a notch. "Well, yesterday, you had a chance to practice what you preach, and instead you just went off, without a thought for me. It hurt me to be left out. As if I didn't matter to Ben. As if I didn't matter to you."

"Of course you matter," Cal said, a strange roughness to his voice. "Why else would this whole thing feel so complicated?"

But Jorie had arrived at some conclusions of her own. "Let me uncomplicate this whole thing," she said, too calmly. "Ben needs you right now. Nothing else is as important as helping Ben get better."

"You're right," Cal said.

She turned back to the window. "Maybe the timing of this is a blessing. No one needs to know that a courtship has been broken."

Cal walked up to her and reached out a hand as if he was going to touch her, then thought better of it. He had a little trouble with his voice when he asked, "Are we broken, Jorie?"

She turned to him. Cal stared at her, his face settling into deep lines, and

Jorie stared back, her head held high, erect. A silence drew out between them, underscored by the drumroll of rain hitting the roof above their heads.

Cal was the first to drop his eyes. "On Sunday, Bud said he'd drive us over to see Ben. If you want to see him. But I can't promise the doctor will let you into his room. He's a little protective, that doctor. Doesn't understand how important family is. I'm anxious to get Ben home as soon as possible. I know he'll get better if he can just come home."

Jorie gave a firm nod. "I'll be there on Sunday."

Cal picked up his hat and walked to the door. As he reached the doorjamb, he turned around. "It's a miracle, really. Like Lazarus, raised from the dead." He put his hat on and adjusted the brim, before walking out in the rain.

"But Lazarus came back whole," Jorie said, so softly Cal wasn't sure if she actually said it or if he had just thought it himself.

13

The following Sunday afternoon, Dr. Doyle led Matthew, Cal, and Jorie to Ben's door while Bud took Maggie and Ephraim to the cafeteria. The doctor explained that they shouldn't expect any response, that they should not cry or put any emotional pressure on Ben. "I recommend that you, Matthew, or you, Mr. Zook, go in first and talk to him for a few minutes. Prepare him for meeting someone else. Matthew said you're his girlfriend, right?" He looked to Jorie to respond, but she didn't answer.

Matthew cringed. Why did he ever tell the doctor that? And he didn't *say* "girlfriend," he said "girl."

"We're his family," Cal said. "We're all family. I'll go in first."

After Cal went into Ben's room, the doctor turned to Matthew. "What, is he like the patriarch of the clan?"

Matthew rolled his eyes at Jorie, as if to say, "English." Then he grinned. "Well, yeah, I guess you could say that. Cal is the head of our family."

A few minutes later, Cal came out and motioned to Jorie to go in. She put her hand on the doorknob and paused. Her heart was racing, part excitement, part dread. She still couldn't believe Ben—her Ben with his laughing eyes and teasing ways—was alive, right behind that door. And as happy as she was that he was alive, she worried terribly about what kind of condition he

405

was in. Cal sounded so confident about Ben getting well, but she wasn't so sure. She'd heard stories of soldiers coming home, forever changed.

Cal placed a reassuring hand on her shoulder and squeezed gently. "It will be good medicine for him to see you, Jorie."

She closed the door behind her and looked across the room at Ben, seated in a chair facing the window. He didn't notice that she had come in. His chin was tucked to his chest and his eyes were closed, but his fingers were tapping the arm of the chair. He looked thin, terribly thin. His skin, normally tanned from the sun, was milk pale. His head—that beautiful head of dark, wavy hair—was nearly shaved, just a bristle remained like the bits of an old broom. She felt a fist tighten around her heart and hot tears sting her eyes. She wiped them away, took a deep breath, and went to his side.

When she spoke, her voice was hoarse. "It's really you. It's really our Ben."

As soon as she said the words, something cold seemed to shiver across his face. She had the impression that, in his mind, he had just seen something, or thought something, that hurt him terribly. The tension was too much and she felt her eyes well up with tears again. She fought them back. She wanted to touch him, just touch him. Just lay her hand against his cheek.

Instead, she pulled up a chair and tried to think of something to say— something that would speak to his heart. All week long, Jorie thought up a dozen things to tell him, but now, none of them made it past the end of her tongue. Finally, she decided to talk to him as if she were writing a letter to him. She had written often while he was in Vietnam, though he seldom wrote back. She told him about her teaching job and about the foals they were expecting at Stoney Creek. She explained that they had a new veterinarian, one who actually knew about horses. "He's been such a help. Knows horses better than Atlee." She smiled. "You always said that once I got started on my Percherons, I could talk the ears off of a donkey."

Ben kept his head down, but she had a sense that he was listening.

"My grandmother still thinks she can heal anyone and everyone. She gave Fannie Byler a remedy to lose weight and Fannie promptly gained ten pounds. Why, Mammi is working on something for you, right now—" Jorie caught herself. She sighed. She really didn't know what else to say. "That Dr. Doyle, he warned me not to stay too long, so I'll say goodbye. For now."

She rested her hand on his forearm, but he flinched, so she took her hand away. At that, he lifted his eyes and looked at her, briefly, before closing them again.

"God is watching over you, bringing you back to us, Ben," she said, answering him as if he had asked her a question. "A sparrow doesn't fall from the sky without God knowing of it. Even you, Benjamin Zook."

While Jorie was in Ben's room, Cal remained in the hallway, pressing Dr. Doyle to release Ben.

"Why?" the doctor asked. "You can see for yourself that he's barely functioning."

"With all the pills you keep tossing down his throat, how could any man function?" Cal asked. As soon as the words left his mouth, he knew he shouldn't have said them. It wasn't like him to be sarcastic, but he and this doctor were on opposite ends.

Narrowing his eyes slightly, the doctor said, "The medications help stabilize him." He looked as if he was trying hard to keep his temper under control.

"You've had him more than a week now. There's been no real improvement to speak of."

"That's not true," Dr. Doyle said, squaring his shoulders. "He's speaking now. Says a few words when he wants something. And he's taking long walks each day."

"His nightmares are getting worse, according to Matthew."

"Those are called flashbacks and they're to be expected." The doctor put his pen back in his coat pocket. "You've got to give us time." He turned to go but then spun around. "Look, Mr. Zook, your brother is psychologically damaged. He may never get well. You need to keep your expectations in line with reality."

"I do, I do." Cal patted the doctor on the back. "I call it faith."

Later that day, when Bud dropped Jorie off at Stoney Creek, Marge and Atlee met her at the door.

"How did Ben seem to you?" Marge asked, concerned.

"He didn't seem to recognize me, if that's what you meant." Jorie hung her bonnet on the peg. "But he looked better than I expected." She sat in a chair. "It was his eyes that worried me the most. He was Ben, but not Ben."

Her grandmother was bustling around the kitchen, gathering ingredients to prepare biscuits. "That Caleb, the firstborn, he's the pick of that Zook litter. Always the serious one, deliberate and thoughtful, even as a boy." Marge scooped flour into a wooden bowl. "Well, if I were you, I'd be sweet-talking that Caleb into romancing you before Ben snaps out of his funk."

Atlee sighed. "I'd hardly call it a funk, Marge. Our Jorie knows what she's doing. Leave her be."

Jorie was watching her grandmother mix ingredients for the biscuits with a growing spike of concern. Marge made biscuits once or twice a week from a family recipe that she knew by heart. Today, after measuring the dry ingredients—flour, baking soda, and salt—she grabbed a can of tuna fish and started to open it. She was just about to dump the can into the flour when Jorie jumped up and held her wrist.

"I don't think tuna fish is supposed to go in the biscuits," she said gently.

Marge blinked a few times at the can of tuna fish in her hand, as if she didn't know how it got there. "Oh my," she said, flustered. "Oh my. I can't talk and cook anymore." She put the can down. "Maybe you could finish those biscuits, Jorie, while I go take down the laundry before it rains." Marge washed her hands in the sink, dried them on her apron, and hurried outside, avoiding Atlee and Jorie's eyes.

Atlee watched Marge go and Jorie wondered what was going through his head. Her grandfather wasn't one for sharing his thoughts. Quietly, she asked, "Do you think she should see a doctor?"

Atlee jerked his head back toward Jorie. "No. She's just a little overtired lately, is all." He got up and went to the barn, his place of refuge.

Jorie turned her attention back to the wooden bowl and added the liquid ingredients to the flour to make dough. As she gently kneaded, she set aside her worries of her grandmother and picked up her worries about Ben. Cal had prepared her well. She didn't expect much of a response from Ben and she didn't get one. She felt a twinge of sorrow for Matthew, that first day, seeing Ben without being prepared for what he was like. Ben didn't really seem to recognize her, not at first, anyway. When it was time to leave, she squeezed his hands in hers and she felt a squeeze in return, ever so slightly. But, maybe not. Maybe she was just wishing for some glimmer of recognition.

She thought back to one of the last times she had seen him. He had just returned from the Armed Forces Recruiting Office with the news that he was being sent to Vietnam as a stretcher bearer.

"You have to go back and make them change it, Ben!" she had said when he told her.

"No," he said, too calmly. "I want to go, Jorie. It's my only chance to see the world."

"You did this on purpose, didn't you? You signed up to go!" She was furious with him.

Ben gave her a cat-in-the-cream smile. "Aw, Jorie, you won't tell, will you?"

She was silent for a long moment, gathering her thoughts. It was so like Ben, to act on impulse before the fire in his belly had time to cool down. "I won't tell, but I won't be waiting for you either. You put yourself in this situation. You'll be sorry for it one day."

Now, those words seemed prophetic.

At the time, though, Ben only laughed and slipped his arms around her waist to pull her close for a kiss to say goodbye. "If you marry some hapless farmer while I'm gone, then you'll be the sorry one, Jorie King."

But she wasn't going to marry some hapless farmer. She was going to marry Caleb Zook, a fine man. A wonderful man. At least, she *was* going to marry him until Ben returned.

Now, she didn't know what was going to become of them.

Later that week, Matthew slid open the barn door at Beacon Hollow and shouted, "Cal! Cal! Where are you?"

Cal and Ephraim came out of the tack room, surprised to see Matthew. "What are you doing here? How did you get here?"

"Hitchhiked," he said, still out of breath. "You're not going to like what I have to tell you."

Cal pointed to a hay bale. "Sit down and catch your breath."

Matthew sat down, his hands on his knees. "They're giving treatments to

Ben. Twice, now. It's making him seem weird too. He's back to just staring out the window."

"What kind of treatments?"

"It's called electroshock therapy. The doctor zaps Ben's brain with electric jolts to make him forget things."

Ephraim's eyes went wide. "L-like a l-lightning bolt?"

Cal took a deep breath and looked at the clock in the barn. "Let's go get Bud." He turned to Ephraim. "Can you handle the milking, Ephraim? I may not be back in time. You can ask Amos Esh or Samuel Riehl for help."

Ephraim nodded. "I c-can handle it."

"You can't forget and get to them late. You know they'll try to step on your feet when they see you coming with the milking pump." Cal's face filled with worry. "Maybe you should stay here, Matthew."

"I can't, Cal," Matthew said. "I need to work in the morning."

"I said I c-can handle it, C-Cal," Ephraim said more forcefully. "I've done M-Matthew's j-job since he l-left."

Matthew looked at the earnest face on his little brother's face. It seemed that every time he came home, Ephraim had grown another couple of inches. He wasn't a little boy anymore. "He can do it, Cal."

Cal nodded. "Of course you can. It's a big job, though, thirty cows. Keep Maggie in the house while you're milking." He squeezed Ephraim's shoulder. "Just don't be late for them and you shouldn't have any problem."

Cal told Bud and Matthew to wait in the car in the parking lot of the Veterans Hospital, he would only be a few moments. The truth was, he wanted to keep Matthew out of this and not jeopardize his job. Cal walked past Lottie at the nurses' station and went straight to Ben's room, scooped him up from the chair in his large arms, and carried him out like a rag doll.

Lottie must have alerted Dr. Doyle because he appeared out of nowhere and stopped Cal in the hallway. "Hold on there, Mr. Zook. You can't just take a patient out without being released."

"Yes, I can," Cal said, shifting Ben's featherlight body for a standoff.

"No, you can't," Dr. Doyle insisted. "There are procedures!"

"You didn't ask me about any procedures before you gave my brother this electric therapy."

"It's part of our treatment here. We've been doing ECT for two decades now with remarkable results. It helps the patients forget unpleasant memories."

Cal peered seriously at the doctor. "We are shaped by our life experiences, both good and bad."

The doctor blanched. "ECT is not a moral issue. It's a medical treatment."

"It isn't right to play God and suppress a man's memory."

"We're just trying to help these men live as normal a life as they possibly can."

Cal shook his head. "Now, Doctor, I do appreciate that you are trying to help Ben. I really do. But if I don't even have electricity in my home, why would I let you put it into my brother's head?"

The doctor held his breath for a long moment, then gave a loud exhale. "Mr. Zook, you remind me at times of a granite wall. An unmovable granite wall."

" 'They that trust in the Lord shall be as mount Zion, which cannot be removed.'"

The doctor gave Cal a look as if he thought he might belong on the ward too. Then he shook his head and looked through Ben's file, scanning pages until he found what he was looking for. "Fine!" He slammed the folder shut. "Your brother's service date was officially over a few weeks ago, anyway. If you want him, he's yours."

"Just like that?" Cal asked, a broad smile covering his face.

"Sign off on paperwork and he's all yours." The doctor brushed the palms of his hands. "I wash my hands of him." He sighed. "Would you at least put him in a wheelchair when you take him out of here."

After signing release papers, Lottie handed Cal a white paper bag filled with amber-colored bottles. "These are all of his medications," she said. "They're clearly labeled. Little orange ones are sleeping pills. Blue ones are antidepressants. Big pink ones are tranquilizers."

Cal thanked her for her kindness to Ben. Lottie leaned down, planted a kiss on Ben's forehead, and disappeared down the hallway, her rubber soles squeaking on the tiled floor.

As they passed through the front door of the hospital, Cal tossed the bag of pills in the nearest garbage can.

Dusk set in early on that late winter afternoon. It was nearly dark when Bud drove back into the drive at Beacon Hollow. Maggie had heard the car and ran out to greet them. Cal jumped out of the passenger side and opened the back door, helping Ben ease out of the car the way he helped the aunties step down from the buggy. Then Cal picked him up and carried him to the house. He smiled when he saw the wide-eyed look on Maggie's small face.

"This is your uncle, Maggie, come home."

14

These last few days Ben had spent a good part of the time in bed. Maggie and Ephraim took turns reading to him, which, Cal thought, seemed to comfort him. Lizzie made all kinds of tempting treats to coax him to eat and he did try to oblige her, though Cal knew he didn't have much appetite. He hadn't come downstairs for meals yet, nor did he participate in evening prayers. But there was a little improvement, Cal noticed, with each passing day. He thought it had to do with getting Ben off of all of those drugs. Ben didn't say much, but he was starting to answer questions, as long as they weren't too penetrating. Cal had the feeling that he just didn't remember much. But once, Cal made the mistake of referring to Vietnam, and he could see Ben recoil and close himself off, as real as if he had blown out the light in a lantern. In that instant, though, Cal caught a glimpse of the horror that lived within him.

After Ben had been at Beacon Hollow over a week, Cal heard him get up and go downstairs in the middle of the night, then the kitchen door—a stubborn door to close—was pulled shut. Cal looked out his window and saw Ben, in the bright moonlight, walk down the long drive of Beacon Hollow toward the road. He watched him for a long while, unsure if he should go after him or leave him be. He finally decided to let Ben have this time to heal. He had to trust in the Lord to take care of him, to take care of them all.

❧❧

Every day after school, Jorie stopped by Beacon Hollow to see Ben, but he was always upstairs, sleeping. He had been back well over a week now. Ephraim had told her that he stayed mostly in bed, though he was starting to take meals with the family.

During breakfast one morning, Marge said she was planning to pay a call to Ben. She had been brewing up a curative for him and was eager to try it out.

"Please, Jorie, go with her," Atlee whispered when Marge was out of earshot. "It makes her happy to think she can doctor him."

As soon as school let out, Jorie walked her grandmother over to Beacon Hollow. She was relieved that she didn't see Cal anywhere, though she hadn't really expected to. She knew he was busy plowing the fields for spring planting. They hadn't spoken much in the last few weeks, and the silence that was wedged between them felt like it was stretching them further and further apart.

Jorie and Marge had just climbed the kitchen steps when Lizzie threw open the door, welcoming them in. "You're just in time!" she called out. "Freshly made doughnuts! Made from my secret recipe. I call them 'Sleeper, Awake! Doughnuts.'"

Jorie and Marge took off their bonnets and capes and handed them to Lizzie.

"I've been pulling out all the stops, making the most tempting, best-smelling food I can think of, trying to lure that Ben downstairs." Lizzie smiled, conspiratorially. "And it's been working! For two days now, he's been coming down, about this time of day." She glanced up the stairs. "Just see if it doesn't work!"

"Have you been having many visitors?" Marge asked, raising an eyebrow at Jorie, who had told her grandmother that no one was visiting Ben yet.

"Gobs! Of course, Cal's been real protective of Ben and doesn't let anybody go upstairs poking their nose at him. That Ben, he's as skittish as a newborn lamb. But yesterday, he was down here and didn't even skedaddle when the aunties came calling." Lizzie poured the coffee into three cups. She stopped and got a fourth. "You just wait and see. He'll be down. No one can resist my doughnuts." She took a dishrag and whirled it around the kitchen, fanning the smell up the stairs.

Jorie had to hold back a laugh as Ephraim and Maggie came galloping up the basement stairs, following their noses. They were all talking together at the kitchen table, dipping the doughnuts in coffee or milk, when suddenly Jorie felt someone's eyes on her. She glanced toward the stairs.

There was Ben. She almost gasped at the sight of him: he looked thin, so thin, and pale, with dark circles under his eyes. And his eyes—usually so bright, filled with mischief—they looked flat and empty. Jorie put down her doughnut and went to him.

"Jorie," he said so softly she thought she might have imagined it.

She reached out a hand for his. "I saw you in the hospital awhile ago, but I don't know if you remember that I came."

"I remember," he said. His voice cracked a little, rusty from lack of use. They held each others' gaze for a long while, when suddenly the kitchen door opened and Cal walked in. He stopped abruptly when he saw Jorie. A look of unspeakable sadness came over his face, but then he recovered almost instantly and the look vanished, replaced with a gentle smile.

"Marge, Jorie, glad you came," Cal said, but avoided their eyes when he spoke. "Those doughnuts can be smelled in the next town over, Lizzie. They drive a man to distraction." He washed up at the kitchen sink. "Please, sit down, ladies. Ben, have a doughnut before they get cold." He tossed a doughnut to Ben, who caught it, then grabbed one for himself and went to the door.

"Cal, stay and join us," Jorie said.

"Can't," he said, stopping at the doorjamb. "Time to start the milking."

Automatically, Ephraim scraped the chair back as he rose to join Cal.

"I'll come too," Maggie said.

Cal warded them off. "Ephraim, finish your doughnuts first. And Maggie, you stay. Practice being a host."

Maggie rolled her eyes and plopped back in the chair as her father closed the door behind him.

Ben sat at the table as Lizzie poured a cup of coffee for him. His hands were restless, drawing circles in the oilcloth. Everyone else was distracted by Ephraim, stuffing his mouth full of doughnuts, washing them down with milk, wiping his mouth with his sleeve before bolting out the door. Maggie watched him go, looking like she'd rather be in the barn.

An awkward silence fell over the table, until Marge opened the bag she brought with her. "Now Ben, I've been working on some remedies for you."

She pulled out bottles of mixed dried herbs. "Steep them, like a tea. One fourth teaspoon to one cup of hot water should do. This one is to help you sleep. And this one is to give you energy. And this one will cure fever, stomach pain, and diarrhea. It's a mixture of cayenne pepper and salt. In fact, it'll cure constipation too."

Ben's eyes went wide at that and Jorie nearly laughed out loud.

"Uh, thank you, Marge. Valuable stuff," he said and wiggled his eyebrows at Jorie. She did laugh then. It was something Ben used to do at her during church meetings when the preacher said something very serious that he thought was ridiculous.

Marge continued to pull out bottles of herbs, describing the contents, until Jorie could see a wave of exhaustion roll over Ben. His face suddenly seemed haggard, almost gray. "If you'll excuse me, ladies, I'm a little worn out." He went back upstairs, holding on to the rail as if he didn't quite trust his own balance.

After he left, Lizzie looked at Jorie's face. "Now don't go feeling too badly. The aunties wore him out in just a few minutes. And that was the most words I've heard out of him all week."

Jorie smiled and plucked their bonnets and capes off of the wall pegs. "We should be going too, Lizzie. My grandfather likes his dinner at the same time, every night."

As she helped her grandmother down the steps on the front lawn, she glanced up at the second story of the farmhouse and saw Ben at the window. She waved to him. When she turned back, there was Cal, standing at the open barn door, watching her. When their eyes met, he dropped his head and turned to go into the barn.

"How does he seem to you?" Cal asked Jorie two weeks later when he stopped by the schoolhouse late one afternoon on a cold, wet day. "Ben, I mean. I was just wondering what you thought. How does he seem?"

Jorie was surprised to see him. Cal had been studiously avoiding being alone with her since Ben returned home. Any conversation between them was drawn and tight, carefully guarded. She saw him from a distance when she stopped by Beacon Hollow to see Ben, which was often. It was hard to see Cal but not be able to chat like they used to, laugh like they used to, and share private smiles like they used to.

"At times he seems like the old Ben." She hesitated. "But . . ."

"But other times, he seems like a stranger."

She nodded.

"He has terrible nightmares. I wake him up but he can't remember a thing. Or he doesn't want to tell me." Cal paced up and down the aisle. "Then he goes out walking in the night. I have no idea where he goes . . . just walking. When he comes back, he sleeps away most of the day."

"He's certainly getting better each time I see him. He's gaining weight and his color is better. His eyes seem brighter too."

"He seems angry," Cal said. He looked so discouraged.

"Maybe. But underneath the anger, I think he's wounded."

Cal took his hat off and spun it around in his hands. "Do you think it was a mistake, taking him out of the hospital?"

Jorie shrugged. "I'm not sure the hospital was going to ever be able to fix him." She wasn't sure any of them could. She picked up her books and headed to the door.

Cal followed her outside, waiting while she locked up.

"How could this have happened, Jorie? How could Ben have veered so far off course? I spend more time worrying about Ben than I do Maggie and Ephraim and Matthew altogether." He started to say something else, then stopped and looked away.

She wondered what he was about to say. Was he going to say that he worried about her too? That he missed her? Did he ever wonder whether they would be able to find their way to each other? Did he even want her anymore? But she didn't say anything. She let the silence between them lay there. Silence that was heavy and full of words that weren't being said.

He looked up at the sky, then right back at her, and she saw all she needed to see.

Spring weather was always unsettled. One day in mid-April, the rain came in waves, beating down all morning. Just as the first grade finished reciting addition facts, Maggie asked if she could go to the outhouse.

Jorie glanced out the window. It was like someone was pouring an ocean's worth of water on the ground. "Maggie, you need to wait until the rain has passed. You'll get as soaked as if you'd jumped in the creek."

"But I can't wait!" Maggie had one leg crossed over the other and was squeezing tight.

"Try thinking about something else," Jorie said firmly. She gathered the second grade to the front of the classroom, when suddenly the room became dim. She lit a lantern and hung it from the ceiling—something she only did on the darkest of winter days. Thunder rumbled in the distance, then a blazing white light pierced the sky.

One of the boys called out, "One one thousand, two one thousand, three one thousand," until a great clap of thunder shocked him silent. Jorie went to the window and studied the clouds. To the north, the sky had an eerie greenish-blue glow. To the east, heavy, low clouds were scudding over the fields. The boys had noticed the strange-looking sky, too, and were hanging by the window. "Let's get back to work," she told them. She gave them a look that meant no kidding around. She was accustomed to thunder and lightning storms, but something felt portentous to her.

"It's going to be a wild one," Eli Schlabach said with a grin.

The sky split with a resounding crash of thunder, so loud it shook the lantern. "That's it," Jorie said. "Down we go."

The basement stairs were on the back porch. As she herded the children down the concrete steps, she spotted Cal running toward her at full speed. "Get in there. Fast. Bud heard on the news that four storms are coming in from different directions."

"It's miles away. Not at all dangerous," Eli said with great authority, as if he could predict where storms would collide.

"I think it's heading north," Ray added, suddenly another expert weatherman.

Once inside, they squinted at the clouds through the dusty basement transom windows as Cal latched the basement doors shut.

"Where's Maggie?" Cal asked, eyes sweeping over the frightened children.

For an instant, Jorie froze in a sick panic. "Outhouse!"

She leaped forward, unlatched the door, and dashed up the concrete steps, Cal racing behind her. It was hard to walk in a straight line because of the wind, and they held hands for stability, fighting their way across the schoolyard. When they reached the outhouse, Cal yanked open the door and found Maggie huddled in the corner, terrified.

When Maggie saw her father, she flew into his arms. He snatched her up and held her tight to his chest as he carried her to the basement steps.

Cal handed Maggie to Jorie and yanked the basement doors shut. It took numerous times, fighting the gusts of wind. "Jorie! Jorie! I need your help."

While he held the doors, she jerked the latch shut. Satisfied, they went back down into the basement. The rain fell heavy and loud, drowning out conversation. Jorie made all of the children sit down in the corner, supposedly the safest place to be. Everyone sat but Cal. He stood looking out the transom window. There was a blue-white flash, dazzlingly bright, and what sounded like a bomb going off. Then they heard a loud crack and the sound of splitting timber, followed by a crash.

He turned to look at Jorie at the exact moment that she looked at him. "Lightning struck the elm tree."

The wind continued to blow, not in fits and gusts, but with sustained howls that made her wonder if the schoolhouse windows might shatter from the pressure. Jorie didn't know how much time had passed until the wind died down and the rain slowed its pounding. When sunlight streaked through the transom window, Cal still made them wait. He kept peering out the window to see as far as he could see, making sure they weren't getting fooled by the eye of the storm, that it had truly passed them by. Then he gave a nod and the boys jumped up to unlatch the basement doors.

"That was a doozy!" Eli hollered, leaping outside to survey the destruction.

Jorie walked around the sides of the schoolhouse, picking her way carefully over the broken glass of the windows. When she came to the far side, she gasped. An enormous branch of the elm tree had dropped directly onto the outhouse, destroying it. The roof was torn off, the sides were split apart. She stood there for a moment, gripping her elbows, heart pounding.

Cal came around the corner, holding Maggie by the hand, and stopped abruptly when he saw the obliterated outhouse. He looked at Jorie with a stunned expression and then turned to the children. "All of you, get your coats and lunch pails and go straight home so your parents know you're safe."

As soon as the children were gone, all but Maggie, he turned to Jorie. "How could you have let Maggie go outside with that weather brewing?"

Jorie looked at Maggie, who tucked her chin to her chest.

Ephraim came running around the corner and skidded to a stop when he saw the outhouse. "Cal, that c-could have b-been our Maggie!"

"But it wasn't," Cal said sharply. "The good Lord protected her. Ephraim, take Maggie and get started home. I'll catch up."

He handed Maggie off to Ephraim. She kept her head low as she passed Jorie.

When Jorie and Cal were left alone, he turned to her with angry eyes. "How could you be so careless? What kind of teacher sends a child out in that weather and then *forgets* about her?" His glance shifted over Jorie's shoulder. "Esther, quit your eavesdropping and get home. Now!"

Esther gasped at Cal's sharp scolding, burst into tears, then turned and ran.

"Jorie!" Cal barked in a cold, steely voice that made her flinch. "Have you nothing to say for yourself?"

Words felt stuck in Jorie's throat. She couldn't stop staring at the outhouse. What if the lightning strike had happened a few minutes earlier? What if Maggie *had* been in it? She felt as if she was stuck in a bad dream. She couldn't even think to defend herself; her heart was pounding so loud she could hear it in the quiet. She only closed her eyes, aware that Cal was waiting for an answer. A ragged silence fell between them and the crack that had started with Ben's return split into a chasm.

"Cal!" Ephraim burst around the corner, panting. "Cal, you've g-got to come! Lizzie is d-down the road. She says to t-tell you to c-come q-quick. Ben is acting as c-crazy as a M-March hare. He's hollering at the s-sky and c-cussing at it."

Cal ran back to Beacon Hollow and found Ben outside, down by the willow tree, soaked to the skin, but no longer shaking his fist at the sky like Lizzie described. Instead, he was on his knees, tears streaming down his face, breathing hard. Cal told Ephraim and Maggie and Lizzie to go in the house and leave them alone, and he just sat down next to Ben. Waiting, just waiting. He was waiting for Ben to spill out whatever it was that was eating at him.

After a time, Ben's breathing returned to normal and he seemed calmer. He eased back to sit on his feet. Finally, he wiped his face with the back of his sleeve. "That thunder, it just . . . it sounded like gunshots," was all he offered as an explanation.

"That Dr. Doyle mentioned something about how noises could trigger flashbacks," Cal said quietly. "But it was just a bad storm." He knew not to ask anything, that it could cause Ben to clam up, but he hoped he might elaborate.

He didn't. Ben gazed out at the field. "Your wheat's ruined."

Cal groaned as he took in the sight. Just this morning he had thanked God for the fields that were greening with the first shoots of spring. Those green shoots were now flattened. The center of the field, always a low spot, looked like a muddy pond.

Ben slowly eased himself to a stand.

Well, Cal thought, as they walked back to the house, *I can thank God for Maggie's narrow escape in spite of the storm. And because of the storm, I can thank God that Ben is out of bed and talking. Two miracles in one day.*

As Cal finished milking the last cow that afternoon, he was grateful for the routine of work in his life. It gave him deep satisfaction, to end each day caring for his dairy. As he looked over each cow, checking each one to make sure she was settled for the night, he realized that work was the best medicine God could give a man. He had a sense, maybe an answer to a prayer he hadn't yet asked, that it was time to ask more of Ben. He decided that he would give Ben and Ephraim the job of building a new outhouse and repairing the windows to the schoolhouse.

When Cal came inside, he found Ben seated at the kitchen table. Maggie was setting the table for dinner. Ephraim was still out in the barn, sweeping up, and Lizzie was stirring the stew she had made.

Washing his hands at the sink, Cal felt such gratitude to the Lord for the comforts of a home. "Ben, I could sure use your help building a new outhouse for the school. You and Ephraim could take it on tomorrow. I can get the lumber from town in the morning and get you set up." He turned around, drying his hands on a rag. "You were always the best carpenter of us all."

Ben had been drawing circles in the tablecloth with his fingers. Cal wondered how he could live with such restlessness inside himself. It would, he thought, be like trying to stare into the sun. But after Cal asked him the question, Ben's hands stopped.

"Remember when you broke your thumb?" Ben asked.

Cal tilted his head, stunned. "I hadn't thought about that in years." He lifted his hand and spread out his fingers. His thumb remained slightly bent; it hadn't healed properly and he couldn't straighten it fully. They had been young boys when it happened, younger than Ephraim. They were at a barn raising and were given the job of pounding in nails that men had started. Ben tried to turn it into a race, like always, and Cal had ended up hitting his hand so hard it broke his thumb.

Laughter burst out of Cal, surprising him. It stemmed from the memory, and from the joy that Ben was finally rejoining the human race. Once started, Cal couldn't stop. He laughed so hard he buckled at the waist. Ben couldn't help but laugh in return, which got Maggie giggling, and soon, Lizzie joined in. When Ephraim came inside, he looked at all of them as if they had lost their senses, which only got them laughing more.

Wiping his face with his hands, Cal realized he hadn't laughed so hard in a long, long time, and it felt good, so good.

Sylvia had never seen her daughter in such a state. As soon as Esther arrived home from school, she explained—between sobs—all that had gone on that afternoon, claiming it had given her a horrendous headache. Sylvia made a cup of chamomile tea for her and sent her straight to bed to rest. Esther was such a delicate child and not only did she have to endure a terrifying electrical storm, but then she was unjustly snapped at by Caleb Zook! In all the years Sylvia had known him, she had never heard a harsh word out of that man's mouth. Until today. It grieved her, because she knew he was under terrible stress. How close they came to losing Maggie today! All because of Jorie King's poor judgment. She whispered a quick word of thanks to the Lord Almighty that he protected Maggie.

She glanced at the kitchen clock on the wall and plucked her bonnet off the hook. There was just enough time before dinner to go speak to the deacon about this troubling situation. Something *had* to be done.

Early the next morning, Cal drove the wagon to the schoolhouse and dropped Ben and Ephraim off to dismantle what remained of the outhouse. He hadn't expected to see Jorie there so early. When she heard the wagon, she came outside to see what was going on.

"We'll have this outhouse rebuilt today and the windows replaced," Cal told her, "so school won't be disrupted. And if it's all right with you, Ephraim will help Ben with the building today."

She nodded but didn't say anything more to him. There was a hardness between them, he knew, from yesterday. He should be quick to forgive, but he wasn't quite ready to overlook what a close call Maggie had experienced. And Jorie wasn't exactly feeling too friendly with him, he could tell. She avoided him. In fact, her eyes, he noticed, were on Ben, as if she still couldn't believe he was here, among them. He couldn't blame her; he felt the same way.

By the time Cal returned from the hardware store with lumber and supplies, the school day was under way. The boys kept popping their heads out the window to catch sight of the legendary Benjamin Zook, the Amish man who had gone to Vietnam and died, only to be back among the living. He was pleased to see how effectively Jorie reeled them back in. From what he could observe, the scholars went through their day with routine, giving Jorie respect.

During lunch, Ben pitched softball to the children in the schoolyard while Jorie watched and cheered. Once, the ball landed near her and she lobbed it overhead to Ben at the pitcher's mound, laughing in that soft way she had, like honey pouring out of a jar. Cal tried to concentrate on measuring a board, but his eyes kept riveting toward Jorie. The wind lifted a stray lock of her copper-colored hair and laid it across her cheek. Absently she coiled it and tucked it back beneath her prayer cap.

Cal continued working during the softball game until Maggie ran up to him and pulled him by the hand to come pinch hit for her team. When Cal went up to bat, he swung the bat a few times to warm up.

"Take all the warm-up swings you need, Cal," Ben said in his teasing voice. "You still can't touch my pitch." Ben wound up and fired, frowning when Cal hit a foul ball. "Strike one!" Ben called out.

The second ball went past Cal so hard and fast that he swung and missed. Jorie clapped her hands together like a young girl.

Cal looked at Jorie and thought her eyes were shining bright and soft as spring sunshine. He knew she was trying hard not to laugh at him.

A look of boyish mischievousness flashed across Ben's face. He rubbed the ball in his hands, eyed Cal carefully, and threw a pitch that nailed him on the forehead, knocking him down. There was a moment of stunned silence before Jorie raced to Cal's side and knelt beside him.

"Cal, are you all right?" Concern covered her face.

Cal was flat on his back, dazed, looking up at the sky, seeing stars. He wasn't sure what stung more, the bruise on his forehead or the one on his foolish pride.

"Ben, how could you do such a thing?" Jorie accused when he came over to examine Cal.

Cal pushed himself up as far as his knees. "It was an accident, that's all," he said.

Ben helped Cal to his feet and patted him on his back. "See? He's fine." He turned to Ephraim. "Let's go finish building that outhouse."

Even though Cal wouldn't have admitted so to Jorie, he was pretty sure that Ben aimed that softball to intentionally hit him. Ben always had flawless aim.

As long as Cal could remember, Ben turned everything into contests between them. He seemed determined to one-up Cal, and Cal always obliged him, content to let Ben triumph. He didn't feel a rivalry toward Ben, which only seemed to exacerbate the situation. Ben was like that, quick to anger. Usually, just as quick to get over it.

But Cal sensed that Ben had been changed, altered deep, by whatever had happened to him in Vietnam, and in some way that he didn't understand. Ben couldn't concentrate on a task. He was never still or calm, as if he was trying to distract himself from letting his mind settle on something disturbing. He was constantly on edge. During evening prayers, Ben acted bored or fidgety, uncomfortable.

It worried Cal, because even though Ben was acting more like himself every day, something about him remained more lost. Lost to their family, lost to the church. Cal hoped and prayed that he wasn't lost to God.

15

Late one evening, a couple of weeks after the great storm, Jorie woke to the sound of someone pounding on the kitchen door. She threw on a robe and hurried downstairs. Standing outside was Ben. Next to him was Marge, in her nightgown and bare feet, wrapped in Ben's coat.

"Missing someone?" Ben asked, as casually as if he had found a stray cat.

"Mammi! *What* are you doing?" Jorie asked, pulling her grandmother inside.

"I thought I heard the rooster crow, so I went to get the eggs from the henhouse," Marge said. She held up an empty basket. "But then I got a little turned around."

"She was down by her roadside stand, setting up for the day," Ben added.

Marge handed Ben back his coat, scowling at him. "So I was a little early for the day's business."

"I'll say!" Ben laughed. "About two months early."

Marge put her hands on her hips and glared at him, annoyed. Then her face softened. "Oh, you still look positively wrung out, Ben." She brightened. "I have just the thing for you. A spring tonic that thins the blood and will have you fit as a fiddle in no time. It's made of sassafras tea, from the inner bark of the root that makes the finest tea. The very best flavor is stored in the root when the tree is dormant. And . . ." Her voice trailed off, as if she couldn't remember what she was talking about. She was silent uncomfortably long, almost as though she had forgotten Ben and Jorie were there. Then she remembered herself with a start. She lifted a finger in the air. "And I've got some new remedies too. I'll go get them." She went to the stairwell and slowly walked up the steps.

Jorie turned to Ben, feeling thoroughly bewildered by her grandmother's odd behavior.

Ben, though, was amused. "She told me about a pinworm cure she named Devil's Bait." He wiggled his eyebrows. "I pray I'll never need it."

Jorie plopped down on a kitchen chair. "I don't know what's wrong with her lately."

Ben sat down next to her. "Aw, Jorie. She's always been a bit of a . . . character."

Jorie winced. "This is different. She's never been like this."

"Haven't you taken her to a doctor?"

"My grandfather doesn't think it's necessary."

Ben's eyes went up the stairwell. "Well, sure. He slept through her night sojourn."

The wind pushed the door open, blowing in a gust of cold air before Jorie jumped up to shut it. "The hinges on this door are practically falling off."

Ben stared at the door for a long moment, mesmerized.

The strange look on his face puzzled her. "What is it, Ben?"

Still staring at the door, he said, "I'm starting to remember things, more and more. It's like a fog, lifting slowly."

Softly, she asked, "What are you remembering right now?"

It was awhile before he answered her. "When I was in the looney bin, the first one, the one in Bangkok, there was a row of doors right by my bed. The doors barely hung on these old rusty hinges. All day long, I stared at those doors, all hanging on those fragile hinges. That's what my mind was like. Hanging on a fragile hinge. Still clinging, still holding on, but with a big gust of wind . . . *whoosh!* Anything could happen." He turned his gaze from the door back to her, looking directly into Jorie's eyes with a hint of pity.

He held her gaze until the truth of what he said hit her. Her grandmother's mind was coming unhinged.

Ben reached over and covered her hand with his.

A spring storm came through in the middle of the night. Lightning flashed through the sky and thunder rattled the glass in the windows. In the morning, the storm had lapsed into slow, even sheets of rain that paused for a minute or an hour, but soon returned. Cal took out his list of chores and divided them up among Ephraim and Ben. The two went out to the barn to muck out the horse stalls and the stanchions of the dairy cows.

Ben took the nine-tine pitchfork off the wall and handed the four-tine pitchfork to Ephraim. "Some things just never change."

Ephraim looked around for the wheelbarrow.

"Seems like I've been doing this my whole life," Ben said, sliding open the door to a horse stall.

Ephraim snorted. "L-long as we k-keep f-feeding them, we'll k-keep c-cleaning up after 'em."

"And just what is Cal doing while we're doing this work?"

Ephraim gave him a sharp look. Ben's hostile tone caught him off-guard. "He's p-paying bills. S-So?"

"Just seems like he gives us a laundry list of hard things to do while he does the easy stuff."

Ephraim never thought about chores like that, like they had a value as-signed to them. There were just things that had to get done and they all had to do them. He'd seen Cal muck out the stalls plenty of times.

Bud walked in as they were just about to get started. "Hello, boys. Ben, you're looking more like yourself every time I see you." He walked over to the workbench. "I wonder if I could borrow Cal's split maul?"

Ben opened up a drawer at the workbench and pulled out the maul. "Here it is. Let me sharpen the edge for you." He went to the grind wheel and poured some water on it. "Bud, why would you call it Cal's split maul?"

Bud watched as Ben started the wheel rolling and ran the maul's edge along it. "What *should* I call it?"

"Why not Beacon Hollow's split maul? Why does it have to be Cal's?"

Bud gave Ben a strange look. "What does it matter?"

Ben finished sharpening the edge, wiped it with a rag, and handed it to Bud. "Just wondered, that's all."

"I suppose I call it Cal's because he's the one who's been taking care of this place since your dad passed."

"Now, that's my point," Ben said. "If Dad hadn't passed when he did, Beacon Hollow wouldn't be Cal's." He turned to Ephraim. "Rightly so, it should be Ephraim's one day. The Amish pass the farm to the youngest son."

Ephraim looked at Ben. "Cal always s-says we'll d-divide it or f-figure it out when the t-time comes."

Ben shrugged. "Maybe so. Maybe not."

Bud raised an eyebrow. "Like I said, Ben, you're more like your old self every time I see you."

A perfect fingernail moon shone down from the midnight sky onto the Kings' dark farmhouse. Jorie woke with a start, knowing that something was stirring in the barn. She dressed quickly, grabbed a flashlight and a blanket, and hurried to the barn. As soon as she slid open the barn door, she knew what sound had woken her: a horse was set to foal. All of the horses were shuffling nervously in their stalls. She walked down the corridor to the foaling stalls, past each pregnant mare—with their enormously swollen bellies—and stopped when she came to Fancy. The horse was pawing almost frantically in the straw with her forefeet to make a nest. Fancy was a maiden mare and Jorie knew it could be a long night ahead, but she didn't mind. She loved the barn at night. She loved the barn during the day too, but at night, it felt like a different world. The sweet scent of hay and oats, the sour tang of manure, the richness of leather harnesses, the gentle sounds of the horses, shuffling and snorting.

She lit a lantern and hung it on a hook, then checked and rechecked the foaling basket stuffed with all sorts of useful birthing objects—towels, scissors, iodine, rubbing alcohol, garbage bags, thermometer, twine, clamps. Her concentration was interrupted by the rumble of the barn door sliding open. She slipped the lantern off its hook and walked to the center of the barn.

"Daadi?" she called out, sure that Atlee had come.

"It's me, Jorie. It's Ben."

At the sound of Ben's deep voice, her heart missed a beat. She waved the lantern in front of her, casting a light over him. "Why, Ben! What on earth are you doing here?"

"I was out walking and saw the light in your barn. Thought maybe something was wrong."

She pointed toward Fancy's stall. "A mare is set to foal."

"Want me to go get the vet?" he asked.

"I don't see any signs of trouble so far." Jorie walked back to Fancy's stall and put the lantern on the hook. Ben followed her. "As long as things seem to be progressing, I'd rather let nature be her midwife."

She leaned her arms against the top of the stall railing as she watched Fancy lay down on her side, her hind legs stiffen and start to quiver. Signs that hard labor had begun. Standing behind Jorie, Ben raised his arm and leaned against the post. As focused on Fancy as Jorie was, she was aware of how close Ben was to her. He smelled of laurel soap and the crisp night air.

A thin white bubble—the amniotic sac—appeared in the opening under Fancy's tail, then disappeared. She lifted her head as a contraction hit. Her neck stretched out, her upper lip peeled back, her whole body strained, her eyes bulged. When the contraction ended, Fancy groaned and dropped her head into the straw. Yet for all of her laboring, the mare was silent, except for a grunt deep in her throat.

"Why doesn't she just let loose a whinny?" Ben asked quietly.

Jorie lifted her head to look at him and was surprised to see he appeared to be suffering right alongside the mare. "Probably just an instinct, so that wild animals won't know she's given birth."

Fancy's opening widened, and more of the white membrane appeared. Jorie could see the emerging foal's front hooves, then a small nose. Relief flooded through her. This foal knew how to make a proper appearance. A loud *whoosh* broke the quiet, and the black mass slid out of the womb like a chute, landing in the nest of hay that Fancy had prepared. Jorie grabbed a towel, slipped quietly into the stall, and rubbed the foal's head and body roughly, trying to wipe the amnion away from its nostrils. She laughed as the foal came to life, lifting its head and gasping for air.

Fancy turned her long neck, stretched her nose out toward her baby, sniffed, snorted, and rumbled in recognition. Then she came to life, heaving and shuddering and scrambling to her feet, eager to nuzzle and lick her baby.

"A filly," Ben said quietly. "Solid black. You should name her Indigo." His eyes were riveted to the sight. "It's the most beautiful thing I've ever seen."

Jorie glanced at Ben, who was watching Fancy try to nudge her foal to its feet by pushing up on its little rump. A gentleness came over his face, softening his features. This was how she loved him best, with tenderness in his eyes. He could be kind, so kind.

As soon as the filly was on her feet, nursing, Jorie went to get a bucket of fresh water and some oats for Fancy while Ben cleaned up the stall. Afterward, they watched the mother and foal for a long time. The barn had quieted down and the animals had gone back to sleep.

She let her gaze roam lovingly over the interior of the barn. "I love this quiet."

Ben blanched, as if she had said something profane. "I can't stand it," he said, surprising her with its sharp, bitter tone. "The quiet makes me crazy. And I can't stand how time goes so slowly. Everything is always the same. Every day like the one before. Every year looks just like the one before."

That was exactly what Jorie loved about her life. The days, how they could flow one into the other the way a river flowed into an ocean. The slow, steady passing of time was a sweet comfort to her.

A barn owl, high in the rafters, hooted. Another hooted back. Jorie lifted her eyes to try and see where they were perched. "Give yourself time, Ben."

"For what?" he asked with a sharp bite of a laugh. "For wanting to be a farmer so I can spend the rest of my days looking at the wrong end of a horse?"

A sickening jolt rocked through Jorie. After all Ben had been through these last two years, all he had seen of the outside world, he hadn't changed. Not really. These were the same endless loops of conversations that she had with him before he left. She would try to convince him of all that was right and good about their life, and he would dismiss her thoughts with a careless shrug.

She remembered one time, after Communion, when he was as cranky as a bear with a toothache. "Ritual! That's all it is," he had complained. "Year in, year out, wash somebody's stinking feet and you're good to go for another year."

"But that's not it at all," she tried to explain. "The foot washing is meant to show our humility toward each other. We stoop—we don't even kneel for it. It's to remind us of when the Lord washed his disciples' feet—even Judas Iscariot's feet. Think about it, Ben. Our God is a *foot washing God.*"

But Ben wouldn't listen to her and eventually she gave up trying to convince him. Besides, it wouldn't do any good. It never did. Ben's mind, once made up, was hard to change. He was like Cal in that way. But Cal's way of thinking was solid and reliable, like a straightly plowed furrow. Ben's thoughts zigged and zagged, first one direction, then another, as if he couldn't quite make up his mind which direction he was heading but he was definitely in motion.

There were so many things she could say to Ben in this moment. She chose what seemed the easiest, the safest. "Well, morning will be here soon. Wouldn't be right to have the teacher nodding off during a spelling bee." She took the lantern down off of its hook and blew it out. "Do you need my flashlight to find your way home?" She held it out to him.

He leaned toward her, taking care not to touch her. She stared up into his face, a face that was so dear to her.

Then he looked down at the flashlight in her hand. "Jorie, I feel like I'm suffocating."

She took a step closer to him. "Ben, what's troubling you?"

He cupped her face with his hands and his gaze wandered all over her face—eyes, cheeks, mouth—as if he was memorizing every feature. She thought he was going to kiss her, but he released her, passed around her, and slid open the door, waiting for her to follow him before he closed it behind her.

Then, without a word, he simply walked away under a sliver of a new moon.

"Uh-oh, looks like trouble just arrived," Lizzie said as she peered out the kitchen window of Beacon Hollow.

When Cal saw who climbed out of the buggy, he braced himself. Sylvia and Jonas, Samuel, and Isaac were heading to the door, somber looks on their faces. He asked Lizzie if she could get some coffee brewing and went out to welcome his company.

A few moments later, seated around the kitchen table with steaming cups of coffee, Samuel and Isaac launched into a long discussion about the weather and what the *Farmer's Almanac* predicted for the next few months. Cal knew they hadn't come to discuss the weather, but he also knew that

Isaac needed time to get to his point. It concerned him that Sylvia was a part of this. It occurred to him that Isaac, in his own polite way, was waiting until Lizzie left the room.

Cal went over to the sink, where Lizzie was washing breakfast dishes, to quietly ask if she'd mind getting the laundry in before it rained. "There's not a cloud in the sky!" she objected. Then, her eyes went wide as silver dollars as she grasped what he meant. "But you never can tell about Pennsylvania springtimes, can you?"

After Lizzie went outside, Isaac sat back in his chair and spoke. "Sylvia told me about what happened in the schoolhouse. During the big storm."

"Oh?" Cal asked, lifting his eyebrows. "Because I'm pretty sure Sylvia wasn't there. I was, though."

Sylvia's face tightened. "Esther told me all about it, about how Jorie let Maggie go to the outhouse in the middle of a raging storm."

"That's not the way it went, Sylvia," Cal said. "Maggie went out before the big storm hit."

"Esther said she completely forgot about Maggie," Sylvia continued as if such a detail was minor. "According to Esther, you said so yourself. She said you called Jorie careless."

And what could Cal say to that? He wanted to defend Jorie, but the truth was, it bothered him greatly that she had been so neglectful with his daughter.

"This is just *another* reason why Maggie should be living with me," Sylvia said. "I owe it to my sister to see that her daughter is growing up well cared for."

For a moment Cal looked as if he was about to say something unpleasant—he was clearly fairly angry himself—but finally his face relaxed and he said, "Maggie is growing up just fine, Sylvia."

Isaac raised his hand. "Sylvia, you agreed to not say a word if you came this morning."

"Then why are you here, Isaac?" Cal asked frankly. "Why are you all here this morning?"

Jonas spoke up first. "We have decided that, come the end of May, Jorie King will not be asked to return to teach next year."

Cal leaned back in his chair. "All because of a big storm."

"Not at all," Jonas said. "That was just the last straw. We have had complaints all year long."

"From Esther?" Cal said with more sarcasm than he should have allowed himself.

Sylvia's eyebrows lifted.

Jonas leaned forward in his chair and pointed a finger at the table. "Let's start with renting a cottage to Dr. Robinson without consulting Isaac first."

"She spoke to me about it," Cal said. "And what she did was the right thing. We've all benefited from the doctor. You have, in particular, Jonas, when your prize cow had a nasty case of mastitis recently." He turned to Samuel, hoping he could count on him to reason with Jonas, but Samuel avoided his eyes. "So what else?"

"They haven't gotten through a single textbook yet!" Sylvia said. "Last week she sent the entire eighth grade outside on the porch with books and told them to read, read, read!"

"Thank you, Sylvia," Isaac said in a longsuffering voice. He turned to Cal. "Now Caleb, you have admitted yourself that she spends more time out of the classroom than in it."

"I might do the same thing if I had a classroom made up of seventeen boys." He folded his arms against his chest. "So, Isaac, do you agree with this?"

Isaac placed his hands on the table. "I have a doubt or two about whether those scholars are being well prepared to pass the state exam."

"There's still a month to go," Jonas said. "There's time for a new teacher to bring them up to speed."

Isaac lifted his hands. "We will allow Jorie King to finish what she started this year. But then, Caleb, after the exam, you need to tell her that she won't be coming back next year."

"Me? Why me?" Cal asked.

"You're on the school board. And you were the one so doggoned determined to hire her," Jonas said, eyes narrowed. "So you need to finish what you started."

"That's enough," Isaac said in a dismissive tone. "We've said what we came to say." He stood. "It's time we went on our way."

16

Matthew couldn't believe the improvement in Ben in the last week. He could hardly wait to tell Lottie and Dr. Doyle when he went back to work on Monday. *Especially* Dr. Doyle. He had the gall to call Cal "selfish and irresponsible" for taking Ben away like he did, but that just showed how little the doctor knew. Cal was the most responsible, most unselfish person on this earth.

Sometimes, Matthew thought, a little too responsible and a little too unselfish.

At lunch on Sunday following church, Matthew could see that something was definitely amiss between Jorie and Cal. Jorie served the men at the table seated far away from Cal. More than a few times that day, Matthew caught Cal watching her with sorrow in his eyes.

At rare moments, Matthew thought, you could catch a person in an unguarded moment. What he thought and how he felt showed on his face for a brief second, before passing away.

It hurt him to see Cal suffering. First he lost Mary Ann, now he was losing Jorie. Not that Matthew knew that for sure, but he knew Ben's effect on others, especially women. It had always been that way. Ben had an easy, charming way about him that drew women to him like bees to a flower. Even Lizzie seemed to light up like a firefly when Ben was around. And she was still making every sweet and cake and pie she knew how to make, just to entice Ben to eat.

Lizzie had never baked Matthew a thing. Not one blessed thing.

That evening, at the singing for the young folks, Matthew made a point of getting on Lizzie's volleyball team. He tried to be thoughtful and set up shots for her, but she never seemed to notice that he was going out of his way for her. In fact, she seemed to be going out of her way to ignore him. He was getting tired of being treated as if he was nearly invisible.

Afterward, he saw Mose Riehl head toward Lizzie, probably to ask her if she wanted a ride home. He made a quick beeline for Lizzie and reached her side just as she was opening her mouth to answer Mose.

"She can't. She's going home with me," Matthew said firmly.

"Oh I am, am I?" Lizzie said, eyes narrowed, hands hooked on her hips.

"Yes," Matthew said, trying to look as cool as a cucumber even though his heart was pounding. "You are."

Lizzie stared defiantly at Matthew, then turned to Mose's befuddled look, then back to Matthew. "Well." She lifted her chin a notch. "I guess I am, then."

Matthew smiled. Things were looking up.

Cal woke earlier than usual and slipped outside. The morning air was crisp and clear, like pure water from a spring. It would be a warm, sunny day, a good day for plowing the north field and getting it ready to plant corn. After a substantial breakfast, Cal and Ben hitched up their large draft horses to the metal plows and led them out to the field. Cal started on one end of the field, Ben on the other. They could have plowed separate fields, but this was the way their father had taught them. Working together made the work go faster, Samuel Zook had often said.

When the horses met in the middle, Cal and Ben stopped to rest the teams. They sat against the fence that separated Bud's property from Beacon Hollow's. The hum of Bud's tractor plowing a nearby field underscored the quiet.

Cal drew in the scent of the early morning. The distant whiff of manure from a neighboring farm drifted his way, mingling with the aroma of thawing earth. Of spring. He lifted his face to the sun and reveled in it. "Smell that, Ben? *What* a fragrance. Freshly plowed dirt." He handed Ben the water jug.

Ben rolled his eyes. "I'd like it a whole lot more if I were sitting on Bud's tractor." He took a long drink of water. "Those English have a way of making easy work out of hard things." He gave a sideways glance to Cal. "Have you given any more thought to no-till farming? Sure beats plowing."

"I enjoy plowing," Cal said, stretching out his long legs. "No matter which angle I look from, I fail to see the benefits of using chemicals on fields."

A few days ago a salesman from a large chemical company had paid a call at Beacon Hollow, trying to convince Cal and Ben of the merits of no-till farming. "I know you Amish have unscientific minds," the salesman had said, "so you need to rely on outside experts to understand proper soil management."

Kindly overlooking the salesman's patronizing remark about his intelligence, Cal listened patiently to a lecture on the virtues of no-till farming.

"You can get twice the output from half the work," the salesman explained. "It will free you up to get off the farm and go work in a factory. You'll make extra income."

When Cal asked the salesman why he assumed extra income would improve the quality of life, the man had no answer and soon left.

But ever since Ben heard the salesman's pitch, he kept badgering Cal to consider no-till farming. "Why can't you just give something new a try?" Ben asked, tipping his straw hat over his eyes to shade them. "Just because generations of Amish have farmed one way, it doesn't mean there isn't something new to learn."

"Generations of Amish have developed a way of farming that is proven, that is excellent. And our way doesn't harm the environment, either." Cal rose to his feet, looking out to the edges of his fields. He waved his arm in a large arc. "There's the Kings' farm, and Bud's, and along the treetops you can see the barn roofs of other neighbors. Many of those herbicides that the salesman was trying to sell are suspected carcinogens. If I used those herbicides on my fields, every time it rained, those chemicals would leach into the streams and creeks that run into our neighbors' properties." He turned to Ben. "Tell me this: how can we love our neighbor and do such a thing?"

Ben closed his eyes and lifted one shoulder in a careless shrug. "Beats the drudgery of plowing."

One fine sunny morning, Jorie had just finished first and second grade arithmetic recitation when the door opened and in walked Cal. Behind him was a short, slight, unhappy man who seemed to have the weight of the world's troubles on his bony shoulders. Cal motioned to Jorie to come to the door.

"Jorie, this is Harry Whitehall." As they shook hands, Cal added, "The public school superintendent."

The scholars, especially the eighth graders, turned toward Mr. Whitehall with wide, worried eyes.

Mr. Whitehall, ignoring the dramatic effect his appearance created, merely walked to the front of the classroom and started unloading the contents of his dark leather bulging briefcase, filled with whatever a public school superintendent carried with him. He started to unpack reams of paper and peered at the back of the classroom, toward the large eighth grade, who sat stiffly at their desks, like cottontails caught in the glare of a lantern. "Are you ready, class, for your exam?"

Jorie glared at Cal and hurried to the front of the class to talk to Mr. Whitehall. "Perhaps if we had some notice . . ."

"Were you not informed that your class would be tested, come May?" Mr. Whitehall asked her.

"Yes, I knew." Jorie lifted her eyebrows at Cal, hoping he would intervene, but he raised the palms of his hands, helpless.

Unconcerned, Mr. Whitehall continued unpacking. "Well, then. Is it not the month of May?"

"Yes, but it's only May 2nd!" Jorie said. "I expected the test to be closer to the end of the month—"

Mr. Whitehall held up a hand to stop her. "We've agreed that it is, indeed, the month of May. So let's stop wasting time and begin."

Jorie turned to the row of eighth grade boys, who stared back at her with blank looks. She felt a great sinking feeling in her stomach. She exhaled, resigned. "Perhaps I should take the other classes out so that you can have the classroom to yourself."

Mr. Whitehall waved her away. "Do with them whatever you want."

"How long will you need?" she asked.

He managed a thin smile for her. "As long as it takes."

Jorie told the rest of the scholars to take their tablets and lunches and go sit under the large maple tree. She gathered some books and walked past the eighth grade, giving them encouraging looks.

When she passed Ephraim's desk, she stopped and leaned over to whisper, "I'm counting on you, Ephraim, to boost the average for the rest of the class."

He whipped his head up in alarm.

She squeezed his shoulder. "You can do it. The Lord gave you a good mind and he will not fail you."

Ephraim dropped his head on the desk with a clunk. She patted him on the back and went outside. Waiting outside the door, Cal intercepted her.

"You could have warned me," she hissed at Cal.

"I didn't know he was coming!" Cal said, clearly uncomfortable. "He just showed up at the house, not thirty minutes ago."

Cal took a step toward Jorie and she took a step back but hit the porch railing. She was stuck. He was so close that Jorie saw the darker blue flecks in his eyes and the lines around his mouth and a few gray hairs at his temple that she hadn't noticed before. Had those gray hairs just sprouted in the last few months, brought on by all of the burdens he had been carrying? The sight of those gray hairs made her resolve weaken. She felt that same tenderness for him begin to melt her heart. She wanted to reach out and touch him, to let him know that everything was going to turn out all right.

But it wasn't.

The superintendent was here and her eighth graders were probably going to flunk the test and ... then ... there was Ben. She didn't even want to get started on Ben—her feelings for him were as tangled up inside as one of Marge's balls of yarn. She didn't even know where to find a loose end to start unraveling the snarled mess, and she was even more uncertain about where it would end.

She lifted her eyes and looked right at Cal. His light blue eyes were searching her face and they were soft, so soft. So very soft.

She had to remind herself to breathe.

A shout from the playground distracted them and Jorie used the moment to slip around Cal. Before she stepped off the porch, she turned back to him. "Have you asked Maggie what's been troubling her lately?"

Cal looked surprised by the question. His eyes searched out Maggie on the playground. He found her crouched under the elm tree, playing tic-tac-toe in the dirt, alone. "Well, no. What makes you ask?"

Jorie looked at him as if it was the most obvious thing in the world. "Haven't you noticed? She's stopped humming."

In the middle of May, spring weather finally arrived. One warm evening, Atlee noticed Marge walking across the driveway from the barn to the house. "What were you doing out there at this time of night?" Atlee asked her, holding the kitchen door open for her.

"I just wanted to see little Indigo," Marge answered. "She might be the prettiest foal we've ever had."

Atlee looked worried. "You locked up, didn't you?"

"Of course I did," Marge said, clearly annoyed.

Atlee glanced at Jorie and she gave a slight nod of her head. When it came to horses, she could read her grandfather so well that he didn't even need to utter a word. As she watched her grandmother climb the stairs to go to bed, Jorie got up to go check that the barn had, indeed, been locked up. Just as she put her hand on the kitchen door, she heard strange noises coming from the barn. Something was wrong with the horses. She could hear neighing and stamping, much more than was normal at night.

Alarmed, Atlee grabbed his gun and followed Jorie outside. She reached the barn first and found the door wide open. The horses were in their stalls, pacing and huffing in alarm. At the end of the dark corridor was Fancy, out of her stall, rearing and kicking out at something in the shadows. Jorie aimed the flashlight at the end of the corridor and felt her heart skip a beat. There was a cougar with its mouth around Indigo's head. Atlee pushed Jorie into Fancy's stall and shot his rifle into the rafters, shocking the cougar. It dropped Indigo and darted past them, disappearing out the open barn door and into the woods.

Atlee grabbed Fancy's enormous-sized halter to get her back in her stall so that Jorie was able to get to Indigo. The foal lay quivering on the ground, panting quick short breaths. Blood was everywhere. Jorie worried the foal was going into shock. Telling herself over and over not to panic, she found some blankets in the tack room and covered Indigo.

"Stay here by her and I'll run to get Dr. Robinson," she told her grandfather, who looked as if he might be going into shock himself.

The story of the cougar attack spread quickly throughout the neighborhood.

"Dr. Robinson was able to save Indigo's life," Jorie told Ephraim when he came to see the injured foal the next day. "She's probably going to be blind in one eye, and we have to watch her carefully for infection in the next few weeks, but if all goes well, she might still be able to be a broodmare."

"It's all m-my fault," Ephraim told Jorie, when he saw the foal's eye, covered in a white bandage.

"How could it possibly be your fault, Ephraim?" Jorie asked. "It was my grandmother's doing. She opened Fancy's stall to pat the foal and forgot to close it—the barn door too. She wasn't thinking straight." Marge had slept soundly through the entire night's drama.

And what a heartbreaking drama, for so many reasons. Dr. Robinson sedated Indigo to sew and bandage her wounds, gave her a shot of an antibiotic, and explained to Jorie and Atlee that the foal would be blind in one eye. The cougar's teeth had punctured the sclera. But even more upsetting than the foal's injury was the reason that it had happened. Jorie and Atlee sat at the kitchen table until nearly dawn, still in shock over what had occurred and all that it meant. She would never forget the defeated look on her grandfather's face, or the way his voice broke when he finally admitted, "My darling is losing her mind."

Indigo sneezed, shaking Jorie to the present. Ephraim had opened the bag he had brought with him and was handing her his sketch pad. Jorie flipped the cover and slowly went through the pages. On page after page were sketches of the cougar, caught in different poses. In flight, crouching before pouncing, standing at the top of a rock ledge, peering over the ridge. Jorie didn't say a word. Toward the end, the pages included two kits.

"I'm the one who's b-been f-feeding the c-cougar. I thought if I c-could f-feed her, she wouldn't be t-taking our livestock. But L-Lizzie started to n-notice that our f-freezer was emptying out and I c-couldn't t-tell Cal what I was d-doing b-because he would m-make me stop. So I tried g-getting the cougar squirrels and c-cottontails with my slingshot. But then she had her k-kits. She m-must b-be so hungry that she needs m-more than I c-could hunt for her."

Confused, Jorie told him to slow down. "Take a deep breath and start at the beginning."

The entire story spilled out, starting with the circus, including the day that Cal was beaten. When he was finally finished, Jorie put her arm around his shoulder. "Aw, Ephraim. She's a wild creature. You'll never be able to change the nature of a wild animal, no matter how kind or loving you are. She was just born to be wild and free."

Matthew practically ran from the bus stop to Beacon Hollow but slowed as he reached the rise. He couldn't wait to see Lizzie again but didn't want to seem too eager. He took the kitchen steps two at a time, opened the door, and worked to keep a grin off of his face when he saw her standing by the stove. He dropped his sack off with a thud, hoping she would turn to look at him. Instead, she slammed the spatula on the counter and turned her attention to chopping tomatoes.

"Lizzie, I'm home."

She ignored him and kept chopping.

He took a step toward her. "Uh, is everything all right?"

She spun toward him with the sharp edge of the knife pointed right at him. "*You* tell *me*, Matthew Zook!"

He took a step back. "Did I do something to make you mad?" He couldn't imagine what he could have done. They had fun on the way home from the volleyball game, laughing and teasing each other. When he said goodbye, everything was fine between them. More than fine. She even let him hold her hand when he walked her to the house.

She took a step toward him; the knife was still in her hand. "After you dropped me at home from the volleyball game last week, did you or did you not take Sarah Bender home in your buggy?"

He gave a faint, guilty smile and took another step back, for safety's sake. "I did."

She turned back to the counter and started chopping the tomatoes with a vengeance.

Matthew watched her for a moment. She finished the tomatoes and turned her attention to cracking eggs in a bowl. She cracked an egg against a bowl so hard that half of it landed on the counter. Matthew grinned. *Well, what do you know? Lizzie is jealous—of a girl like horse-faced Sarah!* "I was heading home and passed Sarah's buggy. Her horse had gone lame, so I tied her horse to the back of my buggy and took her home." He took a step closer. "That's all."

With one arm, Lizzie held the bowl of eggs against her body; with the other hand, she was whipping them senseless. "Sarah told . . . everybody! They're all teasing her, saying you're sweet on her."

Matthew took one step closer to Lizzie. No one might ever call her pretty, but she was a girl full of strength: a high forehead, a strong jaw, wide cheekbones, large brown eyes. Why did he once think her eyes were too big for her face? Those eyes were wonderful: large and luminous. And it shamed him to think he used to call her Fat Lizzie. She wasn't fat—not fat at all. As far as he could tell, she had curves in all the right places. He gazed at her fondly.

When he spoke, his voice was hoarse. "I'm not sweet on anybody but you, Lizzie Glick."

Lizzie stopped stirring and was still for a long moment. She put the egg bowl down and turned to face Matthew. They stared at one another in silence for a long moment. Matthew leaned forward to kiss her, but she deftly picked up a plate of freshly baked cookies, putting it between them. He looked down at the plate, picked up a cookie, and took a bite.

"So, do you like it?" she asked, eyes dancing. "It's a recipe I made up this morning. I call it my Green-Eyed Monster Cookies."

"Very nice," Matthew said, his voice quiet, his eyes locked on Lizzie's. "Very, very nice."

Jorie sat on the porch steps, her arms wrapped around her bent legs, her eyes turned up to the sky, to the lovely, wispy cirrus clouds that looked like the flowing tails of running horses. Mares' tails. The sunshine felt so good after such a long, gray winter. Slowly, she tipped her head back and let herself be drawn, up, up, up into the periwinkle blue of the sky.

Suddenly a deep and familiar voice broke the silence. "Thoreau once said a cloudless sky is like a meadow without flowers and a sea without sails."

Jorie had to squint against the sun to see Ben. He stood leaning against the white picket fencing that surrounded the farmhouse, one booted foot crossed over the other, his straw hat dangling from his fingers. In his hand was a book to lend to her. It was one of their favorite things to do—share books and discuss them. Oh, the arguments they would have over plots and themes! It made her smile to think of those times.

She watched Ben carefully. There was something in his expression: a longing? Sadness? Something else too. She wished she could tell what was going on in that head of his. And what a head—despite being too thin, he had an arresting face. Angular cheekbones, dark eyebrows rimming those penetrating eyes. Those eyes . . . Her grandmother said recently that Ben had cold eyes. Those eyes weren't cold, certainly not when they were looking at her. Not cold at all.

Jorie smiled. "I'd have to agree with Mr. Thoreau. Cloud watching can be addictive."

He walked over and handed her the book *To Kill a Mockingbird* by Harper Lee, then sat down beside her, stretched out his long legs, and leaned back on his elbows.

"What do you think about when you look up at that big sky?" she asked him.

"Truth be told, I think about what a fool I am," he said. "Before I went away, I looked up at that sky and felt desperate to see the edge of the world." He glanced at her. "So I did. And the sky looks just as blue and welcoming and innocent over there as it does here." He scraped a hand over his jaw. "But it isn't."

She wondered what kinds of things he *did* see over there, in Vietnam, but didn't dare ask. He could be like a skittish sheep if asked too many questions. They used to be able to talk about all kinds of things, but that was long ago. She didn't even know if she knew him anymore. There were complexities to Ben that she just couldn't seem to puzzle out. His experience in Vietnam had left a taint on him, wounds and scars that couldn't be seen but were just as real as if they were on the flesh. Yet there was still laughter in him, and unexpected wells of gentleness. She let the silence lay between them. Sometimes, she thought, silence was the only thing that could bring two people together.

"Have you ever seen a Greyhound track, Jorie?" He gave a short laugh. "No, of course not. I saw one once. These witless greyhound dogs go around and around a track, trying to catch this rabbit running along the fence line. A mechanical rabbit!" He paused. "That's what I feel like, like one of those stupid dogs. I get so close, but I never seem to catch the prize."

For a moment Jorie stared at him in wonder. "But Ben, they're not *meant* to catch it."

The easy charm had vanished. He looked aloof and formidable, eyes narrowed in a silent accusation. Then he pushed himself upright, his boots hitting the porch step with a soft thud. He stood and walked away without a word to her.

Ephraim was cleaning out the buggy by the back of the barn one afternoon when a car pulled into Beacon Hollow's drive. It was driving fast and came to a sharp stop by the farmhouse. He dropped the sponge in the bucket with a splash and walked to the car curiously, surprised to see his brother Ben jump out and wave to him.

"Ephraim, come with me! I need you to show us where the new vet's office is." Ben's voice grew impatient, frustrated that Ephraim wasn't hurrying. "Come on—we've got an emergency."

Ephraim had skidded to a halt when he saw the driver of the car: Jerry Gingerich. Ben pulled Ephraim's arm and practically pushed him in the backseat of the car.

Jerry turned the car around to head back to the road. "Which way, kid?"

Ephraim didn't answer until Ben turned to him. "Over at the K-Kings' old c-cottage on the m-main r-road."

Jerry turned right and gunned the engine, causing Ephraim to slide against the door. He heard an odd moaning sound and peered over the front seat. There was Rex, covered with a bloody towel, his tongue lolling out of his mouth.

"At his house?" Ben asked.

"No one will r-rent him office s-space," Ephraim said, glaring at Jerry. "What happened to R-Rex?"

"Jerry's dog took a slug in its leg when we were hunting," Ben said.

As they approached the cottage, he pointed to the drive. Jerry pulled in, parked the car, and scooped up Rex in his arms. He ran to the door and knocked until Mrs. Robinson opened it and let him in.

Ben turned to Ephraim in the backseat. "Poor Jerry. Not sure that dog can be saved. That bullet chewed up its leg pretty bad."

"W-what were you h-hunting?" Ephraim asked.

Ben motioned to him to get out of the car. He pointed, proudly, to the rack on top. He pulled back a covering and there, roped down, was the beautiful cougar, dead. "We got that big cat," Ben said with evident pride. "Shot it myself. It won't be going after anybody else's livestock this summer, that's for sure."

Ephraim whirled around and exploded in rage. "H-how c-could you?"

Ben looked surprised. "How could I? Easily. I talked Jerry Gingerich into going with me. He's the best tracker in town. After hearing about Jorie's foal, I had to do something." He pulled the cloth back over the cougar and tied the edge to the rack. "She'll be pretty darn pleased about this kill."

"You d-did this to impress Jorie?" Ephraim asked.

"Well, sure. I guess that was part of it. But Stoney Creek is close to Beacon Hollow, Ephraim. It wouldn't be long until we started losing stock too. If anybody would know how to track a cat, it would be Jerry Gingerich."

Ephraim wiped his eyes with his sleeves. He hated tears, they made him feel weak.

"Aw, Ephraim," Ben started, "I know you got a soft spot for critters, but someone needed to get rid of that cat."

"W-why did you ever come back? Why didn't you j-just s-stay away? You ruin everything!" The words had startled Ephraim coming out of his own mouth, and they just kept coming. "You d-don't understand how th-things are, but you c-come here and you act l-like you own the p-place and you own everybody."

A tight look came over Ben's face, as if he were suffering a hurt somewhere. "What are you talking about?"

"How c-could you b-be friends with Jerry? He tried to b-beat the l-living t-tar out of Cal! You d-don't care about C-Cal. You're always trying to hurt him. You even threw that s-softball right at his head on p-purpose. I know you d-did. You're even t-taking Jorie away from him! And you d-don't even care about her! If you d-did, you would have m-married her years ago! You just d-don't want C-Cal to have her."

Ben grabbed Ephraim's shirt in one hand. "What do you mean by that?"

"Excuse me?" Mrs. Robinson asked. Her eyes darted anxiously between the two of them. "We need a little help in here. Would you mind coming in to be with your friend while my husband is examining the dog's injuries? He's a little . . . distraught."

Ben released Ephraim; they eyed each other warily but followed Mrs. Robinson into the cottage. There, huddled in the corner of the room, was Jerry, weeping.

17

A few days later, Ben and Cal were alone, having lunch in the kitchen. Lizzie was upstairs changing linens on beds.

"Cal," Ben said. "How difficult would it be to get at my share of Beacon Hollow? In cash?"

Cal looked at him, startled. "Very difficult."

"I need the cash to start a business."

Cal leaned back in his chair. "What kind of business?"

"A friend and I were talking about taking folks out during deer hunting season."

"For the sport of it?"

"Yeah, I guess."

Cal shook his head. "That's not our way. We don't kill for the sport of it."

Ben took in a deep breath, as if he expected as much from Cal.

"Why would you need money for that, anyway?"

"In the off season, we thought we'd lease land for a rifle range."

"Who is this 'we'?"

"Jerry Gingerich." Ben frowned. "Look—I don't know what went on between you and Jerry, but he's been a friend to me. A real good friend."

Cal had to work hard not to make a disparaging comment about Jerry. If he even started . . . no, he checked himself. He shouldn't even go down that path. He had to trust in God's justice. "We Plain folk don't start businesses with the English. You know that."

"Well, I'm *not* planning on being a farmer," Ben said. "So you can get that notion out of your mind right now."

"If you want a business, then do something that's truly needed. Something you're skilled at. You're an able carpenter."

"Maybe. Maybe I'll think about it. But I still need the money now."

"Why?"

"I'm thinking to buy a house in town, for me and Jorie to live in."

Cal kept his eyes down. "You aren't even a church member yet, Ben. Aren't you getting a little ahead of yourself?"

Ben flashed him a dazzling smile. "Gotta start somewhere, brother Cal."

"What makes you think Jorie would leave her grandparents and her Percherons?"

Ben lifted a dark eyebrow. "Because . . . it's *me* doing the asking."

Cal looked straight at Ben. Sometimes he had the feeling that Ben really didn't know Jorie at all. He leaned toward him, placing his elbows on the table. "Ben, you're in a tremendous hurry to do everything but sit down and face your demons."

Ben rose to his feet so abruptly that his chair tipped over backward. He glared at Cal. "You'd do anything to keep me down, wouldn't you?"

"What?"

"You know what your problem is, Cal? Just because you had to step into Dad's shoes when he died, you resent the rest of us for having time to be young." Ben turned and left, slamming the door behind him.

Cal got up to pick up Ben's chair, exasperated. Ben had always been one to flirt with the wild side. His mother used to say Ben was born looking for a rule to break. When their parents were killed, Ben went even further on the precipice. It was Jorie who seemed to temper him and keep him from going too far. Now, it seemed that as Ben's body grew healthy, his mind grew dark and anxious. There were times when Cal thought Ben seemed as tightly wound as a coiled spring.

Standing at the kitchen window, Cal watched Ben storm off down the drive, hands jammed in his pockets, head down. Cal felt a little sorry he hadn't kept those prescription drugs from the Veterans Hospital. He thought maybe Ben could use a sedative or two. He rubbed his knotted fist against his stomach. Or maybe he would take one himself. Dealing with his brother's moodiness was starting to give him an ulcer. He offered a quick apology to the Lord for such an ungrateful heart. Just a few months ago, he had been praising the Lord for bringing Ben home.

Later that week, after giving the matter considerable prayer, Cal drove the buggy into town and stopped by the bank to empty out his savings account. The amount wasn't entirely a quarter of what Beacon Hollow was worth, but it was close. If this would be a way to keep Ben in Stoney Ridge, close to his Amish roots, then Cal would gladly hand it over. He had always known Ben wouldn't be a farmer; his brother just didn't have the patience for it. It made him heartsick to think of Ben going into business with the likes of Jerry Gingerich, but Cal believed a man had to make his own decisions. And mistakes.

When Cal returned to Beacon Hollow, he put the cash in an envelope and laid it on Ben's pillow. Not much later, he heard a loud whoop of happiness coming from Ben's room. Ben burst downstairs and found him at his desk. "Thank you, brother Caleb! You won't be sorry." Ben pulled on his hat and coat and hurried out the door.

"Ben!" Cal called after him.

Ben stopped and turned.

"Ask Jorie about being the keeper of the song."

Ben looked confused.

"Just . . . just ask her."

As Jorie stepped out the side door with an empty laundry basket anchored on her hip, she drew in the scent of the late May afternoon. The fragrance of the grape arbor that wrapped around the back porch drifted her way. She folded the dry laundry as she took it off the line and was about to bend over to lift the basket when she spotted Ben ambling toward her. She smiled.

"A day like this is so good, don't you find it so?" she asked when he reached her. She looked up at the puffy white clouds that danced in the sky. "It just sings with the promise of summer. It makes a person want to praise God, and thank him for giving you the life to enjoy it."

When he didn't answer her, she turned to face him. The gentle wind fluttered her cap strings. He took one in each hand and pulled them down until they were stretched taut, then flashed her a dazzling half-smile that made her weak in the knees.

"Cal said to ask you about being the keeper of the song. What does that mean?"

She studied him for a long moment, puzzled. Why *that* question? Cal's telling me something, Jorie thought: something has happened with Ben. "It means that we are carrying on for those we love. Caring for Beacon Hollow is the keeper of your folks' song. I'm the keeper of my grandfather's song."

Ben stared at her with such fierce intensity that she could almost feel it, like a warm gust of breath on her flesh. "Let's get married, Jorie." There was a strange gravelly sound to his voice.

She was shocked silent. That was the *last* thing she expected to come out of Ben's mouth. She had been waiting for years for this moment, and now that it was here, she didn't know what to do with it.

He took her hands in his. "I've been working on a plan. It's all figured out. I'm going to start a business."

"You're what?" She was stunned.

"I've got the money from Cal. My partner and I—we're just finalizing details now."

She shook her head. "Wait a minute. Cal knows about this?"

"Yeah."

"And he supports you in this . . . this business?"

An annoyed look crossed through his eyes. "I don't need Cal's approval, if that's what you mean."

"Why would Cal give you money?"

"He just gave me what's due me. My quarter of Beacon Hollow."

She cocked her head. "Who is your business partner?"

He looked past her to the horse in the pasture. "Jerry Gingerich."

She yanked her hands away as if he had blasphemed. She couldn't believe what she was hearing. "How could you do such a thing to Cal? To Matthew and Ephraim?"

"I'm not doing anything *to* them! I'm trying to make a life for *us*."

"You can't go into business with the English."

Ben's eyes grew unnaturally hard, set above a stern mouth. She suddenly realized that he didn't consider himself an Amish man.

"You know I would never consider marrying someone who isn't a church member. You know what that would mean."

His eyebrows slammed together. "That was *your* doing! I *told* you not to get baptized, but you went ahead and did it while I was gone! You made this so much harder for us!"

"For us?" She tried to draw in a breath, but it caught in her throat. "For us? You mean, harder for you." She splayed her hand against her heart. "I know what I want, I know who I am."

"Jorie," he said again, impatient now. "I'm finally ready to get married." His face went soft and his voice grew sweet. "You want this too. I know you do."

Did she? She had known him all her life, had loved him for years, almost like a habit, and yet she had no idea at all whether or not she loved him anymore.

She wasn't looking at him, but she could feel his gaze hard on her, as if he could will the words into being. He never expected her to turn him down. Ben was used to getting what he wanted.

She fumbled to find the words for a long moment. When she found them, she risked a look at him. "Oh Ben, I can't fix what's ailing you."

Ben's face clouded over. At first, his eyes flashed with anger. Then they grew soft again. "Yes, Jorie, you can." He bent over and took her face in his hands, his thumbs lightly tracing the hollows in her cheeks. "You *can* fix me. You're the only one who can. Marry me, Jorie. I count on you. I always have. I don't know what I would do . . . if I didn't have you by my side. I *need* you." His voice broke on those last three words. He still had her face cupped in his hands. He leaned closer now and kissed her, a kiss from his heart that said so much more than words could ever tell her.

But it only told her what she didn't want to hear.

Sylvia pounded the bread dough again and again, trying to get it to that point when it would be smooth and elastic, ready for its final rising. She supposed it was a silly thing to be doing so late in the afternoon—it wouldn't be ready to bake until midnight—but she needed something to occupy her head and hands. If she slowed down, her prickling conscience caught up with her.

When the lump of dough finally passed inspection, she put it into a greased bowl and covered it with a damp towel. She looked around the room for a place for it to rise, deciding on the tabletop by the window where sunlight streamed in. It was a small kitchen for such a big house—barely large enough to hold the rectangular oak table with eight ladder-back chairs. Plenty of seats for the children she was going to have with Noah . . . until he died so unexpectedly on that dreadful winter day, at the young age of thirty-eight. It still irked her that no doctor could figure out what killed Noah. She knew *someone*—she was pretty sure it was Benjamin Zook—had started a nasty rumor that Noah was henpecked to death.

For four long years, that big table held only two people: Esther and her. Thank God for her daughter, her Esther.

But it wasn't too late to give Esther a sister or brother. Sylvia was still a young woman, only thirty-four, still beautiful. She was aware of the approving looks of men, Plain or English, though she knew it was vain to derive pleasure from those looks.

She had finally decided that she was ready to marry again, but he had to be somebody worthy, a man she could look up to. Someone who would hold the Word of God high in their home.

Someone like Caleb Zook.

Of course, she had never thought of Caleb in *that* way before her sister passed. The day that she saw Maggie dressed as . . . a *boy*! It still galled her. In that instant, she knew what had to happen. It was her God-given duty: her role in life was to take care of people. She was born to it. She was at her best in that role.

If she and Cal married, Maggie would have a mother, Esther would have a father. It just made perfect sense. Why, she could probably put an end to Ephraim's annoying habit of stammering too.

She knew she suited Caleb better than any one of those spinsters who signed up for the aunties' Saturday Night Supper List. Even though she disapproved of that ridiculous form of matchmaking, she had recently decided that she would add her name to the list in the next available opening.

It would be a way to let Caleb know she would be willing to consider him as a husband.

But first . . . she needed to make sure that Jorie King would keep her attention on Benjamin Zook where it belonged.

Earlier today, Sylvia drove past Beacon Hollow and happened to see Benjamin out by the barn. Impulsively, she turned her horse into the drive. She thought it to be high time that someone let Benjamin know what had been going on while he was serving his country in Vietnam: Jorie had been working her wiles on his eldest brother.

She told Benjamin all about the way Jorie was trying to tempt Caleb—sending him special smiles in church, taking him on picnics. Oh, Jorie thought no one knew she was trying to snare Caleb, but Sylvia was wise to it. She had seen the two of them, more than a few times, walking together. Talking together. Laughing together.

Benjamin didn't even look at her as she spoke, didn't ask a single question. But she knew he was listening, because she could see he was shifting his weight restlessly and his facial expression set like concrete. Those were signs of a man trying to hold his temper, she remembered that from her Noah.

"I wouldn't put it past her if she let her hair down for him too."

At least, that was what she *meant* to say. What came out was more like, "She let her hair down for him too." She felt just the tiniest pang of guilt over stretching the truth like that—she had never lied before in her entire life—but every time that guilty twinge poked her conscience, she dismissed it. After all, she wouldn't put it past Jorie to flaunt that flaming red hair. And besides, that tiny piece of information set Benjamin off. His eyes glowed edgy and wild and his big hands clenched and unclenched.

Oh, it was definitely the right thing to do.

Sylvia went outside to wait for Esther's arrival from school. As she sat on the porch chair, she closed her eyes, sorely aware of the emptiness, the loneliness in her heart.

Jorie couldn't shake the feeling that something about this day felt different. She sensed a strange restlessness, as if something was about to happen that would change things forever. She was glad when four o'clock finally came and all of the scholars ran home, even Maggie, who usually stayed to help her clean up. She had just finished wiping down the blackboard when she heard the door click shut. She turned to see who was there. It was Cal, standing in the middle of the aisle, looking so big and tall next to the small desks.

And sad.

Cal looked so sad. She couldn't bear to see him looking like that. They stared at one another in silence for a moment. Then she took a step toward him, and then another. She reached out her hand to him, and he met it halfway with his own, entwining their fingers. They stayed that way awhile, touching in silence. Then he gave a little tug, pulling her closer, and she came toward him.

He brushed his knuckles along her jaw, so lightly it was as if he'd only thought about touching her. "Jorie," he said again, so softly it was as if he'd only imagined saying it.

She heard in his whisper, she saw on his face, the same longings that cried from her heart.

But she knew why Cal was here. She could read it on his face. He had come to tell her goodbye.

She shook her head and the tears splattered. She squeezed her eyes tightly shut, trying to hold them back. He still had her face cupped in his hands. He leaned closer now and brushed his mouth across hers, almost with reverence. He started to pull away, but she reached up and wrapped her arms around his neck, holding him, holding him as tight as she could until his arms folded around her. She laid her head on his shoulder, and he rested his chin on her head. She didn't know how long they stayed that way.

It was the sound of a shout that pulled them apart. "Ich mache dich dod!" *I'll kill you!* Ben had come into the schoolhouse and witnessed their embrace. He lunged toward Cal, grabbed him by the shoulder, and spun him around to hit him in the jaw.

Cal fell backward against a desk.

"Get up! Get up and fight like a man!"

Cal struggled to his feet as Ben kicked him down again.

"Halt! Halt jetzt!" *Stop it! Stop it this instant!* Jorie tried to put herself between Ben and Cal, but Ben pushed her off. "Was is loss mit dir?" *What is wrong with you?*

455

Ben's eyes were as black as thunder. "Me? Me?! My brother and my girl, kissing behind my back! Du settscht dich scheme!" *You ought to be ashamed!*

"We were doing nothing of the sort!" Jorie said. "We were . . . we were saying goodbye."

"Why should I believe that?" Ben yelled, his voice tinged with the deepest betrayal. "You *always* wanted him. You wanted *me* to be him. You're probably thrilled that Mary Ann made this easy for you and died."

"Don't you say those terrible things!" Jorie shouted.

"I thought I *knew* you." His voice whipped around Jorie like an arctic blast. "I thought I understood *us*. Sylvia told me! She said you let down your *hair* for him!"

"That's enough, Ben!" Cal said, wiping blood from his mouth. "You're talking crazy."

He whirled around to face his brother. "And you! You don't care about Jorie! You're just trying to take her because Mary Ann told you to. I know that, for a fact! I read her letter! It was in that box of Mary Ann's things. The one you gave to Maggie."

Cal's fists clenched at his side, as if he was barely holding himself back from throttling Ben.

Ben whirled back toward Jorie. "He was only courting you because Mary Ann told him to. And because Sylvia threatened to take Maggie." He pointed a finger at Cal, as if he were a child that needed scolding. "I heard! I heard it all! Right after the big storm, when the bishop came to tell you to fire Jorie from her teaching job." He spun around to Jorie. "Did Cal tell you that yet? That you're fired? The bishop is willing to let you finish the term but then"—he drew an imaginary line across his throat—"you're axed." He spun around to Cal. "Tell her, Cal. Tell her the truth."

Cal's face went still. Tension prickled the air.

Jorie's eyes darted between Cal's and Ben's. The fact that Cal didn't deny it told her that Ben was speaking the truth. She shook her head, not understanding, not knowing them. She backed up a few steps, nearly tripping over something, then made herself walk out slowly with her head up. At the doorway she looked back at them as though she were about to add one last thing, then she thought better of it and turned and walked down the road.

She walked all the way to Stoney Creek, into the barn, all the way into the middle of it, and just stood, gripping her elbows as if she was trying to hold herself in one piece. Dust motes danced in the shaft of sunlight that shot through the open doorway. She swallowed and drew in a deep breath, taking in the comforting smell of animals and hay. She told herself not to cry, but in the next instant, scalding tears pushed against her eyes. Soon, she was sobbing.

When she was done, a huge sigh from her heart escaped her body, a sigh so deep and long she felt it as a breath she had been holding for years.

Ever since she first loved Ben.

"For such a peaceable man, you sure get the daylights walloped out of you on a regular basis," Matthew said as he prepared an ice pack for Cal's swollen eye.

"Matthew," Cal said wearily, "don't blaspheme." Cal was sitting at the kitchen table at Beacon Hollow, staring at the salt and pepper shakers on the center of the table.

"You might need some stitches for that cut on your eyebrow," Matthew said as he handed Cal the ice pack. "You gonna let me know why your face came to look like a side of butchered beef?"

Cal sighed. "Ben and I had a . . . misunderstanding."

"Ben did this to you?" Matthew whistled. "Guess the Army taught him a few things." He leaned back in the chair. "I suppose Ben isn't looking any worse for the wear."

"I didn't hit him back, if that's what you're implying."

"It is," Matthew said. "Any idea where Ben went off to?"

"No," Cal said. "I don't even know if he's coming back." But surely he would. They were bound, he and his brothers, with ties strengthened by life and love and God, too strong to break. Surely, surely, they were bound too tightly to be broken apart.

Matthew leaned forward on his elbows. "I'm guessing that this had something to do with our Jorie."

"It's a long story," Cal said, shifting the ice pack to the cut on his eyebrow.

"I've got time, at least until the cows start bawling like they're fit to be tied and need me to ease their misery."

Cal didn't tell Matthew everything, but he did tell him about the big storm and that he was told to fire Jorie. "The look on Jorie's face when Ben told her she had been fired . . . I'll never forget it." He shuddered. "Wouldn't surprise me if she never wants anything to do with a Zook—any of us Zooks—ever again." Cal saw Matthew wince. It felt so wrong, hurting people like this. Every morning, Cal prayed to God that he would be a blessing to others. Instead, he was causing pain.

"So what are you going to do?"

"I'm going to do the right thing."

"Well, sure. But what is that?"

Cal sighed. "That's what I don't know yet."

Matthew dropped his chin to his chest. "Must be hard, caring about them both."

Cal was surprised by his younger brother's sensitivity—a characteristic with which Matthew wasn't overly endowed. The thought pleased Cal. Maybe his brother was turning into a man. "You're in the same spot, though, aren't you? Wanting the best for both Ben and me."

"I guess I am." Matthew looked up. "The thing is, I want you and Jorie to end up together because she's so right for you. She's smart enough and she speaks her mind and, well, she'd be a good wife to you. And Maggie and Ephraim are crazy about her. But there's a part of me that wants Ben to have her too, because . . ."

"Because he needs her," Cal said with a heavy heart.

"Yeah. I guess there's the rub. He needs her more."

18

That night, Ben still hadn't returned. After everyone had gone to bed, Cal opened his Bible at the kitchen table, hoping God's Word could provide some guidance through this mess. Communion would be coming in a few weeks. This was a season of making amends, of setting things right between people. He had always loved Communion for that very reason. But this spring, he would need to set things right with a long list of people: Sylvia, Ben, smooth over that nettlesome tension with Jonas, and now Jorie. He wondered if things would ever be right again with Ben or with Jorie. Two people he cared about deeply and yet he didn't know what to do. Loving Ben meant not loving Jorie. And loving Jorie meant not loving Ben.

He heard a scuffling noise and turned around to see Ephraim and Maggie standing at the bottom of the steps in their nightclothes. Ephraim was holding Maggie's hand, but she was hidden behind him.

"Cal," Ephraim said. "We got something to t-tell you."

Cal turned his chair to face them. "Something that's troubling you?"

Ephraim pulled Maggie forward to stand side by side. "Matthew t-told us. He said Jorie was g-going to be f-fired. Cuz of the b-big storm."

Cal rolled his eyes. "Is nothing private in this household?"

Ephraim looked at Maggie, who kept her gaze on her bare feet. "Jorie t-told her not to go."

"Who?"

Ephraim waited.

459

Maggie pushed her glasses up on her nose. "Me," she answered, as her eyes welled up with tears. "Jorie told me not to go. To wait until the storm was over. But I couldn't wait. I slipped out when she wasn't looking."

Cal raked a hand through his hair.

"I didn't mean to get Jorie fired," Maggie said. "I just had to go to the outhouse, real bad."

Cal grimaced and rubbed his forehead. "Maggie, in the morning you're going to tell this story to the bishop. He needs to hear this. We have to put things right."

She cringed, scrunching her small shoulders, then gave a nod.

"I'll c-come too," Ephraim whispered to her.

Cal had just finished mixing feed in the barn when he heard the familiar clip-clop of a horse driving a buggy. He wiped his hands on a rag and went out the side door to see Isaac's mare slow her gait as she reached the steep incline of Beacon Hollow's long drive. Seated next to Isaac in the buggy was the superintendent of public schools, Mr. Whitehall. Cal wrapped the mare's reins around the hitching post and helped Isaac climb down from the buggy.

Isaac's sparse eyebrows shot up when he saw Cal's black eye. "Looks like you met up with a grizzly bear, Caleb," he said in his quiet, slow way.

"Something like that," Cal said.

The superintendent didn't even notice Cal's eye. He had a big smile on his face. "I thought that buggy ride would rattle my bones, but it was smooth as molasses." He shook Cal's hand. "I'm learning that it's high time I unlearned some assumptions."

Cal gave Isaac a questioning glance. The superintendent looked the same but acted like a different man entirely than the one who gave the eighth graders their exam just a few weeks ago.

Isaac's face was unreadable. "Caleb, Mr. Whitehall has some news to tell you."

Mr. Whitehall lifted a knee to prop open his briefcase and pulled out some papers. "We just received the scoring from the state exam."

Cal straightened his back, bracing himself for bad news.

Mr. Whitehall practically burst forth with the news. "The eighth grade at the one-room schoolhouse at Stoney Ridge earned the top marks in the state!"

Cal thought he hadn't heard correctly. He looked to Isaac for confirmation and noticed his pleased look.

"You don't say," Cal said, working to keep a grin off of his face.

Mr. Whitehall thrust the report at him. "Not only top marks, but a full five percentage points higher than any other public school. In the entire state of Pennsylvania!" He laughed gleefully, as if he had been a proponent of one-room schoolhouses all along. "In fact, you've got one pupil who beat out everyone, in every subject! A perfect score! Reading comprehension, mathematics, science!" He slapped his knee. "Imagine, nearly 100 percent on the *science* exam from a boy in an *Amish* schoolhouse!"

Isaac leaned over toward Cal. "Ephraim," he said quietly. "It was our Ephraim who earned those high marks."

Cal didn't know what to say. He let the news soak over him. He felt so pleased for Ephraim, and for Jorie too, who had brought the best out of Ephraim. Even his stuttering had improved lately. It was just what Mary Ann had said would happen: Jorie would be the best choice. For Ephraim, for Maggie. For him too, though that prospect seemed markedly dim.

"The bishop and I are stopping by to see that schoolteacher of yours next. I want her to speak at a conference in Harrisburg and give suggestions to the public school teachers about making improvements."

Cal exchanged a look with Isaac, sharing a thought. They wouldn't stop Mr. Whitehall from asking, but they knew Jorie would never agree to such a prideful thing.

Isaac took off his hat and scratched his head. "Uh, Caleb, have you already spoken to Jorie about the teaching job for next year?"

"In a manner of speaking, yes, she knows," Cal said.

"Oh dear," Isaac said, looking worried. "I suppose I have a little smoothing over to do."

"Speaking of that, Isaac," Cal said, "if you have a minute to spare, Maggie would like to speak to you. She's in the kitchen, waiting." Peering out the kitchen window with wide, worried eyes were Maggie and Ephraim.

Cal knew Jorie well enough to know that she would be in the barn after sunset, checking on each horse one last time before locking things up for the night. He found her in the stall of a mother and new foal. He couldn't help but smile when he saw her standing by her feather-footed Percherons. She looked tiny next to the giant horses. Even the foal—only a few days old—was nearly as tall as she was.

"So school is over for another year."

She glanced up when she heard his voice. It was getting dark, too dark now to see her face, and he was glad for it. Maybe, without realizing it, he had even planned it that way.

"Maggie and Ephraim were both down in the mouth the day after school let out. Ephraim, in particular. He's done with his formal schooling."

It was more than the last day of school that had Maggie and Ephraim upset. Esther had told everyone that Jorie had been fired. Some—even Ray Smucker, Maggie said—had tears rolling down their cheeks as they helped clean out the schoolhouse on the last day and pack up Jorie's belongings.

Jorie continued to handle the foal, brushing it gently, stroking its back, lifting its hooves one at a time. He knew it was part of a daily ritual she had, to make sure the foal was comfortable with a human touch.

"I owe you an apology, Jorie."

Finally, she spoke. "For what in particular?"

He was surprised that she didn't sound mad, for she had every right to be. "Accusing you of neglecting Maggie. Last night she told me what really happened." He looked embarrassed. "It's why she stopped humming. She was feeling guilty."

"I don't deny that it hurt me you wouldn't have more faith in me than that," Jorie said. "But . . . apology accepted." She slid the stall open to slip out, then shut it and locked it tight. She stood and looked at him, knowing he had more to say.

He wondered what she was thinking; he knew there was a deep hurting behind those blue eyes. "Maybe you shouldn't forgive me so easily. I've made quite a few mistakes lately."

She walked past each stall, checking its lock to make sure each was tightly hitched. "Was everything Ben said true?"

He fell into step beside her. "He got things mixed up, but there was some truth in it. It's true that Mary Ann had chosen you for my wife. But that wasn't why I asked you to marry me." He stopped himself. "That's not really the whole truth. At first, I didn't want to even consider you because of the very reason that people were telling me I ought to. But then Sylvia started talking about taking Maggie from me and I panicked. That was the first time I asked you to marry me."

She finished checking the last latch and turned toward him, listening. He couldn't read what she was thinking; her face remained expressionless.

"The second time I asked you, I really believed that you were the right one for us. For Maggie, for Ephraim, for me."

She just kept looking at him with mild interest.

"The third time, that was when I asked you for me, Jorie. Just for me." His voice broke a little as he added, "To be the wife of my heart." He walked up to her. "I'm sorry that I hurt you, especially what I said to you after the storm. I knew better. Look how each horse gets tended to every night—I don't know why I didn't think you'd do the same for your scholars. For Maggie, in particular."

He saw her expression soften, ever so slightly, and took a step closer to her. "I think I just wanted a reason to be angry with you. It felt easier to be angry with you than . . . to try and stop loving you. Knowing it's really Ben you love."

There, he said it. And she didn't deny it. It pained him to even say it aloud, that she loved Ben, but at least the truth was out in the open. He turned to go and stopped when he heard her speak.

"You're not the only one who's been making mistakes."

He spun around to face her, but she avoided his eyes, fixing her gaze down on her clasped hands.

"Ben was right, Cal." Her voice broke over the words. "He was right about me wanting him to be more like you." She lifted her eyes to meet his. "Don't misunderstand. I never coveted my friend's husband. I never, ever wanted Mary Ann to be gone. Never that." She looked away. "But I can't deny that I've always thought . . . highly of you. And then, this winter, that feeling grew into something else." She tucked her chin to her chest. "But feelings can't be the only thing that guides us, can they?" She lifted her face, her expression strong and clear.

She was so strong, his Jorie, the strongest person he had ever known. But he reminded himself that she wasn't his Jorie . . . she was Ben's Jorie. He wiped the tears off of her cheeks with a gentle brush of his hands—not the touch of a lover but that of a friend.

On an unseasonably hot afternoon in early June, Jorie led two mares and their foals out to pasture. As she closed the gate behind her, she stopped to watch the foals chase each other in play. It was a sight that never failed to pull at her heart. What was it about being young that brought such joy and abandon, even to animals?

She heard someone call her name and turned to see Ben standing there. She hadn't seen him since that awful day at the schoolhouse, when he raised his fists against Cal. He looked like he hadn't slept in a few days; his beard was scruffy and his eyes were rimmed with dark circles. He looked so hurt, so frightened and broken, and she found she couldn't bear it. She knew she should be angry with him, but it was no use. She felt her anger slip away, like an ocean wave from a shoreline.

Ben stared at her for what seemed like forever.

She came up to him, her gaze moving over his troubled face.

"Don't," he said. "Don't come any closer, Jorie."

She took a step toward him and he flinched, backing away again, lifting his palms to stop her.

"I lost all of my inheritance—every cent of Cal's savings—in a card game. Every blasted dollar."

She took his hand in hers as if she were cradling a wounded bird.

"Please, Jorie. Please. Don't touch me. I'm filthy," he said. He tried to pull his hand free, but she tightened her grip. She wanted to comfort him and he made it so hard.

She took a step closer and wrapped her arms around his waist and pressed her face against his chest. He started to cry then and let her hold him until he stopped. After she released him, she struggled to find words to fill the silence and break the uneasiness that lay between them.

All that she could think to say was, "Please. Go to Cal. Talk to him."

It was so hot that the thick air shimmered in waves before Cal's eyes. Sweat dripped off his hair and down his neck. He was planting a section of the vegetable garden to cultivate for fall vegetables when he looked up and saw Ben. It had been more than a week since Ben had disappeared. Cal dropped the shovel, wiped his forehead with a rag, and walked up to his brother.

"A garden's the sign that life keeps going on, that people are home and happy to be there," Ben said, his hat brim covering his eyes. "Isn't that what Mom always said?"

Cal nodded.

Ben lifted his head and peered at Cal's eye. "You did more damage to my hand than I did to your eye." He held out his hand. His knuckles were still bruised and scabbed.

Such a terrible thing, Cal thought, an Amish man bearing marks of violence on his hands. "Oh, you gave me a shiner. Folks at church wanted to ask but didn't dare."

A smile tugged at the corners of Ben's mouth.

"Have you seen Jorie yet?"

"Yes." Ben's smile faded. "I'm sorry, Cal. Sorry for all of the trouble I've brought on you. I've just been so . . ."

"Angry."

"Yes. Angry. Since the war."

"It's not just the war, Ben. You've been angry a long time. You've been clinging to your anger with every ounce of humanity left in your body."

Ben's chin lifted a notch. "It wasn't easy following you, Cal. You cast a deep shadow for me. For Matthew and Ephraim too."

Cal choked down a retaliation, which would have been futile. "Don't go making me an excuse for your choices."

"What's that supposed to mean?" Ben said, his voice tinged with irritation.

Cal took off his hat and spun it around in his hands. He was trying to remain calm, but he had some things to say to Ben, things that would be hard for him to hear. "You're always looking for a shortcut. You lead Jorie into thinking you'll marry her, but never quite get around to it. You stay as close to being Amish as you can, but never choose to baptize. You find the one loophole to being a conscientious objector and make the rest of us think you've been cuckolded."

Ben looked away. "So Jorie told you," he said, his voice flat.

"Es macht nix aus," Cal said, frustration in his voice. *It doesn't matter.* "You've *got* to stop blaming others. Blaming me, blaming Jorie, blaming the Army."

Cal saw something shift over Ben's face. It looked as if he wanted those secrets spilled, like it would be a relief to spew it all out.

Ben let out a deep breath. "Have you ever found yourself in a situation when you did one thing that led to another? And that led to another thing? Until suddenly you find yourself at a place where there is no going back, and no escaping."

Now, *finally*, Ben was talking from the heart. Cal pointed to a tree with a large canopy. "Let's get out of this hot sun and sit."

After they sat under the shade of the tree, Cal waited patiently for Ben to start talking.

"I had a friend in Vietnam. Another Amish guy like me, a stretcher bearer." Ben's voice was rough, as if his throat kept tightening up, choking off the words.

The humidity of the warm day was oppressive, even in the shade, but Cal thought Ben looked as if he felt cold. His face had grown pale and his hands were trembling.

"We nearly had the same name too. Benjamin S. Zook. His 'S' was for Simeon, mine was Samuel. We had been put together in the same company because of our last names. One day, this Ben and I were taking supplies to the field medic. There'd been sniper activity in the area, so the captain insisted we carry weapons. Small guns. My friend and I talked about it, what to do. He said he wouldn't carry a gun, no matter what. But I slipped the gun into my pocket." Ben sat forward, elbows resting on his knees, eyes fastened on the garden. "We got a little lost on the trail, the overgrowth was so dense. Suddenly, we were face-to-face with an NVC—a North Viet Cong—holding a rifle to our faces. Ben—the other Ben—started saying the Lord's Prayer, like a chant, especially the part about loving our enemies. And that sniper, he walked around Ben, as if he was listening to him, then he gave him a big smile—I'll never forget that smile—and shot him dead. One bullet to the forehead. By the time he turned toward me, I had slipped my hand into my pocket, pulled out the gun, and fired it. I did it without thinking, like it was a survival instinct. Like I was hunting in the woods with you and Dad. I killed him, Cal. I . . . *killed* . . . a man." He covered his face with his hands.

Cal felt shock jolt through him, to think his brother—for that matter, to think *any* Amish man—took the life of another . . . he felt sick with disgust. But he worked to keep his face empty of judgment. This was why his people avoided war, for just such a thing as this. Who knew how he would have reacted had he been in the same situation?

Ben dropped his hands and lifted his head to the sky. "I was stunned by what I had done. I just stood there, watching blood pour out of that sniper's neck . . . like a kitchen faucet. A soldier heard the gun shots and came to help. He found me with those two dead bodies around me. He saw the dead sniper and congratulated me. He *congratulated* me! Told me I'd be getting a medal. For *killing*. He ran back to get the captain and that was when I switched dog tags with my friend. I knew I would be viewed as a hero and I couldn't stomach it." He gave Cal a sideways glance. "I wasn't thinking straight. I didn't even consider that folks back home would be told I was dead. I only thought about getting a medal for *killing* a man. I tried to put it out of my mind, that killing, but it kept coming back at me. I couldn't sleep, and pretty soon I was acting like a nutcase. Couldn't even get out of bed one morning. That was when I got shipped off to the looney bin in Thailand. The doctors kept slapping me with different diagnoses, different labels. First it was a nervous breakdown, then combat trauma, then a clinical depression."

He rubbed his face with his hands, wiping away tears. "They were all wrong. It was dread and fear and guilt—most of all, the guilt—that was churning around inside my belly for so long I just couldn't take it anymore." Emptied of words now, he rubbed his eyes with the arm of his shirt. "So tell me, Cal. *How* do I get rid of this crushing guilt?" His voice broke on the words.

Cal spun his straw hat in his hands around and around, thinking hard. He took his time answering. "God doesn't convict us of sin just to make us feel guilty. Conviction is meant to move us to confession and repentance. After confession comes forgiveness. It's like the sun shining after a summer storm. There is peace and joy to be found in God. And there is forgiveness and eternal life. It's never too late to make your soul whole. You've been dwelling on your sin and forgetting that we have a gracious God who loves to forgive the repentant sinner."

Ben dropped his head, hiding his eyes beneath the brim of his hat. "So you think it was a sin, killing that sniper?" His voice turned hard and cold again. "He would have killed me, you know. Is that what you preferred?"

Cal's gaze shifted to the road to watch a buggy with a high-stepping gelding drive by. He felt as if he was on the edge of a precipice—one wrong move and the conversation could slip down the wrong path. "I don't judge you, if that's what you're asking. But I don't think killing that sniper is all that's troubling you."

Ben looked away.

"Somewhere there is a family who doesn't know what has happened to their son. You need to find them and tell them all that happened. I think Matthew would know how to track them down."

Ben fell silent, but Cal didn't mind. Silence was good. When Ben finally glanced over at him, a question in his eyes, Cal added, "I don't know what's the cause of the hardness between you and Ephraim, but you need to make things right. He's a sensitive boy, Ben. You've done something that has made him feel betrayed."

Ben gave a quick nod but didn't explain. "What else? Go on. I know you've got something else you're itching to say."

Cal nearly smiled. They knew each other so well. "It's high time you start being the man God created you to be." He leaned his elbows on his knees. "Think about all of the experiences God gave you—the good ones and the bad ones—and let God *use* them, Ben. Stop trying to hide from your past. Give your past to God."

He stood, put his hat on his head, and adjusted the brim. "Ben, this time in Vietnam, all that happened over there—it's a chapter, not the whole book."

Ephraim had gotten in the habit of stopping by Dr. Robinson's office when he was passing by the cottage and saw his car. Mrs. Robinson said she appreciated his help, cleaning out the animal cages—their patients, she called them. Dr. Robinson even let Ephraim sew a couple of stitches on an ear of an anesthetized cat that had gotten into a fight. Not too bad for a first time, the doctor had said, but he took out the stitches and redid them.

Today, when he was at the Robinsons' feeding the cat with the sewn-up ear, Jerry Gingerich dropped by to pick up Rex. He couldn't believe how Jerry practically gushed over Dr. Robinson, shaking his hand, thanking him again and again for saving Rex's leg. It made Ephraim feel uncomfortable. It was easier to hate Jerry than to see something good in him.

On the way back to Beacon Hollow, Ephraim was coming up the drive as Ben was walking down. Ephraim scowled when he saw him and crossed to the other side of the drive, ignoring him, but Ben blocked his path.

"Ephraim, I'm sorry about the cougar," Ben said. "I really am. I wish I could make it up to you somehow."

Ephraim gave him a suspicious look, wondering how sincere he was. He actually looked quite contrite. "Then help me k-keep the c-cougar k-kits safe from Jerry Gingerich. He's going out t-tonight to trap them and k-kill them, I heard him say s-so himself, just now, over at Dr. Robinson's."

Ben tilted his head. "You know where the kits are?"

Ephraim nodded. "I've been f-feeding them every d-day since you murdered their mother."

Ben winced. "Sheesh, you put it like that, Ephraim, it makes me sound heartless." He folded his arms across his chest. "Even if we built a cage for them, they're going to grow. They're not pets. They need to be free and wild."

Ephraim turned away. "You s-said you wanted to help m-make things right."

Ben sighed. "But I can't help you do something stupid." He leaned his elbows against the fence with one boot heel resting on the low railing. He was quiet for a while, then slapped his hat against his knees. "Why not? I've done plenty of stupid things." He pushed himself up with his foot. His hand fell on Ephraim's head, propelling him up the drive. "Let's go trap us some cougar babies."

Before sundown, Ephraim and Ben had two cougar kits, safe and sound and mewling in a burlap sack, and headed back to Beacon Hollow through the Deep Woods. When they emerged at the opening of the woods, Ben said, "Ephraim, go to Jorie's with this sack and tell her what's happened. She'll know what to do."

"Aren't you c-coming with me?"

"I can't, little brother. There are a few things I need to take care of." He patted Ephraim on the back. "Jorie will know what to do." He looked out at the setting sun. "I have no idea what that will be, but she'll figure it out. She's always had a sense of knowing what to do."

He started down the road, then spun around as if he'd just remembered something. He reached in his pocket and handed Ephraim a folded piece of paper. "Give her this."

Ten minutes later, when Ephraim knocked on Jorie's door and showed her the wiggling sack, she couldn't believe her eyes. "Oh, the poor darlings, they must be hungry."

As soon as Ephraim heard her call them darlings, he knew that Ben, for once, had given him good advice. These kits weren't darlings, they were monsters. He had cuts and scratches all over his hands and face to prove it.

"What do you think we should feed them?" she asked.

"They l-like p-peanut butter sandwiches."

Jorie looked at him as if he were crazy. "How about milk?"

Ephraim shrugged.

"I'll be right back," Jorie said. She came back a few minutes later with two large bottles used for foals, filled with cow's milk. "Let's go down to the barn and find an empty stall so you can let them out of this sack."

In the barn, the horses sniffed the air—detecting the smell of an enemy—and started making nervous sounds but settled down as Jorie called to them in her soothing voice. She pointed to an empty corner stall. Ephraim slid it open and closed it behind them, setting the sack on the floor so the kits could scramble out.

After watching them explore the stall for a few minutes, Jorie handed him a bottle and said, "You grab one, I'll take the other." She picked up a kit like she'd been doing it her whole life, cradled it in her arms, and tipped the bottle into the gaping, eager mouth. "Drink up, little one, drink up," she crooned, tickling it under its little mouth.

Ephraim was amazed at Jorie's gentle way with animals, even a wild cougar kit. But then again, Jorie always seemed to amaze him. In his mind, there was nothing she couldn't do. He picked up the other kit and tried to imitate her. They sat there, quietly letting the kits drink from their bottles, until the sucking slowed and the kits fell asleep, milk dribbling down their chins.

Softly, Jorie said, "Maybe Dr. Robinson knows of a zoo that might like two baby cougars."

Ephraim shook his head. "Please, n-not a zoo. No c-cages. They n-need to be free."

"Maybe a wildlife reserve then. Someplace where they could roam but be protected too."

He thought that sounded like a good idea.

"We need to do this right away, Ephraim. As long as you can stay here in the stall, the horses won't get anxious. I'll run over to Dr. Robinson and tell him the situation. I'm hoping he'll be willing to come and get them before my grandparents get back from town. If my grandfather catches wind of these cougars, he'll have their hides tanned and hanging on the walls by breakfast." She carefully tucked the sleeping kit into a nest made of hay.

If Jerry Gingerich found out what I've done, Ephraim thought, *he would probably tan my hide.* The thought made him smile.

Dr. Robinson made a few phone calls and found a place for the kits to live. He and Jorie returned an hour later with two crates in the back of his station wagon.

"Tomorrow, Ephraim, I'm going to meet with a friend of mine with the Audubon Society of Western Pennsylvania. They have a nature reserve in Butler County where the kits might be able to live."

"You're s-sure?" Ephraim asked. "They won't end up in a z-zoo?"

"I give you my promise," Dr. Robinson said. "I kind of feel responsible, anyway. I'm the one who started this by giving you those circus tickets."

Ephraim went to the back of the station wagon to say goodbye to the kits. Jorie saw him wipe his eyes with his sleeve. After Dr. Robinson left, Ephraim handed her a note. "It's from B-Ben."

Ephraim waited expectantly, so Jorie read it aloud:

Dear Jorie,

I'm going away for a while to sort a few things out. I'm going to get my head fixed.

Love, Ben

"That would be g-good, w-wouldn't it?" he asked, but she didn't answer.

19

Communion was held late that year because the bishop's spring cold turned into a bout of pneumonia, and both Samuel and Cal knew they needed to wait for Isaac. The preparation service, the Attnungsgemee, held two weeks before Communion, was quite strenuous and physically draining for the ministers, who not only preached long sermons but needed to give emotional support to the members as well. The Attnungsgemee was an all-day meeting, filled with importance. The Ordnung, the rules and practices of their district, was presented by the ministers, and each member was asked if he was in agreement with it, at peace in the brotherhood, and whether anything "stood in the way" of entering into the Communion service. Great emphasis was placed on the importance of preparing one's heart for this holy service. Sins were confessed, and grudges—less obvious but just as dangerous—were settled between members. It was this *intention* that Cal loved. A reminder that folks should be keeping short accounts with each other, to not let bitter feelings take root. Mary Ann used to call it internal spring cleaning, and she was right, in a way. It was a cleansing ritual.

Communion would be scheduled two weeks' hence, but only if the members were in full agreement. Maggie and Ephraim always looked forward to Communion because they would be left at home without any adult supervision. Lizzie, having joined the church last fall, planned to attend too.

Cal loved the day of Communion. It occurred twice a year, after a day of fasting. To him, it was layered with symbolism. By starting the day hungry and weak, aware of his humble state, he felt he entered into the suffering and death of Jesus Christ. The long day ended in joy, with a full stomach, and with vivid gratitude and remembrance for Christ's death on the cross. The Communion service always reinforced the unity and commitment of the church members, binding them together.

Toward the end of the day, Cal read John 13, about Jesus washing the disciples' feet, while Jonas and a few helpers carried in towels and pails of water. Isaac announced a hymn and the men began to remove their shoes and stockings, to wash each other's feet. The women, in the next room, followed the same pattern. They worked in pairs and were reminded by Isaac to wash the feet of the person sitting next to them. But from the corner of his eye, Cal saw Jorie purposefully make her way around two rows of benches to reach Sylvia. Jorie stooped down low, and gently washed Sylvia's feet.

And he fell in love with Jorie all over again.

One July morning, Cal asked Ephraim and Maggie to run over to Bud's and call Dr. Robinson to see if he could drop by to check on one of the dairy cows later today.

"Bud? We're here!" Maggie started into the kitchen, but Ephraim held her back, waiting for Bud to invite them in.

No answer returned except an odd blurping sound.

A chill ran through Ephraim. "Bud?" he ventured. "C-can we c-come in?"

Ephraim told Maggie to stay there and approached the doorway with slow, unsteady steps. He quickly found the reason Bud hadn't answered him. Bud was collapsed forward in his chair, his strong arms outstretched across the table, his head turned toward the door and his lifeless eyes opened wide. It took Ephraim a moment to recognize the blurping sound as coffee percolating in its pot. Cold toast had popped out of the toaster.

Ephraim gulped so hard he practically choked. He went back outside and told Maggie in a clear, calm voice, "Go get Cal."

Bud's son was notified and he swooped in to take care of his father's effects. Cal met with Bud's son right away and offered him full price for the farm. He had always hoped to buy that property for his brothers' sake, but there was more to it than that. Keeping Bud's farm intact was his way of honoring his good friend. He'd known Bud all his life; he was nearly like family to him.

At the hardware store, when they heard Ron Harding say that Bud's son had sold off the Deep Woods, Cal saw Ephraim wipe hot tears from his eyes with the back of his coat sleeve.

"I couldn't afford anything more, Ephraim," Cal said on the ride home. "Those woods can't be farmed. I had to take out a loan for Bud's farm as it was, and I had never wanted to take a loan out for anything." He balked at the notion of a mortgage. He had been saving his money to buy farms for his brothers ever since his folks passed—but now that money was gone. He had no choice but to take on a mortgage. He knew Bud's son had wanted to sell the land to a housing developer. But he couldn't rationalize the debt he would take on if he tried to buy up the Deep Woods.

Still, Cal had the same gut-wrenching sense of loss as Ephraim. Those woods meant something special to each one of them. When he heard that the timber had been sold, he felt a stab of concern. He knew their Deep Woods was doomed.

"Everything keeps changing, in ways I don't like," Maggie complained to Cal and Ephraim. "Ben's gone, Matthew doesn't come home, Jorie doesn't come around." She lowered her voice so her father wouldn't hear her. "Only that Elsie lady."

Everyone in the district was talking about Elsie Lapp, the aunties' newest find. Elsie had come to Stoney Ridge from Somerset County for the summer, staying with her brother Jonas and his family. "She's 'the one' for you," Ada told Cal.

"The very one," Florence echoed.

So convinced were they, Elsie was automatically signed up for four Saturday nights, which meant all of June and July. "She's supposed to head home by the end of July," Ada explained to Cal. "If you're going to court her, you need to hop to it."

"Try harder," Florence added, more firmly. "We're running clean out of prospects."

Late Friday afternoon, Ephraim saw a row of trucks carrying bulldozers as they drove past Bud's farm.

Cal came up behind him, watching the parade. "Come Monday morning, our Deep Woods will be history," he said solemnly, as much to himself as to Ephraim.

After milking the cows the next afternoon, Cal promised Ephraim and Maggie a hike through the woods, their last. Just as they walked out of the farmhouse, the aunties and Elsie drove up.

"Oh no," Maggie groaned. "Does this mean we can't go on our hike?"

Ephraim looked up at Cal.

"I'd forgotten . . . ," Cal said, swallowing hard. "I forgot it was a Supper Night."

"Aw, Cal," Ephraim said.

"We're still going on our hike," Cal said, squaring his shoulders. "We need to admire those woods for the last time." He walked out to meet the buggy and help the ladies down. "I promised Ephraim and Maggie a hike into the woods before dinner. Would you mind, Elsie, if we put off dinner for another hour or so?"

"No," Elsie said. "In fact, I'd like to join you."

Surprised, Cal handed the basket of food to Ephraim to take inside. "Tell Lizzie that she's going to be in charge of the aunties for a while," he whispered.

After getting the aunties settled in the living room with Lizzie hovering around them like a bee over a field of flowers, they set off on their hike. When they came to the edge of the woods, they followed the flow of the stream. It led them to a stand of sugar maples, along with a few oak and hickory trees. At the east edge of the grove was a small cemetery where a pioneer family had been buried. Ephraim had forgotten about that cemetery; he hadn't ventured to that part of the Deep Woods for a long time. He had only been in the area where his cougar lived.

"Look, Maggie." Ephraim pointed out two small graves of children who had died of scarlet fever, one day apart.

"I can almost see the grieving family," Cal said quietly as he brushed off the moss on the graves.

Elsie gave Cal a strange look. "So can I."

Ephraim decided, at that moment, that maybe Elsie wasn't so bad. Maybe the aunties had finally stumbled on someone who would be good for Cal. They rested for a while in the cool shade of the cemetery trees.

"D-do you think they'll s-spare these trees?" Ephraim asked Cal.

"Surely so," Cal said. "Surely they wouldn't take trees that were nourished on the pioneer family."

As they walked through the woods, Ephraim took the lead, blazing a trail to his favorite place, underneath the ancient beech tree where his father had carved his initials when he was a boy. When Ephraim pointed it out, they all stopped and stared for a long while. Ephraim eyes glistened a little, but so did Cal's, he noticed.

"Just the tree I wanted to say goodbye to," said a quiet voice.

"Jorie!" Maggie ran over to her and grabbed her hands.

Ephraim was so happy to see her that his hat slipped off when he nearly tripped over a tree root to get to her side. "W-what are you d-doing here?"

"Same as you, wanting to take one last walk in these woods," she said, tousling his hair.

It was so hot that his hair stuck straight up, making Maggie giggle. She interrupted the uncomfortable silence, dragging Jorie over to the beech tree to point out her grandfather's carving.

"I wish it could be saved," Jorie said.

"You must be that schoolteacher everyone talks about," Elsie said kindly. "Folks say you're a wonderful teacher."

"This is . . . I'm sorry . . . Jorie King . . . this is . . ." Cal turned to Elsie with a blank look on his face, his cheeks stained with red.

Elsie looked at Cal, a little nonplussed. "I'm Elsie Lapp, Jonas's sister."

Jorie stuck out her hand to shake Elsie's. "Pleased to meet you, Elsie," she said, sounding like she meant it.

Ephraim wondered what was running through Jorie's mind. She looked as pleased as could be to come across them in the woods. Cal, on the other hand, looked as if he had been caught with his fingers in the cookie jar.

Early Monday morning, the quiet of the countryside was shattered by the snarl of chain saws. Soon afterward came the whine of power log skidders. Throughout that week, Ephraim came to shudder when the sound of a saw shut off, knowing that what would follow would be the thunderous crash of a tree falling. At the end of each summer day, smoke-belching diesel trucks rumbled past Beacon Hollow laden with mammoth logs.

Last night, Cal had stood with Ephraim and watched the trucks go by. He said something that gave Ephraim an unforgettable twinge, a sense that something major was ending. "What nature had taken more than three centuries to create, man will undo in a few weeks' time."

Jorie couldn't stop thinking about Elsie Lapp. She had told her she was pleased to meet her, but she wasn't. She had watched Cal and Elsie in the Deep Woods, unobserved, for a long while before she made her presence known. Elsie was fine-boned, tall, and blond. She had a gentle voice, soft spoken and polite. She suited Cal well, that was plain to see. Jorie noticed that she even leaned slightly toward Cal as they stood side by side, staring at the beech tree. She fit against his side as neatly as a matched puzzle piece. Anyone watching them would think they were already a family. The sight of it nearly broke Jorie's heart, until she reminded herself that God always had a plan. For her too.

But for the life of her, she just didn't know what that plan might be.

Rain was coming. The clouds were low and dark and the wind had kicked up, mercifully cooling the air. Jorie went out to bring the horses in from the pasture before the rain began. Something had set the foals off and they were galloping around the pasture, all thundering legs and raised tails. She stopped to watch the impressive sight. The Lord had seen fit to bless them with five healthy foals this spring when one mare, Stella, delivered twins. Those five foals, including Indigo—who had healed up quickly from her eye injury—galloped from one end of the pasture to another, headed straight toward the fence. At the very last second, they would change direction as one, like a flock of starlings. It was when they galloped back toward the other end of the pasture that she noticed Ben, standing with one leg bent, leaning against the fence like he always did, with a book in his hand to loan. He was waiting for her.

The sight of him caught her breath and made her feel a little dizzy, the way she used to feel when he came calling. "Hello, stranger," she said, walking up to him.

He looked much better. Gone was that haunted look. His features—just a little too sharp when he was so underweight—had softened. His dark hair had grown in, full and thick and wavy, the way she loved it. A hundred memories rushed at her—the way his hair had always smelled of laurel soap, the small scar under one eye, the lazy way he leaned against a fence, as if he had all the time in the world.

"Hello, Jorie." He pushed himself off the fence and handed the book to her. She glanced down at the title—*The Winter of Our Discontent* by John Steinbeck. "Walk with me?"

He reached out a hand for hers as they walked down the long lane that led to the road.

"Where have you been?" she asked.

"Over in Lebanon, staying with Matthew. I've been having a bunch of tests from that shrink, Dr. Doyle. He pronounced me 'officially cured.'"

He gave her a dazzling smile. She had always liked his smile best of all. It had a touch of sweet whimsicality about it.

"Said he's going to send all of his worst nutcases out to Beacon Hollow."

At the end of the drive, he stopped, released her hand, and leaned his back against the fence.

He looked out over the green pastures where the Percherons were grazing. "I'm sorry for those terrible things I said to you. I shouldn't have said what I said. About you being glad Mary Ann passed. I know that wasn't true."

She looked away.

"I'm sorry, too, for telling you about getting fired. That wasn't my place."

She smiled at that. "The bishop wants to rehire me. Said he'd even give me a raise for doing such a good job."

Ben looked pleased. "You gonna take it?"

"I don't know."

"But . . . I thought you loved teaching."

"Oh, I do! It's been such a wonderful experience. I love it more than I could ever have imagined. Even some of the scholars who are hardest to love—Ray and Esther—they have grown dear to me." She sighed. "My grandmother needs more help. We took her to a doctor last week. He thinks she has . . . he thinks she has senile dementia. She's going to require more help. My grandfather . . . he needs me."

"You're the Keeper of Atlee's song, huh?"

She nodded.

Ben smiled a sad smile. "Ironic, isn't it? I've been trying so hard to forget my life while poor Marge is trying so hard to remember hers." He exhaled a deep sigh. "It's been hard, being back."

"I know. It's an adjustment."

Ben turned around and placed his hands on the top of the fence. "It's more than an adjustment, Jorie."

"You've got to give yourself time."

"Time isn't going to make a difference." He turned to her. "There's something I came to talk to you about. I've been thinking of going back to Vietnam. Still as a C.O. Maybe as a medic."

Jorie was shocked. "*What?* How could you even consider such a thing?"

"To finish what I started." He gave her a wry smile. "It's been pointed out to me by my wise older brother that I am not very good at that."

"Ben, give yourself some time to think that over."

"The thing is . . . the thing is, Jorie, I've already done it. I signed up to serve." He bit his lip. "I'm leaving today." He jerked his chin toward the road. "When the bus comes."

"Oh," she whispered, stunned. "Oh." She noticed a suitcase leaning against the mailbox and stared at it for a while. "Have you told Cal?"

"Yes. I've already said my goodbyes." He sighed. "I wish I were the kind of man you deserve, Jorie. The man you wanted me to be. I wish I wanted to be a farmer, an Amish farmer, and wanted to stay here at Beacon Hollow the rest of my life. But I can't be something I'm not." He took his hat off and raked his hand through his hair. "You don't have to say anything. I know it's a shock."

She peered into his face, searching it out. Something was different in him. A wound had healed. "I guess that's what surprises me. I'm shocked

. . . but not shocked. I think, deep down, I always have known you weren't here to stay."

He risked a look at her. "Think you'll be able to forgive me?"

He didn't understand; he'd always had such trouble understanding her and her faith. She reached out her hand for his. "Oh, Ben. I already have."

They stood there for a long while, neither one wanting to let go. They heard the whine of the bus as it started to chug up the hill, and Ben's eyes started glistening, but he released her hand and bent down to pick up his suitcase.

"Jorie," he said, as the blunt nose of the bus appeared over the rise. "I hope I haven't messed things up so badly with Cal that you can't find your way back to each other." The bus slowed to a creaky stop.

She looked down at her shoes. "He and Elsie . . ."

"Jonas's sister? Nah." He gave a short laugh. "You know our Cal. Takes him awhile to make up his mind, but once he's done it, not even a stick of dynamite can budge him loose." He put his suitcase down again and faced her. "Cal loves you, better than I ever could."

Her eyes filled with tears. "May the Lord bless you and keep you safe, Ben Zook."

He reached his hand out to caress her cheek. "And may he do the same to you, Jorie King." He held her gaze for a long time, a look of settled peace, then picked up his suitcase and hopped up on the bus.

Jorie watched as Ben wound his way to a seat and waved at him until the bus disappeared around the bend. For a long time afterward, she stood watching the empty road, gripping her elbows, offering a prayer to the Lord over Ben and his future. To her, Ben seemed unfinished and rough-hewn, a man still waiting to happen.

Then she thought she heard someone call her name, just a gentle whisper on someone's lips. She thought she only imagined it, but then she heard it again and turned toward the sound. There she saw a man.

It was Cal, standing at the turnoff to Beacon Hollow with his broad shoulders squared straight, spinning the brim of his straw hat around and around in his hands, his eyes soft around the edges. He was waiting for her, like he had been doing for months now.

Her heart stood still.

He smiled.

She started walking to him, slowly at first, then faster and faster. Soon, she broke into a run.

And then she was in his arms.

Acknowledgments

I'd like to express my deep appreciation to my first draft readers—Lindsey Ciraulo, Wendy How, Nyna Dolby—who read the manuscript with tough and loving eyes and generously shared their insights.

As always, enormous gratitude to my agent, Joyce Hart of The Hartline Literary Agency, for being so helpful and steadfast.

A heartfelt thank-you to the entire staff of Revell Books, for making each book they publish the best it can possibly be. A book passes through many hands—editing and marketing and sales—before it ends up on a bookshelf: Erin Bartels, Michele Misiak, Deonne Beron, Claudia Marsh, Carmen Seachrist, Twila Brothers Bennett, Cheryl Van Andel . . . and so many others. Barb Barnes, whose deft, perceptive editorial touch was invaluable. And a special thank-you to my acquisitions editor, Andrea Doering, whose insightful questions helped craft the story more effectively. It is a privilege to work with all of you.

Above all, thanks and praise to the Lord God for giving me an opportunity to share the wonder of His reconciling love through story.

The SEARCH

For Steve,
who has been such a supportive and kind husband
that nobody would believe it if I were
to write him into a book!
Thank you with all of my heart.

1

$\mathcal{I}$t was a June morning, hazy with summer's heat, and Billy Lapp was already bone tired. Only one person on earth could wear out an eighteen-year-old farm boy, and Billy happened to be her hired hand. For over two weeks now, Bertha Riehl had met him at the barn door of Rose Hill Farm with a to-do list that seemed to grow longer with each passing hour. Bertha's granddaughter, Bess, was coming for a summer visit, and Bertha wanted the farm so spic-and-span clean a body could eat off the barn floor. Which, Billy knew, meant he would be the one scrubbing that barn floor until it shone.

He didn't know why Bertha felt her farm needed sprucing up. So sauwer wie gschleckt. *It was as clean as a whistle.* The vegetable garden ran neat and tidy from the kitchen steps down to the greenhouse, beside the yard where she stretched her clothesline. Why, hardly a rose petal dared to wilt without Bertha flying out to the fields with a pair of pruning shears in her big hands. And besides that, folks visited each other all the time. But then Billy remembered that something was not quite right between Bertha and Jonah, her son, Bess's father. He had left years before. Billy didn't know what had caused the rift, but he knew enough not to ask. Bertha could be private like that, keeping her business to herself.

"Could you tell me something about Bess?" Billy had asked Bertha the other day as he helped her turn the mattress in the spare bedroom she was readying for Bess.

Bertha flipped her end of the mattress and let it slip into the wooden bed frame with a soft sough. "Like what?"

"Well, how old is Bess now?" He vaguely remembered a towheaded, skinny wisp of a girl coming in from Ohio a few years back when Samuel, Bertha's husband, passed.

Bertha raised an eyebrow at him, as if she thought his motives were highly suspect. "Old enough," she said, lifting her big chin. "But too young for you."

Billy sputtered. "I wasn't asking for that. Besides, me and Betsy—" He stopped abruptly. He knew how Bertha Riehl felt about his Betsy Mast, and he didn't want another lecture about thinking with your head and not your nether regions, a comment at which he took offense. But that was Bertha Riehl for you. She didn't mince words and she didn't hold back her opinions. And she had plenty of both.

On this sunny day, Bertha handed him a broom. "When you're done sweeping out the hay loft, you need to clean out the ashes in the chimbley place." She bent over to pick up her favorite rooster, a fourteen-year-old leghorn named Otto, who followed her around the farm. Bertha tucked Otto under her arm, football-style, and headed up the hill to the farmhouse. Her left side was flanked by Boomer, a big black dog who had appeared one day and never left.

"You gonna finally cook that ol' rooster for dinner, Bertha?" Billy said, grinning.

"Been giving it some serious thought," she called over her shoulder, stroking Otto's feathers like he was a pampered housecat.

Bertha was always threatening Otto was going to end up as Sunday's stew, but Billy knew better. Bertha Riehl was all bluff and bluster. Well, mostly bluff and bluster. He couldn't deny she had a way of intimidating folks that was a wonder to behold. It had happened to Billy only once, when he made the mistake of asking her if she was six feet tall. Bertha planted her fists on her deluxe-sized hips and narrowed her eyes at him. "I am five feet twelve inches." Then she stared him down until he was sure he had shrunk an inch or two, right in front of her.

From the kitchen door of the sprawling brick-and-frame farmhouse, Bertha turned and hollered at Billy. "Es is noch lang net faercih wann's yuscht halwe gedus is!" *Half done is far from done!*

He dashed into the barn and picked up where he left off, sweeping the concrete floor with a dash and a fury. One thing to be grateful for, he thought as hay and dust flew up around him, the day of Bess's arrival had finally come.

Jonah Riehl was seeing his daughter, Bess, off at the bus station in Berlin, Ohio. He handed her a ham sandwich for lunch and bus fare for the return ticket home. Bess would be spending the entire summer at his mother's farm in Stoney Ridge, Pennsylvania. His mother had written recently to say she had suffered through some female surgery and could Bess please come? She was in dire need of someone to help.

Jonah knew it couldn't be true that his mother needed help. Bertha had lived in Stoney Ridge all of her life and had plenty of sisters, cousins, and neighbors she could count on. Wasn't that what being Plain was all about?

And yet he couldn't rest easy telling his mother that Bess wouldn't come this summer. His mother was getting up there in years, and she was the type who had never been young to begin with. A few years back, Jonah's father, Samuel, had an accident while cutting timber. A big tree fell into a smaller tree, and the smaller trunk snapped under the weight, striking Samuel with terrific force in the forehead. He died seven days later. After his father's funeral, Jonah had invited his mother to come live with them in Ohio. She said no, she wanted to stay on the home place. Still, he knew his mother had a difficult time, losing her partner of so many years. Bertha Riehl did like she always did: she dug in her heels and made do with life as it was.

So, in the end, Jonah showed Bess the letter from his mother.

"The whole summer?" Bess shook her head. "I can't leave you, Dad. You need me around here."

He couldn't deny that. It was just the two of them rattling around in the house. He hadn't wanted to think of summer without his Bess—much less about the fact that she was growing up so quickly. It wouldn't be long before boys would start buzzing around her. Too soon, she would have a life of her own. It was the natural order of things, he knew, the way things were meant to be, but it still grieved him to think of it. So much so that he had written a letter to his mother to say he couldn't spare Bess.

That very afternoon, before he had a chance to mail the letter, Bess came home from school and announced a change of heart. She would go to Stoney Ridge, after all. "It's the right thing to do, and you're always telling me that we need to do the right thing," she said with a dramatic flair.

It still puzzled him why she had flip-flopped on the topic.

Now the loudspeaker was announcing the bus's departure, and Jonah's eyes got blurry. "Be careful, Bess," he said, "because—"

"—because you think I'm five, not fifteen." She smiled at him.

Jonah clamped his mouth shut. Bess teased him that each time he said goodbye to her, even as she left for school each morning, he would add the caution, "Be careful, because . . ." *Because . . . I won't be there to protect you. Because . . . accidents happen.* He knew that to be true. At any given moment, anything at all could happen. He brushed a few stray hairs from her forehead and gave her shoulders a quick squeeze, his way of saying that he loved her and would miss her.

As the bus pulled out of the station and Bess waved goodbye to her father, it was her turn for blurry eyes. She had visited Stoney Ridge only one other time, for her grandfather's funeral. That time, her father was with her. Now, it was just her. At the other end of the trip—Mammi. And no Daadi to soften her grandmother's rough edges. Bess had adored her grandfather. He came to visit them in Ohio every other year—as often as he could. He was a tenderhearted man, as lean and lanky as Mammi was wide and round.

As Bess watched the phone lines swoop up and down to each pole along the road, she remembered what wouldn't be there—no phone in the barn, like at home. No bicycles, only scooters. And no indoor plumbing. When she asked her father why her grandmother still used a privy despite knowing that their district allowed plumbing, he told her that his mother was a woman who held on tight to the old ways. "If it isn't broke, why fix it?" was her life motto, he said.

Hours later, when the Greyhound bus pulled into Stoney Ridge, Bess climbed down the steps onto the sidewalk. The driver yanked her suitcase from the belly of the bus and thumped it down next to her. There Bess stood at the end of the world with all her worldly possessions. Her suitcase and Blackie, her cat.

Blackie had traveled in a picnic hamper and spent most of the trip trying to claw his way out. As Bess set down the hamper and looked around, a small knot of fear rose in her throat. She assumed her grandmother would be here waiting for her. What if she had forgotten Bess was coming? What if no one came to meet her? How would she ever find the farmhouse? Maybe her grandmother had gotten even sicker since her female surgery. Maybe Bess had come too late and Mammi had up and died. Bess had to shield her eyes from the late afternoon sun, beating down on her. She was tired from the long, hot ride and briefly thought about getting back on the stuffy bus to head home. Home to her father, Ohio, and all that was familiar.

Bess sat down on top of her suitcase. These were the moments in life when she wondered if her mother was up there in heaven looking down at her now and maybe trying to figure out how to help her. She loved imagining what her mother was like, what she'd say or do. She never tired of hearing stories about her from her father. She hoped that she might be able to find out even more from her grandmother this summer. That is, assuming she could ever locate Mammi. She shaded her eyes to look as far down the street as she could.

Bess let out a sigh of relief when she saw a horse and a gray-topped buggy veering around the corner. The buggy tipped so far to the right, Bess worried it might topple right over. The horse stopped abruptly right next to Bess, and the buggy tipped even more sharply as her grandmother disembarked. Land sakes, but she was enormous. Bess hadn't seen Mammi in three years, and she was even bigger. Taller still with her large black bonnet. She had several chins with wattles like a turkey. She drew nearer to Bess till she blotted out the sun.

"Where's your father?" Mammi asked, looking up and down the platform.

"He didn't come," Bess said. "I'm old enough to travel alone."

For a long moment, Mammi stared at her. Then something passed through those dark brown eyes, something Bess couldn't quite make out. Irritation? Or disappointment, maybe? Whatever it was, she shook it off in a flash.

"Old enough, are you?" Mammi hooked her hands on her hips and looked Bess up and down. "You look like you need a dose of salts and a square meal." The picnic hamper in Bess's hand quivered and Mammi noticed. She pointed to it. "What's that?"

"Blackie," Bess said. "My cat."

"Hoo-boy," Mammi said. "Better be a good mouser."

With a powerful arm, she swung Bess's suitcase aboard the buggy, lifting it high as if it was a feather. "Well, make haste." She climbed into the buggy and Bess hurried to join her. A big black dog with a muzzle of white hair sat in the back and leaned his head forward to sniff Bess. He must have decided Bess passed inspection because he gave her ear a lick. "That's Boomer," Mammi said. "He showed up out of the blue one day after my Samuel passed."

"Boomer?" Bess asked, trying to push the dog back. "Where'd you get a name like Boomer?" The dog sniffed out the hamper with great interest. Blackie let out a hissing sound and Boomer drew back.

Mammi shrugged. "Wait'll you hear his bark. Sounds like a blast of dynamite."

Boomer settled down onto the buggy floor and fell asleep.

"A good guard dog," Bess said, trying to be friendly.

Mammi snorted, but she dropped a big hand to stroke Boomer's head. "The day that dog barks at anything worth barking at is the day there'll be white blackbirds in the sky."

"Mammi, do you want me to drive? You must not be feeling too well after your female surgery and all." Bess hoped she might say yes. She enjoyed driving horses. Some of her fondest memories were sitting with her father on the plow, holding the giant draft horses' reins in her small hands, his big hands covering hers.

"Female surgery?" Mammi gave her a blank look. "Oh. Oh! Had my teeth pulled." She opened her mouth wide and clicked her teeth. "Store-bought choppers. As good as new."

Then what am I doing here? Bess wondered.

Mammi slapped the horse's reins and it took off with a start, as if they were heading to a fire. But instead of turning down the road that would take them to Rose Hill Farm, Mammi steered the horse to a little bakery called The Sweet Tooth. She stopped under a shade tree and wrapped the reins on a low-hanging branch. "Bet you're hungry. Let's go get us something to eat." She turned to Boomer, who had a hope to go in with her. She waved her finger at him to say no. Boomer hung his head and settled back down for another nap.

Bess *was* hungry. The last few months, she had grown so quickly, she was always hungry. But it surprised her that Mammi was willing to shell out money to pay for premade food. Her father said that his mother's cooking skills surpassed most everyone in the county. And she was thrifty! Mammi never bought anything new or threw anything away; even her letters were written on the backs of old bills.

Bess followed and waited in line behind Mammi at the bakery counter. An older woman standing at the counter gave a double take when she saw Mammi. The woman had a massive pile of braided hair, like a coiled snake, on top of her head. Bess wondered how she managed to sleep at night.

The woman recovered from her surprise. She put a hand to her chest. "Bertha Riehl, as I live and breathe."

"Dottie Stroot," Mammi said. "And I hope you are still living and breathing."

"Have you finally decided to let me sell your rose petal jam in my bakery?"

"I have not," Mammi said firmly.

Mrs. Stroot sighed. "Folks are asking me for it all the time, Bertha. They can't always find you to buy it up at the farm."

"I'm busy."

"I'd give you a generous cut."

"For my own jam?" Mammi stared her down, and Bess saw Mrs. Stroot start to crumble.

In a longsuffering voice, Mrs. Stroot asked, "Is there something you came in for today?"

"I want to talk to that one." Mammi pointed in the kitchen area, to the back of a girl in an apron and uniform who was putting a pie in a pink box, then carefully tying it with string.

Mrs. Stroot looked puzzled but called out, "Lainey. This lady wants you to wait on her." An oven buzzer went off and Mrs. Stroot quickly forgot Mammi to hurry to the kitchen.

Without looking up, the girl named Lainey called out, "Be with you in a minute." Bess saw her write something on top of the pink box and slip the cap back on her pen. The girl whirled around to face Mammi and froze. Then she stiffened up straight and swallowed hard. Bess was getting the feeling that people often had to swallow hard when they encountered her grandmother. She felt the same way.

"Bertha Riehl," Lainey said, faint and far off.

Bess had it wrong. Lainey wasn't a girl at all. She was a small woman, probably in her mid-twenties. She was very pretty. Her hair—nearly coal black—was cut short and curly. Her thickly lashed eyes were the color of blueberries that grew in her father's garden. Her complexion was perfection, as delicate as bone china.

"Lainey O'Toole," Mammi said flatly in return. "Last time I laid eyes on you, you were ten years old and so thin I could almost see the sun shining through you. You've gone and grown up."

Lainey swallowed again. "It's good to see you, Bertha."

"This here is Bess." Mammi indicated Bess with a thumb, without saying she was her granddaughter. Mammi never told more than the minimum.

Lainey gave Bess a brief nod, then turned back to Mammi. "I've been meaning to pay you a call since I came back to Stoney Ridge."

"Good. I'll expect you for Sunday noon dinner." Mammi looked through the glass counter. She pointed to a cherry tart. "You make those?"

Lainey nodded. "Just this morning."

"I'll have one. Make it two. And a cup of coffee." She glanced at Bess. "What about you?"

"A Danish please," Bess answered. "And a coffee too."

"Make it milk," Mammi said. "And best stick to those cherry tarts. If those are as good as I remember, you'd be a fool to miss 'em." She paid Lainey for the baked goods and took her coffee to a small table by the window.

Bess asked her grandmother how she knew her.

"Who?" Mammi asked, the picture of surprise.

"The bakery lady. Lainey."

"She grew up around here. Then she left."

Mammi didn't offer up another word. She ate with the fork in one hand, the knife in the other, polished off her two cherry tarts and then eyed Bess's. Bess quickly stuffed it into her mouth. It was the finest cherry tart she had ever tasted, with a crumbly crust and cherries that were sugared just right and still tart. Soon, Mammi was ready to go, and she looked at Bess pointedly. Bess guessed that when Mammi was ready, she'd better be.

That was another odd thing about Mammi—as big as she was, she could move like greased lightning. In a twinkling, she was at the door, pointing at Lainey. "Sunday noon, then." It was a statement, not a question.

The bakery lady looked a little pale but gave a nod.

Lainey O'Toole watched Bertha Riehl walk out the door and climb into the buggy. Bertha had always been a big, husky woman, now even bigger than Lainey remembered. Older, too, but she still moved along like a ship under full sail. And beside her was the young girl with platinum blond hair under an organza prayer cap that was shaped differently from the Lancaster heart-shaped cap. She had white lashes that framed her wide blue eyes. They made an odd pair. The girl turned back to wave at Lainey, as if she knew she was being watched. That young girl seemed as jumpy as a cricket. But those blue eyes—they were the color of a sapphire.

As surprised as Lainey was to see Bertha Riehl walk into the bakery, she was relieved too. She had wanted to see Bertha again and wasn't sure how to go about it. She'd already been in Stoney Ridge for two weeks and hadn't mustered up the courage to head to Rose Hill Farm. Bertha wasn't the kind of woman you could just walk up to and start asking personal questions. She could just imagine the way Bertha would stare her down, until Lainey's mind would go blank and she would forget why she was there. Like it did only fifteen minutes ago, when she turned and found herself face-to-face with her in the bakery.

Still, there were things only Bertha could tell her. It was the reason she was in Stoney Ridge in the first place.

Lainey had a plan. She was on her way to attend the Culinary Institute of America in upstate New York—she had scrimped and saved every penny for tuition since she was eighteen. She finally had enough money, was accepted, and was eager for her new life to begin. The school term didn't start until September, but she wanted to find a place to live and get settled. She thought she could pick up a waitress job to tide her over. Lainey liked planning her future. It was a trick she had learned years ago. Making plans gave her great comfort; she always felt better with a plan in place—like she had some control over her life.

Two weeks ago, Lainey packed up everything she owned and said a teary goodbye to her two best friends, Robin and Ally. She was going to make a quick pass through Stoney Ridge on her way to New York. At least, it was going to be a quick stop until her eleven-year-old VW Beetle sputtered to its death in front of The Sweet Tooth and she went inside to borrow the phone. Apparently, the bakery owner had just put up a sign for help wanted and assumed Lainey had come in to apply.

"Can you bake?" the owner, Mrs. Stroot, asked.

"Once I won first prize at the county fair for my cherry tart," Lainey said truthfully. She was just about to explain that she only came in to make a phone call, when Mrs. Stroot cut her off and gave a decided nod.

"You're hired," Mrs. Stroot said. "I'm desperate. My best girl quit this morning and my other best girl is out with bunion surgery. I'm busier than a one-armed wallpaper hanger. Here's an apron and there's the kitchen."

Lainey tried, several times, to inject that she wasn't going to be in town very long, but Mrs. Stroot was more of a talker than a listener. She pointed to a building across the street as she dialed the phone. "See that brick building across the street? The landlord happens to be my very own sister—" she held a finger in the air when someone answered the phone—"Ellie? I found you a boarder for that room you got available. What's that? Turn your telly down." She rolled her eyes at Lainey and whispered, "She doesn't appreciate being interrupted during *General Hospital*." Ellie must have said something because Mrs. Stroot's attention riveted back to the phone. "A lady boarder. Uh-huh, uh-huh." She covered the mouthpiece. "Do you smoke?"

Lainey shook her head.

"No, Ellie. She doesn't smoke." Mrs. Stroot covered the mouthpiece again. "Any pets?"

Lainey shook her head again.

"Weekly or monthly?"

"Weekly," Lainey said. "Definitely weekly. I don't plan to be here long, you see . . ." She gave up. Mrs. Stroot wasn't listening. She was asking her sister for today's update on *General Hospital*.

Lainey had to admit that God had a funny way of answering her prayers. As she set out on her road trip to New York, she had prayed that God would direct her path while she drove through Stoney Ridge. She wanted to visit only one person—Bertha Riehl. Here she was, just a few hours later, and she was employed—even though she wasn't looking for a job. And it happened to be doing the one thing in the world that Lainey loved to do: bake.

Less than ten minutes after arriving in Stoney Ridge, Lainey had a place to live and a job to bring in some cash so she wouldn't have to dig into her culinary school tuition money. Her car, the mechanic said, was a lost cause. She thought that was God's idea of a joke. He directed her path all right. To a dead stop.

The house was painfully quiet. Jonah glanced at the clock in the kitchen and counted forward an hour. Bess would be in Stoney Ridge by now, probably at Rose Hill Farm. There were hundreds of reminders of his daughter throughout the house, more than he had ever been conscious of. Dozens of images of Bess at different ages rolled through his mind: taking her first wobbly steps as a toddler, dashing to the mailbox each afternoon to meet the mailman, running barefoot from house to barn and back to house.

Taking a sip of coffee from his mug, he lifted the pages on the calendar hanging by the window and counted off. Just twelve weeks to go and she'd be back.

He wondered how Bess and his mother would be getting along. He hoped Bess would let him know just how sick his mother was. He felt worried about her, and that was a new feeling for him. In the letter, his mother said she was pining for her granddaughter and off her feed. It troubled him, that letter. It wasn't like his mother to pine. Or to be off her feed. She had a mighty appetite. He never remembered her ailing, not once, not even with a head cold.

He sighed. Something wasn't adding up. Either his mother's health was truly a concern or . . . she was up to something.

Just then, Jonah saw his neighbor and particular friend, Sallie Stutzman, coming up the drive with a casserole dish in her arms. He set down the coffee cup and went to see what Sallie had in that dish. It had been only a few hours since Bess had left, and he was already tired of his own cooking. And he was lonely.

Bess was a quick learner. After one buggy ride with her grandmother, she had already figured that she should hold tight to the edge of the seat so she wouldn't slide off and land on the buggy floor when Mammi took the curves. Her grandmother drove through those country roads like a teenage boy, the buggy leaning precariously to the side. She made a tight right turn and, suddenly, there it was: Rose Hill Farm.

The farm sat in a gentle valley surrounded by rolling hills, with fields fed by a secluded, spring-fed pond. The farmhouse—a rambling house with white clapboard siding and a brick foundation—was even prettier than Bess remembered. Three years ago, when she was here for her grandfather's funeral, she remembered being impressed by the neatness of the fields, the trimmed hedges, and the cherry trees that bordered the drive. It was the same today. Her grandmother may be ancient, but she had kept up the farm in good condition, that was plain to see.

A perfume wafted past Bess, and her eyes traveled to the fields that surrounded the house: acres and acres of blooming roses in what used to be pastures. The roses were at their peak. Pinks and reds and yellows and oranges blurred together to create a collage of color. Bess remembered that her grandmother had written awhile back that she had started a small business selling rose petal jams and jellies. But *this*—this was more than a small business.

Mammi stopped the horse under a shade tree next to a hitching rail. "We'd best get to work."

Oh no. Bess clutched her forehead. "On my first day here?"

Mammi lifted a sparse eyebrow. "Es hot sich noch niemand dodschafft." *Nobody ever worked to death.*

Boomer let out an ear-busting woof and leaped out of the buggy to run to the fields. Mammi hopped out of the buggy and reached a large hand to pull Bess forward by the arm. She stopped dead and aimed a stern look at Bess. "A little work might put a little muscle on them bones."

There were moments, like this one, when Bess thought it would be simpler to be English. On the bus this morning, a little girl wanted her mother to give her a snack, and when her mother refused she broke down and bawled. That's just what Bess would like to do right now, break down and bawl. Of course, she couldn't.

But oh! she was hot and tired from the bus trip and frustrated at what she had just figured out. She came to Stoney Ridge on a mission of mercy for her ailing grandmother, and the truth was that she was nothing more than another pair of hands—to pick roses. For an entire summer! Her father was right. Her grandmother was sneaky. Bess wished she had just stayed home and worked with her father on their farm. She missed him terribly. Far more than she had expected she would.

Bess heard Boomer bark again and she looked to see why the dog was causing such a ruckus. Boomer was standing on his hind legs, licking the face of a boy—or was it a young man?—and ended up knocking off his straw hat.

"That's Billy Lapp," Mammi said. "He's my hired help."

The boy pushed Boomer off of him and reached down to pat the dog's big head. Then he bent down and picked up his straw hat, knocking it on his knee a few times to shake off the dirt. Billy Lapp looked to be about seventeen or eighteen years old. Man-sized. When he stood and his eyes met hers, Bess felt her heart give a simple thump. Clearly Amish by his clothes and haircut, he was tall, broad-shouldered, with curly brown hair and roguish eyes rimmed with dark eyebrows. Hands down, he was the best-looking boy Bess had ever laid eyes on. Her heart was beating so strangely now, she thought she might fall down and faint.

Things were looking up.

2

By the time Bess woke the next morning, she could hear Mammi banging pots and pans down in the kitchen. She dressed fast, already worried by yesterday's hints that her grandmother thought she had a lazy streak. She flew down the stairs expecting to encounter a hands-on-the-hips disapproving frown, but Mammi stood in front of the range at her usual place, on gray-speckled linoleum that was worn to the floorboards. With her thumb, she pointed to the table, already set with two places. Bess slipped into her chair and Mammi slid a belly-busting breakfast in front of her.

"How do you like your eggs poached?"

"Is there more than one kind of poached egg?" Bess asked.

"Runny, soft, or hard?"

Bess looked startled. "My yolks always end up hard."

Her grandmother flipped an egg timer. "Three minutes for runny, four for soft, five for hard."

"Dad and I poach eggs for fifteen minutes."

Mammi snorted. "A yolk like that could double for a rubber ball."

Bess grinned. Blackie had done just that with a yolk, patting it around on the ground with his paws. Her father had suggested Blackie be included in a game of kickball after church one Sunday.

Where was Blackie, anyway? He had disappeared the moment he was let out of that hamper and caught full sight of Boomer, head to tail. Mammi told her not to worry, that Blackie would find a place to live in the barn.

Bess was horrified. She tried to explain that Blackie was a house cat and Mammi only scoffed. "Animals belong outside." Boomer apparently didn't qualify as an animal, because he had followed Mammi right into the house and stayed by her side like a shadow.

They bowed their heads and then dug into the meal. They ate in silence for a long while until Mammi asked, "What's your father got growing in his fields right now?"

Bess cracked the poached egg with her spoon and pulled off the shell in pieces. "He's leased out the fields to a neighbor."

Mammi broke up her egg over a piece of toast so that the yellow yolk oozed over it. "He's not farming?"

Bess looked up, surprised. "Well, his bad back made it too hard for him. So last year he started a furniture-making business and it's done well. He has orders piled up for months." Bess poured molasses into her oatmeal. She would have thought Mammi would have known such a thing. She seemed to know everything, often before it happened. But her grandmother was stunned to silence, a silence so thick that Bess could hear a wasp buzzing on the windowsill.

Mammi remained deep in thought. "It wonders me. To think of my Jonah without a farm to tend." She took off her spectacles and polished them. Then she reached into her apron pocket and pulled out a handkerchief to blow her nose. A loud honk that rattled the windows. "Allergies," she muttered, but Bess couldn't be fooled that easily. It shocked her, finding a tender spot in her grandmother. Mammi quickly recovered. She handed Bess a jar of pale pink jam. "Put that on your toast."

Bess spread some on it and took a bite. Her eyes went wide. "Oh Mammi. Oh my. Oh my goodness. Is this your rose petal jam?"

"It is," Mammi said. "It's the food of angels, if they have a choice."

Bess took more jam from the jar and spread it all over her toast, right to the edges. She took a large bite and chewed thoughtfully. It was the most delicate, delicious flavor she had ever tasted.

Mammi tried to hide a smile at Bess's rapturous expression with a swallow of coffee. "So what else is your dad doing?"

"Not much," she said, reaching for a spoonful of jam. "Well, except . . . he's given some thought lately to getting married again."

Mammi raised an eyebrow. "About time."

She shrugged. "You know Dad. He acts like a sheep that spooks and runs off at the slightest mention of marriage. He says it's because his heart belonged only to my mother."

Mammi nodded.

Bess took a bite of toast. She took another bite, chewed, and swallowed, then frowned. "But there's a neighbor lady who's wearing down his matrimonial resistance." She hoped the glum note didn't sound in her voice.

"En grossi Fraa un en grossi Scheier sin kem Mann ken Schaade." *A big wife and a big barn will do a man no harm.*

Bess shrugged. "It's not that. I want Dad to find a wife . . ."

She felt Mammi staring at her, hard. "What's wrong with her?"

"Oh, nothing. She's . . . real cheerful. And talkative. Cheerful and talkative." *Professionally cheerful.*

Mammi raised an eyebrow. "Our Jonah is a catch."

Bess knew that. Her dad was a fine-looking man. Even her friends said so. And he was young, only thirty-five. He was well thought of in their community, by men and women alike, and nearly every single female in their district—plus two neighboring districts—had set their cap for him. Cookies and pies, invitations to dinners and picnics, one father even boldly hinted to Jonah that his dairy farm would be passed down to his only daughter if Jonah married her. But Jonah never took the bait.

Until now.

That was half the reason Bess decided to come to Stoney Ridge this summer. Her father was spending time with Sallie Stutzman, a man-hungry widow with twin six-year-old boys—and the whole notion turned Bess's stomach inside out. Sallie had a heart of gold, everyone said so, but her very presence set Bess's teeth on edge. It wasn't that there was anything wrong with Sallie, other than the fact that she never stopped talking. *Not ever.* She even talked to herself if no one was around to listen.

Bess had a hope that her father would fall in love again, and she just didn't think he was in love with Sallie. That didn't seem to be a worry for Sallie, though. Bess saw how she was weaving her way into her dad's life. She asked him for rides to church and frolics, so often that other people assumed they were a couple since they always arrived together. Sallie stopped by every day with a casserole or cake or pie. The everydayness of it all was what made the difference between Sallie and other persistent female suitors. Even Bess found herself counting on Sallie's fine cooking. Sallie usually dropped broad hints about how it would be so much easier to cook for Jonah and Bess in their own kitchen. About how their new cookstove was so much more reliable than her old temperamental one.

Her father always paled a little when Sallie dropped those hints. Sallie kept at it, though. Bess overheard her point out to her father that every girl needed a mother, and poor Bess—poor Bess, she always called her, as if it was one word—had gone without one far too long. She needed a mother's love before it was too late.

And what could her father say to that? Sallie's dogged determination was causing her father to weaken. Just last week, he asked Bess what she would think about having a little brother or two around the house.

The truth of the matter was that Bess thought it would be a terrible idea. Sallie's twins weren't like most Plain boys. Sallie's twins were as tricky as a box of monkeys. Their idea of fun was spreading Vaseline on Bess's toilet seat. But to her father, she only said, "Well, now, that's certainly something that needs serious thought." *Long and hard.*

Her father grew pensive at her response. And that was the moment when Bess decided to come to Stoney Ridge for the summer. She may not be able to stop a marriage with Sallie from happening, but she didn't want to watch it happen.

Bess suddenly realized that Mammi's gaze was fixed on her, and she was sure her grandmother could read the dark thoughts that were darting through her mind. Her cheeks grew warm and she looked out the window. Billy was coming up the drive and gave a wave to them before he disappeared into the barn.

Mammi smacked her palms down on the table. "We got us some roses to tend." She was on her feet now, making short work of the dishes.

Not ten minutes later, they joined Billy out in the rose fields. Mammi repeated the rose petal–picking instructions she had given out yesterday. Bess didn't interrupt her to say she understood; after all, her grandmother was older than the hills.

"The best time is in the late morning, after the dew has dried and before the strong afternoon sun." Gently, Mammi held a large pink rose with the tips of her fingers and pulled it off the base. "Trim the white sections with scissors—this will save you time." She quickly snipped the white part off of each petal and then let them shower into the basket by her feet. "Next, cut the stem to the next five leaves. That's where the next bud will form."

It amazed Bess to see Mammi's chapped, man-sized hands handling the roses like they were made of spun sugar. Her own hands looked like a child's next to her grandmother's. And she was embarrassed by how soft her hands were. As careful as she tried to be, thorns kept pricking her. Within fifteen minutes, her hands were covered in cuts and scratches. And how her back ached, bent doubled over!

When they had harvested a large basketful, Mammi gave a nod to Bess to come along, and they went to the barn. Boomer trotted behind, never more than a few feet away from Mammi. Inside, Bess stopped abruptly when she noticed that the cow stanchions and horse stalls were empty. There were no animals other than Frieda, the buggy horse. She had been so distracted by the sight of Billy Lapp yesterday that she hadn't even gone into the barn.

"What happened to the animals?" The last time she was here, this barn had been filled with horses, mules, cows, and even two ugly sows.

"Couldn't take care of them without my Samuel, so I sold them at auction," Mammi said matter-of-factly. "I buy milk from a neighbor. Still have my ladies, though." She meant her hens. She loved those chickens and called each one by name. She slid the door shut behind Bess. In the center of the barn were rows of sawhorses with screen doors laid on top. "This is how we dry the petals. Lay 'em out so they can air dry. No overlaps or else they'll mold. They need to get as crisp as cornflakes."

"Why don't you just put them out in the sun to dry?" Bess asked. "That's what we do with apricots and peaches. Apples, even."

"No. I keep them in the barn and out of direct sunlight."

"Have you ever thought about drying them in a warm oven?" Bess asked. "Once when it rained all summer, Dad put sliced up fruit in the oven to finish drying." She felt pleased with her suggestion. Maybe that was one way she could be helpful to her grandmother this summer: by pointing out ways to improve the farm. Being fifteen, Bess had some pretty good ideas about modernizing, and her grandmother had lived here since Noah's ark reached Mt. Ararat. She could use Bess's help with such things. *Like indoor plumbing.*

Mammi cast her a look as if she might be addle-brained. "Might work for fruit but not for my roses. You'll lose oil. Lose oil and you'll lose fragrance." She straightened and pressed a hand against the small of her back. "Go bring me another basketful." She handed the empty basket back to Bess. "Be quick about it. We can't pick flowers in the afternoon. It's gonna be hotter than hinges today."

Bess took the basket and went out to join Billy in the fields. Yesterday, he had left soon after she arrived so she hadn't had time to get acquainted with him. Mammi said he usually only worked a few hours a day, then needed to get home to tend to his father's farm. Bess was looking forward to getting to know Billy. She followed behind him as he worked. He culled roses from the right row of bushes, she from the left. She could see he was concentrating on the work. He kept peering at the roses as if he was learning something from them. She racked her brains for an interesting thing to say, but nothing bubbled up to the surface. Finally, Billy stopped for a moment to gaze at a golden eagle flying overhead and seemed surprised to discover she was there.

"So, Bess, where are you from?" he asked.

"Berlin, Ohio."

Billy went back to examining roses, so Bess hastened to add, "Some folks think it's Ber-Lin, like the place in Germany. But it's really pronounced Burrr-lin. Folks changed the way they pronounced it during World War I, so it would seem less German." She could tell Billy wasn't really listening. Silence fell again. She tried to come up with a topic that would create conversation. Something that would make him notice her and realize she was bright, intelligent, deep. Nothing came to mind.

He stopped at a bush and examined a few blossoms, then started picking them. "You sure don't look anything like your grandmother."

That was a good thing, in her mind. Mammi must be nearly six feet tall and half as wide.

He eyed her bright blue dress. "Is it different in Ohio? Being Amish?"

"What do you mean?" She shrugged one shoulder. "Amish is Amish."

He snorted. "That's like saying roses are roses." He put a hand on his lower back and stretched, looking out at the wide variety of blooms. "What color is your buggy?"

"Black." So maybe there were differences. Lancaster buggies had gray tops.

"Some folks think Ohio churches are more worldly than ours." He shook the basket so the petals spread out. "Can you ride bicycles?"

"Yes."

"Telephones?"

"Only in the barn."

"You drive a car?"

"Gosh, no." Billy looked so disappointed that she added, "Once I drove a neighbor's tractor, though. And I take a bus to the public school."

He whipped his head up. "You go to public school?"

"High school." Bess had just sailed through ninth grade and was in shooting distance of high school in Berlin. All that stood in the way was that dreaded algebra class. That was the other half of the reason she changed her mind about spending the summer at Mammi's. On the day she took her final exam for algebra, she decided Stoney Ridge didn't sound so bad, after all. And if she hurried about it, she could leave Berlin before report cards would be mailed home, which suited her just fine. That way, she wasn't being deceitful. She didn't know for sure that she had failed the class. She had a pretty good idea that she did, but until that report card arrived, there was a slight hope she had squeaked by. And had she failed, well, if she were in Pennsylvania, then she couldn't possibly attend summer school in Ohio.

She searched for something—anything—to pique Billy's interest. "My dad got arrested for letting me skip school," she blurted out. Then she clapped her hand against her mouth. Why in the world did she say *that*?

Billy spun around to look straight at her.

Oh my! but he was fine looking. Those dark brown eyes nearly undid her. She felt her cheeks grow warm. "Last September, Dad said I didn't have to go to school anymore. Kids in the county right next to ours had stopped going the spring before and no one bothered them, so a few families in our district decided to quit too. But it didn't work. The truant officer came knocking on the door and took Dad to the county jail."

"What happened then?"

"He was fined and let go. And now I have to go until I'm sixteen. Ohio law." Her dad wasn't going to mess with the law anymore, he'd said more than once when she tried to convince him to let her stay home. "I can't imagine stopping school at the eighth grade." She couldn't imagine it, but she sure would enjoy it. She had often thought she had about all the education she could absorb. Especially math.

A look came over Billy's face, as if he thought she might be a very dense child. "What makes you think an education has to stop?"

That was a new thought for Bess. She gave his backside a sharp look. A book stuck out of his back pocket. She never thought it any fun to be bothering about books when you didn't have to. "My teachers say you need a formal education to get ahead in the world." Now, why did she say that? Why did her mouth not seem to be connected to her brain today?

Billy took his time answering. He pulled a few more rose blooms, snipped the petals, and tossed them in the basket. Then he lifted his chin and looked at her. "I guess it all depends on which world."

They picked blossoms in silence for a long while. When the basket was full of rose petals, he picked it up and leaned it against his hip. "Have you followed the Wisconsin trial?"

"No."

He shook his head as if she had just arrived from the moon. "*Wisconsin vs. Yoder*. It's a big court case going on in Wisconsin right now. Might bring about changes for us."

She hated to seem ignorant, but curiosity won out over pride. "What sort of changes?"

"It's possible that we won't have to attend public schools. That we could have our own schools right in our districts. Schools that would stop at eighth grade."

Such a thought made Bess's heart sing with gladness. She . . . would . . . be . . . done . . . with . . . algebra!

He handed her the basket to take into the barn. She broke into a skip on the way there, so thrilled by the news of *Wisconsin vs. Yoder*.

Billy and Bess picked rose petals for a few more hours. The sun had already begun to punish them when Billy said it was time to quit.

"I'll be on my way," Billy told Mammi as he handed her the last basket. He put his straw hat back on. "But I'll be over tomorrow morning, first thing."

He nodded goodbye and tipped his hat slightly in Bess's direction, which made her knees feel weak. The boys in Berlin would never dream of tipping their hats to a girl.

Mammi watched him go and said to no one in particular, "He's a good one, that boy."

Bess wanted to ask Mammi more about Billy Lapp, but then she thought better of it. Mammi saved herself a lot of bother by not being the kind of person who answered nosy questions.

Mammi closed the sliding door of the barn to keep it cooler inside. "After lunch," she said, "we got us an errand to do."

A few hours later, Bess hurried to keep up behind Mammi as she breezed through the Veterans Hospital in Lebanon. On the bus ride there, Mammi told her they were going to pay a visit to her brother, Simon, who was seriously ailing. Bess had heard terrifying stories about Simon, bits and pieces of his life woven together from tales her cousins whispered to her at her grandfather's funeral. She knew he was Mammi's only brother, was the youngest in the family, had always been a black sheep, and—worst of all—that he had been shunned.

But Simon was nothing like Bess expected.

She had prepared herself for a hulking brute of a man, with eyes narrowed into slits and teeth sharpened into points and horns sprouted on his head. A monster.

Instead, before her was a tired, pale-skinned old man who looked as if he was weary of living and ready to die.

Bess and Mammi stood by Simon's bedside in the ward, trying to determine if he was awake or asleep. Bess had a fleeting thought that he might have passed.

She looked at her grandmother and whispered, "Should I get a nurse?"

Mammi ignored her and leaned over him. "Wake up, Simon!" she boomed, and the room echoed.

Simon's eyes flew open. "Oh Lordy. It's the town do-gooder." He glanced at the basket Mammi held in her hands. "Did you bring your jam?"

"I did," Mammi said.

"Homemade bread?"

"It's in there." She put the basket on his bedside table. "You always did take better care of your belly than your soul."

Simon squinted at Bess. "Who's that?"

"That's Bess," Mammi answered. She eased her big self into a hard-backed plastic chair.

"Jonah—your nephew—he's my father," Bess filled in. She shifted her weight awkwardly from foot to foot while standing at the end of the bed. There wasn't any other chair to sit in. "So I guess that makes you my great uncle."

Simon's eyes opened wide, full of mockery, as he looked Bess over. "Another holy howler." He looked at her long and hard with cold blue eyes.

She'd never seen eyes so cold. There was a touch of meanness in his thin smile. Bess felt a bead of sweat run down the valley between her shoulder blades.

Mammi was watching her. "Bess, en rauher Glotz nemmt'n rauher Keidel." *A rough log requires a rough wedge.* "Never forget that."

How could Bess remember it when she couldn't even understand it? Bess looked at her, confused, but Mammi had turned her attention back to her brother.

"Simon, you never did know beans from honey," Mammi said. "If you could put two and two together, you'd figure out by now that Bess is a relation."

"So?" Simon asked.

"So mebbe she'd be willing to get a blood test and see if she can help you out. Mebbe her bone marrow could be a match for you."

Bess's eyes went wide as quarters.

"If she's willing, that is," Mammi repeated, avoiding Bess's eyes.

The ride home on the bus was a silent one.

Mammi had been told by the nurse that since Bess was underage, the hospital required a parent's consent before her blood could be tested. Mammi hadn't expected that, Bess could tell. But Bess was thoroughly relieved. It wasn't easy to say no to Mammi, and yet she wasn't at all sure she wanted to have her blood tested. The blood test was pretty simple, she knew that, but what if she were a match? Giving blood was one thing. Bone marrow was entirely different. She wasn't even sure what that meant and didn't want to ask. Her only experience with bone marrow was to cook up a pot of soup and simmer the bones for a good long while. Besides, even if Simon was her great uncle, he was not a nice man. He was downright mean-hearted. Maybe it all worked out just fine, Bess decided happily. Since she was only fifteen and her father was in Ohio—with no intention to come to Pennsylvania—there was no possible way she could have a blood test. Bess looked out the window and smiled. Things had a way of working out.

"Bess," Mammi asked, one sparse eyebrow raised, "have you ever driven a car?"

Bess shook her head. "Just a tractor."

Mammi gave up a rare smile. "Same thing. When we get back to Stoney Ridge, we got us another errand to do."

Lainey O'Toole reread the letter she had written to her friends one more time before licking the envelope and sealing it shut. She had written and rewritten this letter during her break today until it sounded just right.

Dear Robin and Ally,

A moment of silence, please, for the passing of my Beetle. It sputtered to a stop in a little town called Stoney Ridge, but it didn't die in vain. It took its final breath in front of a bakery called The Sweet Tooth just as the owner put out a help wanted sign. I kid you not! One thing led to another and . . . well, instead of hunting for a temporary job in upstate New York, circumstances dictate that I am going to spend the summer here. But do not worry! It is just a short-term turn of events.

Love you tons and miss you more,
Lainey

P.S. Did I ever mention that my mother and I had lived in Stoney Ridge until I turned ten?

Satisfied, Lainey dropped the envelope into the mailbox before she crossed the street to head to her little rented room.

When the bus dropped Bess and Mammi off in Stoney Ridge, Mammi told her to keep up as she made her way through the streets. Finally, her grandmother found what she was looking for. She made a beeline straight to the sheriff's car, parked by the hardware store.

Mammi peered in the open window of the sheriff's car and saw the keys dangling in the ignition. She turned to Bess. "Come on, big talker. Show me what you know."

Bess's jaw dropped open. "Mammi, you don't mean . . ."

"I do." Mammi got into the passenger seat. "Sheriff won't mind a bit. We're good friends. I've known that boy since he was in diapers."

"Still . . ." Her father was forever warning her to avoid stepping into moral mud puddles, and here she was jumping headfirst into one of his mother's own making!

Mammi reached over and pushed open the driver's side door. Cautiously, Bess slipped in.

She glanced at her grandmother with a worried look. "Seems like there are rules . . ."

Mammi turned to give Bess one of her surprised looks. "Es is en schlechdi Ruhl as net zqwee Wege schafft. *It's a bad rule that doesn't work both ways.* "Never forget that." She looked straight ahead. "Let's go."

Bess sighed and prayed God would understand. She turned the ignition and the car roared to life. She opened her mouth to try once more to talk her grandmother out of this notion, but Mammi only pointed down the road. "That way."

As if Bess was driving a car made of eggshells, she shifted the gear, took her foot off the brake, and the car lurched forward. This wasn't at all like driving a tractor in an open field. She was terrified she would hit something or somebody. She drove so slowly that a few shopkeepers came outside and stared at the sight of two Plain women inching a police car down the street.

"That'll do," Mammi said after one block. "Park it over there." She pointed to the curb.

Bess pulled over and shifted the gear to park. The car lurched to a halt and the engine died. She exhaled with relief. She knew she could start the car, but she wasn't quite sure about stopping it. Her grandmother's eyes were on the rearview mirror. On her face was another of those rare smiles. Running up the road was the portly sheriff, waving his fists in the air. Mammi opened the door and climbed out of the car, prepared to meet the sheriff head-on. Bess slowly stepped out, wondering how many years a car thief would spend in prison.

The sheriff slowed to a jog and reached them, panting heavily. "Miz Riehl! What the Sam Hill were you thinking?"

"Hello there, Johnny," Mammi said, friendly as anything. "Have you met my granddaughter?"

Still panting, the sheriff looked Bess up and down without a smile.

Bess stood there, nearly dying of shame.

The sheriff hooked his hands on his hips. "*Why* would you take my police car?"

Mammi looked unusually innocent. "Bess here is visiting from Ohio. She's driven a tractor before. We just got to wondering—"

We? Bess wondered.

"—if it seemed like the same thing . . . driving a car or driving a tractor. I don't know too many folks with cars. So I figured you wouldn't mind if we borrowed yours."

"Borrowed the car? Miz Riehl, what you did was to steal a police officer's car! That's larceny! I could have you arrested."

Mammi nodded agreeably. "So be it." She stretched out her hands so that he could handcuff her.

The sheriff looked down at her fists thrust in front of him, then looked up at her, bewildered. "Miz Riehl, I'm *not* going to throw a widder lady into the pokey."

"The law is the law," Mammi said. "But I get one phone call."

"Miz Riehl, I just don't want you moving my patrol car."

"Stealing," Mammi said. "You called it stealing."

The sheriff sighed, exasperated. "Seeing as how it was recovered and no harm was done, I'll just give you a warning this time." He got in the car, closed the door, and stuck his head out the window, jutting his round chin in Bess's direction. "I've got my eye on you, young lady. You should know I got E.S.P. Extrasensory perception. I see things before they happen." He glared at her. "I don't know what kinds of trouble Amish teens get into in Ohio, but you can't get away with those shenanigans in Stoney Ridge." He looked disgusted and shook his head. "Hoodwinking a sweet little old lady into taking a joyride. You oughta be ashamed."

Bess's eyes went wide with disbelief. *Mammi? A sweet little old lady?*

Mammi frowned. Then she marched through town and down the road that led to Rose Hill Farm. Bess hurried to keep up with her, wondering what in the world her grandmother was up to and how she could ever explain this to her father.

3

Dear Dad,

Mammi and I are getting along fine, just fine. She seems to be fully recovered from her female surgery. I didn't realize that pulling a tooth or two would be considered female surgery, but she said it definitely falls under that category. And one thing I'm learning about her, it's best to just agree.

 Did you know Mammi's rose business is taking over Daadi's pasture land? Those roses of hers—they're something else. In full bloom! Lots and lots of rose blossoms. To handpick and hand trim. Each and every day. My hands have been pricked by so many thorns they look like a pin cushion.

    Love,
    Bess

Jonah was rubbing a final coat of stain on a picnic table ordered by Mrs. Petersheim. She was one of his best customers, and he had promised to deliver the table for a family reunion she had planned this weekend. The humidity was working against him and the stain wasn't absorbing like it should. He put down the rag and opened the workshop door to let the breeze in. It had been a hot June. Even after thirteen years, he still wasn't quite used to the extremes of Ohio weather. Hotter in the summer than Pennsylvania and colder in the winter. He stood by the door, looking out over the fields of oats planted by his neighbor. It still ate at him, to not be able to work his fields anymore. He missed farming. Like his father, he had always marked his year by his growing crops. He planted alfalfa on the day after the new moon. Then oats and clover went in. Corn in April, when the sap was rising in the maple trees. The seasons turned like a wheel.

It used to give him great satisfaction to see crops growing in the fields, as if he was part of something bigger. But he didn't have the physical capability to farm anymore. He had tried to keep up for years now, but it was too much for him. He wasn't the same man he was before the accident. The doctor warned him he would end up in a wheelchair if he kept asking too much from his back. "Jonah," the doctor said, "if I were you, I would consider that limp a small price to pay for still being alive."

A small price to pay? What about losing the only woman you've ever loved? What about trying to raise a child alone? What about the fact that his daughter never knew her mother?

He had worked so hard to honor Rebecca's memory and raise Bess the way she would have wanted her raised. He created a new life for himself and Bess, and the Lord had blessed his efforts. When he finally decided to lease the fields and try his hand at furniture making, the business took off. So much so that he had taken on a partner, Mose Weaver. Mose was a lifelong bachelor, an older, quiet man who spoke with a lisp when he talked, which was seldom. Most knew Mose was silent as a tomb, a man of deep thoughts, none of them revealed. Some thought that was because he had no thoughts at all, but Jonah knew better. Mose lived with his parents, worked hard, and wanted for little. He was a fine business partner for Jonah. There was more than enough work for both of them.

Jonah had no complaints about his life. But with Bess gone this summer, and with the painful awareness that she was growing up, he knew that things were going to be changing soon. He never did like change.

And what would life look like after Bess was raised? Sallie was forever pointing that out, as if he didn't wonder about it himself.

Jonah wiped the sweat off the back of his neck. Sallie had been making loud suggestions lately about getting married. He was fond of Sallie, but the thought of getting married made his throat tighten up. There had been a time, four or five years ago, when Jonah had tried to find a new mother for Bess, but his heart wasn't in it. He wanted to love again the way he had loved Rebecca.

Sallie had different ideas about marriage. She had been a widow for less than a year and was already moving on with her life, eager to marry again. That was one thing he admired about her. She didn't hold on to the past. Just last night, she had told him that she never expected a second marriage to be like the first. "There's no feeling like that first love, when you're young and carefree and life seems filled with possibilities," she said. "But that doesn't mean that a real good friendship isn't a fine start for a marriage."

Sallie thought his ideas of marriage were unrealistic. And she should know—she'd been married twice before.

Her boys needed a father, she had told him frankly, and his Bess needed a mother. It made perfect sense, she said.

He picked up the rag and dipped it in the can of stain, ready to finish up that table for Mrs. Petersheim. Maybe Sallie was right.

The Sunday after Bess arrived in Stoney Ridge was an off-Sunday, so no church would be held. Earlier this morning, a chicken—whose pet name was Delilah—lost its head when Mammi had picked it out specially and wrung its neck off. It happened so fast that Bess felt woozy. Mammi was feeding her ladies by tossing cracked corn on the ground, making little clucking sounds at them. Suddenly, she reached down and picked up a chicken by the neck and spun it over her head, snapping its neck. Within seconds she had it on a tree stump. After plucking off the feathers and saving them in her pillow bag, Mammi dipped those chicken parts in buttermilk and bread crumbs, fried it, whipped up biscuits to mop up the gravy, added snap beans and sliced tomatoes from the garden. Bess was sure she'd never seen a chicken go from the yard to the table so quickly. It was record time.

Mammi asked her to set the table and get it all ready for Sunday dinner, so Bess took out three servings of utensils.

Without looking up from the fry pan, Mammi said, "Make it for four."

"Why four?" Bess asked.

"You never know," Mammi answered with an air of mystery. She tucked in a wisp of gray hair that escaped her cap. In English she added, "Mebbe I got extra-century perception like the sheriff."

So Bess set the table for four. What was the point of asking?

Jonah loved this time of year. On the way to pick up Sallie and her boys for church on Sunday morning, he passed by a neighbor's house and saw the straight rows of crops in the fields, tended lovingly. He loved summer best of all. The first fruits of summer gardens would be making an appearance for lunch after meeting: deep red beefsteak tomatoes, sliced thick; cucumber salad; a pyramid of pickled peaches; bowls of luscious, plump strawberries. Yes, this was a good time of year.

He was especially looking forward to meeting today. It had been nearly a week since Bess had left, and he was starting to talk to himself just like Sallie did, he was *that* hungry for company. He felt a familiar warm feeling spread over him as he pulled into Noah Miller's yard: dozens of buggies were lined up, shoulder to shoulder, like pigs at a feeding trough.

After meeting, the men and boys ate first at the set-up tables, then cleared out of the way so the women could eat. A softball game had been started by the big boys and Jonah watched for a while. He noticed Sallie's twins were sent off to the outfield to catch fly balls. They had been pestering the big boys until they were finally given a job to do and could be out of harm's way.

Jonah walked over to join Mose, standing with a few other men under the shade of a large oak tree. Jonah half listened to the men's grave analysis about the weather they'd been having. Too little rain, they worried, a drought in the making. But then, farmers always worried about the weather. He could hear the murmur of women's voices—including Sallie's laugh, for she was always laughing—through the open kitchen window, along with the clinking of plates and forks, the thumping of bowls and platters onto the tabletops to be taken home.

Young Levi Miller sidled up to him, kicking at the ground. Levi was an awkward boy, but he adored Bess, and for that, Jonah admired him. "Any word?" Levi asked in a low voice. He began to blush, a bright red trickling its way up from his collar to the middle of his ears. They were sizable ears. They stood straight out at the side of his head.

Jonah smiled. "Nothing yet. But I'm sure she's having a good summer."

Levi was crestfallen. "All summer? Bess is going to be there all summer?"

Jonah felt the same way.

Mose placed his large and gentle hand on Levi's shoulder and steered him to the softball game. He helped Levi find a spot in line to have a turn at the bat, then he jogged to the outfield to help Sallie's boys field balls.

Without a car, Lainey O'Toole had no option but to walk the entire way to Bertha Riehl's farmhouse. In her arms was a pink box—a lattice-topped gooseberry pie she had made last night at the bakery. She knew the way to Rose Hill Farm as if she'd been there yesterday. As she turned onto Stone-leaf Road, she slowed her pace and turned down the dirt lane that led to the cottage where she had lived with her mother and her stepfather. The cottage was set back from the road. When she saw it, her heart slowed and pounded. It had been fifteen years since she laid eyes on it. She squared her shoulders and approached the cottage. Her throat felt tight and a weight settled on her chest. She looked up at the worn clapboards, without a speck of paint, the rusted gutters, broken windows covered with nailed boards. It was even shabbier close up than it looked from the road. Like nobody cared.

She stopped for a moment and took her time looking. When she was little, she had tried to imagine it was pretty, but now she saw that it had always been just a poor man's house, with crooked shutters and a sagging front porch. The porch roof had a vicious slant to it, as if a strong burst of wind might carry it away. An old grape arbor, overgrown like everything else, sat at the end of a broken flagstone path. A crow shrieked in the distance and a few more answered back by telling it off. A mother deer and her baby were grazing under a tree and lifted their heads at the same time, startled to see someone in the yard. They froze, their stiff forelegs splayed out to the sides like stilts. They inspected Lainey with their black-tipped ears, worried she might be a threat. Then finally, deeming her harmless, they looked away and resumed grazing. Otherwise, the place looked lifeless.

She walked up on the front porch and tested the door handle. It wasn't locked, but she didn't go in. It was hard to even imagine walking through the door, so she stepped back and peered in the windows. There was nothing to see there, just an old, forgotten cottage, yet she had the strangest feeling about it. Like she was home.

She stepped off the porch onto the walkway and nearly tripped on a fallen-over For Sale sign. She tried to set it upright, then made her way through the weeds, back to the road that led to the Riehls' farmhouse.

Lainey smiled when she saw the old hand-painted sign hanging on Rose Hill Farm's mailbox: "ROSES FOR SALE. NO SUNDAY SALES." She'd forgotten all about that sign. It had always seemed odd to folks that a woman like Bertha Riehl—as tough as old boots—grew delicate roses to sell. Samuel Riehl was the tenderhearted one, most folks presumed. But Lainey knew better. Bertha Riehl might be tough on the outside, but she was as soft as a marshmallow on the inside.

She walked slowly past the leafed-out cherry trees that lined the long drive, mesmerized by the sight of endless rosebushes in full bloom. Those roses were the most glorious sight she had ever seen in her life. She felt sure that the path to the Pearly Gates of Heaven couldn't be any more inviting than the one leading up to Rose Hill Farm.

Lainey saw Bertha first. She was shaking out a wet dishrag to dry on the kitchen porch railing. Lainey stopped at the bottom of the porch steps and looked up at the big woman, wearing a shapeless plum-colored dress with a black apron stretched around her vast girth. "I've never seen such beauty, this side of heaven. It's like . . . God is showing off a little." She looked out toward the barn. "You've added so many roses. Doesn't your husband object to your converting his pastures to roses?"

"Samuel passed three years ago come October the tenth," Bertha said in a matter-of-fact voice. "I couldn't keep up the farm, but I could do one thing."

Lainey smiled. "Grow roses."

"That's right. And now I'm selling jam made from my mother's rugosas over there." She pointed to shrubs of pink, multiflowered roses.

"I remember those rugosas," Lainey said. "I remember your jam."

Bertha nodded. "I keep adding more and more stock. Filling the pastures with roses. I got a hired boy who has a knack for grafting roses, so he started grafting those rugosas onto heartier root stock." She nodded in the direction of a small greenhouse next to the barn. "Folks come from all over to buy my rosebushes and now they're after my jam and tea."

Lainey nodded. "Mrs. Stroot is hoping I'll talk you into selling some at The Sweet Tooth. She wants me to find out what you'd say to a barter arrangement."

"Such as?" Bertha lifted an eyebrow. She was interested, Lainey could see.

"Maybe you could have your pick of things from the bakery—like a credit—in exchange for letting her sell the jam and tea."

Bertha sized that up for a long moment. "Tell Dottie Stroot I'll think it over."

Lainey felt pleased. She had expected a flat-out no.

Bertha eyed the pink bakery box in Lainey's hands. "What's in there?"

"Gooseberry pie. Your favorite, if I remember right."

"You do." Bertha turned to go back to the house and Lainey took that as an invitation to follow.

Lainey was surprised to see the same young girl standing in the kitchen who had come with Bertha into the bakery the other day. Today she was steeping teabags in a blue speckled pitcher. "You're Bess, aren't you?" she asked. "Have you been working for Bertha for a long time?"

"Just this week, but it seems like forever and a day," Bess said. She held up a hand covered with Band-Aids. "She's wearing me to a frazzle."

Bertha looked unimpressed. "The poor child hardly knows a tea rose from a China rose."

Bess hooted. "But you're giving me a crash course on all things roses." She took out some glasses, filled them with ice, and set them on the counter, next to the pitcher. "Help yourself to the sugar. I like sweet tea, myself." She pointed to the sugar bowl.

"Too much sugar will make your teeth fall out like a picket fence," Bertha said. "I never have it, myself."

"Except for every day," Bess muttered.

"Mebbe just a little on Sundays," Bertha said, spooning heaps of sugar into her glass.

Lainey noticed Bess rolling her eyes and had to bite her lip to keep from smiling. When she first met Bess at the bakery, she thought she had seemed frightened of Bertha. Today, though, she was clearly at ease, gently teasing and joking with her. Lainey could tell Bertha enjoyed Bess's company too, though she would probably never say so. Bess was like a filly, all legs and arms. Watching Bess reminded Lainey of herself at that age, when she had grown several inches in one year and became awkward and clumsy, as if she couldn't get used to the new dimensions of her body.

Bess was pouring Bertha a second glass of iced tea when the kitchen door opened and in walked a very good-looking young man, straw hat in hand. He looked curiously at Lainey, then his gaze turned to Bertha. "Am I late?"

"Right on time," Bertha answered. "The very pineapple of punctuation." And with that, the glass slipped out of Bess's hand, shattered on the floor, and spilled tea everywhere.

Billy knelt down and began to carefully pick up broken glass. Lainey and Bess grabbed dishtowels to mop up the tea.

"Being barefooted, I ought not to help," Bertha said, sprawled in her chair, the picture of ease. "But I don't mind having a floor mopped clean, now that Bess's cat has moved in."

Lainey hadn't seen any sign of a cat, just a big dog sleeping in the corner and a rooster standing guard just outside the kitchen door.

As soon as the broken glass was picked up and the tea wiped clean, they sat down to dinner. The chicken was delicious, but Lainey had little appetite for it. Too nervous. She needed to have a talk with Bertha. How could she bring up anything private with Bess and Billy here? Bess, Lainey noticed, never gave up another word once Billy arrived. Lainey caught her studying Billy, aware of his every word and movement. Lainey fought back a smile. She was glad she wasn't fifteen anymore. Billy and Bertha seemed to be completely unaware of Lainey's anxiety or Bess's discomfort. They ate everything but the pattern on the plate.

Billy concentrated on his food until the subject of grafting roses was brought up, then he didn't stop talking. "Some rose varieties put on a lot of top growth and few roots, which makes them liable to be weak-wooded and short-lived," he said to Lainey with professorial patience, as if she had asked. "But we can graft that rose onto a better taproot so that it puts down a good deal of roots. Doing that makes a rose plant liable to be long-lived, grow better and bigger blooms, and be more resistant to stresses and strains, like a hard freeze."

"Where'd you learn how to graft roses, Billy?" Lainey asked when he finally stopped talking long enough to fill his mouth with roast chicken.

He shrugged and looked over at Bertha. "She told me if I could figure out how to graft, I could have a job. So I went to the library and read up on it and gave it a whirl." He spooned the rest of the pickled peaches onto his plate and looked around the table to see if there was anything left to polish off.

"Gave it a whirl?" Lainey asked in disbelief. "Why, I've heard people go to college to learn how to graft plants!"

"His mother was a Zook," Bertha said, as if that explained everything.

Billy looked embarrassed but pleased. "Roses aren't difficult to graft because they're compatible with nearly all other roses."

When Bertha served the gooseberry pie, silence fell over the table. Lainey started to worry that something was wrong until Billy looked up and said, "This is the best pie I've ever had. Better even than yours, Bertha, if you'll pardon me for saying so."

"Pardon accepted," Bertha said, helping herself to a second slice. "You're right. This pie is unparalyzed."

Bess's spoon froze, midair. She looked at Bertha, confused. Lainey swallowed a smile. Only Billy took it in stride, as if accustomed to Bertha's way of twisting English words around.

"I taught Lainey how to make a flaky pastry shell when she could barely reach over the counter," Bertha said.

Now it was Billy's turn to be surprised. He looked at Lainey, curious.

"It's true," Lainey said. "I used to live nearby. Bertha would let me come visit and help her in the kitchen. She taught me how to bake. Once she could get that black iron range fired up, she could do some serious cooking."

"Still can," Bertha said between bites.

They wolfed down the pie so quickly that Lainey knew it was good. Just as Billy had his eye on another helping, a horse nickered from the barn. Lainey looked out the window. A horse and buggy had turned into the drive, and Bertha's horse knew company was coming. Lainey had forgotten how horses always seemed to know things that people didn't.

Billy jumped up from the table. "That'll be my cousin, Maggie. She was coming by to get me for a youth gathering at the Smuckers' this afternoon."

"Good," Bertha said. "It will give Bess a chance to meet some other young folk."

Billy froze. A look of mild panic lit his eyes. He spoke hesitantly. "She seems awful young for a gathering—"

"I'm nearly sixteen!" Bess said indignantly.

Billy looked unconvinced.

Bertha waved that concern away. "Die Yunge kenne aa alt waerre." *The young may grow old too.*

That only confused Billy.

"Besides, your Maggie Zook is only twelve or thirteen and she's welcome," Bertha said.

"But . . . it's Maggie! You know Maggie. She's thirteen going on thirty. Besides, she's the bishop's daughter. Who's going to tell her she can't go?"

As Bess saw Billy's hesitation, her face clouded over. Bravely, she lifted her chin. "Actually, I had plans of my own this afternoon."

"Like what?" Bertha asked.

Bess looked around the kitchen until her eyes rested on a jar of homemade jam. "You were going to show me how to make rose petal jam."

"Can't," Bertha said. "It's Sunday."

Billy still looked uncomfortable. He scratched the top of his head. "She really shouldn't . . ."

"Sure she should," Bertha said, clamping her granite jaw. "Besides, Lainey and I got us some visiting to do." She shot him a deeply dangerous look.

Defeated, Billy slumped to the wall, plucked his hat from the peg, and held the door open for Bess. She grabbed her bonnet and brushed past him, head held high.

Lainey went to the window to watch them drive off in Maggie's buggy. When they were out of sight, she turned to Bertha, who was still seated at the table, halfway through a third slab of pie.

Lainey sat back down at the table. "There's something I'd like to tell you."

Bertha picked up the blue speckled pitcher and refilled their glasses. Then she added three teaspoons of sugar into her glass and stirred. "What's that?"

"I've never thanked you for helping me like you did, years ago. You always made me feel welcome in your home, and you took an interest in me and helped me and my mother out. It's thanks to you that I'm a Christian today."

Bertha picked a loose thread from her apron front.

Lainey could have been talking about the weather. She tried again. "Bess is a lovely companion for you."

"She's a nervous little thing. Jumpy as a dog with fleas. But time will fix that."

Then quiet fell again. How could Lainey shift this conversation in the right direction without making Bertha suspicious? A stray thought fluttered through her mind, something she hadn't noticed before. She cocked her head. "When Bess left just now, she called you Mammi."

"So she did." Bertha took a sip from her glass.

"Isn't that the Deitsch word for grandmother? I . . . thought she was your hired girl."

Bertha snorted. "Not hired. Doubt I'd hire her—she oozes away like a barn cat when there are chores to be done." She looked straight at Lainey. "But she is my girl. My only grandchild."

Lainey was confused. "I thought Jonah and Rebecca and their daughter were in Ohio."

Bertha smoothed her skirt and pulled in her lips. "Rebecca died in that buggy accident, long ago."

"Oh no," Lainey said. That news was a shock to her. "I'm so sorry. I didn't . . . I thought she had survived it." She stood and went to the window, then turned to Bertha, confused. "So Jonah remarried?"

Bertha shook her head. "Not yet. Far as I know."

"Are you . . . ?" Lainey's voice cracked and she had to start over. "You can't mean that Bess is Jonah's daughter? That girl with the blond hair?"

Bertha nodded. "Bald as an egg until she was two years old."

Understanding flooded through Lainey and she felt her face grow warm as blood rushed to her head. She sat down in the chair to steady herself. "I never knew her name," she said in a faraway voice. "I knew Rebecca had her baby, but I never knew the baby's name. It was the same week my mother died . . ." The words got stuck in her throat and she couldn't continue.

Bertha leaned back in her chair and crossed her arms over her chest. "Jonah and Rebecca's baby was named Bess, so that's what he called this little girl." She took a deep breath. "That's what he called the little baby girl you switched on us, Lainey. Fifteen years ago."

Lainey felt as if her heart was pounding so loudly that Bertha must be able to hear it. She looked down at her lap and saw that her hands were trembling. It was such a hot day, but she was suddenly cold. For a brief second, the room started to spin and she thought she might faint. "How long . . . ?" Her voice drizzled off.

"How long have I known?" Bertha leaned forward, cool as custard, to take a sip of iced tea. "From the moment I arrived at the hospital, after the accident." She smoothed out the oilcloth on the table. "Think I wouldn't know my own grandbaby? And Mrs. Hertz told me—told the whole town—about your baby sister's passing and you getting shipped off to a foster home. Wasn't beyond my apprehension to put two and two together."

Lainey chanced a look at Bertha. "Samuel knew too?"

For the first time, Bertha seemed mildly distressed. She slipped off her spectacles and polished them. Then she blew her nose, loud. "That rain we had last night was hard on my sciences."

Lainey frowned. "Your what?"

"My sciences." She gave her nose a honk.

"I think you mean your sinuses."

Bertha huffed a small laugh. "That's what I said." She stuffed her handkerchief in her apron pocket.

Lainey tried again. "Did Samuel know?"

Bertha took her time answering. "No. The very week Rebecca had her baby, Samuel's brother in Somerset was laid up in the hospital for a bleeding ulcer. Samuel went to go help finish up spring planting on his brother's farm. He hadn't laid eyes on his own granddaughter yet. But he came back as soon as I sent word about the accident."

Lainey felt the words lock in her throat. "Why . . . why didn't you ever tell?"

"When Jonah found out that Rebecca had died, it was like the light had gone out of him. His back was broke to smithereens."

Lainey's eyes went round as quarters. "He's paralyzed?"

"No. His spiney cord wasn't hurt, but his lower back was broke. He had to learn to walk all over again. Knowing Bess needed him was all that kept him going."

Lainey stared at Bertha for a long time. She rubbed her forehead. "Are you saying that Jonah doesn't know?"

Bertha shook her head and looked away. "You know how fast babies change and grow. By the time Jonah was able to see her and hold her, she was already holding her head up and rolling over." She sighed. "But Jonah never knew. I planned to tell him. I meant to. But there never seemed to be a good time. And then weeks and months turned into years."

Lainey closed her eyes and squeezed her fists tight. She should have realized! She should have known! The color of Bess's hair—white blond—and those turquoise eyes. Simon's hair color. Simon's eyes. She looked at Bertha. "So . . . Bess . . . is my half sister?"

As Bertha nodded, a single tear fell on Lainey's cheek, followed by another and another, until she couldn't hold them back anymore. She covered her face with her hands and wept.

When Bertha Riehl invited Billy for Sunday lunch, even then, he felt a pang of unease. He should have known that she would have something up her sleeve. She had a reputation for doing the unexpected. He had been working for her for over two years now, and she had never once invited him for Sunday dinner . . . until today. Normally, he got a kick out of Bertha's unpredictable methods of getting what she wanted. But he had never been the object of her finagling. He liked working for her. She paid him well, and he knew she needed his help around Rose Hill Farm. But now he was stuck babysitting her granddaughter for the rest of the afternoon—a girl who acted as nervous as a cottontail and had a hard time stringing more than two words together that made any sense. He found younger girls to be tiresome: they giggled a lot and refused to take anything seriously.

A horrible thought darted through his mind. He hoped Bertha wasn't trying her hand at matchmaking. He was real fond of Bertha, even if she was crafty, and he didn't want to lose this job. It was more than a job to him. It was his future. This was what he wanted to do with his life. He could never work up much enthusiasm pushing a plow behind a team of mules, but this—experimenting to create a better plant—this felt like something he was born to do. He studied books about roses, he wrote away to experts and asked their opinions, and he kept precise records—something Bertha had no interest in. It was a sin to be prideful and he was careful not to indulge in it, but it did please him when folks said they drove long distances to buy rose stock from Rose Hill Farm. Last week, an English lady came all the way from Pittsburgh because someone at Penn State told her this was the only place to buy a rose that smelled like one grown a hundred years ago. "The hybrids might be the rage," the lady told Billy, "but they have no fragrance. But these roses"—she scanned the fields—"you can tell they're grown with passion."

How his father and older brothers would laugh at that comment. They thought his ideas were nonsense, so he stopped doing experiments and bringing his horticulture books home from the library. But his mother had understood. She and Bertha had been good friends and neighbors. His mother must have told Bertha the kinds of things Billy liked to learn about, because at his mother's funeral, she asked him to come work at Rose Hill Farm.

But as much as he liked and admired Bertha Riehl, as much passion as he felt for the roses, he knew he would never be passionate about this skinny girl sitting on the buggy seat next to his cousin Maggie. He guessed Bess could hardly weigh ninety-nine pounds soaking wet. She had an unnaturally scrubbed look, like she'd been dipped in a bottle of bleach and came out with ultra blond hair and white eyelashes. And that anxious-to-please expression on her face made him nervous.

He was glad his cousin was with them. Maggie could talk to a brick wall and never notice it wasn't answering back. At least he was off the hook from trying to come up with any more painful attempts at conversation, like he had to do—just out of politeness—when Bess was out helping him pick roses.

Still, the least he could do was to be nice, for Bertha's sake, so he took the long way to the Smuckers to show Bess his favorite spot on earth, Blue Lake Pond. A little jewel of a pond with pine trees that lined the shores. It was deserted, just as he expected. That was another thing he loved about this lake. He stopped the horse, hopped down, and tied its reins to a tree branch. He took a few steps and then stopped to wave to the girls. "Well, come on."

"Not me. I'm going to stay here," Maggie said, pushing her glasses up on the bridge of her nose. "I don't want to get my shoes dirty."

"Suit yourself," he said. "What about you, Bess? Every visitor to Stoney Ridge needs to get acquainted with Blue Lake Pond."

Thrown that small morsel of encouragement, Bess leaped off the buggy and trotted behind Billy.

Down by the shoreline, he put his hands on his hips and inhaled deeply. "This is the best lake in the county. In all of Pennsylvania. I spend every free hour on these shores—swimming in the summer, skating in the winter. Fishing in between." He picked up a rock and skimmed it across the pond. He gave Bess a sideways glance. "Me and my friend Andy go skinny-dipping here every summer." He paused for her reaction.

Bess's eyes went wide and her cheeks flamed scarlet.

Billy grinned.

Clearly mortified, Bess turned away from him and walked along the shore. Billy kept skimming rocks. After a while, she stopped to look up in the treetops. "It's the quietest place in the world."

"Sure is. Quiet and peaceful."

"I didn't mean it that way. I meant it in a strange way."

He tilted his head. "What's so strange about a quiet lake?"

"There are no birds singing."

He searched the skies and the trees. "Huh. You're right." He shrugged. "Maybe it's the time of day."

She walked further along the shoreline. "You'd think there'd be some sign of wildlife. A loon or a duck or a goose. Even a crow or scrub jay." She looked all around. "Nothing."

Maggie hollered to them she wanted to get to the Smuckers' before the gathering was over, if they wouldn't mind, so they turned around to walk back to the buggy. Before Billy left the shoreline, though, he shielded his eyes from the sun and scanned the lake. He saw plenty of dragonflies skating over the surface of the pond, but he was looking for some sign or sound of a bird in the trees or skies. Not one.

Billy disappeared to join his friends the minute they hitched the horse at the Smuckers', but Maggie stuck to Bess like glue. She reminded Bess of a pixie, small and dark, with eyes darting here and there, forever watchful. She could talk a person to death. Bess didn't mind at all; she'd grown accustomed to half listening after being around Sallie Stutzman so much. As they walked around the yard and watched some boys pegging out a game of horseshoes, Maggie pointed out names and gave Bess the full rundown on each person. Bess nodded, vaguely interested, but she kept one eye on Billy the entire time.

Someone tapped Bess on the shoulder. "*Who* are you staring at?"

Bess whirled around to face a tall, shapely girl with sandy-blond hair and dark brown eyes. If it weren't for the fact that she was glowering at Bess, she could even be called attractive.

Maggie intervened. She hooked her arm through Bess's and pulled her along. "I should have warned you about Esther Swartzentruber. She set her sights on Billy awhile back and hasn't let go. Well, most every girl has her sights on Billy, but Esther is the only one bold enough to tell everyone. She watches him like a hawk." She looked back at Esther who was scowling at both of them. "With you here, Bess, I think it's going to be a real fun summer. Esther thinks she's got all the boys pining for her, but look at how they're sizing you up like a hog at auction."

Bess was absolutely sure no boy was looking at her, but such a loyal remark earned Maggie a spot in her heart.

Right at that moment, a buggy wheeled into the driveway and pulled to a stop. Out poured four girls. It was the fourth girl who caught Bess's eye. Actually, it was Billy's reaction to Girl #4 that she noticed. He stopped playing horseshoes and walked over to greet Girl #4, lingering over her. But who wouldn't? She was *that* pretty.

Maggie leaned over and whispered, "That's Betsy Mast. Every boy in Lancaster County is wild over her."

A wave of pure jealousy came over Bess, shaming her. She said nothing. She was afraid it might show in her voice.

"How could they not be?" Maggie continued. "Look at her big eyes and gigantic pouty lips. Her chest looks like the prow of a ship! I call her Busty Mast. Have you ever seen such enormous—" She clasped her hand over her mouth. "Oh, I *shouldn't* have said that! Jorie—she's my stepmom—she's always telling me to think before I speak. But my mouth does run away from me."

Bess looked down at her own flat chest and up again at Betsy Mast. She sighed.

"Fellows sure do seem to love the prows of ships. They're always talking about them." Maggie spoke in a wise, mature woman-of-the-world voice and patted Bess's shoulder. "I know these things." She gave a sly grin. "I have a gift for eavesdropping."

For the rest of the afternoon, Billy hovered around Betsy like a bee around a flower.

For hours, listening to crickets in the thick, muggy silence, Lainey lay in bed and stared at the ceiling. Bess was her sister. *Bess was her sister!* She still couldn't believe it. She never dreamed she would see her again. Her thoughts bounced back to that terrible night, when she made a snap decision that altered lives. She had made a bold promise to her mother, who lay dying just two weeks before, that she would take care of her baby sister, Colleen. But within a few days, Lainey was overwhelmed and exhausted. And sad. Terribly sad. She missed her mother. She had found a small amount of cash tucked in the back of her mother's dresser drawer, but that was disappearing quickly after buying two weeks of baby formula. By now, she had been sure Simon would have returned. She was starting to panic.

When she heard the screech of tires and the horse whinnying and then that horrible crashing sound, she grabbed her baby sister out of the cradle and ran outside to see what had happened. The buggy had flipped to its side. She bolted over to it and her heart lurched with recognition—Rebecca and Jonah Riehl. She called their names, but they didn't respond. They both looked pale and still. Rebecca was bleeding from her ear.

The truck driver who had hit the buggy climbed out of his cab. He walked up to Lainey in shock. "I didn't see them! It was so dark and I was trying to pass . . ." He looked as if he expected her to tell him what to do next.

Lainey took a deep breath. "Go down the street until you come to the intersection. Find the gas station and call for an ambulance."

The man just stood there, looking at the horse trying frantically to get up, panting heavily. Its leg was twisted grotesquely. Then the man looked at the buggy, at the bodies in it, as if he couldn't believe his eyes.

"Go!" Lainey shouted, pointing her small finger down the road.

The man backed up, staggering, then started to run down the road.

Lainey heard a sound and turned to Rebecca, whose eyes opened halfway. "Mein Boppli," Rebecca whispered. "Meine Dochder." *My baby. My daughter.*

Lainey looked around and found a small bundle, thrown from the buggy. She hurried to the bundle and felt her stomach reel. The baby looked nearly identical to her own baby sister—same size, bald like Colleen, the same wide blue eyes. The face was unmarked, but the baby's chest appeared to have caved in. Her eyes were wide open, showing no signs of life. There was no breath. She didn't blink at all, even when Lainey touched her cheek. She put her hand on the baby's tiny chest but couldn't find any heartbeat. She had seen enough of farm life to know that this baby was dead. She heard the horse whimper in pain and shock—she would never forget that sorrowful sound as long as she lived—and she looked back at the buggy, at Jonah and Rebecca, and then down at the dead baby. Nausea rose in her throat and she coughed, retching. There weren't many times she wished Simon were home, but she wanted him here now, to help her. She was frightened, so frightened, and didn't know what to do next.

Lainey heard Rebecca call out. How could she tell Rebecca that her baby was dead? Slowly, she walked back to the buggy and saw Rebecca's eyes flicker open again. Impulsively, hoping to give Rebecca comfort, she tucked Colleen into her arms. "She's here, Rebecca," Lainey lied. "She's just fine."

Rebecca's eyes tried to open, but Lainey could see she was fading. "Denki," she murmured. *Thank you.*

Lainey hoped that truck driver could figure out where the gas station was. She stayed by the buggy, telling Rebecca and Jonah to hold on, that help was coming. When she heard an ambulance siren in the distance, she exhaled with relief. As she reached down to pick up Colleen, she had a heart-thudding moment. Her infant sister looked up at her with wide blue eyes, oddly serene and peaceful despite this gruesome scene.

A plan took shape in Lainey's ten-year-old mind.

She saw the red flash of the ambulance's siren as it turned onto the street. Then she kissed her sister goodbye and picked up Rebecca's baby before running into the house. She spent the next hour by the window, shaking like a leaf, watching the ambulance workers and the police. She tucked Rebecca's dead baby in her sister's cradle and curled up in the corner of the old brown couch that smelled like mold. When she heard a single gunshot ring out— knowing the policeman had to put down the horse—she threw up again.

She didn't sleep at all that night. As soon as dawn broke, she walked down the road to tell her nearest neighbor, Mrs. Hertz, that her baby sister had died in the night, peaceful as can be, in her sleep. Surely God would punish her for all of these lies she was telling. Surely somebody was going to figure out what she had done. But all Mrs. Hertz said was, "God was merciful, Lainey. He knew no child should have to endure Simon Troyer as a father." She grabbed Lainey into her generous-sized bosom for a hug. "I never did understand why your sweet mama ever married that poor excuse for a man, anyhows."

They both knew the answer. A single mother, poor as a church mouse, didn't have a whole lot of choices in 1957.

Mrs. Hertz made one call to the county coroner and the next one to a county social worker. A bead of sweat trickled down Lainey's neck when the coroner arrived. She was petrified he might ask questions about the baby's death, but he just came and took the baby away, like he did two weeks before when her mother passed. She figured the coroner didn't concern himself with poor folks like them. In fact, he acted as disinterested as Simon had the night Lainey's mother lay dying. The day after his wife was buried, Simon told Lainey to take care of the baby and he went off deer hunting, though that couldn't be right because it wasn't hunting season. But maybe he *was* deer hunting. Rules were always optional for Simon.

As the coroner left, the social worker arrived. She took one look at Lainey's living conditions, at the absence of any adult in the home, and whisked her off to a foster home. When Simon didn't appear at the court date to claim Lainey, she became a ward of the state of Pennsylvania. She lived in three different foster homes until she was eighteen. After graduating from high school, she was on her own. She worked for a department store in Harrisburg and saved her money. She had a plan. Her two friends, Robin and Ally, gave her a hard time for being so serious and saving every penny, but Lainey knew what could happen to girls without goals and dreams. Her mother had warned her. She wanted a different life for herself.

All the while, Lainey had never forgotten her baby sister. Giving Colleen up was the hardest, best thing Lainey had ever done. Not a day went by when she didn't wonder a dozen questions about her sister—what did she look like? was she happy?—but she didn't feel plagued with guilt about whether it was the right thing to do. She couldn't think of a better life for a child than to grow up Amish. And now God in his mercy was giving her a chance to see that her sister had a childhood just as she had hoped for her: happy and loved.

Lainey gave up trying to sleep and went to the window to open it wider. The room she had rented from Mrs. Stroot's sister faced west and was hot and stuffy by evening. She sat on the sill for a while, looking up at a sliver of the new moon. Her feelings felt jumbled. She had come to Stoney Ridge to try to find out information from Bertha about how her sister was doing, but she never planned to reveal her secret. She never wanted to upset her sister's life.

Today, that noble intention turned upside down.

Bertha said she was going to tell Bess and Jonah the truth this summer. It was high time. Bertha said when she saw Lainey in town a few weeks ago, she decided she would do all she could to get Bess out here as soon as she could. Now the time was right, she said. Maybe not today, but soon.

At least Bess would be here all summer. And so would Lainey.

Lainey's thoughts bounced to Jonah. Bertha didn't offer up much information about him—typical of her—but she did say that Bess was his only family. Lainey was sorry to hear that Rebecca hadn't survived the accident. Rebecca had always been kind to Lainey. It gave Lainey comfort to think she might have given her peace in those last moments, laying Colleen in her arms. She remembered Rebecca had been a beauty—small and delicate. It was plain to see how much she and Jonah loved each other. She had thought they were the luckiest two people on earth . . . until the accident.

As she thought about all Bertha had told her today, she found it hard to believe. But life could be like that, she had learned. A single decision, a moment in time, and the ground could shift beneath your feet.

4

When Bess came into the kitchen the next morning, Mammi was pouring batter on the waffle iron while the coffee perked. Mammi had finally relented to Bess's pleading and allowed her to drink coffee, as long as it was half milk. Peering out the window, Bess noticed Billy was already out in the fields among the roses. Unlike other mornings, she wasn't in any hurry to join him. She picked up her fork as Mammi brought her a waffle, then put it down as Mammi sat down and bowed her head. Mammi's prayers were never short.

When Mammi lifted her head, she said matter-of-factly, "You got in awful late."

Bess poured syrup over her waffle. "By nine. You were asleep in the rocker. I didn't know if I should wake you to outen the lights." She had decided against it when she realized that her grandmother had taken out her false teeth. The sight made Bess shudder. Mammi's mouth had looked like a shrunken apple.

"I never sleep."

Bess rolled her eyes.

"Did you have a good time?"

Bess nodded, distracted, and chewed slowly.

"Then why are you sitting there with a face as long as a wet week?"

Bess rested her chin on her propped-up hand. "I'm all at sea."

"What's making you so mixed up?"

"Do you know a girl named Betsy Mast?"

Mammi raised an eyebrow at Bess, then her gaze shifted through the window to Billy in the fields, bent over a blooming rose. "Es schlackt net allemol ei as es dunnert." *Lightning doesn't strike every time it thunders.*

"I'm not so sure, Mammi. You know boys." Bess sighed dramatically and took a sip of her coffee-laced milk.

Mammi nodded. "Boys are trouble. But girls is worse." She started filling up the sink with soapy water.

Bess gave up a smile, in spite of her grim mood.

One sure way of surviving heartache was to stay busy, Mammi told her, and shooed her out to join Billy by the roses. Bess picked up a basket on the porch and slowly went out to the field.

Last night, with her chin propped on the windowsill watching the moon rise, she had given her runaway feelings about Billy some serious thought. She'd barely known him a week. Now was the time to reel her heart back in, before she found herself falling off the edge of no return—the way Billy's face looked when he caught sight of Betsy Mast.

So that's the way things were going to be. She thought she had found the man of her dreams . . . but it was only an illusion. A tragic illusion. She sat in the moonlight and shed a tear or two. It didn't take much to set her off, now that she was fifteen. Her feelings were as tender and easily bruised as a ripe summer peach. Even Blackie, her cat, had declared his independence and had taken up barn living. She shed a tear for Blackie too. She missed her father, missed her home and her own bed. She even might miss Sallie and her boys a little. *No, scratch that.* But she did regret ever coming to Stoney Ridge. Even summer school looked more appealing than being stuck here, picking roses near a beautiful boy who hardly noticed her. She sighed, deeply grieved, and climbed back into bed, sure she would never sleep. She turned over once, and it was morning.

As Bess walked out to the roses, she decided that she would avoid Billy as much as possible, picking roses in rows far from him. She bent down to examine a blossom.

"Hey, what are you doing way over there?" Billy called out to her.

She bounced back up.

He picked up his basket and joined her in the row she was working on, making her heart turn in somersaults. "You were right about birds missing from the lake. I went back later last night, to see if I could hear any owls hooting. Nothing. What do you make of that?"

What did she make of that? Looking into his dark eyes, she couldn't make sense of anything. She couldn't think of a single thing to say—she was that tongue-tied around him. He looked particularly fine today too, with his cheeks turning pink from the sun and his shirtsleeves rolled up on his forearms. The wind lifted his hair. He looked so handsome she wanted to reach out and stroke his cheek. Her spirits soared.

Billy Lapp wasn't making it easy for her to fall out of love with him.

Jonah walked out to the shop in his barn, reviewing the facts for the hundredth time. He had tossed and turned last night trying to figure it out. What exactly had happened last night to lead Sallie to the conclusion that they now had an Understanding? He had dropped her and her boys off after church, and she had invited him to stay for dinner. There was nothing different about that scenario. He and Bess had often taken Sunday suppers at Sallie's. He remembered saying that the house was awful quiet without Bess. Then, as he said good night, Sallie told him that she was just thrilled they had an Understanding. He was mystified. What had he said?

The morning was so warm that he opened up both doors in his workshop to have air circulate through. As he slid open the barn door, a thought seized him. Sallie was so . . . overly blessed . . . with the gift of conversation that he often found himself not really listening to her. Maybe he was asking himself the wrong question. Maybe the question wasn't what he had said. Maybe it was: what had he not said in reply?

When Lainey heard the bakery door jingle, she looked up, surprised to see Bess. Her blond hair was covered by a bandanna knotted at the nape of her neck, just below her hair bun. She wore a lavender dress under her white apron and she was barefooted.

"My grandmother has a craving for your cherry tarts and sent me down to get some," Bess said, peering into the bakery counter. She looked up, disappointed. "But they're all gone!"

The store was empty and Mrs. Stroot had gone home, so Lainey grabbed the chance to encourage Bess to stay. "I was just going to whip some up. What would you think about staying to help?"

Bess looked delighted. "I'd love to! Mammi is canning zucchini, and the kitchen is so hot that it's steaming the calendar right off the wall. One thing I've learned, if I don't make myself scarce, Mammi will find me some chores." She followed Lainey to the back of the bakery.

Lainey pointed Bess to the sink to wash her hands while she got out the flour and sugar and lard. She felt her heart pounding hard and tried to calm herself. It still seemed like a miracle to her, to think that her sister was right there beside her.

Mammi was waiting out on the porch, arms akimbo, when Bess drove up the drive to Rose Hill Farm. Bess felt a little nervous because she'd been much longer than she said she would.

"Where have you been?" Mammi asked when Bess pulled the buggy horse to a stop by the barn.

"Lainey taught me how to make cherry tarts!" Bess handed Mammi a big pink box before she got out of the buggy, which, she thought, was a smart move. "The bakery was empty and she was just about to make a fresh batch. So she asked if I could help and I thought you wouldn't mind, seeing as how you love them so much."

Mammi opened the box and looked over the tarts. "Well, as long as you were helping her and doing something useful." She took a bite out of a tart and closed her eyes, as if she were tasting heaven.

"Lainey didn't even let me pay for them. She said I earned my keep and she hoped I'd come back again. She said late in the day the bakery is usually empty and she could use my help." Bess hopped down from the buggy and started to unbuckle the tracings on the horse. "Would you mind if I go see Lainey at the bakery now and then? Dad would sure love it if I could bake something new. I told her you wouldn't mind. You don't, do you, Mammi?" She backed the buggy up from behind the horse and leaned it upright against the barn.

There was no answer, so Bess chanced a look at her grandmother. Mammi's mouth was too filled with another cherry tart to talk.

Three o'clock in the afternoon had become Lainey's favorite time of the day. For the past two weeks, like clockwork, Bess came through the door for another baking lesson. Normally, Mrs. Stroot closed the bakery at three, but when Bess started coming by at that time, Lainey asked if she would mind if the store stayed open a little longer. "I'm here anyway, getting ready for the next day," she told Mrs. Stroot, "and each afternoon we end up selling a few more baked goods. Better first-good than day-old prices."

Mrs. Stroot couldn't argue with logic that turned a profit, but she did say she needed to go home and start dinner for Mr. Stroot. Lainey promised her that she would lock up. So each afternoon, Bess drove Bertha's buggy to the bakery, parked the horse under the shade tree, and spent two hours with Lainey, baking and talking. More talking than baking.

Oh, the things she was discovering about Bess! She learned about Jonah and how he was going to marry his neighbor, Sallie Stutzman, who had twin boys no one could tell apart. And she learned about the boy at school who liked Bess overly much. "Levi Miller is nothing but a bother and a nuisance, Lainey. So . . . childish," Bess said, sounding so very adult. "But we're the only two Amish ninth graders at our public school, so he thinks we're destined for each other." And with that, Bess made a sour face.

There were also things about Bess that Lainey picked up without being told. Earlier in the week, Bess was in the middle of mixing cookie dough when she froze, eyes wide, as she stared out the window. Eventually, she turned back to the cookie dough, but sadness covered her like a blanket. Carefully, Lainey craned her neck to see what had caught Bess's eye out the window. It was that young fellow who worked for Bertha, Billy Lapp, carrying packages for a very attractive Amish girl.

"You're every bit as pretty as she is, Bess," Lainey said. She wasn't just saying that. Bess was going to be a beauty. She was unusual looking, with lovely cheekbones and skin like peaches and cream. And those eyes! They were extraordinary. When she wore a dress of a particular shade of blue, those eyes looked like the waters of a tropical island.

"No. I'm not," Bess said, sounding miserable. "It's hard on an ordinary moth when a beautiful butterfly comes around."

Lainey couldn't help but laugh. "Give yourself a little time. You just turned fifteen!"

Sadly, Bess said, "I don't have time. The summer is flying by."

Lainey's stomach gripped tight. She didn't want to think about that.

Bess looked up at her, a question on her face. "How did you know how old I am?"

And Lainey had no answer for her.

Over two weeks had passed since the Understanding, as Jonah came to think of it, had been formalized with Sallie. By Sallie. He still felt a little stunned, yet the idea of marrying again wasn't altogether unpleasant. It was starting to grow on him, the way Sallie sort of grew on a fellow. She was cheerful, that Sallie. And her boys certainly did need a father's influence. Sallie thought their antics were adorable, but most people ran the other way when they caught sight of those twins. Just the other day, they stripped Jonah's tree of apples and tossed them at passing cars. Mose caught them in the act and quietly took them home to Sallie. If Jonah had caught them, he would have wanted to tan their hides. Yes, those boys needed a father. And living alone this summer gave him a pretty good idea of what the future would hold for him once Bess was grown and gone. He hated it.

Over a month had passed since Lainey had arrived in Stoney Ridge. This July afternoon Bess came into The Sweet Tooth looking pale and worried, with arms crossed tightly in front of her as if she were shivering despite summer's muggy warmth. Lainey tried to teach her how to roll a pie crust, but she could see Bess couldn't concentrate. Bess kept rolling and rolling until the crust was so thin, it was nearly see-through.

Lainey quickly rolled it into a ball and put it in the refrigerator to chill. "You can't let pastry get warm. The shortening needs to be in layers when it bakes, not mixed in."

Bess looked as if the thought of ruining the pastry made her want to cry.

"Is something troubling you, Bess?" At first, Lainey was sure it had something to do with Billy Lapp. But then she had a horrible premonition that maybe Bertha had finally told her the truth.

"No. Yes." Bess's eyes met Lainey's, wide and sea blue. "I'm dying."

"What do you mean?"

"I'm bleeding to death."

Lainey looked her up and down. She didn't see any signs of hemorrhaging. "Where?"

Bess pointed to her stomach. "Here."

"Your stomach?"

Bess shook her head. She pointed lower.

"Oh," Lainey said. Then her eyes went wide as it dawned on her. "Oh!" She put her hands on Bess's shoulders. "Oh Bess, you're not dying. Hasn't anyone ever told you about getting the monthly visit from Flo?"

Bess looked at her, confused. "From who?"

Of course she hadn't been told! She had no mother. Her father certainly wouldn't discuss such a personal thing. Lainey went to the door and locked it, turning the closed sign over. She sat down and patted the chair next to her. "Let's have a talk."

Later that afternoon, as soon as Bess returned to Rose Hill Farm, Mammi showed her a black bonnet she had made for her.

"It's bigger than a coal scuttle!" Bess said miserably. "Mammi, are you trying to turn me into Lancaster Amish?" Her Ohio bonnet was much smaller.

"Nothing of the sort," Mammi said, tying the ribbons under Bess's chin.

Bess could hardly see from side to side. "I feel like a horse wearing blinders."

Mammi didn't pay any attention. "We got us another errand in town."

"Oh Mammi," Bess said, too worried to stir. She didn't think this day could get any worse, but it just had.

Sure enough, Mammi was on a mission to search out that poor sheriff's car. Mammi spotted the empty car out in front of the five-and-dime store and pulled the buggy over.

"Why? Why are you doing this?" Bess asked.

"I got my reasons."

"Then why don't you do the driving?"

"Can't," Mammi said. "I'd be put under the ban." She gave a sideways glance to Bess. "You're safe."

Bess sighed and got into the driver's side. Refusing Mammi anything never worked. She started up the car and drove down the road, a little faster this time—after all, she might as well enjoy this—until Mammi pointed to an empty parking spot and Bess pulled over.

Just like last time, the sheriff came running up the street, huffing and puffing. "Dadblast it, Miz Riehl! You did it again!"

"Did what?" Mammi asked, the very picture of surprise. She pushed open the passenger door and eased out of the car. Bess hopped out and stood beside her.

The sheriff's face turned purple-red. "Now, Miz Riehl, don't be like that."

Out of nowhere, Billy Lapp stepped in front of Mammi and Bess and made a patting gesture with both hands. "You'll have to excuse Bertha Riehl, Sheriff Kauffman. She's feeling her age these days." He made a clocklike motion around his ears with his hands. "I'll make sure these ladies get right on home so they don't cause any more trouble for you."

The sheriff turned to Billy with one hand on his gun holster. "You do that. And make sure that yellow-haired gal stops tempting her granny to a life of crime."

Mammi glared at Billy as he steered them by their elbows to the buggy. Billy tried to help her into the buggy, but she batted away his hand. "Feeling my age, am I?"

He rolled his eyes. "I was only trying to keep you out of jail. What were you thinking?" Mammi wouldn't answer, so he turned to Bess. "And just what do you think you're doing? Why would you ever drive off in a sheriff's car?" He reached out a hand to help her climb up in the buggy.

Still mindful of seeing Billy drive Betsy Mast in his courting buggy the other day, Bess shook his hand off her arm. "We have our reasons," she said huffily as she climbed into the buggy. As soon as they had left the main street, she turned to her grandmother. "Just what *are* our reasons?"

"Why, no reason at all," was all Mammi said, jutting out her big chin.

Later that week, Bess was in the barn, spreading rose petals. She took off her bandanna and wiped her forehead and neck. It was already hot and only nine in the morning. She opened the barn doors to get a crosswind and leaned against the doorjamb for a moment. She scanned the farm as she tied her bandanna in a knot at the nape of her neck. She saw Billy in the fields, Mammi in the kitchen. Hot breezes sighed in the cornfield across the road. A row of crows on the fence line told each other off. A woodpecker was hard at work somewhere high in a treetop. The morning was going on around them.

Suddenly she heard Billy holler like he'd seen a ghost. "Aphids! Bertha! We got aphids!"

The kitchen door blew open and Bertha stood there, arms akimbo. "Aphids?!" She marched out to the rose fields like a general to the front lines. She bent over the rose that Billy was working on, then looked around her. "Why, they're everywhere!"

From the look on her face, Mammi had just declared war on the aphids. She pointed at Billy. "Scoot uptown and bring me back Coca-Cola. Bring back as much as you can carry." She turned on Bess, who was walking over to see the aphid invasion up close. "Run in the kitchen and get five dollars from my special hiding place. You go with Billy to help him carry the soda pop."

By the time Bess figured out that Mammi's special hiding place for her money was an empty Folger's coffee tin—the same place her father kept his money—Billy had the horse harnessed to its traces and was waiting for her. She hurried to join him, delighted at the turn of events that gave her time alone with him. Usually, Mammi was within shouting distance and added her two cents to their conversation. Bess tried to think of something interesting to say, something witty and wise. Just last night, she had been working out a few imaginary conversations with Billy, just in case an opportunity like this—driving together in a buggy—presented itself. But now her mind was empty. She couldn't think of a single thing to say. They were getting close to the store when she blurted out, "Why Coca-Cola?"

"Kills aphids," Billy said without even glancing at her. And then he fell silent.

"What do you suppose it's doing to your belly?" Bess said quietly.

Billy turned to her, a surprised look on his face, before bursting out with a laugh. "Good point." He flashed a dazzling smile at her. His smile seemed as if he had never smiled for anyone else in the world.

Bess felt pleased. She had made Billy Lapp laugh.

Satisfied that the aphids were done in, Mammi spent the rest of the afternoon on another project. Instead of drying the rose petals from today's pickings, she said she was using them to make rose water. She filled a pot with clean rose petals. Then she poured boiling water over them and covered the pot with a lid. She turned off the heat and let the petals stand until they cooled.

Before bedtime, Bess helped Mammi strain the petals from the water. They ended up with the most beautifully colored liquid a person would ever see. The liquid would be kept in the cooler and used whenever they would bake something that called for rose water, and Mammi would sell it in small mason jars. "And we'll charge double at Dottie Stroot's," she told Bess.

Some nights, like tonight, it was so hot that Bess couldn't sleep. She threw off her sheets and went downstairs, finding her way by touch because it was so dark. She opened the back door and stepped into the yard. Boomer followed her out and disappeared into the shadows.

She stood still for a moment. Ohio summers were even hotter, lacking the fresh breeze that seemed to always come through Stoney Ridge. There was just a sliver of a moon and the night was not totally black. She could make out vague shapes: the henhouse, the barn, the greenhouse, the cherry trees.

Blackie slid out of nowhere and wove himself between her legs. Bess picked him up. "You're getting fat! You must be feasting on barn mice."

Blackie jumped down and oozed away, insulted.

She looked up at the velvety night sky, filled with star diamonds. It was a peaceful time. She still went back and forth about being there, but tonight she was glad to be here in Stoney Ridge with her grandmother.

She thought of the things she had already learned to do this summer: how to pick roses and get rid of aphids, how to dry rose petals to make tea and jam, how to make rose water. And how to make a fair profit. How to bake a cherry pie. Mammi told her that was just the beginning of things she needed to learn.

How much more learning can I take? she wondered as she rubbed her head.

Later that week, Mammi made one more valiant effort to steal the sheriff's car. Bess tried to talk her out of it all the way into Stoney Ridge, but Mammi went right on merrily ahead with her plan.

"But why, Mammi? You're going to give that sheriff a heart attack! Why would you want to kill the poor man?"

Mammi set her jaw in that stubborn way and wouldn't answer.

This time, as Bess coaxed the sheriff's car slowly onto the road, Mammi flipped a switch and the siren went on. In the rearview mirror, Bess saw the sheriff run out of the bank and into the road. She pulled the car over and hung her head. Her grandmother was certifiably crazy and she was the accomplice.

The sheriff opened the passenger door for Mammi and helped her out. "Miz Riehl, you are turning into a one-woman crime wave."

Mammi's eyes were circles of astonishment. Stoically, she stiffened her arms and offered her wrists to the sheriff for handcuffing. "Do what you must, Johnny."

Now a crowd started to gather. The sheriff paled. "Aw, Miz Riehl, don't make me do this."

"You are sworn to uphold the law." Mammi clucked her tongue. "Think of all them voters, watching their tax dollars at work. You can't be playing favorites."

"Dadblast it, Miz Riehl! If I didn't know better, I would say you are trying to get yourself thrown in the clink." His face was shading purple.

"Nothing of the sort! But I do get one phone call."

The sheriff narrowed his eyes and thought hard for a moment. "Get in the patrol car, Miz Riehl. You too, missy." He meant Bess.

Mammi slid into the back of the patrol car and patted on the seat beside her for Bess. Bess wanted to die, right there on the spot. But Mammi looked as content as a cat sitting in cream.

The sheriff drove them to his office and took them inside. He pointed to two chairs by his desk. "Can I get you two anything to drink?"

"Nothing for me," Mammi said politely, lowering herself into a chair, "but my Bess here would like a soda pop."

Bess didn't want a soda pop, the way her stomach was turning itself inside out. The sheriff went to the back of his office and brought back a warm Tab. He eased himself down into his chair and leaned back, lacing his fingers behind his head. "Now, Miz Riehl. Let's cut the cackle and come straight to the point. Who do you want to call?"

"Oh, I don't want to call anyone," Mammi said. She pointed at him. "But you can call someone."

The sheriff picked up the receiver. "What's the number?"

Mammi turned to Bess. "What's the phone number to Jonah's barn?"

Bess's jaw dropped open. "Oh no, Mammi, no! You can't tell Dad about us getting arrested! He'll be on the next bus to Stoney Ridge!"

Mammi pushed a few loose gray wisps of hair back into her prayer cap. "Do tell."

5

As Jonah hung up the phone on the wall of the workshop in his barn, he had to sit down. He couldn't believe what he had just heard from the sheriff. His mother and his daughter were in jail for stealing a police car. In jail! If he hadn't recognized the sheriff's voice, he would have even thought it might be a prank call. Bess had been in Stoney Ridge for only a few weeks. What in blazes had been going on back there?

He had to get there. He had to go, get Bess, and bring her home. As soon as possible. The thought of his precious daughter locked up in a city jail, surrounded by drug addicts and cat burglars and pickpockets and murderers, sickened him. He shuddered. Then he had a comforting thought. No one would bother her as long as his mother was nearby.

He went in search of Mose to tell him that he would be in charge of the furniture business for the next few days.

When Mammi and Bess returned to Rose Hill Farm that afternoon, freed from the sheriff after promising that they would stop taking his car, they found a bucket of water sitting on the porch, two big catfish, mad as hornets, swimming inside. "They are sure ugly fish," Mammi said, "but they make good eatings." She picked up the bucket and took it in the house, but turned toward Bess at the door. "My ladies need feeding. And take the big pail for eggs. Lift *every* hen."

Bess always gathered every one she found, but maybe some days she didn't look as hard as she might. She picked up the pail by the kitchen door and turned to Mammi. "Aren't you wondering where those fish came from?"

"Billy left 'em," Mammi said. "He's done it before."

Bess took off her big black bonnet and hung it on the porch railing. She walked across the yard to the henhouse, cataloging her woes. Her father, understandably, had been astounded to hear that she was at the police station and said he was on his way to Stoney Ridge. He would probably be here by morning, if not late tonight, to take her home. Just when she was starting to feel encouraged about her developing friendship with Billy Lapp.

On the buggy ride back to Rose Hill Farm, Bess had fought back tears. She asked her grandmother, why didn't she just say she wanted to send her home? Why go to all that trouble to aggravate the poor sheriff?

Mammi gave her a look of pure astonishment. "I *don't* want you going home." She turned her gaze to the back of the horse. "I want my boy to *come* home."

"But why?"

"It's high time." Then her jaw clamped shut in Mammi's own stubborn way and she didn't give up another word all the way home.

What troubled Bess the most was that she understood Mammi's logic. In fact, even more worrisome, she thought it was pretty smart. Her father wouldn't have come back to Stoney Ridge under any other circumstance than an emergency. And finding out his daughter was thrown in jail for stealing a sheriff's car would definitely constitute an emergency.

She got a scoop of cracked corn from the feed bin and tossed it around the ground as the chickens tried to peck at her bare toes. Life just wasn't fair, wasn't fair at all. Under the late afternoon sky, all life seemed wrung out.

From the kitchen window came the smell of catfish sizzling in the frying pan. Suddenly, Billy came flying out of the barn, pounding for the house, face first, bellowing like a calf, "No! No! Don't eat it!"

With eyes as big as quarters, Bess watched him jump the steps into the kitchen. She threw the corn on the ground and ran up to the house. Inside, Billy grabbed the frying pan from a startled Mammi and tossed it into the sink. Then he yelped in pain, "Eyeow!" and hopped on one leg. He had burnt his hands from picking up the pan without a rag.

With unusual presence of mind, Bess thrust his hands in the bucket of water the catfish had been in. "*What* is the matter with you?"

He yanked his hands up and she pushed them back in the water. "Those fish. Something's wrong with them. I shouldn't have left 'em on the porch, but that black cat of Bess's was eyeing them in the barn."

"What makes you think something is wrong with them?" Bess asked. She was putting ice from the icebox into a rag and tying it up to make an ice pack.

"Didn't you see them?" he asked.

"They were just as ugly as any other catfish," Mammi offered.

"They didn't have whiskers," he said, taking the ice pack that Bess offered to him. He leaned against the counter, holding the ice pack between his hands. "And one was missing its eyes. A few weeks ago Bess noticed that birds weren't singing at the lake. So I've been back a few times. She's right. There's no birds up there anymore. And this time, I found these fish up on the shore, practically dead. Something's wrong with that lake."

"Blue Lake Pond?" Mammi put a hand against her chest. "That place is teeming with wildlife. My Samuel used to say he only needed to hold out a pail on the shore and fish would jump in."

"Not anymore," Billy said mournfully.

"What were you planning to do with the catfish?" Bess asked.

"I don't know," he said. "I hadn't gotten that far."

"Something like that happened in Berlin. A company dumped chemicals in a lake. Birds ate the fish and they ended up with strange-looking babies."

Billy's dark eyebrows shot up. "Someone is *polluting* the lake."

"Maybe so," Bess said. "But you need proof." She held up some B&W salve to put on his hands.

He held out his palms. "I don't know what shocks me more." He looked at Bess as she put a dab of salve on his hands. "Someone ruining my lake—" he gave her a sly grin—"or hearing you speak a full entire paragraph that makes sense."

Mammi snorted. "Come around here for breakfast sometime. She babbles like a brook. A person can hardly drink a cup of coffee in peace."

Bess wrapped a rag around Billy's hand and tied it so tight he yelped like a snake bit him and yanked it away from her.

"So how am I going to get some evidence that someone is polluting my lake?" he asked.

Bess put the salve back in the kitchen drawer. "You have to go out there and look for tracks. Maybe even stay out there awhile and watch, at different times of the day. Even at night."

"Trapping!" Mammi said happily, clapping her big red hands together. "Haven't gone trapping in years. Used to be my favorite thing in the world. We'll go tonight."

Later that evening, Jonah Riehl was on the bus heading to Pennsylvania. He gave Mose a note to give to Sallie, telling her he had a sudden errand to attend to. He didn't explain the circumstances. He felt too ashamed of what had happened. He leaned against the window on the bus and tried to sleep, but his thoughts kept him awake. He had been back in Stoney Ridge only once in the last fifteen years—for his father's funeral—since he left it that year after Rebecca died.

It was the trial that made him decide to leave Stoney Ridge for good.

The truck driver who crashed into the buggy, killing Rebecca, had been driving under the influence of alcohol that night. Jonah had to testify against him. It tore Jonah up—he was grieving so deeply for his Rebecca, yet he couldn't ignore the anguish in the truck driver's eyes. He saw the driver's wife at the trial every single day, looking as if she was barely holding herself together in one piece. Who was he to ever judge another man? If he couldn't forgive that man for what he had done, how could he ever expect God to forgive him? In a letter presented by Jonah's bishop, he had asked the judge for mercy. "He has suffered, and suffered heavily. It was a tragedy, not a crime. Sending the defendant to prison would serve no good purpose, and I plead leniency for him."

The state was less generous. The truck driver was sentenced to six years in prison for reckless driving and involuntary manslaughter.

Jonah also asked the judge to dismiss a petition for a wrongful death settlement because he was receiving all the financial help he needed from the church. The judge looked at him as if he thought Jonah might have endured more than broken bones in the accident—maybe he had been brain damaged.

The insurance company representing the truck that had struck their buggy and killed Rebecca had offered Jonah a settlement of $150,000. Jonah returned the check to the insurance company with a statement: "I'm not seeking revenge. Our Bible says revenge is not for us."

Someone in the insurance company, astounded by Jonah's letter and returned check, leaked it to the press. Newspaper writers and photographers swarmed to Rose Hill Farm like bees to a flower. Jonah couldn't even go out of his house without someone trying to take his picture and ask for comments. He thought it would blow over, but the story was picked up and reported across the nation. He received hundreds of letters expressing sympathy. And then ordinary folks started arriving at Rose Hill Farm, knocking on their door and wanting to see Bess. That was when he couldn't take it any longer. Every day brought reminders of what he had lost. It was just too painful to stay in Stoney Ridge. Even more so because he knew better. His people were known for yielding and accepting God's will. Yet, deep inside, he was angry with God for what had happened. It made it worse still for him to be among his people and feel like an outsider.

His father understood why he had to move, but his mother didn't. She felt that family belonged together, through thick or thin. Maybe that was why he agreed to let Bess go this summer. It was time to smooth things out with his mother.

His eyes jerked open. How could he possibly smooth things out when his mother got his daughter tossed into jail?

When a round and creamy moon rose above the barn later that evening, Billy came back to Rose Hill Farm to pick up Mammi and Bess in his open courting buggy. It was so small that it tilted to one side when Mammi climbed up on it. Bess was squished between Mammi and Billy and tried not to notice how good Billy smelled—like pine soap. He led the horse up to the turnoff to the lake and drove the buggy to the edge of the trees. Then he hopped out. "I thought we would walk the perimeter and see if we find anything out of the ordinary."

Bess climbed out behind him.

"I'd better stay alert for us all and keep a lookout on things at this end of the lake," Mammi said, stretching out in the buggy seat. She yawned. "I've got eyes like an eagle and ears like an Indian scout." She dropped right off.

Billy and Bess had hardly gone a few hundred yards when they heard the rhythm of Mammi's snores echoing off the still lake water.

"She's as loud as an air compressor," Billy said.

"This is just the prelude snore," Bess said. "Wait till you hear what it sounds like when she's sleeping deep. She rattles the windows. And if you think that's loud, you should stand clear of her sneezes. If I sneezed like Mammi did, I would fly apart."

A laugh burst out of Billy and he stopped to turn around and look at Bess, amazed. "It's nice to hear you finally talking, Bess. Kinda made me nervous at first when I thought we were going to be stuck picking rose petals together all summer."

Bess's knees suddenly felt as quivery as Mammi's green Jell-O salad. Her heart was pounding so loudly she was sure it drowned out her grandmother's snores. She hurried to keep up with Billy's long strides. There weren't many perfect moments in life, she thought happily, but this was surely one of them. Here she was with Billy Lapp, on a moonlit summer night, at a beautiful lake.

"Whatever happened with that lake in Berlin?" Billy said, turning his head slightly to call back to her.

Oh. Apparently she wasn't exactly on the top of his mind like he was on hers. "Well, someone found out it was the chemical company that was dumping their waste in the lake. So then the state of Ohio got involved and the chemical company was fined a bunch of money and had to clean up the lake. Took a few years to come back, but now it's just like it was before."

"How did the state of Ohio get involved?" Billy asked.

"I guess someone notified the police."

Billy stopped abruptly. "Oh," he said flatly. He looked crestfallen.

"What's the matter?"

"Even if we found something tonight, I'm not sure what I would do with the information. You know I can't go running to the police."

Bess snorted. "Tell that to Mammi."

Billy took a few steps and whirled around. "This is no joking matter, Bess. What's the point of trying to find out who's polluting the lake if we can't turn them in?"

"Well, how are you going to protect the lake if you don't find out what's causing a problem?" She walked a few steps to catch up with him. "Maybe you're getting ahead of yourself, assuming it's a person doing wrong. Could be something else entirely."

"Like what?"

"Well, like algae growing. In science class, I learned about some kinds of algae that grow so thick they wipe out any oxygen in a pond, so all the plants and fish die. That might explain what happened to the birds. No fish, no birds." Bess liked science much better than math.

Billy took off his hat and ran a hand through his hair. Then he put his hat back on. "I guess what you're saying is not to get ahead of myself." He started walking again, scanning the shore for some sign of human activity. Too soon, they had walked the rim of the lake and were back at the buggy. Mammi's head was rolled back and she was sawing logs. Billy helped Bess up into the buggy, which startled Mammi out of her deep slumber.

"Sorry to wake you," Bess said.

"I was just resting my eyes," Mammi said. "Find anything suspicious-looking?"

"Nothing," Billy said, untying the horse's reins from the tree. "Not a thing."

"What about that?" Mammi pointed behind Billy. There, on the ground, was a pile of sawdust in between two wheel ruts, as if it had spilled from the back of a vehicle.

Billy bent down and rubbed the sawdust between his fingers. "It's fresh. I can smell the sap." He picked up some more and looked up at the trees. "It's not from these pines. It's from a different wood. Someone brought it here."

"Could sawdust ruin a lake?" Bess asked.

"If there's enough of it," he said.

"I'm feeling a little peckish." Mammi rubbed her big red hands together. "And when I get hungry, I get cranky."

And heaven knows, Bess thought, they couldn't have *that*.

Jonah got off of the bus in Stoney Ridge at five in the morning. He walked down Main Street straight to the sheriff's office, but the doors were locked and it was pitch black inside. The town was silent. It drove him crazy knowing that Bess was just yards away from him, locked up in a dirty jail cell. Frustrated, he turned and bumped right into a young English woman as she came around the corner.

"I'm sorry," Jonah apologized and picked up the purse she had dropped. "What are you doing out at this hour of the morning?" he asked. The birds weren't even singing yet.

She looked at him cautiously, then seemed to relax as he handed her the purse. "I work at the bakery. This is when the workday starts. What about you?"

He pointed up the street toward the bus stop. "I just got off the bus. Waiting for the sheriff to arrive."

"You might have a long wait. His hours can be very . . . casual."

Her gaze took in his straw hat and his jawline beard. Her face was lit softly by the streetlight and she smiled. To his surprise, so did he.

"You look pretty harmless. Why don't you wait for the sheriff in the bakery?" She crossed the street and unlocked the door to The Sweet Tooth, then turned on the lights.

He followed her inside but stood by the door. She put on her apron and turned on the lights in the kitchen. He hadn't really noticed what she looked like out in the dark street. He didn't usually pay much attention to English women, but there was something appealing about this one. That face . . . it seemed vaguely familiar. Where had he seen her? He studied the woman more closely as she bustled around in the kitchen. There was a cautious quality in her eyes that made him suspect she'd seen more of life than she wanted to. He felt as if he'd met her before, but of course that was impossible. She was quite a lovely woman, he realized, with fragile, finely carved features and a long, slender neck. And she had been kind to him, even after he nearly knocked her down in the street.

She poked her head out from the kitchen. "If you don't mind waiting a minute, I'll start the coffee."

"I don't mind," he said. He was famished. He hadn't eaten dinner last night; he was too busy trying to pack and get to the bus station in time. He sat down in a chair at a small table and stretched out his legs.

She set down a mug of coffee and a cinnamon roll on Jonah's table.

"Cream and sugar?" she asked, glancing at him. Then she got a startled look on her face and froze.

He felt a spike of concern, wondering what had caused her to suddenly look so alarmed. Had he done something wrong? She dropped her eyes to the floor and spun around, returning to the kitchen to get started on the day's baking.

Jonah decided he should leave, that he must have made her uncomfortable, but she started to ply him with questions. Where had he come from? What was it like living there? She was mixing dough and rolling it out and the oven was starting to send out some delicious smells. Before he knew it, she was asking about his family and he found himself answering. He began to talk: slowly at first, like a rusted pump, then things started spilling out of him in a rush.

"Rebecca and I met when we were both only sixteen. She lived in a neighboring district. I courted her for four years, driving my buggy two hours each way to see her on Saturday nights. Sometimes, I would barely arrive home in time to help my father milk the cows on Sunday morning." He gazed into his coffee mug as the bakery lady refilled it. She poured herself a cup and slipped into a chair across from him, listening carefully.

As Jonah lifted the coffee mug to his lips, his mind floated to a different time. "As soon as her father gave us his blessing, we married. Rebecca came to live at Rose Hill Farm and a year after that, our Bess arrived." He glanced up at the bakery lady, wondering if she was listening to him only out of politeness, but the look on her face suggested otherwise, as if she was anxious for him to continue. "Most men wanted a son, but I was glad the Lord gave us a daughter. I knew Bess would be good company for Rebecca." He stopped then and looked out the window at the empty street. "You see, I thought there would be plenty of time for sons. But there wasn't."

"Life can be that way. Things have a way of not turning out the way we expect." She said it so softly, he wondered if it was more his thought than her voice he'd heard.

Jonah caught her gaze and gently smiled. "No, you're right about that."

Then, in a voice that hurt him with its gentleness, she asked, "How did she die?"

His smile faded and he took his time answering. He'd never spoken aloud of Rebecca's accident, not with his parents or Bess, nor Mose. Not even with Sallie. Yet on this morning, the morning he returned to Stoney Ridge, he found himself wanting to talk about Rebecca. "It was a warm April night, just a week or so after Bess had been born. Rebecca wanted to go visit her folks—they were moving to Indiana—and truth be told, my mother was making Rebecca go a little stir crazy. She was always afraid of my mother, was Rebecca." He gave up a slight smile. "My mother can be a little . . . overbearing."

The bakery lady nodded sympathetically, as if she understood perfectly.

"The baby was in Rebecca's arms, sound asleep, and Rebecca had nodded off. The baby's blanket had slipped to the floor. I reached down to pick it up. I took my eyes off the road for just a moment . . ." His voice drizzled off and he closed his eyes tight. "It was the last thing I remember." He covered his face with his hand, but just for a moment. He came to himself with a start and glanced cautiously at the bakery lady. She didn't say a word, but the look in her eyes, it nearly took his breath away. It wasn't pity, nor was it sorrow. It was . . . empathy. As if she understood what a horrific moment that was for him, and how that moment had changed his life.

He hadn't meant to reveal so much to an English stranger. It shocked him, the things that spilled out of him in the predawn of that day. Maybe he was just overly tired and overly worried about Bess and his mother, but talking to that bakery lady felt like a tonic. His heart felt lighter than it had in years.

But this lady had work to do and he had stayed long enough. He stood to leave. "I don't even know your name," he said at the door. "I'm Jonah Riehl."

"I know," she said, giving him a level look. "I know who you are." She put out her hand to shake his.

He took her hand in his. It surprised him, how soft and small it was.

She took a deep breath. "My name is Lainey O'Toole."

Jonah's dark eyebrows lifted in surprise. "Lainey? Lainey O'Toole. I remember you. You were just a slip of a girl. Simon's stepdaughter."

She nodded.

"You disappeared. After your mother died."

She nodded again.

"What happened to you?"

"I became a long-term houseguest of the state of Pennsylvania."

He must have looked confused because she hastened to add, "Foster care system. Until I was eighteen."

He leaned against the doorjamb. "What then?" Jonah asked. He was sincerely interested.

"I worked at a department store in customer service. That's a fancy way of saying I listened to people complain. I didn't want to do that forever and a day, so I saved my money to go to culinary school."

"I remember you and my mother baking together in the kitchen at Rose Hill Farm." Those eyes of hers, they were mesmerizing. Full of wonder and wisdom for a woman barely twenty-five, if he counted back correctly. "Are you back home now, for good?"

She didn't answer right away. "I'm trying to do good while I'm here." She gave him an enigmatic smile then. She had flour on her cheek, and without thinking, he almost brushed it away. It shocked him that he would even consider touching a woman like that. There were ten years between them, and a world of differences in every way that mattered.

Still, something about Lainey O'Toole stirred him. He remembered her as a small, worried-looking girl. Simon was a bad-tempered man, lazy and cynical. Even though he lived down the street and passed the house almost daily, Jonah kept a wide path from Simon, and his parents shunned him completely. Jonah saw Lainey's mother only a few times, tossing food out for chickens that lived under the front porch. He remembered her as a faded-looking woman who had probably been pretty in her youth. Lainey used to slip up to the fence that lined the house, quiet as a cat, and just watch him and his father work in the fields or around the barn. It wasn't long before his mother coaxed Lainey into the kitchen, teaching her how to bake. Just taking an interest in her, because no one else seemed to.

And here Lainey O'Toole was, a grown woman, standing in front of him. "Jonah . . . ," Lainey started. Just as she opened her mouth to say something, the sheriff drove by in his patrol car. She snapped her mouth shut.

And now his thoughts shifted to Bess. "I'd better go. Thank you, Lainey O'Toole." He held her eyes as he put his straw hat back on his head, then tipped his head to her and hurried down to the sheriff's office.

Jonah Riehl had a crooked gait. The good leg did most of the work while the weaker one shuffled to keep up, twisting stiffly from the hip. Lainey knew, from Bertha, that was a lasting result of the accident. Her heart swelled with compassion for the man as she watched him walk down the street, leaning on his cane.

She had nearly told Jonah about Bess. That first Sunday afternoon, when Bertha told her she knew Bess wasn't Jonah's daughter, she had made Lainey promise not to tell him or to tell Bess, either. "I'm the one who needs to do the telling," Bertha insisted. "And I will. When the time is right."

Lainey had agreed, reluctantly. Now she regretted that promise. She hadn't expected to be spending so much time with Bess, nor did she ever dream she would meet Jonah face-to-face.

It took her awhile to recognize him this morning, yet once she did, she saw him as he was fifteen years ago, with laughing eyes and a quick wit. When she was just a girl, he used to tease her like a big brother. Never mean-spirited, though. She remembered how kind he was . . . so very kind. He was still kind. And he still had that wavy dark hair, snapping brown eyes, and good-looking face, slightly disfigured by a broken nose. She remembered the day it was broken. He was pitching in a softball game and got hit in the face by a ball. She'd watched from afar and thought she'd never seen a nose bleed so much.

As she saw Jonah head into the sheriff's office, she leaned against the doorjamb and crossed her arms. This summer was turning into something she had never expected. Everything—all of her carefully designed plans—was turning upside down. Would things right themselves again? The oven buzzer went off and she went to check on the bread. Or maybe, she thought as she pulled the loaves from the oven, maybe things had been upside down and were turning right side up.

She set the loaves on cooling racks and pulled off her oven mitts. Either way, she had trusted God with all of this years ago, when she was only ten. And she wasn't going to stop trusting him now. She would see it through.

While Bess was making her bed, she heard a car turn onto the driveway of Rose Hill Farm. She looked out the window and felt her stomach twist into a knot. It was the sheriff. With her father.

She ran downstairs to tell Mammi but found her already on the front porch, ready to greet her son. Like she had been expecting him all along. Bess went outside and stood behind Mammi as the sheriff's car came to a stop and her father opened the door. He climbed out, pulled his suitcase from the backseat, and turned to the sheriff to shake his hand.

"My work here is done," the sheriff said, leaning out the car window. "Stay out of trouble, Miz Riehl." He pointed to Bess. "You too." He made a motion with his hand, two fingers splayed, pointing from his eyes, as if to say "I'm watching you."

After he drove off, Jonah took a few strides to the kitchen porch.

"Jonah," Mammi said calmly.

"So, Mom," Jonah said, just as calmly. "Care to tell me what's been going on?"

Then an awkward silence fell, until Billy appeared out of nowhere. "If they're not going to tell you, I will. Bess had a notion to take the sheriff's car out for a few spins," he said. "Three times, from what I hear."

Bess popped out from behind Mammi and glared at Billy. What had she *ever* seen in him?

"Billy," Mammi said firmly. "Time to move the bees out to the fields. Take Bess with you." She turned to Bess. "Get your bonnet. You'll need it."

Bess went into the kitchen and grabbed her big black bonnet from the wall peg. As she passed by her father, he held his arm out wide to her. "Don't I even get a hello?"

She leaned into him and felt a wave of relief that he was here. She hadn't realized how much she missed him. He wasn't nearly as upset about the police car borrowing as she had expected him to be. But then, her father wasn't quick tempered. She had never seen him angry, not once. Still, she would know if he was upset with her. This morning he looked relaxed, even a little pleased to be here in Stoney Ridge. She hadn't expected *that*.

"Maybe when you're done with moving your grandmother's bees," Jonah said with one dark brow raised, "we can talk about your algebra grade."

She dropped her head. She hadn't expected *that* either.

In the barn, before getting anywhere close to the beehives, Billy rolled down his sleeves, then tucked his pants into his boots. He took out a roll of mosquito netting and covered his hat and face with it. "Better cover up good, Bess," he said, but she didn't appreciate his advice. Billy lifted the mosquito netting to help her wrap it, but she turned away from him. "Bess, don't be childish. You have to protect yourself." He turned her by the shoulders to face him. As he wrapped the netting around her bonnet, she kept her eyes on the ground. "What are you so peeved about, anyway? I was only telling the truth."

She locked eyes with him. "Well, you were wrong. It was Mammi who wanted me to borrow that sheriff's car. I tried talking her out of it . . . but you know my grandmother."

Billy tucked the netting into the back of her apron. "No kidding? That's too bad." He sounded genuinely disappointed. "A couple of fellows were asking me all about you. They think you must act all quiet and shy, but underneath . . . they say . . . sie is voll Schpank." *She is daring.*

Oh no. That meant that everyone in town knew about Mammi's car thievery. "Tell them I'm neither." She pushed his hand away from her waist and rolled her eyes. They both looked ridiculous, covered up with so much mosquito netting, and she couldn't help but laugh at the sight, which got Billy grinning.

"Well, I'll pass that information along." He put the netting on the shelf and picked up a matchbox and the smoker, then placed it on the wheelbarrow. "So what's this about algebra?"

"I see no reason to study math," she said firmly. "No reason in the world."

"I love math," Billy said.

Bess looked at him. "What is there to love?"

"Math is . . . entirely predictable," he said. "There's always a right answer."

"Only for those who make sense of it in the first place."

"You're not looking at it in the right way. Math is based on all the patterns around us. They are constant and repetitious and dependable, like . . ." He looked out the barn window. "Like rows in the fields, ripples in a stream, veins on a leaf, snowflakes. Man-made or natural, those patterns are there. Math is always the same."

She had never thought of math like that. She didn't like to think about math at all.

Billy picked up the wheelbarrow handles and pushed it out the barn door.

He waited until Bess joined him, then slid it shut behind her. They walked down the path to the rose fields. "Isn't there anything about learning you love?" he asked.

"Words, I guess. How you can tell by the root the way words get started in the first place. And then how they change over time."

"See? Not so different. You're looking for patterns too."

She pondered that for a while and decided he was probably right, but she still felt suspicious about math.

"Since you're over being mad, I need some advice."

Her heart skipped a beat. Billy came to her for advice? Her madness melted away. "What kind of advice?"

"I'll tell you more when we're done. I need to concentrate." Billy pushed the wheelbarrow down to the beehives in the back of one rose field. As they approached the hives, the buzz grew louder. He lit the smoker and waved it all around the stack of hives. She noticed that he sang softly to the bees as he worked. It touched her, that gentle singing. It was one of the hymns from church, sung in a slow, mournful way. He told her his singing calmed the bees; that they were smart creatures and appreciated a good tenor voice when they heard it. She rolled her eyes at that but couldn't hold back a smile.

Carefully, Billy lifted a hive onto the wheelbarrow as Bess held it steady. A few stray bees buzzed around them, curious. They rotated the hives among the fields where the roses were in bloom. It made for more honey, Bertha had taught him. The bees didn't have to work so hard on the gathering and could concentrate their energies on the honey making. He took one more hive and gently placed it on the wheelbarrow. When he was finished, he emptied out the smoker and they headed to the barn. About halfway there, Billy stopped to make sure the bees weren't swarming, indignant that their homes had been moved. Satisfied, he told Bess she could take off the netting now.

He helped her unwind it from around her bonnet, carefully rolling it up again to reuse. "Yesterday afternoon, I went to the lake and saw the truck dumping the sawdust. Backed right up to the shoreline and lifted the truck bed up and dumped. Deep enough so that it all sank."

She pulled the big gloves from her hands. "Did you say anything to the driver?"

He shook his head. "No. I stayed out of sight."

"What are you going to do with that information?"

"That's what I don't know. That's the part I need your advice about."

Her heart skipped another beat. Maybe Billy was finally starting to notice her. She admired how much he cared about the lake. He was genuinely troubled about it.

"If I tell my father about it, he'll only say that we need to let English problems be English problems, and Amish problems be Amish problems."

"Is that what you think?" she asked.

"I can't just do nothing and let the lake die. God gave us this earth to care for properly. But my father is right about one thing too. It's not my place to get the law involved. It's not our way to demand justice. We leave those matters in God's hands."

Bess shrugged. "It's just letting consequences have a place. There's nothing wrong with that."

"Still," he said, hesitating, and she knew. These kinds of situations were complicated. How could they care for God's earth and not want the lake to be protected? And yet by protecting the lake, they would need to get involved with the law. Billy lifted the wheelbarrow handles and started walking carefully to the rose fields. Bess followed behind, thinking hard.

She stopped as a new idea bubbled up. "Maybe there's something in between."

He turned his chin toward her. "I'm listening."

She took a few steps to catch up to him. "Every afternoon, I've been going to the bakery to visit with Lainey. There's a newspaperman—Eddie Beaker—who comes in after three so he can buy Danish for half off. He's always asking Lainey if she's heard any big news stories. Even not-so-big stories. Any story at all, he said. Just yesterday I heard him complaining to her that he doesn't like summer. Said it's too hot and it always makes for slow news months."

Billy stopped and spun around to face her. "You think maybe he could break the story?"

She nodded. "Mammi says Eddie Beaker is 'a wolf in cheap clothing.'"

Billy smiled, then stroked his chin. "Bess Riehl, du bischt voll Schpank." He tapped his forehead. "Und du bischt en schmaerdes Maedel." *You are daring. And you're a smart girl.*

Jonah leaned against the doorjamb at Rose Hill Farm and looked around the kitchen. It hadn't changed, which comforted him somehow. The wrinkled linoleum floor, the pale green walls and ceiling. Even the bird clock on the wall was the one he had grown up with. He used to think that clock was irritating. Now, it seemed endearing. "I see that the early rain has been good for the roses."

"Now we need sunshine to keep them dry and blooming," his mother completed his thought.

He hung his cane on the wall peg and put his straw hat on top, then sat in a chair. It was the same chair he had always sat in. He knew it would always be his chair. His place in the family. "Bess seems happy. She's as brown as a berry. Looks like she's gaining some weight from your good cooking."

Bertha nodded in agreement. "She came here looking as brittle as a bird. Now she's as fat as a spring robin."

Hardly that, Jonah thought, as Bertha poured two cups of coffee. But Bess's appearance had changed. In just a few weeks, she seemed older, more mature. "The sheriff gave me his side of the story. Mind filling me in on yours?"

Bertha eased into her chair. "I had to do something that would get you back here."

"Why didn't you just ask?"

"I did," she said flatly. "Been asking for years."

So she had. Jonah leaned back. "What is so all-fired important that you need me to be back in Stoney Ridge? Right now?"

His mother took her time answering. She sipped her coffee, added sugar and milk, stirred, then sipped it again. "Simon's dying."

Jonah snorted. "Impossible. Dying would take too much work. He'll outlive us all."

"He's dying all right."

"Where is he? The cottage looked empty."

"He lost that years ago when the bank took it. It's been up for sale for a long time. He's at the Veterans Hospital over in Lebanon."

Jonah sighed. "What's he dying of?"

"Some kind of cancer. Hopscotch disease."

"Hodgkin's?"

"That's what I said." Bertha stood and went to the window, crossing her arms against her chest. "Them doctors are looking for family members. They want bone marrow for him." She turned back to Jonah. "They think it might cure him."

"Don't tell me you're getting tested to give your brother—a man who has done nothing for anybody his whole livelong life—don't tell me you're planning to give him your bone marrow?"

"I tried. I'd give it to him if I could. But I'm not a match." She sat down in the chair. "But you might be." She looked into her coffee cup and swirled it around. "And so might our Bess."

"Bess?" Jonah looked up in surprise. "She's a distant relation to him." He easily dismissed that notion. "What about your sisters? Why don't they get tested?"

"Two did. Three refused because he's still shunned. The two that did—Martha and Annie—they aren't a match." Before Jonah could even ask, she answered. "And their husbands won't let their children or grandchildren test for it."

"Because he's been shunned."

Bertha nodded. "You and Bess . . . you're his last chance."

Jonah exhaled. "What makes you think Simon would accept my bone marrow, even if I were a match? You always said he was as cranky as a handle on a churn."

"You leave Simon to me," she said in a final way.

On the following Sunday, before church, Jonah was buckling the tracings on the buggy horse. Bess and his mother were upstairs getting ready to leave. His mind was a million miles away from churchgoing. He was thinking about what his mother had told him yesterday, about wanting him to take a blood test to try to cure Simon from his cancer. His mother rarely spoke of her brother—Simon had been excommunicated from the church years ago. He wasn't included in family gatherings, his name wasn't spoken, and he was ignored when he was seen, which was often.

Jonah could never figure out why Simon stayed in Stoney Ridge. He moved there right after he was discharged from the army due to an injury. Simon had been drafted in World War II and served as a conscientious objector, stationed as a maintenance worker in a base camp in Arkansas. He was accidentally shot in the foot. He claimed he was cleaning a gun, but the story was vague and changed each time he told it. Samuel, Jonah's father, said it probably went more like this: Simon was doing something he shouldn't have been, like hunting when he was supposed to be on duty, then blamed the Army for the accident. Using his disability pension, Simon bought a run-down home near his sister's farm and ran it down even further. It was as if he enjoyed being a thorn in everyone's side. But . . . that would be Simon. His father said Simon was born with a chip on his shoulder.

Jonah slipped the last buckle together on the bridle and looked up over the horse's mane to see Lainey O'Toole walking toward him.

"Bess invited me," she said, as she took in his confused look. "To church."

"Our church?" he asked, wondering why Bess would have put Lainey in such an unfair position. She might have meant well, but Lainey shouldn't feel obligated to come. "Our church . . . the service lasts for three hours." He knew enough about the English to know they zoomed in and out of church in scarcely an hour's time. Why, the first hymn was just wrapping up after an hour in an Amish church.

Lainey shrugged. "I'm used to that. The church I've been going to the last few years has long services, plus Sunday school."

"The preachers speak in Deitsch."

"I remember. I used to go with your mother." She smiled. "As I recall, those preachers can get a good deal across with just their tone of voice."

A laugh burst out of Jonah. She surprised him, this young woman.

"I can still understand a little bit of Deitsch. Growing up in Stoney Ridge . . . living with Simon those few years, I picked up a bit."

Jonah looked past her to the rose fields, then turned back to her. "Du bisch so schee." *You are so lovely.* Did he *really* just say that? Oh please no. He suddenly felt like Levi Miller, self-conscious and bashful and blurting out ridiculous, awkward compliments.

She gave him a blank look. "I guess I don't remember as much as I thought."

Oh, thank you, Lord! "I said, 'Well then, hop up.'" He offered her his hand

and helped her into the buggy. He happened to notice that she smelled as sweet as a lemon blossom.

This was how church was meant to be—pure and simple, Lainey thought as she followed behind Bertha and Bess. This must have been what church was like for the first disciples—no fancy church building with a steeple that grazed the sky. Just a home, shared, to worship in. And God was there.

Today, church was merely a well-swept barn. But God was here. She could feel his presence.

It was such a hot and humid July morning that the host—the Zooks of Beacon Hollow—decided to hold the meeting in the barn, where it would be cooler. The sliding doors were left wide open to let the breeze waft through.

Lainey sat in the back row bench on the women's side, in between Bess and Bertha. Bess whispered to her that they had to sit in the back row because no one wanted to sit behind Bertha—she was too big. She also warned Lainey to watch her head. "Barn swallows might swoop in and steal your hair for their nest if they're in the mood. I've seen it happen. Just two weeks ago, to Eli Smucker's chin whiskers—"

Bertha leaned over and laid a calming hand on Bess, who snapped her lips shut and tucked her chin to her chest.

Lainey had to bite her lip to stop from grinning. She could barely contain the happiness she felt. It nearly spilled out of her. There was no place in the world she would rather be than where she was right that minute. It was a miracle of miracles. On one side of her was Bertha, a woman who had always been good to her, and on the other side was Bess, her very own sister. She could hardly hold back her feelings of praising God.

And to add to her happiness, she was still feeling a little dazed that Jonah had told her she was lovely. She was so startled by it that she pretended she didn't understand him. But she did. It was a phrase Simon said to her mother in those rare moments when he was at his best. Hearing it from Jonah made her stomach feel funny. She glanced at him across the large room. His dark head was bowed, preparing for worship, she knew. Unlike her mind, which seemed to be darting around the room like one of those barn swallows. Where had these new thoughts about Jonah come from? He had always been just

Jonah to her, Bertha's son. She remembered that she had thought he was a good-looking young man. She had never been crazy about those scraggly Amish beards. Jonah's was a full, soft brown beard that he had worn since he was twenty. She thought back to being disappointed when he started to grow that beard after he married Rebecca and covered up that fine square chin. His face had so many other interesting features, though, such as high cheekbones and gentle brown eyes that looked at her with warm concern.

Then, as if Jonah had read her mind, he looked up and caught her eye, and she felt a nervous quiver in her belly. She reached down to smooth out her dress as a small, elderly man stood up. A perfect, pure note, as dazzling as a sunrise, floated from his open mouth. The men joined in, then the women, all singing the same slow tune, the same quavery note, almost a chanting. Two hundred voices rising to the barn rafters. They sang for the longest time. Then they stopped, as if God himself was the choir director and signaled to everyone the end of the hymn.

As Lainey inhaled the familiar barn smells of hay and animals, and heard that long, sad hymn, she felt a tidal wave of long-buried emotion. Songs and smells could bring a person back to a moment in time more than anything else. It was amazing how much could be conjured with just a few notes or a solitary whiff. Her thoughts drifted to the church service she had attended with Bertha just a few weeks before her mother had died. The wind that morning had the barest thread of warmth to it. It smelled of the thawing earth, of spring. Lainey suddenly realized that was the last true moment of childhood. The last moment she had been thoroughly happy. A sadness welled up inside her. She shut her eyes and pressed her fingers to her lips. She didn't want to cry, not here. Not now.

And then came the preaching. She was fine through the first sermon, given by an elderly minister. That sermon was told in a preacher's voice, hollow and joyless. It was the second sermon, given by Caleb Zook. She vaguely remembered him as a friend of Jonah's. Caleb was the bishop now, married to the small, copper-haired woman sitting in front of Lainey, who had a baby in her arms and a toddler by her side. Lainey was amazed at how quiet her children were, how quiet all of the children were. When it was Caleb Zook's turn to stand and preach, his eyes grazed the room and rested on his wife's face. Some kind of silent communication passed between them, because he shifted his eyes and noticed Lainey sitting in the back row. He delivered his sermon in English. For some reason, such kindness touched her deeply and made her eyes well with tears. An odd pang of longing pierced her heart. She felt overcome with a desire to belong to this—to these people—forever.

The woman with the child on her hip kept her back turned, slowly ladling the apple butter into small bowls. Bess wanted her to hurry, so she could take out the platter with bread and apple butter and serve the farthest table, where Billy happened to be sitting with his friends after the church service ended. Billy had smiled at her during the sermon. Twice. She thought that when he smiled, he really meant it.

She glanced nervously over at Billy. Sometimes, for no reason, looking at him made her chest ache. It was the tall, strong, splendid sight of him, she supposed.

Bess cleared her throat, hoping the woman would notice she was there, waiting. But this woman could not be hurried. Bess chanced another look in Billy's direction and her heart sunk. Sure enough, Betsy Mast had gotten there first. She was leaning over Billy's shoulder, filling his glass with sweet tea. The dreamy look on Billy's face as he looked up at Betsy made Bess think about dumping the bowl of apple butter right on his head.

The woman spun around and handed Bess a platter of freshly sliced bread. Bess went to find where her father was sitting instead, to serve him. She looked all over and couldn't find him, so she set the bowl and platter at the nearest table. Then she spotted Jonah, still over by the barn, leaning one arm against the door, engrossed in a conversation with Lainey O'Toole. The way Jonah was looking at Lainey—standing a full foot taller than she did, his head bent down as if he didn't want to miss a word she was saying—something about the sight caught Bess in the heart. She stopped and stared. She'd never seen her father pay such rapt attention to a woman.

Her grandmother came up behind her and silently watched. Then she took in a deep breath and let it out with, "Hoo-boy. Didn't see that coming."

6

On Sunday evening, Jonah told Bertha he had decided to get the test to see if his bone marrow could be a match for Simon. "I'll have the test and wait for the results. But I'm not bringing any of this up to Bess," he told her. "There's no reason to. If I'm not a match, that will be the end of it. I won't let Bess get tested. She's barely related to Simon. The chance of being a match is remote."

Bertha gave a brief nod of her head. "One thing at a time."

He wasn't quite sure what she meant by that, but he needed to turn in for the night. He stood to leave but turned around to face her. "Mom, why are you going to such lengths for someone like Simon?"

"He's the only brother I got," was all she said.

That comment struck him as forever odd. It was similar to what Lainey said at church this morning when he told her that his mother lured him here to be a bone marrow transplant for Simon. She said that Bertha had told her all about Simon's illness, but she hadn't had the courage to see him yet. "I'd like to go with you to see him," Lainey told him. "It's my day off, if you don't mind going tomorrow."

"Are you sure?" he asked her. He knew Simon had treated her badly. Everybody knew. It amazed him that she would even bother with Simon.

"He's the only father I've known," was how she answered him.

So early Monday morning, Jonah met Lainey in front of the bakery and they walked to the bus station to catch the first bus from Stoney Ridge to Lebanon. He felt a little uncomfortable at first, spending an entire day traveling with an English woman, but she soon put him at ease. She started by asking him questions about Bess. It was as if she couldn't get enough of hearing stories about their life in Ohio. He found himself telling her all kinds of stories . . . Bess's first day of school when she came home and told him she quit, that one day was enough. Levi Miller, who overly liked her and left wilted flowers for her in the mailbox until the mailman complained. Her cat, Blackie, who seemed to have abandoned her at Rose Hill Farm and taken up the life of a barn cat. They both started laughing then and couldn't stop. He hadn't laughed that often in a long time, and it felt so good.

Just being with Lainey felt good. He hadn't enjoyed another woman's company so much since . . . well, since he first met Rebecca, he realized with a start. He had taken one look at Rebecca, in her pale green dress that set off her hazel eyes, and he knew she was the one for him. He never wavered, not once. He just knew.

And here he was, with feelings stirring for Lainey. Yet this made no sense. No sense at all. It was downright wrong. Lainey was English. Besides, he felt with a sting of guilt, there was the Understanding he had with Sallie. Oh, this was wrong, wrong, wrong.

And yet . . . he couldn't take his eyes off of Lainey. He found himself memorizing every feature, every expression, of her lovely face. He marveled at her beauty, her glorious black hair that curled around her head like a wreath.

The hour-and-a-half bus ride to Lebanon flew by, and soon they were standing at a nurse's station in the hospital, filling out reams of paperwork. Then they had a long wait until a phlebotomist would be free to draw Jonah's blood for the donor test, so the nurse pointed them to the waiting room.

Lainey looked at Jonah. "Maybe I'll go see Simon while you're waiting to get your blood drawn."

"Not without me," Jonah said firmly. It worried him, having her meet up with Simon after all these years. He remembered Simon to be unpredictable. Granted, his love for the drink had much to do with those moods. But even at his best, Simon was not a pleasant person.

There was something in Lainey's expression right then—a sadness? A longing? He couldn't quite tell. Then she gave him one of her inscrutable smiles and sat down in the plastic chair. He sat down next to her.

"Jonah, why would you be willing to share your bone marrow with Simon?"

He set his cane on the empty chair next to him. "I guess I'm doing it for my mother. Since he was shunned all those years, there hasn't been much we could do for him. But this . . . well, maybe this would give Simon the push he needs to return to the church." He crossed his arms against his chest. "That's what she's hoping, anyway, to encourage him to make things right with God before it's too late."

"Did you ever know that Bertha used to bring us meals on a regular basis?" Lainey asked. "And she would slip my mother money to pay bills."

"What?" Jonah was stunned. "My parents . . . ?"

"No. Not your father. Only your mother." Lainey tilted her head. "Your mother . . . she's something else."

Jonah couldn't believe it. No Amish from their church went near Simon. To do so would risk their own good standing. They were quiet for a long time after that, until he finally asked, "So are you in Stoney Ridge this summer to see Simon?"

Her head was bowed as she quietly said, "He's part of the reason. I need to tell him something." She lifted her head and looked him in the eye, as if there was something she wanted to say. He'd had that feeling before when he was with her . . . as if there was something she was holding back. But then, how could he really know that? He was just getting to know her.

If Simon was part of the reason she was back in Stoney Ridge, what was the other part? He was just about to ask when a large graying woman in a nurse's uniform pointed at him from the door to the lab. "Jonah Riehl?"

He nodded.

"In here. Now." Her lips compressed into a flat line. "Hope you got big-sized veins cuz I've had too many folks in here today with itty bitty veins. Had to poke 'em a hundred times."

His dark eyebrows shot up in alarm. "I'll be back soon," he told Lainey. "Real soon, I hope."

Fifteen minutes later, he came out, unrolling his sleeve. He looked around the waiting room for Lainey, but she was gone.

As soon as Jonah left with the nurse, Lainey went to find Simon. She finally located him on a ward for terminally ill patients. He was at the far end of the ward, and she felt herself trembling as she approached him. When she was about ten feet away, she stopped and watched him for a while. He was sleeping and looked so peaceful. Simon had been handsome before alcohol had thickened his face. He had good features, high cheekbones, and deep-set eyes. Once, he had been a big man. Now, he seemed shriveled, like a grape left out in the sun. His face, once smooth and glossy, was like old shoe leather.

She used to be terrified of him. He could be sweet and charming, but then something minor could trigger an explosive rage.

She remembered one time when she served him a piece of cake she had made and waited by his side, hoping to see if he liked it. He had eaten it in its entirety. Then, instead of complimenting her, he yanked the blue ribbon she won at the county fair for her cherry tart off of the refrigerator and tore it into pieces. "You were getting too fond of that ribbon. Don't you think I've noticed?"

She didn't answer him, which had enraged him.

"Pride goeth before a fall. You should be ashamed!"

She glanced at her mother for help, but her mother looked away. "You're right," Lainey said meekly. "I was too fond of winning that ribbon."

Afterward, her mother had tried to explain to her that it was getting injured in the war that had made Simon so quick to anger. Lainey wasn't so sure. She thought he was born mad, though he was the only Amish-born person she'd ever known who had a temper on him. They were gentle people, she knew that to be true. Gentle like Jonah.

Simon opened his eyes and stared at her. Then recognition dawned in his eyes. Those eyes—icy blue—combined with his mane of thick white hair had always reminded Lainey of a Siberian Husky. "Elaine?"

Elaine, her mother. Lainey supposed she did resemble her mother, at least in coloring. Certainly more than Bess did. Bess took after Simon, that was plain to see. "No, Simon. I'm not Elaine. She died over fifteen years ago. I'm Lainey, her daughter."

Simon peered at her, trying to comprehend what she was saying. He was very ill, she could tell that. "I got married once," he said. "Long time ago, she left me. That's when my life took a turn."

"She didn't leave you, Simon. She died having your baby."

He closed his eyes and was quiet for a moment. After a while, he opened

573

one eye. "I don't suppose you have something to drink?" he asked her, licking his lips.

"There's some water by your bedside." She went to it and poured a glass, then held it out to him.

"I was hoping for something a little stronger," he said, brushing her hand away that held the water glass. "Course, I don't drink much as a habit. Don't have the taste for it."

She knew that was a lie. Simon drank like a fish.

He put his head back down on the pillow and gazed at her. "So, you're Lainey. All growed up."

She nodded.

"I don't have money, if that's what you're after."

"I don't want your money, Simon."

"You must want something. Showing up after all these years, without a word. You're after something. Everybody wants something."

"I don't want anything from you. I wanted to tell you that . . . I forgive you. That's all." She exhaled. "I just want you to know that I forgive you."

He snorted. "For what?"

She dropped her head and didn't see him grab her arm until he had it tight in his grip.

"For what?" he snarled, like an angry dog. "I put a roof over your head and food in your mouth. You weren't even my kid. You should be thanking me."

His grip was weaker than she would have expected. She peeled his fingers off of her arm as calmly as if she was peeling a banana, and stepped back. "You can't hurt me anymore." She took in a deep breath. "No matter what you think, Simon, you do need to be forgiven. And no matter what, I do forgive you."

He seemed not to care in the least. He pointed to the door. "Don't let the door hit you where the dog bit you," was all he said.

His sarcasm slapped her with surprise. She lifted her chin and marched toward the door. Her shoes made a clicking sound down the ward. As soon as she went through the door, she leaned against the wall, trying to compose herself. Hadn't she thought this all through before she even asked Jonah if she could join him today? Hadn't she reminded herself, over and over, not to expect anything back from Simon? And yet, here she was, deeply disappointed.

She found herself shivering, as if she was very cold. She heard someone call her name, so softly she thought she might have imagined it. But there was Jonah, walking down the hall toward her. When he saw the look on her face, he held out his arms to her. She burst into tears and sank into him.

Dear Jonah,

Your note said you would be gone only a few days. It has now been nearly a week and I haven't heard a word from you. Should I be planting celery? Can't have an Amish wedding without celery!

Affectionately,
Sallie

"Today's the day, Bess," Billy said when she came into the greenhouse to bring him a glass of lemonade. "We're going to the bakery today to talk to Eddie Beaker."

Bess's eyes went wide. "We? What do you mean, we?"

He took a sip of his lemonade and wiped his mouth with the back of his hand. "You've met him. I don't have any idea who he is."

"I haven't *met* him. Lainey pointed him out, that's all. And you can figure out who he is. He wears a plaid blazer and his hair is slicked back with Crisco and he chews on a cold cigar." She shook her head. "You go. He gives me the creeps."

Billy blew air out through his lips like an exasperated horse.

"What would we say, anyway?"

"Bess, think," he said patiently, as if she were a schoolchild stumped on an easy problem. "We need to be talking about the lake just loud enough so that he overhears us. He needs to think it's his story to break."

She bit her lip. He made it sound simple, but she knew it wouldn't be. It was just like Mammi and the sheriff's car. Same thing.

"Come on, Bess," he said, as she hesitated. "We've got to try and save our lake! You're the one who found out it was polluted in the first place!"

The way he was looking at her, so passionate and fired up, made her fall in love with him all over again. And he had said "our lake," like it belonged to just the two of them. "Fine," she said. "I'll tell Mammi that we're going to buy some cherry tarts from Lainey. She'll be thrilled."

But there were no cherry tarts at The Sweet Tooth today. It was Lainey's day off, Bess and Billy discovered unhappily when they arrived at the bakery five minutes before three. Mrs. Stroot was trying to lock up for the day and seemed anxious for them to leave. Billy stood in front of the counter, stalling for time, pretending that he couldn't make up his mind about what to buy. Bess kept looking down the street to see a man in a big plaid jacket head this way. Finally, just as Mrs. Stroot was about to shoo them out, in came Eddie Beaker. It was just like Bess had told Billy, he was chewing a cold cigar.

"You go first," Billy told Eddie as he walked up to the glass counter. "I'm still thinking it over."

Mrs. Stroot rolled her eyes.

Eddie pointed to the Danish. "How much?"

"Ten percent discount," Mrs. Stroot bargained.

"Make it half off and I'll take them all," he growled.

As Mrs. Stroot sighed deeply and started to pack the Danish in a box, Billy unrolled his spiel. "I was planning to go fishing, but there's just no fish at Blue Lake Pond." He motioned with Bess to pick up his lead.

"Still none?" Bess asked, too loudly.

"Just the dead ones on the shore," he said.

"Such a pity," Bess said. "And all of those birds gone too." She wished Lainey were here. She would have been able to engage Eddie Beaker into the conversation. He seemed far more interested in the Danish than in the missing wildlife.

Billy sidled closer to Eddie Beaker. "It's the strangest thing. Ever since that paper mill went in, there's been less and less wildlife up there. Now, there's virtually none. Can't figure it out." He looked at Eddie Beaker to see if he was taking the bait. What more of a morsel could he toss to a reporter hungry for news?

Eddie Beaker pulled out his wallet to pay Mrs. Stroot. He handed her a few dollars, took the change, put it in his pocket, and left the bakery.

Billy exchanged a defeated look with Bess. "Let's go home."

Mrs. Stroot groaned.

Bess woke to the sound of bacon sputtering and popping in the pan. She lay in bed and smiled. Mammi said she would be making pancakes with maple syrup today.

Bess was delighted that her father wasn't talking about returning to Ohio anytime soon. She had assumed they would be heading back as soon as possible, but no. Jonah had told her that he was waiting on blood test results to see if he could help out Mammi's brother with his cancer. And happily, there was no mention of Bess as a donor.

She was glad she didn't have to worry about returning to Ohio. She had enough worries on her plate without adding more.

Her main worry was Billy Lapp. He'd taken up the outrageous notion that Bess could give him advice about how to get Betsy to stop flirting with other boys and just concentrate on him. "I know she's sweet on me," he told her just that afternoon while they were bagging up dried rose petals from the drying frames.

Bess listened sympathetically with her face and about a third of her mind. The rest of her thoughts were on memorizing Billy's face. "How do you know that?" She bent down to scratch a mosquito bite on her ankle until it bled. "Well?" she asked defiantly.

"She tells me so."

Bess straightened up and rolled her eyes to the highest heaven at that comment. "If she's telling that to you, Billy, she's telling that to all the boys."

He scrunched up his handsome face. "Nah. You don't know Betsy like I do."

How could Billy be so smart in rose grafting and mathematics and so dumb when it came to understanding women? The way the male sex thought had her stumped.

Bess had tried to have a conversation with Betsy Mast after church the other day, just out of curiosity. She couldn't deny that Betsy was exceptionally pretty—even more so, up close—but she had a breathy, baby voice and answered questions with questions. Bess asked her if her parents were farmers, and she responded by saying, "Aren't all Amish farmers?" Well, no,

Bess told her. Some build furniture, like her father. One fellow manufactures windows. Others even work in factories. Betsy looked at her as if she was describing life on another planet. Bess wasn't sure if Betsy's lantern in her attic wasn't lit or if she was just trying to pretend she was interested when she wasn't.

Billy nudged Bess to bring her back to his problem at hand. "What do you think I should do? Should I tell her I want her to stop seeing other fellows?"

They were working side by side. She enjoyed being this close to him. He smelled of earth and sweat and roses. "I don't know, Billy."

He lifted a frame and leaned it against the wall. "Sure you do. You're a girl, aren't you?"

Charming. At least he had noticed that.

"You can't *make* someone like you." She knew that to be true. "There was a boy in Ohio who drove me cuckoo, he liked me so much. Kept trying to walk with me to school and hold my hand and talked about getting married someday. He hung around me like a summer cold. He even had our children's names picked out. All ten of them!" She shuddered. "If he had just left me alone, maybe I would have taken notice of him." Probably not, though. Everything about Levi Miller was annoying to her.

Billy lifted the last empty frame and set it against the wall. He swiveled around on his heels, his head cocked. "Okay, I'll try it! I knew you'd have an idea of what to do. You're a peach." He smiled, exposing two rows of very white, straight teeth. Possibly one of his best features, Bess assessed. Either that or the cleft in his chin.

Bess turned away. *Don't tell me I'm a peach*, she thought. *Tell me I'm ... what? Beautiful? Hardly. The love of your life? That would be Betsy Mast. A loyal friend? Oh, that sounds like a pet dog.* So what did she want? Why was she so determined to keep on loving him, knowing that he loved another?

She had no answer.

In the middle of her musings, Billy surprised her with a loud and brotherly buss on her forehead. He grabbed his hat and waved goodbye as he left the barn for the day. She went to the open barn door and watched him walk down the drive, hat slightly tilted back on his head, whistling a tune as if he didn't have a care in the world. Blackie—fatter than ever from hunting all those barn mice and birds and other things Bess didn't want to think about—came out of his hiding place and wound himself around her legs. She bent down to pick him up, the traitor.

She wasn't sure what she had said that gave Billy a better plan to woo Betsy, but she knew she wasn't going to wash that kiss off of her forehead for a very long time.

Billy hurried through his chores that afternoon to get home, shower, and change, so he could hightail it over to the volleyball game at the Yoders'. He was grateful to Bess for giving him such good advice. Bess was turning out to be a valuable resource. He hadn't really had a friend who was a girl before. Bess was easy for him to talk to, maybe because she was a good listener. When Bess told him the story about the fellow who overly liked her, it hit him like a two-by-four. That was just the way he'd been acting toward Betsy.

It made so much sense. Betsy was more than a year older than he was. The last time he had tried to talk to her about courting, she tilted her head and asked him how old he was.

"Eighteen," he said. "Nearly nineteen."

Betsy gave him a patronizing look. "You can't even call yourself a man yet."

"Years aren't everything," Billy said. "I'm taller and stronger than most grown men."

Betsy had smiled and let him kiss her on the cheek, but he knew she never took him seriously. Of course not. He'd been acting immature, fawning and obsequious. Girls didn't like that, Bess had told him. That came as a surprise, but most things about girls came as a surprise to him.

Starting tonight, he was going to ignore Betsy. Not talk to her. Not even look at her.

When Billy arrived at the Yoders', he found his friends huddled together in a sad circle. "Who died?" he asked his best friend, Andy Yoder, who claimed to also be head over heels in love with Betsy. But Billy wasn't at all concerned. Andy was always in love with somebody.

"Haven't you heard? Betsy Mast ran off. We think she's with an English fellow who works at the Hay & Grain. Guess they've been planning it for months now." Andy looked as if his world had just imploded. "She's just been using all of us as decoys, so her folks wouldn't catch on."

❊❊

That night, Bess was sleeping deeply until a noise woke her. She opened her eyes and tried to listen carefully to the night sounds. She wasn't entirely used to Rose Hill Farm yet, the way the walls creaked or the sounds of the night birds, different from Ohio birds. At first she thought the sound must have been Mammi's snoring, but then she heard something else. Something thumped the roof by her window. She hoped it was a roof rat. Or maybe Blackie, finally coming out of that barn for a visit. Where was Boomer when she needed him? Probably snoring right along in rhythm with Mammi.

She tiptoed out of bed and looked out the window. Sometimes at night the leaves rustled branches at the window, but she didn't see leaves or branches. A shape was down there and it scared her half to death. She was just about to scream when she heard the shape calling up to her.

It was Billy, below her window, waving to her. He cupped his hands around his mouth and whispered loudly, "Get dressed and come down! I need to talk to you!"

Bess's heart sang. She never dressed faster in her life. She stuck herself twice as she pinned her dress together. She bunched up her hair into a sloppy bun and jammed her prayer cap over it, then quietly tiptoed down the stairs and slipped out the side door.

Billy was pacing the yard, arms crossed against his chest. When he saw her, he stopped and motioned to her to come. "Let's go to the pond."

He had left his horse and courting buggy on the road so that he wouldn't waken Mammi and Jonah, he said, so they hurried down the drive and climbed in. Bess looked back once, but the large farmhouse looked silent. Billy slapped the horse's reins and kept his eyes straight ahead. He didn't say a word, but Bess didn't care. Here she was on a perfect, moonlit summer night, being secretly courted by Billy Lapp. This was the most wonderful, splendid moment of her life. She wanted to remember every detail of the evening so she could relive it during dreary moments—math class came to mind—when she returned, inevitably, to Ohio. The night was dark, so she chanced a glance at Billy, admiring the determined way his jaw was sticking out, the stern set of his mouth, his two dark eyebrows furrowing together.

All of a sudden, Bess's dreamy hopes evaporated, like steam rising from a tea cup. She felt something was wrong, but then she was always feeling that and it never was. "Billy, is something bothering you?"

He took in a deep breath. "She's gone, Bess. She ran off with an English fellow who worked at the Hay & Grain." He wiped his eyes with the back of his sleeve.

"Who?"

"For crying out loud, Bess! Who do you think? Betsy!" He jerked the horse's reins to sharply turn right onto the path that led to Blue Lake Pond. He pulled back on the reins and stopped the horse at the end of the level space, then hopped down and tied the reins to a tree. He sauntered down to the water's edge, looking bereft.

Bess stayed in the buggy, watching him, half furious, half delighted. A part of her was disappointed that Billy used her as a listening post for his troubles. The part that felt delighted Betsy was gone made her feel shamed. What kind of person took delight in another person's downfall? She knew that wasn't right and she breathed a quick apology to the Lord for her sinful thoughts. But from the start she knew what kind of girl Betsy was, that she never did care about Billy or see how special he was. Betsy Mast wasn't good enough for Billy Lapp. Then she caught herself. That, too, was a sinful thought, and she had to apologize again to the Lord.

Goodness. Love was a tricky business.

She could see that Billy was suffering, and she tried not to be too glad for it. She sighed and hopped down from the buggy to join him.

"This is the worst summer on record," he said mournfully. "My lake is ruined. My love life is ruined." The words gushed out of him, heartfelt. He pressed a fist to his breast. "I love her so, it's like a constant pain, right here in my chest." He glanced at Bess. "You probably don't understand that kind of love."

Oh, I understand it all right, Bess thought. Love that burns so hot and fast it makes you act crazier than popping corn on a skillet.

He was sitting at the water's edge with his elbows leaning on his knees. "It's your fault, you know."

Her jaw dropped open.

"It is. If you had only given me the idea of ignoring her before today, maybe she would have taken me more seriously." Billy looked up at the moon. "I should have told her how much I loved her. How I was planning on marrying her. I shouldn't have waited."

Bess rolled her eyes. One minute he's ignoring Betsy. The next minute he's professing undying love.

"It's just that . . . I've never felt like that about anyone before. And I'm sure she was in love with me. I'm just sure of it."

Bess plopped down on the shore next to him. "Lainey said she's seen Betsy zooming around town in that English fellow's sports car all summer."

Billy froze. "That's not true."

"Lainey wouldn't lie about that," she said softly. "And you must know she was spending time in other boys' courting buggies." She looked away. "Even I knew that, and I've only been here a little over a month."

"That is a lie!" Billy shouted.

"No, it is not. You know it's the truth. I've seen Betsy in Andy's buggy and Jake's buggy and—"

Billy scrambled to a stand. "Aw, you don't know what you're talking about! She told me to my face that she was pining only for me!"

Bess rose to her feet and brushed off her dress. "Billy . . . you must have had some inkling—"

"Why am I even trying to talk to you about this? You're nothing but a child! What would you know about love?" He spun around and marched to the buggy.

Bess opened her mouth, snapped it shut. How *dare* he call her a child! She stomped up to the buggy. "Betsy Mast was never sweet on you! You got caught up like all the others with her . . . her curves and big lips and wavy hair. There was nothing in the attic." She tapped on her forehead. "Kissing don't last. Brains beats kissing every time."

Billy stared at her, as if he was trying to absorb what she had said. Finally, she threw up her hands in the air, turned, and marched up to the road to walk back to Rose Hill Farm.

She was halfway down the dark road and thought she heard a rustling noise in the berry bushes along the road. She stopped, slowly turned, looked back. The movement behind her also stopped. Each time she paused, it happened. Was Billy really going to let her walk all of the way home by herself? She was determined not to look behind her to see if he was coming, but now she was sure she heard a loud scruffling noise. Why, it was as loud as a bear, she started to think, though she had never actually come face-to-face with a bear. Bears liked berry bushes, she knew that for a fact. Yes, it definitely sounded like something was following her. A spooky owl hooted, wind cracked in the trees, and something else made a slithery noise that she hoped wasn't a snake, because she was afraid of snakes.

Just when she was about to run for her life, she heard the gentle clip-clop of Billy's horse pull up the road.

When he was beside her, he called out in his soft, manly voice, "Bess, hop in."

She continued walking quickly up the road, stubborn but pleased he had come for her.

Billy slowed the horse to a stop and jumped out, putting his hand on her shoulder to turn her to face him. "Bess. Don't be like that. I'm sorry I called you a child. I'm just . . . upset."

He looked so heartbroken and sad that her madness dissolved. He guided her back to the buggy and helped her up. They rode home silently, and he let her off at the edge of the drive so she could sneak back in the house.

Morning came too early. Bess couldn't stop yawning throughout Jonah's prayer before breakfast. Mammi handed her a cup of coffee without any milk in it. When Bess looked into the cup, puzzled, Mammi said in her matter-of-fact way, "Awful hard to sleep with a full moon blasting through the window. Goings-on outside look as bright as daylight."

Bess froze. Her eyes darted between Jonah, who was spooning strawberries onto his hot waffle, and her grandmother, quietly sipping her coffee with a look on her face of pure innocence. There was no end to what Mammi knew.

7

The weather all week was sunny and mild with no sign of rain. Late one afternoon, Lainey found Caleb Zook out in his cornfield, walking among the rustling whispers of the stalks. He was a tall man, yet the green stalks nearly reached his chin. He waved when he saw her and came through the path to meet her by the fence.

"We met at church on Sunday," she said, putting out her hand to shake his. "I'm Lainey O'Toole."

"I remember." He smiled. "I remember you as a girl too. Bertha brought you to church now and then."

His warmth surprised her. She would have thought a bishop would act stern and serious and cold with an Englisher. But Caleb Zook wasn't cold. Not cold at all. "I was hoping to have a talk with you sometime."

"Now is as good as any," he said kindly, though she knew she had interrupted him. "Shall we walk?" He hopped over the fence and joined her along the road. "What's on your mind?"

"There's something I've been thinking about. I've given it a lot of prayer, and thought, and more prayer. And more thought." She had too. It was something she couldn't get out of her mind. The more she tried, the more she felt God pointing her in this direction. And it was a frightening direction. She wouldn't be in charge of her life, not anymore.

He cocked his head, listening intently.

"I want to become Amish."

Caleb took off his hat and spun it around in his hands. "You want to become Amish?" he asked her. "Amish go English, but English don't go Amish. At least, not very often. I can only think of a few converts." He looked up at the sky. "Oh, lots of folks come and say they want a simpler life, but they don't last more than a few months. It's just too hard on them. The language, living without modern conveniences. They just didn't understand what they'd be giving up."

"Their independence," she said quietly.

"Yes. Exactly that." He looked at her, impressed. "Folks don't realize that being Amish is much more than simple living. It's giving up self for the good of the community. It's giving up individual rights because you're part of a whole. It's called Gelassenheit. There's not really a way to say what it means in English."

She nodded. "I know enough about the Amish to know what you're getting at. But that's the very reason I want to become Amish." Her gaze shifted past him to the corn in the fields, swaying in the wind. "For just that very reason—to be part of a whole. To belong." She crossed her arms against her chest. "I don't know if you can understand this, but I've never really belonged to anyone or anything. Until I was ten, I watched all of your families, always wishing I were part of one."

Caleb listened, spinning his hat. "Have you thought of joining an English church? Wouldn't that give you what you're looking for?"

She dropped her chin to her chest. "I've always belonged to God. He's been the one thing I've been able to count on. I've always gone to church, even on my own, even when I was living with different foster families." She lifted her head. "But there's still a part of me that wants something more. I thought finding a career would be the answer, so I saved up my money for culinary school. That's where I was heading when I ended up in Stoney Ridge this summer. But now that I'm here, I know it's something else that I want." She swept her arm out in an arc and gathered her fist to her chest. "I want this." She owed so much to the Amish. It was through them, years ago, when her sorry childhood was at its bleakest point, that she met the Lord. It was one of those mornings when Bertha let her tag along to church. Lainey couldn't understand much of the service, but there came a moment when she knew God loved her. It was during a hymn, a long, mournful Amish hymn, and it was as real as if God spoke to her, telling her that he knew her and loved her and not to worry. He would be watching out for her. She couldn't explain how or why, but she knew it was true, and that assurance had never left her.

Caleb looked at her with great sincerity. "Being Plain . . . it's not easy, Lainey, even for those of us born to it."

"I know more about being Amish than you might think," she said. "Do you remember Simon, Bertha's brother?"

He dropped his eyes. "Of course."

"Simon had it all wrong, about being Amish." Caleb was about to interrupt, but she put a hand up to stop him. She knew what he was going to say. "Oh, I know he was excommunicated. But he was raised Amish and thought he understood what it meant. He emphasized all the wrong things. He would rail against pride and then scold my mother for decorating a birthday cake for me with icing. He would say God was watching everything we did, like an angry parent, then he would go out drinking until the wee hours."

She could see Caleb wasn't sure what she was trying to say. She tried to make it more clear, but this was hard. She was telling him things she had never told anyone else. "Even back then, I knew he was missing the heart of it all. He didn't understand God the way I knew him, not at all."

Caleb raked a hand through his hair. "I have to ask. Does this have anything to do with Jonah Riehl?"

She looked at him, stunned.

"I noticed the two of you talking together after church on Sunday."

Her eyes went wide with disbelief. Why would talking together make the bishop think she wanted to join the church? "No! For heaven's sake, no! Nothing could be further from the truth. Jonah will be leaving for Ohio any day now. Bess said he's planning to marry someone there. I'm staying right here, in Stoney Ridge."

Caleb spun his straw hat around in his hands, around and around. She could see he was thinking hard. "Spend one week without using electricity."

Lainey's eyes went wide. "What will I tell Mrs. Stroot at The Sweet Tooth?"

He smiled. "No. Not at the bakery. But at home. You might find yourself heavy-hearted in your soul for machine-washed clothes and flipping on a light switch and other things in life that you have taken for granted."

Lainey was sure she wouldn't be so heavy-hearted. She had grown up poor, accustomed to going without luxuries. "Before I came to Stoney Ridge, I worked at a department store, listening to people's complaints about the products they bought." She shook her head. "All day long, I listened to complaints. It struck me one day that people were hoping these products—these things—would bring them happiness and satisfaction. But they never did." She looked up at him. "Because they can't."

Caleb listened carefully to her. "One week without electricity. Then we'll talk again." He put his hat back on his head and laid his hand on the fence post. Before turning to go back to work, he added, "For now, Lainey, I'd like you to keep this to yourself. Just something between you and the Lord God to work out. I'll be praying too."

She did write weekly to her two friends, Robin and Ally, but she would never dare tell them about this new plan. They would think she was certifiably crazy. "Bess knows."

Caleb tilted his head and smiled approvingly. "Then we'll keep this between the three of us." He jumped back over the fence.

Lainey watched the top of his straw hat until he disappeared among the cornstalks before she started back down the road. The funny thing was, going Amish was Bess's idea in the first place, a week or so before Lainey went to church with her. Bess and Lainey were baking muffins one afternoon at the bakery and talking about what they imagined a perfect life to be. Lainey described growing up Amish, and Bess looked at her, surprised. "Well, why don't you become Amish, then?" Lainey laughed, but Bess persisted. "I mean it. Why not?"

Lainey hadn't taken her seriously, but she hadn't stopped thinking about it ever since. And then when she went to church last week, she felt an even stronger pull. So then she started to pray about it, long and hard, asking God to tell her all the reasons why she *shouldn't* become Amish. But all she sensed from God was the same question Bess had posed, "Why not?"

She ran through all the logical things: she didn't know their customs or language, she didn't dress Plain, she would have to give up modern conveniences. Many things that she took for granted would be forbidden, like listening to the radio or watching television for entertainment. Then there were the deeper aspects to being Amish: humility and obedience to authority and denying self. Those weren't exactly popular concepts in the world she lived in.

It didn't make any sense, yet she couldn't deny what was stirring in her heart: a deep-down longing to join the Amish church and community. She wanted a place amongst them.

For the rest of the week, Bess avoided Billy as best she could, but he was so sulky, he didn't even notice.

"That boy looks like he's been poked in a private place," Mammi noted, watching him walk to the barn one morning. She finished drying the last dish at the kitchen sink and hung the dish towel to dry. "Anything to do with Betsy Mast running off?"

How did Mammi know everything that went on in this town? "It's not fair! It's just not fair," Bess cried, dropping her head on her arms at the kitchen table. "How could he be so sweet on a girl who would leave her church and family?"

Mammi shot her a warning glance. They should be worried that Betsy's soul was in peril, not throw stones at her. Bess knew that, but it was hard not to feel despair over the situation.

"The only fair I know hands out ribbons for canned pickles and prize tomatoes," Mammi said calmly. She eased her big self down onto a kitchen chair. "Things happen for a reason. Best to leave it in the Lord's hands."

"Do you think Billy will pine after her *forever*?" Bess glanced out the window as he came out of the barn and went over to the greenhouse.

"Forever is a big word for a fifteen-year-old. No sense tearing through life like you plan on living out the whole thing before you hit twenty." She leaned back. Bess was sure she heard the chair groan. "But he's no fool, that Billy Lapp."

Bess had no desire to listen to Billy's woes about Betsy Mast, but the situation at Blue Lake Pond was another matter entirely. Last night, lying in bed, she gave the matter serious thought and had a brainstorm. In the morning, she took out a sheet of white paper and started to write. She described the vanishing wildlife, the sawdust on the shoreline, the truck seen coming in and out dropping a load of paper pulp. She even included the license plate of the truck. She signed the letter, A Friend of the Lake. She addressed the letter to the *Stoney Ridge Times*, attention: Letter to the Editor, put a stamp on it, and tucked it in the mailbox so the postman would pick it up. She hoped the good Lord would understand that she wasn't just doing this to help Billy Lapp. She really did care about that lake.

Then she waited. And waited. But there was no sign of any activity at Blue Lake Pond other than the truck dropping paper pulp into it on a regular basis.

After lunch one day, Bess and Mammi washed the dishes and swept the room, and now Mammi was mending a torn dress hem while Bess was cutting scrap material into quilt pieces. They sat close to the window for better light—it was raining again. Jonah was in the greenhouse fixing a broken window.

"Mammi, I've been thinking," Bess said.

"Mebbe you should have tried that in math class," Mammi said.

Bess paid no attention. She was getting used to her grandmother. "I just don't know what else we can do about Blue Lake Pond. Billy and I have tried to get the attention of the right people, and they just don't seem to care."

Mammi's brow was furrowed and she rubbed her forehead, thinking hard. Then a look came over her. You had to study hard to see any expression at all on Mammi's face, but it was a look Bess was coming to know. She could tell Mammi was having one of her sudden thoughts. Mammi slammed her palms down on the table, stood, grabbed her bonnet off of the hook, and opened the door. "You coming?"

Bess followed behind her to help get the buggy ready. It wasn't long before Mammi went flying into town and pulled the horse to a stop at the sheriff's office.

Bess's heart nearly stopped. "Oh no. Oh no no no. I am not telling that sheriff about this. I don't want to get the law involved and then have to testify and . . . oh no." Bess crossed her arms against her chest. "I am staying right here."

"Suit yourself," Mammi said agreeably. "Here he comes now."

From across the street came Sheriff Johnny Kauffman. "Well, well, well. It's Miz Riehl and her granddaughter. Out on another crime spree?"

Mammi ignored his question. "Johnny, it's time you came out to dinner at Rose Hill Farm. I was thinking catfish. Battered and fried."

The sheriff's eyebrows shot up. He was practically licking his chops. "Your cooking is legendary, Miz Riehl."

"Saturday lunch then. We'll be looking for you." She climbed back in the buggy. "You wouldn't mind bringing the catfish, would you? You being such a dedicated fisherman and all. From Blue Lake Pond? No better catfish than Blue Lake Pond."

The sheriff looked pleased. "I haven't been out that way all summer." He clapped his hands together. "What time you want me at your farm?"

Mammi whispered to Bess in Deitsch, "What time does that paper truck make the drop?"

"Two on Saturdays," Bess whispered back.

"Twelve noon," Mammi said decidedly. "I want those catfish still jumping."

"I'll be there, Miz Riehl." He looked pleased. "You can count on it."

As they drove off, Bess tried to object, but Mammi waved her off. "You leave him to me."

Bess spent the drive home trying to think up Mammi-proof, ironclad excuses to absent herself from Saturday's lunch. *Nothing.* Nothing came to mind.

On Saturday morning, Mammi picked out two plump chickens to roast. By eleven, they were plucked, dressed, and in the oven. At twelve thirty, the sheriff turned into the drive at Rose Hill Farm and parked, all riled up.

"There wasn't a fish to bite," he told Mammi. "Something's *wrong* with that lake."

"Do tell," Mammi said, looking surprised. "Why, just last week, Billy Lapp said there's no birds out there anymore." She shook her head. "It's a misery, all right."

"She means mystery," Bess whispered to the sheriff.

"No, she's right," the sheriff said, looking quite bothered. "It *is* a misery. I sure was looking forward to Bertha Riehl's catfish, battered and fried."

"We'll have to make do with chicken," Mammi said. "Bess, go call your dad from the barn. Tell him dinner is ready."

The sheriff ate heartily, but as he left, Bess and Mammi noticed he turned left instead of going right into town. Mammi said she had a hunch he was heading back out to Blue Lake Pond.

Early Wednesday morning, Billy came running up to Rose Hill Farm, hollering for Bess at the top of his lungs. Bess and Jonah and Bertha were having breakfast. He burst into the kitchen.

"Look at this, Bess!" He held a newspaper up in his hands. The headline read "Schwartz Paper Company Fined for Poisoning Blue Lake Pond."

"Somehow, it worked!" Billy was overjoyed. "That Eddie Beaker took the bait!"

Jonah asked what bait he was talking about and Billy tried to explain. Bess opened her mouth to interrupt and point out that the story wasn't written by Eddie Beaker at all but by another reporter. But before she could cut a word in edgewise, Mammi shot her a silencing glance.

Jonah read the article aloud: "'The Schwartz Paper Company has been fined for discharging millions of gallons of untreated paper pulp into surface water at Blue Lake Pond. Sheriff John Kauffman of Stoney Ridge blew the whistle on one of the worst pollution offenders in Lancaster County. While fishing one day, he noticed that the lake seemed to be absent of fish. The sheriff began an investigation and discovered that the Schwartz Paper Company had been dumping gallons of untreated pulp straight from their mill into Blue Lake Pond.'" His voice picked up the pace as he read through the more factual parts of the story: "'Tremendous amounts of material discharged into the lake used up the oxygen in the water. Fish and aquatic life died from lack of oxygen. Mill wastewater also carries large amounts of suspended solids, such as wood fiber, that could smother underwater habitat for scores of fish and invertebrates such as insects and mussels . . .'" His voice trailed off. He scanned to the end of the article. "The company has admitted negligence and will pay the costs to return the lake to its original pristine condition." Jonah put the paper on the table and looked up. "The sheriff's been given a special commendation from the governor."

After Billy had left the kitchen, Jonah stroked his beard. "Curious, isn't it? Sheriff was here on Saturday. Story broke on Monday." He cast a sideways glance at his mother.

Mammi paid no attention. She stifled a rare smile and appeared pretty satisfied with the way things had turned out. "Well. That's that." She nodded, as if a great mystery had been solved.

Jonah had to leave a contact number for the hospital to call about the results of the blood test, and Lainey had offered the bakery's phone number since Bertha didn't have a phone. Plus, she said, someone was at The Sweet Tooth most every day. So Jonah had quickly slipped into the habit of dropping by the bakery very early in the morning—just to see if the hospital had called—when the town was still sleeping and Lainey was already at work. He would sit at the table by the window while she baked, and they would talk. Too soon, they would hear the noises of Stoney Ridge waking up, of the squeaky bicycle wheels that belonged to the paperboy as he rode down the street and the thump of the newspaper as it hit the shop doors. Of a car engine sputtering to life. Of a dog barking excitedly and another answering back. And then Jonah would get to his feet and prepare to go. He had to make himself leave. It seemed to him that the sweet smells that came out of that bakery—well, they could make a man forget everything in the world and follow its fragrance wherever it led.

As he shaved his cheeks, getting ready to head out the door this morning, his eyes fell on Sallie's letter, received just yesterday. It made his stomach hurt a little.

Dear Jonah,

It has been more than two weeks since you left for Pennsylvania. Mose Weaver is working full-time taking care of your furniture business. I'm worried about the poor man, he works so hard. You left an abundance of undone work for him. I need to bring him lunch each day just to keep up his strength so that your business doesn't suffer.

Fondly,
Sallie

P.S. I went ahead and planted celery. It is starting to come up. Plenty for the food, plenty for the table decorations.

He thought he would try to call the shop today and speak to Mose, just to make sure he wasn't overwhelmed by the workload. He was going to need to stay in Stoney Ridge awhile longer. For his mother's sake. For Bess's sake.

Oh, who was he kidding? It was for his sake. He couldn't get Lainey O'Toole out of his mind. It thrilled him to death. It worried him to death.

8

Early one morning, Mammi stood at the foot of the stairs to give Bess a wake-up call. She banged a spoon against a metal pan. "And bring down your sheets," she hollered up the stairs.

"I'm doing the laundry today," Bess hollered back down the stairs. Lainey had the morning off and was coming over. For once, Bess knew something that her grandmother didn't know. Lainey had told her she spoke to the bishop about going Amish, and Bess was so thrilled by the notion that she quickly offered to help. Today, she was going to give her a lesson on how to work a wringer machine. They had talked yesterday and picked out today for a laundry lesson because Jonah would be gone all day at an auction with Caleb Zook. And Mammi had plans to go to a neighbor's for a quilting frolic. Lainey wanted to keep quiet about her interest in going Amish. Bess wasn't sure why it was so important to keep it mum—she thought it was *wonderful* news—but she respected Lainey's wish.

"Good! I'll go back to bed and sleep till noon!" Mammi called out.

"Thought you didn't sleep at all!" Bess yelled back with a smile in her voice.

"Mebbe I'll just have to give it a try one of these days. See what Ohio folks find so appealing about it."

Bess laughed out loud. She looked out the window and saw her grandmother cross the yard to go to the henhouse, as she did every morning. A feeling of love for Mammi swept over her. How could she have ever been so frightened of her? She thought of those first few days when she arrived at

Rose Hill Farm. She had been deathly worried her grandmother would be relentless about her getting a blood test for bone marrow to help Simon, but she never mentioned it after that first time. Not even when her father arrived in Stoney Ridge. She knew her grandmother continued to visit Simon at the hospital once a week, but she never discussed him with Bess. She didn't even ask Bess to go with her. In fact, Bess had nearly forgotten about Simon.

When her grandmother disappeared into the henhouse, Bess turned her attention back to her project. She had just finished writing out another list of Deitsch vocabulary words for Lainey to memorize. She looked the list up and down. Earth. *Erd.* Mountain. *Berig.* Ocean. *See.* It struck Bess that this might have been what Adam and Eve felt like, having to learn the names of everything. The first job God gave Adam: inventing language. *Not* math. She'd have to remember to point that out to Billy Lapp.

She folded up the list and stuffed it in her pocket. She glanced out the window again and saw Lainey coming up the street with a pink bakery box in her arms. Mammi saw her too. Good. Maybe Mammi would be too busy thinking about what was in that box to wonder why Lainey was here.

Not likely. Her grandmother didn't miss a thing.

Lainey had spent a week now going without any electricity in her little rental room. She had to admit, it was harder than she thought it would be. Bess was a big help, showing her that it didn't have to mean living *without* power—she just had to do things differently. Bess loaned her a gas lamp with a fierce-looking fabric wick and showed her how to fill it with kerosene. They bought a little propane camper stove to use for heating food.

"It's a small version of what we use," Bess told her. "If you can start getting comfortable with kerosene and propane, you'll find that most everything else comes easily."

Lainey had tried to make chicken corn rivel soup for dinner last night using the propane stove. The soup wasn't so bad, but the rivels were inedible. Instead of turning out like dumplings, they tasted like lumps of school paste.

One thing that took getting used to was sitting in a room so dimly lit. She kept the gas lamp close to her so she could read, and it cast its glow in a circle around her while the rest of the room remained dark. It seemed so different from the English way of lighting up the entire room and then some, especially on a rainy day.

Bess gave her fifty words to learn each day, then quizzed her on them and corrected her pronunciation. She said the easiest way to learn a language was to be just like a toddler again, matching words for objects, so your ear became attuned. Bess was a hard taskmaster, Lainey thought with a smile. Lainey had taken German in high school, so she had a head start, but Deitsch was a dialect of German. Similar but different. Everything was slightly skewed, like how you felt when you looked in a wavy mirror.

This morning, she followed Bess down to the basement. Two large galvanized tubs were waiting, side by side, filled with hot water that Bess had brought down from the kitchen. On one of the tubs was fastened a wringer.

Bess tossed in some shavings of Mammi's soap and swirled it around until it lathered. "Mammi's soap lathers up real good. Vile smelling, but it does lather up."

Bess took a sheet and placed it in the tub. Lainey's eyes went wide when she saw Bess pick up a plunger to swirl the water.

"I've only used that to unclog a toilet," Lainey said.

Bess snorted. "Not around here. Mammi still uses a privy." She rolled her eyes. "I've tried talking her into letting Dad put in indoor plumbing till I'm blue in the face. Now it's Dad's turn to persuade her." After a few minutes of plunging, Bess fed the sheet through the wringer, then put it in the second tub to rinse it. Again, she plunged and plunged, then fed the sheet into the wringer.

Lainey helped with the next sheets. By the end of wringing them, she was panting hard. "This takes some muscle, doesn't it?"

Bess laughed at that. "This is just bedding for three people. Imagine what it's like for most Amish families."

Now Lainey understood why she saw clotheslines up at Amish farmhouses every day of the week except Sunday. It must take an Amish housewife hours every day to keep a family in clean clothes.

Bess looked up at her over the wringer. "How do you do your laundry?"

"At the Laundromat. You have to sit there for a few hours so no one steals your clothes."

Bess's head snapped up. Lainey could see that the thought shocked her.

Stories about the English fascinated Bess. To her, they seemed so complex, so filled with odd contradictions. Lainey knew what Bess was thinking: how could it be better to use electricity when it meant you had to worry about your clothes getting stolen?

By the time they got the big basket of sheets outside and hung on the line, the sheets were half dry and Bess and Lainey were wet through. Lainey's black hair hung in damp tendrils. Bess's blond hair was flying every which way out from under her prayer cap.

Lainey slipped a clothespin on the last sheet. The wind pushed against the damp sheet, making it fluff and lull in the air like a sail on a ship. The scent of roses lingered around them. For some odd reason, the morning's work was deeply satisfying. Far more satisfying than she ever felt at a desk, listening to people complain about their purchases. Their stuff. She wondered what Robin and Ally would say to that. They loved their stuff.

The Amish used time in a different way, Lainey thought, walking back to town after the laundry lesson with Bess. As she had watched Bess work, she noticed that her movements were unhurried. She never seemed to be rushing through a task so she could get on to something else, something better. To Bess, it was all good, all worth her time. Lainey thought of how she and her English friends would jam their schedules full so they could fit in more. And yet they were always running out of time! The Amish had the same amount of hours in a day, lived busy, productive lives, but somehow they seemed to have an abundance of time for all that really mattered. Lately, she felt as if she were on a fence, in between Amish and English worlds. Watching, evaluating. With every passing day, Lainey felt herself drawing closer to the Amish way.

Jonah had come up with an idea to build Mammi a roadside stand so folks wouldn't always be wandering up to the farmhouse. Bess knew Mammi didn't like to have English strangers wandering around Rose Hill Farm, mostly because they interrupted her work and they talked too long. Mammi was so pleased with Jonah's suggestion that she decided to expand her line of rose products to sell at the stand. Besides rosebushes, she sold rose petal jam, rose petal tea, potpourri, rose water, and now, she decided, she would add rose-scented soap.

Mammi had always made her own lye soap. It smelled like woodsmoke and could take the top layer of skin right off of a person. Bess thought it was a fine idea to try rose-scented soap.

Jonah told her that if she wanted to sell the soap, she should probably stop using animal fat and switch to vegetable shortening or coconut oil. Mammi looked shocked, and it wasn't often that she could be shocked.

"Where did you learn so much about soap making?" Mammi asked Jonah.

He told her he might have learned a thing or two in his life, and Bess thought he was starting to sound an awful lot like his mother.

When Mammi started to collect ingredients around the barn workshop for her rose soap project, Bess had a hunch she was going to have the raw end of this new business prospect.

To be sure, the very next morning Mammi set Bess to the chore of cleaning out the old soap kettle. That ancient kettle hadn't been thoroughly scraped out since it was new. Bess had to roll the cast iron kettle in the grass and climb halfway in with a wire brush to loosen the clinging, foul-smelling lye soap. Even Boomer wouldn't come near her. Blackie came to investigate, then scampered away before slowing to a stiff walk, his white-tipped tail arrogantly upstanding.

Near the barn, in the shade of a big tree, Billy was helping Jonah build the roadside stand. He walked past her once or twice and shook his head. It was hot and sticky work, and by the end Bess reeked of old lye soap.

When the kettle was finally scraped clean to her grandmother's satisfaction, Mammi brought out the ingredients for the rose soap. She cooked the soap outside, over an open fire, despite weather that had turned beastly hot and humid. The air felt so heavy it was hard to breathe, but Mammi soldiered on, which meant Bess had to also. Mammi experimented until she was satisfied with the right blends. Using rose water instead of plain water at the end of mixing the glycerin and oils together gave it a heavenly scent. Mammi wanted to get it perfect before they poured the soap into molds and let it cure in the barn for a few weeks. At last, she had the perfect combination.

"I need a victim," Mammi said, eyeing Bess's prayer cap. "Let's wash your hair."

Bess smelled of such sour smoke that she was happy to get her hair washed, but she hoped to high heaven Mammi's soap wouldn't leave her bald in the process. Mammi brought out a new wash pan and filled it with fresh water from the pump. Jonah and Billy had finished the stand and were building a foundation for it down by the end of the drive, so the two women had plenty of privacy. Bess pulled out her pins to let down her hair. Her hair fell to her waist. She bent over a big washtub and Mammi lathered her head.

"That burning your scalp at all?" she asked Bess.

"So far, so good," Bess said. Actually, it felt good, so good, with gentle suds and a sweet smell.

Mammi rinsed out her hair with clean water, again and again, until it squeaked. Then she took the tub and leaned it upright against the house before she went back inside. Bess wrung out her hair and let the air dry it. She sat very still, with her back to a tree, staring into the sky as she combed her hair out. The clouds were scudding overhead. There was quiet, and soft summer air, and time to think. She closed her eyes, just for a moment, and drifted to sleep.

Moments later, or maybe an hour, she opened her eyes and there was Billy. He was smiling at her with his thrilling white smile. She hoped her white blond hair looked like shining waves of water, blowing gently in the breeze.

Her eyes closed again, and when she opened them, he was gone.

Early the next morning, Lainey waited for Jonah to come into the bakery. She kept peering out the window, looking for him. She smiled when she saw him turn the corner. She looked forward to their visits and was surprised at how comfortable it felt to be with him. She had a cup of coffee ready for him and let him sit down before she gave him the message from the hospital.

She sat down across from him. "They said you're not a match. You have three HLAs that match, but Simon needs six HLAs." She scrunched up her face. "I'm not really sure what that means."

Jonah stirred his coffee solemnly. "It means that even though we have the same blood type, there are different antigens in the blood."

She thought he would be relieved by the news, but instead, he seemed distressed. They amazed her, these Amish. They genuinely cared about people who were difficult to care for. The timer for the oven went off and she picked up her mitts to take the Morning Glory muffins out. She was ashamed to realize that she wasn't sure she would give Simon her bone marrow, at least not as readily as Bertha and Jonah had offered theirs. Had she really forgiven him, then? Or was it a conditional forgiveness? Only good as long as he didn't ask anything of her. Was that truly forgiveness?

Jonah was watching her face as she took the muffins out of the pan. He stood and came to her. "What's troubling you?"

She finished setting the hot muffins on a cooling rack. "I told Simon I forgave him for being such a pitiful father. But the truth is, I'd only given him a small piece of forgiveness. The part that benefited me. I released my anger toward him for how he treated me and my mother. But I don't want the best for him." She took off the mitts and placed them on the counter. "I'm not even sure if I care if he lives or dies." She looked away. "That must shock you."

He leaned his back against the counter, his arms crossing his chest. "It doesn't shock me. I remember Simon's drinking and his get-rich-quick schemes. And his temper." He locked eyes with her then, and before she knew it, he brushed a curl of her hair away from her eyes.

His touch was so gentle, feathersoft, it nearly undid her. She was finding herself attracted to Jonah despite her best efforts to ignore—even stamp out—those feelings. Falling for Jonah didn't make any sense. But still, there was . . . just . . . something about him. She felt so safe with him, as if she could be entirely herself. She had never felt this way about a man before. But she couldn't forget about the Sallie woman back in Ohio. Jonah had never mentioned her to Lainey, and Bess didn't mention her either, other than that one time. But Lainey hadn't forgotten.

She tucked her hair behind her ear. "I'm amazed you don't feel relieved that you're not a match."

"I'm not relieved." He crossed his arms again. "I wish I had been a match. Since I'm not, my mother will be after me to get Bess tested. She's brought it up nearly every day. I keep telling her there's no way it would work. Bess is Simon's grandniece. But you know my mother. She gets like a dog with a bone over things."

Lainey felt a cold shock run through her. She turned away from Jonah so quickly that she dropped the empty muffin pan and it clattered as it hit the ground, echoing throughout the bakery.

Billy had offered to show Bess how to graft roses, so when the weather cooled off one day in late July, with gray skies threatening rain, he told her today was the day. Good grafting weather. He showed her how to pick out the strongest rootstock, healthy and undamaged. Then they went out to the rose fields to cut some slips.

"Your grandmother said she has an order for ten plants of white sweetheart roses," Billy said. He pointed out the best plant. Then he pulled out his knife and made slanted cuts from branches, quickly wrapping them in a wet dishrag. "Don't want the cut pieces to dry out."

Raindrops started to splatter their faces as they hurried back into the greenhouse. Inside, the air was warm and musty. Billy made an assembly line with rootstocks and slips. First, he dipped the slips into a powdery substance to help the root take, then carefully matched each slip to a rootstock branch before wrapping it with gauze. "Roots may not be glamorous, and they aren't even seen, but they're the source of a rose's strength," he told her, as if he were a teacher and she a student.

"Like people," Bess murmured.

"How's that?" he asked absently.

"It was in one of the sermons last week. 'If our roots go deep in the knowledge of God and our lives are hidden in Christ, we'll be strong. More likely to survive the storms of adversity.'" She surprised even herself by remembering what the minister had said. It was Lainey's influence. The more time she spent with Lainey, the more interested she became in spiritual things. Lainey quizzed Bess and Jonah after each church service. She understood more and more Deitsch now and was eager to piece together what she was learning. Her enthusiasm was contagious. "I'm thinking of joining the church," Bess said aloud to Billy. She had been considering it, but it gave her a shiver to say it aloud. It seemed more real.

Billy glanced at her. "I already did. Last year." He put away the powder. "If you know it's right for you, no point in putting it off, is the way I see it." He brushed one palm against the other. "But you are awful young. Not sure the bishop would allow it."

She rolled her eyes at that slight. She was, after all, nearly sixteen. She doubted Billy was much older when he became a member. He had joined at a younger age than most boys did, but that didn't surprise her. Billy wasn't like most boys. In many ways, he seemed already grown-up, solid and unwavering. Except when it came to girls. In that area, Bess thought, his judgment was quite poor. Abominable.

Billy liked to talk while he worked, and Bess loved listening to him. Today, he told her that he wanted to buy his own farm as soon as he turned twenty-one. "No mortgage, either. I've been saving every penny. I want to own my land free and clear. You see, land is a trust, Bess," he said, starting to sound like a preacher. "I think it's something you hold onto for a lifetime. Something a man passes on to his sons. And his sons pass on to their sons. Land should be cared for and improved in every generation—just the way your grandparents have done here at Rose Hill Farm—and that way, we're passing on a legacy."

Bess studied Billy as he worked. She felt keenly aware of every detail. She liked being this close to him. The rain was coming down hard now, soughing on the roof above them. She pretended for a moment that she and Billy were married, working side by side on their farm. Talking together, laughing together, making plans together. She wished this moment wouldn't come to an end, wished she could stretch the morning and make it last forever. Why was it that three hours in school felt like a week, but three hours with Billy Lapp felt like mere minutes?

The morning melted away too soon. The rain ceased and a bright sun flooded the space with light as Bess fell more in love with Billy than ever. Unfortunately, he showed no sign of feeling anything more for her than a kind of platonic friendship. But he hadn't mentioned Betsy Mast all morning. That thought made Bess happy.

And then it was noon and Mammi was calling to Bess to stop for lunch, which meant Billy would head home. She sighed. Time spent with Billy was always over too soon.

Dear Robin and Ally,

Work at the bakery is going well here in Stoney Ridge. So well that I've even given some thought to postponing culinary school. But don't worry; I haven't decided anything for sure.

Love,
Lainey

At lunch one day, Bess mentioned to Mammi and her father that Lainey would be dropping by later in the afternoon. Afterward, as Bess was washing dishes at the kitchen sink, she happened to glance out the window and notice her father by the pump. His head was under the pump. Then he skinned off his shirt and was washing his entire upper region. He was soaping seriously and Bess grinned. Her dad had never said so, but she had a sneaking suspicion that he and Lainey were growing sweet on each other. They shared smiles with their eyes and stole glances at each other when they thought no one was looking. But Bess saw and it suited her just fine. She had a hope for her father and Lainey, but she knew it was best to keep that thought quiet. She knew when to leave things be.

When Lainey arrived at Rose Hill Farm, Mammi was over at the Yoders', helping to clean the house for church that weekend. Another neighbor had come to ask for Jonah's help to catch a runaway horse. The house was empty but for Bess and Lainey. This afternoon was working out better than Bess had even hoped.

She told Lainey she was going to teach her how to sew using a treadle sewing machine.

Lainey looked dubious. "I can't even sew a button on my blouse."

"Good news," Bess said. "No buttons." She laid out a few yards of dusty plum–colored fabric and spread a thin tissue pattern over it. As soon as she had smoothed it all out over the fabric, she pinned one edge and pointed to Lainey to start on the other side.

"What are we making?"

Bess smiled mysteriously. "A dress."

After cutting out the pieces, Bess threaded the machine and started to push the pedal with her foot, causing the needle to go up and down at a steady speed. She sewed one seam and then turned it over to Lainey. "You do the other side. Just sew a straight line."

It took awhile for Lainey to get the rhythm, to pump her foot steadily so the machine would work. "You made it seem so easy, Bess. It's harder than it looks!" But then it came together. She held up the shapeless dress. "Done!"

"Not hardly," Bess said. She took two sleeves and pinned them to the main section. "Watch carefully. Curves are trickier." She whipped off one sleeve and let Lainey take her place.

After Lainey finished, Bess held it up and frowned. "Pull out the stitches and we'll do it again."

So Lainey did. Two more times until Bess was satisfied. They worked the rest of the afternoon and took the dress downstairs to press out the wrinkles.

Bess showed Lainey how to light the pilot light for the Coleman iron. They drank sweet tea while they worked in the kitchen. Lainey ironed the dress and held it up for Bess's approval. "There you go! A new dress for you."

Bess shook her head. "Not for me. It's for you."

Lainey looked stunned, so Bess added, "I don't know if or when you feel the time will be right to start wearing our garb, but I thought it would be good for you to have a dress. For when you're ready."

Lainey looked at the dress. "Should I try it on?"

Bess nodded, pleased. "There are pins on my bureau top."

Lainey felt strange, taking off her blouse and skirt and putting on this Amish dress for the first time. She wasn't even sure what kind of underwear they wore. She forgot to ask Bess. Did women even wear brassieres? Well, she would be wearing one today, that's for sure. One step at a time.

She slipped the dress on and tried to figure out how the pins should be placed so they wouldn't work themselves loose. She had heard a taxi driver who came into the bakery complain about all the loose pins he found in his cab's backseat after driving Amish women on errands. She folded the front pieces across each other and tried not to jab herself as she pinned them shut. Bess and Bertha never seemed to complain about the pins, but she knew they would take getting used to. Laid out on the bed were a prayer cap and a white apron. Lainey smiled. Bess had this all planned out ahead of time. She hesitated for a moment, but then decided to try them. She slipped the prayer cap on her head. It perched uneasily on her curls. She was growing out her hair, but she knew the covering probably looked silly. She tried to tuck her hair back under the cap. She had watched Bess do it one day and was shocked to see how long her hair was. Below her waist! She told Lainey it had never been cut.

Lainey put pins through the cap to hold it in place, the way she'd seen Bess do it. Then she pinned the apron into place and turned around slowly, trying to decide if she felt any different. She had pins holding her together from head to waist. There wasn't a mirror, so she wasn't as self-conscious. She had been wearing less and less makeup the last few weeks and hadn't even missed it. Well, the first day or two she had felt practically naked, but then she relaxed. She even started to like feeling less made-up, more natural. Maybe that's another secret the Amish have, she realized. If you aren't looking in mirrors all the time, you aren't thinking about how you look all the time. Your mind is freed up for other things.

She went downstairs to show Bess. Moving quietly as she always did, she found Bess washing dishes by the kitchen sink and said, "Well, what do you think?"

Bess whirled around, startled, dripping soapy suds on the floor. "Oh Lainey! Seller Frack bekummt dich!" *That dress becomes you!* Then her eyes darted nervously to the other side of the room.

Lainey looked to see what had distracted Bess. Jonah was standing by the door, staring at her. "Ya. Ich geb ihr allfat recht." *Yes, I agree with her.* His smile got lost somewhere in that quiet moment.

Now, Lainey felt different.

Dear Jonah,

It has been over four weeks since you left. Mose has been working as hard as a pack of mules for you, but he did take time out to stake the tomato plants in the garden for me. And take us for a picnic down by Miller's Pond. And he built a treehouse for the boys with leftover wood from the furniture-making business. He said you wouldn't object. Would you?

> *Yours truly,*
> *Sallie*

P.S. The celery patch is nearly six inches tall!

It took Jonah a few days to get up his nerve to tell his mother about the blood test not being a match for Simon. He had dreaded this conversation. He waited until Bess had gone to the barn, and then he quietly told her. He sat sprawled in his chair, one arm hooked over the back.

"I know," Bertha said. "They sent a letter with the results." Out of her apron pocket she pulled a letter from the hospital.

Jonah closed his eyes. "How long have you known?"

Bertha looked up at the ceiling. "Let's see. A week."

Jonah rubbed his forehead. "I know what you're thinking. And I'm not going to agree to it."

"Bess is old enough to make the decision for herself."

"She's still a child."

"Fifteen years old is no child. Why, when I was a girl—"

"I know, I know," Jonah interrupted. He'd grown up hearing plenty of hardship stories that started with that sentence. "There's a remote chance, anyway, that Bess would be a match. Why take the risk?"

Bertha slapped her palms on the table and glared at him. "Why not?"

Right then, Jonah realized that the simplest, easiest thing to do would be to have Bess take a blood test. That way, the results would show his mother what he already knew—that Bess could not possibly be a match. "Okay." He surrendered his hands in the air. "If she agrees to it, Bess can have the test."

He thought his mother would be ecstatic or, at the very least, satisfied. He was giving her what she wanted. Instead, her gaze shifted to the window. From the look on her face, it seemed as if she just had a sense of something dreadful coming to pass.

That night, Jonah asked Bess to sit out on the porch with him to watch the sunset. She knew he had something on his mind. It was a clear night. They watched the sun dip below the horizon and the sky turn a bruised blue. Then he told her about his mother wanting her to get the blood test. Bess sat on the porch steps, hugging her legs, with her chin leaning on top of her knees as she listened to him.

"I want you to pray about this tonight. I don't want you feeling any pressure to have the test."

Bess turned her head toward him. "You were willing to give Simon your marrow, weren't you?"

Jonah nodded. His heart ached in a sweet way when he saw the earnest look on her face. "I was willing, but that doesn't mean you have to. The blood test is pretty simple, just a prick in your arm. The marrow test is a much more complicated procedure. You'd have to have general anesthesia and stay in the hospital, and it will be a little painful. The chance of you being a match is highly unlikely. I can almost rule it out. It's just that your grandmother . . . well, you know how she can be once she gets an idea in her head."

Bess lifted her eyebrows. "Sie is so schtarrkeppich as an Esel." *She is as stubborn as a mule.*

This time Jonah had no trouble smiling. "It seems very important to Mammi that we at least rule it out."

Bess shrugged. "I guess I can understand that. Simon is her brother."

"But that doesn't mean you have to do this, Bess. If you'd rather not, I would never make you do it, no matter what Mammi has to say about that."

"But you were willing. To give Simon your bone marrow."

"I was willing."

"And Mammi was willing?"

Jonah nodded again. He knew his daughter's tender heart. "Bess, I don't know if he . . . deserves such mercy." He told her the entire story, all that he knew, about Lainey and her mother and how Simon treated them. He was surprised to realize that Lainey had never mentioned Simon to Bess. He knew the two had grown close this summer. He could see Bess was shocked when she learned Simon was Lainey's stepfather. She grew quiet for a long time. Jonah wondered why Lainey had never told her, but then he decided that she was probably protecting Bess. Knowing what he knew of Lainey, he thought she was trying not to influence Bess one way or the other.

They sat quietly for a long time, watching the stars fill the sky. Finally, Bess lifted her head and gave him a soulful look. "Simon may not deserve our mercy, but Lainey is always telling me God has a different perspective on mercy."

Those words cut into him as real as a sharp knife. That old disquiet filled him again, gripping his chest like an actual pain. He had discovered something about himself this summer—something that shamed him deeply. He had believed in God all of his life, but did he truly believe God was sovereign over all? Did he believe that God's ways were truly merciful?

Fifteen years ago, he would have said yes. But after the accident that killed Rebecca, a part of him had stopped counting on God the way he had before. As if God couldn't entirely be trusted.

And so Jonah had run. He had run from God, the same way he had run from his memories. It was too difficult to remain in Stoney Ridge, driving by the accident site nearly every day where Rebecca had died, constantly reminded of what he had lost.

Lainey had just as many reasons to leave Stoney Ridge as he did, yet here she was. Back, facing the very things that haunted her. She was even willing to face Simon in the hospital. When she had come out of Simon's ward into the hallway, the look on her face nearly sliced his heart in two. It was filled with sorrow, but not for herself.

It was filled with sorrow for Simon's lost soul.

Billy hadn't been planning to go to the gathering tonight. It was Bertha Riehl who pinned him to the wall to go and take Bess along too. That woman had a way of getting what she wanted. She didn't ask directly, she just stared at you until your knees buckled and you caved in.

He wasn't in much of a party mood, and hadn't been, and probably never would be again, since Betsy Mast's departure. He still couldn't believe she had up and gone. He had had so many plans for their future together. As soon as he turned twenty-one, he was going to buy some land to farm. He knew just the kind of house he wanted to build for himself and Betsy: it would have a southern exposure, and a barn on a right angle, and a pond to fish and swim in. A pond that would be safe from polluters.

In his vision, his father and brothers would see what he had done— bought a parcel of fine land, married the most sought-after girl in the district, started a thriving business—and they would treat him with respect, not just as the baby of the family. Der Kaschde. *The runt of the litter*, his brothers called him.

But that dream was gone now. What irked him most was that he thought he knew Betsy. He thought she would want the same things. It still stunned him that she was gone. She had left her family, her church. She had left him for another man.

Bess had told him once that he had made up the idea of Betsy in his head. Maybe he didn't really know her at all, she pointed out.

He glanced over at his cousin Maggie, talking a mile a minute, and Bess on the other side of her. Bess was in a cranky mood today. The day had started out fine. She had been helping him get some plants ready to sell to a customer this morning, and he told her his latest theories on Betsy's departure. She grew quieter and quieter, like she was getting a headache, and didn't say goodbye to him when her grandmother called her in for lunch. Girls could be like that, he was learning. Moody and unpredictable.

As soon as they reached the yard where the gathering was held, Billy jumped down, tied up the horse, and sauntered off to join his friends at a game of volleyball. He didn't even notice where Maggie and Bess had gone until Andy Yoder pulled him aside.

"Who's that?" Andy pointed across the yard to a tight knot of girls.

"Who?"

"The blond."

"The skinny one? That's Bess. Bertha Riehl's granddaughter."

Andy snorted a laugh. "Maybe you need eyeglasses. She ain't so skinny now. Seems like she's got a different shape up above." He handed the volleyball to Billy and walked across the yard to meet Bess.

Billy watched Andy make his way to sit next to Bess. It occurred to him that Bess was going to be quite a nice-looking girl. It was a thought he'd never had.

After volleyball and dinner, then hymn singing, Billy was ready to go home. When he found Maggie, he told her to go get Bess and he would meet them at his buggy.

"She already left," Maggie told him. "With Andy Yoder."

Bess woke up in the morning with a firm resolution: last night was the final time she would cry herself to sleep over Billy. She could feel how swollen her eyes were and wondered if she could sneak out to the garden to snatch a cucumber without Mammi spotting her. She had heard girls talk about putting cucumbers on their eyes as a cure. She tiptoed down into the kitchen and was glad to find it empty. She was just about to open the side door when she spotted Mammi, picking beans and filling up her apron, talking to Billy in the garden. Bess couldn't go out there now.

Maybe pickles would work. She grabbed a jar from the pantry and hurried back upstairs. She opened the pickle jar and lay down on the bed, placing a sliced pickle over each eye. Within seconds, her eyes were stinging from the vinegar. She jumped up and reached for a pitcher of water. What a terrible idea! Her eyes were bloodshot now and even more swollen-looking than before. A sharp scent of dill and vinegar hung in the air.

An hour later, she was in the barn spreading rose petals when Billy came in with a freshly filled basket. "Where do you want them?"

She kept her head low and pointed to an empty tray.

He carefully spread the petals out, single layer, on the screen. "So Andy Yoder took you home last night?"

She shrugged. That was her business and no one else's.

"You could have at least told me. I wasted time looking for you."

Bess looked up, pleased. "You did?"

"Sure." Billy shook out the basket and set it on a shelf with the other baskets. "Last thing I want is to have your grandmother sore at me for not bringing you home."

Charming. "Well, she's not sore at you." She gave him a sideways glance. "She thinks Andy Yoder is a fine fellow."

"Bertha Riehl said that?" he asked, amazed. "Andy isn't very selective about girls. He'll take any female who smiles his way."

She brushed past him to go to the farmhouse.

He sniffed the air as she walked by him. "Strange. I keep getting a whiff of pickles."

Jonah was about to turn off the kerosene lamp in the kitchen and head to bed when a knock on the door surprised him. He opened the door to find Lainey standing there in the moonlight.

"Jonah, I would have come sooner, but I was working late tonight in the bakery for a big order tomorrow. A call came for you today. From the hospital." She bit her lip. "Bess is a perfect match for Simon. Six for six."

Jonah was stunned. "How could that be? How could that possibly be true?"

Lainey looked past him with a hard stare.

Jonah turned to see what she was looking at. His mother was on the bottom stair. It looked as if she had come down, overheard them, and was starting to tiptoe back up.

"Tell him, Bertha," Lainey said in a firm voice.

Bertha stopped in her tracks.

"Tell me what?" Jonah asked, looking from his mother to Lainey and back again.

Lainey and Bertha locked gazes. "If you don't tell him, I will."

"Oh, I'll tell him. I said I would and I will." Bertha scowled at Lainey but sat down at the kitchen table.

The tendon of his mother's jaw was working, so Jonah knew to prepare himself for a revelation.

Bertha looked at him carefully, paused a long while to gather her thoughts, then slapped her palms on the table and turned to Lainey. "Fine. You tell him."

Lainey gave Bertha a look as if she couldn't believe what a coward she was. She dropped her head and let out a deep breath. She pulled out a chair across from Jonah. "This is a story that goes back to that night fifteen years ago when you and Rebecca and . . . your baby . . . were in that horrible accident."

Jonah stiffened.

But Lainey didn't waver. She told him the entire story, she didn't leave anything out. When she was done, she looked directly at him. "I switched those babies, Jonah. Your baby for my little sister."

Jonah was stunned silent. The kitchen was so quiet that the sound of a fly buzzing against the window echoed through the room. He stared at Lainey as if she had been speaking in a foreign language. The full realization of what she said slowly started to dawn on him. *No. It couldn't be. It couldn't possibly be true.* He had trouble speaking—the words tangled up in his throat, and he had to stop and unravel them before he could say what he needed to say.

In a hoarse voice, he spoke at last. "You were only ten. You must not be remembering clearly. You must have it mixed up."

"I remember it right, Jonah," Lainey said softly. "I'll never forget that night."

"But . . . how? How could you . . . how would you even know if a baby was dead?" He leaned forward in his chair. "Maybe she wasn't. Maybe—"

Lainey shook her head. "She died instantly. I know I was young, but I knew she was gone." Her eyes welled with tears.

In a tight voice he said, "But I was told my daughter was completely unhurt. I was told it was a miracle."

"I put my baby sister in Rebecca's arms—to bring her comfort—and waited until I heard the sirens. I just stayed right by the two of you, telling you over and over again not to quit. Not to give up. But by the time the ambulance arrived, I had made a decision."

Silence fell over the table. Jonah's mind struggled to grasp what Lainey was saying. He grabbed hold of the table, feeling like the victim of a hurricane, his life strewn to pieces. Everything seemed to be floating.

Bess wasn't really his daughter. It shocked him to the core.

Then he had an even greater shock. His eyes met his mother's and he realized that she wasn't at all surprised. She *knew* this. She knew this!

As if Bertha could read his thoughts, she crossed her arms defensively against her chest. "Yes, I knew about this, Jonah. I knew. The night of the accident, I went to the hospital and found out Rebecca had passed and you were in bad shape. They said the baby had come through the accident unharmed. A miracle, they called it. They kept her overnight for observation. Then the next day, she was given to me to take home. But she wasn't our Bess. By that time, I had already heard about Lainey's sister's passing and put two and two together. I went to the county morgue, to be sure. I planned on telling you, but it got harder and harder, and then . . ." Her voice drizzled off.

He lifted his eyes to look at his mother. "And now you've finally come clean because of Simon."

Slowly, Bertha nodded. "When Lainey showed up out of the clear blue sky, I knew the time had come."

"How could you do that? How could you lie to me for fifteen years?"

"Some things are just worth a little bit of trouble."

Jonah exploded. He rose to his feet and leaned his palms against the table. "Don't you dare make this sound like something trivial!"

Bertha didn't back down. She looked straight at him. "You needed that baby, Jonah." She pointed a strong finger on the table. "And she needed you."

Once again, silence covered the room. In a voice so calm he hardly recognized it, he said, "Tomorrow, Bess and I will return to Ohio. This topic is closed. Forever." He stared at Lainey, hard, for a long moment, then reached for his cane and went up the stairs.

At breakfast, Bess could tell that something had happened between her father and grandmother, but she had no idea what had made her father decide to leave Stoney Ridge so suddenly. It saddened her when he told her at breakfast. She tried to object, but she could read the stubborn look on his face. There was no changing his mind. And Mammi, as usual, wasn't talking.

Bess went up to her room to pack up her belongings. As she folded her dresses and aprons into her small suitcase, she could hardly believe how attached she had grown to Mammi, to Lainey, to Rose Hill Farm. To Billy. It had been only two months, yet she felt as if she belonged here. As if this was her home.

She heard her father call to her to come downstairs. She looked around the room one last time to brand the image on her memory: the pale green walls rimmed with pegs for clothing. The scratched-up wooden floors. The small wooden bed with Mammi's handmade starburst pattern quilt on top, the nightstand with a glass oil lamp, the windowsill where she sat some nights, watching the moon rise and cast shadows over the rose fields. She sighed and trudged down the steps.

Billy was out front, waiting for them by the buggy. Jonah had asked him to drive them to the bus station to catch the noon bus. She walked up to him and he took the suitcase from her.

"What's going on with your dad?" he whispered. "What's the big rush to leave town?"

Bess shrugged. "Just needs to get back to his business, I guess," she said nonchalantly. Bess felt a small sense of dignity rise up in her. After all, Billy had disappointed her tremendously. Maybe it was good that she was leaving. Maybe he would pine for her. Maybe he'd even write long letters to her.

"I'll go scrounge up that black cat of yours," he said, heading over to the barn.

Blackie! She'd nearly forgotten him.

Mammi and Jonah came out to the buggy.

"What's keeping Billy?" Jonah asked, looking anxiously at the barn.

Not a moment later, Billy let out a large whoop. He came outside, cradling two small kittens in his arms, with an angry Blackie trailing behind. "Hey, Bess! So much for your scientific skills! I thought you said your cat was a boy!" he cried out, laughing.

Bess ran over to see the kittens. Blackie curled around her legs. She looked back at her father. "I can't take them! They're hardly a day or two old!"

"They'll stay," Mammi said decisively. "Their mother stays too. She's a decent mouser after all."

Bess gave each kitten a kiss and let Billy take them back to the barn where he found them. She reached down to stroke Blackie, but he . . . she . . . glared at her and hurried after her kittens.

Bess watched them go and turned to say goodbye to Mammi. When their eyes met, Bess felt tears choke in her throat. She ran to her grandmother and threw her arms around her big shoulders. She felt Mammi's arms reach up to pat her on her back. When Bess finally let go, Mammi took off her spectacles, breathed on them, and rubbed them with her apron. Needed polishing, she said.

Jonah offered his mother a stiff handshake. Mammi held onto his hand extra long, Bess noticed, as if she didn't want to let go.

But Jonah was undeterred. He went to the buggy just as a pony and cart pulled up the drive. It was Andy Yoder, carrying a bouquet of wildflowers in his arms.

When he reached the yard, he reined the pony over to the buggy and jumped off the cart. "What's going on?"

"They're heading back to Ohio," Mammi said, glaring at Jonah.

Andy looked horrified. "But why?" When no one answered, he looked to Bess, but she only shrugged. Then he turned to Jonah. "Well, could I at least speak to Bess? Privately?"

Jonah rubbed his forehead as if he had a headache coming on, but he climbed into the buggy. Mammi stayed put.

Andy gave a sideways glance at Mammi before thrusting the wildflowers at Bess. "What would you say if I wrote to you? Would you write back?"

Billy came out of the barn and stopped abruptly when he saw Andy handing the wildflowers to Bess. "We'd better get going if you want to make that noon bus, Jonah," he said in a loud voice. He climbed into the buggy.

"He's right, Bess," Jonah called out.

Andy looked stricken. Bess got into the buggy and sat in the backseat.

"Write to me, Bess!" Andy yelled as Billy slapped the reins to get the horse moving.

Bess leaned a hand out the window to wave to Mammi and Andy and the rose fields and the house and Blackie.

When Billy turned left onto the road, Bess said to her father, "I want to say goodbye to Lainey."

"No time," Jonah answered, eyes on the road. He spoke sharply but without conviction.

"We're going right past the bakery and it won't take but a minute," she said firmly.

Jonah didn't respond, so Billy pulled the horse to the hitching post. Lainey came out as if she had been expecting them. Bess ran into her outstretched arms.

"I don't know why he's doing this, Lainey!" Bess whispered. "Something's happened to make him upset."

Lainey didn't answer at first. Then she pulled back and held Bess's arms. "Being here . . . it's hard for your father. It brings up a lot of sad memories. Things he'd rather forget about. Give him time. He'll come around." She hugged Bess again and released her.

Jonah came toward them. "Bess, hop in the buggy. I'll be there in a moment."

Bess went to the buggy to wait with Billy. She kept her eyes on her father. Lainey was saying something to him, but he didn't say anything back. He looked away while she spoke, as if he didn't really want to hear it.

"He'll be in love with a new girl by week's end," Billy said crisply.

Bess's gaze was fixed on her father and Lainey. "I don't think so. I've never seen him like this."

"What do you mean? He's like this all the time."

She turned to Billy. "Who?"

"Andy Yoder. He's girl crazy."

Bess rolled her eyes.

"I'm only looking out for your welfare."

Bess turned back to her father and Lainey. He was saying something to her now, something that made Lainey look hurt. He returned to the buggy and gave a nod to Billy to get going. Bess waved to Lainey, who blew a kiss at her and waved back, slow and sad.

Jonah and Bess's quick departure left Billy with a vague unease, as if he had left the barn door open or forgot to water the new rose graftings. Something just didn't feel right. What was Jonah's big hurry about, anyway? Billy clucked to old Frieda to get her moving faster. This horse moved plenty fast for Bertha but acted like a tired old nag for everybody else.

His thoughts drifted to the way Jonah and Lainey looked—so serious—when they were talking to each other outside the bakery. If he didn't know better, he would say they looked like their hearts were breaking. But that couldn't be right. A straight-up fellow like Jonah Riehl would never get involved with an English girl. Bertha Riehl would have him drawn and quartered.

But what did he know about love? He thought Betsy was straight up, and he sure was wrong about that. *Oh Betsy, Betsy, I thought I knew you,* Billy lamented as the horse plodded along.

He felt himself slipping back into what Bess called his Betsy funk. He tried to snap out of it by thinking again about Jonah and Bess and Lainey. Bess had been trying to figure out what Jonah and Lainey were saying to each other while he was trying to warn Bess not to count on Andy's devotion for longer than a minute. Bess was awfully innocent about boys, though she didn't seem to appreciate his warning. She had told him to hush.

"They're saying something important," she scolded him, watching Jonah and Lainey. She squinted her eyes, trying to lip-read. "She's asking him if it would have been better to be raised by *that* man. He's telling her that he thinks living with the truth would have been better. No . . . best." She shrugged and blew out a breath. "*What* is going on with those two?"

As Billy turned the horse right into Rose Hill Farm, he felt an odd feeling stir in the pit of his stomach. It surprised him, that feeling. Bess wouldn't be there anymore.

Gone would be their daily challenge: he would give her a math problem to figure out, only to have her give him a vocabulary word that he had to puzzle over. She didn't think she was very smart, but he thought differently. She knew about things he'd never heard of: Latin names of birds that visited the rose fields. She would hold her head in dismay as he butchered the pronunciation. She said he did to Latin what her grandmother did to English. Bess was interested in everything: how to graft a rose, how to gather honeycombs without making the bees mad, even how to track animals. He never knew anyone with such curiosity. He thought about how her eyes always widened when she thought deeply. He would wait and lean in her direction, as a sunflower would follow the sun, for whatever illumination was sure to follow.

He felt a strange ache in his heart, a different kind of ache than Betsy Mast's devastating betrayal. He was going to miss Bess.

9

ess had never seen her father like this before.

Jonah was carrying a burden, heavyhearted. He hardly said more than a few words during the long bus ride to Ohio. When they returned to the house late that night, Sallie rushed right over and Bess's heart sank to her knees. Bess fled upstairs to open up the windows, she told Sallie, and let the house cool off. It was so hot and stuffy inside that candles had melted in their holders. She didn't intend to eavesdrop, but Sallie and Jonah were outside on the porch, right below her window.

"My oh my, but you gave me a start!" Sallie was saying. "I was beginning to think you weren't coming back at all! Not at all!" She spoke so quickly that her words blurred together.

Jonah said something so quietly that Bess couldn't make out what he said.

"If you were much later, I was afraid we'd have to wait until December to get married. But November will still work. Not a minute too soon, mind you. We're already way behind schedule. Not to worry, not to worry! It will all get done!" She started listing out all that she had already done—made a list of people to invite, made a list of foods to prepare, decide which house to live in . . . but that could be discussion for another day, she told Jonah. Then Sallie gave up a rare pause. "You do still want to get married, don't you, Jonah?"

There was silence down below. *Oh please, Dad. Please, please say no!*

"Yes," Jonah finally answered, loud and clear. "Of course."

Bess's heart sank. She tiptoed to another room to open the windows and get a cross breeze. She knew when to leave things be.

Maybe, Lainey thought, maybe it was just as well that Jonah had left before anything more serious developed between them. She had a lot of thinking to do about her future, and being around Jonah made her mind a little scrambled. She didn't like feeling scrambled. She liked having plans laid out, even and straight. Not that plans couldn't be changed. They could.

In fact, she was changing her plans this very day.

Earlier today, Lainey had met with the realtor, Ira Gingrich, wanting to have an informal conversation about the purchase of Simon's former house. She had thought long and hard about this. She prayed about it every time she walked past the cottage. She felt as if there was something about that cottage she couldn't ignore—as if it was a metaphor for how she felt about her life. God was in the business of restoring things. People too. The old could be made new.

Ira Gingrich was a plump, easygoing man with pink skin and white hair, who sat with his hands resting on his belly. The house had been on the market for three years, without a bite, he said sadly. When Lainey made a ridiculously low offer on it as a joke, he squinted at her in confusion. Then a sudden smile creased his face.

"Sold!" he shouted and jumped to his feet, thrusting his hand out to grab Lainey's and pump it up and down.

Stunned speechless, she was suddenly the owner of a dilapidated, run-down, neglected house sorely in need of some love and attention.

That night, in her little room, she went over her finances and felt rather pleased. The money she had saved up for culinary school would suffice as a down payment. She thought she would talk to Billy about doing some renovations for her. She had a lot of confidence in Billy's abilities. She had noticed how carefully he worked at Rose Hill Farm. If he didn't know how to do something, he would find out. She figured out that her bakery hours would cover her mortgage payments . . . just barely. Even still, she didn't regret this turn of events. Not at all. For the first time in her life, she had a home of her own. And she hoped and prayed that Jonah would come to his senses and at least let her be a sister to Bess. She had squelched the hope that was stirring within her heart for Jonah.

It was probably a good thing that he left when he did, she told herself. Over and over and over. After all, she thought, it made things simpler.

Ira Gingrich sped up escrow so Lainey would close on the house by Friday. Bertha observed that nobody had ever seen Ira Gingrich move this fast, not even at quitting time at the bank. She said he was moving that escrow through like a greased sow before Lainey could think twice and change her mind. Lainey started a list of things she would need: a bed, sheets, a table, chairs. She wondered if Bertha might have a few extra pieces of furniture to loan in that big attic at Rose Hill Farm.

By the time Friday dawned, Lainey woke up more excited than she had ever felt about anything in all her life. She wished she could be sharing the day with Bess and Jonah. Instead of missing them less, she found she was missing them more. Especially Jonah. Every morning when she went to the bakery, she expected him to be there, waiting for her. And often at night, as she had closed up shop, he would happen to stop by to walk her home. She hadn't even realized how often Jonah filled her thoughts. It worried her. She had only known him a month's time. Was Caleb Zook right? Was she planning to get baptized for Jonah's sake?

No. She had an unwavering certainty that it was more than that. She had been longing for something all of her life . . . and when her VW Beetle died on Main Street in Stoney Ridge, it wasn't long before she knew she had found what she had been looking for. She wasn't one to think that only the Amish were Christians . . . she'd been around too many types of people to know that God cared about the interior condition of a person's heart, not their exterior labels. But for her, she knew she worshiped God best here. What she liked best was that being Amish, to her, meant that every part of her life was a testimony to God.

She had given away her clothes and makeup and was wearing the garb now. Even at the bakery. Mrs. Stroot took one look at her, shook her head, and blamed Bertha Riehl. It took Lainey a few days to feel comfortable, to get used to startled stares. After a while, she decided that the reason the

Amish wore Plain clothes was to identify them as belonging to God. So each time she was reminded she was dressing differently from others, it drew her attention to God. She liked that.

As she was dressing this morning for work, it dawned on her that she had an answer to the bishop's nettlesome question: if Jonah Riehl was the reason she was going Amish, that reason was gone. Most likely, he was planning his autumn wedding to that Sallie woman in Ohio whom Bess had mentioned once or twice.

And still, Lainey was determined to become Amish.

Bertha Riehl burst into the bakery midafternoon on Friday as Lainey was pulling chocolate chip cookies out of the oven. "Been to see Simon. He's only got a few weeks left. They said we should take him on home. Let him die in peace."

Lainey set the trays on the counter to cool. She took off the mitts. "You're awfully kind to do that, Bertha." She slid a spatula under each cookie to loosen it.

Bertha eyed the cookies. "Do what?"

Lainey put a warm cookie on a plate and handed it to Bertha. "For taking in your brother. For seeing him out."

Bertha took a bite of the cookie. With a full mouth, she said, "I'm doing nothing of the kind."

Lainey looked up, surprised. "Where will he go?"

Bertha kept her head down over her plate with the cookie.

The terrible truth dawned on Lainey. "Oh Bertha, you can't be thinking I would take him in!"

Bertha snapped her head up. "Why not? You got a house now."

"But . . . but . . . why can't *you* have him?"

There was never a more surprised look on a person's face. "Simon was shunned."

"That was so long ago! The bishop would certainly understand. Simon is dying!"

Bertha nodded. "Mebbe so. But my Samuel wouldn't hear of it. If he were still living, it would give him a cardinal arrest."

That remark didn't surprise Lainey. It was always Bertha who had come visiting, bringing casseroles and tucking money under the sugar bowl. Never Samuel. People often made the mistake of blurring the Amish together, assuming that because they dressed alike and looked alike, their thoughts ran alike. But that assumption was wrong. Bertha and Samuel Riehl were as different as two people could be. She remembered every detail of Samuel: the clear-rimmed glasses and broad smile, the grandfatherly bald head like a warm, bright lightbulb. He seemed so trustworthy and kind, and he was, as long as it fit inside the Amish box.

Lainey came to herself with a start. While Jonah had his father's warmth, he also had his father's strict observance to rules. How had she not seen this before? Now she understood why Jonah left Stoney Ridge so abruptly after learning Simon was the real father of Bess. He was his father's son.

A combined sigh of impatience and exasperation from Bertha jolted Lainey back to her present dilemma. "Bertha, that house is a disaster. It's not safe! There's no way anyone could live in it . . . for weeks! Maybe months! I don't even take possession of it until the end of today."

"We'll help."

Lainey didn't know what to say. Her stomach twisted up in a firm knot. "I have to think about this, Bertha. You can't just bully me into it."

Bertha lifted her eyebrows as if she couldn't imagine what Lainey was talking about. "Just don't take too long. He's getting ejected from the hospital next Friday," she said at the door.

"What if Simon doesn't agree? Have you thought of that?"

"You leave Simon to me," she said. "He may be a tough caricature, but he's still my baby brother."

Lainey covered her face with her hands. When Bertha Riehl got her mind set on something, you'd just as well prepare to see it through.

Ira Gingrich handed Lainey the keys as soon as he received her cashier's check. She left his office holding those keys so tightly that they made a red indentation in her palm. Ever since Bertha had paid her that visit to the bakery and told her she should take in Simon, she had been filled with doubts about buying this cottage. She had an inner debate with herself. If our possessions belong to the Lord, why is it so hard to share them with others in need? And Simon certainly needed *someone*.

But then she would go back to wondering why *she* needed to be the one to help him. She began to question if becoming Amish was such a wise thing, after all. If they believed so strongly in community, why would she be left on her own to take care of Simon? Maybe she had glamorized being Amish. Maybe it wasn't any different than so many other Christian churches. Big intentions, little action. A mile wide and an inch deep.

She walked to the cottage and stood outside of it. A small bead of sweat trickled down her back. What had she gotten herself into? And was it too late to get out of it?

She heard a noise, like a very loud woodpecker, coming from inside the house. Slowly, she went up to the porch. The noise was definitely coming from inside. It sounded like a team of woodpeckers. She was just about to push the door when it flew open. There stood Billy with a hammer in his hand and nails in his mouth.

He took the nails out of his mouth and grinned. "Saw you standing out front with a dazed look on your face."

Behind him came Bertha, with a broom in her hands. Past the two of them were a few other men whom Lainey had seen at church. Through the front room, Lainey could see some women scrubbing the kitchen.

"What's going on?" Lainey asked.

"Billy's fixing loose cupboards in the kitchen. Them two men are working on the chimbley. I'm cleaning with them ladies." She spread her big arm out. "It's called a working bee. More are coming tomorrow." She took in Lainey's stunned look. "It's what we do."

Lainey clapped her hands to her cheeks. "I don't know what to say."

"I told you we'd help," Bertha said, starting to sweep the cobwebs out of the ceiling corners.

"But . . . I didn't really expect it. It's just so touching. So . . ."

Billy shrugged. "Amish," he said. As if that explained everything.

Lainey nodded as tears started to well in her eyes.

"It certainly gives a person something to compensate about," Bertha added. She gave up a rare smile.

"It does, Bertha," Lainey said, talking through her tears. "It definitely gives a person something to compensate about." That clinched it for her. Any lingering doubts she had just vanished. She wasn't alone. She would tell Caleb Zook this very weekend that she wanted to be baptized as soon as possible.

Bess watched the clouds float across a sky so bright a blue it shimmered, and her thoughts turned to home. But it wasn't Berlin, Ohio, that she was thinking of. She was thinking of Rose Hill Farm. She felt as unsettled as a yanked-up weed.

This summer, she had grown to love her grandmother. She began to notice how hard Mammi worked and how old she was getting. She wanted to be there with her, helping her grow roses and make jam and tea and rose water and soap. It troubled her to think of Mammi alone on that big farm.

She was worried about her father too. She had thought if she left him be, he would work himself through this sulky mood. But two weeks had passed and he was still moving through each day in slow motion, as if weighed down by something. By contrast, Sallie was moving like a runaway train with their wedding plans.

Tonight, as they finished up another silent dinner, she spoke up. "I got a letter from Lainey today."

Her father didn't respond, didn't even look at her. Bess decided to give him most of the details anyway.

"She said Simon is nearly dead. The hospital, according to Mammi, is ejecting him by week's end." Bess hoped her father would react, reminded of his mother's way of mangling English words.

The ghost of a smile flickered across Jonah's face, but he didn't make a comment. He moved his fork around on his pie plate.

"I'm not sure I should be telling you this, but I'm not sure I shouldn't, either. Lainey is getting baptized this fall. She's becoming Amish."

Jonah stilled, but he kept his eyes downcast. "She is, is she?"

Bess nodded. "All summer long I've been teaching her how to do things without electricity. And I was teaching her Deitsch."

Jonah took that information in silently. He avoided Bess's eyes.

She bit her lip. "Dad, won't you please tell me why we left Stoney Ridge so suddenly?"

Jonah's face set in warning lines. Bess could see the shutters coming down. He eased back in his chair. "Things are . . . complicated, Bess."

"Maybe if you told me about it, I could help you uncomplicate things."

Jonah gave her a slight smile. "Things happened long ago that you wouldn't understand."

She felt offended. Nothing irked Bess more than when someone inferred she was a child. Usually, that someone was Billy Lapp. "Try me."

"Oh Bess . . . some things are best put away." He dropped his chin to his chest as if he was fighting something inside himself. He was quiet for a long while and Bess let him be. She knew not to push him. He was like Mammi that way. He let his fork drop on his plate. "Your blood test came back as a perfect match for Simon."

She *knew* it! She just knew this had something to do with that blood test. Her father was so protective of her. She looked into his kind, dark eyes and reached out for his hand. She took a deep breath. "Then we need to go back to Stoney Ridge. As soon as possible. I want to give my bone marrow to Simon."

Jonah looked at her, horrified. His voice nearly broke on the words. "Why? Why would you do that? It's a painful procedure. And for a man who . . . a man like him." He raked a hand through his hair, as if he was struggling with how to grapple with this. "Maybe it's just consequences for the life he's led. I'm not at all sure we should interfere. Maybe it's Simon's time to pass. Maybe it's . . . God's will."

Bess's gaze shifted out the window. "I asked Lainey what she remembered about Simon. She said he slept till noon, then took a nap. He could lie as smooth as new cream. And that was on his good days. When he got to drinking spirits, she said he was like another person. So mean he could make angels weep. Once he made her kneel on uncooked rice until she had cuts in her knees." She turned back to Jonah. "I asked Mammi what made him so mean and she said he was just born that way."

She got up out of her seat and went to put the dishes in the sink. "Lainey bought Simon's old house with her cooking school money. She's taking him in. To die." She filled up the sink with hot water and added dish soap. She swirled the water with her hand to make it sudsy. "I guess if Lainey can do that, after how he treated her, if she can forgive him . . . well, if my bone marrow could give him a chance to live and maybe to love God through it . . . then I should at least offer it to him." She wiped her hands on a rag and turned to her father. "I *need* to do this, Dad."

Jonah rubbed his face with his hands for the longest time. Finally, he stood, walked over to her, and put his arms around her. Bess burrowed her face into his shoulder.

"We'll leave in the morning," he finally said in a husky voice.

Jonah looked out the window as the bus drove over the bridge into West Virginia. Bess had drifted off to sleep and was starting to lean her head against his shoulder. He felt such tenderness toward her. She was hardly the same girl he sent off in a bus to visit his mother. He had always thought of Bess as excitable as a hen walking on hot coals, never able to keep still, always jumping up with some further excitement. Yet gentle too. He had worried that others might take advantage of Bess's gentle ways. A part of him felt his mother had taken advantage of her, deciding she was a last-ditch cure for Simon. He felt a hardness toward his mother that plagued him.

But it was starting to dawn on Jonah that he didn't need to worry about Bess the way he used to. Next to him was a calm, assured young woman who knew her mind. She had grown up, slower than she wanted, faster than he realized.

Bess jolted awake and looked at him as if she hadn't been asleep at all but had been thinking. "Don't you wonder how two people from one family—like Mammi and Simon—could begin their lives at the same point and somehow take turns that would lead them to such very different lives? I mean, are we born who we are, or does life make us that way?"

That is an eternal question, Jonah thought, as he watched Bess drift back to sleep. *Take you and Lainey. You started in the same point, took a turn, and then seem to be ending up leading very similar lives.*

They arrived at Stoney Ridge not long after dawn. Bess wanted to see Lainey first thing, hoping she'd already be at the bakery. Jonah said to go ahead without him. He had an errand of his own. He walked Bess to Main

Street, saw the lights on in The Sweet Tooth, and then told her he would meet her later at Rose Hill Farm.

She didn't ask him any questions, but she did put a reassuring hand on his shoulder. "Everything is going to turn out fine, Dad."

When did they switch roles? he wondered as he walked the road that led to Caleb Zook's farmhouse, Beacon Hollow. When did Bess become the parent and he become the child?

Jonah found Caleb in the dairy barn, just as he had expected. The cows had been milked and Caleb was stacking the emptied-out milk cans into the sink to be washed. Jonah stood for a while, watching him work. Caleb had been Jonah's closest childhood friend. They did everything together—hunt and fish, swim, skip school. They stood together as witnesses for each others' weddings. And Caleb was by his side to help him when Rebecca died. When Jonah moved to Ohio, they lost touch. *No,* he corrected himself. *I lost touch. With everything and everyone from Stoney Ridge.*

Caleb rinsed out the last bucket and hung it upside down on a wall hook to dry. That was when he noticed Jonah. "Well, well. Skin me for a polecat." Caleb looked pleased. He picked up a rag and dried his hands as he walked over to Jonah. "Heard you had returned to Ohio."

"I did," Jonah said. "Now I'm back." He shook Caleb's hand. "Would you have time for a talk?"

"For you, Jonah, I have all the time in the world." Caleb led Jonah down to two lawn chairs that sat under the willow tree, along the creek that ran parallel to the road.

Jonah watched the water make its way around rocks. Caleb didn't press him, and Jonah expected that. Caleb always had a way of knowing how to work with others. When Jonah heard Caleb had become a minister, then a bishop, he knew the Lord had chosen well for the district.

A mother sheep bleated for her lambs, and the two hurried to find her. The sun was just starting to rise as Jonah took a deep breath. "Caleb, I learned something that has turned my world upside down."

Caleb leaned back in his chair. "Well, my friend, let's see if we can make things right side up again."

Jonah spilled out the entire story, leaving nothing out. Caleb didn't say a word. He just sat there, letting Jonah work through his tangled thoughts and feelings.

"This summer," Jonah said, "it's like I've woken up after a long sleep." There'd been joy this summer, in seeing his mother and Bess grow so close, and in meeting Lainey, he told Caleb. But there was pain too, as he was reminded of Rebecca and the life they should have had together. And now, there was fear. He hadn't been able to tell Bess the whole truth, about Simon being her father. What if he did tell her and she told Simon? If Simon did get well, would he take Bess away from him?

"Lainey was only ten years old and she was trying to give her sister a better life. She was keeping a promise to her mother. I understand that." Jonah looked up at the sky. "But my mother! She knew, yet she didn't tell me the truth." He wiped his eyes with his palms. "How do I forgive her for that, Caleb? How do I forgive my mother for coaxing Bess here this summer to be a bone marrow donor for Simon?"

Caleb took his straw hat off of his head and spun it around in his hands. Finally, he looked over, past Jonah, to the large vegetable garden on the side of the house. "I've been trying something new this summer. I've got a compost pile working just for kitchen scraps."

Jonah looked sideways at him, alarmed. Did Caleb not hear him? What did a compost pile have to do with all that had just spilled out of him?

Caleb leaned forward in his chair. "Composting is a miracle, really. It starts out with carrot scrapings and coffee grinds and banana peels. And then you give it time and the sun warms it and God turns all of that rubbish into something wonderful and useful. Something we can use and spread in the garden."

Jonah tilted his head. "You're trying to make an analogy of composting to the lie I've been living with for fifteen years?"

"I guess I am." Caleb smiled and set his hat on his knee. "The funny thing about composting is that it ends up benefiting us. Nothing is beyond God's ability to repair. Even kitchen scraps. He is all-powerful."

Jonah glared at him. "So you're saying that I just forgive and forget?" He thrust his fist against his chest. He felt so angry. He felt so cheated. "Something as big as the fact that this child I've been raising isn't really mine?"

"Isn't she?" Caleb asked, holding Jonah's fixed gaze. "Could Bess really be any more your daughter?"

Jonah dropped his eyes to the ground. Caleb was right. Bess *was* his daughter. He had to fight back a lump in his throat.

"Nothing can ever change that, Jonah."

Jonah looked down at the creek. "You probably want me to tell Bess the whole story."

"I'm not the one to tell you what to say or what not to say. You'll have to pray long and hard about that matter. I do understand that it's heavy information for a child to bear."

"She's not a child any longer. She's grown up years this summer."

Caleb smiled. "There are seasons in our life that are like that."

The sun was up now, filtering through the trees, creating shadows over the creek.

"As far as forgiving your mother," Caleb said, "Peter asked Jesus, how many times should he forgive another? Peter wanted a statistical count. And Jesus responded with a story. 'Not seven times, but, I tell you, seventy times seven.' Jesus was teaching him that we don't live by careful bookkeeping. Through God's mercy, bookkeeping has given way to extravagant generosity." He paused for a moment. "So this is your story, my friend."

They spoke no words for a long while, and yet the silence didn't seem uncompanionable.

Then Caleb placed a hand on Jonah's shoulder and added, "There's someone else you need to think about forgiving."

Jonah looked at him with a question.

"Yourself," he said softly. "For the buggy accident."

Jonah winced. He started to protest, to give the pat answers that he always gave—God was in control. God knew best. God has a purpose in all things. But he couldn't say the words. He stopped and leaned forward, resting his elbows on his knees, holding his head in his hands. "I should have prevented it. I should have been paying closer attention to the road." His voice grew hoarse. "It's hard enough to accept that I could have prevented Rebecca's death . . . now I've learned that my daughter died in that accident too. I was responsible for them." He covered his face with his hands and his shoulders started to shake. Something broke loose inside of him and he began to weep. He couldn't even remember the last time he cried. He didn't even cry when he learned that Rebecca had passed. He just felt numb. But now, this morning, he felt fresh, raw, searing pain, as if the accident had just happened. He was spilling out grief he had stored for fifteen years, his chest heaving and racking with sobs.

Caleb sat quietly until Jonah's tears were spent. Finally, he spoke. "You didn't cause that accident, Jonah. It's hard to understand why God allowed it, but we trust in God's sovereignty. Your wife and baby's lives were complete. And now we trust they are in the presence of our Almighty Lord." The faint clang of a dinner bell floated down to the creek. He rose to his feet. "Breakfast is ready. Jorie's probably wondering where I've disappeared to. I know she'd be pleased to have you join us."

"Thanks, Caleb. Another time."

Jonah started to rise, but Caleb put his hand on his shoulder. "Why don't you stay here awhile and talk this all out with the Lord? I find it's my favorite place to hammer things out with him."

As Jonah eased back down, he asked Caleb, "So you think Bess should give Simon her bone marrow? A man such as him?" He looked away. "You remember, Caleb, how he treated Lainey and her mother. How the sparkle drained from them." And what life would have been like for his Bess, too, had she been raised by Simon. Lainey had pointed that out to him, but he hadn't listened to her.

Caleb rubbed his forehead. "Are we going to be part of condemning a man? Or are we going to be a part of releasing him from condemnation?" He sat back down again. "Jonah, we want to share in this world, of forgiving and being forgiven. Even such a man as Simon."

It wasn't easy, though. Even for Caleb. Jonah could see this was a temptation for both of them, to let consequences fall as they would. To let Simon pass away without a hand of kindness offered to him. Except for the hand of Bertha. Suddenly, Jonah felt a slight softening toward his mother. He realized how hard this must be for her, what a difficult spot she was in. Despite everything, Simon was her brother.

Caleb added, "You probably know this, but Lainey O'Toole is planning to be baptized."

"Bess told me," Jonah said.

"When she first came to me a while back, I told her to go without electricity for a week. That usually changes folks' minds right off. They miss their radio and hair dryer and television too much. But she didn't bat an eye. She's been learning our language and choring without modern convenience. Even still, I had to make sure she wasn't doing this on a whim."

He nodded.

"I asked her why, and she told me she truly believes that she can serve and love God best by being Plain." Caleb lifted his eyebrows. "Sure wish some of our members felt that way. Quite a few of them claim to be meditating during church." He raised his eyebrows. "An activity that looks suspiciously similar to dozing." He rose to his feet. "God always has a plan, doesn't he?"

Jonah looked up at Caleb and did his best to offer up a slight smile. He wished he had Caleb's unwavering faith. Ever since Rebecca—and his baby—had died, he had been able to summon only a pale shadow of the faith he once had. For how could a loving God let a twenty-year-old young mother and her newborn baby die in a careless accident? If God was sovereign, then his sovereignty seemed frightening. It was a question Jonah had never been able to work through to a comfortable solution.

Caleb watched him carefully, as if reading his thoughts. "God may allow tragedy, Jonah, just like he allowed his Son to have a tragic death." He leaned closer to Jonah. "But God is a redeemer. Never, ever forget that truth."

Once a week, on her day off from the bakery, Lainey traveled to Lebanon to visit Simon. She brought him baked goods and a magazine or a puzzle. He was not looking well. He had become even more pale and thin, with dark circles under his eyes. Today, she found him on the patio, getting some sun. Simon, who had always looked so sure of himself, seemed hollow and fragile.

He opened one eye when he heard her. "What's in the box?" he asked in a gruff voice.

"Doughnuts. Jelly filled. Your favorite, if I remember right."

"I never liked doughnuts." He held out his hand, palm up, for a doughnut. She opened the box and handed him one. He ate it carefully, as if he had sores in his mouth, and jelly dripped down his chin. She wiped it off with a tissue and he let her. It amazed her to see Simon helpless. "So the nurse said they're going to release you."

He narrowed his eyes. "They just want the bed. Government can't bother themselves with a dying vet. Even one with a purple heart."

Lainey tried not to roll her eyes. She had heard that purple heart line many times before. "It was Bertha who talked them into releasing you. She thought you'd be better off in a home."

"I'm staying right here. I got my rights."

She knew the truth was that he had no place to go. He was a pathetic, lonely old man who was dying. She looked at him with eyes that were not hard or cold. She saw him objectively. "I'd like you to come home with me."

Simon didn't move a muscle. He didn't even blink.

"I bought the old cottage and neighbors helped fix it up. We're going to rent a hospital bed for you and keep it downstairs in the living room, so you feel like you're part of things."

He eyed her suspiciously. "If you're looking for money, I told you I ain't got none."

She smiled. "I don't want your money, Simon, even if you had any."

"Then why would you be bothering with a sick old man?"

That was a question she had asked herself and prayed over ever since Bertha suggested—no, informed her—she should take in Simon. She finally decided the answer was because she was able to make something right in at least one tiny corner of the vast house of wrongs. It was another thing she was learning from the Amish. "Everybody needs somebody in this world to help them through. I guess you're stuck with me." *And I'm stuck with you,* she thought but kindly didn't say.

Simon tucked his chin to his chest. She thought his hands were trembling a little. Maybe not. Then he lifted his head. "I like my coffee strong, and served right at six a.m."

A laugh burst out of Lainey. "Oh, I see you're already giving orders." She stood. "I'll go talk to the nurses about getting you released."

He put his hand on her forearm to stop her. He looked up at her, and for the first time she could remember, he didn't look full of mockery. He looked scared. "Lainey, why?"

She patted his hand, the way she would a child. "Your debt is canceled, Simon. That's why."

Jonah hadn't seen Lainey yet. Nor had Bess. When he returned to Rose Hill Farm after talking to Caleb, Bess was already there. Apparently, it was Lainey's day off from the bakery and Bess couldn't find her anywhere.

By late afternoon, Jonah drove the buggy down to Lainey's cottage to see if she had returned yet. There was no answer at the door. It amazed him to see that cottage transformed. It had been well worthwhile to fix it up. It was starting to look the way it was probably intended to look, years ago, when it was first built by the original owners. It was a lovely little house, with good bones and a solid foundation. He could still smell the fresh paint. New windowpanes replaced the broken ones.

He sat on the porch steps to wait for her. He had been worried to hear that she was going to live in this house—the one where her mother had died in childbirth. He put a hand to his forehead. She died delivering his Bess! Right here. Another discovery that hadn't occurred to him. How could Lainey live in a house that sheltered so many unhappy memories? He couldn't have done it.

His back was stiff from sitting for so long, so he got up to stretch. He hoped she would return soon. Soon it would be more dark than day. He walked down the pathway and around to the back of the house. He peered inside the window and recognized some furniture and an old rug from Rose Hill Farm's attic. He should have known his mother had a hand in this. He walked all around the perimeter of the house, stopping by a small, newly planted rose garden. He smiled. More evidence of Bertha Riehl. He walked around to the front and then he saw Lainey. She stood by the road, watching him, wearing a Plain dress—lavender that brought out her eyes. Her hands were clasped before her to keep them steady.

"Lainey," Jonah said softly as he approached her.

"You came back," Lainey said. "There's so much I need to explain—"

"Would you take me to see my child's grave?"

She nodded. "We can go right now."

They didn't speak in the buggy as Jonah drove them to the town cemetery.

Lainey led him straight to the back where her mother was buried. A small grave marker was next to it. He could see that the two graves had been recently weeded. They looked cared for. By Lainey, no doubt.

"I'll give you some privacy," she said quietly, and went to wait in the buggy.

Jonah knelt in front of his daughter's grave. And for the second time that day, he wept.

As Jonah drove away from her cottage, Lainey stood by the road and watched until his buggy had dipped over the rise and was out of sight. They had stayed at the cemetery and talked for hours. It was as if they were filling each other in on the last fifteen years of their lives. They talked until the shadows got longer and still had more to say to each other. It wasn't until long after the dusk turned to darkness and the stars came out in the clear sky that Jonah said he should be getting back to Rose Hill Farm. But he didn't look at all as if he wanted to leave.

10

The next morning was a church Sunday. Bess dressed quickly and offered to go down the road to pick up Lainey and come back for her father and grandmother, but Jonah said he wouldn't mind going. He said old Frieda needed a little warming up, but Bess wasn't so sure. Her dad came back late last night, whistling. Even Mammi noticed how happy he seemed. You had to know Mammi pretty well to decipher a difference in expression, but Bess thought she hadn't stopped looking pleased ever since she and Jonah had arrived.

Bess wished her father would hurry old Frieda along. She hadn't seen Billy at Rose Hill Farm yesterday. She knew he would be at church this morning, and so she took extra care with her hair. She even pulled a few strands loose behind her cap and tried to curl them into tight ringlets. She didn't think anyone would see since they sat in the back bench, but she hoped maybe Billy might notice. Betsy Mast often had corkscrew curls slipping under her cap and down her neck. But then, Betsy had thick, curly hair, and Bess's hair was thin and straight.

She spotted Billy by the barn the minute they arrived at the Smuckers'. He was surrounded by a group of friends; they were laughing over some joke. Mammi took her time getting out of the buggy from the backseat, which gave Bess a chance to furtively glance at the boys while pretending to help her down. She saw Andy Yoder spot her with a delighted look on his face.

Billy hadn't noticed her yet. He had turned around to talk to someone else. As soon as Bess climbed out of the buggy, Andy was at her elbow.

"Bess! You're back! Hallelujah! You look . . . wonderful." Andy's admiration was unqualified. "I was just this minute trying to talk Billy into making a trip to Ohio to see you! But he made it sound like we were going to the far side of the moon."

Bess stifled a smile. Andy was the kind of person that sometimes told you unexpected things.

"Don't listen to a word this fellow tells you," Billy said, approaching them from behind.

Bess whirled around to face Billy. "Which words?" Her heart was pounding like an Indian war drum. She was sure Billy could hear it.

Billy looked at her as if he was seeing her for the first time. For a few seconds, he was literally unable to find words. "The second part," he said simply.

Then it was as if the mist had cleared and they went back to their old ways.

"Missed picking rose petals, did you?" he asked.

She grinned and held out her palms. "Especially the thorns. When the last cut healed, I told Dad we needed to return. My hands looked too good."

Billy and Andy peered at her hands as if they were made of fine china.

Jonah handed the reins of the horse to one of the Smucker sons and interrupted them. "Well, boys—"

Bess cringed at the undue emphasis her father placed on the word "boys." Couldn't he see that Billy was a man?

"—it's time we went in to the service." Jonah put a hand protectively on Bess's shoulder to steer her to the house for meeting.

Around three o'clock, they left the Smuckers' to return to Rose Hill Farm. Bess invited Lainey to join them for supper, and Jonah couldn't hold back a smile. As he turned the buggy into the drive, he felt a jolt. Bess let out a gasp.

There, on the front porch, patiently waiting, was planted Sallie Stutzman, her twin sons, and Mose Weaver.

Jonah swallowed hard. In his haste, he had completely forgotten to tell Sallie and Mose that he and Bess were leaving.

Over breakfast on Monday, Bess asked her grandmother if she would take her to see Simon in Lebanon as soon as it was convenient. Mammi said it was convenient right now and grabbed her bonnet to head out the door. Sallie and her boys and Mose were staying at Rose Hill Farm, and Sallie's "cheerfulness," Mammi said, was making her dizzy.

They didn't talk much on the bus ride. Something was building inside of Bess, something she had discovered last night as she watched everyone at dinner. She was so sure she was right that she felt as if she might explode. Finally, she blurted out, "Oh Mammi! Whatever are we going to do?!"

Mammi had been looking out the window. She turned to Bess as if she had forgotten she was there. "About what?"

About *what*? Wasn't it obvious? "Dad loves Lainey and Sallie loves Dad and Mose loves Sallie and Lainey loves Dad! If we don't do something quick, the wedding is going to happen because Dad is too honorable to tell Sallie no. That's what!" Sallie hadn't stopped talking about the wedding last night. That dinner was one of the most painful moments of Bess's life. Her father looked stricken, Mose kept looking at Sallie with this terrible longing—Bess knew Mose well enough to know that his mild look held *terrible* longing—and Lainey! Poor Lainey! She hardly said a word. When Jonah offered to drive her home, she refused him, flat out.

Mammi turned back to the window and exhaled. "We let nature take its course. *That's* what." She patted Bess's leg. "That's what we do. Never forget that."

Bess turned that thought over and over in her mind, not at all convinced it was the best plan. Didn't Mammi care? Didn't she want her dad to be happy?

Just before they reached Lebanon, Mammi asked, "Does that little round gal ever stop talking?"

"No," Bess said glumly. "She never does."

"Them two boys ever stop wiggling?"

Bess shook her head. "Not even in church."

"Does that tall fellow ever say a word?"

Bess scratched her prayer cap. "None that I recall."

"Hoo-boy," Mammi said. "Nature has her work cut out for her."

After they arrived at the hospital, Mammi went in search of a bathroom and Bess knew *that* could be a long wait, so she decided to go ahead to Simon's ward. She tiptoed up to his bed. She could see he had grown much weaker than the other time she had visited. Sweat gleamed on his face, like he was feverish.

"If you're another vampire, go away," Simon muttered without opening an eye. "I don't have any more blood to give."

"But I'm not . . . I'm not a vampire," Bess said. "It's me. It's Bess. Bertha's granddaughter. Jonah's daughter."

"Well, well. It's the holy howler." He groaned. "If Bertha sent you here to get me to confess my sins before I kick the bucket . . . tell her no thanks."

"She didn't," Bess said quietly.

Simon didn't respond.

"Would it be such a bad thing, though, to confess your sins?"

Now he looked at her. "It wouldn't be if I didn't enjoy sinning so much."

Bess had never heard of anyone who enjoyed sinning. She gave him a look of great sadness. "I'll pray for you, for your soul."

"Have at it," Simon said mockingly. "I'm afraid all those childhood lessons in holiness slid off me like hot butter off the griddle." He pointed to the door. "Now go look for where the carpenter made a hole."

She supposed that was his rather impolite way of telling her he wanted her to leave him alone. For a brief moment, she thought about not going through with the bone marrow operation. Simon would never appreciate the gift.

And yet, she wasn't doing it for him. She was doing it for God. And for Mammi. She bit her lip. "I came here today to tell you some good news. It turns out we're a match, you and I. I can give you my bone marrow."

Simon lay very silent, but he was listening, she could tell that.

"So instead of going home with Lainey to d—," Bess gulped back the word, "um, you're going to be getting some medicine to help your body get ready for the transplant. In another week or so, I'll have the procedure. Harvesting the marrow, they call it. Then they'll give it to you and, hopefully, it will cure you right up."

He still didn't look at her. He didn't say a word.

"I guess it won't be that fast," Bess said, rambling now. "Sounds like it will take a while to graft. They called it grafting, which is interesting, because that's what we do with the roses at Rose Hill Farm. We graft them onto better rootstock. Then they're stronger and healthier. I guess that's just what it will be like for you. You'll get stronger and healthier. That's the plan, anyway." She ran out of things to say. "I just wanted to tell you the news myself."

Simon lifted his chin. "I'll have to think on it."

"Well, think a little faster," Mammi said. She had come into the ward and eased into a chair beside Bess.

Simon frowned at his sister. She frowned back at him.

"Well, Bess," he said, "don't expect me to thank you."

Bess lifted her chin a notch. "I don't. I don't expect a thing."

"Good. As long as we're clear on that." But he did look at her, right in the eyes.

Bess held his gaze. "We're clear on that."

"Simon, anybody ever tell you it's hard to put a foot in a shut mouth?" Mammi said, standing to leave.

Everything was happening so fast that Jonah didn't know what to do. Sallie had settled into Rose Hill Farm like she wasn't going to budge. The dining room table was covered with wedding invitations that she was busy addressing. Mose, too, seemed to be in no hurry to leave, and even though the fate of their business troubled Jonah, he was thankful for Mose's presence. Mose acted like a self-appointed shepherd to those boys, and it was a good thing. They *were* little monsters, just as Bess had said. How had he never noticed? The first day, they ran their scooters into his mother's most cherished rugosa and broke the bush at the stem.

His mother went so still it scared him, like the quiet right before an Ohio tornado hit. When she finally spoke, it was in a chilling voice. "Bess, go get Billy Lapp. Tell him we got us an emergency."

The second day, those boys knocked over a shelf of freshly canned rose petal jam in the barn when they were horsing around. The third day, they forgot to latch Frieda's stall and she wandered into the vegetable garden, trampling a row of tomato plants.

And he would never forget the look on Lainey's face when she was introduced to Sallie on Sunday. He had never mentioned Sallie to Lainey . . . it never occurred to him to mention her. But Sallie started right off with wedding talk, and Lainey responded with forced cheer, like daffodils in January. When he offered to give her a ride home—hoping for a chance to explain—she gave him a firm "No."

It made him feel sick to his stomach.

Dear Robin and Ally,

I haven't written in a while because so many changes have been happening so quickly and I didn't know where to begin. First of all, I bought a cottage with my savings. A fixer-upper would be a generous description. It's the home I lived in as a child. And I am going to be taking in my stepfather, Simon Troyer. He's been quite ill. I've told you about Bess. We've grown as close as . . . well, she's like a sister to me.

And to answer your question about men: no. There are no men of interest in Stoney Ridge. None whatsoever.

Love, Lainey

For the actual bone marrow transplant, Simon had been moved from the Veterans Hospital down to the hospital in Lancaster, where a specialist worked who was skilled at performing the relatively new procedure. Bess would be given a general anesthesia, and the marrow would be removed from her hip bone. She would stay one night, just for observation, and be allowed to go home the next morning.

The night before the operation was scheduled for Bess was one of those hot late-August nights that never cooled off. She had trouble sleeping, so she got up and went outside to get some fresh air. She sat on the porch steps and gazed at the stars. Somehow, the night sky gave her a sense of the majesty of God. She seemed so small and he seemed so big. In the distance, a horse whinnied and another answered.

"Bess?"

She looked out toward the yard and saw the silhouette of a person. "Billy! What are you doing here?"

Billy hesitated. "I forgot my books." He looked toward the barn. "In the barn. I forgot my books." He kept his books in Bertha's barn because his brothers teased him for being a bookworm.

"And you couldn't wait until morning to read?"

"No. I was right in the middle of a good part. What are you doing out here?"

"Couldn't sleep."

He walked up to her. "It's a brave thing you're doing. Giving Simon your bone marrow."

"I'm not at all brave," she answered truthfully.

"Are you scared? About tomorrow?"

She squeezed her elbows. "Maybe a little."

"Think it will hurt?"

"I'm not too worried about the pain. They said it's not much more than a bad fall on ice. I've suffered through plenty of those. It's more . . ."

He sat beside her on the porch steps. "What?"

"Well, I've never had general anesthesia before. Where do you go, when you're put to sleep like that? I won't even dream, the nurse said. I mean, where does your soul go?"

Billy didn't answer for a long time. "Caleb Zook said once that our great hope is when we're absent from the body, we're present with the Lord." He looked over at her.

She thought about that for a while in the quiet of the night. That answer satisfied her. It gave her peace. "Thank you, Billy."

"Bess?" Billy asked, husky-voiced.

She turned her face to him to see what he wanted. He held her face in both his hands and kissed her very softly on the lips. Then he drew away. She could hardly breathe, so stunned by the kiss.

He tucked a loose strand of hair under her cap, and then gently grazed her cheek with the back of his hand. "Good night." He stood and took a few steps down the walkway before turning slightly. "I'll see you in the morning. I'm going to the hospital."

His tone was so sweet that it made her heart flutter. She was just about to tell him that he forgot his books again, but then she realized that he hadn't come over for the books at all. Billy had come over this night because he was worried about her. It gave her the shivers, even on a hot night like this.

It was the longest day Jonah had ever known. As soon as Bess arrived at the admitting office, the hospital machinery moved into action. She was whisked away in a wheelchair with barely time enough to wave goodbye to everyone who had come with her that morning: Bertha, Billy, Sallie and her boys, Mose. And Lainey, who was keeping a considerable distance from Jonah.

Jonah waited with Bess in the pre-op room. Machines hummed softly and white-soled shoes whispered up and down the halls. A nurse came into the room. "We just got word that the doctor is getting prepped." After she left, Jonah and Bess sat in silence. Suddenly, this was real.

Jonah leaned down to smooth her hair from her face. "You," he pronounced, "will wake up and still be the same girl who cannot be bothered to study for a math test and vanishes when there are chores to do and goes to sleep reading with the light on." But all he heard himself say was the first part of the sentence: "You will wake up and be the same girl . . ." That's all he was praying for.

The anesthesiologist came in and put the mask over Bess's mouth and nose. He told Jonah to count aloud to Bess, but instead, Jonah recited the Lord's Prayer in Deitsch. It was Caleb Zook's suggestion. He recommended having Bess hear the words "Thy will be done" before she fell asleep. When her eyes drifted shut, the nurse ushered him out to the waiting room.

Lainey looked so worried that Jonah wanted to take her in his arms and tell her everything would be all right. But of course he couldn't.

And there was part of him that wasn't sure everything would be all right. A terrible fear came over Jonah, a feeling he struggled to disown. He knew he must yield absolutely to God's will and trust in his ultimate mercy. "Not my will but Thine be done," he had told Bess before she slipped into unconsciousness. He had spent a lifetime reciting that prayer and wanted to believe it. But the fear of God's will was there, nonetheless. He still struggled against yielding to God's will, and he prayed desperately that God would bring Bess back to him, whole and well.

He looked over at his mother, sitting in a plastic chair with her head tucked down and her hands clasped together in her lap. He wondered if she felt worried too. She was more a woman of action than of words and worry. Her eyes were closed, either praying or meditating or . . . she let out a loud snore. A laugh burst out of him, Lainey too. He looked at her then; his brown eyes met hers, and they shared a smile. Sallie had been telling Mose something and caught the look that passed between Lainey and Jonah.

She stopped talking. Sallie Stutzman stopped talking. Her eyes darted back and forth between the two of them.

Jonah felt like he was a boy caught with his hand in the cookie jar. Guilt washed over him and he made sure he didn't look in Lainey's direction again.

It seemed like an eternity, but it was really less than an hour before the doctor came to the waiting room, searching out Jonah. The doctor seemed a little startled to find a large group of Amish jump to their feet, eyes fixed on him.

"She's fine," the doctor reassured everyone. "Bess is awake now. We're just going to observe her for a while, make sure no complications develop, and then we'll put her in a regular room for the night."

"Can I see her?" Billy asked.

Jonah turned to Billy with an eyebrow raised.

"Uh, I mean, can her father see her?" Billy stumbled.

"In a little while," the doctor explained.

"What about Simon?" Bertha asked. "When will he be getting Bess's marrow?" Simon had been in isolation for over a week and hadn't been allowed any visitors because of risk of infection.

Jonah felt shamed. He hadn't even given a passing thought to Simon. *Forgive me, Lord*, he prayed quickly.

"It's actually easier for him to receive the marrow than it was for Bess to give it," the doctor said. "A needle is inserted into the cavity of the rear hip bone where a large quantity of bone marrow is located."

The doctor became quite animated with such a rapt audience. "We harvested about one to two quarts of marrow and blood. Bone marrow is actually a spongey material, found inside the bones. While this may sound like a lot, it really represents only about 2 percent of a person's bone marrow, which the body replaces in four weeks."

Billy looked as white as a sheet. Bertha told him to go sit down and put his head between his knees so he wouldn't faint.

"Men don't faint," he said in a weak and pale voice, but he let her help him to a chair. "They might pass out, but they don't faint."

"Whatever handle you want to call it by, you look like you're just about to do it," Bertha told him.

"Everything's getting ready for Simon now, and I'm going to head in and take care of that." The doctor clapped his hands together. "Hopefully, the donation will 'take' and make its way into the central shaft of larger bones to restore stem cell function."

Billy groaned, then stood abruptly and hurried down the hall, in need of a men's room.

Bertha watched him weave down the hall and shook her head. "That poor boy's going off his feed again."

Early the next morning, Billy went over to Rose Hill Farm to finish chores as fast as he could. Billy had told Bertha he would take her to the hospital to meet everyone for Bess's release this afternoon. For the last two days, he had felt an odd anxiety and he hadn't been sleeping well, as if something wasn't quite right and he didn't know what.

He was walking up the tree-lined drive when he heard Boomer barking up a fury in the rose fields. He glanced at the house and was surprised there was no buttery glow from a lantern light in the kitchen. Usually, he could see Bertha at the stove and smell something delicious frying. Even though he had just eaten a full breakfast at home, his stomach would begin to rumble in happy anticipation. Not today, though. The farmhouse looked dark and cold.

He jogged over to see what Boomer's ruckus was about, then slowed as he approached him. A chill ran down his spine when he saw the frantic, wild-eyed look in the dog's eyes.

Then he discovered what Boomer was troubled about. Bertha Riehl was lying on her side, as if she had laid down to take a nap among her roses. Billy rushed to her and rolled her on her back. Her eyes were closed, her lips were blue, her face was white, and he could see she wasn't breathing. She'd been gone for a while. She had been out spraying Coca-Cola on her roses when she passed. She looked utterly at peace. He held her hand for a while, tears streaming down his face, unsure of what to do next. Boomer rested his big woolly head on Billy's shoulder.

Billy took a few deep breaths, trying to steady himself, and went up to the farmhouse. He was looking for Jonah, before he remembered Jonah was spending the night at the hospital with Bess. It looked like their company— Sallie and her boys and that Mose—were gone too. Probably at the hospital, Billy figured. Billy rubbed his face with his hands. His father would know what to do. He hated leaving Bertha like this, but he couldn't move her on his own. Boomer was standing guard by her. He bolted down the drive and ran home to fetch his father.

Billy knew word would trickle quickly through the community about the passing of Bertha Riehl. He had to act fast to get to the hospital in Lancaster as quickly as he could. His father tried to insist they get Caleb Zook to tell Jonah and Bess the news about Bertha. "That's what bishops are for," he told Billy. "They know best how to say these things."

Billy was tempted, but he knew, deep down, he needed to be the one to go. Part of being a man was not avoiding hard things. He changed clothes and his father drove him into town to catch the bus to Lancaster.

"Maybe I should go with you," he told Billy.

"No, I need to do this myself." Billy wasn't sure how he was going to break the news to Jonah about Bertha's passing. But he had to get to them before they returned to Rose Hill Farm and found a group of women gathered, preparing the house for the viewing.

Just before he hopped on the bus, his father stopped him by placing a hand on his shoulder. Billy turned to him, and his father didn't say anything, but there was something in his eyes—a look that said he was pleased with him. He couldn't remember ever seeing that look from his father before.

Not an hour later, Billy arrived at the hospital and found Jonah and Lainey and everyone else sitting in the waiting room.

"Billy!" Lainey said when she spotted him. Then she grew solemn, sensing from the look on his face that something had happened. "What's wrong?"

Billy sat near them, struggling to speak. Lainey took hold of his hand to give him strength. "It's Bertha," Billy started, then tears filled his eyes. "She's gone." He had to stop and wipe his eyes with the back of his sleeve. "I found her in the roses." He covered his face then, unable to continue.

Jonah heard the words come out of Billy's mouth, but he couldn't understand them. It was as if everything had stopped. The sound of the nurses' shoes as they hurried up the hallways, the clocks ticking, the elevator opening and shutting. He looked at Billy and felt pity for him. Poor Billy. He was suffering. And then he looked at Lainey, with tears running down her cheeks. Sallie started to tell Mose a list of things they needed to do for the funeral. It was like Jonah's mind had shut down and he wasn't able to process the meaning behind the sentence, "She's gone."

His mother had passed? She was dead?

Like a fog lifting, the full meaning behind those words started to sink in to him. Then the pain rushed at him, as real as an ocean wave, and he felt the tears come. Billy crouched down beside him and Jonah put his hand on Billy's head. They sat there for a long while, until a nurse came and timidly interrupted to let them know Bess was ready to go now.

Jonah nodded and wiped his face with his handkerchief. "I need to tell her."

"I'll go with you," Lainey offered.

"*I* should go," Sallie said as she rose to her feet.

"No," Lainey said, giving Sallie a firm look. "No. I'll go."

Sallie looked confused, then hurt, but Mose put a gentle hand on her arm. Jonah didn't have the presence of mind to do anything more.

Before walking into Bess's room, Jonah took a deep breath and prayed for God's strength. Bess had grown so close to his mother this summer. More and more, she was acting like her too. She even cooked like his mother. He opened the door a crack and saw her waiting by the window, dressed and ready to go.

"How are you feeling?" Lainey asked her.

"Not too bad," Bess said. "A little sore. They won't let me see Simon, but they did tell me it went well for him."

Jonah nodded. "So I heard."

Bess picked up her bonnet and cape. "Let's go home."

Jonah pulled up a chair for Lainey to sit in. "Bess, something has happened."

Bess looked curiously at her father. Then she gasped. "It's Simon. He's dead, isn't he? All this effort, and he's dead."

"No. Simon is fine." In a twist of irony, Simon *was* fine and his mother was dead. Jonah pulled the curtain around her bed to give them privacy from the other patients. Then he leaned a hip against the bed frame, crossed his arms against his chest, and lifted his face to Bess. Gently, he told her that her grandmother had passed this morning while she was out tending the roses. He waited, expecting her to break down.

Bess turned to face the window. She hugged her elbows as if she was holding herself together.

Lainey walked up to Bess and put her hands on her shoulders. Softly she said, "It was your grandmother's time. She'd done everything she needed to do. She brought Simon back to his family. She brought you and your dad back to Stoney Ridge." Lainey turned Bess around to look at her. Bess was dry-eyed. "God's timing is always perfect. You see that, don't you? Her life was complete." She spoke with conviction.

Jonah remained silent as Lainey said those words. He was amazed by her, nearly in awe. But it distressed him to see Bess so quiet. It wasn't like her. Two years ago, when their pet dog had been hit by a car, she had cried for two days straight. "Are you all right, Bess?"

Bess nodded but didn't say a word.

"When you're ready," Jonah said, "Billy is waiting for us in the hallway."

"I'm ready now," was all Bess said in a voice unfamiliar to him.

It was afternoon by the time they returned to Rose Hill Farm. The hardest moment of all came as the taxi drove up the driveway. Knowing Mammi wasn't there—and wouldn't be there ever again—made Bess feel an unbearable pain in her chest, as real as if she had been stabbed.

Everyone in the taxi was aware of Mammi's absence. She saw the tight set of her father's jaw. Billy kept his chin tucked to his chest, Lainey just went ahead and let the tears flow. Sallie was quiet, which was a great blessing. Even her boys seemed to know they needed to be calm and still, but it helped to have Mose sit between them in the back of the station wagon.

Rose Hill Farm wasn't empty. The news had spread quickly throughout Stoney Ridge. Friends and neighbors were in and around the farmhouse, cleaning it from top to bottom in preparation for the viewing and the funeral. The women fussed over Bess, but all she wanted was to go upstairs and lie down on her bed. She was stiff and exhausted after an uncomfortable night. Her hip felt sore and so did her heart—aching for her grandmother. It was the bitterest kind of heartache she had ever felt—an ache that burned and gnawed. She hoped that tears would come in solitude and help wash away the pain. It seemed a terrible thing that she couldn't shed a tear for Mammi. She had loved her grandmother more than she had even realized. She knelt by her window and looked out over the rose fields, wondering where it was that her grandmother had lay down and died. But still no tears came, only the same horrible ache of grief.

When she finally went downstairs, she learned that the undertaker had returned her grandmother's body. The women had dressed Mammi in burial clothes and laid her out in the front room. One had stopped all of the clocks in the house at the early morning hour they assumed Bertha had died. They would be restarted after the burial.

Bess walked slowly into the front room. Mammi didn't look like Mammi, she thought as she stood next to her grandmother's still body, lying on the dining room table. Jonah came up behind her and put his hands on her shoulders.

"She's really gone," Bess whispered. "You can tell. Whatever it was that made her Mammi is gone."

"Gone from us, but gone to God," Jonah told her.

At first, Boomer seemed to be in everyone's way, all the time. Bess knew he was looking for Mammi, and it nearly broke her heart. She knew what he was thinking: almost everyone else in Stoney Ridge seemed to be in and out of Rose Hill Farm, doing errands of kindness, but there was no sign of his mistress.

Later that day, Boomer went missing. Bess called for him and put food and water out on the porch, hoping he would return. He seemed to have disappeared.

It was a muggy, rainy day when Bertha Riehl was buried, three days after she passed. Jonah and Bess stood by Bertha's graveside and viewed her for the last time in the large, plain pine coffin.

Jonah stood looking down at his mother. Her face was relaxed and serene, but Bess was right—whatever it was that made her Bertha—her soul? her pneuma?—it was gone. *Our bodies are just a shell, a house, for our eternal souls.*

How differently he would have done things if he'd known his mother was slated for death this summer. How much time he had wasted. He felt moved with a deep grief for the years lost between them. And yet, on its heels came a quiet joy. Coming back to Stoney Ridge last week had been no accident. He and his mother, in the end, they made their peace. Just in time.

He saw Billy lean close to Bess and whisper, "Are you okay?"

Bess nodded without looking up. She was calmer than Jonah would have thought possible, considering. His mother would be proud of her.

The lid of the coffin was nailed shut and lowered into the ground; the young men—Billy was one of them—picked up their shovels to heave dirt. When the first loud clump of dirt hit the coffin, Bess broke down with a loud sob. Jonah took a step toward her, but Billy had already handed his shovel to another boy and was at Bess's side. He patted her on the back to comfort her, handed her his handkerchief, then as her weeping grew worse, he steered her by the shoulders to lead her to his buggy.

On the drive back to Rose Hill Farm, Billy couldn't find any good words to ease Bess's sorrow. Several times he almost had the right thing. But always he stopped. He couldn't bear it any longer. He turned the buggy down a side road and pulled the horse to a full stop. "Go ahead, Bess," he said as he put his arms around her. "Cry it all out. I'm here. No one's here to see. Have a good cry."

And so she clung to him and wept and wept until he thought that her body would never stop shaking with the sobs and the grief. He didn't think a body could have so many tears to cry, but maybe girls were made with more tear ducts. It was good, though, to have her finally show some emotion. It worried him to see her tearless. It just didn't seem like Bess.

"It's not that I'm crying for Mammi, Billy," she said between sobs. "I know she's in a better place. And she's with Daadi now. I'm crying for me. What will I do without her?"

Finally, the wave of sorrow subsided and Bess's sobs turned to sniffles. When he thought she seemed all wrung out, with not another tear left to shed, he wiped her face with his sleeve and took her home.

As soon as the house had emptied out that evening, Jonah went outside to get some fresh air. He checked that Frieda had water and alfalfa hay, then lingered in the barn for a while. He swept the floor of rose petals and knocked down a few spiderwebs. He just didn't want to go inside. Sallie would be waiting for him and he couldn't face her. He couldn't deny that she had been a wonderful help these last few days. She seemed to know how to get things done in a matter-of-fact, efficient way.

But all he could think about was how much he wanted to be with Lainey. To talk to her about his mother. About Bess. About Simon. About everything. She had participated in every part of the viewing and the funeral, was accepted by the community as nearly one of them—he noticed that folks weren't switching to English anymore when she came in a room. And he would be forever grateful for the support she had provided to his Bess.

But Lainey continued to avoid him. He couldn't blame her at all, but he didn't think he could abide much more of it.

Jonah hung up the broom and slid the door open to find Sallie walking toward the barn in the dusk. "Shall we walk awhile?" she asked him.

They headed down the drive to the road without saying a word to each other. The strange thing, he realized, was not that he wasn't talking. It was that Sallie wasn't talking. In fact, now that he thought about it, she hadn't said much at all lately. She was as silent as a Sunday afternoon. Then, with a start, he realized why.

She knew.

"Sallie," he started.

She held up a hand to stop him from continuing. "Tomorrow, Mose and I and the boys, we're heading back to Ohio. School starts soon for my boys and I don't want any trouble with that terrible truant officer. And Mose is awfully worried about the business."

Jonah knew that wasn't true. Mose didn't worry about a thing. Sallie was only being kind.

"Sallie," he started again.

She held up another hand. "I'm sorry, Jonah. I just don't think things are going to work out for us. I need a man who . . ."

Who wants to be married to you? Who wants to be a father to your boys? Or maybe, Jonah thought, cheeks burning, *who isn't in love with someone else?*

". . . who isn't quite as complicated."

Jonah stopped short. A laugh burst out of him, the first laugh in a very long time. It surprised him, that laugh. He felt as if a tremendous burden had lifted. "You're right, Sallie. You deserve someone who isn't as complicated as me." He *was* complicated. He spent fifteen years grieving, then finally fell in love with someone new—a woman who wasn't even Amish. Not yet, anyway.

Sallie smiled at him then, a genuine smile. All was well. As they headed back to Rose Hill Farm, she started to tell him about something cute one of her boys had said today. And she didn't stop talking all the way up the drive. Jonah found that he didn't mind a bit.

11

At Billy and Maggie's urging, Bess went to the youth gathering on Saturday evening, a few days after Mammi had been buried. She wasn't in much of a mood for socializing—though her spirits had risen temporarily after Sallie left for Ohio and she learned that the wedding was off for good. Her father had seemed anxious to have her go out tonight. He said it would do her good to get out of the house. She couldn't deny that she always enjoyed watching Billy play volleyball. He was such a good athlete. He had been so kind and attentive to her this last week. It made the upheaval of the last week more bearable. She still struggled with the reality of Mammi's passing, and she missed her dearly. She kept repeating to herself Lainey's reminder: her grandmother's life was complete. This was God's time to call Mammi home.

Bess sat on a rock in the shade by herself, content to be left alone, half paying attention to the game until it came to an abrupt halt. Billy held the ball in his hands, as if frozen. His eyes were glued on a buggy that had just pulled into the yard. Bess's gaze shifted from Billy to the buggy. A clump of girls had arrived and spilled out of the buggy, one by one. The last girl climbed out, scanned the yard, then flashed a dazzling smile when her eyes rested on Billy. It was an awful, heart-stopping moment for Bess as she recognized Betsy Mast, looking fresh and lovely in a pink dress.

Billy dropped the ball and made his way over to Betsy. His back was to Bess and she couldn't imagine what he was saying to her, but she could see

Betsy's face clearly. Betsy's eyes sparkled as she laughed and joked with him. Bess's heart sank.

Everyone at the youth gathering learned about Betsy's return in record time, though what they heard bore little relation to the facts. Maggie said that the English boy had refused to marry Betsy and dumped her back at her parents' farm. Andy heard that Betsy tired of the English life and wanted to return to her Amish roots. Someone else said that Betsy heard Billy Lapp had made clear his feelings for Bess at her grandmother's funeral—and hightailed it back to stake her claim on him.

Bess spent the rest of the evening doing her very best to appear at ease, but she kept one eye on Billy and Betsy. At first, she noticed that Betsy was her usual flirtatious self, tilting her head, looking up at Billy from the corner of her eyes, playfully striking him in mock punishment for something he said. As the sun went down, they stood off by themselves. Betsy became serious, speaking to him insistently while he seemed to protest innocence. They both looked at Bess, and she guessed they were talking about her.

Was that good? she wondered. *Probably not.*

Betsy could see that Billy's mind was on other things. They were in his buggy after the youth gathering, parked by the shoreline of Blue Lake Pond. Andy had offered to take Maggie and Bess home, and he was grateful for it. Billy needed time to talk to Betsy alone. His mind was darting in a hundred different directions, like a moth to a flame. Betsy shifted a little closer to him on the buggy seat as she tried to explain again why she had left suddenly and why she had returned.

"What about that English fellow?" he asked her. He'd asked her twice before, but she kept changing the subject, turning it around to accuse him of flirting with Bess.

"You're not going to listen to rumors, are you?" She sidled a little closer to him. "He just gave me a ride to see a friend." She put a hand on his forearm. "I needed to see the other side, Billy. Just to see, before bending at the knee. You understand, don't you?"

She batted her long eyelashes at him, and he knew he couldn't stay mad for long. She really was a beautiful girl. He saw her familiar features as if for the first time, and he was enchanted again by her sparkling green eyes, her dainty nose, and the determined set of her jaw. Her mouth, he realized, did not quite fit the rest of her face: those lips were too full. It was a mouth made for kissing, and the thought that he might never kiss it again filled him with despair.

Maybe he could understand why she left, after all. Everybody had doubts. Wasn't it better to work that all through before getting baptized? That was what the ministers had told him before he was baptized. Better to not take the vow than to take it and break it. "So are you planning, then, to join the church this fall?"

Betsy was looking up at Billy with her red lips in a big *O* of surprise. "Why do you ask, Billy?" Then she leaned up against him and put her lips on his and he felt his mind start to spin. Kissing Betsy always had that effect on him.

Later, after he dropped her at home and was driving the buggy back to his farm, he realized that she had answered his question with a question and given him no answer at all.

As soon as Bess had left with Billy and Maggie to go to the youth gathering, Jonah hurried to Lainey's cottage. Yesterday, he had said goodbye to Sallie and her boys and Mose, and he wanted to be the one to tell Lainey the news of their departure, before Bess had a chance to tell her at church tomorrow. He found her in the backyard of her cottage, trying to turn sod over with a shovel.

"What are you doing?" he asked.

She looked up, surprised to see him, and wiped her forehead with her sleeve. "Making a space for a vegetable garden." Then she turned her attention back to the sod.

It was hard work, what she was doing. But that wouldn't stop Lainey, he realized as he watched her huff and puff. If she made up her mind to do something, she would see it through.

"Maybe I could help," he offered.

She gave him a sideways glance. "No, thank you." Her tone was crisp.

He came closer and put a hand on the shovel's handle. "The place you've chosen gets too much afternoon shade. A vegetable garden needs at least six hours of sunlight a day." He scanned the yard. "Over there, away from the cottage, would be better."

She blew air out of her mouth, exasperated. "You're right."

She released her grip on the shovel and sat down on the porch steps. He set the shovel against the house and sat down next to her.

"I'll dig the sod for you. This week. Right now, even."

"I can get Billy to do it. You've got your . . . houseguests . . . to tend to."

He glanced at her. "Lainey, she . . . they . . . they're gone. Sallie and Mose and her boys . . . they went back to Ohio." He dropped his cane, leaned back against his elbows, and stretched out his legs, crossing one ankle over the other. "Autumn is coming, and Sallie's boys need to start school and Mose needs to tend the business. I need to stay here and see to my mother's estate." He lifted his head. "Sallie and I . . . we had a talk the other night. There isn't any Understanding between us . . . not anymore."

Lainey stared at her balled fists in her lap.

"It's for the best," Jonah continued, his voice steady and strong. "We have different . . . ideas of marriage. We want different . . ." We want different people, he wanted to say, but he didn't finish the sentence. He glanced at her between sentences, wondering what she was thinking. Unlike Bess, whose every thought revealed itself on her face, Lainey was hard to read. She was cautious and careful about her feelings. He watched her intently, waiting for a response.

Lainey lifted her head and looked at the area Jonah had pointed out as a good spot for a vegetable garden. "Maybe . . . maybe that might be a better spot for the garden."

"It's important to start with the right spot," Jonah added with a smile, not at all sure they were talking about a garden plot. He rose to his feet and reached for the shovel. "The right spot makes all the difference."

He took off his jacket and threw it on the ground, then marked out the space for the garden before he began to dig. Lainey found a spade and worked alongside him, breaking up clumps of grass.

Jonah felt happy and whole for the first time in what felt like forever. The deep calm had been missing before, but not now. Not anymore.

Yesterday afternoon, Lainey had been stunned when Jonah told her that Cheerful Sallie had returned to Ohio. As he spoke, she kept thinking this was a moment when people pinch themselves in case they're dreaming. She kept her hands in a tight ball and pinched the inside of her palms, just to make sure. And it hurt! she found, relieved.

He had dug up a patch of earth for her to make a garden and agreed to stay for dinner in lieu of payment, and soon everything slipped back to normal between them. He stayed after dinner and helped her with dishes, leaving only when he thought Bess might be due in from the gathering. She could tell he didn't want to leave, and knowing that made her heart sing.

And today, Jonah said he wanted to go with her to the hospital to learn about all of the postoperative treatment that Simon's convalescence would require. She was pretty sure Jonah must think she was crazy to take him in, but he didn't say so. Instead, he helped her think through the details she would need for Simon, such as ordering a hospital bed. And then he listened endlessly as she described her plan to start a pie-baking business. She wouldn't be able to work at the bakery anymore because she needed to be available for Simon. Mrs. Stroot crumbled when she had told her this morning that she was quitting the bakery. She crumbled even more when Lainey told her she planned to bake pies from her home.

"You'll run me clean out of business!" Mrs. Stroot had wailed.

"I'd never do that to you, Mrs. Stroot! Never! How could I possibly hurt a person who has been so good to me? I thought I'd only make pies on days when the bakery is closed. I just need enough money to cover the mortgage."

Mrs. Stroot shook her head and wiped her tears. She gave Lainey a satisfied smile. "I have a better idea. I'll buy your pies and sell them here. Fifty-fifty."

They shook on the arrangement, and Lainey had her first customer.

Lainey could hardly wait to tell Jonah about the conversation with Mrs. Stroot. He had barely lighted from the buggy when she rushed to meet him with her news. "She wants me to bake pies for her every week! She said I could vary the fillings by what's in season. And we even talked about down the road. That's what she called it. 'If this works out, Lainey, down the road, we can think about adding your signature cinnamon rolls.'"

She looked at him with her black eyebrows raised in delight above her wide blue eyes.

The brackets around Jonah's mouth deepened ever so slightly, and his eyes tightened at the corners. Quietly he said, "Well then, perhaps we should see about getting you an oven."

Her face fell. She hadn't thought about such practicalities. It was so like her, to jump into a lake before she learned to swim. Her enthusiasm for her plans always did carry her away. Of course she would need an oven! And a refrigerator. And a stove top. Her kitchen was sparse, only a table and two chairs, provided by Bertha. "I'll have to go to Lancaster for that."

Jonah tilted his head. "Are you thinking you'll use electricity? The cottage isn't set up." Then his gaze shifted beyond her.

She knew what was behind that question. She had planned to be baptized this fall, but that had to be postponed because of Simon. If she were baptized, she would have to shun Simon. She would wait.

Jonah had never asked her about joining the church. She was getting to know him well enough to know that he was watching and waiting, letting time provide the answer. "No. Not electricity. Bess has been teaching me how to cook on a propane stove top. And how to use a woodstove too."

Jonah looked back at her. "You could get those things, used, at an auction."

She nodded. "Then I'll go to an auction."

Jonah stifled a patronizing smile. "Make out a list and I'll get what you need."

"I can take care of these things." *I can take care of myself*, was what she meant.

Jonah gave a short laugh. "Might be a little hard to purchase items at an Amish auction, Lainey. You don't speak Deitsch."

Now her spine stiffened. "I'm learning." But she was a long, long way from being fluent.

He walked up to her. "I'm offering to help. Would it be so hard to accept it?" He searched her eyes.

Yes, she thought, suddenly shy. *More than you could imagine.* She'd always had a hard time accepting help from others. Depending on others. Trusting others.

But she was trying to get past that obstacle. It was part of what she was learning this summer. How could she become Amish if she didn't learn how to rely on her community? It would be like missing the forest for the trees.

She wiped her hand on her apron and held it out to him to shake. "Then I accept your help."

Jonah looked at her extended hand, then took her hand in his. They remained that way for only the briefest moment, touching palm to palm; she was the one to pull away.

She gave him a shy smile. "Thank you."

Dear Robin and Ally,

Isn't the start of autumn wonderful? The air is getting crisp in the morning and evening, and apples are falling off the trees! Don't you just love autumn?

So . . . perhaps there is a man of interest in Lancaster County after all.

Love,
Lainey
P.S. By the way, did I happen to mention that I'm becoming Amish?

Jonah took the time to find out what the state requirements would be to get permits and a license for a commercial kitchen. Then he drove a wagon to an auction and purchased a used propane refrigerator and stovetop oven, delivered them to Lainey's cottage one hazy and humid September afternoon, and hooked them up for her. The sky had begun to cloud over and the kitchen grew dim, so Lainey held a lamp over his head while he worked. She studied his face in the shifting light of the flame. Once, he caught her eye and smiled. She considered how attractive he was—the type of man who was clearly comfortable in his own skin and had grown up unaffected by his good looks.

When he finished, he stood and turned on the gas to the stove. When she saw the pilot light fire up, she clapped her hands together and said, "How can I ever thank you?"

Jonah looked down at her. He was quite a bit taller than she was. "I should be thanking you, Lainey."

She wanted to ask why but could see he had something on his mind. He seemed to be carefully arranging his thoughts, so she remained quiet.

"There's something I've been meaning to tell you. The night of that accident, when you stayed by the buggy until the ambulance arrived. You kept saying not to give up . . ." He swallowed hard. "I remember. I remember hearing your voice and I held on to those words. They helped me stay alive." His eyes became glassy with tears and he wiped them away with a laugh. "I can't stop tearing up this summer. It's like I'm shedding a lifetime of bottled tears."

They locked eyes for a long moment, then she leaned toward him. She stroked his face softly. He caught her hand and held it to his lips. He kissed it with his head bent over it so that she couldn't see his eyes.

A month had passed since Simon's bone marrow transplant. Jonah and Lainey were seated in hard plastic chairs in an office as a nurse explained what to expect after Simon was discharged. His blood counts were returning to safe levels, the nurse said.

"Does that mean the bone marrow transplant worked?" Jonah asked.

"The transplanted marrow seems to be engrafting," the nurse said. "We're cautiously optimistic. But I have to warn you that recovery can be like a roller-coaster ride. The patient may be irritable and unpleasant with the caregiver. Helplessness is also a common feeling among bone marrow transplant patients, which can breed further feelings of anger or resentment."

"Even more than usual?" Lainey asked.

"One day a patient may feel much better, only to awake the next day feeling as sick as ever." She gave Lainey a bright smile. "So if his daily blood samples continue to show that he's producing normal red blood cells, he can go home by the end of this week."

"So soon?" Lainey asked in a dull, polite way.

"By the end of this week," the nurse repeated cheerfully.

Jonah had a funny feeling the staff was eager to have Simon leave.

"In the first several weeks," the nurse continued, "he'll be weak and tired and will want to sleep and rest frequently. He'll need to return to the hospital for frequent follow-up visits for medication, blood transfusions, and monitoring."

"And then?" Jonah asked. "How long until he can take care of himself?"

"Recovery from a bone marrow transplant is lengthy and can take up to six months to resume normal activities, including returning to full-time work."

Jonah and Lainey exchanged a look of shock. Six months!

"During the first three months after the transplant, he'll be vulnerable to complications due to the fact that his white blood cell counts will be very low and incapable of providing normal protection against everyday viruses and bacteria. So he'll have to avoid crowded public places such as movie theatres and grocery stores to avoid contact with potential infection." The nurse clapped the file shut. "And he really shouldn't have any friends visiting for a while."

Jonah's eyebrows shot up. "Well, *that* shouldn't be a problem. Simon has no friends."

That made the nurse burst out with a laugh. "Will wonders never cease?"

The first morning after Simon was released from the hospital and moved into Lainey's house, he rang a bell at five in the morning to wake her to help him find the bathroom. At six, he rang it again for coffee. At seven, he complained that the eggs she had scrambled for him were cold.

Bess came by in the early afternoon to see if Lainey needed any help. Stoney Ridge was experiencing an Indian summer, and it was too hot to pick rose blooms. Jonah wanted to keep the rose petal harvest going, though he still hadn't decided what to do about Rose Hill Farm or their home in Ohio, either. The roses were in their second bloom, and they had to work quickly in this heat to get those roses picked and dried. Lainey smiled to see the Band-Aids covering Bess's hands.

Lainey made Simon lunch, went back to the kitchen to clean up, only to have Simon ring the bell again. "I don't like crust on my sandwiches," he complained to her. "I don't like crunchy peanut butter, only smooth. I asked for a Coke, not milk. Do you think I'm a six-year-old?"

Lainey took his plate back to the kitchen and cut the crust off of his sandwich, then took it back to him with a Coke.

Bess sat in the front room and watched this ongoing interaction. The third time Simon rang the bell to complain, Bess stood abruptly and held a hand in the air to stop Lainey from taking his plate back to the kitchen. "So, you don't like your lunch?" Bess's voice was dangerously calm.

"Dang right I don't like that lunch. Didn't like breakfast, neither." Simon turned to Lainey. "And I didn't like the coffee. I told you I want it strong."

Bess picked up the bell, walked to the door, opened it, threw the bell outside, and closed the door.

Simon did not make any further comments through the rest of lunch. He didn't thank Lainey for it, but he didn't complain about it, either.

For the next few hours, Bess helped Lainey roll out pie crusts in the kitchen, and they talked quietly to each other as they worked, while Simon rested. Finally, sounding hurt that he was being left out of the conversation, Simon called to them to ask what kind of pies they were baking. Bess had just taken a pie out of the oven and stood at the door, holding it in her hands with hot mitts. "Apple and pumpkin."

Lainey pulled out a rack for Bess to set the pies on and asked Simon what his favorite pie was.

He scowled at her. "I only like two kinds of pie: hot and cold."

Bess and Lainey laughed at that, genuinely laughed, and Simon's mournful, hound-dog face brightened a bit.

Not much later, Lainey and Bess were cleaning up the mess they'd made in the kitchen when an ear-busting woof came from the front of the cottage. Bess dropped the wet dishrag and hurried to open the front door.

"Don't open that door!" Simon hollered from his bed. "We're getting bombed!"

"That's no bomb! That's Boomer!" Bess said, clapping her hands in delight. She threw open the door and in charged Boomer, looking a little thinner and smelling pretty bad. He jumped up on Bess, then Lainey, then put his dirty front paws on Simon's bed.

"Get that mutt out of here," Simon yelled. "He smells like he was on the wrong end of a fight with a polecat!"

"This is Mammi's dog, Simon," Bess said. "His name is Boomer. He's been out mourning for Mammi. But now he's back. We'll give him a bath and he'll be as good as new."

"Fat chance of that," Simon muttered.

"If you wouldn't mind keeping Simon company for a few minutes," Lainey told Bess after they gave Boomer a bath, "I've got some laundry hanging that I need to take down." She picked up an empty laundry basket and went to the backyard. Having a house of one's own took getting used to, Lainey had quickly realized. There was always some little thing to be done. It wasn't a big house, but there were plenty of chores.

She took her time taking the dry clothes off the line. Hanging laundry was something she found she enjoyed doing. Pinning clothes up and letting the sun permeate them with its warmth was so much better than sitting in a dark Laundromat guarding a machine. Bess had told her once that working is a form of prayer. At first, Lainey had trouble understanding that. But now, she could see it. She thought it meant the kind of work that came from caring for others.

When Lainey came back inside, she found Bess helping Simon drink from a glass of water. It was touching to see Bess, this child who had grown up with another life and another father, reaching out to this man. When Bess tossed that bell out the front door, it was like Lainey was watching some other girl entirely. Bess was so confident and clear about how to handle Simon. She handled him better than Lainey ever did. In fact, it just occurred to Lainey, she handled him the way Bertha used to. Bertha never stood for any of Simon's bluster.

Lainey tiptoed to the bedroom to fold the clothes. When she came back out, she found Simon had drifted off, and Bess was curled up in a corner of the couch, sound asleep. Boomer was on the foot of Simon's bed, snoring.

Later that week, Bess stood on the porch at Rose Hill Farm and waved goodbye to Andy Yoder after he had dropped off a bushel of ripe apples from his family's orchard. Before turning onto the road, Andy looked back and yanked off his straw hat. He stood on the wagon seat, holding the horse's reins in one hand, waving his hat in a big arc with the other.

The thing about Andy Yoder, Bess was finding, was that you just couldn't put him off. He was cheerful and funny and full of life, and totally convinced that she loved him. Which of course she didn't. It wasn't that she was immune to Andy's charms; it felt nice to be admired. He told her today that he thought she looked like an angel: smooth skin with large, bright eyes and a mouth shaped like a bow. He stared at her mouth when he said it, and it made her stomach do a flip-flop. Andy was like that: chock-full of sweet words and lingering gazes and always willing to share every thought.

But as fun as Andy was, Bess knew her heart belonged to Billy. Each day, they worked in the rose fields or in the greenhouse and talked about all kinds of things. Conversation was so easy between them, even their good-natured arguments. Sometimes, when he was in a professorial mood, she couldn't understand half of what he said. Her thoughts often wandered to imagining that this would be their life: the two of them living side by side, day by day, for always.

Esther Swartzentruber told her at church that Billy was spending a lot of time with Betsy Mast, but Bess knew it couldn't be so. Not after that week when she had the surgery and he had kissed her, ever so gently, and had been worried for her. Not after he had comforted her when her grandmother died. Even Mammi had said Billy Lapp was no fool. Surely, Esther was just spreading rumors.

Bess reached down and hoisted the basket of apples onto her hip. Mammi also used to say that a rumor was "something with truth on the trail," and a flicker of fear ran through her.

Billy Lapp wiped his brow. He had worked a few hours at Rose Hill Farm, teaching Jonah about Bertha's rose business, then spent another hour replacing shingles on Lainey O'Toole's roof. He still needed to get home and help his brothers with the oat shocks. Threshing day was tomorrow, and they needed to knock the shocks down to ready the rows for pitching. Billy had done some research to calculate the best time to harvest the oats. He'd recommended this week to schedule their farm for the community's threshing rotation, and for the first time ever, his father had listened to him. The weather cooperated, and this oat harvest looked to be one of the best they'd had in years. Just this morning, his father was discussing tomorrow's pitching and had given him a nod of approval in front of everyone. That was no small thing.

Billy hopped down from the roof and packed up his tools. Then he told Lainey he was heading home, and she handed him a slab of blueberry peach pie she had just pulled from the oven. It was a recipe of her mother's, she said, and she was trying to improve it.

Billy looked up at the sky and was relieved to see the clouds didn't look as threatening as they had an hour ago. If they worked fast, they might be able to get the north field finished before it got too dark. And wouldn't his dad be pleased with that?

He took a bite of Lainey's blueberry peach pie, then another. It was delicious, that pie. It struck him that Bertha had done the same thing with her roses: took something old and made it new. Maybe that's what life was all about—taking the lot you were given and making it better, he thought, finishing off the rest of that pie slab in two bites as he hurried down the road.

The nurse had been right about the roller coaster of emotions Simon would experience, yet that was nothing new to anyone who had dealings with him. At times, Lainey could see that he was making an effort to be pleasant. Or at least, not unpleasant. And then, hours later, it was as if he used up all of the niceness he had, which wasn't in great supply to begin with. He would slip back to constant complaining, mostly about her cooking. Lainey could brush off most of Simon's insults but not those about her cooking. That area was off-limits. She told him that he was welcome to cook for himself.

He gave her a hard look. "You're in no position to be giving me lectures."

There was a moment's silence.

Lainey thought of what Bess would say. She pulled up a highback chair and sat next to him. "The truth of it is that I am in a position to be giving you a lecture. The way I see it, you have two choices. You can stay here, but only if you stop complaining about every little thing. Or . . ."

He narrowed his eyes.

"Or you are free to leave." Lainey was firm.

She had him there. He had no place to go.

He glared angrily at her. "Women are the devil." He said it at least three times a day.

And yet it was Jonah who had the most difficulty tolerating Simon. He dropped by the cottage often, to help Lainey with house repairs or to take her on an errand to town. But he was cool to Simon and had little patience for him. If Simon dared make a vague complaint against Lainey, Jonah would put up a hand to cut him off. In turn, Simon acted cautious around Jonah, as if he knew not to cross him.

As Simon's health improved, he liked to talk. While Lainey worked in the kitchen, he would tell her stories about all of the near riches he'd had in his business dealings. Since she was in the other room and working on her pies, she was able to only half listen. But Jonah didn't want to hear the stories, even if he was working on a house repair in another room and Simon was in the front room. He never said a word, but he would quietly get up and go outside.

One afternoon, Lainey followed Jonah outside to the vegetable garden. He had given her some spinach seedlings to get in the ground, but she hadn't had a chance yet. He picked up a hoe and raked a neat furrow. She put a hand on his shoulder and he stopped digging.

"I just can't listen to him, Lainey. This chasing after rainbows and borrowing money from people—never paying anyone back. Simon's spent a lifetime living on the near brink of disaster. It just sickens me to think this would have been the life my Bess would have had."

"But she didn't," Lainey said quietly. "She grew up with you. The life she's had with you is the only life she's ever known."

He finished marking the row. "I can't seem to find a way to tell Bess. I can't see what good would be served if she were to know Simon was her father."

"Is that what you're concerned about? Whether it would be good for Bess to know?"

"I don't want her to be hurt. Or confused."

Lainey sat down on the back step and patted the step in silent invitation for Jonah to sit beside her. He lay the hoe on the ground and sat down. "I'm not sure it's up to us to decide whether truth is good for us or not. Truth is just . . . truth. I guess it's how we respond to it that makes it good or bad."

Jonah looked away. "Lainey, why are you doing this?" He took off his black hat and raked a hand through his hair. "I have an easier time forgiving the truck driver—a stranger—who caused the accident that killed Rebecca and our baby, than I do Simon, for abandoning you and Bess like he did."

Lainey didn't answer for a while. "That truck driver was remorseful. Forgiveness comes a little easier when a person asks to be forgiven."

"Maybe. But that doesn't explain you. You're not even Amish, yet you're able to give Simon something I—who lived my whole life in the Amish church—can't." He turned to her. "Why?"

Lainey lifted her head to the sky. "For a long time, I felt abandoned. And so lonely. I still do, at times. I think it will always be my Achilles heel. But a few years ago, I went to a church service and the pastor happened to be preaching on the difference between divine forgiveness and human forgiveness. I knew I couldn't forgive others without God's help. He said that we fail in the work of grace and love when there is too much of us and not enough of God. That thought stayed with me. Too much of me and not enough of God. Once I understood that and asked for God's help, I was able to forgive Simon and stop condemning him." They sat together there for a long time before Lainey added, "I learned how to love from watching your mother. I know she could scare a body half to death, but a person knew she could fail and still be loved. I think even Simon knew that about your mother. I think that's why he never left Stoney Ridge. She might have been the only person who really loved him."

Jonah tucked his chin. "Rebecca was always frightened by my mother."

Jonah was bringing up Rebecca's name more and more and it made Lainey glad. She wanted him to feel comfortable talking about her. She didn't want him to feel as if he had to forget her.

He glanced at her. "You never were frightened by my mother, were you? Even as a young girl."

"I always knew there was a tender heart inside that gruff exterior."

Lainey smiled at him, and Jonah smiled back at her.

She reached out and jostled his knee. "Listen. Simon's still telling the story."

Sure enough, they could hear Simon's voice through the window, carrying on as if they were still in the kitchen. Jonah gave a short laugh. "Are you seeing much improvement in him? Other than his talking voice is back in working order?"

"Little by little. He's not needing as much sleep. He took a walk to the end of the road yesterday."

Jonah tucked a curl behind her ear and stood to leave. "Good. Maybe there is an end in sight.".

And then what? Lainey wondered, watching Jonah head out to the street toward Rose Hill Farm.

Caleb Zook made a point of stopping by to see Simon every Sunday afternoon. Lainey was amazed. Caleb had no responsibility for Simon since he had been shunned. But Jonah said Caleb was like that. He said Caleb had always managed to be sincere about his faith without becoming legalistic. It wasn't that rules were optional to Caleb. She noticed that he didn't entirely ignore Simon's shunning: he didn't sit at their table for a meal with Simon. Once she offered a plate of cookies to the two of them while they were talking in the living room, but Caleb politely turned her down. Jonah told her later that Caleb shouldn't be offered food from the same plate that had been handed to Simon. And Caleb didn't touch Simon, not even a handshake. But he still showed genuine concern and interest in him. He seemed to believe that there was something to redeem in Simon.

All men of God should be like Caleb Zook, Lainey thought more than once.

"Do you really believe Simon can change?" Lainey asked him one Sunday as she walked with him out to his buggy after he had paid a call on Simon. "Or are you just saying that because you're the bishop and that's what you're supposed to think?"

Caleb laughed at her candor. "Simon always was chock-full of brag and fight." He put on his hat. "But, yes, I think he can change if he wants to. God wants all men to come to him."

Lainey wanted to ask him more but waited to see if he was in a hurry to leave. When he didn't get in the buggy right away, she blurted out, "What made Simon the way he is?" It was a question Lainey had often wondered and wished she had asked Bertha. She did ask Jonah once, but he had no idea. As long as he could remember, Simon was just thought of as the black sheep.

Caleb leaned against the buggy, one long leg crossed over the other, his arms crossed against his chest, that black hat still shadowing his face. "I'm not sure there's an easy answer to that question. I don't think there's one event. But I do recall my mother saying that Simon's mother died bringing him into the world, and his father was a hard man to please." He stopped as a thought seemed to come to him. "A little like Billy's father. Always wondered if that might be why Bertha took such an interest in Billy." He stared down the road for a moment, then turned back to Lainey. "Simon was the last child and only boy in a string of females, and life seemed to be a little more difficult for him—learning in school, getting along with others, learning a trade. He grew up being told he couldn't do anything right. Maybe there came a point when he believed it. It became a way of life for him. A habit. Maybe it was easier to just go ahead and disappoint people in advance. Maybe that's how he has felt about God." He unknotted the buggy reins from the fence. "He's softening, though. Little by little. Bertha would say, 'En Baam fallt net uff der eracht Hack.' *One stroke fells not an oak.*"

Lainey frowned. "Bertha also said, 'You can't make good hay from poor grass.'"

Caleb grinned. "Now, now. How could a man be at death's doorstep and not have some change in his heart?"

Lainey was unconvinced. To her, Simon didn't seem capable of change.

Caleb caught the look on her face. "Let me put it another way. Before Simon's body could accept Bess's bone marrow, the doctors had to kill off his own marrow. Only then would his body be able to accept the new marrow, Bess's sacrifice. There's a spiritual part of this. The way I see it, he's a new man. It's just taking awhile to break those old habits, to kill off that old marrow. That old way of life."

That was a new thought to her.

"But," Caleb warned, "it might take time." He shrugged. "No matter. God has plenty of time. It's one thing he's never short of."

Lainey rolled her eyes. "God might have time, but I'm running out of it. Patience too. It's like trying to take care of a bear with a toothache."

Caleb laughed. "Lainey, now that Simon is getting more energy, maybe you should think about putting him to work for you." He climbed into the buggy. "Work does a soul good. Even a tough old codger like Simon."

As she watched his buggy drive down the road, she wondered if what Caleb said could possibly be true. Could Bess's sacrifice to Simon be changing him, inside out?

She heard Simon's voice yelling for her to hurry his dinner. *Fat chance.*

12

*J*onah and Lainey were heading back to the cottage from buying supplies in town. They were on the top of the rise when Rose Hill Farm came into view. This was Lainey's favorite vantage point. She could barely make out the rooftop of her cottage down below, hidden by trees, but it gave her comfort to realize how close their homes were. Suddenly a car honked loudly and careened around the buggy, upsetting the horse so that Jonah pulled quickly over to the side of the road and stopped.

"Dutt's weh?" he asked Lainey. *Does anything hurt?*

"A little scared but not hurt," she said.

He raised his eyebrows. "You understood?"

She lifted her chin. "I understand a lot more than you might think."

He grinned at her. "I'm sure you do." He looked back at the horse. "I haven't known Frieda to rear before."

Lainey looked up the road at the small speck of a black car, now far up the road. "It wasn't Frieda's fault. It was that car's."

Jonah got out of the buggy to calm the horse down. When they arrived at the cottage, they found that little black car parked out front.

"Oh no," Lainey said, worried. She hopped out of the buggy and hurried inside while Jonah hitched the horse to the fence.

There in the living room were her English friends, Robin and Ally. Simon, looking delighted to be in the company of two young women, was entertaining them with stories.

It was Robin who recognized Lainey first. Robin was not quite beautiful, and certainly not pretty, but men had always been attracted to her. She had a straight nose and a strong jaw, and her green eyes were large and clear. She was not smiling when she saw her friend; in fact, she wore a slight frown. She was studying Lainey, her gaze moving slowly over her prayer cap, her blue Plain dress and white apron, then back up to her starched white cap again. "You look so . . ."

"Plain?" Lainey offered.

"Then it's true," Robin said. "What you wrote to us. We thought you were joking. They've got you in their clutches. It's a cult, just like he said."

"*Who* said such a thing?" Lainey asked.

"Him," Ally answered, pointing to Simon. Ally was round and pleasant looking. There was something friendly and understanding about her face.

Lainey glared at Simon. "Don't listen to him. He's always saying crazy things. Being Amish is not a cult."

"It's a cult of the worst sort!" Simon said. "Seems all sweet and rosy as long as a fellow toes the Amish line. But just put a toe over the line a very little bit and folks will come down on you like a wolf on the fold." He folded his arms across his chest. "If that's not a cult, I don't know what is."

Ally was staring out the front window at Jonah, who was looking over the black car. "Who's he?"

"That's her boyfriend!" Simon called out. "He's been bringing twigs and leaves and starting to build a love nest, just like a couple of doves in springtime." He made a sweeping gesture with his hand. "She's getting baptized just so she can throw me out on the streets. Shunning me just like the rest of 'em."

Lainey lifted her palms and looked at Simon. "Why do you say these things?" She had told him once that she would postpone her baptism until he recovered and could live on his own, just to avoid any complications of his shunning. How had he twisted that around?

Robin walked up to the window and stood next to Ally to peer at Jonah. Lainey looked over their shoulders. Seeing him at a distance the way a stranger might see him, she felt a surge of tenderness for him. He was such a fine-looking man.

"Oh sheesh," Robin said. "She's gone off the deep end for sure. It's worse than we thought."

Jonah had a pretty good idea to whom the black car belonged. Lainey had told him about her two English friends she used to live with, that they were good-hearted but ran a little wild. He saw the two of them watching him from the window. He took his time getting the horse some water, stalling, trying to settle his unease. Would Lainey be tempted by her friends to return to the world?

Maybe this was good, he tried telling himself as he emptied the water bucket. Now was the time for Lainey to find out if an Amish life was what she truly wanted. To be sure she was hearing God's guidance correctly. And before his feelings for her were at the point of no return, he had to admit, hoping he hadn't already passed it. Cautiously, he approached the cottage porch.

Lainey met him outside. "My friends are here." She had an uncomfortable look on her face. "They think I've gone crazy."

Jonah looked down at her earnest face and tried to hold back a grin. "Have you?"

Her face relaxed into a smile. "No more than usual."

When she smiled like that, with her full-lipped mouth, it always made Jonah think of kissing her. He was seized by an urge to take her in his arms, but instead he reined in those stray thoughts and said, "Then let them see that. They're here because they care about you. Let them see you're still you."

Lainey nodded and turned to go into the house. She stopped and whirled back around. "I just . . . apologize in advance for anything they say that might be considered . . . offensive."

Jonah gave her a reassuring smile and followed behind her into the house.

Lainey gestured toward Jonah. "Robin, Ally, this is my friend Jonah Riehl."

There was an awkward silence as the two women looked him up and down. Then the taller of the two, the woman whose mouth was pursed tightly—Robin—took a few strides forward to shake his hand. The gesture struck him as insincere; he could see a mocking intelligence in her eyes. He turned to the other woman to shake her hand. Ally had a small, round face on top of a small, round body. The image of a sparrow following behind a raptor flickered through his mind.

"I noticed one of your car tires is nearly flat," Jonah said.

"We've been running on three tires since we hit Lancaster," Robin said, as if it didn't seem to matter.

"If you have a spare, I could change it out for you," he offered.

Robin exchanged a curious glance with Ally. "I thought you Amish folks didn't want anything to do with cars."

Now it was Jonah's turn to exchange a glance with Lainey. "Knowing about something and using it are two different matters." He took off his coat and tossed it on a chair, then rolled up his sleeves and went out to the car.

After Jonah went outside, Ally turned to Lainey. "That sweet old man was just about to rustle something up for us in the kitchen. We're starving!"

Sweet old man? Simon? Lainey heard a curse fly out of the kitchen and hurried in to find Simon in the middle of frying up a loaf of scrapple. He was rubbing butter on his hand. A curl of black smoke was rising up from the frying pan. Lainey grabbed a dishcloth and pulled the heavy cast iron pan off of the burner.

"Scrapple?" she asked Simon as she put his hand under cool water. "Why would you offer scrapple to my friends at this time of day?" She cracked the window open to fan out the smoke.

"They wanted something Penn Dutch," he said, carefully examining his hand.

"Fine," Lainey said, pulling forks out of a drawer. "If that's what they wanted, then that's what they'll get." She had just bought a loaf of scrapple in town because Simon had pestered her to get some for breakfast.

It irked her to see Simon bend over backward, acting as charming as could be toward her two friends. To her, he always sounded quarrelsome, even if he wasn't. Why, he had never even cooked before! She pulled plates from the cupboard and napkins and took them to the table. By the time she got everyone something to drink, Jonah had returned from changing the tire. He took one look at the burnt scrapple and said he should be leaving.

"Please, Jonah. Don't go. Sit down and visit." She wanted him to get to know her friends and for them to get to know him. Plus, Simon was on better behavior when Jonah was around. She pointed to the place she had set for him at the table.

Too late, Lainey remembered that Jonah couldn't sit at the same table with Simon. He hesitated, an uncomfortable look passed over his face, until she jumped up and offered him a glass of iced tea. Then, instead of sitting down, she nonchalantly leaned against the kitchen counter and he followed her lead. She had seen Caleb do the same thing once. Still respecting the rules of the church, but without making a scene or being rude to others.

Jonah took a sip of iced tea. "So, what is it you two do in Harrisburg?"

"We're cosmetologists," Ally said.

"They study the stars," Simon said to Jonah, thumping the bottom of the ketchup bottle over his plate.

Robin snorted and Lainey exchanged an amused glance with Jonah. "That would be cosmology," Lainey whispered to Simon.

"Same thing," Simon said.

"Not hardly," Robin said. "We work at a beauty salon."

"Ha!" Simon said. "It is the same thing. You're turning coal into diamonds!" He grinned at his own joke.

For some reason, it irritated Lainey even more that Simon could laugh off Robin's correction. If she had corrected him, he would have barked at her.

Ally poked carefully at the scrapple with her fork. "What's in this?"

"Offal," Simon said, sawing a piece of scrapple with his fork.

Ally looked up. "Awful?"

"Yup," Simon said. "Hog offal. Heads, heart, liver, and other scraps. All mixed together with cornmeal and flour." He took a bite and chewed it. "Guess that's why they call it scrapple."

Robin made a face. "It sounds awful!"

"Yup," Simon said. "That's what I've been telling you. Offal."

Lainey gave a sideways glance with a smile to Jonah, and Jonah smiled back at her. An intimacy passed between them that shut everybody else out. It only lasted a moment, but no one at the table missed it.

After Jonah left, Lainey showed Robin and Ally upstairs to the spare bedroom. She felt as if she should brace herself, now that they were alone.

"Why, this room is as bare looking as the downstairs!" Robin said, walking into it. There were two twin beds covered with handmade quilts, and a simple nightstand between them. No curtains on the windows, no rugs on the floor, no pictures or posters on the wall. It was a Plain room.

Lainey looked around the room as Robin and Ally did, then her gaze came back to her friends. As they stared at each other, the air seemed to acquire a prickly tension but the silence dragged out.

Finally Robin let out an exaggerated sigh. "You can't actually be thinking of wanting to marry that simple farmer, can you?" she asked, flopping on the twin bed. "Why, he even smells like a farm!"

Lainey liked the way Jonah smelled—of hard-work sweat. It blended with the other scents of summer, of sweet clover and mown hay. He had spent the morning helping a neighbor thresh in his fields.

"Simon told us that Jonah's house doesn't have toilets," Ally said, eyes as big as saucers. "Or running water."

Lainey winced. "Rose Hill Farm belonged to his mother and she died recently. He's installing indoor plumbing right now." It was the very first project Jonah started work on after his mother had passed, and Bess couldn't have been happier.

Ally sat down on the other bed. "Has he told you he loves you?"

"Not in so many words," Lainey said, handing them towels. "The Amish don't use terms of endearment the way we—you—do. They show how they feel about someone by example." Like the time Jonah cut a cord of wood for her and stacked it neatly into a pile by her front door. She thought of him preparing the vegetable garden for her, then helping her to plant. Or accompanying her on medical appointments for Simon. Even changing her friends' tire today, without being given a word of thanks. Were those things not evidence of love? She knew her thoughts showed on her face, and her cheeks grew warm. "Jonah Riehl will make someone a fine husband," she added. She wasn't sure why she felt as if she needed to defend him.

"Oh, will he really?" Robin asked in mock amazement. "I'll grant you this . . . if he shaved off that beard and took a shower and got a haircut and wore a T-shirt and blue jeans, he could be a looker. But what about that cane? And his limp? How old is this guy, anyway?"

"Not old at all," Lainey said in a crisp tone. She thought Jonah was quite marvelous just the way he was: wise and kind and wonderful.

Robin stood and pointed a finger at Lainey. "And you? You always told us you weren't the marrying kind. Not Lainey O'Toole!"

Robin's words rankled Lainey. It was true, she had said many times marriage wasn't for her. Hadn't she thought this whole thing through a hundred thousand times before? But that was before she met Jonah and grew to care for him. It was a frightening thing—to realize that you wanted to love and be loved more than you could have ever imagined.

"Do you actually think he's going to marry you?" Ally asked. "Wouldn't he be driven off for marrying someone out of his commune?"

Lainey stiffened. "No one ever said anything about getting married." That was the truth. Jonah had never hinted at marriage in any way, shape, or form. He seemed to carefully avoid any discussion of their future. She didn't know if he was planning to return to Ohio or stay here in Stoney Ridge. All she knew for sure was that Sallie Stutzman had married his business partner, Mose, and he didn't seem bothered by the news. Lainey often wondered if Jonah even thought about marrying her at all; she thought about it all the time. "And the Amish do not live in communes. Nor is it a cult."

"But what about culinary school?" Ally asked. "You scrimped and saved for years! It was your dream!"

Lainey shrugged. "I've learned more about cooking in the last few months here than I ever could in a formal school. Here, food means more than nourishing a body. Sharing a meal nourishes a community. It's like women are feeding a big family."

"That's another thing Simon told us about," Ally said. "Amish women are oppressed. They're always serving the men and the men are controlling and mean-spirited. The women can't speak their mind and they have to do whatever their husband tells them to and they have no self-esteem and they have at least a dozen babies—"

"And you . . . Miss Independent!" Robin interrupted. "How many times have you given us a lecture about respecting ourselves and not falling in love with every guy that looks our way? About how we should have goals and plans? And how a man would only derail our dreams?"

Ally nodded in silent agreement.

Robin lifted her hands in the air. "But along comes a guy in a beard and a buggy—who walks with a cane and has a teenaged daughter, no less—and Lainey falls for him, hook, line, and sinker." She looked back at Ally as if to say "what is the world coming to?" then turned to face Lainey. "Well, honey, if you're not derailed, I don't know what is."

Lainey sat down on the bed. "Listen, you two. I'm *going* to become Amish. Not *because* of Jonah. This has nothing to do with Jonah."

Robin and Ally exchanged a doubtful glance.

"I'm becoming Amish because that's what I think God wants me to do." Once she said it aloud, she realized that was exactly what it was. She truly believed God was leading her in this direction.

Robin put her hands on her temples, as if she had a headache. "I'd like to think your bonnet is on too tight, but you always did go a little overboard with the God stuff. I never imagined you'd go this far."

Stung, Lainey felt no need to reply. Without a word, she rose to leave and went downstairs to start dinner. Still upset, she decided to go sit on the porch steps for a few minutes of solitude and watch the sunset. Why did it seem that when a person really started listening to God, others assumed that person had gone off the deep end? Maybe because God does lead us into unusual places. She looked up at the streaks of red that blazed out from the dying sun. What was it Jonah said? Red sky at night is a farmer's delight. Red sky at morning, a farmer takes warning.

The wind unfurled strands of her loosely pinned hair and pressed her dress to her legs. She smoothed out the apron over the blue dress Bess had made for her. Maybe she shouldn't be so hard on Robin and Ally for their concern. If someone had told her six months ago that she'd be dressing in simple garb and living a Plain life, falling in love with a Plain man, making a life in Stoney Ridge, she would have laughed out loud.

But she was here and so very glad to be . . . where life was simple, where people cared for each others' needs, where faith in God and life blended together as one. This was where she belonged.

She noticed the first star appear on the horizon. Looking up at the bruised blue of the evening sky for a few minutes—at the vast and empty sky—always cut human problems down to size. A short laugh burst out of her as she rose to her feet. *Maybe it is a little crazy.* But it was a crazy that suited her.

All through dinner and into the evening, Robin and Ally tried to convince Lainey to return to Harrisburg with them, but she wouldn't budge. She tried to explain her feelings, but they couldn't see her point of view.

"Can't you just be happy for me?" Lainey asked them at last. "I'm still me. I might be wearing a Plain dress and living without modern conveniences—"

"I'll say," Robin interrupted with a sneer.

"—but I'm really, truly happy." Lainey could tell that they still didn't believe her, and it hurt her. The three of them had been friends since high school; Robin and Ally were the closest thing to a family that she'd ever had. The way they looked at her—especially Robin, but Ally always followed Robin's lead—was almost as if she had to choose one or the other, the Amish life or her old friends. Why did it have to be that way?

She would have thought it to be the other way around, that Jonah might frown on her English friends. She knew there were some Amish who avoided the English as much as possible, as if they might be corroded by worldly rust. Jonah didn't seem to share that belief. As he left her cottage yesterday afternoon, he had quietly suggested to her that she might bring them to Rose Hill Farm tomorrow afternoon. He said he wanted them to meet Bess.

On Sunday morning, Lainey tiptoed into their room at seven to ask if they would join her for church. She thought that maybe, if they could see the gathering for themselves, if they could see the kindness and the sincerity of the people, then they would understand why she felt so drawn to this community. If they could only see what a wonderful father Jonah was to Bess, then maybe they could see why she cared for him. And if they could meet Bess, they would understand why Lainey wanted to be close to her. She wanted Robin and Ally to come to her church because it was becoming so much a part of her, the backbone of her life.

Robin opened one eye and said emphatically, "No. Way."

Bess couldn't wait to meet Lainey's English friends. Her father had told her what he knew about them, but it wasn't much. Lainey had mentioned their names to Bess once or twice, but then she would change the subject, as if she just wasn't sure how to combine her past with her present. Bess was curious about them. She knew they were important to Lainey, and she was eager to know everything she could about her. Lainey fascinated Bess.

After a light lunch that followed church, Bess, Jonah, and Lainey returned to the cottage. As Jonah hitched the horse's reins to the fence post, they heard Simon singing. It sounded slurry and strange and off-key. And loud. Very, very loud. Jonah motioned for the two to stay put while he went inside. He opened the door carefully, then pushed it wide.

He looked back at Lainey with a look of sheer disgust. "Er is gsoffe." *He is drunk.* Jonah's patience for Simon hung by a thread.

Lainey and Bess went to the door. A near empty bottle of an amber-colored liquid was on the floor and Simon was sprawled on the couch, singing at the top of his lungs. The smell of alcohol oozed from him, sour as old sweat. His eyes shone too brightly.

Lainey stomped over to him and picked up the bottle. "Where did you get this?"

Simon's chest heaved as he drew in a ragged breath. "Don't even think about sharing," he said, slurring his sibilants.

"Your English friends is my guess," Jonah said. He took the bottle from Lainey and poured it out on the grass.

"Did Robin and Ally give that to you?" Lainey asked.

"They . . . might have . . . left it behind," Simon said. "They went into town to get a new tire, then came back and waited for you, but you took too long. They had to get to Philly by nightfall for a rock concert. Said to say goodbye." He waved his hand carelessly in the air.

Silence covered the room. Bess saw the disappointed look on Lainey's face. Jonah saw it too. How could her friends leave like that?

But then Lainey stiffened her spine. "Did you ask them to buy you that booze?" she asked.

"All of you, quit looking down your noses at me!" Simon snapped. "People been looking down their pointy little judgmental noses at me for as long as I can remember. Nobody believes in me! Nobody has ever been in my corner!"

Eventually his voice grew slower, his hand movements less exaggerated. His arms fell to his sides, and soon his head began to hang as if it were a great weight. Then he stopped altogether. His face was white, but he was not going to ask for mercy, or understanding, or a second chance.

Bess felt a surge of pity for him. She took in his thin, greasy hair and his long, white narrow face. There was some sincerity in the way he spoke. If this was his version of his life, then this was his life.

"Very well, then," Lainey said. Something in her tone made them all look at her. "You should leave now, Simon. If that's how you feel, if that's what you think—after all Bertha went through to bring Jonah and Bess here, and after all Bess went through to donate her bone marrow, and after all I've been doing just to get your sorry hide healthy—if that's how you feel, you should leave this afternoon."

It was more decisive even than Bess would have been. She looked at Lainey in admiration. So did Jonah. There was no hate, no revenge in her tone. Just a simple statement of the position. It startled Simon just as much.

Something clicked then. Simon knew she meant it. He looked at them, one by one, as if he had never seen any of them before. Defeated, he retreated.

Simon turned a corner after Robin and Ally's visit. He grew noticeably stronger and healthier. He stayed in the spare bedroom now and cheered when the truck drove away with the rented hospital bed. He still napped quite a bit, but his face gained color and he was filling out some.

But Lainey's determination to become Amish felt tangled up after her friends' visit. It was the seeds of doubt about Jonah they had planted that ate at her. They were shocked that he had never said he loved her nor hinted at a life together. Ever since, it had bothered her too.

She knew it was silly to think that words alone would reveal if a man loved a woman. How many times had she mopped up her friends' messes after they had their hearts broken by a man who had professed love? Too many times to count. Words were cheap, she knew that.

But there was a part of her that longed to know how Jonah truly felt about her. Did he care about her the way she cared for him? She knew he had a lot to do to sort out Rose Hill Farm, but she wondered if he was planning to return to Ohio soon. What about his business there?

Would he ever tell her he loved her?

Did he need to?

She felt as if she was staring at a fork in a road. One way of thinking was the English way: that words expressed how a person felt.

The other road was the Amish way: that action took the place of words.

It was her friends' visit that showed her how truly English she was. Becoming Amish was so much more than learning their language and their ways. It was changing how she perceived things, even small things. Things like terms of endearment.

If she felt this way about hearing the words "I love you," how many more things were there that she didn't even understand yet? Like being submissive to a husband. What if a husband made wrong decisions? And Robin was right about one thing: Amish women always served the men first. She'd seen Amish women out in the fields, working side by side with their husbands, but she'd never seen an Amish man in the kitchen. Why did Amish men seem to have a complete pass on domestic duties? And what about her little pie business? She loved to bake. How could she keep her business if she had a dozen babies?

She kept these internal musings to herself, but whenever she was alone, the doubts slipped back, as persistent as a buzzing fly that needed shooing away.

Maybe this path wasn't right for her, after all. Maybe becoming Amish was really impossible for an English person. Maybe it wasn't too late for her to leave and return to her original plan—to attend culinary school.

And have a life of independence. Unencumbered.

Alone.

After Sallie had left for Ohio, Jonah told Bess that they needed to stay for a while to clean out Rose Hill Farm and straighten out Mammi's affairs. Bess was thrilled. She loved Stoney Ridge. She adored Lainey. She was hopelessly in love with Billy. And, to add icing to the cake, it meant she could avoid repeating algebra. But it also meant they had a big job to tackle. Mammi never threw anything away. Each day, Bess and Jonah tried to clean something out—a closet, a desk, a bureau. Bess felt as if she was having an opportunity to peek in on her grandparents' lives. Especially Mammi's. She cherished anything that helped explain her grandmother to her. Mammi seemed the sort who'd never really been young, yet here Bess was, finding letters and notes Mammi had written and received years and years ago.

She missed Mammi more than she could have ever imagined. She hated waking up to the shock of remembering that she was gone. Tears would come to her eyes at unexpected moments during the day, then they would disappear just as quickly. But always, like a shadow, there remained a sharp tug of loss.

Her deepest regret was that she was just starting to understand her grandmother and her unexpected ways . . . and then she was gone. Bess had never lost anyone close to her in such a sudden death. This must have been what her father felt after her mother died in that accident. Like a fresh wound that was slow to heal.

But God's ways were always best. She knew that to be true.

One evening, Jonah had already gone to bed but Bess was wide awake. She decided to brew herself a pot of chamomile tea. Once the kettle boiled, she went out into the garden, mug in hand. There would be a hard frost tonight, the first one of autumn. She drew the cold air into her lungs, and when she breathed out again, her breath hung in the air for a moment in a thin white cloud, quickly gone. The air had a touch of wood smoke in it from somebody's fire. She shivered and turned to go back inside.

Bess decided to finish cleaning one last desk drawer before going to bed. She found an unmarked large envelope and opened it. In it were yellowed newspaper clippings. That struck Bess as strange, because her grandmother didn't read anything but the Amish newspaper, *The Budget*, and these were clippings from the *Stoney Ridge Times*. She picked up the lantern and went to the kitchen table. She laid the clippings out on the table. As she realized what she was reading, she started to tremble. The articles were about the buggy accident that killed her mother. There was even a grainy but gruesome black-and-white picture. She saw the mangled buggy and the horse lying still in the background. She held it up to the light. She could hardly make it out in the background, but an ambulance had its back doors wide open. She touched the picture gently. Was that her mother on the stretcher?

There were other clippings too. Ongoing ones of the trial her father had to testify in against the driver who rammed into the buggy. It touched her deeply to see the quotes her father had made. He was just a young man, only twenty-one years old, newly widowed, with a child to raise. Yet he was quoted with such clarity and rightness. And then there were other clippings—ones that described how stunned the nation was to learn of a man who turned down an insurance settlement. There were pictures of her dad in the article. She could tell he was trying to keep his head down, away from the cameras. No wonder her father had felt the need to leave Stoney Ridge. He was such a private man.

She gathered up the clippings to slip back in the envelope. One small clipping dropped on the floor. She stooped to pick it up and held it by the light. It was a death notice, only one paragraph long, of a newborn baby that had died of sudden infant death syndrome. *Parents: Elaine O'Toole Troyer (deceased) and Simon Troyer. Surviving sibling: Lainey O'Toole.*

She read it again and again, confused. Lainey had never mentioned having a sister. She wondered why Mammi would have kept that clipping. Was it because it was Simon's only child? But why in this envelope? Then she noticed the date. Lainey's baby sister had died the same day as the buggy accident. She slipped the clipping back into the envelope. Tomorrow, she would ask Lainey about it.

13

*L*ainey heard the rumble of thunder in the distance and hurried outside to take the laundry down before the rain began. The air had grown thick and heavy this afternoon, signs of a storm coming. Lightning cracked again, this time much closer. So close her ears hurt. She knew this rainstorm would hit with a fury. She looked up to see Bess hopping over the fence to join her. Under Bess's arm was a large manila envelope.

"What are you doing here in this weather?" Lainey asked her, folding a stiff towel. When Bess didn't answer, she tossed the towel in the laundry basket and turned to face her.

Bess had an odd look on her face. "I was cleaning out Mammi's desk and I found this." She handed Lainey the manila envelope. "Open it."

Lainey sat down on the back steps to the kitchen and opened the envelope. She drew in a quick breath when she read the headlines on the yellowed newspaper clippings. She flipped through the clippings and stopped when she saw the obituary about Colleen. She glanced up in alarm.

Bess pointed to that clipping. "Why would my grandmother have kept that? Why . . . in that very envelope?"

Lainey's heart felt fierce with panic. It was time for Bess to know the truth, she was sure of it. Bertha Riehl had felt the same way. Jonah should have told her long ago. It was time.

But it should be Jonah telling her this truth.

She patted the seat beside her, but Bess shook her head. Lainey bowed her head and was silent for a moment, offered up a silent prayer for God to give her the right words, then she lifted her chin and met Bess with a level gaze. "There's a story I need to tell you. It's about you and me. About Jonah and Rebecca." She told Bess everything, every detail. She kept looking up to see how Bess was taking the news. Bess stood with her arms crossed tightly against her chest, an inscrutable expression of calm on her face. Lainey rose to her feet and reached a hand out to touch her. "Bess, can you tell me what's running through your mind?"

Bess kept her gaze on the fluttering sheets, as if concentrating on how the gusts of the wind lifted them.

"Bess?" Then Lainey heard Simon shouting for her from inside the house. She tried to ignore it, but the calls grew louder and louder. She sighed. "Let me just check on Simon and I'll be right back."

She went inside to discover Simon ranting about a window left open. The wind was giving him a chill, he complained. She slammed the window shut, rolled her eyes at Simon, and went back outside to finish her conversation with Bess.

But when she went back outside, Bess was gone.

Lainey hurried to Rose Hill Farm to tell Jonah that she had told Bess the truth: that Simon was actually Bess's father. She found him feeding hay to Frieda in the barn.

Jonah was stunned. For a long time he said nothing, seeming unable to take it in. The rain was coming down harder now and pounded the metal roof like a drum. Then, as the truth of it dawned on him, he looked bewildered. "You told her about Simon?" he asked her.

"She asked me, Jonah. She had a bundle of newspaper clippings that your mother had saved. In it was one about the death of Simon's baby. She asked me specifically if I had any idea why Bertha had saved that clipping."

His face had gone all white and taut. "But why? Why would you tell her?"

Lainey waited a heartbeat before she said, "I wasn't going to lie to her."

"You could have waited."

"For how long, Jonah? When were you ever going to tell her? You've been avoiding this conversation for months!"

"Maybe she didn't *need* to know. Maybe some things are best left alone."

He looked so anguished. She wanted to put her arm around his wide shoulders, to try to console him with her touch. But he seemed suddenly brittle, as if he might break if she were to touch him. She was desperate to give him some kind of comfort, but she didn't know how. What could she say to him in these circumstances? Every phrase that came to mind seemed inadequate.

He turned to face her. "Where did she go? She must be upset."

"I don't know where she went, but she wasn't upset," Lainey said, her voice surprisingly soft. "She really wasn't."

He glared at her. "How could she *not* be upset?"

She folded her arms against her chest. "You underestimate her, Jonah."

"Oh? You think you know Bess so well after just a few months?" Now he was clearly livid. "Then where *is* she?"

That, Lainey couldn't answer.

"In this pouring rain, why isn't she home? Where is my daughter?" He grabbed a bridle and went to Frieda's stall, quickly slipping the bit into the horse's mouth and buckling the buckles. He led her by the reins out of the stall and toward the door. Just as he was about to leave the barn, he turned to Lainey and looked at her with anger in his eyes.

"If something happens to her, Lainey . . . if anything . . ." He shook his head as if to stop himself from saying more, then left.

The rain hit with a fury. It was cold and sharp and falling sideways in the fierce wind. Jonah barely noticed it. When he heard what Lainey had done, he felt such panic grip his chest that for a moment he couldn't breathe. He was furious with Lainey. She had no right!

"Bess is *my* child!" he said aloud. The words tore out of him, from some deep place, some old, long-buried hurt. He had to find Bess and explain. But where could she possibly be? He felt as if the world had become very fragile. Very dangerous.

As he rode the horse past the Lapp farm, it occurred to him that Billy might have an idea where Bess might be. The two had spent hours together this summer and it had given Jonah cause for concern. Bess was too young to be thinking seriously about boys. Then, suddenly, a well of hope bubbled up. Maybe Bess went to Billy to find comfort.

He turned the horse around and galloped toward the Lapp farmhouse.

As soon as Billy saw the frantic look on Jonah's face and heard that Bess had gone missing—that she was upset about something—he had a pretty good idea of where she would have gone.

"Give me an hour," he told Jonah. "If I'm not back in an hour—no, give me an hour and a half—then you can go looking. But there's no sense in both of us getting soaked to the skin. I think I know where she is." He grabbed a slicker and went to the barn.

Jonah followed behind him. "Then tell me and I'll go find her."

"It's too hard to find. Trust me, Jonah." Billy saddled up his pony. "You go home in case she returns there." He rode away before Jonah could object.

About a month ago, he and Bess had found an abandoned crow's nest at Blue Lake Pond, high on a ledge but protected from the rain by the branches of a sheltering tree. He knew she was there, as sure as if he could see her. When he got to the lake, he tied the pony's reins to a tree trunk. The wind was lashing through the trees, and the pony shifted its weight from foot to foot, uneasy, but the fury of the rain had eased up. Billy hiked up to the ledge, slipping a few times. There on the ledge, shivering and drenched, was Bess, hugging her knees to her chest. When he called her name, she looked up, startled, and put her fingers to her lips. She pointed to the nest. There was a black crow, staring down at both of them.

"I've been watching her land in that tree. She thinks she owns it, that it's her tree. She takes off and lands again, watching me watching her. That's what crows do. She's living her crow life," she said softly, eyes fixed on the bird.

Billy sat down next to her. "Your dad is steaming like a kettle. Said something has upset you."

"I'm not upset."

With a measured glance, he realized she was speaking the truth. She didn't seem at all upset. Wet, cold, and shivering, but she was calm. She had a look on her face that seemed peaceful. Andy always said she looked like an angel, and right now, he was right.

She turned her face to the sky, like a flower, and smiled softly. "Billy, isn't it a wonder? That the crow is here? God made nature so things can get fixed again." She turned to him. "Blue Lake Pond will have birds and fish again."

He'd been so relieved that Bess was where he thought she'd be, he hadn't even given the appearance of the crow a second thought. "Why, you're right." He scanned the lake and heard a woodpecker somewhere, hard at work, hammering a tree. He smiled.

"God does it with people too. Makes it so that they can find their way back to him." She rested her chin on her knees. "You know what I love about looking up at the sky? It helps me to remember that I am so incredibly small and God is so immense." She lifted her face to the sky. "Behind those clouds is an ocean of stars, limitless in its infinity, so large, so large, that any of our problems, even the greatest of them, is a small thing."

Billy wasn't really sure what she was talking about, but the day was dying and they were wet and cold. He knew Jonah was out of his mind with worry. He stood and gave her his hand. "Maybe you can save your philosophizing for home, by a warm fire, in dry clothes."

Jonah had given Billy an hour, like he agreed, but now that hour was up and he was going to find his Bess. He was putting on a rainproof cloak and his black hat when he saw a pony heading up the drive with two figures on its back. He ran out the door and down the porch steps. He could see them now, Billy in front with Bess holding on to him from behind. A powerful wave of relief flooded over him, like the relief that follows the first rainstorm after a long summer drought—swift, complete, overwhelming.

The first thing Jonah did was to wrap Bess in a large towel and make her sit down by the fire.

"I'm sorry to worry you, Dad," she told him, and she saw tears prickle his eyes.

He brought her a cup of hot tea and kept fussing over her as she tried to explain how she felt. She could see he was worried sick. Billy had warned her as he left to return home.

Bess knew she should have been shocked by what Lainey told her today, or at least terribly upset. But instead, she was filled with a strange sense of destiny, as if God had spared her for a reason. She told Jonah she felt blessed, having him for a father, and that only made his eyes water up again.

"It's like the roses, Dad. I'm a branch that's been grafted onto this good tree. Your tree. An Amish tree. And the great root of God sustains us." That thought had come to her while she was sitting on the ledge, and she had rolled it over and over in her mind. She liked how it sounded.

Her father bowed his head. She wished she could make him understand that it was all right. That everything was going to be all right in the end, just like Mammi had said it would be.

She went to him and knelt down by his chair, putting a hand over his. "Please don't blame Lainey, Dad. She was only telling me the truth." There was something else that occurred to her on that ledge, something wondrous. A wide smile broke over her face. "Dad, do you realize that Lainey is my half sister?"

Lainey knocked tentatively on the door to Rose Hill Farm, unsure of what kind of reception she would get from Jonah. A few hours ago, he had seemed so angry with her, and—from his point of view—she couldn't really blame him. Nor did she agree with him. But she had to know that Bess was home safely.

"Lainey," Jonah said as he opened the door. He put a hand to his forehead. "I was going to come down tonight. Bess is here. She's fine. She's safe."

Lainey exhaled with relief. "Good. I mean, I'm glad she's home." She turned to leave.

"You . . . were right. She wasn't upset. Not upset at all."

She turned and looked at him. "But you didn't believe me."

He looked uncomfortable, but he didn't dispute her. "She's upstairs, changing into dry clothes. Would you come in and wait for her?" His eyes were pleading.

"No. But tell her I stopped by." She saw a hurt look cross his face, and straightaway she wished she had not sounded so curt. All that mattered right now was that Bess was home.

She started to leave, but Jonah touched her arm lightly to stop her. His voice dropped to a whisper. "She said that she felt as if God had a purpose in all of that. By protecting her."

Lainey gave him a direct look. "She's absolutely right."

Jonah took a step closer to her. "Lainey. I'm sorry for doubting your judgment. Your judgment is far better than mine about these matters."

"We can talk about it tomorrow."

"I didn't want to lose Bess."

"You love your daughter." Her voice was flat—without salience. "It's normal to want to hold on tight to those we love."

"Maybe there's such a thing as holding on too tightly." He looked away. "Tonight I wondered if God might be testing me, the way he tested Abraham with Isaac." He folded his arms against his chest. "As if he wants me to figure out if I trust him completely or not."

Lainey softened a little. "It's the worst place to be, half trusting, half not."

He rubbed his forehead. "That's where I've been for the last fifteen years. Stuck right in that very place. The worst place to be. I haven't really been living, I've just been tiptoeing around, trying to avert disaster."

"It doesn't work," Lainey said, quiet but firm. "You just end up missing the life you have." Through the window, she saw Bess come down the kitchen stairs and look around the room for her father. "Go. Talk to her."

Jonah reached out his hands to her. "Come in with me. Let's talk to her together."

Lainey hesitated. Doubts about Jonah had been buzzing around her all afternoon. She shook her head. "No. I'd better get back."

Jonah watched her carefully. Her words and posturing were bold, but only skin deep. As if she was on a precipice. "Lainey, please?" His question, and the gentleness in his voice, disarmed her. He kept his hands extended, waiting for her to take a step toward him. Just waiting.

A silence came between them then. A silence she could feel, for it was thick with words that had never been spoken.

Jonah's face opened for an instant: trust and hope.

She felt a sense of perspective wash over her. This was *Jonah*. Her Jonah. Jonah wasn't the kind of man Robin and Ally thought him to be— mean-spirited and controlling. Why, in fact, she suddenly realized they were describing a man like Simon! Jonah wasn't like Simon, not at all. Just the opposite. He asked her opinion about things and really wanted to know her thoughts. He helped her set up her pie business. Why had she allowed Robin and Ally to influence what she knew to be true? How could she have let that happen? Her friends said Amish women had no self-esteem. If only they had met Bertha Riehl! Bertha had a stronger self-esteem than anyone she'd ever known. And Bertha was Amish to the core.

Lainey's heart lifted. She knew Jonah's heart—knew it in some fundamental, important way. Yet she'd held herself back from him, not trusting this love that had come so unexpectedly, from such an unexpected source. She looked at him long and hard, tears in her eyes, then reached out and tangled her fingers with his. He tugged on her hands and drew her close. She felt his arms go round her, and they clung to each other as if it were the most natural thing in the world.

On Tuesday evening, Mrs. Stroot dropped by Lainey's cottage with an order for one hundred little six-inch pumpkin pies and seventy nine-inch pecan pies for the Stoney Ridge Veteran's Day Parade, to be delivered on Friday afternoon. Lainey was thrilled and quickly agreed when Mrs. Stroot told her about the order. She needed the money; setting up a home business had cost more than she expected, and her savings account was dwindling rapidly.

The gray light of an autumn dawn was beginning to appear at the window as Lainey sat at the kitchen table the next morning and decided she must have temporarily lost her mind. How could she possibly bake that many pies in such a short amount of time? She was still getting accustomed to a propane stove. Not every pie turned out like the one before. Even with Bess's help, she was facing a daunting task. She sat at the kitchen table, notepad in her hand, and tried to make a list of all of the ingredients she would need. Then she put the pencil down and stared at a point on the ceiling.

"I can't do it," she said to herself. "It's my own fault. I got greedy. I thought I could do it, but I can't."

"Yes, you can," Simon said.

Lainey hadn't even noticed that he had come into the kitchen for coffee and had been watching her. "My pies are too inconsistent. I would need to make double the quantity, just to make sure I have ones to sell."

Simon lifted one shoulder in a careless shrug. "I'd sooner have a slice of your worst pie than anyone else's best."

Lainey's head snapped up. She couldn't believe her ears. Was Simon actually paying her a compliment? She couldn't quite tell.

He looked away, embarrassed. "Keep writing that list. I'll head into town and get the supplies. You better get moving."

Tears came into her eyes. "Simon . . . I don't know what to say . . ."

"Don't say anything or I'll take back my offer," he groused, but he looked pleased.

There followed two of the busiest days Lainey had ever known in her life, and certainly so for Simon. The two of them, plus Bess and even Jonah, rolled out endless mounds of pastry dough, cracked open pecan shells for the nuts until their fingers were stained and blistered, stirred fillings, and sampled the results. The kitchen, in a white fog of flour, had a heavenly scent of vanilla and cloves and pumpkin and blackstrap molasses. The pies were laid out on baking racks, like little works of art. Lainey displayed a streak of perfectionism; only the best would be delivered to Mrs. Stroot. She had to keep sending Simon up to the store for ten-pound bags of sugar and another big can or two of Crisco. He went without complaint, which amazed her. He drove Jonah's horse and buggy as if he'd done it every day of his life. Boomer rode along as shotgun, just the way he had accompanied Bertha. Simon liked to gripe about Boomer, but he whistled for the big dog to come along whenever he was going anywhere.

By Friday morning, Lainey had the pies ready for delivery in pink boxes that Mrs. Stroot had provided. Jonah and Simon, with Boomer shadowing him, took the pies over to the lunch grounds for the parade. Then they came back for the pies that didn't make the cut and delivered those to grateful neighbors.

"She's been working me like a whole pack of bird dogs," Simon groused to Caleb on Sunday afternoon. "She's aiming to put me back in the hospital and kill me for certain." Boomer lay sprawled right by Simon's side.

Lainey was used to him now and paid no attention to his tone of voice. "Don't you lie to the bishop, Simon," Lainey called out from the kitchen.

She wiped her hands on her apron and leaned against the doorjamb. "But I will say you've been a big help. I couldn't have done that big order for Mrs. Stroot this week without you."

Simon turned to Caleb. "That's the gospel truth. I saved the day." He stroked Boomer's big head.

Then Simon smiled—for the first time, thought Lainey—and it was not a smile that lasted long. But still, Simon had smiled.

Billy tossed some pebbles up at Bess's window late one evening. He cupped his hands around his mouth and whispered loudly, "Can you come down?"

Bess's heart left the ground and sailed into the night sky. She dressed quickly and hurried downstairs. Maggie had said she was pretty sure he was courting Betsy again, but Bess didn't believe it. Would he be coming to see her now, if he were still interested in Betsy?

She opened the kitchen door as quietly as she could and met him at the bottom of the stairs. She stopped on the last step so she was eye level to him. She couldn't pretend; she was thrilled to see him. But her delight seemed to distress him. A flicker of fear came and went through her, but she dismissed it.

"Oh Bess," he said, taking her hand and holding it to his face.

Bess's intuition rang an alarm. Something was badly wrong, she felt sure, though she did not know what. She looked into his eyes. His face was working with emotion. He was struggling for words. She could almost hear him trying out different words in his head.

"I need to tell you something. I want you to hear it from me first." He swallowed hard. "It's about me. About me and Betsy. We're going to get married. Soon. Betsy doesn't want to wait."

So it was true. Bess said nothing, unable to take it in. She blinked away tears and looked down to hide her confusing emotions. Then one strong feeling broke through: disappointment that felt like a knife wound.

Billy grasped her arms and pulled her close to him. "You know, don't you? That you've meant something special to me?"

He kissed her mouth. It was a new kind of kiss, different from the one he had given her the night before her surgery. It was as if he was determined to remember the moment. She realized, with dismay, that he was thinking this would be their last kiss.

She clung to him, wanting it to go on forever, but all too soon he drew away and turned to go down the drive. Bess stared at him as he walked away, chin to chest, hands jammed in his pockets, beautiful in the moonlight. So this is what it felt like to have your heart break.

When Billy was out of sight, Bess went back to the house, up to her room, closed the door behind her, and lay down on the bed. Her body started to shake with sobs. Once she started to cry, it was hard to stop. She cried because she had lost Billy for good. She cried because life seemed so unfair sometimes. She cried because she missed Mammi. She wanted her grandmother.

Billy walked home from Rose Hill Farm that night feeling lower than any man on earth. He hated hurting Bess like that. Her face looked so trusting, so eager to please, when she first came outside to him tonight. Unfortunately, she looked particularly pretty. Her soft white skin seemed to glow, and the light blue dress she was wearing made her eyes the color of a tropical sea.

Then, after he told her about planning to marry Betsy, her face looked as pained as if he had wounded her. It tugged at his heart, and tears came to his eyes. He had to look away so that she would not see. He wished she would have yelled at him or thrown something at him. The disappointed look on her face cut him to the quick. He had dreaded telling her about him and Betsy. What he truly feared, he realized, was hurting Bess. He could bear her anger; it was her pain he could not face.

She must have heard some gossip about him and Betsy. She must have noticed how he had been unable to meet her eye the last few weeks. But she seemed shocked by his news. It shamed him, how she always believed the best in him.

Could he be in love with two different girls at the same time? And such different girls. Bess was so full of curiosity, eyes as big as saucers, and her face would light up with excitement over new things. He found himself thinking of her at the oddest moments, when he saw a soaring Cooper's hawk or found a hummingbird's nest with that delicate fir bark lining its cup. He'd never forget how thrilled she was when he brought her the newspaper clipping that the United States Supreme Court agreed to hear the case of *Wisconsin vs. Yoder*. With her face lit up with happiness, she kissed the clipping and declared she was never going to have to step into a school again as long as she lived. He thought it was ironic that she was so glad to be done with school. She was the smartest girl he knew.

But then there was Betsy. He'd been crazy about Betsy for as long as he could remember. Finally, she seemed to be equally as smitten with him. They kissed every chance they got: behind the barn at gatherings, when they met on the road, in the buggy, and—best of all—when he was at her house and her parents went off to bed and they found themselves alone. He thought about kissing her before he dropped off to sleep, and it filled his mind as soon as he woke up. He lived for those moments.

So why did he often feel a painful jumble of anxiety?

He rubbed his hands over his face, exasperated. What was wrong with him? What kind of man was he?

He would have liked to have slowed things down with Betsy, but she seemed insistent to get baptized and married soon. Six months ago, he would've jumped at the chance to hear Betsy Mast say she would marry him. Now, it made his stomach twist up in a tight knot. In fact, it suddenly occurred to him that he hadn't actually *asked* Betsy to marry him. They were necking down by the pond and she started talking about how nice it would be to not have to stop but to wake up in each others' arms every morning. He must have murmured that he agreed because next thing he knew, they had a meeting set up with the bishop. He knew he had to talk to Bess before they spoke to Caleb Zook.

Billy loosened his collar. Lately it felt like it was cutting off his air supply.

Jonah could see that Bess was hurting. She was quiet and pale and her eyes were swollen like she'd been crying. These were the moments when he longed for a wife. Bess needed a mother. He hoped she would talk to Lainey about whatever was bothering her, but Lainey was taking Simon to the hospital today for a checkup. Usually, that meant a long day.

When Billy came by early today to say that he needed to quit working at Rose Hill Farm, Jonah put two and two together and had a pretty good idea about what was troubling Bess. Last week, Lainey had tipped him off that she had seen Billy with a girl in his courting buggy a couple of times lately.

He found Bess in the barn, Boomer by her side, gathering up the dry petals and stuffing them into bags. They sounded like crackly tissue paper as she stuffed. His heart went out to her. Her head was down and her shoulders slumped. He saw a dried tear on her cheek.

"Bess, I need to tell you something."

She kept working, kept her head down.

"There's something I've discovered that you and I have in common." It was never easy for him to say things out of his heart, but there was something he needed to say. "When we love someone, we love them with our whole heart."

She put the bag down and bent down to pat Boomer.

It's funny, he thought, that it's always easier to talk about important matters with our eyes turned away. He let his cane slip to the floor, leaned his hip against the table that held the rose petals, and folded his arms against his chest. "I've learned something this summer. I've learned that I have a tendency to make a person I love too important. They start filling the spot that only God should hold in my life. I did it with Rebecca, and when she passed, I felt that great void for far too long. I've done it with you, and when I found out that Simon was your father, I felt that void again." He chanced a look at her. "The Lord has to keep teaching me the same lesson. To hold on a little more lightly to others and to trust him in a deeper way."

He crossed one boot over the other. "Lainey is a good example for us. She's always depended on God in just the right way." He was a better person for knowing her. Lainey had an ability to make him revise his stiff attitudes—like his attitude about Simon. Or about telling Bess the truth. It was an uncomfortable process, but she was so often right. And he had nearly lost her, that night. He had held himself so close and tight, so afraid to love again after Rebecca died. "When we left to go back to Ohio, Lainey was sorry and she missed us, but she wasn't devastated. She left us in God's care." He looked up at Bess. "And the Lord brought us back here, didn't he?" But he knew that things rarely turned out nice and neatly in this life.

Bess stood and picked up a handful of rose petals, letting them slip through her fingers back onto the table. "I don't think the Lord is going to bring Billy and me back together. He's marrying Betsy Mast."

So *that's* what had happened. Jonah put his large hand over Bess's. He wished he had better words, softer ones. "Then we can trust in God's plan for Billy and Betsy. And trust God has another plan for you. A good plan."

With that, Bess dove into his arms. They stood there for a while, with Jonah's chin resting on her head, until Boomer stood abruptly, hackles raised, and let out a huge bark. He tore outside and kept barking as he ran down the drive.

"Someone must be coming," Jonah said. "I'll go see who Boomer is scaring half to death." Before he turned to go, he stroked her cheek with the back of his hand. "Things have a way of turning out in the end."

She gave him a slight smile. "That's what Mammi used to say."

The taxi had dropped Lainey and Simon back at her cottage from the hospital. Lainey was so happy she felt as if she were floating. She made Simon a cup of his favorite tea and told him she would be back soon, that she had an errand. She hurried up the hill to Rose Hill Farm, practically bursting with happiness. She stopped to pet Boomer at the bottom of the hill and when she looked up, there was Jonah. She walked up to him, a smile wreathing her face.

"Simon's well, Jonah. He was given the all clear by the doctors! He still has to be tested every six months, but he can go back to living a normal life . . . whatever normal means for Simon Troyer."

Jonah put his arms around her waist and swung her in the air, laughing. "We can finally make plans!"

"What kind of plans?" she asked him boldly when he set her down. She needed to know.

He took in a deep breath. "Plans to marry, you and me," he said in a voice as dry as toast. "That is, if you're willing to have me."

When she didn't answer, his face grew worried. He suddenly looked so earnest and vulnerable and sincere that any doubts if he loved her evaporated, like steam from a cup of hot tea. In its place swept a feeling of assurance, of safety, of tenderness, and an overwhelming love. The love she felt for him was so strong it burned her every breath.

The next moment she was in his arms and they were kissing. She thought she must be dreaming, but she felt the grip of his strong arms around her, felt the passion and warmth of his kiss. She didn't need to hear him say the words "I love you." She knew.

From the side door of the barn, Bess watched her father with Lainey. She couldn't hear what was being said, but she could tell they were happy. And in love, that was plain to see. Her grandmother had spotted that from the first time they laid eyes on each other.

Boomer came charging back up the hill to join Bess and collapsed by her feet, panting heavily. When Bess saw her father bend down to kiss Lainey, she turned and closed the barn door. She knew when to leave things be. She smiled, though, as she went back to work. Wouldn't Mammi have been pleased by this turn of events?

Caleb Zook said no to Billy and Betsy's engagement. He explained gently that he felt they needed more time, especially after Betsy's very recent time spent running around. This time next year, if they still felt the same way, then he would be pleased to marry them. After Betsy went through instructions for baptism, of course.

Billy was visibly relieved. He even felt as if his shirt collar wasn't tightening up on him, like he'd been feeling for a few weeks now. He tried to encourage Betsy on the buggy ride home, but she was stunned silent.

When they got to her parents' home, she stayed in the buggy, her eyes on the back end of the horse, and calmly said, "We should elope."

There wasn't much Billy would refuse Betsy, but that was one thing he was firm about. "Oh no. We don't go against the bishop. I don't aim to start a marriage off on the wrong foot." He glanced at her. "To tell you the truth, I agree with Caleb. I always hoped to marry you, Betsy, but I imagined it in a few more years, after I turned twenty-one." He gently stroked her cheek. "We've got our whole lives ahead of us."

She kept her chin tucked to her chest. "My whole life starts now." She turned to him then and gave him a deep, searching look. "You're a very nice boy, Billy. But you're still just a boy." Then she hopped out of the buggy without a word and walked to her house.

He had the strangest feeling that she was saying one thing but trying to tell him something else entirely.

⁂

The next week, Betsy Mast left again. Maggie hurried over to Rose Hill Farm to tell Bess the news. She found Bess in the backyard, taking down laundry from the clothesline just as the gray sky began to darken to twilight.

"Betsy's gone to stay with an aunt in Maryland."

"Oh," Bess said.

"An *aunt*," Maggie stressed, whispering in a low, conspiratorial voice.

"So you said."

"She's having a baby, Bess." Maggie's eyes were bright with the scandalous details.

Bess gasped. "You shouldn't be spreading tales, Maggie."

"I'm doing no such thing! I overheard her father talking to my dad. And my dad is the bishop, you know!"

Bess was so surprised that for a second she froze. "Billy's baby." *My Billy.*

Maggie buried her face in her hands. "No, Bess. *Not* Billy's. *Think!* That English boy at the Hay and Grain! He just used her and dumped her. He had no intention to marry her. That's why she came back. She was trying to trick our Billy into marrying her!"

But Bess knew better. "Billy might not have known all the details, but he was still willing, Maggie." She felt a little sorry for Billy. She even felt a surge of pity for Betsy. Life hadn't turned out the way Betsy had expected.

Maggie put her hands on her hips. "Are you trying to tell me that you're over Billy?"

"I guess I am." And oddly, Bess meant it.

She remembered how she had ached all over at the very thought of him. That soul-deep ache—it was less painful now.

14

*J*onah walked up and down the sidewalk in Harrisburg, trying to get the nerve to walk into the Shear Delight Hair Salon. He had never been inside such a place—had never even noticed them before—and he felt a little terrified. He could see women of all ages seated in chairs with large plastic capes around them. Some were sitting under enormous metal globes. He walked past one more time, steeling himself, took a deep breath, and went inside.

The receptionist took one look at this tall, lanky Plain man with a black hat on and her mouth fell open. As she recovered herself she blurted out, "Here for a trim?"

"No!" Jonah answered, flustered. "No . . . I'm here to see, um, Robin and Ally." He pointed to them toward the back of the long room.

"They're with clients right now. Have a seat and I'll tell them you're here."

Jonah sat down next to an elderly woman with blue-ish colored hair. The woman kept staring at Jonah. He was accustomed to stares by the English, but he felt his cheeks grow warm. Or maybe it was the sour stink of the place. He had never smelled such toxic fumes before; they made his eyes start to water. He thought the smell of a hog farm was the worst smell on earth, but this hair salon was inching it out. He picked up a magazine, opened it, and quickly dropped it back on the table when he saw the contents in it. He crossed his legs, then uncrossed them, then rubbed his hands together, then tried to look out the window. The blue-haired woman continued to stare at him.

Finally, he heard Robin's voice ring out loudly from the back of the store. "No way! An orthodox rabbi is here? For us?"

He turned his head toward Robin's station and rose to his feet as he saw her make her way toward him. He reached out a hand to shake hers, but her hands were covered with black mud.

She lifted her hands in the air. "Sorry. I'm doing a dye job on Mrs. Feinbaum."

He could tell she didn't recognize him, but Ally did. She had walked up behind Robin and peered over her shoulder.

"Jonah!" She elbowed Robin. "This is Lainey's boyfriend." She turned anxiously to Jonah. "Is Lainey all right?"

"She's fine," Jonah said. "I was hoping I could speak to you both. Just for a moment."

Ally and Robin exchanged a look. A woman in a chair with black mud covering her head was calling for Robin in a worried voice. "I gotta finish up Mrs. Feinbaum, then I can take a break," Robin said.

Jonah nodded and went back to sit down.

The blue-haired woman continued to stare. "You a Quaker?" she asked in a reedy voice.

"No," Jonah said. "Amish."

The woman frowned. "You don't pay taxes."

"Yes, I do," Jonah said patiently.

"You don't fight in the military."

"That's true. But we do serve. As conscientious objectors."

"Still. Not the same."

Jonah hoped the conversation could end with that.

"I don't understand how you can live in this country and reap all the benefits and not do your part."

Jonah sighed. The fumes in the salon were giving him a headache. He hoped this errand would turn out well. He was starting to think it was a terrible idea.

Just as the blue-haired woman opened her mouth to provide Jonah with another opinion, Ally and Robin approached. He leapt to his feet.

"I've only got ten minutes before I need to rinse Mrs. Feinbaum," Robin said.

Jonah glanced at the blue-haired woman, who was still glaring at him. "Could we go outside?"

Out on the sidewalk, Jonah explained that he and Lainey were planning to be married soon.

Robin frowned. "I figured as much."

"I came to invite you both to the wedding," Jonah said.

"Where's Lainey?" Ally asked. "Why didn't she come?"

"She doesn't know I'm here," Jonah said. "When you left . . . without saying goodbye, I think she felt a little hurt."

"Couldn't be helped," Robin said brusquely. "Your church service took too long. We had to go."

"Robin," Ally said in a coaxing tone. She was weakening, Jonah could see by her expression. She looked at him. "That's awful sweet of you, to come all this way."

"You are Lainey's family," he said. "Just because Lainey is choosing"— he emphasized that word—"to become Amish, it doesn't mean you won't continue to be an important part of her life. She . . . we . . . want you to be there. At the wedding. And in her life. In our life."

"Aw," Ally said. Her face got all soft and tender. "You really love her, don't you?"

Robin rolled her eyes. "I gotta get back to Mrs. Feinbaum." She bit her lip. "We'll think about it." She put her hand on the door handle to the hair salon. "I think she's gonna wake up one day and regret this whole ridiculous phase she's going through. And then what?"

Ally waited until Robin went inside. "Don't mind her, Jonah. She's bitter because she just found out her boyfriend has been cheating on her. As soon as she gets over that, she'll be happier that Lainey has found true love."

"Then, you'll come to the wedding?" he asked.

"Oh . . . I don't know about that. I guess it depends how long it will take Robin to get over things." She scrunched up her face. "I've found it's always best to wait until Robin's not riled up. Then I'll try talking to her." She turned to go inside. "No promises. But . . . I'll try."

She pulled the door open wide so the blue-haired lady could leave.

Jonah saw the lady aim for his direction and he decided now would be an excellent time to return to the bus station and wait for the bus to Stoney Ridge.

Jonah and Lainey decided to let Simon stay in the cottage after they married, with the understanding that he had to take good care of it and he had to start going to church.

Simon looked grieved and shook his fist. "Here it comes. I knew it! I *knew* it! It's blackmail!"

"We're not telling you to go to the Amish church," Jonah explained, "unless, of course, that's where God's leading you. But you have to go to some church. You have to worship God."

"That's out-and-out blackmail!"

But they held firm and he reluctantly agreed to the conditions.

As Lainey dressed for church one Sunday morning in mid-December, she realized that she no longer felt strange in Plain clothing. In fact, she would feel strange if she weren't wearing it. When she was in town last week, she noticed the types of clothing that young girls wore, even in winter: miniskirts, low-cut tops. Six months ago she wouldn't have thought twice about how much skin showed. Now she felt embarrassed for them.

When Jonah and Bess came by to pick her up, she asked Simon—as she always did—if he would like to join them for church. He was seated at the kitchen table, drinking coffee.

He gave her the same answer he had given her for three or four months, "Now, why would I want to do that?"

If she had time to spare, she would try, always without success, to give him reasons why he should come. But today, this special day, she had no time to waste.

She hurried out to the buggy and smiled when she saw Bess and Jonah. She squeezed Bess's hand. She was so glad they were sharing this day. Today, they were going to be baptized.

"I only wish Mammi were here," Bess said quietly.

"Knowing my mother," Jonah said, "she had a hunch this is how things would work out." He smiled at both of them. "Probably planned it all along."

For the last few weeks, Lainey and Bess had been attending a class of instruction, studying the Confession of Faith, with the ministers. Yesterday, they had one more opportunity to meet with the ministers and "turn back" if they so desired. The ministers, including the bishop, had emphasized that to them again and again: it was better not to make a vow than to make a vow and later break it. But Lainey and Bess had no doubts.

It was a solemn morning. Lainey and Bess wore new clothing they had made specially: black dresses, black prayer caps, long white organdy aprons, white organdy capes, black stockings, and stiff black oxfords. They filed in and took their seats in the center section near the minister's bench. They sat silently through the service, heads bowed, in anticipation. When the time came, the deacon left the service and returned with a small pail of water and a tin cup. Caleb turned to Lainey and Bess. He reminded the applicants that the vow they were about to make would be made not to the ministers or to the church but to God. He asked them to kneel if it was still their desire to become members of the body of Christ.

So Bess and Lainey knelt.

Caleb asked them a few simple questions, which they answered. Then, the deacon's wife untied the ribbons from Lainey's cap and removed the cap from her head. Caleb Zook laid his hands upon her head, "Upon your faith, which you have confessed before God and these many witnesses, you are baptized in the name of the Father, the Son, and the Holy Spirit, Amen." The deacon poured water into Caleb's hands, cupped above Lainey, who was still kneeling, and it trickled down over her hair and face.

Then it was Bess's turn.

When the rite of baptism was completed, Caleb took the hand first of Bess, then Lainey, and said, "In the name of the Lord and the Church, we extend to you the hand of fellowship, rise up."

As they stood, the deacon's wife greeted them with a holy kiss and retied their prayer caps, one by one. Lainey searched for Jonah's face as she waited for Bess's prayer cap to be retied. Their eyes met and locked, and she was completely undone when she saw the tears streaming down his face.

Jonah's heart felt pierced. He had prayed for this moment for fifteen years. To watch Bess, his daughter, bend at the knee, and then to have Lainey, his soon-to-be bride, do the same, felt like a perfect and holy moment. As if the heavens parted and he had a brief glimpse into the great and wondrous plans of God, weaving all things together for good. He would never, ever forget this day.

It was a powerful moment for a parent to watch his child join the church. He couldn't help thinking of the little girl Bess used to be. He wished she could have stayed a little girl, but she was growing up. Growing into a lovely, wise young woman.

He could hardly wait for Caleb to conclude the service and announce his and Lainey's wedding plans. They were going to be married on a Thursday, the week before Christmas, at Rose Hill Farm. He felt a growing impatience, eager for Caleb to wrap up.

Caleb wasn't usually long-winded, but today he seemed to be drawing out his sermon, a long admonishment to the congregation to be helpful to new members. Then he began to give instructions to Lainey and Bess to be faithful to the church and to the ministry. Jonah felt a little relieved when he concluded the sermon with Romans 6. Caleb kept making furtive glances toward the door. Jonah didn't think anyone else noticed, but he was puzzled by it. It seemed as if Caleb was going to preach forever today. Then the other ministers offered their statements of approval of Caleb's message, but Caleb had run over so long that they were mercifully brief. Finally, Caleb rose to his feet and asked everyone to kneel for prayer. Just as he finished the prayer, Jonah thought he heard the door squeak open, cautiously. He opened his eyes and saw Caleb motion to someone with his hand.

All eyes turned to the door. It was Simon. Bess let out a gasp, and Lainey and Jonah exchanged a baffled look as Simon made his way down the aisle to the bishop, head held high. Boomer trailed along behind him. Caleb extended his hand to Simon, as if he had been expecting him. Slowly, Simon knelt, facing the church, facing his family. Boomer settled down beside him as if he had found the perfect spot for a winter's nap. Caleb read a short message from the Bible, about how the faithful shepherd didn't rest until he found that one lost sheep.

And then it grew quiet.

In a quavering voice, Simon said, "I am that lost sheep. I have sinned against the Lord God. I confess to the sin of pride. I confess to the sin of drunkenness. Oh, and laziness too. I've got a nasty temper on me. I wasn't much of a husband to my Elaine." He glanced over at Lainey. "I might not be much of a father, neither." He looked up at the ceiling rafters. "And there might be a few other sins I'd like to keep private between just me and the Lord." He wiped tears off his face with the back of his sleeve. "But I want a fresh start. I'm ready to repent."

Caleb placed his hands on top of Simon's head. "After a sinner was brought to the Lord Jesus Christ to repent, he told the sinner, 'Go and sin no more.'" Caleb helped Simon rise to his feet. "This is our brother, Simon, home for good." He reminded the church members that Simon was now a member in good standing. "Geduh is geduh." *What is done and past cannot be called again.* His sins would not be spoken of. The Lord God had wiped them clean, he said. They were gone.

Caleb then announced the upcoming wedding of Jonah Riehl and Lainey O'Toole. As folks turned toward Jonah, he thought he probably looked like a fool, grinning from ear to ear. But he didn't care. This was quite a day.

"Let us sing our closing hymn," Caleb said, with one hand clasped on Simon's shoulder. With the other hand, he motioned to the Vorsinger.

As if the cue from Caleb was meant for him to set the key, Boomer let out a bark and, in a rare moment, the church rocked with happy laughter.

A week before Jonah and Lainey's wedding, on a gray midwinter day, Caleb Zook dropped by Rose Hill Farm, looking for Bess. He found her in the greenhouse where she was checking to see that young rose graftings were protected from the cold.

He walked around the greenhouse, examining the plants. Bess was surprised to see him and wondered briefly if she had done something wrong. In Ohio, the bishop didn't tend to call very often unless there was some unpleasant business to deal with. She could tell Caleb Zook had something on his mind and it was making her nervous. He slowly made his way to where Bess was working. She was wrapping plants in burlap and tying them with twine.

"So, Bess, have you thought about whether you're going to let Simon know that he's your real father?"

Bess froze. She hadn't expected *that*. She looked at him. "You told me that could be my decision."

"I still stand by that."

She went back to wrapping the roses. "Jonah is my real father."

Caleb took off his hat. "Yes, but—"

"I guess that's my answer," Bess interrupted. She surprised herself. Normally, she would never speak so forthrightly to an elder, much less interrupt one. But there was something about Caleb Zook that made her feel as if she could speak her mind to him. "Simon might be my actual father, but Jonah is my *real* father. Day in and day out, year after year. I just don't think Simon needs to know anything different." She gave him a direct look. "I have prayed long and hard about this, and for now, I would like to keep my secret."

Caleb looked at her for a long while, then put his wide-brimmed black felt hat back on his head. "Then that's how we'll leave things." He turned to go but stopped at the door and put his hand on the doorjamb. He looked back at her. "For what it's worth, I think you're right. For now. Maybe for a long, long time. Someday, though, I hope Simon will be told. It would be nice for him to know that his life has counted for something good in this world."

Jonah and Lainey's wedding day was sunny but bitter cold. Several friends came from Ohio for the event, including Mose and Sallie—now newlyweds—and Sallie's rambunctious twins, plus Levi Miller, the boy who liked Bess overly much. His head and body were finally growing to fit his ears, Bess had noticed, relieved, when she laid eyes on him yesterday. And his hair didn't stick straight up anymore. It usually looked like somebody had just held him under the water pump.

The furniture at Rose Hill Farm had been moved from the first floor to the second and the entire house had been cleaned. Tables were provided so that the meal would be served inside, but the barn would be where the wedding service would be held. The church wagon brought the wooden benches to fill the now bare floor. The church wagon provided dishes, glasses, and silverware, but one neighbor loaned their good dishes—with a pink rose pattern—for all of the tables. Other neighbors pooled their water glasses, pitchers for lemonade and coffee, cups and saucers, and small glass dishes for pickles and condiments.

Jonah and Lainey didn't have any frills, but Bess was allowed to order paper napkins engraved with the name of the bride, groom, and wedding date: JONAH AND LAINEY RIEHL, DECEMBER 16, 1971. The Eck, the special corner table, was the place for the bride, groom, and the witnesses, Bess and Simon. It was draped with a royal blue tablecloth and held a small two-tier wedding cake that Lainey had made and iced herself.

For the last few days, it seemed nearly every female member of the church had been at Rose Hill Farm. These experienced cooks, all red with heat and hurry, were preparing the meals to serve to 250 guests. The menu for the noon meal included roast duck and chicken, mashed potatoes and gravy, dressing, cold ham, coleslaw, corn, homemade bread, two kinds of jelly in cut-glass dishes, and a variety of cakes and cookies. A second meal would be served later. Smaller though, since most folks would have need to return home for choring.

That morning, Bess helped Lainey get ready upstairs. Lainey had made the dark blue dress herself. She tried to pin the white cap on, but she kept dropping pins on the floor.

"Look at me, Bess! My hands are trembling!"

Bess laughed. "It's an important day! You're entitled to be a little nervous."

She scooped up the pins from the floor and picked up a comb to brush Lainey's hair into a bun. It was growing longer now and could at least be gathered into a small knot, but curls were always escaping along the nape of her neck. Bess sighed. Those were just the kinds of curls she had always wished she had. She placed the cap gently over Lainey's head and pinned it into place.

They heard a car pull into the drive. Lainey went over to the window and gave a short gasp. Bess came up behind her. "Why, that's . . . that's Robin's car. Look! There they are! Robin and Ally!" She turned to Bess. "Did you . . . ?"

Bess shook her head and smiled. "Not me. It was Dad's idea. He went all the way to Harrisburg to invite them to come. Said they're like family to you and it wouldn't be a wedding day without them." She laughed. "Can you imagine Dad in a beauty salon?"

Lainey clapped her hands together. "Oh Bess. I never dreamed that God would give me all of this. You. Jonah. Simon. I never thought I'd have a family of my own."

Bess sat on the bed. "I think Mammi knew. But then she claimed to know when anyone in this town so much as sneezed."

Lainey sat next to her. "You're right. I think somehow she did. She always seemed to know things—"

"—even before they happened," Bess finished.

They both laughed and stopped quickly when a knock came on the door.

"Bishop said it's time," someone said from the other side. "We're just waiting on the bride."

Late that evening, after most folks had gone home, the young people piled into a couple of buggies and went down to Blue Lake Pond for a bonfire on the shore. The air was biting cold and the wind stung Bess's ears as she walked across the crunchy frosted shoreline to the huge blazing fire. The boys were still dressed in their Sunday best: black and white, with vests. The girls were trim and neat with crisply pressed white aprons under their dark capes. Before Bess sat down, she glanced behind the bonfire to the lake that unfolded before her, silvered by frost and moonlight.

Andy and Levi made a space for her between them. Exhausted but happy, Bess plopped down on the ground. She was surrounded by so many friends, new and old, all sitting in a great circle. It was peaceful here and she felt content.

The clouds that had been in front of the moon scudded past, and for a few minutes it was almost as bright as daylight. Bess noticed someone come up tentatively behind the circle, waiting, as if he wasn't sure he belonged. It was Billy Lapp. She had seen him once or twice at church but hadn't spoken to him since Betsy had left. He had been at the wedding service today, and she saw him sitting with Andy and other friends for the meals, but Bess was busy helping Lainey and her father.

A few people waved to Billy, but he held back and didn't join in. His eyes sought out Bess's before joining the circle. She smiled at him. Her welcome was real.

Somebody moved over to make space and Billy sat down in the casual way he always sat: legs apart, elbows on his knees. Andy Yoder began to sing and the others joined in. Their breath streamed out in white ribbons.

Bess's gaze returned to the fire. She listened to the voices in the dark, happy to know that Billy was a part of things, spending time with all of their friends around the fire. But she was even happier to realize he no longer gave her such a stomach-dropping feeling. It wasn't so long ago that being in such close proximity to Billy would have a physical effect on her. Her stomach would quiver, her cheeks would grow warm, her heart would pound, and her imagination would run away from her. Thoughts of Billy had filled her mind from the moment she woke until she fell asleep. She even imagined his face in the clouds, or in a fire such as this, or in the shimmering reflection off Blue Lake Pond. That was the way it had been for a very long time, ever since she had first met him.

Tonight, all she saw in the fire were flames and smoke and sparks. She looked up at the sky. Nowhere in the clouds did she see the handsome face of Billy Lapp.

Billy had been watching her. When he caught her eye, he pointed subtly toward the trees—a signal to meet him. Out of curiosity—or was it habit?—she slipped away to join him. They walked along the shoreline until they were out of view of the others.

Billy stopped and turned to her. He swallowed hard. "Bess, would you let me take you home afterward?"

Bess looked at him, her eyes went all around the face that she had loved so much, every line, every crease of the skin so dear to her.

If she agreed to go home with him tonight, it would be so easy. They would be back to where they had been before. In time, Betsy Mast would be forgotten.

But Bess would always wonder. What would happen if Betsy came back again? Or if she had never left? It was too much to ask. Bess didn't want to wonder and doubt and worry anymore.

"No, Billy." Her voice was gentle and polite and sincere. "But thank you anyway."

His face was surprised and sad. More sad than surprised.

He began to say something.

"Bess, I do care for you . . ." Then he stopped.

Bess waited quietly. His words drifted on the still night air.

"I never meant to . . ." He stopped again.

"It's all right, Billy," Bess said. "Really." It *was* all right. "Mammi used to tell me: 'Gut Ding will Weile haben.'" *Good things take time.* She used to think Mammi meant food—like not rushing the making of a pie crust—but now Bess realized she meant other good things too. Like love. And the mending of a broken heart.

Maybe someday, when the time was right, Bess and Billy would find their way to each other. But maybe not. That time would be far off in the invisible future. And if there was one thing Bess had learned she couldn't see at the age of fifteen, it was ahead.

She thought she saw tears in Billy's eyes and looked away quickly. Then she walked quietly past him to go back to the fire to join her friends.

Acknowledgments

I'd like to express my deep appreciation to my family, near and far. To my sister, Wendy, and daughter, Lindsey, and good friend, Nyna Dolby, who generously shared their insights and also read an early draft of this manuscript. A heartfelt thanks for reading this manuscript with tough and loving eyes, offering candor and guidance. As always, enormous gratitude to my agent, Joyce Hart, for being so wise, warm, and steadfast. I'm very grateful to all the people at Revell, especially my editors, Andrea Doering and Barb Barnes, who make my books so much better.

And above all, abiding gratitude goes to the Lord God, for his wisdom on matters seen and unseen.

Coming Spring 2015 from

SUZANNE
WOODS FISHER

Anna's Crossing:
An Amish Beginnings Novel

Revell

a division of Baker Publishing Group
www.RevellBooks.com

1

APRIL 15, 1737

It would be a hard crossing, they'd been warned. Eight weeks in a wooden tub with no guarantee they'd ever get there. Anna König crouched beside a bed of roses, breathing deeply of the freshly turned loam. She had done all she could to avoid this treacherous sea journey, and yet here she was, digging up her rose to take along with her. She jabbed her shovel in the ground, mulling all the reasons this voyage was fraught with ill.

It meant leaving behind her grandparents, her home, her church in Ixheim, Germany. Her people. It would be the end of everything she'd ever known and loved.

"Some endings are really beginnings," her grandfather had said when she told him that Christian Müller, the minister, had asked—no, insisted—she join the departing families. "If you don't remember anything I've ever tried to teach you, remember that."

Despite misgivings and forebodings, Anna relented. How do you say no to a minister? She was the only one who could speak and understand English. And that's why she was stabbing the earth with her shovel, digging up her most precious rose to take on the journey, hoping that the hard winter and late-to-come spring meant its roots would still be dormant. If she was going to go to this strange New World, she was going to bring this rose. And she was going. Tomorrow.

Tomorrow! Just that one word was like the crack of doom.

Anna had begged her grandparents to join the emigrating group, but they wouldn't budge. "It's a young man's sport, that sea journey," her grandfather said, shaking his head, ending the discussion. She couldn't argue that point. The voyage was filled with risks and dangers and uncertainties, especially for the very young and very old.

Anna sat back on her heels and looked around. In a few years, who would be left in Ixheim? Who would care for her grandparents in their final days? Who would bury them and tend their graves? Tears welled and she squeezed her eyes shut, trying to will them away.

This little valley that hugged the Rhine River was supposed to be their home, for good, for always. Here, they had tried to live in peace, keeping to themselves in secluded hills and valleys, where they could farm the land and their sheep could graze and they could go about their daily life of work and worship without worry or hassle. This valley was dear to her, peaceful and pastoral.

Yet beneath the surface, life had started to change. A new baron held the Amish in disdain; much of the old conviviality of the village was disappearing. It was time to leave, the bishop had decided, before tensions escalated as they had in Switzerland, years ago.

Carefully, Anna wrapped the root ball of the dug-up rose in burlap. She glanced around the garden, filled with her grandmother's roses. Their survival was a testament to her people's story: roots that adapted to whatever soil they were transplanted into, thorns that bespoke of the pain they bore, blossoms each spring that declared God's power to bring new life from death. As long as the roses survived, her grandmother said, so would our people. Her grandfather would scoff and call her a superstitious old woman, but Anna understood what she meant. The roses were a living witness to survival.

The sounds of hooting and hollering boys stormed into her thoughtful moment. She caught sight first of eight-year-old Felix, galloping toward her, followed by his older brother Johann. Felix frightened the chickens that scratched in the garden's dirt, scattering them in a squawking cloud of flapping wings and molting feathers.

"A letter from Papa!" Felix shouted.

Behind him came Johann, holding his father's letter in the air, red faced and breathing hard from the exertion of climbing the hill. His eyes, bright from anticipation, fastened on Anna's face. "My father wrote there are twice as many immigrants leaving for Port Philadelphia this year as last. And last year was three times as many as the year before. He said we must make haste to join him in Penn's Woods and settle the land."

"Just think, Anna. Deer, turkey, rabbits, all easy to obtain. And with a little more effort—" he pretended to aim and shoot a rifle at an imaginary beast—"elk and wild boar to put up for winter provisions." Naturally, Johann, at age thirteen, knew everything.

But Anna, practical and skeptical and older than Johann by six years, held a different point of view. "I hear that the New World is a land of poisonous snakes, lions, tigers. And black bears and mountain lions. Grey wolves sweep down from the mountains in packs." A wolf pack frightened her most of all. When the wolves here grew desperate for food, they would attack her woollies.

Johann wasn't listening. He never listened to her objections about America. "Good water springs, lumber for building cabins."

"I've heard stories that settlers have seen red men. Many times."

Johann shook his head as he came up to Anna in the rose garden. "Friendly Indians. Curious ones. Fascinated with shiny brass kitchen kettles and knick-knacks. Papa said he has found a place for us to settle." His eyes took on a faraway look and she knew he was off in his head to America to join his father. Jacob Bauer, the bishop of their church, had gone ahead to the New World last spring, to claim land and purchase warrants for those who intended to join him this year.

Anna turned to Felix and couldn't hold back a grin. A riot of curly hair peeped from beneath a tattered black felt hat, blue eyes sparkled with excitement, and a big smile showed more spaces than teeth.

The Bauer boys were like brothers to her. Felix was round and sturdy, with carrot red hair that matched his temperament. Johann, blond and thin, had never been hale and was afflicted with severe asthma. His heart and body might not be strong, that Johann, but his mind made up for it. What he carried around in that head of his was what mattered.

Now Felix was another story. Two black crows cackled from a nearby tree and he stared at them with a distant look in his eyes. "There's a crow's nest on the ship that's so high, you can see the curve of the earth."

Smiling inside, Anna said to him, "It's really that high?"

"Even higher." With a sweep of his hand Felix showed the curve of the earth. "Johann told me so."

Anna didn't know where Johann got his information. He'd had no schooling and owned no books except the Bible, but he knew all sorts of things. Solid-gold facts, he called them. She didn't care if they were true or not; she believed them all.

Then the twinkle in Felix's eyes faded. "It's a great pity I won't be able to find out for myself."

"The Bakers changed their mind and aren't going, so Felix wants to stay behind too," Johann explained. "That means that Catrina Müller is the only one aboard close to Felix's age."

Felix's scowl deepened. "I'm not going if I have to be stuck on a ship with her. I'll stay here and live with the Bakers."

"I don't think you have much of a choice, Felix." *Nor do I.* Anna would never voice it aloud, but she dreaded the thought of spending the next few months in confined quarters with Catrina and her mother, Maria. Those two had a way of draining the very oxygen from the air. She set down her shovel. "Is your mother ready to go?"

Felix shrugged. "She's packing dishes into barrels."

"She must be eager to see your father."

He tilted his head. "She's humming. That's good. She wants to see Papa." Then he took off running along the narrow sheep's trail that led up the hill.

"I wish I could find a reason to go. Better yet, to stay."

"Change is coming, Anna," Johann said with annoying professorial patience. "It's in the air. We can't stay here and live like sheep in a pasture."

Anna looked up at the hillside. "I like sheep."

He crossed his arms in a stubborn pose. "I mean there is a whole new world out there. Just think of the mountains and valleys and unknown places we'll see."

"Filled with savages and the beasts. Your father has said as much in his letters."

"He also says there is land waiting for us which has never before been claimed, surveyed, or deeded. Land, Anna. We can live in safety. We can *own* land."

"Maybe there's no place that's truly safe for us."

He shook his head hard. "That's not what William Penn said. He offered a place where we can go and live in peace."

Johann didn't understand. He was moving toward someone—his father. His mother and brother would be traveling with him. Anna was moving away from those she loved. "My grandmother says it's wicked to want more than you have. She wants to just stay put and thank God."

Johann laughed. "Your grandmother is a frightened old lady who's had a hard life. Doesn't mean you should be scared of new things."

"I'm not." *Yes, I am.*

"Everything changes. That's the way of life. This Greek fellow Heraclitus said there is nothing permanent except change, and I think he was right." He leaned forward and whispered in a conspiratorial voice, "Your grandmother has made Maria promise to find you a husband in the New World. She said that Ixheim has only old toothless men and young toothless boys." He lifted his voice an octave or two, warbling, to mimic her grandmother. "Anna must have Her Chance! She is pushing twenty without a man in sight."

Anna laid the rosebush in her basket and stood, sobered by the thought. With each passing birthday, her grandmother grew increasingly distressed. The New World, she decided, was Anna's only hope to find a like-minded bachelor.

Johann was watching her carefully, and then his eyes took on that teasing look of his. "If there's no one in the New World who passes Maria's muster, and if you don't mind holding off a few years, I suppose I could marry you."

She laughed then, and her mood shifted instantly from solemn to light-hearted, as it always did when she was around Johann. "I'll keep such a heartwarming proposal in mind."

"With fair wind and God's favor," Johann said, with his usual abundance of optimism, "we'll reach Port Philadelphia by the end of July."

When Anna pointed out that he was basing that assumption on all conditions being ideal and how rarely things ever turned out that way, he rolled his eyes in exasperation. "It's God's will. Of that my father and Christian have no doubt."

And how does anyone object to that? How in the world?

He wiggled his eyebrows and winked at her, then hurried up the hillside to join Felix, who was already on the top, to reach the shortcut that took them back to their house. Midway up the hill, Johann stopped and bent over to catch his breath. When he topped the hill, he turned and doffed his hat at her, flourishing it before him as if he were going to sweep the floor. She grinned, and then her grin faded as he disappeared down the other side of the hill and she was left with only her worries for company.

Tomorrow. Tomorrow!

Like it or not, the journey would begin. They would travel down the Rhine River to Rotterdam, board the vessel a shipping agent had arranged as passage for them, and then they'd be off to the New World.

Anna stretched her back and moved out of the shade to feel the afternoon sun on her face. The muscles in her arms and shoulders ached from spearing the shovel into the cold earth, but it was a pleasant ache. She'd always loved working outside, much more than she did the washing and cooking and keeping up of the house, the woman's work. The drudgery, she thought, and quickly sent an apology to the Lord for her ungrateful heart.

A furious honking of geese in the sky disrupted her reverie. Heading north for summer, she presumed. Her gaze traveled up the green hillside dotted with ruffs of gray wool. Her woollies, each one known to her by name. Her heart was suddenly too full for words as she let her gaze roam lovingly over the land she knew as home: over the rounded haystacks, the neat lambing sheds, the creek that ran almost the year round. The steep hills that brought an early sunset in summer and broke the wind in winter. It grieved her that she wouldn't be here this year for spring, as the lambs came and the wool was sheared and the ewes were mated and then the lambs would come again. She gazed at the hills, trying to engrave it in her memory. Where would she be next spring? She wondered what home would look like, feel like, smell like. She glanced down at her basket and gripped the leather handle, hard. At least she had her rose. If it survived, so would she.

A few hours later, Anna heard the whinny of a horse and came out of the house to see who was driving up the path. She shielded her eyes from the sun and saw Christian Müller on a wagon seat, Felix beside him. She noticed the somber look on Christian's usually cheerful face, the way Felix's small head was bowed. She crossed her arms, gripping her elbows. The wind, raw and cold, twisted her skirts around her legs. *Something's wrong.*

There came a stillness as if the whole world were holding its breath.

Let it be nothing, she entreated silently, let it be another meeting tonight to talk about the journey, or to let her know that Johann stopped to visit a friend. Let it be something silly. With every squeak of the wheels, she felt the lump in her throat grow bigger, the apprehension build.

A gust of wind swirled up the hill, flapping Anna's dress like a sheet on a clothesline, whipping the strings of her prayer cap against her neck, and she shivered.

Christian hauled back on the reins and set the brake on the wagon. Slowly, he climbed down and waited beside the wagon, bearded chin on his chest. Felix jumped off the seat and threw his arms around Anna's waist, shuddering with sobs.

Anna's gaze moved over Christian's pale face. Behind him, in the back of the wagon, was the shape of a body, covered by a gray wool blanket.

"Christian, who is it?" An icy feeling started in Anna's stomach and traveled up her spine. "Ch-Christian?" she whispered again, her eyes wide, her throat hot and tight. It was then she saw tears running down Christian's cheeks. The awful reality started to hit her full force and she pressed a fist to her lips. *Dear God,* she thought. *Dear God, how can this be?*

Christian turned away with his chin tucked down, then, almost lovingly, gently folded back the top of the blanket. His eyes lifted to meet hers. "The Lord has seen fit to take our young Johann from us."

2

JUNE 26, 1737

Bairn rounded the stern of the square-rigged ship. What a beauty she was! The *Charming Nancy* was a typical merchant vessel of her day: square-rigged and beak bowed, with high, castle-like superstructures fore and aft that protected her cargo and crew in the worst weather. Maybe she wasn't the prettiest ship sailing the seas. No doubt she wasn't the youngest, and that did spike concern for Bairn. Even the sturdiest sail ship lasted only twenty years and the *Charming Nancy* was inching close to that age. She was worn and creaky, leaky as a sieve, and beating against the wind would be a painfully inefficient endeavor, but to him, serving as ship's carpenter, she was magnificent.

"Bairn!" A familiar voice boomed from the bow of the ship.

Bairn shielded his eyes from the sun to see the ship's new commanding officer, Captain Charles Stedman, scowling down at him from the fo'c'sle deck. The captain tried very hard to look the part of a cultured, confident sea captain, like his much esteemed older brother John, but never seemed to quite manage it. He was short and slender, with bushy side-whiskers, dressed elegantly with a whiskey-colored velvet vest, a tricornered black hat, and a white silk tie. "Make haste! Supervise the hold and see to it that no one is slacking!" The captain pointed to a stack of cargo that had been on the same spot on the deck since this morning.

Bairn felt heat rise up his neck, but he smiled amicably enough and tipped his hat in a feigned sign of respect. "Aye, Captain!" He had been supervising the loading of the hold—that's why he was standing at the hatch next to that very stack of cargo. But he knew the captain liked to sound off to deckhands to show he was in charge.

Bairn's gaze shifted to the first mate by the captain's side, Mr. Pocock. He shared officers' quarters with the first mate, an Englishman who was long past the prime of his life, with saggy, tired blue eyes, sun-leathered skin, and a belly that hung over the waistband of his black breeches. Mr. Pocock had little to say unless you made the regrettable error of asking him about his gout. On that topic, he had plenty to say.

A light cross-course breeze blew in from the channel, pushing away the thin, acrid smell of tar and pitch from the docks that hung in the humid air. Bairn scrutinized the cargo that the stevedores were loading into the hold—the lowest part of the ship that stored most of the passengers' household goods, tools, and supplies, as well as the ship's supply of food, cordage, canvas, gunpowder. The capstan, a type of winch fitted with holes in which long bars were inserted, was used to hoist the cargo and other heavy loads down into the hold. By pushing on the bars, stevedores hauled in a rope wound around the capstan, moving the load up or down.

Earlier this morning, Bairn walked through the lower deck of the *Charming Nancy*. If he closed his eyes in the dark space and breathed deeply, he thought he could still smell the faint scent of wines and woolens of their recent cargo in the moist air, masking the stench of the bilge below.

Ships were ballasted with a noxious mix of sand and gravel that rattled and swished about the bilge for years, growing increasingly more foul as it absorbed the waste of life on board. The only place where the air was completely free of the smell of the bilge was the windward forecastle deck, the fo'c'sle deck, and this small space was sacred to the captain.

Bairn pitied the crew for their quarters in the fo'c'sle, below deck. Even more, he pitied the passengers who would be living in the lower deck. The stink of the bilge that pervaded the ship was strongest there. The *Charming Nancy* had spent most of her life going back and forth across the Atlantic with goods from England to trade in the colonies and vice versa, cargos that didn't care about stink. No longer.

The Rotterdam shippers had discovered that there was more money to be made shuttling Germans to the colonies of Georgia, Virginia, and New York. And now their attention had riveted to the surest of all markets, Pennsylvania.

Over the last few weeks, as the *Charming Nancy* was anchored in Rotterdam, Bairn's days were spent making repairs and adjustments to the old ship. He corrected the fitting of the bowsprit so rainwater no longer leaked into the seamen's living quarters. That should set him in good standing with the crew and make up for the more onerous task Captain Stedman had asked of him: the building of double bedsteads in the lower deck to allow for increased capacity of passengers in the ship. The poor souls would be fitted in like sardines in a tin.

"I got me a bad feeling about this trip. A real bad feeling."

Bairn spun around to face Decker. His eyes narrowed in perplexity as he studied the irritating seaman. Decker bullied the crew, caused malice and rancor, but he was a skilled craftsman and the captain had recently promoted him to carpenter's apprentice—against Bairn's objection. "Decker, ye need to stop worryin' others with yer odd dreams. Ye sound fey. Ye've got the crew nervous as a scalded cat."

"It's not just my dreams. I saw Queenie under a tub this mornin'. 'Tis an omen. You know what 'at means."

To Decker, it was a portent of magnitudinous proportions: death was imminent. To Bairn, it meant the ship's black cat, Queenie, never the brightest of felines to start with, had gotten herself trapped under a tub.

Something shiny caught his eye. Decker was wearing polished black shoes with silver buckles. Bairn tilted his head. "New shoes?"

Decker clicked his heels together. "Aye. Bought 'em off a shoemaker in Rotterdam. Seein' as how I'm an officer now, I thought I should look the part."

Bairn rolled his eyes. "Yer naught but an apprentice, Decker."

"The shoemaker said the buckles would ward off bad luck."

"Why don't ye just admit ya don't want to haul bodies across the sea and stop scarin' the deckhands. Half the crew went jobbin' with other ships once ye started spoutin' off with yer crazy dreams and superstitious nonsense."

"I don't deny I'd rather tote silent cargo than tend to complainin' Germans, but 'at's only part of the reason. You know as well as I do that havin' women on board is bad luck. And the captain's tryin' to jam more bodies down here than the ship can hold."

Decker was a provoking fellow, always firing at people with hammer and tongs, but on this particular topic of overcrowding, Bairn couldn't fault him. He was helpless to do anything about it, though. "Yer a free agent, Decker. Ye can always sign on another ship." He knew Decker would never leave the *Charming Nancy*. The lure of the promotion was too appealing.

Decker's gaze shifted across the harbor to the tall ships that lined the docks. "Problem is, I dunno any captain out there who isn't doing the exact same thing."

"Well, then, until ya make up yer mind, see that ye finish the double bedsteads."

Decker shot him a dark frown and stomped away.

Bairn inflated his cheeks and blew the air out in a gusty sigh. Decker's foreboding nettled him. While he felt a great loyalty to Captain Stedman, the overcrowding of the ships was a valid worry—not only would it strain the timbers and seams of the *Charming Nancy*, but the additional provisions needed to keep the passengers fed would add critical weight to the ship. The *St. Andrew*, the ship under Captain John Stedman's command, had already left Rotterdam with far more passengers than was safe. Bed shelves were stacked two and three deep. A man's nose would brush the bottom of the next fellow's bunk.

Opportunity drove the overcrowding, both for the passengers and the captain. Whether a man traveled in the Great Cabin or the lower deck, each had an ambition to get to the New World, where milk and honey flowed and all men could become rich.

The number of German immigrants arriving in Philadelphia had grown sevenfold in the last two years. The journey was a perilous one and many didn't survive—though that didn't stop the shipping agents and the captains from collecting their passage. Dead or alive upon arrival, each body owed its fare.

Bairn knew food and fresh water for such an enormous quantity of people would be jeopardized due to space constraints. And what would they do if they experienced delays? He'd heard macabre tales of passengers starving to death. If a ship took much more than eight weeks to cross the ocean, no doubt they would run out of provisions.

Weeks ago, when Captain Stedman had ordered the refitting of the lower deck, Bairn had cautiously objected. You had to tread carefully when you questioned the captain. His word, and mostly his ego, ruled the ship. As expected, Bairn's protest was quickly shot down. "I'll do the fashin' for me ship, lad," the captain said.

Lad. Boy. *Bairn.* A Scottish word for "child." That was the captain's way of reminding him of his place.

Everything in life boiled down to money, that truth Bairn had observed in his two-and-twenty years on earth, the last eleven of which were spent at sea. And he couldn't deny that it was the very thing that drove him, as well. There was nothing more important to Bairn than making money.

And yet, at least for him, something else hung in the balance with the *Charming Nancy.* Captain Stedman had strongly hinted that after this voyage he might expect a promotion to first mate, the top boatswain. A few years as first mate, then he would be ready to captain his own ship. Better still, he would have funds saved to become an investor like his benefactors, the Stedman brothers. Captain Charles often boasted that he was an investor of eleven ships. Captain John never boasted, which indicated to Bairn that he was an investor in far more.

Wouldn't life be sweet to hold that kind of wealth one day? Bairn had it all worked out: With a bit of luck and fair winds, he would be commanding a ship like the *Charming Nancy* with her hold filled with freshly sawn timber, saltpeter, iron, sugar, hempen yarn, and more—stamped and bound for England. Come spring, he would fill the ship with Germans from Rotterdam and return to Port Philadelphia. His ambition lured him onward and the cycle would begin again.

Bairn had a passionate, bone-deep desire to become wealthy. Nay, extraordinarily wealthy. And with the influx of German immigrants pouring out of Rotterdam to the New World, he was riding the top of a wave.

He saw Decker's black cat sashay over to him and curl around his boot leg, tail swishing, so he bent down to scoop her up. "Omen, me eye," he told her. "Yer naught but a curious cat."

728

JUNE 27, 1737

This Rotterdam was a poor place, and Anna longed to go home.

Weeks and weeks had passed since she had left Ixheim. Her heart still ached and her eyes filled with tears when she least expected it. In their haste to depart, there wasn't time to properly grieve Johann Bauer's unexpected passing. In Christian's eyes, it was a clear sign of more cruelty to come—aimed at the Bauer family—and confirmed that departure could not and should not be delayed.

Johann was buried the morning after his death, and the families left, in a somber mood, to meet the boat on the Rhine by high noon. Dorothea, his mother, was still in shock, barely spoke, hardly ate. She was just going through the motions of living. She stayed close to Anna, but her mind was elsewhere. Felix hadn't smiled or laughed since that pivotal afternoon in the rose garden.

The Amish group had traveled down the Rhine from Heilbronn to Rotterdam by ship, docking at each custom house so agents could board and examine their goods for taxation. Valuable time was lost—the entire month of May and part of June.

Maria Müller, Christian's wife, was outraged by the endless delays. "Twenty-six custom houses down the Rhine," she said at every meal, as if they all hadn't been there. "Twenty-six! What should have taken one week took six. Nothing but thievery, those tax collectors." Maria sniffed. "Highway robbery."

Christian tried to ward off his wife's tirade. "Remember, dear, we were helpless to do anything about it."

He knew, as they all did, that this initial complaint was Maria's prelude that led straight into the next grievance. "And as soon as we do arrive in Rotterdam, they shoo us off to stay . . . here!" She lifted a palm in the air and waved it in a circle, then heaved a loud sigh of disgust. "In squalor and filth."

Maria could be taxing, but she said things that everyone else was thinking. It *was* a disgusting place, Anna heartily agreed. An overcrowded makeshift tent city. Government officials of Rotterdam had sent them off to a holding area in the vicinity of the ruins of St. Elbrecht's chapel below Kralingen because emigrants weren't permitted to remain in the city.

"And they said *we* might bring disease," Maria endlessly recalled. "Dirt and filth. Hmmph. As if we would bring anything but cleanliness and godliness."

And patience.

They were waiting until passage to America could be arranged between a Neulander—a recruiter—and a shipping agent. More precious time slipping through their hands. Worse, their funds were slipping away too.

Last night brought good news. The Neulander found them in the tent city to tell them he had been able to secure their passage on the vessel *Charming Nancy*. His name was Georg Schultz and he certainly didn't look the part of a man of influence. He was the fattest man Anna had ever seen, doughy and white as a dumpling, a three-hundred-pound dumpling. He was almost perfectly round. Just over five feet tall, with an oddly shaped head that seemed too small for his body and a gray beard elegantly trimmed to a point. But as soon as he spoke of the bounty of land that waited for them in America, Anna realized why Georg Schultz had a reputation for a surprisingly compelling gift of persuasion. "Land as far as the eye can see," he said, describing the scene as if it were right in front of them. "Rich, dark soil, babbling brooks with fresh clean water, virgin timber that tickles the sky, waiting for you to claim it and tame it."

Anna served as interpreter for Georg Schultz, who spoke a crisp and polished high German, and refused to lower himself to speak the peasant farmers' dialects, like that of her people. In between translations, she stirred a large kettle of stew. Georg sidled over to the kettle and took a whiff of the stew. He stood uncomfortably close to Anna, giving her a slow once-over. The eyes in her mind narrowed and she moved a few steps away.

"In Penn's Woods," Georg said, "one might travel about a whole year without spending a penny. It's customary when one comes with his horse to a house, the traveler is asked if he wishes to have something to eat. If one wishes to stay overnight to the morrow, he and his horse are harbored free of charge." He moved closer to Anna. "He is invited to take his seat at the table and take his luck at the pot."

The breath of that man! It could peel the varnish off a table. Anna set the wooden spoon in the kettle and stepped back yet again from Georg. "I think perhaps you are hinting for an invitation to a meal."

"A tongue as tart as a green apple, I see." Georg burst out with a laugh. "I'd be delighted." His eyes swept down her figure and returned to rest at her chest.

She spun on her heel to turn her back on him. Him and his roving eyes.

Georg moved around their temporary dwelling and frowned at the sight of the bulky household goods, the chimney backs and scythes, shovels and iron pots and frying pans, crosscut saws, axes and hatches. "So much, so much. This will cost you a fortune to transport." He pointed to Christian. "I have a suggestion that will save you money. And time." He clapped his pudgy hands. "Time and money!" He wheeled around to find Anna. "Girl! Come translate."

Anna explained what Georg had in mind and Christian's eyes lit up at the thought of saving money.

"I will trade your used goods for new ones of the same kind," Georg said. "I can get the same items in lots of dozens, tightly packed so it won't look like you have as much. You won't run the risk of the captain refusing your passage." He peered at Christian, who was looking to Anna to explain. "They can do that, you know. Refuse your passage. The captain's word is law." Georg folded his large arms over his chest. "And that would mean you must wait for another ship. Soon it will be late in the season." He glanced around the tent. "It would be a pity to lose a chance to sail with Captain Stedman."

That name meant something to Christian. His eyes went wide. "We are sailing under John Stedman?"

"Well, close," Georg said, wagging his big chins. "Captain Charles Stedman. John Stedman's brother." John Stedman had a reputation among the Palatinate Mennonites as a blue-water captain, and word had trickled to the tiny Amish church of Ixheim. Captain Stedman had safely transported hundreds of German Mennonites from the Rhine Valley to the colonies. Christian excused himself and drew into a knot with a group of men, standing shoulder to shoulder, to confer.

Anna watched Georg Schultz observe them and wondered if he looked at the men of her church and assumed they were all alike, long beards jerking, big felt hats flapping in the wind. From where she stood, they certainly looked alike, sounded alike, acted alike. But Anna could see how different they really were: Josef Gerber, a bulky, gentle man with a toddler in each arm, both tow-headed, with straight-edge bangs above their nearly white eyebrows. Flat-faced Simon Miller, his hair and beard black as a crow. Lean and lanky Isaac Mast. Next to him was his gangly, sixteen-year-old son Peter, a fuzz of whiskers circling his chin to celebrate his recent wedding to Lizzie. And then there was Christian, their leader, bald and bespectacled with a long beard on his chin that was as tangled as a bird's nest. The men's heads bent together to hear Christian, shorter than all of them, and quieter too, but when he spoke, others always listened.

Yes, the men were different in many ways, but underneath they were much the same, in all the things that mattered most: faith and family and tradition.

Just then, as if they'd been given some invisible signal, there was a great nodding of heads and dipping of beards. Christian strode over to Georg Schultz to give him permission to trade off most of their household goods. Pleased, Georg Schultz promised him new goods would be waiting at the docks tomorrow to be loaded into the hold of the *Charming Nancy*.

Anna hoped Georg Schultz's word could be trusted, as they were entirely dependent on the Neulander. She thought back to warnings Jacob Bauer had written about Neulanders: they received a handsome commission on each passenger they brought to the ship, as well as free passage, so they were not always a reliable source of information.

That night, as Anna lay on her pallet, she could hear the familiar voices of Christian and a few other men as they sat by the fire, talking over the day, in good spirits now that the journey was finally getting under way. Dorothea slept peacefully beside her. Even Felix seemed cheerful tonight. Anna felt the opposite—a rush of loneliness and longing.

As she looked up at the stars, sparkly diamonds on black velvet, she tried to come up with a plan to get back home.

June 28, 1737

Felix Bauer thought he might explode from nervous excitement. Any day now—maybe tomorrow—they would be climbing aboard a boat—a ship!—and sail to the other side of the world.

He wished his mother and Anna were more excited about this sea journey.

His mother, well, he wasn't sure she knew or even cared where she was since they had left Ixheim. And Anna tried to act like they were off on a jaunt to a neighbor's house, nothing more. But Felix saw through her. She was no Catrina Müller, putting on performances. Anna had only one or two faces, maybe three, nothing hidden, nothing exaggerated. She never once said how exciting the trip would be. She just said that going was something whose time had come. That it had to be done.

Maria Müller, Catrina's mother, had no hesitation about sharing her opinion. She didn't want to leave Ixheim and didn't mind if everybody knew her feelings. It struck Felix as funny when Maria would start out saying, "I've kept quiet long enough" and then out would come another list of worries about the journey ahead. She liked to repeat horror stories she'd heard from some of the Mennonites who were waiting in the tent city, like they were, to book passage on a ship. "Esther Wenger heard of a ship that ran completely out of food," Maria told Christian. "They left Rotterdam with one hundred fifty on board, they arrived with only fifty persons alive." Felix lurked nearby, fascinated by the gruesome tale. "In the end, they had to eat rats. Rats!"

Christian's spectacles flashed her a warning, but by suppertime, everybody knew everything. The notion of running out of food was a particularly frightful one, stirring up the mothers, so Christian decided that as a safety measure, they would take additional provisions on the ship. "We will not go hungry," he reassured the anxious mothers. That afternoon, he and Josef Gerber set out to buy smoked meat, cheese, butter, peas, barley, and Zwieback from the stores in Rotterdam that catered to ship passengers. Felix tagged along to carry the purchases, happy to have an excuse to get away from Catrina, who was always pestering him about one thing or another.

Christian Müller, Felix observed, had an impressive way of ignoring his wife. He would tilt his head and nod as if he was listening carefully to Maria's woes, then turn his attention to something else entirely. Felix would like to try to manage the horrible Catrina as skillfully, especially since he would be stuck with her for the next few months. Just this morning, he had stopped peeling potatoes for one moment—hardly *one* minute—because he had spotted a long line of ants and wondered where they were headed.

Catrina noticed. "Felix needs help," she said in a loud voice.

"I do not!" Felix said, but what he was thinking was, *A pox on her!* He picked up his peeling knife, sat down again with the stupid potatoes, crossed his eyes at Catrina, and she promptly told her mother.

Catrina was born with an eyeball that was kind of lazy. Instead of looking where it should be looking, it floated off to the side. She'd done lots of things to make it better, but none of them worked. She tried exercises where she had to look that way, then this way, then that way, up and down, down and up, but the eye always floated away. Anna's grandmother gave her a patch to wear on her other eye to make the lazy one work, but that didn't do the job either. Felix had perfected a way to get even with Catrina: whenever she talked to him, he would act flustered, as if he didn't know which eye to look at, which made her all the madder.

Catrina Müller was the only blight on this trip.

No. There was one more. His worry about his mother. She was quiet and sad and would eat hardly at all. And she was always tired. She would sleep the day away if Anna let her. When she was awake, there was fear in her eyes, fear of the far-off. Felix did what he could to cheer his mother up, but nothing seemed to help. Anna said that being reunited with his father was the only thing that would help his mother. But that was still a long time away.

Tonight, Felix stayed up practically all night long picturing what lay ahead. First, he considered the other side of the world: America. It was hard to have an idea of what it would be like—in his mind, the world he knew in Ixheim kept fanning out around him. So he would shift his imagination to the world nearly at hand—the sea journey. He saw himself high in the crow's nest on the ship, shielding his eyes from the sun with one hand, searching, searching, searching for the first sign of land. He spotted pirates and whales, and the captain praised his keen eyesight. He shimmied down the long poles, just like the other sailors did, and climbed the ropes like a monkey. Even better, he saw himself behind the big wheel in a ferocious storm, saving the ship from running aground.

All winter, Johann had read stories of sailing on the high seas, spinning tales and igniting his imagination of what the journey to the New World would be like. Whenever he thought of Johann, dozens of times a day, his stomach hurt. When he had something he wanted to tell Johann and had to remind himself that his brother wasn't here anymore, his head hurt. When he thought of all that Johann was missing, his heart hurt.

One thing hadn't changed. Felix would see his father at the end of this adventure. He imagined his father—a big, tall man with a long salt-and-pepper beard—waiting on the dock for their ship to sail in. Felix would spot him first, naturally, and gallop down the gangplank into his arms, stretched out wide for his son to run into them. Everything would be all right again.

Almost everything.

3

JUNE 29, 1737

There were so many rivers here, fast-flowing streams in a hurry to wind around the city triangle of Rotterdam and spill into the sea. Anna followed in the long line of Amish who followed Christian Müller, and remembered that Johann had told her on a cold winter afternoon that Rotterdam was once nothing but a small fishing village. "Now it's the main access from Europe to England."

And now to America.

Anna had never been to a city. She had never been anywhere but her small German village. Now, standing on a rise that overlooked Rotterdam, looking out at the great hulls of ships in the harbor, the tall buildings that impaled the smoke and steam and heat haze, listening to the cacophony of shouting people and squeaking chains, she didn't know whether she found it beautiful or frightening. It was a much bigger world than she had thought possible.

Today, at long last, they were finally going to board the ship and set sail for the New World. Georg Schultz had been surprisingly true to his word. Yesterday, their household belongings had been placed in the hold of the ship for ballast as Christian and Josef Gerber and Isaac Mast counted everything.

The only belonging Anna cared about was her rose, wrapped carefully in burlap that she moistened with water each day. This rose would *not* be kept deep in the ship's dark hold. She kept it with her, in a basket by her side, at all times.

As they left the tent city to head toward Rotterdam's harbor, Anna noticed a group of women drenching their dirty linen in the river and slapping it against the rocks. The women, with their sleeves rolled up to reveal strong, red arms, skirts pulled high, feet bare to spare their shoes, were gossiping, cackling, singing as they washed. Anna felt a sweeping sense of loss, missing all that was familiar. Simple everyday tasks—washing clothes in the kettle with her grandmother, hanging them on a wooden clothesline, bringing the sheep down the hillside, gardening beside her grandfather—they seemed so precious to her. When would life feel familiar again? Would it ever?

"Anna? Are you all right?" Felix stood in front of her, alarm sparking in his blue eyes. "Is your leg hurting?"

She walked with a slight limp, a remnant from a childhood accident, but that wasn't the reason she had slowed to a stop without realizing it and had fallen behind. "I'm thinking too much is all." Gently she brushed the hair out of his eyes. She hardly had to reach down to do so anymore, he was getting that big. He would be nine years old come winter. "Where is your hat?"

Felix's hands flew up to his bare head. "Oh no! It must have blown off!"

"So, boy, you finally noticed," Maria Müller said, holding out Felix's black hat. A woman of considerable girth, she consistently lagged behind the others and brought up the rear of the group. Fitting, Anna thought, because she knew Maria was unhappy about leaving home. Christian, her husband, discouraged her from sharing her reluctance with others. That didn't stop Maria. If any thought crossed through her mind, it was shared with all.

Anna took the hat from Maria and plopped it on Felix's head. She gave him a look. "You must not lose it. Your mother has no extra money to replace it."

All the Amish had barely enough money left to book their passage on a merchant ship—at least one thousand guilders per person.

At least Felix knew better than to fuss right then, with Maria looming, for he had a contrite look on his face without his usual commotion.

As they neared the wharves, the streets grew more congested, packed with people buying and selling, begging and thieving. Church bells clamored from every street corner, vendors bargained, dogs barked, cats slithered, shoppers stomped about on thick clogs, holding their hems up from mud puddles.

Anna's nose filled with the smells of coils of sausage ropes, bins of produce, bags of spices, beeswax candles, fine perfumes, sides of raw meat. Peddlers called out their wares: turnips, spring carrots only slightly withered, salted cod, salt-cured pork, salted beef, salt! "Vissen, Vissen!" a rosy-cheeked gray-haired woman shouted with a tray of silvery dried fish, laid out like knives, hanging from her neck.

Carrying their handheld belongings in the stifling, humid heat, the Amish walked on the market fringe toward the docks, staring up at the great hulls of ships. Soon the air brought a new scent Anna didn't recognize: a salty, briny, tangy smell. The sea. How curious!

When they reached the docks, they found a port busy with afternoon activity. Orders were shouted, drums rolled, pulleys squeaked, timbers creaked, waves lapped against the pilings. Even Anna, who knew nothing about ships and sailors and sea journeys, could sense excitement in the air.

It took a number of tries with Dutch dockworkers to find out where the *Charming Nancy* was docked, but the Amish eventually made their way toward the ship through a jumble of barrels, shipping crates, stacked cargo, impatient seamen.

And then they got their first glimpse of the ship that was to sail with them to America. There, at the far end of a dock, rocking gently on the waves of the harbor, was the *Charming Nancy*.

Light rain had been spattering on the deck on and off since morning, but the clouds were beginning to burn off. There was an urgency to get the voyage under way as Captain Stedman intended to sail on today's outgoing tide. Sweaty stevedores filled the hold with trunks and crates and barrels as Bairn leaned over the open hatch. It was critical that the hold be well packed, highly organized, and expertly balanced to keep the keel settled deep in the water. Additional provisions would be acquired in England; afterward, there wouldn't be room in the hold to swing a cat by the tail.

Employing nearly the full extent of his Dutch vocabulary, Bairn shouted that the hold looked good and to keep going. Like he did in every port, he had picked up enough foreign language to communicate what needed to be said to the stevedores. He climbed the ladder to the lower deck, where the passengers would stay. If all went well, this would be the last time he would be in that section until the ship reached Port Philadelphia. He, as ship's carpenter, along with the first mate and the captain, would never venture down below except for an emergency. The captain's Great Cabin and the officers' quarters might be small, but they were in the stern of the ship where fresh air came in through the windows, providing relief from the pervasive stench of the lower deck and bilge, and they were protected from crashing waves.

Bairn climbed the companionway stairs to the upper deck. He heard a strange squeal—an animal in distress—and bolted over to the railing. He watched in disbelief as he saw a stevedore try to lead a large pig up the gangplank with a rope around its neck. The pig wasn't cooperating. It eased back on its haunches and then down on its forelegs, refusing to budge off the dock, squealing unhappily. Bairn gripped the rail and leaned over the edge, watching the scene unfold with amusement. The stevedore tried to pick the pig up, but two hundred pounds of hog was too much for even the goliath strength of the man. The pig buried its head under its front legs. The stevedore pushed the pig from behind and Bairn started chuckling. When the stevedore tried rolling the pig up the gangplank, he burst out laughing.

If he wasn't in a hurry to get this ship loaded and ready to sail the channel, he could have stood there all afternoon, enjoying the sight. Instead, he went to the galley and took a handful of oats from the crock, then went down the gangplank. The stevedore had worked himself to a frenzy. Bairn held one hand up to stop him from his wrestling match with the pig. He took the rope leash from the stevedore and spread oats up the gangplank. Like a docile dog on a lead, the pig followed the oats trail straight up the gangplank. When it reached the deck, Bairn tied the pig's rope to a bollard. The stevedore ambled up the gangplank with an embarrassed look on his red face. "Ye need to think the way a pig thinks to get it to do what ye want it to do.'"

The stevedore didn't comprehend what Bairn was saying, but he understood that he meant him no disrespect. He shrugged, then grinned, and Bairn smiled with him.

"Bairn! Get the captain and get down here!"

He spun around to locate the voice and saw the recruiter, Georg Schultz. If there was anyone who could set his teeth on edge, it was Schultz. To most,

Schultz appeared to be a carefree fellow: a cockalorum, a jolly little man who drank for the pleasure of it. Bairn knew those small eyes bespoke a cunning shrewdness; he knew that every action Schultz took was motivated by money. He was a cagey character who was able to import a steady stream of innocent Germans, vetting them with visions of a land of milk and honey, just waiting to be enjoyed on the other side of the ocean. Ultimately bilking them out of their hard-earned savings. Along the way he alienated more than a few people, but Schultz managed to keep the ship captains happy by filling the lower decks with passengers.

Down on the dock, Schultz was waving frantically to Bairn. Beside him was a long line of bonneted and bearded people in dark, somber clothing, milling silently about on the dock, peering up at the ship. They were known on the docks as the Peculiar People. He scrutinized the faces, wondering what they were thinking as they waited to board. Did they feel fearful? Anxious? Certainly, they must be judgmental of the profane deckhands. But he read no hostility, no contempt, little anxiety, mostly simple curiosity.

Why should it matter? The passengers meant nothing to him.

Yet try as he did to ignore it, Bairn experienced the stirrings of uneasiness in his midsection, as he always did when he came across these odd people—a prickling, a plucking in his chest.

Waiting, waiting, waiting. Anna kept one eye on Dorothea and the other on Felix as they stood on the dock, absolutely sure that one or the other would end up in the dark water and neither of them knew how to swim. Felix had an abundance of curiosity and a dearth of common sense, and Dorothea was still muddled in a fog. Never emotionally sturdy, the death of Johann took her over the edge.

Felix's stomach grumbled loudly. "How much longer? I'm getting hungry." His stomach was a bottomless pit.

"It shouldn't be too much longer," Anna said. Her heart ached in a sweet way as she watched relief ease his face. As she saw him bend down to throw a pebble at a seagull, she wished for the hundredth time that Johann were with him. Felix seemed so lonely. The only other child close to his age was Catrina Müller, and she was a sore trial to him.

And suddenly Georg Schultz appeared in front of her. Again the hackling feeling. He wanted her to interpret as he spoke to Christian. "Guilders, Christian," Anna relayed. "He wants you to prepay the freight. Full freight for each adult, half-freight for each child from age four to fifteen. No charge for those under four."

Alarm flickered through Christian's eyes. "I wasn't anticipating a charge for children. We spent more than expected when we bought extra provisions in Rotterdam yesterday. If we pay now, we will have nothing left." He rubbed his forehead. "What can be done?"

Think, Anna. Think. She looked Georg Schultz in the eye. "We will pay half-freight now, and the remainder when we arrive safely in Philadelphia. We want to ensure that we will be well cared for."

Georg Schultz pointed to her and growled low in his throat, "Kommst du mit."

She followed him up the gangplank and noticed an official-looking figure standing at the top of the gangplank, watching her approach with sharp, penetrating eyes. For a split second he reminded her of Felix's father, bishop Jacob Bauer—treetop tall, muscular, wide-beamed shoulders. Then the moment passed and she saw how very different from the bishop he really was. Jacob was plain and humble and holy. There was nothing plain nor humble nor holy about this man.

This man was dressed impeccably in a sturdy, long-sleeved coat that hugged his ribs, a crisp white linen shirt, tight-fitting breeches that tucked into polished knee-high black boots. Sun-streaked, amber-gold hair threaded with red, kept long and held back in the traditional seaman's queue. High cheekbones framed by side whiskers, boxy jaw, and cold slate-gray eyes. His skin was nut-brown from days in the sun, or perhaps from his heritage. While he appeared young, his seaman's stance, so solid, so self-confident, and his style of dress sent a simple message: that he was in charge, and that he was all business.

Georg Schultz, intimidated by no one, barely came to the middle of his chest. "Bairn, where is the captain?"

The man propped his shoulders against the polished oak and crossed his arms over his broad chest, as though preparing for a long chat. "He's in the Great Cabin. Not t'be disturbed. What do ye want, Schultz?" Behind him, sailors hurried from one end of the deck to the other, exchanging words, issuing orders. Now and then, the man would bark an order to the sailors who hurried past him. This man, Anna thought, had the kind of authority that shut you up fast if you were a young sailor inclined to challenge something he had just said.

He glanced at her then, the hard line of his jaw softening just a little, looking down at her with an inscrutable gaze, making her feel even smaller and more awkward.

Had he noticed she was taking a survey of his person? Her neck heated, and she lowered her gaze yet still felt his intense scrutiny. Why was he staring at her? Perhaps there was something on her face. Her skin itched by suggestion, and she brushed self-conscious fingers across her cheeks.

He straightened to his full height. Goodness, he was tall. The tallest man she'd ever seen. He spoke English with a distinctive accent that she couldn't quite place, shortening words and lilting the end of a sentence. Northern England, perhaps, or Scottish. Her grandfather would have been able to pinpoint it.

Georg Schultz pointed a thumb at Anna. "She says they won't pay full fare until we reach Philadelphia. Only half fare for now."

A frown settled over the man's features, and he hooked his thumbs in his waistcoat pockets as he studied Anna. "The captain won't like hearin' that the passengers cannae pay passage."

"I didn't say we *couldn't*. We will pay. You can be assured of that." She looked down, afraid he'd read the truth in her eyes, more than she was ready to reveal. She felt no such assurance that the Amish would be solvent by the end of the journey, not after how their coffers had been diminished down the Rhine. But if they ended up in a desperate situation, she felt sure that Jacob Bauer would find a way to provide passage once they reached America.

He was still staring at her, she suddenly realized, though with a bemused look on his face. "Ye speak English quite well."

Georg Schultz answered for her, folding his pudgy arms over his chest. "The only one of this batch of Peculiars who can speak it."

"How did ye learn?"

"My grandfather. He served in the military in Switzerland."

"A man of yer . . . people . . . knew both plow and sword?"

She knew he had barely stopped himself from saying the word Peculiar. She'd heard the dockworkers mutter the disparage. "My grandfather had no choice but to serve. And he was clever at learning languages."

"And taught them ta his family."

"Yes." Anna's grandfather was convinced that their people must be wise to the ways of the world, wise as serpents and innocent as doves, especially in the skill of communication. No one in Ixheim shared his conviction, but he was adamant that his granddaughter would speak, read, and write English, German, French.

"Then what is yer reasonin' ta only pay half fare?"

"We want to be sure we will be treated well. Good food and clean water."

The man gave her a skeptical glance. "Lassie, if yer people cannae pay passage, the ship 'twill become a market. Buyers in Port Philadelphia will find out how much each person owes. Those who cannae pay their debts are called 'redemptioners.' They haggle with the buyers fer so many years labor ta pay off the debt. The redemptioner belongs ta the buyer until that debt is paid off. *Belongs*, like a slave. It happens. Quite a lot. Ta men, women. Ta children too."

The muscles in Anna's midsection tensed. She bit her lip. Her expression must have registered the sting of his words, for he softened.

"Even if a person doesn't survive the journey, the passage will be owed. 'Tis unfortunate, but it happens more often than ye might imagine."

Their eyes met, locked, held. His gaze was like granite. "I understand."

"Yer basket," he said. "It should go down in the hold. Ta save room. Ye'll want every spare inch down in the lower deck."

"No," Anna said.

"All nonessentials belong in the hold." He bent over to take the basket, but Anna's grip on it tightened.

"No," Anna repeated. "This basket *is* essential." She stared at his calloused hand that covered hers, refusing to let go, then peered up at the man, so incredibly tall, it put a crick in her neck. Up close he was larger than life and even more intimidating. For a moment she couldn't blink, breathe or move.

He released his grip on the basket. "What's in it, then?"

She tried to speak, but it was as if those stormy dark eyes had fused the words to her throat. She finally swallowed hard. His bold gaze and the scent of sandalwood from his clothing did funny things to her stomach.

He angled her a glance with the barest of smiles. "Now, I know ye can talk, because ye've already bargained yer way across the ocean."

She coughed, clearing the knot of awkwardness from her throat as she tightened her grip on her basket. "A rose. It is precious to me." Her lips compressed into a straight line and one hand was on her hip. It was the look and stance she used when someone thought she was too young to know what she was doing, which happened rather a lot back in Ixheim.

"A rose?" A shadow of something passed through his eyes, then vanished like vapor, making her think she'd imagined it. Next he surprised Anna with his terse, dismissive words. "I'll inform the captain of yer predicament." He turned and strode down the ship's deck.

As Anna followed down the gangplank behind Georg Schultz, her thoughts remained with that tall arrogant man in the fancy frock. She snapped a glance over her shoulder. "If he's not the captain, then who is he?"

"He's the ship's carpenter. A boatswain." Georg Schultz held up three thick fingers. "Third in command."

At the bottom of the gangplank, Anna explained the arrangement to Christian and waited as he pulled out a leather pouch. The money was counted and handed to Georg Schultz. When the ship's carpenter shouted down to load the passengers, they lined up behind the large group of Mennonites to walk up the gangplank. The mighty Mennonites, was how Anna thought of them. There were so many of them! Twice, perhaps thrice as many as there were Amish. Tensions between the Mennonites and the followers of Jacob Amman were thorny at best. How would they survive living together in such close quarters? Anna gazed at the ship as she took her place in line, sticking closely to Dorothea, who held Felix's hand in a death grip.

If all went well, this ship would be home for the next two months. If all did not go well, it could be longer. Maria liked to remind everyone of another of Esther Wenger's horrifying tale: a ship's passage that took nine months. Nine months! Three quarters of a year. The thought made Anna shudder. But then she'd also heard Maria speak of a journey that took only four weeks. She was counting on the latter—a swift passage, blessed by God.

Once on the ship, they were led straight down the companionway into the lower deck. Anna's eyes took awhile to adjust to the dim lighting. She helped Dorothea climb down the last few steps as Felix disappeared to explore the lower deck. Christian went quickly ahead in the cavernous space, pointing out sleeping shelves, nooks and crannies where families could claim space near the bow of the ship because the mighty Mennonites had claimed all available space in the stern. It was quickly apparent that passengers outnumbered beds.

The beds bore little resemblance to the kind found in Anna's home in Ixheim. These were wooden bunks, six feet long, three feet high, open at both ends. They were set in rows, side by side, and stacked to the ceiling. No more than two persons were supposed to be assigned to one bunk—according to Esther Wenger, who told Maria—but Georg Schulz insisted that each family was only allowed one bunk. Georg, first down the companionway, took the largest one, nearest the stern of the ship and closest to a hatch. For the Gerbers and the Müllers and the Masts and others, one family per bunk would mean crowding four or five or six into one bed. Anna looked toward the stern and saw a Mennonite family of ten settling in. Ten in one bed!

Maria was directing traffic. "You, Josef, you take your family over there. Conrad—you take your brood and go over there. You'll be cozy as a yolk in an egg." Her eyes swept the area until she found what she was looking for: a corner berth, the roomiest area for trunks and packages to be stored.

"And here is where Christian and I will sleep," she continued. "Anna, you and Dorothea and Felix should use pallets and sleep over there." She pointed to the gun deck, where a cannon was pointed through a square hole. "The air will be good for Felix. Growing boys need fresh air. Yes, you'll be most comfortable there."

"Of course, Maria," Anna said. *I sincerely doubt it, Maria*, she thought. As she placed her basket on the ground, she peered out the small opening at the open sea. How wet and cold could this area get when a storm blew in?

Catrina stood in front of Anna with her arms on her hips, though at the age of ten she had no hips to speak of. "Where did Felix go to?" She pursed her thin lips together. "Being a boy, and a most bothersome one at that, he'll need to be watched every moment so that he doesn't go straight into the sea and end up as food for the fishes." That was Catrina all over: huffy and prone to hysterics, always first with the alarm whether it was valid or not.

Dorothea and Anna exchanged a glance. Never far from Dorothea's mind was the fear that Felix could fall overboard. Any number of disasters could befall a boy on a boat. Especially a boy who does not think.

"Catrina, thank you for your concern," Anna said, "but you don't need to trouble yourself over Felix's whereabouts. His mother and I keep a careful eye on him at all times."

"I try to set a good example for the children." Catrina drew herself up importantly and sniffed. "Somebody has to."

"But . . . where is Felix, Anna?" Dorothea looked around the lower deck anxiously.

Oh no. Where did that boy go? Then Anna spotted a shock of red hair over by a cannon portal, examining the cannon balls, stacked in a pyramid. She pointed him out to Dorothea and watched her visibly relax.

As soon as Anna spread out their pallets and laid quilts down, Dorothea sat and held her quilt and rocked back and forth, staring out the small portal opening of the cannon, a forlorn figure. Anna hoped she would improve in spirits by the time they reached Port Philadelphia, or Jacob Bauer would be in for a shock to see the condition of his wife. It was just like last time, after Dorothea received the news that her oldest son Hans had passed. In her grief, she had become a hollow ghost of a person.

Anna still wasn't convinced of the wisdom of including Dorothea in this journey; she was still so fragile in her sorrowing over Johann, but Christian made the decision to bring her. "Jacob is expecting to see Felix and Dorothea," he said. "He's been there for a year now, purchasing land for each of us. It would be worse to have the family remain separated."

But he did agree that Dorothea needed minding, not to mention Felix who minded no one—and those caretaking chores were assigned to Anna.

Anna thought about the last conversation she had with her grandfather. "I'll be back," she told him.

"Girl, there's no turning back in life. But don't you worry. The Lord is watching over us."

Her grandmother told her it was bad luck to look back, that if you looked back it meant you'd never return. So as Anna walked down the muddy path to meet Christian and the others, she didn't look back. Tears streamed down her face, but she didn't look back. She was *going* to return.

Anna checked on Felix, who was hanging over the rails of the pig stall trying to pat the pig. The poor pig. It looked as bewildered and lost as everyone else, but at least Felix had found something to amuse himself. She thought there might be a little extra space near the pig and chickens to try to hold English classes for Felix and the Müller girls and anyone else who might be interested. She had brought a few books with her for that purpose. Learning English was one thing she could do to help prepare them for their new life. Though Felix was interested in everything *but* his lessons.

She had hoped there might be some Mennonite boys close to Felix's age, but there were just a few school-age girls and he wanted nothing to do with girls. The rest were toddlers. So many toddlers! Too many for a peaceful journey.

Maria was fussing over how to fit her trunk under the bunk, so Anna went to help her and then returned to Dorothea. Surely more cramped, uncomfortable quarters couldn't be found. The dark, damp lower deck was only five feet high. She pitied the men who would spend their days hunched over. By the time they reached Port Philadelphia, their backs would resemble question marks.

Wooden crates, boxes, sacks, bundles of food crammed the narrow aisle. Somewhere up front, a small child wailed relentlessly. And the lower deck was filthy. They would need to spend these first few days cleaning and scrubbing. At least, Anna thought, there would be something to do.

She'd heard the carpenter say that when the tide turned in their favor, it would be time to depart. Removing his hat, Christian bowed his head and fell down to his knees on the deck, as did everyone present, including the Mennonites. He offered up one of the most heartfelt prayers Anna ever heard him pray, fervently asking the Lord for blessings on this journey.

Longing for home filled Anna's heart. She felt an overwhelming need to know they'd be safe, that the next haven would indeed be welcoming, but there were few guarantees.

At sunset, the sky turned a miraculous color of pink and gold, shining off the water. She peeked out the small window and hoped it meant God's blessing on them.

Soon, the *Charming Nancy* sailed into the channel with the lights of Rotterdam blazing brightly behind them. It was a whole world, this ship, and they would sail to America in its very bowels.

Suzanne Woods Fisher is the author of the bestselling Lancaster County Secrets and Stoney Ridge Seasons series. *The Search* received a 2012 Carol Award, *The Waiting* was a finalist for the 2011 Christy Award, and *The Choice* was a finalist for the 2011 Carol Award. Suzanne's grandfather was raised in the Old Order German Baptist Brethren Church in Franklin County, Pennsylvania. Her interest in living a simple, faith-filled life began with her Dunkard cousins. Suzanne is also the author of the bestselling *Amish Peace: Simple Wisdom for a Complicated World* and *Amish Proverbs: Words of Wisdom from the Simple Life*, both finalists for the ECPA Book of the Year award, and *Amish Values for Your Family: What We Can Learn from the Simple Life*. She has an app, Amish Wisdom, to deliver a proverb a day to your iPhone, iPad, or Android. Visit her at www.suzannewoodsfisher.com to find out more.

Suzanne lives with her family and big yellow dogs in the San Francisco Bay Area.

Meet Suzanne
online at

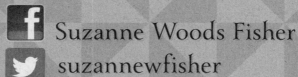 Suzanne Woods Fisher

 suzannewfisher

www.SuzanneWoodsFisher.com

Download the

Free **Amish Wisdom** App

WELCOME TO A PLACE OF UNCONDITIONAL LOVE AND UNEXPECTED BLESSINGS

Don't miss the Stoney Ridge Seasons series!